DEPARTMENT 19
BATTLE LINES

First published in hardback in Great Britain by HarperCollins *Children's Books* in 2013
This edition published in Great Britain by HarperCollins *Children's Books* in 2013

HarperCollins *Children's Books* is a division of HarperCollins*Publishers* Ltd,
77–85 Fulham Palace Road, Hammersmith, London, W6 8JB.

Follow Will Hill on twitter
@willhillauthor

www.department19exists.com
www.facebook.com/department19exists

1

ISBN 978-0-00-735453-5

Typeset in Berylium by Palimpsest Book Production Limited, Falkirk, Stirlingshire
Printed and bound in England by Clays Ltd, St Ives plc

DEPARTMENT 19
BATTLE LINES

WILL HILL

HarperCollins *Children's Books*

ACKNOWLEDGEMENTS

My agent Charlie Campbell and UK editor Nick Lake, without whom these books wouldn't exist.

My lovely US editor Laura Arnold, for her endless transatlantic enthusiasm.

Everyone at HarperCollins and Razorbill, for everything they do.

My wonderful publishers around the world, for spreading the word in so many languages.

Sarah, for putting up with me.

My friends and family, for their understanding and encouragement.

And most importantly, everyone who has spent their time and money on these books. It never ceases to amaze me, and I will never take your support for granted. Thank you.

Will Hill
London, February 2013

For Sarah,

who knew what writers were like, but managed to look past it

The earth had a single light afar,

A flickering, human pathetic light,

That was maintained against the night,

It seemed to me, by the people there,

With a Godforsaken brute despair.

Robert Frost

We seem to be drifting into unknown places and unknown

ways; into a whole world of dark and dreadful things.

Jonathan Harker

MEMORANDUM

From: Office of the Director of the Joint Intelligence Committee

Subject: Revised classifications of the British governmental departments

Security: TOP SECRET

DEPARTMENT 1	Office of the Prime Minister
DEPARTMENT 2	Cabinet Office
DEPARTMENT 3	Home Office
DEPARTMENT 4	Foreign and Commonwealth Office
DEPARTMENT 5	Ministry of Defence
DEPARTMENT 6	British Army
DEPARTMENT 7	Royal Navy
DEPARTMENT 8	Her Majesty's Diplomatic Service
DEPARTMENT 9	Her Majesty's Treasury
DEPARTMENT 10	Department for Transport
DEPARTMENT 11	Attorney General's Office
DEPARTMENT 12	Ministry of Justice
DEPARTMENT 13	Military Intelligence, Section 5 (MI5)
DEPARTMENT 14	Secret Intelligence Service (SIS)
DEPARTMENT 15	Royal Air Force
DEPARTMENT 16	Northern Ireland Office
DEPARTMENT 17	Scotland Office
DEPARTMENT 18	Wales Office
DEPARTMENT 19	**CLASSIFIED**
DEPARTMENT 20	Territorial Police Forces
DEPARTMENT 21	Department of Health
DEPARTMENT 22	Government Communication Headquarters (GCHQ)
DEPARTMENT 23	Joint Intelligence Committee (JIC)

PROLOGUE

In the village of Crowthorne is an alarm.

A direct copy of a World War Two air-raid siren, it is bright red, and sits atop a pole two metres above the ground.

The alarm is connected by an underground network of wires to Broadmoor Hospital, the sprawling estate of red-brick buildings that sits above the village, and which is home to almost three hundred of the United Kingdom's most dangerous, damaged citizens.

It is designed to alert anyone within a twenty-five-mile radius to an escape from the hospital, and has been sounded only five times in earnest in more than fifty years.

Ben Dawson had been asleep for about forty-five minutes when the siren burst into life. He jerked up from a dream about sleep, the kind of long, deep, uninterrupted sleep that had been impossible in the six weeks since Isla was born, and felt his wife raise her head slowly from her pillow.

"The baby OK?" she slurred.

"It's not Isla," he replied. "It's the siren."

"Siren?"

"The bloody Broadmoor siren," he snapped. It was deafening, a two-tone scream that made his chest tighten with anger.

"What time is it?" asked Maggie, forcing her eyes open and looking at him.

Ben flicked on his bedside lamp, wincing as the light hit his eyes, and checked the clock.

"Quarter to four," he groaned.

Not fair, he thought. *It's just not fair.*

Then he heard a second sound, in between the peals of the alarm; a high, determined crying from the room above their bedroom. Ben swore and swung his legs out from under the duvet.

"Stay there," said Maggie, pushing herself to the edge of the bed. "It's my turn."

Ben slid his feet into his trainers and pulled a jumper over his head. "You see to Isla. I'm going outside, see if anyone else is awake."

"OK," said Maggie, stumbling through the bedroom door. She was barely awake, moving with the robotic lurch of new parents everywhere. Ben heard her footsteps on the stairs, heard her begin to gently shush their daughter.

Ben felt no fear at the sound of the siren. He had been up to the hospital several times, had seen the electric fences and the gateposts and the sturdy buildings themselves, and was not the slightest bit concerned about the possibility of a breakout. There had been several, over the years; the escape of John Straffen in 1952, who had climbed over the wall while on cleaning duties in the yard and murdered a young girl from Farley Hill, was the reason the siren system had been built. But the last time anyone had made it out had been almost twenty years ago, and security had been increased and expanded since then. Instead, as he stomped down the stairs towards the front door, knowing the baby was already awake so it didn't matter, what Ben was mainly feeling was frustration.

The last six weeks had been nothing like the parenting books had suggested, or as their friends had described. He had expected to be tired, expected to be grumpy and stressed, but nothing had prepared him for how he actually felt.

He was utterly, physically, exhausted.

Isla was beautiful, and he felt things he had never felt before when he looked at her; *that* part was exactly as advertised, he had been glad to realise. But she cried, loudly and endlessly. He and Maggie took it in turns to go and check on her, to warm bottles or burp her or just rock her in their arms. Eventually, her eyes would flutter closed, and they would place her back in her cot, and creep back to their own bed. If they were lucky, they might get two hours of uninterrupted sleep before the crying began again.

Ben shoved open the front door. The night air was warm and still, and the siren was much louder outside. He walked out on to the narrow cobbled street and saw lights on in the majority of his neighbours' homes. As he lit a cigarette from the pack he kept for emergencies, like when he had been woken up for the third time before it was even four o'clock, doors began to open and pale figures in pyjamas and dressing gowns began to appear.

"What on earth is going on?" demanded one of the figures, a large, broad man with a huge, bald dome of a head that gleamed in the light. "Why doesn't someone turn it off?"

Charlie Walsh lived next door to Ben and Maggie. Ben glanced at him as he made his way over, then returned his gaze to the hill above the village. The hulking shape of the hospital was visible as a distant black outline in the centre of a faint yellow glow.

"I don't think you can," Ben replied. "I'm pretty sure you can only turn it off at the hospital."

"Then maybe someone should go up there and see what's happening?"

"Maybe someone should," replied Ben.

"All right then," said Charlie. "I'll come with you."

Ben stared at his neighbour. He wanted nothing more than to go back upstairs, wrap his pillow round his head, and wait for the terrible ringing to stop. But that was now no longer an option.

"Fine," he snapped, and strode back into his house to grab the car keys from the table in the hall.

A minute later the two men were speeding out of what passed for central Crowthorne in Ben's silver Range Rover, heading up the hill towards the hospital.

Behind the desk in Crowthorne's tiny police station, Andy Myers was trying to hear the voice on the other end of the phone over the deafening howl of the siren.

Crowthorne police station was rated Tier 1 by the Thames Valley Police, which meant that its front desk was staffed entirely by volunteers. There were twelve of them, mostly retirees, who took turns to field the small number of enquiries that came in from local residents – everything from minor incidents of graffiti and vandalism, to requests for advice on traffic accidents. The station was not manned overnight, but one of the volunteers was always on call. Tonight, Andy Myers had drawn the short straw.

He had dragged himself from the warmth of his bed when the siren burst into life, grumbling, stretching, and feeling every single one of his sixty-eight years. The space in the bed beside him was cold and empty; his wife, Glenda, had occupied it for more than thirty years before cancer had claimed her the previous summer. Since then Andy, who had spent his working years in the brokerage houses of the City of London, had been looking for ways to fill the hole in his life that she had left behind. Volunteering at the police station was just one of the ways he tried to do so; he was also on the board of the local Rotary Club, an active member of the Village Green Association and secretary of Crowthorne Cricket Club.

He dressed quickly and made the five-minute walk to the station. He did not hurry; he was no more concerned about the possibility of an escape than Ben Dawson was. But there were protocols in the event of the siren sounding, and Andy Myers was a great believer in protocol.

He walked into the station's car park, wincing at the bellowing noise from the siren that stood behind the building. It was little more than a converted house, sitting at the end of a row of terraces. He unlocked the door and went inside, flopped down into the worn leather chair behind the desk, reached for the phone, and dialled a number.

The official response to a suspected escape from Broadmoor was twofold: it required all local schools to keep children inside and under direct supervision of staff until parents could arrive to take them home, and it called for the establishment of a ring of roadblocks at a ten-mile radius from the hospital. Crowthorne station had a single police car, an ageing Ford Focus that was sitting outside, so Andy's only duty was to call the Major Incident Response Team in Reading and request instructions.

"Say again, sir?" he shouted, over the din of the siren. "You want me to do what?"

"Drive up there," yelled the voice on the other end of the phone. "Go and see what the hell is going on. We're sending units out to set up the roadblocks, but we can call them back if this is a false alarm."

"What are they saying up on the hill?" shouted Andy.

"No answer," replied the officer. "We think their system's crashed, or gone daft, or something. Get up there, talk to the duty nurse, then radio in and tell us what's happening. Clear?"

"Yes, sir," shouted Andy Myers, and hung up the phone.

He swore heartily, the way that had always made Glenda widen her eyes at him in warning, and grabbed the Ford's keys from the hook above the desk. He locked up the station, climbed into the car, and pulled out of the car park. As he reached the edge of Crowthorne, he flicked on the lights and the siren, even though it would be impossible to hear over the blare of the alarms. Then he pressed down on the accelerator and pointed the little Ford along the same road that Ben Dawson's Range Rover had taken, less than five minutes earlier.

Charlie Walsh fiddled with the radio as Ben drove, flicking from one station to the next until Ben gave him a sharp sideways look and he turned it off. They drove on in silence, climbing the wide, shallow hill that dominated the countryside for miles around, until the Range Rover sped smoothly round the final bend and Broadmoor lay before them.

It had been opened in 1863 as Broadmoor Criminal Lunatic Asylum, terminology long since considered offensive. In the modern era it had been expanded to the size of a small village, a sprawl of low concrete buildings and trailers, of metal sheds and covered walkways. But the main buildings, where the inmates were housed and treated, were the same now as they had been more than a hundred and fifty years earlier: squat, Gothic structures of orange-red brick and grey tiled roofs that revealed their original purpose. The buildings looked, in every way, like those of a prison.

Ben slowed the car as they approached the outer fence. The tall metal mesh, easily seven metres high, topped with razor wire and electrified along its entire length, marked the edge of the exclusion zone that surrounded the hospital; inside it, tall brick walls, security patrols, deadlock doors and barred windows were designed to make sure that no inmate got anywhere near the fence. If they did, there was a sharp, unpleasant shock waiting for them.

The gate in the middle of the fence was standing open.

It ran on wheels, dividing in the middle, powered by an automated system operated from the security control room. There was a small box beside the gate containing a telephone, but it was rarely needed; very few people arrived at Broadmoor unannounced.

Ben pointed the Range Rover between the open gates and drove slowly forward.

"I don't like this," said Charlie Walsh. "We should go back. Let's let the police deal with it."

"We're here now," said Ben. "We might as well take a look."

Beyond the electrical fence the road rose slightly to the main entrance of the hospital. The gatehouse resembled a medieval keep: two towers flanking a vast black gate, above which was set a severe-looking clock, fashioned in black and gold. The outer buildings of the hospital extended away from the gatehouse on both sides, merging into the looming ward buildings and the towering inner wall. The gatehouse gave the impression of being impregnable.

Unless the gate was open, as it was now.

Ben drove slowly through it, unease crawling in his stomach. The gates to Broadmoor were never open, and even if there had been a malfunction in the electric fence, they should never have been able to get this close to the gatehouse without being intercepted. That both gates should be standing open was unthinkable. And Ben noticed something else. He pressed the button on the door handle that lowered his window, felt the mild night air flood into the car, and listened.

The siren screamed into the car, rising and falling. But beyond it, in the gaps, there was no sound.

The hospital was usually a hive of activity and noise, even this early in the morning. There should have been the sounds of footsteps, the barking of the security guards' dogs, the chatter of the nightshift employees.

But there was nothing.

"What are you listening to?" shouted Charlie Walsh, making himself heard over the alarm. "What can you hear?"

"Nothing," shouted Ben. "Nothing at all."

He wound the window back up and gently pressed the accelerator. The big car crept through the gate; beyond it were two small guard posts, plastic boxes like the kind that stand at the entrance to toll roads. He peered into the one on his side as the car rolled slowly past. It was empty. There was no sign of movement, although there was a dark shape on the rear wall, like a tin of paint had been thrown against it.

"What about your side?" he asked. "Anyone there?"

"No one," replied Charlie and, for the first time, Ben heard the fear in his neighbour's voice. "There's no one here, Ben. Where the hell are they all?"

"I don't know."

They drove silently into the courtyard beyond the gatehouse. Modern administrative units stood on either side, but rising in front of them was the original Broadmoor building, a towering, imposing structure of dark orange bricks. There was a wide set of steps leading up to an ornate front door, and it was on these steps that Ben saw something out of place.

He stamped on the brakes of the Range Rover, throwing Charlie Walsh forward against his seat belt, causing him to yell out in alarm.

"What the hell—"

"Quiet," interrupted Ben. He flicked the car's headlights to full beam, illuminating the courtyard.

Lying on the stone steps was a man wearing a white hospital gown, much of which was soaked crimson.

"Oh God," whispered Charlie. "Oh God, Ben, I don't want to be here any more. Let's get out of here."

Ben didn't reply. He was leaning towards the windscreen, craning his neck upwards, awfully sure of what he was going to see. He heard his muscles creak, then saw it.

On the fourth floor, directly above where the man was lying, one of the windows was open to the night, its reinforced glass missing.

"He jumped," whispered Ben. "You can see the broken window. He jumped out."

Walsh leant forward, but his shoulders and neck were too wide to see where Ben was pointing. He slumped back in his seat, breathing hard.

"He's dead, Ben," he said, his voice wavering. "There's nothing we can do for him. We go home and we call the police and they can send an ambulance up here. Please, Ben, let's go. Please."

"Why is he just lying there?" wondered Ben aloud. "Why didn't anyone try to help him? Where are all the nurses?"

"I don't know!" screeched Charlie. "I want to go home, Ben, I want to go right now!"

Ben looked at his neighbour. The man appeared to be on the verge of a panic attack, his chest heaving, his eyes wide and bulging. And he was right, there was nothing they could do for the man: the puddle of blood beneath him was shockingly large. But everything about the hospital felt wrong to Ben. It wasn't just the open gates; it was too quiet, too empty, and now one of its patients was lying dead in the courtyard and no one seemed to have even noticed.

He unfastened his seat belt, reached out, and opened the door beside him.

Charlie let out a yelp. "What are you doing?" he shouted, over the deafening siren.

Ben ignored him. He stepped out of the car in something close to a trance, his mind racing with what he was seeing all around him, turning it over and over like a puzzle whose solution was dancing just out of reach. Distantly, he heard the passenger door open and Charlie Walsh step nervously on to the cobblestones.

"Get back in the car, Ben," he yelled. "Please."

The pleading in the man's voice brought Ben to his senses and he shook his head, as if to clear it.

"OK," he shouted, and saw Charlie Walsh's face crumple with relief. "Sorry, mate. Let's go."

He climbed back into the driver's seat and was pulling the door shut when the dead body stood up and looked at them.

It was a man in his late twenties or early thirties. His gown looked as though it had been dipped in dark red paint, and his left arm was pointing away from his body at an unnatural angle, but his face wore a wide, hungry smile and his eyes glowed the colour of lava.

Charlie Walsh let out a high, trembling scream, and pressed his hands against the dashboard as though trying to push himself backwards, away from the nightmare thing before him. Ben just stared, his eyes bulging, unable to comprehend what he was seeing. Then the blood-soaked figure ran forward, leapt on to the bonnet of the Range Rover, and smashed its fist through the glass of the windscreen.

Ben's paralysis broke as Walsh screamed again. The noise of the siren burst into the car through the broken windscreen, deafening them both. The man with the red eyes shoved his arm through the glass, tearing his skin to ribbons; blood splashed into the air as the man's fingers slid across Ben's throat, then lunged for Walsh's face. The man was yelling so loudly that he was audible over the din of the alarm, shouting words that were unintelligible to Ben's ears, his mouth working furiously, spit and blood pattering down on to the glass as he fought to reach the two men inside the car.

Then his grasping, searching fingers closed on Charlie Walsh's lower lip. With a primal roar, the crimson, glowing monstrosity tore it from the man's face with a sound like ripping paper. Blood burst from the wound, spraying on to the dashboard and windscreen, and Walsh's screams reached a terrible new pitch.

Ben shoved the Range Rover's gear stick into reverse and floored the accelerator. Walsh was thrown forward in his seat and for a terrible second the patient's fingers closed on his throat. Then momentum hauled him back, and he fell heavily on to the cobblestones of the courtyard. He was on his feet again instantly, bathed in the blinding gleam of the car's headlights as it hurtled backwards. Ben looked over his shoulder and saw the open gate approaching, dangerously fast. There was no time to correct their course; he could only hope that he had not turned the steering wheel since driving them into this terrible place.

There was a screech of metal as the car shot between the gateposts and a huge shower of sparks on the passenger's side as the panels tore along the brick wall. Charlie Walsh, who was sobbing between screams, wearing the look of a man who expects to wake up from a nightmare at any moment, leapt in his seat and almost fell on to Ben, who shoved him roughly back. Then the screeching stopped, and they were through the gate. Ben slammed on the brakes and hauled the steering wheel around. The tyres smoked and squealed, until the big car was facing the right way down the road they had driven up, only minutes earlier. There was a thud behind them, and Ben glanced into the rear-view mirror as he shoved the car back into drive and floored the accelerator again.

The blood-soaked patient, who had torn Ben's neighbour's lip from his face as though it was nothing, had run headlong into the back of the car. There was a bright spray of blood across the rear window at the point of impact. The car leapt forward and Ben saw the man lying in the road; he seemed to have knocked himself out. But, as he looked at the fallen patient, he caught sight of something else that almost stopped his heart.

Dark shapes were dropping steadily into the courtyard, before moving quickly towards the gate. Ben pressed the window's button again and, over the howl of the siren, he could hear, very faintly, the crunch of breaking glass and a low, swelling roar, like the noise made by a pack of animals. He was still looking in the rear-view mirror as the car accelerated through the outer gate and down the hill; as a result, he didn't see the glow of blue and red emerging from around the sharp bend in front of them.

Andy Myers gritted his teeth and pressed his foot down more firmly on the accelerator. The siren was deafening, even from inside the car; the old vehicle's windows and doors were not as airtight as they had once been, and the sound was so loud the windows might as well have been rolled down. He was looking forward to finding out from the duty nurse exactly what was going on, radioing it in, and getting back to bed. There was a cricket match at noon and he was already glumly aware that very few of the club's players were going to be rested and at their best.

He turned the wheel gently, sending the car neatly round the bend that would take him on to the final approach to the hospital. Then everything in front of him was blinding light, and he had the briefest of moments to wonder where it was coming from before the Range Rover slammed into his car head-on.

"Look out!" screamed Charlie Walsh, the words mangled by his missing lower lip.

Ben dragged his gaze away from the rear-view mirror, aware that something had moved at the edges of his vision. Then red and blue light filled the windscreen, there was a sickening crunch of metal, and everything went black.

Ben emerged into a world of chaos.

His eyes flickered open and pain shot through his head as the siren pounded into it. Slowly, ever so slowly, he turned to look at Charlie Walsh.

His neighbour hung in his seat belt, his head lowered, his eyes closed. His face was covered in blood and a ridge of swelling was already beginning to rise across his forehead. As Ben watched, a small bubble of blood inflated and popped in Charlie's ruined mouth, followed by a second, and a third.

He's alive, he thought. *Thank God.*

Ben looked down at himself and felt relief wash over him; the big car's roll cage had held. There was a bulge behind the pedals where the engine block had been forced back by the collision, but it had not broken through; it would have crushed the lower half of his body to jelly if it had. Blood was falling steadily from his nose and he could see the dent in the dashboard where he must have been thrown against it. His head thumped with pain and he found he couldn't think straight; he tried, but the thoughts drifted away from him, as insubstantial as smoke on the wind. He reached out with a shaking hand and opened the car door. He made to get out, but a sheet of agony bloomed up from his left ankle, and he screamed. Ben looked down, and saw that his foot was twisted almost ninety degrees to one side. The sight was so alien, so terrible, that he vomited into his lap, unable to stop himself.

Ben fumbled his mobile phone out of his pocket and dialled Maggie's number. He knew he should phone the police, but for some reason he felt unwilling to do so. Something had happened before the crash, although he wasn't sure what it was. Had there been another car? Had he *hit* another car? He held the phone to his ear as he peered through the broken windscreen. There were pieces of metal strewn across the road. He leant further forward, dimly aware that the car seemed to be higher than usual, that his view of the road was different, and saw a twisted hunk of metal lying beneath his front wheels. Ben stared at it blankly, until his eyes picked out a smashed pair of lights sticking out of the wreckage, one red, one blue, and everything flooded back to him.

The hospital, the man, Charlie Walsh's lip, the police car and—

He froze.

Oh God. The patients. The breaking glass. Behind me.

The siren screamed and roared, and he could hear Maggie's voice shouting down the phone, but could not make his mouth work to answer her. He forced himself to look into the rear-view mirror and saw a red glow descending the hill towards him, a pulsing, shifting mass of crimson that seemed to originate from a hundred pairs of glowing points of light.

"Run," he croaked into the phone. "Take Isla and run."

52 DAYS TILL ZERO HOUR

1

THE NEXT GENERATION

Jamie Carpenter was so focused on the violence playing out before him that he didn't notice his console's message tone until the third beep.

"Take five," he called, pulling the metal rectangle from its loop on his belt, and heard two simultaneous groans of relief. Jamie thumbed READ on the console's touch screen, and read the short message that appeared.

NS303-67-J/LIVE_BRIEFING/OR/ASAP

The message was simple, but it still caused Jamie a momentary pang of sorrow. It was an order for him to immediately attend a briefing in the Ops Room, similar to dozens of other orders that had appeared on his console's screen in the months since he had arrived in the Loop, the classified base that was the heart of Department 19. But this one had been sent only to him; his Operator number was there on the screen in black and white. The previous orders had almost all been sent with the prefix G-17, the Operational Squad that he had led until a month or so ago, the squad that had comprised himself, Larissa Kinley and Kate Randall.

Their squad had been disbanded in the aftermath of Valeri Rusmanov's attack on the Loop, so that their combined experience could be put to wider use helping the Department heal and rebuild. It had been one of Interim Director Cal Holmwood's first commands, and although it was one that Jamie understood, it had still felt like the three of them were being punished for being good at what they did. Holmwood had assured them that that was not the case, but how they felt was ultimately of little importance: it was an order and they would follow it.

"Sir?"

The voice trembled, and Jamie looked up from his console. He was sitting on a bench at the edge of the Playground, the wide circular room on Level F of the Loop in which generations of Operators had been trained, sweating and bleeding on its hard shiny floor. For the last fifteen years or so, the room had been the domain of Terry, the tall, barrel-chested instructor who was standing in the middle of the gleaming floor with his hands folded across his chest. But it was not he who had spoken; the voice belonged to John Morton, who was slumped on the ground and looking over at Jamie with wide eyes.

Morton was breathing heavily and bleeding from half a dozen places, most seriously from where the instructor's weathered knuckles had split his bottom lip open. He was sat on the floor, his legs crossed, his arms resting on his knees, his face so pale that Jamie thought he might be on the verge of throwing up. The blood from his lip was dripping steadily, pooling between his legs.

"Nothing for you to worry about," replied Jamie. "I have to head upstairs for a bit."

"Everything OK, sir?" asked a second voice, and Jamie turned his head towards its source. Sitting apart from Morton was a dark-haired woman whose name was Lizzy Ellison. She was almost as pale as Morton and she too was bleeding, from a wide cut above her left eye and from somewhere inside her mouth, but her voice was steady.

"Fine," said Jamie, giving them both a quick, narrow smile. "At least, as far as I know it is. Terry?"

"Yes, sir?" replied the instructor. The huge man had taken advantage of the momentary pause in the training to give his mind a moment to clear, and a small smile of pride had emerged on his face as he looked at Jamie Carpenter. It seemed to Terry as though it had been mere days since the boy had arrived in the Playground, nervous and skinny and completely disoriented, but with a streak of bitter determination that had been immediately obvious to Terry, a veteran reader of people. Now he emerged from his thoughts, pushing the smile away as he answered the calm, deadly Operator the boy had so quickly become.

"CQD, please," said Jamie. "Again."

Both Morton and Ellison let out low groans, their eyes flickering wildly from Jamie to each other, then up to the imposing figure of the instructor.

"Of course, sir," replied Terry, and turned towards the two trainees, a wide smile of anticipation on his face.

Jamie strode along the corridor towards the lift that would take him up through the base to the Ops Room.

He felt a momentary pang of guilt as he thought about the brutal physical programme Terry was putting Morton and Ellison through; Close Quarters Defence was a regime of violence and exhaustion that he would in all likelihood remember until the end of his days. But he quickly pushed the feeling aside. Recruits were broken down and rebuilt: that was the way it was done, the way it had always been done, and he knew that the understanding his two new provisional squad members would gain from their ordeal would serve them well out in the world, where violence and danger beyond anything they had known lurked around what often seemed like every corner. The darkness that Blacklight had kept at bay for so long was now threatening to overwhelm them, and there was no time to be wasted on the hurt feelings and bloodied bodies of the new intake of recruits.

Jamie was cautiously hopeful about the two potential Operators who had been thrust into his care, a situation that never ceased to amuse him. Both were older than him and far more experienced in the outside world. Inside the Loop, however, their experience counted for nothing and Jamie was an almost legendary figure; they both looked at him with barely concealed awe.

John Morton was twenty-one years old and had been recruited personally by Major Paul Turner. He had been about to be transferred to the First Battalion of the Parachute Regiment, and had already been marked out as a soldier likely to one day undergo the gruelling selection process that would see him join the SAS, the British Army's elite special forces unit. Turner had become aware of him through his old colleagues at Hereford and had stepped in quickly to derail the young man's career path. Less than a day later, Morton had arrived at the Loop with a look of wonder similar to the one that had been a fixture on Jamie's own face barely six months earlier.

Lizzy Ellison was twenty-three, two years older than her training mate and more than five years older than Jamie. She had been an agent in SIS, the Secret Intelligence Service that had previously been known as MI6, and what she had done there was classified at a level accessible only by the Director General of the SIS and the Chief of the General Staff. Jamie had not asked her, although the time would come when he would do so; he had learnt from personal experience that secrets within a squad could be dangerous. But for the time being, he was content to let her past remain a secret for a single reason: Angela Darcy, the beautiful, fearsome Operator who had accompanied Jamie on his desperate rescue mission to Paris only a month or so earlier, who had also once been SIS and was, he thought, the most deadly and calmly predatory human being he had ever known, knew who Ellison was. He didn't know how, but it was enough; if she had appeared on the radar of Angela Darcy, who had spent her pre-Blacklight career wading through blood that was often elbow-deep, then he would not push her to reveal her secrets.

Not yet, at least.

The lift doors slid open and Jamie stepped inside, pressing the button marked 0. As the lift began to ascend, he wondered what Cal Holmwood might want this time.

It often felt as though he spent more time in the Ops Room than in the small quarters where he occasionally found the opportunity to sleep. It was an oval room in the centre of the only above-ground level of the Loop, and it was where the Priority Level missions were briefed and despatched. In the month that had followed the attack on the Loop and the abduction of Henry Seward, the Department's veteran Director, it had become the hub of the entire base, as every mission had become Priority Level. It was exceedingly rare to find good news waiting there.

Jamie leant against the cool metal wall of the lift and let his mind drift; as was so often the case, his thoughts were quickly full of his friends. The catastrophic attack on the Loop by Valeri and his vampire army had affected them all profoundly; Kate was still struggling to come to terms with the death of Shaun, the young Operator who had been her boyfriend, and had made a decision in recent days that Jamie had pleaded with her to reconsider. Matt was buried deep in the bowels of the Loop, spending every waking second staring at a computer screen. And Larissa, the vampire girl who had become the most important thing in the world to Jamie, was gone.

The lift door slid open again, and he walked slowly down the Level 0 corridor. He paused outside the door to the Ops Room, took a deep breath, then stepped inside.

Gathered round the long row of tables in the centre of the room was a group of dark figures.

Cal Holmwood stood at the head, with Jack Williams at his side. Arrayed along the sides of the table, their attention focused on the Interim Director, stood Patrick Williams, Dominique Saint-Jacques, Jacob Scott, Andrew Jarvis, Richard Brennan and a Communications Division Operator called Amy Andrews. She had been recently added to the Task Force, along with Dominique and Angela Darcy, who appeared to be absent; in the aftermath of Valeri's attack, it had been expanded to include at least one representative from every Division in the Department.

As Jamie sat down, he noted that Paul Turner was also missing, although this no longer qualified as surprising.

"Lieutenant Carpenter," said Cal Holmwood. "How are your recruits coming along?"

"Pretty well, sir," replied Jamie. "Terry's making sure they realise what they've signed up for."

Cal Holmwood smiled grimly. "I'm glad to hear it. They're going to see for themselves in a few hours."

Jamie frowned. The Blacklight training programme had once taken thirteen months to complete, on top of the elite-level training that the majority of recruits had already undertaken before they were even made aware of the Department's existence. But circumstances had made this impossible, and what was being carried out in the Playground now was the very definition of a crash course. It was far from ideal, from anyone's perspective, but it was unavoidable: the Department had been hurt, and hurt badly.

There were rooms on the residential levels that had been occupied by Operators who were never going to return to them, unused desks in the Surveillance, Security and Intelligence Divisions, Operational Squads that had lost one, two, or in some awful cases, all three of their members. These empty spaces, these holes in the fabric of the Department, would not be filled easily, even by the new men and women who were being recruited specifically to do so. Friends, colleagues, even family members had been lost, and rookies would not take their places, even though they were vital: restoring the Department to something approaching full strength was of paramount importance.

The countdown to Zero Hour would not wait for them to be ready.

Nonetheless, Jamie did not believe the members of his new squad were; he had not been intending to take them out for another week, at least.

"Why, sir?" he asked, looking at the Interim Director. "What's happened?"

Holmwood glanced over at Jack Williams. "Jack?"

Jamie's friend nodded. "Thank you, sir," he said. "In the Security Officer's absence, I've been asked to brief you all on the events of last night." He tapped a series of commands into the console in front of him, and the Operators turned their attention to the screen set high on the wall. A window opened and grainy CCTV images filled the screen: running figures in white coats, leaping, grasping shapes moving among them, tearing and rending. Blood sprayed on to walls and ceilings, and the panicked, pleading eyes of the victims were wide, even in the low-resolution footage.

"This," said Jack, "is D ward of Broadmoor Hospital, one of three secure hospitals that house the most dangerously ill men and women in the country. At 1:47 this morning, a group of vampires broke into the facility, killing every member of staff and releasing every patient from their rooms. We've confronted twenty-nine of them so far and managed to bring two into custody. Every single one has been turned."

There was a sharp communal intake of breath.

"All of them?" asked Patrick Williams, his voice low.

"That's correct," replied his brother.

"This was an attack on us, not on the patients," said Dominique Saint-Jacques. "They turned them all and let them out, didn't they?"

"That appears to be the case," replied Jack. "However, this was not the only incident of its type to take place last night. Vampires also attacked the Florence Supermax facility in Colorado, the Black Dolphin prison in Sol-Iletsk, the C Max in Pretoria, al-Ha'ir prison in Riyadh, Kamunting Detention Centre in Malaysia, Goulburn Correctional Centre in New South Wales, and the Penitenciária Federal de Catanduvas in southern Brazil. There are now more than four thousand maximum-security prisoners unaccounted for, and in every country, those who have been recovered have all been turned. This appears to have been nothing less than a deliberate, coordinated attack on the supernatural Departments of the world."

There was silence as the Operators attempted to absorb the scale of what they were hearing. Jamie looked round the table; Patrick

Williams and Dominique Saint-Jacques were staring steadily at Jack, their expressions calm and neutral, and he felt admiration rise through his chest.

Nothing fazes them, he thought. *Absolutely nothing.*

He was about to return his attention to Jack when he caught sight of Jacob Scott; the Australian Colonel was staring down at the desk, his eyes wide, his face deathly pale. The outspoken veteran Operator looked, to Jamie's untrained eye, as though he was about to have a heart attack; his fists were clenched so tightly that his knuckles had turned bright white.

"This is now this Department's number-one priority," said Cal Holmwood. Jamie dragged his gaze away from Colonel Scott, a frown furrowing his brow, and turned back to the Interim Director. "I'm sure you can see that the potential for public exposure and loss of life is extremely significant. I'm calling back the Field Teams—"

"All of them?" interrupted Jamie. "Even the ones that are looking for Admiral Seward? And Dracula?"

"Major Landis's team will continue to search for Admiral Seward," replied Holmwood, fixing him with a glacial stare. "The rest are coming home until this situation is resolved."

"Dracula is gathering strength," said Jamie. "Right now, while we're sitting here. Surely he's the priority."

"This is *about* Dracula," said Holmwood. "Jack, bring up the gatehouse."

The CCTV footage changed to a view of the arched entry to Broadmoor. Jamie winced. Daubed across the arch, in dripping blood, were two words.

HE RISES

"Even so," he persisted. "If Dracula and Valeri released the prisoners, then we're playing right into their hands."

"Thank you, Lieutenant Carpenter," said Holmwood drily. "We hadn't been able to figure that out for ourselves."

"So why are you doing it then?"

Holmwood looked over at Jack. "Lieutenant Williams? Play the Crowthorne footage, please."

Jack nodded and pressed a series of keys. A new window opened on the wall screen, filled with a stationary image of a picturesque village street. He pressed PLAY and the image began to move, the black and white footage scrolling smoothly. A row of terraced houses was visible, the gardens neat, the pavement beyond the low walls clean and tidy. A small car was parked in the middle of the frame; its windscreen reflected the light of the street lamp that stood above it.

After a few seconds, there was movement. A middle-aged man ran down the centre of the street, his arms flailing, his feet pounding the tarmac. He reached the car and slid into a crouch beside its radiator, facing the way he had come. Moments later a second man strolled into the shot; he wore a long white hospital gown, his feet were bare, and his eyes glowed ferociously. As he approached the parked car, he appeared to be smiling.

The vampire stopped, and for a long moment nothing happened; the two men seemed to be in conversation, regarding each other from opposite ends of the vehicle. Then the vampire reached down and casually flipped the car across the road. It skidded over the tarmac, sending up showers of sparks, before crashing into a garden wall on the other side and coming to a halt.

Gasps filled the air of the Ops Room; Jamie glanced round the table and saw expressions of shock on the faces of his colleagues.

On the screen, the helpless man stood up, entirely exposed, and raised his hands in a futile plea for mercy. The vampire took half a step forward, then blurred across the screen, lifting the man into the air and carrying him out of the frame.

Jack pressed a button and the footage paused, freezing the upturned car where it now lay. The Interim Director turned back to face the Zero Hour Task Force.

"The vampire in that footage had been turned for a maximum of forty-five minutes," he said. "Does anyone want to tell me what's wrong with that picture?"

"Jesus," said Patrick Williams. "He was *strong*."

"And fast," said Dominique. "Too fast."

"Correct," said Holmwood. "The vampires who have been destroyed so far all exhibited strength and speed far beyond what would normally be expected of the newly-turned."

"How come?" asked Amy Andrews.

"We don't know. Science Division is examining the two inmates we've recovered, but they've found nothing so far. But there is obviously something different about these vamps, and there are about three hundred of them out there right now. *That's* why this is our number-one priority, Lieutenant Carpenter, because this Department's mission is to protect the public from the supernatural. Do you understand?"

"I do, sir," said Jamie. "How come the Science Division is examining the captives? Shouldn't that be a Lazarus Project thing?"

Holmwood shook his head. "I don't want Lazarus diverted from its primary task. Dr Cooper is liaising with Professor Karlsson and, if he genuinely needs their help, I've authorised him to ask for it."

"OK," said Jamie.

"Good," said Holmwood. "Anything else?"

"Where's Angela, sir?" asked Jack Williams. "She should be here for this."

"Lieutenant Darcy and her squad are in the field," replied Holmwood. "They were active when the first calls started to come in. They're due back within the hour."

Jack nodded, unable to keep his obvious concern from his face.

"All right," said Holmwood. "Anything else? No? In which case—"

"What about Zero Hour?" said Jamie. "How are we going to protect the public if Dracula is allowed to rise?"

Holmwood fixed Jamie with a cold stare. "The men who escaped from Broadmoor had been removed from society, Lieutenant Carpenter. Many of them suffer from the most severe personality disorders, a large number have long histories of violent and unpredictable behaviour, and the majority are dependent on pharmaceutical assistance. They have been turned in such a way as to make them unusually powerful, something that is worrying and new in itself, and in the next few hours every one of them is going to become insatiably hungry for running blood. If we don't take them down, there might not *be* a public to protect."

Jamie dropped his gaze.

"So what's the plan, sir?" asked Patrick Williams, his voice steady, his jaw set firm.

Cal Holmwood looked at him. "Search and destroy," he replied, softly. "As quickly as possible. It's as simple as that."

Jamie looked at the overturned car on the screen.

Right, he thought. *Simple.*

2

LAZARUS REVAMPED

Matt Browning pushed open the heavy door in the centre of the Level F corridor, as excited as a child on Christmas morning, and saw that, despite the early hour, he was not the first member of the Lazarus Project to arrive for work. Professor Karlsson looked up as he entered, gave him a smile and a brief nod, then returned his attention to a page of text resting on his desk.

He is the boss, thought Matt, smiling to himself. *I suppose I shouldn't be surprised.*

The reconstruction of the Lazarus Project had been undertaken with great urgency in the aftermath of the loss of Admiral Henry Seward. Cal Holmwood had given Matt, its only surviving member, *carte blanche* to make recommendations; he had done so, putting his natural shyness aside once he came to realise that he was not going to get into trouble for saying what he thought. His very first suggestion was that Blacklight make every possible effort to persuade Professor Robert Karlsson, the Director of the Swedish Institute for Genetic Research, to become the new head of the project. He had been aware of Karlsson's work for some time, and considered him one of the cleverest people on the planet, a towering intellect whose area of specialisation was the manipulation of replicator enzymes within DNA, making him the perfect candidate to advance the search for a cure for vampirism.

Holmwood had nodded with polite incomprehension. Four days later Karlsson had arrived at the Loop with a small suitcase and a leather satchel full of portable hard drives. He had been introduced to Matt, listened politely as the teenager gushed at him like an adolescent girl meeting her favourite pop star, then suggested they got to work.

Today was to be the first day of the fully staffed, fully equipped, fully functional second incarnation of the Lazarus Project. Karlsson and Matt had spent the last month recruiting the finest minds from around the globe, rebuilding and expanding the laboratories, and overseeing the installation of the most powerful local computer network in Europe.

Every minute of time that was not consumed by the practicalities of rebuilding was devoted to analysing the data on the hard drive that had been salvaged from Professor Richard Talbot, the former head of the Lazarus Project and a servant of Valeri Rusmanov whose real name they now believed had been Christopher Reynolds. The hard drive had been recovered when Jamie Carpenter shot the treacherous Professor in the head, as Matt lay unconscious on the floor between them. Reynolds had murdered the Project's entire staff, and had been about to kill Matt and make good his escape when Jamie intervened. It was thanks to Reynolds that it had taken a month to re-staff the Project; the background checks carried out on every potential recruit had been thorough to the point of being overtly invasive, as a repeat of the Professor's treachery simply could not be permitted.

Reynolds had been working on vampire genetics for more than a decade, and had acquired the bulk of his data via methods that were as immoral as they were criminal: vivisection, live experimentation, torture. His work, in particular his mapping of the vampire genome and his analysis of the physical effects of vampirism on a turned human being, was proving invaluable to everything the new Lazarus Project was doing. Without it, the scale of the task might well have seemed insurmountable.

With it, there was hope: if nothing else, there was a place to begin.

The process of analysing and building upon the recovered data was already under way; each new member of the Project that arrived had immediately got started. But this morning was to be the official beginning, as it were, and Matt knew full well that the page of text that Karlsson was poring over was the speech he was about to give. He left his boss to it and made his way to one of the desks by the far wall of the wide room. He logged in to the Lazarus Project's secure server, opened the analysis he had been working on until only a few hours earlier, and lost himself in the incredible complexity of the building blocks of the human body.

By ten past seven, all thirty-two members of the Lazarus Project were at their desks. There was a hum of intensity, the buzz of great intellects bent to a single purpose, a purpose as noble as any in the history of scientific research. Matt's gaze was drawn, as it often was, to the narrow, pretty face of Natalia Lenski, the almost superhumanly clever eighteen-year-old Russian who sat five desks away from him. She had been recruited by the SPC, the Russian Supernatural Protection Commissariat, out of the University of Leningrad, where she had been studying for her doctorate, having attained her Master's degree four years earlier, when she was fourteen. Her skin was as pale as Siberian snow, her blonde hair only a shade or two darker. She glanced up from her screen and smiled at him as Matt felt heat roar into his cheeks; his eyes widened and he jerked his head back towards his monitor, mortified.

Oh God. Oh God oh God oh God.

Slowly, millimetre by agonising millimetre, Matt turned his head back in her direction, using the very edges of his peripheral vision, and saw, to his utter horror, that she was still looking at him, the smile on her face unchanged. He was rescued from these terrible, seemingly endless seconds by Professor Karlsson, who chose that precise moment to get to his feet, walk quickly to the front of the room and bang on the nearest desk with his hand. Instantly, the spell was broken; every man and woman in the room, including Natalia, turned their attention towards their Director, who looked distinctly uncomfortable as their gazes settled on him.

"Good morning," he said, his voice unsteady. "It's good to see us all together for the first time. Very good indeed."

There was a murmur of approval from the watching scientists.

"Mr Browning," continued Karlsson, locking eyes with the teenager. "Matt. Could you come up here, please?"

Matt's colleagues turned to him, smiles and expressions of encouragement on their faces, and assumed the crimson hue of his face was the result of being singled out by the Director; only Natalia knew differently. Matt pushed his chair back and got nervously to his feet. He walked slowly to the front of the room and stood stiffly next to Professor Karlsson; his Director was looking at him with an expression of great pride, and Matt felt a smile rise on his face as the heat in his cheeks began to recede. He was suddenly incredibly happy; he felt full of purpose, full of righteous determination.

"Ladies and gentlemen," said Karlsson, looking out across the ranks of the Lazarus Project. "We have in our hands an opportunity to do great good. To save thousands, perhaps millions, of lives and to eradicate a disease more deadly than that being worked on in any laboratory in the world. This Project represents *the* furthest frontier of scientific research, and each and every one of us should be proud at having been given the chance to be a part of it."

Karlsson continued to talk, but Matt was no longer listening. Instead, his thoughts had turned to his mother, to how proud she would be if she could see him and what he was doing, and to the last month, which had been without doubt the happiest of his life.

For the first time in his life, he felt like he belonged. It was a dizzying sensation for Matt, a boy who had spent the majority of his life alone, ashamed of himself and unwilling to put anything more than the absolute minimum of himself forward; long experience had taught him that the more you allowed the world to know about you, the more it would use that information to hurt you. But he no longer believed that. Here, in this strange, unlikely place beneath the forests of eastern England, he had found true friendship, created under the most intense pressure, and a cause to which he was quite prepared to dedicate the rest of his life, if that was what was required.

"Get to work," said Karlsson, and the round of applause that met the end of the Director's speech roused Matt from his thoughts. He joined in, quickly enough that he was sure no one would notice he had been daydreaming, and as the men and women of the Lazarus Project began to return to their work, to the undertaking that each and every one of them had sacrificed the prospect of a normal existence for, Matt saw Natalia Lenski glance in his direction before she turned to her console, her pale cheeks flushed a beautiful, delicate pink.

3

SLOW NEWS DAY

WAPPING, LONDON
THREE MONTHS EARLIER

Kevin McKenna dropped the last of his cigarette into the warm can of lager on his desk and checked his watch.

It was almost nine thirty and he was the only member of *The Globe*'s editorial team still in the office. England were playing Portugal in Oporto and everyone else was either across the road in The Ten Bells, cheering and drinking and swearing, or on their way home, grateful for an excuse to leave the office at a reasonable time without appearing lazy. McKenna wanted to be in the pub with his colleagues, but the phone call he had received an hour earlier had been simply too intriguing to ignore. So, instead, he was sitting in his office with the door shut and the smoke detector unplugged, waiting for a courier to bring him a package from a dead man.

The call had come from a lawyer McKenna didn't know; it wasn't one of the many to whom he regularly passed white envelopes of cash in return for five minutes alone with the case files of celebrity lawsuits and super-injunctions. The man had been polite, and had solemnly informed McKenna that his firm was discharging the estate of the late Mr John Bathurst. There had been a long pause, which McKenna had clearly been expected to fill with gratitude, or sorrow, or both. But he had not known what to say: the name was utterly meaningless.

Then a flash of realisation had hit him, and he had laughed loudly down the phone.

The lawyer's voice, when it reappeared, had a hint of reproach in it, but the man remained smoothly professional. He told McKenna that he had been left an item in Mr Bathurst's will, an envelope, and asked whether he would like it couriered to him. In any other circumstance, McKenna would have told the man to put it in the post and made his way to the pub. Instead, he gave the lawyer *The Globe*'s address and told him he would wait to sign for it.

You're dead and you're still causing me grief, he thought, lighting another cigarette. *Mr John bloody Bathurst.*

There was a simple reason why it had taken him a moment to realise he knew the name of the man who had remembered him in his will: he had only ever heard it spoken aloud a single time, and there was a reason for that as well.

It was Johnny Supernova's real name, and his most closely guarded secret.

There had been a time when Kevin McKenna would have spat in the face of anyone who had dared to suggest that he might one day spend his time writing stories about minor celebrities for a publication as morally bankrupt and pro-establishment as *The Globe*.

This younger, slimmer, angrier version of himself had arrived in London in 1995 at the age of nineteen, his ears ringing with guitar bands and house music and his veins full of working-class fire, to start work as a journalist for legendary left-wing style bible *The*

Gutter. He strolled into the magazine's offices off Pentonville Road to be greeted by a receptionist more beautiful than any girl he had ever seen in his nineteen years in Manchester. She held open the door to the editor's office and gave him a ridiculously provocative smile as he walked through it.

Sitting behind a huge glass desk, on which were arranged glossy colour spreads of the latest issue, was Jeremy Black. He wore a charcoal-grey suit, which McKenna knew without asking would be either Paul Smith or Ozwald Boateng, over a faded tour T-shirt for the Beatles. He glanced up as McKenna stopped in front of his desk.

"Beer?" he asked.

"Sure," replied McKenna. It was barely eleven thirty in the morning, but he had no intention of looking like a lightweight in front of his new boss.

Black reached down and pulled two cans from a fridge that McKenna couldn't see. He handed one over, then leant back in his chair and folded his hands behind his head. "I don't want to see you in here more than a couple of times a week," he said. "If you're in the office, you're not doing your job. Yeah? The stories are out there."

"Got it," replied McKenna, opening his beer and taking a long swig that he hoped was full of casual bravado.

"Leave your copy at reception. I'll give you a call if it's good enough."

"All right."

"I got someone to agree to show you the ropes. He's going to hate you, and he's going to treat you like shit, but he owes me about ten thousand words I've already paid him for, so that's his bad luck. Yours too, probably."

"Who is it?" asked McKenna, as a smile crept on to his boss's face.

Jeremy Black was right: Johnny Supernova did indeed treat him like shit. But McKenna didn't care.

Supernova was a legend, a freewheeling, anarchic genius who roared through the London night like a drug-fuelled hurricane. His writing was a reflection of the man, a furious avalanche of beautifully written invective, shot through with language and imagery that would have embarrassed Caligula: despatches from the bleeding edge of popular culture which served to define the time almost as much as the events they described.

The man himself was small and wiry, with pallid skin and a shock of black hair. He was older than McKenna, almost forty, maybe more. His eyes were narrow and piercing, and his appetites, for drink, drugs and debauchery, were famously prodigious. He greeted McKenna with obvious suspicion when they met for the first time, but allowed him to join him at his table in the Groucho Club, clearly still sufficiently connected to reality that he had no desire to be sued by *The Gutter* for breach of contract.

Back then, at that brief moment of cultural awakening, Johnny Supernova had been king. Pop stars, artists, actors, actresses and directors: they all flowed to his table and fawned over him. Kevin sat at his side, night after night, in the tall building in Soho, basking in his mentor's reflected glory. He was older, and cleverer, and harsher than them all, and as a result, they worshipped him.

But it couldn't last, and it didn't.

The drugs, the booze, the endless girls and boys: all were fuel for the vicious self-loathing that burned inside Johnny Supernova, that drove him to examine the worst depths of human behaviour.

What had been fun became hard to watch as Supernova's edge began to slip, taking with it the hold over the glitterati he had once had. His table became a little more empty, his writing a little more soft, lacking the razor-sharp precision with which it had once slashed at its readers. Excess takes its toll eventually and, when it does, it either happens gradually, slowly, almost imperceptibly, or all at once, like an avalanche. For Johnny Supernova, it was the former. His star faded, rather than burning out.

McKenna was hanging on by his last fingernail by then; the craziness had ceased to be fun and had begun to feel like work. Johnny appeared to be shrinking before his eyes, week on week, month on month. Eventually, in late 2006, McKenna bought him dinner, told him that he was tired, that he wanted a little bit of stability, a little bit of normality, and that he had taken a job at *The Globe*.

The explosion he had expected didn't come.

Instead, Supernova gave him a red-eyed look of disappointment that was infinitely more painful. "You're the worst of them all," he said, his eyes fixed on McKenna's. "You could have been good. You could have *mattered*. But you're just a whore like the rest of them."

They never spoke again.

The phone on McKenna's desk rang, making him jump. He had been lost in the past, drifting through the memories of a man he realised he had almost forgotten.

He reached out and picked up the receiver.

"Courier for you," said the receptionist.

"Send him up," said McKenna.

The courier arrived a minute later. Kevin signed for the package, thanked the man, and settled back in his chair to open it. He tore through the tape and the bubble wrap until he was looking at what

Johnny Supernova had left him: an audio cassette, a thin folder and a sheet of thick creamy paper. McKenna placed the tape and the folder on his desk, lifted the sheet of paper, and read the short message that had been typed on it.

Kevin,

If there is still some tiny worm of integrity in that black void you call a soul, maybe this will give it something to chew on.

Johnny

McKenna couldn't help but smile, despite the insult.

As he read the words, he heard them spoken in Johnny Supernova's thick Mancunian accent, spat out as if they tasted bitter. He realised it had been four years since he had last heard that voice, seen the gaunt, narrow face from which it emerged. Supernova had died three months ago, from a heroin overdose that had surprised precisely no one.

McKenna had been too ashamed to go to the funeral.

He put the note down on his desk, considered the cassette, then decided it would be too much trouble to find a player at this time of night and picked up the folder instead. Inside was a small sheaf of copier paper, almost transparent, with faded black ink punched almost all the way through it. McKenna lifted the first sheet and read the header.

TRANSCRIPT
INTERVIEW WITH ALBERT HARKER. JUNE 12 2002

Barely a decade ago, thought Kevin. *Jesus Christ, it seems so much longer.*

In 2002 Johnny Supernova was past his prime: still famous, still infamous, still relevant, but fading fast, starting to realise, with disappointed bile in his heart, that his angry brand of burn-it-all-down cynicism was becoming a tougher and tougher sell in the New Labour wonderland. McKenna read the header again.

Albert Harker. Never heard of him.

He lifted another can of lager out of the bottom drawer of his desk, lit a new cigarette with the smouldering end of the last one, and began to read.

A minute later he paused, his drink forgotten.

"Jesus," he muttered.

Five minutes later his cigarette burned down to the filter and hung, dead, in the corner of his mouth, spilling ash on to his lap.

McKenna didn't even notice.

THE DESERT SHOULD BE NO PLACE FOR A VAMPIRE

LINCOLN COUNTY, NEVADA, USA,
YESTERDAY

Donny Beltran leant back in his chair and stared up into the dark desert sky. Stars hung above his head, an infinite vista of flickering yellow and milky white that he could have watched for hours had Walt not announced that the burgers were ready, jerking him out of his awe and eliciting a loud rumble from his ample stomach.

Donny picked his chair up, lumbered to his feet and made his way over to where Walt Beauford was plucking burgers from a metal grill and placing them on a plastic plate beside white buns and sachets of ketchup and mustard. He fished another beer out of the cool box as his friend approached; Donny took it, twisted off the cap, and took a long swallow. He belched loudly, wiped his mouth with the back of his hand, and grinned at his friend. The two men settled into their chairs and began to eat their supper; they were completely at ease in each other's company, the result of two and a half decades of friendship that had started at college in

51

California, and had survived the pleasant, unavoidable diversions of marriages and children.

This weekend, though, was sacred.

It was the anniversary of the strange, surreal day in 1997 when they had sold five per cent of their shares in the search engine they had helped found to a private investment group in San Francisco, and realised with genuine bemusement that they had both become millionaires. They had celebrated by taking Donny's old van out to Joshua Tree, where they drank whisky and smoked grass and reminisced, and it was now traditional for them to head into the desert for two days every year.

Donny wolfed his burger down in three bites. Walt ate slowly, savouring each mouthful, and was still finishing his first as his friend was attacking his third. They ate in companionable silence, their eyes fixed on the skies to the west, above the low hills that shielded Area 51 from unwelcome eyes. Their little clockwork radio sat on the desert floor between them; they had found a Las Vegas classic rock station at the edge of the dial and Bruce Springsteen's 'Highway Patrolman' was crackling softly out of the speakers.

Donny finished the last of his burgers, felt his stomach rumble appreciatively, and settled himself in his chair. The two friends would stay like this until they fell asleep. Eventually, one of them would wake up and rouse the other, and they would stumble into their tent to see out the rest of the rapidly cooling night. It was a familiar routine, and one they enjoyed immensely.

"What's that?" asked Walt.

Donny grinned. The first time they had come up here, almost a decade earlier, they had spent most of their first night claiming to see something in the distance, trying to make each other jump. But they had never seen anything in the famous Area 51 skies apart from regular military jets and helicopters, and Donny had no intention of falling for this old routine.

"Nothing," he said, without even turning his head. "Just like it was nothing last year, like it's always been nothing. Don't even try it, Walt."

"I'm serious."

Something in Walt's voice made Donny look round. It wasn't fear, or even unease; it sounded more like incredulity. He turned his head slowly and saw Walt pointing towards the northern horizon. He followed his friend's finger and looked.

In the distance, a tiny red light was moving smoothly through the night sky. It was perhaps half a mile away, little more than a pinprick in the darkness, but it was darting quickly through the air, seeming to change direction rapidly. Then Donny realised something else.

It was moving in their direction.

"What the hell is that?" he said.

"No idea," replied Walt, his gaze fixed on the approaching light. "It's small, whatever it is."

"No sound either," said Donny. "No engine. Listen."

The two friends fell silent. Out on the highway, a car rumbled quickly past. But from the north, the direction the glowing dot was coming from, there was no sound of any kind.

The light swirled and swooped through the sky with dizzying speed. It accelerated in one direction for a second or two, appeared to stop dead and hover, then zoomed away in another direction entirely. It flickered, as though it was rapidly turning on and off, then shot towards the ground, so low that it seemed to scrape the desert floor, before rocketing back into the sky. And it was getting closer, second by second, to the two watching men.

"Can't be a plane," said Donny. "Too quiet. Too quick."

"Maybe a drone?" said Walt. "Some new model?"

"Maybe," replied Donny, but he didn't think so. The speed and the angles of the light's movement were too fast, too sudden, for even the smallest remote aircraft. He stared at the dancing light, fascinated, then felt the breath catch in his throat as it accelerated directly towards them. It swooped low, and now, for the first time, Donny *could* hear something: the rattling of desert sand as whatever it was passed above it at incredible speed. He opened his mouth to say something to Walt, but didn't get the chance.

The glowing red light hurtled through their campsite, barely two metres above their heads. Their barbecue thudded to the ground and their tent fluttered heavily in the rushing air, its canvas sides rattling out a suddenly deafening drumbeat. Plates and cups and empty beer cans leapt into the air and Donny raised a protective arm across his eyes, feeling his weight shift as he did so. His gaze was still fixed on the patch of sky through which the light had passed at incredible, unbelievable speed, and he overbalanced, hearing the plastic of his chair rip as he thudded to the ground. Walt was beside him immediately, dragging him to his feet, then shushing him before he uttered a single word. The two men stood in the middle of their scattered campsite, listening intently, scanning the skies for the red light.

There was no sign of it in any direction.

It was gone.

"What. The. Hell. Was. That?" asked Donny.

"I don't know," replied Walt, his eyes shining with excitement. "I've never seen anything move like that. Never. And I..." He trailed off, still staring up into the sky.

"You what?" asked Donny. He was beginning to smile at the

incredible weirdness of the moment, glad that he had shared it with his friend.

"I thought I... heard something," said Walt. "When it passed through, just for a second. Something crazy."

"What was it?"

"Laughter," said Walt, a smile of embarrassment rising on his face. "It sounded like a girl, laughing."

Fifty metres above their heads, Larissa Kinley floated in the cool air, a smile of unbridled pleasure on her pale, beautiful face.

It had been reckless to swoop through the little campsite, and it was almost certainly a breach of regulations, but she didn't care; she knew full well that neither of the men had been able to see her at the speed she had been moving, just as she knew they wouldn't be able to see her now, even if they happened to look directly at her. The matt-black material of her Blacklight uniform disappeared completely into the darkness of the desert sky. And neither man *was* looking, in any case; they were chatting excitedly to each other, their words perfectly audible to her supernatural ears. She savoured their conversation for a few moments, then spun elegantly in the air and flew slowly back towards the wide white expanse of the dry bed of Groom Lake.

Larissa loved the desert.

Its vast expanse made her feel tiny; made her feel free. She would obviously have been forbidden from flying during the hours of daylight even if doing so wouldn't have caused her to burst into flames, but once the sun was down, she was allowed to take to the skies. Such freedom was wonderful after more than three months in Department 19, where her every movement was scrutinised and subject to seemingly dozens of rules and regulations. Part of it was simple geography: the Loop was hidden away in the middle of one of the most densely populated countries in the world, whereas NS9 sat at the centre of several hundred square miles of land that belonged to the US government, land that no member of the public was permitted to enter. Everyone knew Area 51 existed, but no one knew what really happened there, and the military were quite happy to let the UFO conspiracies run and run; they worked as a fantastically efficient red herring.

She had been in the desert for almost three weeks. When Cal Holmwood had told her that she was being sent on secondment to NS9, she had immediately assumed she was being punished for something. It had seemed unthinkably cruel that the Interim Director, who was fully aware of the situation that had developed between herself and Jamie Carpenter, would send her halfway around the world to do a job that any number of Operators could do just as well. But she was beginning to revise her opinion of his motives.

Larissa missed Jamie and Kate and Matt; her friends made her happy, and Jamie made her positively blissful at times. But they were often the only things inside Blacklight that did. She was a vampire member of an organisation whose sole reason for existing was to destroy vampires, and although she had proved herself time and again since being allowed to join, there were plenty of Operators inside the Loop who still looked at her with barely concealed disgust. Part of it was the fact that she had spent her first days there in a cell on the detention level, part of it was the perception that she had endangered the life of Jamie's mother to serve her own needs, but mostly it was the mere fact of who, and what, she was. She was surrounded by hostility, and suspicion, with no indication that either was going to end any time soon.

At NS9 she had instantly been given a fresh start, the clean slate she knew she would never be granted at the Loop. She had been made to feel welcome and valued, and had made friends, so quickly and naturally that it had surprised her: men and women whose company she enjoyed, who made her feel normal and gave her energetic self-loathing a rest. As she drifted over Papoose Lake, descending slowly towards the wide-open doors of the NS9 hangar, she saw one of them waiting for her in the long rectangle of yellow light. She slipped easily to the ground and smiled at Tim Albertsson, who grinned back at her with his perfectly straight, perfectly white, all-American teeth.

The tall, broad former Navy SEAL was Larissa's handler during her secondment in the desert. He was of Scandinavian descent, as his blond hair and blue eyes would readily attest, and a member of NS9's elite Special Operator programme.

"Nice flight?" he asked.

"Very nice," she replied. "Beautiful in fact. It felt like I could see all the way to the ocean."

"With your eyes, you probably could," said Tim.

Larissa laughed. "Maybe."

"Dinner?" asked Tim. "I'm meeting everyone in the diner."

"I can't right now," replied Larissa. "I've got a meeting with the Director, and I'm going to try to call home in a few hours. But I'll come round if I get time in between."

Tim nodded. "Say hello to Jamie for me if you don't make it," he said.

"I will," said Larissa, knowing that she wouldn't.

"Cool," he said, and smiled widely. "I might see you later then."

"Maybe," she said, and walked into the hangar, her heart thumping in her chest.

*

Larissa waited until the lift began to descend, then leant heavily against the metal wall.

Her heart was refusing to slow down. Part of the reason, she knew, was Tim, with his handsome face and his hair and his casual, easy-going confidence, but it was mostly because of the realisation that had been steadily building inside her for the last week or so. It intensified whenever she was about to speak to Jamie, because it was the one thing she couldn't tell him; the one thing she knew he wouldn't want to hear.

She got out of the lift on Level 1 and floated along the corridor. She never thought twice about flying inside the NS9 base, never felt self-conscious or worried that the next person she saw would give her the look of contempt she had become all too used to. Inside the base that everyone called Dreamland, the only emotion her vampire abilities provoked with any regularity was good-natured jealousy from Operators who wished they had her strength and speed.

Larissa knocked on the door of the Director's quarters and felt it swing slightly open. The door was rarely closed, let alone locked, and she had never seen a single guard stationed outside it; it was just one of the many ways that NS9 differed from Blacklight. She pushed it open, calling General Allen's name as she did so.

"Come on in," shouted a voice.

Larissa floated through the door. The room beyond was square with a wide desk standing to one side. On the wall opposite a vast black screen had been hung, reaching almost from floor to ceiling, and at the back of the room stood a wooden table on which was arranged a silver tray full of bottles: whisky, brandy, vodka, gin. Beneath the table was a small grey fridge that Larissa knew was always full. The table stood between two doors that led into the rest of the General's quarters; above it, the wall was covered with pennants and banners and scarves in the black and gold colours of the West Point football team.

Larissa had spent a number of evenings in this friendly, comfortable room since arriving at NS9. General Allen was a warm, garrulous conversationalist and she enjoyed his company immensely. He regaled her with stories of the men and women she had met during her secondment and the ones she had left behind in England, stories of adventure and daring and blood and death. Last time, he had told tales of Henry Seward and Julian Carpenter, two men for whom the General had enormous affection. She had listened intently as he described the three of them, all young and full of fire, determined to destroy every vampire on the planet; they had fought alongside each other countless times, their paths crossing often enough for the two Englishmen and the American to become friends. They had remained close, even as geography separated them, and it was obvious to Larissa that the loss of Henry Seward had hit General Allen hard, coming as it did less than three years after the death of Julian Carpenter.

Their first conversation had turned into a subtle interrogation of Department 19's ability to find Admiral Seward and bring him home; Larissa got the distinct impression that only protocol was preventing General Allen from shipping the entire NS9 roster to Europe to aid in the search for his lost friend. She had reminded him that he knew Cal Holmwood and Paul Turner were good men, and reassured him that they were doing everything they could; her presence in Nevada was proof that they were keen to restore Blacklight to full strength as quickly as possible so they might better hunt for their lost Director, and Allen had appeared satisfied, at least outwardly.

Larissa floated to the pair of sofas that dominated the centre of the room. They were angled towards the screen with a long wooden coffee table before them; she took a seat and waited for the Director to appear. She was hopeful that General Allen might continue his tales of Jamie's father; she loved hearing them, and had taken to writing them down in a small notebook she kept in her quarters. Her plan was to give the notebook to Jamie when she got home; she hoped it might help him to know the real man his father had been.

A minute or so later one of the doors at the back of the living room opened and General Allen emerged. He was a large man, tall and broad through the shoulders, and carried himself with the upright ease of a lifelong soldier. He was dressed in a white T-shirt and combat trousers and was towelling the last remnants of shaving foam from his ears and chin as he strolled into the room. He saw the vampire girl sitting on the sofa and grinned broadly.

"Larissa," he said. "Good to see you. Drink?"

"Diet Coke, please, sir."

Allen nodded, and took a can from his fridge. He selected a beer for himself, then handed the can and a glass full of ice to Larissa. She thanked him, and poured her drink as the General twisted the cap off his own. He flopped down on to the sofa opposite her and took a long pull from his bottle.

"Tim says you're scaring the hell out of the trainees," he said. "Apparently, a couple of them asked to be transferred back to their units."

"Oh God," said Larissa, her face flushing pink. "I'm sorry, sir. I didn't mean for that to happen."

"Don't worry about it," said the Director, smiling broadly. "They've all been turned down. You opened their eyes, that's all. They'll get over it. And if they can't, they're no use to us."

Larissa nodded. "I suppose not, sir."

"Your Operational reports have also been excellent. Uniformly so."

"That's good to hear, sir."

Allen nodded. "Have you talked to Jamie?"

"Not for a couple of days, sir. I'm going to call him tonight."

"That's good," said General Allen. "It still blows my mind to think about what he did to Alexandru Rusmanov. A kid his age? Unbelievable."

Larissa felt pride explode through her chest. "He doesn't think it was that big a deal, sir," she replied. "He thinks he did what he had to do. I've tried to tell him he's wrong, but he won't hear it."

"He *is* wrong," said General Allen. "Do you know how many Operators have lost their lives to Alexandru over the years? Older, far more experienced men and women than him? Too many to count, Larissa, and every one of them was trying to do what needed doing. Only he actually did it."

Larissa beamed. She loved the awe with which her boyfriend was regarded on this side of the Atlantic, from rookie Operators all the way up to the Director himself. Jamie was nothing short of a legend: the teenager who had destroyed Alexandru Rusmanov, who had taken a squad of men and women into the lair of the oldest vampire in Paris and rescued Victor Frankenstein, who had earned the trust of Henry Seward and the grudging respect of Paul Turner. She felt no jealousy when people asked her about him, just pride, and love.

"I know, sir," she said. "You should tell *him*."

"I will," said General Allen. "One day, I definitely will."

"He'll appreciate it, sir."

"Do you miss him?" asked the Director. "Are you looking forward to going home?"

Larissa considered this: two different questions, with two different answers.

"I miss him," she said.

General Allen nodded. "I'm hearing nothing but great things about you," he said. "Tim's just about ready to adopt you. I'm sure you've noticed."

"That's nice to hear, sir."

"We probably could, you know," said Allen, his grey eyes suddenly fixed on hers. "Arrange a permanent transfer, I mean. What would you think about something like that?"

Larissa felt her stomach churn with desire. She pictured herself flying through the great open spaces surrounding Dreamland, eating and drinking and laughing with her friends in the diner at the edge of the runway, training recruits and helping NS9 on Operations throughout the length and breadth of this vast, unfamiliar country.

"What about Jamie?" she asked. "Could you have him transferred too?"

General Allen laughed. "Nothing would give me greater pleasure, Larissa, I can assure you of that. But I think the chances of Cal Holmwood letting that happen are somewhere very close to zero."

Bob Allen watched as Larissa closed the door behind her, then got up and reached into his fridge for another beer. As he removed the cap, the sense of conflict that always arose in the aftermath of talking to Larissa made its presence known in his stomach, where it twisted gently. His excitement at discussing Blacklight's new generation with the vampire girl was tempered by a sense of guilt, of having betrayed the man who was currently locked in a cell eight floors below his feet.

He had told Larissa the truth: one day he would meet Jamie Carpenter and, when he did, he intended to shake him by the hand

and congratulate him. That wouldn't be enough, but there were no words that were sufficient for what Jamie had done, no way to do it justice. Bob Allen would never have permitted a lone Operator to face a Priority Level 1 vampire, especially not one as old and dangerous as Alexandru Rusmanov; he doubted, in fact, whether he would have sent less than fifty of his finest Operators to face him. But Jamie had faced him alone, with minimal weapons and training, and prevailed.

Yet, despite his genuine admiration, Bob Allen feared Jamie Carpenter. Specifically, he feared how the boy might react if he ever found out the truth: that on both sides of the Atlantic, men he was expected to trust with his life were keeping his father's survival a secret from him.

The Director drained his second beer and headed for the door. At the end of the corridor stood the elevator that would take him down to the detention level, where the man he had described to Larissa as one of his closest friends would be waiting for him, alone in the darkness.

5

EVERYTHING HEALS, IN TIME

Kate Randall wiped her eyes and splashed water on her face. It was the first time she had cried in almost two and a half days, a new personal best since the night a month earlier when she had watched her boyfriend die.

She was standing in the bathroom within the small suite of rooms that had been commandeered by ISAT, the Internal Security Assessment Team. In the centre was the interview room, containing a seat flanked by two metal cabinets of monitoring equipment, a desk and two plastic chairs. Outside the entrance to the interview room was a small lobby, separated from the rest of the Intelligence Division by a heavy steel door, which was accessed by a nine-digit code known only to three people. To the left of the lobby stood a door, leading into a small living room and kitchen. The thin plaster wall of the living room contained two further doors; one led into the small quarters that the ISAT Director had taken to sleeping in, the other into the bathroom where Kate had just stopped crying.

There was a gentle knock on the door behind her.

"One minute," she called.

"Are you all right?" asked a male voice, full of concern.

"I'm fine," she replied. "Just… give me a minute, OK?"

"OK," replied the voice. "We're ready when you are. Take your time."

Kate wiped her eyes a final time.

Get it together, she told herself, sharply. *He needs you.*

She stared at herself for a long moment in the mirror above the sink; she took a deep breath, held it, let it out, then turned and opened the bathroom door. Major Paul Turner was standing in the small ISAT living room, his arms folded across his chest. He smiled at her, almost, but not quite, managing to hide the expression of concern she had seen on his face as she emerged from the bathroom.

"Ready?" he asked.

"Ready," she replied.

Turner clapped her on the shoulder, his hand pausing momentarily before falling away, then led her out into the lobby and through the door to the interview room.

ISAT had been formed in the aftermath of Valeri Rusmanov's attack on the Loop, in response to a claim made by his brother Valentin during the interrogation that had followed his defection to Blacklight.

Paul Turner had asked the ancient vampire whether he had any information regarding the existence of double agents inside the Department. The sad case of Thomas Morris, the former Operator who had betrayed them to Valentin's brother Alexandru and had been responsible for the death of Julian Carpenter, had been assumed to be an isolated incident. Valentin's answer had immediately cast doubt over that assumption; he had claimed to know with absolute certainty that Valeri had maintained *at least* one agent inside the Department since its expansion in the 1920s.

Valentin had been able to offer no support for this claim, no names, no dates, no incriminating evidence, and the thought that it may have been intended to sow distrust within Blacklight had immediately occurred to everyone. But then the Loop had been attacked, by a vampire army that had made its way undetected beneath the radar arrays and through the motion detectors and laser nets, and the double life of Professor Christopher Reynolds had been uncovered; *he* had been in the employ of Valeri Rusmanov his entire life. As Cal Holmwood tried to piece the wounded, reeling Department back together, Paul Turner had approached him and quietly explained that they needed to clean house, as a matter of urgency. Holmwood had agreed and instructed Turner, the Department's Security Officer, to create a team to carry out the task.

"They're going to hate you for this, Paul," warned Holmwood. "But you're right, it needs doing. When you're ready to start interviewing, come and tell me. I'll go first."

Turner agreed, then set about the creation of ISAT, the first internal affairs team in the long, proud history of Blacklight.

Holmwood was right: they hated him for it. The knowledge that he was creating a team to investigate Operators leaked quickly through the Loop, and proved incredibly unpopular; it seemed cruel to subject men and women who had just fought for their lives, who had watched friends and colleagues fall at their sides, to new suspicion. The survivors felt they had proved themselves, that their loyalty had been shown beyond question. Paul Turner understood their position, but didn't care. And the whispered consensus within the Loop was that *why* he didn't care was obvious: as far as Turner was concerned, ISAT was a personal crusade. One of the Operators who died during the attack on the Loop was Shaun Turner, Paul's twenty-one-year-old son, who had also been Kate Randall's boyfriend.

As a result, the first dozen Operators that Turner approached about joining ISAT turned him down flat. They were too scared of the Security Officer, whose glacial grey eyes could turn even the boldest Operator's insides to water, to tell him exactly what they thought of his project, but not to reject his offer. Turner didn't hold it against them; he merely moved on to the next person on his list. He needed only a single Operator to share the ISAT burden, someone who could ensure his actions were above suspicion, and he would ask every single man and woman in the base if necessary. If they all said no, he would go back to the top of his list and ask them all again. But in the end, this proved unnecessary.

Kate told Jamie she was going to volunteer for ISAT before she did so; she wasn't asking his permission, but she didn't want him to find out from someone else. His response had been entirely as she expected.

"You're kidding," he said. "Why the hell would you do that?"

"I have my reasons," she replied, looking him directly in the eye. "I'm sure you can work out what they are."

"Of course I can," he snapped. "Obviously I can. But have you thought this through, Kate? Like, really thought it through? Everyone's going to hate you if you do this. Everyone."

"I don't care," she said. "Let them hate me."

He had tried to talk her out of it for a further half an hour, but once it became clear that she was not going to be persuaded to change her mind, he had done the second thing she had expected: told her that he would stick up for her, no matter what anyone else said or thought. She had thanked him, and given him a long hug that had brought tears to her eyes and a lump to her throat.

Larissa and Matt had both been amazing in the aftermath of Shaun's death, and could empathise with her, up to a point; both were living without the people they loved, in Matt's case voluntarily, in Larissa's as a result of what had been done to her by Grey, the ancient vampire who had turned her. They understood loneliness, and what it meant to miss someone, but they couldn't fully appreciate what she was going through. Jamie was the only one who could, having watched his father die less than three years earlier.

Kate would never have dreamt of suggesting that her loss in any way compared to his. She had only been with Shaun for a couple of months, barely any time at all, even given the hyper-reality of life inside Blacklight. She knew the loss of her boyfriend didn't come close to the loss of his father, and never tried to claim otherwise. But what it did mean was that Jamie understood the thing that she was struggling to find a way past, the same thing that had tormented him in the months that followed Julian Carpenter's death: the fact that Shaun was *gone*, that everything he had ever been, everything he might one day have become, had disappeared into nothing. She was never going to see him again, and neither was anyone else. He wasn't somewhere else, separated from her by distance or protocol or orders.

He was dead and he was never coming back.

Paul Turner's eyes had lit up when Kate entered his office and volunteered for ISAT.

She had spent a lot of time with the Security Officer since Shaun had died, a mutual support system that had been observed with utter bewilderment by the Operators of Blacklight, many of whom had never genuinely allowed for the possibility that Paul Turner might have human emotions. And, in all honesty, Kate had answered his request to see her the day after Shaun's death with a significant amount of trepidation; unlike Jamie, she had never spoken privately with the Security Officer and was not afraid to admit that she was scared of him. But he had welcomed her into his office that dark, terrible day with a warmth that she could never have expected or prepared herself for. He made her tea and asked her about his son; she told him about her boyfriend, and felt unsteady common ground form beneath them.

Kate had, in fact, become immensely fond of Major Turner, and she was increasingly sure the feeling was mutual. The last time she had gone to visit him, he had mentioned the prospect of her coming to meet Shaun's mother once all this horror was over. Caroline Turner, who was Henry Seward's sister as well as Paul's wife, and who therefore must be going through a hell that Kate couldn't even begin to imagine, with her son dead and her brother in the hands of the enemy, had apparently asked repeatedly to meet her. She had accepted gladly, and Turner told her they would arrange it when the time was right. As a result, her appearance at his door on the day she volunteered for ISAT was not a surprise. He had welcomed her in, and listened as she explained why she was there.

"Are you sure?" he asked, when she had finished.

"Yes."

"Thank you," he said, and hugged her. The sensation was so strange that for a long moment she stood stiffly in his arms, before gradually bringing her own up and wrapping them round his broad shoulders.

With Kate on board, ISAT was ready to go in less than a week. The rooms were equipped, the Intelligence Division briefed, and preliminary interviews carried out on the men and women who would be working for the team; this included Kate and Paul Turner, who insisted on going first. By this point, the Intelligence

Division had been carrying out the most invasive background checks in the history of the British Intelligence Services for almost a month; they had been Turner's first order as soon as ISAT was authorised by Cal Holmwood. Turner's was complete and had come back spotless. But the revised checks were only half of the process; the other half was an interview, with the subject attached to a lie-detector machine more sensitive than any available to the public.

The ISAT machines measured the same variables as regular lie detectors – heartrate, breathing patterns, perspiration etc. – but did so with a precision that was unmatched. They returned results that were 99.9 per cent accurate; from a mathematical perspective, they were as close to infallible as it was possible to be. The Intelligence Division staff had attached pads and wires to Paul Turner's body, and Kate had asked him the questions they had devised together; he passed, as no one had ever doubted for a second. Then Kate had taken her turn, followed by the eight members of the Intelligence Division that had been assigned to ISAT. All passed, and Major Turner had sent a message to Interim Director Holmwood, telling him they were ready for him.

That had been yesterday.

Cal Holmwood had also passed, to the surprise of precisely no one, and had given them the final order to begin. To avoid any possible accusations of agenda, they were taking the Operators in computer-randomised order; the first of them, Lieutenant Stephen Marshall, looked up as Kate and Turner entered the interview room. The pads and wires were already attached to his body, and his face bore an expression of outright contempt as they took their seats opposite him.

"Lieutenant Marshall," said Paul Turner. "Do you need anything before we begin?"

Marshall's face curdled with disgust. "Just get on with it," he spat.

"As you wish," replied Turner, and glanced over at Kate. She nodded, then opened her folder of questions to the first page.

"This is ISAT interview 012," she said. "Conducted by Lieutenant Kate Randall, NS303, 78-J in the presence of Major Paul Turner, NS303, 36-A. State your name, please."

"Lieutenant Stephen Marshall."

Kate looked down at the table; set into its surface was a small screen, angled in such a way that it could not be seen by the interviewee. Two grey boxes filled it; these displayed the results of the two sets of monitoring equipment that were humming quietly away on either side of Lieutenant Marshall's chair. After a millisecond or two, both boxes turned bright green. She nodded.

"Please answer the following *incorrectly*," said Kate. "State your gender."

Marshall smiled, slightly. "Female."

Both grey boxes turned red.

"OK," said Kate. "Let's get started. Are you a member of Department 19?"

"Yes."

Green.

"Do you currently hold the rank of Lieutenant?"

"Yes."

Green.

"Are you currently assigned to the Surveillance Division of said Department?"

"Yes."

Green.

"Do you understand that your position involves the acquisition and analysis of data that is classified above Top Secret?"

"Yes."

Green.

"Have you ever used your position for any purpose other than directly specified in your orders?"

Marshall tensed with anger. "No," he said.

Red.

"I would ask you to think very carefully about your last answer," said Paul Turner. "Lieutenant Randall is going to ask you the question again."

Marshall's face began to colour a deep crimson. "This is absolutely—"

"Lieutenant Marshall," interrupted Kate. "Have you ever used your position for any purpose other than directly specified in your orders?"

"Yes," spat Marshall. "You obviously know I have."

Green.

"Please explain the circumstances that led to your last answer," said Kate.

"My girlfriend and I were having problems," said Marshall, his face burning red, his voice like ice. "She was acting weird, being secretive, lying about stuff. So I listened in on a couple of her phone calls."

Green.

"When did this incident take place?" asked Turner, taking over the questioning as Kate sat back in her chair. Marshall stared at her with eyes full of hatred, then turned his attention to the Security Officer.

The first interview, thought Kate. *The very first one and I've already made an enemy. Jamie told me they were going to want my head if I did this.*

She had no idea how right he was.

6

CIVILISED MEN

CHÂTEAU DAUNCY
AQUITAINE, SOUTH-WESTERN FRANCE

"More wine?" The voice was smooth and full of quiet authority.

Admiral Henry Seward nodded, raising his glass with one slightly trembling hand. A servant in immaculate black and white eveningwear, his eyes glowing a faint, respectful red, appeared beside him and filled his glass with wine that was a purple so dark it was almost black. The chateau's cellar contained treasures that would have widened the eyes of even the most experienced sommelier, and bottle after stunning bottle was brought up and decanted every evening in anticipation of dinner, even though the diners never numbered more than three, and usually only two.

Such was again the case this evening.

Henry Seward sat at one end of a long table that could easily have seated twenty, while his dinner companion sat at the other. A small team of vampire servants attended to his every request, looks of devoted terror on their supernatural faces, although Seward knew full well it was not him they were scared of.

The source of their fear was sitting at the other end of the table, a gentle smile on his narrow face.

Vlad Tepes, who had later been known throughout Europe as Vlad Dracul and Vlad the Impaler, and who had eventually come to call himself Count Dracula, sat easily in his chair and regarded his guest. Valeri Rusmanov, who could not be faulted for his loyalty or his diligence, but often left much to be desired when it came to manners and etiquette, referred to Seward only as 'the prisoner', which was unacceptable to Vlad. It was factually accurate, but it created an atmosphere he considered unbecoming of civilised men, men who had commanded armies and fought for what they believed in. So he referred to Henry Seward as his guest, and treated him accordingly during the dinners they shared. The treatment the Director of Department 19 received in the long hours of darkness after the meals were finished was far less civilised, but was a regrettable necessity of the situation. Regrettable from a perspective of manners, that was. From a personal perspective, Vlad found the nightly torture of Henry Seward utterly delightful.

The first vampire looked down the length of the long table at his guest. Seward was clad in a beautiful dark blue suit that Vlad had ordered made for him by one of the finest boutiques in Paris. He had sent one of Valeri's servants north to collect it two days earlier, and had been pleased to see that it fitted his guest like a glove. He had not been sure that it would; Seward was losing weight rapidly, a result of the deprivations and torments that had been inflicted upon him in the last month. And, despite the elegant shimmer of the suit and the soft lines of the shirt and tie beneath it, the damage inflicted during the long nights could not be completely hidden.

Two fingers were now missing from Henry Seward's left hand; they had been broken with hammers and torn off at the end of the day the Blacklight Director had been delivered to the chateau by Valeri, who had worn a grin of immense satisfaction on his craggy, mountainous face as he presented his prize to his master. The stumps were bandaged neatly, and the dressings were changed every day by a vampire servant who had once been a doctor. More bandages, small caps of bright white, covered the tips of five of Seward's remaining fingers, hiding the ragged pink flesh that had been uncovered as his fingernails had been pulled out. It was an ancient torture, one of the very oldest, and although it could not be expected to break a man with as much determination and experience as Henry Seward, it still produced a pitch of scream that was music to Vlad's ears. It was also a good place to start, an early benchmark to establish, from where things would only get worse the longer the victim held out. And, indeed, they had got much, much worse.

Beneath his suit, the Director's body was a horror of bruises, burns and wounds: marks left by simple beatings, by lead pipes and plastic cables, and by pairs of metal clips attached to a car battery. As was appropriate for a man of his standing, Vlad had not inflicted any of this damage himself; instead, he had stood and watched Valeri and two of his servants as they worked, maintaining an air of detached professionalism as the torture was administered. But, beneath his veneer of disinterest, his mind raced with possibilities and his stomach churned with a longing so powerful it was almost physical: a desire to push the others aside, to spill blood and inflict pain with his own bare hands.

Throughout it all, Seward had told them nothing beyond his name and his Blacklight identification number. Vlad was impressed by the man's fortitude, though he knew full well there were things he could order done to his guest that he would have no chance of withstanding. But he was in no hurry; there would come a time when he would need to know everything Seward knew, in case there was something of which Valeri was unaware, but it could wait. His recuperation was progressing well, fuelled by a constant stream of warm running blood. He was now draining three or four human beings every day, each drop of their blood contributing to his gradual return to what he had once been. Valeri sent his servants out each night, and each morning they returned before dawn with victims taken from the surrounding towns and villages. Vlad had ordered them to make sure they spread their hunts far and wide; he had no interest in creating a panic or attracting unnecessary attention to this isolated corner of the world, not when he was so close to regaining the power he had once taken so recklessly for granted. He was not there yet, not by any means, but he was getting closer with each passing day, with each swallowed mouthful of blood. And the exquisite reality of the matter was this: there was, in truth, almost nothing Henry Seward could tell him that he didn't already know.

The Operational frequencies of the various Departments, the access codes to their bases and computer systems, these were things that could have one day been extremely useful to Vlad and Valeri. However, both vampires knew full well that they would all have been changed the minute Henry Seward was taken, rendering his knowledge of them useless.

He must know that too, thought Dracula, his gaze locked on his guest. *Surely he must. Yet he refuses to tell us, regardless. Admirable.*

Until his recovery was complete and he was ready to take direct action, Vlad was content to let Seward believe he was successfully resisting. When that time came, Seward *would* tell him everything, whether he wanted to or not, at which point Vlad would kill whatever

77

was left of the man and send his head to Blacklight on a spike. But for now, he was content to play Seward's game. They would continue attempting to get the Director to give up the information he didn't want to reveal, using what he would allow Seward to believe were his most persuasive methods, and his guest would continue to refuse. It afforded Seward a measure of dignity, and it helped to pierce the boredom that Vlad had felt so keenly since he had been reborn, boredom that was slowly beginning to abate as the recovery of his mind and body gathered pace. It also afforded him an agreeable dinner companion, sparing him the stoic silence of Valeri's company or the embarrassment of dining alone.

At the other end of the table, the servant had finished refilling Seward's glass. Vlad raised his own and waited until his guest did likewise.

"*Noroc*," said the ancient vampire.

"*Noroc*," replied Henry Seward. He had spoken the Romanian toast many times over the last month, evening after evening, glass after glass; it was now almost second nature.

He drained half his wine, looking forward to the numbing effect of the alcohol, feeling his arm tremble as he raised the glass to his lips. It was one of a number of shakes and tremors that had appeared over the last month, one result of the tortures inflicted upon him every night. Another was his inability to sleep, even when the torment was over: his body was always wracked with pain and thrumming with adrenaline, and when sleep did eventually come, it was fitful, full of bad dreams and echoed agony.

Seward was exhausted, in constant pain, and knew his body was beginning to fail him. It wasn't the result of any one particular torture, but the cumulative effect of them all; he had begun to cough up blood in the mornings and see spots of red in the toilet bowl after he urinated. He coughed steadily, and struggled for breath after climbing only a handful of stairs. It was now clear that he didn't have long to live, as he knew very well that Dracula was never going to let him leave this place; he had come to terms with the realisation that he would never see his family and friends again. He also knew, although he didn't think Dracula realised that he did, that he was resisting telling them information that was worthless.

He knew that Dracula believed he was playing with him, letting him be brave and resilient while waiting for the right moment to prise whatever Seward was hiding from his head. But the ancient vampire was wrong: he was holding no secrets, no information that would be of use to them. When the monster unleashed whatever agonies he was holding back, he would tell him everything; when the vampire realised that none of it was useful, Seward would spit blood in his face before he died. In the meantime, he would grit his teeth and take what they gave him, and join his captor in this bizarre facsimile of normality each evening, as though they were two old school friends having dinner at their club.

"What are we having?" he asked, glancing at the hovering vampire servants.

"Wood pigeon, I believe," replied Dracula. "Is that agreeable to you?"

"I'm sure it will be," replied Seward. The food and wine he had eaten and drunk since he had been taken by Valeri, dragged kicking and screaming into the sky as men and women he had once commanded fought for their lives beneath him, had been uniformly excellent. He supposed he should not be surprised: Dracula had been a Prince when he was a man, then a Transylvanian Count as a vampire, and had been used to the very best of everything, throughout both of his lives.

The man and the vampire sat in silence as the servants suddenly burst into action, delivering silver trays to the table and placing them before the two diners. The lids were withdrawn to reveal a delicate *foie gras parfait* and home-made brioche that made Seward's mouth water despite the steady throbs of pain that coursed through his body. He attacked the food, aware of Dracula's faintly reproachful expression, and demolished the plate within a minute. He sat back in his chair, feeling the energy being released by the food in his stomach and the endorphins radiating out from his pituitary gland.

Eating emboldened him. He had allowed the previous dinners to be filled with small talk, with mindless chatter about the modern world, with stories and tales of their pasts; nothing that had any edge, nothing that might cause offence. It was time for that to change.

"You're still weak," he said.

Dracula tilted his head slightly to one side. "I beg your pardon?"

"It was a straightforward statement. You're still weak. Your powers have not fully returned to you."

"What makes you say so?"

Seward looked round the room. "The evidence of my own eyes," he said. "Why else would you be hiding here, surrounded by servants to protect you?"

Dracula frowned. "To protect me?" he said. "They are honoured that I permit them to serve me. It is the highlight of their tiny lives."

Seward smiled. "I'm sure that's what you tell yourself. It must be hard for you to admit that even the weakest vampire in this building could kill you with one hand if he chose to."

Dark red started to bubble in the corners of the first vampire's eyes, and Seward felt a surge of satisfaction in his chest. Then the ancient eyes cleared and Dracula began to laugh, an awful sound that started small, but went on and on, getting louder and louder.

"Wonderful," he said, as his laughter finally stopped. "I understand now. You hoped to annoy me with your comment, yes? You believed that I would consider it impertinent. I am extremely sorry to have disappointed you, my dear Admiral."

Seward swallowed hard. "They'll find you," he said, willing his words to be true. "Blacklight will find you and stop you. Your rise will fail."

"You are like a child," said Dracula, his voice warm and friendly. "You understand nothing. My rise has already begun, my dear Admiral. I am out there in the darkness, as we speak. I am everywhere. I am *legion*."

"What are you talking about?" asked Seward, cold fingers working their way up his spine.

Dracula shook his head. "You will find out soon enough," he said.

The servants scuttled back into the room, removing the plates and placing new cutlery before the vampire and his guest. Then they were gone, as a second team delivered new plates of food.

Dracula lifted the silver lid from the plate before him and favoured Seward with a wide, contented smile.

"As I thought," he said. "Wood pigeon. *Bon appétit.*"

7

SINK OR SWIM

"So where do we start?" asked Patrick Williams.

"Intelligence is putting together probable location lists," replied Holmwood. "We've had every available satellite working outwards from the hospital since early this morning, and we've tracked over a hundred heat blooms. They're where we start."

"OK," said Dominique Saint-Jacques. "Let's get going."

Holmwood nodded. "I'm sending squads out with lists of five likely target locations. I'm authorising daylight operations, so destroy them before the sun goes down if you can. All usual containment protocols remain in place, and I want it made clear to all Operators that these targets are significantly more dangerous than the vampires they usually encounter. I'm putting in place a hard window of eight hours, after which you come home. I don't care whether you've destroyed all five of your targets, or two of them, or none of them. Eight hours, then return to base. Having what's left of this Department exhausted and careless is not an option. Clear?"

"Clear, sir," replied Dominique.

"Excellent. I'm officially activating all Operational Squads that include rookies until this threat has been eliminated, then they go back to training. Look after them out there and bring them back safe. Clear?"

"Yes, sir," chorused the Zero Hour Task Force.

"Good. Dismissed."

Jamie stepped out of the lift and strode along the central corridor of Level B.

Search and destroy, he thought. *Just like that. Search and destroy three hundred super-powerful vampires. No problem at all.*

He had left the Ops Room with his stomach churning uneasily. There was no doubt in his mind that the mass escapes of the previous night had been orchestrated by Dracula, or at the very least by Valeri, and that they had the potential to cause widespread carnage. There was a positive aspect to the move: such a large action, designed so clearly to occupy Department 19 and its counterparts around the world for a significant amount of time, strongly suggested that Dracula was not far in advance of their Zero Hour timeline, if at all. But that was going to be of little comfort to the men and women who were by now already heading out to hunt down the escapee vampires.

Jamie pulled the console from his belt and typed as he walked.

M-3/OP_EXT_L1/LIVEBRIEFING/BR4/ASAP

He pressed SEND and knew that, far below him, in the circular confines of the Playground, the consoles belonging to John Morton and Lizzy Ellison would now be vibrating into life. He wondered how long it would take them to make their way up to Briefing Room 4 on Level 0, and guessed at ten minutes.

It'll probably take them five minutes to find the right room, he thought, smiling to himself. *It used to for me.*

Jamie reached his quarters, pressed his ID against the keypad set into the wall, and pushed his door open when the red light turned green. He flopped down on his bed, grateful for a few minutes' rest; given the situation that Cal Holmwood had described, he doubted there were going to be many similar opportunities in the next few days. Not that there ever really were; life inside Department 19 was physically and mentally exhausting, a result of the high stakes that were constantly in play. If Jamie and his colleagues failed to do their jobs well, people died; it was as simple as that. Every Operator understood this, found a way to process it and carry on, but it was not always easy.

Jamie felt his eyes begin to close, even though he had only woken up three hours earlier, to find a box in the middle of his console's screen telling him that he had a message waiting from Larissa. He had pressed OPEN and read the lines of text that appeared.

Hey! Hope you're OK? Will be awake for the next hour
or so if you're around and fancy giving me a call... x

Jamie had checked the time stamp on the message. It had arrived at 7:30am, when he had apparently been so soundly asleep that he hadn't even heard it beep. He had quickly done the time-zone maths in his head.

Half past eleven in Nevada. Late.

He had considered calling her anyway – he didn't think she would be too annoyed if he woke her up – but had decided to let her sleep. Now, as he contemplated the scale and horror of what he had just been told in the Ops Room, he wished he had made the call; it would have been good to hear a genuinely friendly voice. For a second, he considered walking round and knocking on the door to the quarters next to his own, the quarters occupied, technically at least, by one of his best friends, but knew it would be a waste of time.

Matt Browning was almost never in his room these days, unless he was asleep. Jamie knew he had turned down the chance to move into one of the larger quarters inside the Lazarus security perimeter, and while he admired the reasoning behind his friend's refusal, a spirited attempt to avoid devoting his every waking moment to his work, he thought it had, in fact, been largely pointless. Matt's life now revolved entirely around the Lazarus Project, and that was that. Jamie missed his friend, but wasn't annoyed with him; how could he be, when what Matt had devoted himself to was arguably the most important project being carried out in the whole of Blacklight? However, he did think he should try to press Matt into having a drink in the officers' mess, or at least into sharing a table at lunch; it had been a while since they had talked for longer than a minute or two in a corridor, when both were on their way somewhere else.

On the other hand, it had been barely seventy-two hours since he had talked to Larissa, but he still missed her terribly. They had spoken for almost an hour over a secure video connection, Jamie battered and bloodied by the operation he had just returned from, Larissa bright and smiling, eight hours behind him, her day just getting under way. The pleasure and excitement in her voice as she told him about Dreamland, the NS9 base, and the men and women who inhabited it, was bittersweet to his ears. He knew she had been furious with Holmwood for selecting her for the NS9 secondment, and he knew she missed him as much as he missed her, but she now had a levity about her that he both relished and feared.

He was happy that she was happy: God knows she deserved it after what had happened to her over the last few years, and what had been done to her during the attack on the Loop, when she had been burned down to little more than bones. But he was also jealous of her temporary new life, away from the darkness that surrounded Blacklight, that seemed to follow *him* wherever he went; jealous that she was meeting new people and experiencing new places, new things. And a tiny piece of him, the vicious, self-loathing part that had been birthed by his father's death and nourished by years of bullying and loneliness, kept asking the same two questions, whispering them in the darkest recesses of his mind.

What if she forgets about me? What if she doesn't want to come back?

He pushed such miserable thoughts aside and climbed off his bed. He pulled a bottle of water out of the small fridge beneath his desk and headed out into the corridor, pulling the door to his quarters closed behind him, trying to focus on nothing more than the task at hand.

Jamie logged in to the terminal at the front of Briefing Room 4 and found his squad's target list waiting for him. He moved it up on to the wall screen behind him, and waited for the rest of his newly activated squad to arrive.

They kept him waiting for less than two minutes. Morton and Ellison burst through the door, clad in their dark blue training uniforms, red-faced from what Jamie knew would have been several minutes of running along the curving corridors of Level 0 in search of the right room. They were caked in sweat and drying blood, but their faces wore identical expressions of determined enthusiasm.

"Good to see you both," said Jamie. "Get lost on the way up here?"

Morton looked about to deny it, but Ellison opened her mouth first. "Yes, sir," she said. "The corridors all look the same, sir."

"You'll get used to it," said Jamie, and smiled at his squad mates. "Trust me."

The two rookies nodded, clearly relieved.

"Take a seat," Jamie said, motioning towards the empty plastic chairs that surrounded the long table in the middle of the room. Morton and Ellison did as they were told as Jamie watched them, wondering if he had been so nervous and eager to please when he first arrived at the Loop.

I don't think I was, he thought. *I didn't give a damn about anything apart from my mum. I acted like I owned the place.*

He flushed at the memory, but only slightly. He had done what he needed to do to get his mother back, and that was all that had mattered. He knew he had annoyed plenty of Operators in the process, and that not all of them had forgiven him for what they had perceived as arrogance and a disrespectful attitude.

"Operators," he said, his voice even. "This morning, Interim Director Holmwood authorised MOVING SHADOWS, a Priority Level 1 operation being carried out by the entire active roster of this Department. What you can see on the screen behind me is our little piece of it." He tapped a series of keys on the console's touch screen and the first name on the target list was replaced by a digital scan of a hospital admission record. "Last night," he continued, "an unknown vampire force conducted a mass escape from Broadmoor Hospital in Berkshire. Surveillance footage and satellite thermal imaging suggest that all released patients have been intentionally turned, and Science Division analysis indicates that they are significantly more powerful than usual newly-turned vampires. All of which means we now have almost three hundred potentially highly dangerous vampires on the loose. MOVING SHADOWS is a search and destroy mission, intended to eliminate this new threat in as short a timeframe as possible. Any questions so far?"

Morton raised his hand and Jamie nodded. "Why are you telling us this, sir?" he asked.

"Your training has been suspended," replied Jamie. "As of right now, you are active Operators in Department 19, until such time as this operation is concluded. When it is, you go back to the Playground. But not until then. Do you understand?"

Morton nodded, the colour draining from his face. Ellison looked at him with wide eyes as she raised her hand.

"Yes?" said Jamie.

"You said search and destroy, sir," said Ellison. "Right?"

"That's right."

"How is that going to work?"

"What do you mean?"

"I mean, people are going to expect the patients to be found, sir. The media is going to go absolutely crazy, and the families of the escapees are going to demand to know what happened. We're talking about vulnerable people here, sir, people with severe psychiatric issues."

"Not any more," said Morton. "Now we're talking about vampires."

Ellison shot her squad mate an extremely sharp glance, then returned her attention to Jamie.

"The media doesn't know anything yet," he said. "When it leaks, which we have to assume it will, we'll make sure they don't run it. Anyone who lives near the hospital is being handled, and when it becomes necessary to tell the public about what happened to the patients of Broadmoor, the Security Division will devise a cover story. I've no idea what that will be, before you ask, and it's not something you need to worry about. What you do need to worry about are the five vampires we've been ordered to destroy."

"OK, sir," said Ellison, although unease had clearly settled over her. Morton gave her a furious look, then whispered something Jamie didn't catch. Ellison turned on him, her eyes blazing with anger, and opened her mouth to reply.

"Operators!" barked Jamie, causing them both to jump in their seats. "This is not a training exercise. This is the real thing. You will give me your complete attention right now or I'll assume that you aren't ready for this and send you back downstairs. Is that what you want?"

"No, sir," they chorused.

"Good," replied Jamie. "That's good. Because this is a Priority Level 1 operation, the kind that Operators die on. The footage demonstrating the power of these escaped vampires is extremely disconcerting, so let's focus, shall we? I want us armed and triple-checked and ready to go in one hour, so it might be useful for us to know who the hell we're looking for."

Morton and Ellison leant forward, their attention fully focused on their squad leader. Jamie forced a tension-breaking smile and began to brief them on what was waiting for them beyond the walls of the Loop, knowing even as he did so that nothing he said could truly prepare them.

I'll just be pleased if I bring them both back alive.

8

THE LOST HARKER

THREE MONTHS EARLIER

TRANSCRIPT
INTERVIEW WITH ALBERT HARKER. JUNE 12 2002

(tape begins)

JOHNNY SUPERNOVA: Right, it's on.

ALBERT HARKER: What's on?

JS: The tape recorder. It's recording.

AH: Oh. Fine.

JS: Please say your name for the tape.

AH: Albert Harker.

JS: OK. I'm going to call you Albert, if that's cool?

AH: That's fine.

JS: So. Albert. You approached me and offered me this interview. Why don't you start by telling me why.

AH: Thank you. I wanted to give this interview so that people know the truth.

JS: The truth about what?

AH: About vampires, Mr Supernova. About Blacklight. About my family.

JS: Now you see, my bullshit detector just went off straight away. Because you just said the word vampires.

AH: That's right. I did.

JS: Well, let's get this out there then. Your position, what you're saying to me, is that vampires are real? They exist, right now, in the real world.

AH: That's correct.

JS: And why would you expect me to believe something so ridiculous?

AH: Because it's the truth.

JS: Do you have any proof? Anything to back up your claim?

AH: Just my word.

JS: I sent a car to collect you for this interview from a homeless shelter, Albert. I can see needle tracks on both your arms. And you think I should take your word for something like this?

AH: That's entirely up to you, Mr Supernova. I can't make that decision for you.

JS: Oh, I'll make it for myself, don't you worry about that. So. Before we get on to the supposed existence of these vampires, tell me something else. Tell me how you would be in a position to know about them, if they were real. Because it seems to me like everyone else thinks they're fiction, and I've got to tell you, you're off to a pretty bad start when it comes to being convincing.

AH: You are aware of my surname?

JS: I am.

AH: And, as a journalist, I would presume that you are a well-read man?

JS: I suppose so. Reasonably.

AH: And you don't see the connection?

(pause)

JS: Dracula. You're talking about Dracula?

AH: Very good, Mr Supernova. Dracula, yes. My great-grandfather was Jonathan Harker, the hero of Stoker's story. Which, in truth, was a work of historical fact, rather than the fiction it has been portrayed as.

JS: You take a lot of heroin, don't you, Albert?

AH: That is immaterial.

JS: So Dracula wasn't a story. It really happened. Am I understanding you here?

AH: You are. It happened much as Stoker wrote it down. He overheard the tale from Abraham Van Helsing, who he crossed paths with here in London.

JS: Van Helsing was real too?

AH: Obviously. The sooner you get your head around these simple facts, the quicker and less painful this process will become.

JS: Don't get snippy with me, mate. Remember who's paying who.

AH: I apologise. Yes, Mr Supernova, Van Helsing was real, as was John Seward, and Quincey Morris, and Arthur Holmwood, whose great-grandson sits in the House of Lords as we speak. And so was my great-grandfather. They were all as real as you and I.

JS: Meaning Dracula was real too.

AH: Correct. He was real, and he died, as Stoker described. And my ancestor and his friends came home. But Dracula was not the only vampire in the world, merely the first. Others followed, in time.

JS: And?

AH: And my great-grandfather and his friends were given the authority to deal with them. On behalf of the Empire.

JS: By who?

AH: By Prime Minister William Gladstone. In 1892.

(pause)

JS: You're serious, aren't you? This isn't a wind-up.

AH: I am deadly serious, Mr Supernova. This is the biggest secret in the world, a secret that my family and others have kept for more than a century. And I'm telling it to you.

JS: Why? I mean, apart from the money.

AH: My family and I are... not close.

JS: So you're doing this out of spite? I mean, if this is all real, if you're not crazy, then my guess is you're going to be in a hell of a lot of trouble if I find someone to run this.

AH: That's my problem. But yes, I imagine they won't be thrilled.

JS: Are you in danger? More importantly, am I?

AH: Not as far as I know. But I offer no guarantees, Mr Supernova. Blacklight operates entirely outside the laws that govern you and I.

JS: Blacklight?

AH: The organisation that hunts vampires and keeps them secret. That's not its real name, but is what it has always been called. It evolved from the four men who survived the encounter with Dracula.

JS: What is it?

AH: I've never seen the inside of it. But it's something like a special forces unit for the supernatural.

JS: Whoa, whoa. You've never seen it?

AH: Not from the inside, Mr Supernova. It is the most highly classified organisation in the country. But there are traditions that concern the descendants of the original members, the founders. We are automatically given the chance to join when we turn twenty-one.

JS: And I presume you said no?

AH: I did.

JS: Why?

AH: Because I had no desire to spend my life chasing monsters. And because there are few things I have ever wanted less than to be anything like my father.

(pause)

JS: Why's that, Albert?

AH: Because he was a bully, a sadist and a fraud, who played favourites. He loved my brother while he tolerated me, and made it abundantly clear to everyone.

JS: But when the time came, he still asked you to join this Blacklight?

AH: I have no doubt that it broke his heart to do so. But he was bound by the rules, by the traditions of the organisation he gave his life to. I've come to believe it was the only thing he ever truly cared about. So, yes, when I turned twenty-one, he asked me. I've never seen him happier than when I turned him down.

JS: So how does it work? You wake up on your birthday and your dad comes into your room and says 'Hi, son, by the way, vampires are real, I'm part of a secret organisation that fights them and now you get the chance to be too'?

(Harker laughs)

AH: Pretty much. He used a lot more words than that, most of which were honour, and duty, and sacrifice. But yes, that's about it.

JS: And so you said no. How did he react?

AH: He looked like the cat that got the cream. Then he shouted at me for about an hour, called me a coward and a baby, and told me he was embarrassed that I was his son. It went perfectly for him.

JS: How so?

AH: Because he was allowed to openly hate me, Mr Supernova. I finally gave him a good enough reason, by turning down his life's work. And he didn't have to have me there with him every day. I don't know what he'd have done if I had said yes.

(pause)

JS: But you didn't. So what happened then? He tells you this massive secret, and everyone normally says yes, but you say no. How does that work?

AH: He warned me not to tell anyone what I'd heard, said that they'd lock me up if I did, and that no one would believe me anyway. A couple of days later he brought me a form to sign, some version of the Official Secrets Act. And that was that. We never talked about it again.

JS: You mentioned your brother. He joined?

AH: Of course. Of course he did. He was my father in miniature. He couldn't wait.

JS: So what did you do instead?

AH: Finished university. Moved to London. Discovered drugs. Became very, very fond of them.

JS: How did your family react to that?

AH: They cut me off the first chance they got. Said I was a stain on the family name, that I was no longer welcome at home. They turned their back on me, Mr Supernova.

JS: Bastards.

(pause)

AH: On several occasions I would be at a party, or in a bar, and I would catch someone staring at me, someone who didn't look like they belonged with me and my friends. And a couple of times I got home and knew someone had been in my flat. Nothing was missing or out of place. It was professional work. But I knew. So I suppose they kept an eye on me, in their own way.

JS: Because they were worried you might talk?

AH: I don't know. I imagine so.

JS: But you never did. Until now, at least. Why not?

AH: I wanted to forget everything. I didn't care about their stupid little department, and I doubted anyone would believe me. So I tried to let it go.

JS: Why now then?

AH: Spite, Mr Supernova, as you said. And justice. And because I'm sick of carrying this around with me. I want to be rid of it.

(pause)

JS: This is good stuff, you know? The black sheep son of a noble family cut off and left to rot, heroin, homelessness, people following you, going through your stuff. It's juicy, mate. Very juicy. But there's still one problem.

AH: Which is?

JS: Vampires. Blacklight. I just... I can't see a way that anything you're telling me is the truth.

AH: I understand your position, Mr Supernova. Better than you realise, believe me. But it is the truth. I can tell you what my father told me, and that's all. Beyond that, you're on your own.

JS: Tell me.

AH: I'm afraid I can't duplicate the pathetic awe in my father's voice, but I can still remember most of what he said. I've already told you that Blacklight was founded in the late nineteenth century. Well, in the hundred or so years since, it's changed rather a lot. My father told me it started out as four men in a house on Piccadilly, but now it's more like the SAS, a classified special forces unit that polices the supernatural. I doubt you'll find it mentioned officially anywhere, but you're welcome to try and prove me wrong. As for the vampires? Nobody knows what made Dracula more than human, but what is known is that he was the first. After he died, he left a handful of vampires behind, vampires that he had personally turned. They turned others, and so on, and so on. The rise in vampire numbers is what prompted the expansion of Blacklight.

JS: What about the vampires themselves? Jesus Christ, I can't believe I'm saying that word, but what are they about? They, what, swoop around in the night, changing into bats and wolves?

AH: No, Mr Supernova. The shape-changing was added by Bram Stoker for the entertainment of his readers, as was the susceptibility to crosses and holy water. They don't work. Nor does garlic or running water. The rest of it, though, is true. They're strong, and fast, and vulnerable to sunlight. Their eyes glow red. And they need to drink blood to survive.

JS: What kind of blood?

AH: Any, as far as I am aware.

JS: Human?

AH: Yes. Of course.

JS: So they bite people?

AH: They do. They bite people, and if their victim doesn't die, they turn into a vampire as well.

JS: So why aren't there thousands of them? Why don't I see them on every street corner?

AH: As far as I understand, it's because very few of their victims survive. And because Blacklight works very hard to keep them secret. (pause)

JS: What do you want me to do with all this, Albert?

AH: I don't understand the question.

JS: You're a smart man. You know every editor in the country is going to laugh me out of their office if I write this up and submit it. Nobody is going to believe it. I'm sitting here looking at you and I believe you mean every word you've said, but even I can't accept it as the truth. I just don't see how it can be. How come nobody has ever broken ranks before? Why has no vampire ever come forward? Why aren't the papers full of missing persons and bodies found drained of blood? You see what I'm saying?

AH: You are a journalist, aren't you?

JS: Yeah.

AH: Then do your job. Everything I've told you is the truth. So dig, Mr Supernova. Find out what you can. If you can't find anything to back up what I'm saying, then forget it, with my blessing. But if you can, if you can find any tiny little thing that corroborates what I've told you, you will find yourself in possession of the biggest exclusive in the history of humanity. Surely that's worth a few days of your time, even if all it does is confirm that you were right about me all along. As for why nobody has ever broken ranks? I would imagine that the members of Blacklight would find it very difficult to speak to anyone without being monitored, and even if they did, I'm sure they would swiftly find themselves facing a court-martial. And the vampires? Why would they make themselves known? So that all their potential victims know they exist, so that the government can declare open war on them? And finally, Mr Supernova, I'm sorry to have to tell you that the papers are full of missing persons, and people who have had terrible things done to them. And that's not even allowing for the hundreds of dead and disappeared who never make the pages of the tabloids.

(pause)

JS: I think we're done here, Albert.

AH: I think so too.

JS: Where can I find you? If I need to follow up on any of this.

AH: You can't. If I'm still alive in a few months' time, if neither the vampires nor Blacklight get me, I'll find you.

JS: This is ridiculous. You know that, don't you? It's nuts.

AH: Just do your job, Mr Supernova. That's the only advice I have for you. Treat it like any other story and see what you can turn up.

I wish you the very best of luck, I honestly do.

JS: Cheers. I think.

(tape ends)

Kevin McKenna dropped the transcript on to his desk and exhaled heavily; it felt like he had been holding his breath the entire time he had been reading. The dead cigarette fell from his lips, making him jump; he had forgotten all about it.

Jesus, Johnny, he thought. *How desperate were you?*

The transcript was nonsense, so much so that McKenna felt almost embarrassed for his former mentor. This kind of tattling, tabloid silliness was so far beneath the Johnny Supernova he had once known that it made him genuinely sad.

Things must have been so much worse than I realised. The Johnny I used to know would have laughed this guy out of his flat.

McKenna got up from his chair and flicked through the rest of the folder. It contained four or five pages of notes, written in Johnny Supernova's distinctive sloping scrawl. He gathered them up, held them over the wire rubbish bin that sat beside his desk, then paused.

He left you this in his will. It's disrespectful just to throw it out.

He put the folder back on his desk, grabbed his jacket, and walked quickly out of his office. A minute later he was in the elevator, checking his watch.

Should still be able to catch the second half, he thought.

Then a pang of sadness gripped his heart. He had not really thought about Johnny Supernova in a long time, not even when the obituaries ran in the newspapers and magazines. By then, they had long since ceased to live in the same world.

Goodbye, Johnny. Sleep well, you crazy bastard.

9

THE SHOCK OF THE NEW

STEVENAGE, HERTFORDSHIRE

"I've lost him!" shouted Alex Jacobs. "Next level up!"

Angela Darcy swore and ran for the concrete ramp, John Carlisle keeping pace at her side.

Operational Squad F-5 had been about to head back to the Loop when the call had come through from the Surveillance Division, informing them of a new target. Squad Leader Angela Darcy had asked no questions; she had merely told their driver to head for the new coordinates, as fast as possible.

She was tired, and knew her squad felt the same. They had taken down a vampire in the north London suburbs, a routine operation that had been perfect for Carlisle. The rookie had been with the SBS in Portsmouth until barely a month earlier, when recruitment to replace the men and women lost during Valeri's attack had begun in earnest, and he had been summoned to Blacklight to begin his training. He was doing well under Angela's tutelage; she had been encouraged by the poise and calm he had displayed on his two missions so far, characteristics that she had long since come to take for granted from Alex Jacobs. The quiet, experienced Operator had spent long spells in the Intelligence and Security Divisions, but had requested reinstatement to the active roster immediately after the attack that had hurt the Department so badly. Angela had watched him closely for the first few days, looking for signs of Operational rust, but quickly realised she had nothing to worry about; Jacobs had slipped into the black Operator's uniform as though he had never taken it off.

They had found their target, a disoriented, raving vampire in his early twenties wearing the tattered remains of a white hospital gown, exactly where the Surveillance Division had told them they would: in a rail freight yard outside Stevenage station. Angela had led her squad towards him with their weapons drawn, ready to put one more vampire out of its misery before heading for home and the warm comfort of their beds. The target had backed away from them, his eyes glowing red, twitching and twisting like a cornered animal. Angela had been about to give the order to fire when the vampire, its eyes wide with confused panic, turned, sprinted across the metal rails, and leapt over a brick wall into the second level of the multi-storey car park that served the station.

Angela gasped. The vampire had been little more than a blur, a streak of white that had been gone before she could even tighten her finger on her T-Bone's trigger.

"Jesus," said Carlisle. The rookie was staring up at the looming concrete structure of the car park. "I've never seen anything move that fast."

Jacobs said nothing; he simply turned, raised his visor and gave Angela a look whose meaning was clear.

Neither have I.

Angela felt the faintest flicker of unease in her stomach and pushed it down. "Follow me," she said.

She led them back along the deserted platforms and out of the empty station. The car park rose tall against the night sky, an ugly lump of concrete, lit weakly from within by flickering yellow light.

"Do you think he's still in there?" asked Jacobs.

"I don't know," she replied, her gaze fixed on the towering building. "Let's find out."

Angela's boots thudded on the concrete as she ran up on to the car park's uppermost level. They had chased the vampire up through the structure, getting little more than a glimpse of him on each floor, and she felt a surge of relief as she crested the ramp and surveyed the wide-open area.

No more levels, she thought. *Nowhere for you to go.*

Carlisle and Jacobs arrived beside her, weapons drawn, visors down. There were only a handful of cars parked on this level, spread out between the thick concrete pillars that supported the dilapidated structure. Water dripped steadily from numerous cracks in the ceiling, and the smell of petrol and grease was thick in the air.

"Where is he?" asked Jacobs.

"On this level somewhere," said Angela. "Spread out and find him."

The three black-clad figures moved slowly towards the centre of the car park, spacing out as they walked. Angela was on the left, her T-Bone resting against her shoulder, her breathing shallow and steady. Through the thermographic filter on her visor the car park was a landscape of grey and blue, cold and uninviting.

"Stay alert," she said, via the comms system that linked them together. "Let's take him down clean and easy."

Three pairs of boots clicked quietly across the concrete. In the distance, Angela could hear cars making their way along the bypass, but the car park itself was silent. She felt a chill run up her spine as she remembered the speed the vampire had shown in the train yard, but tried to ignore it.

Nothing to worry about. Just a routine kill.

She looked across the wide concrete space and checked her squad mates. Jacobs was five metres to her right, moving steadily, with Carlisle the same distance again beyond him. A grim smile rose on her face as she watched them, an expression that froze in place as a voice suddenly echoed around them.

"Leave me alone," it growled. "I just want to be left alone."

Angela stopped dead. "Hold," she said, then flicked her visor up as her squad mates did as they were ordered. She surveyed the empty space, looking for the source of the voice, suddenly acutely aware that the structural pillars were more than wide enough for someone to hide behind.

She reached down and twisted the control dial on her belt. "Why don't you come out?" she asked, her amplified voice booming through the car park. "There's nothing to be afraid of."

"I'm not afraid!" screamed the vampire. His voice was shrill, reverberating against the flat concrete walls. "I'm not I'm not I'm not! Leave me alone!"

"We can't do that," she replied, her voice steady. "Just come out."

There was no reply.

Angela scanned the area slowly, looking for any sign of their target. There was nothing: no shadow, no movement, nothing to give away his position. She looked at Jacobs, his T-Bone resting in his hands, then at Carlisle, standing easily between two pillars with his MP5 at his shoulder.

Then something white moved. Her eyes widened and she opened her mouth to speak, but it was already too late.

The vampire emerged from behind one of the concrete pillars, so suddenly it was as though he materialised from thin air. Carlisle began to turn, bringing his gun around, but was far too slow; one of the vampire's fists crashed into his visor with a noise like a clap of thunder. The purple plastic shattered beneath the force of the blow, sending jagged shards into the Operator's face and neck, drawing pulsing blood from innumerable cuts. Carlisle crashed unconscious to the concrete floor, his body spasming, his legs drumming involuntarily on the ground.

The vampire howled, an ear-splitting bellow of triumph, and turned its crimson gaze on Jacobs as the veteran Operator raised his T-Bone.

Alex Jacobs pushed down the fear that was pressing on his heart and slid his finger inside the trigger guard, his attention focused completely on the monster before him. The vampire was almost naked, his modesty spared by the fluttering scraps of what had once been his hospital gown. The man was skinny, almost malnourished, and his shaven head was covered in whirls and loops of pink scar tissue. His eyes blazed red and his mouth hung open, revealing gleaming white fangs.

The T-Bone settled against Jacobs's shoulder; he aimed down the barrel, sighting the centre of the vampire's chest. He began to tighten his finger on the trigger, but before he could exert enough pressure to fire the weapon, he found himself aiming at nothing as the vampire crouched low and came for him.

It surged across the concrete floor and seized his left hand, pushing it up and back. His finger convulsed against the T-Bone's trigger, sending the metal stake slamming into the ceiling before it bounced back down and skittered away. The vampire's grip was impossibly strong, and Jacobs screamed as he felt the bones in his wrist grind together; he beat at the monster with his free hand, but nothing happened. The vampire's face rose up before his own, glowing red and twisted with madness, and Jacobs felt terror explode through him as his hands were gathered together in the crushing, vice-like grip and pulled forward, his body bending involuntarily at the waist as his feet scrabbled against the ground.

Angela Darcy fought back a momentary wave of panic and forced herself to stay calm, to do her job. Her squad had been decimated in what seemed like the blink of an eye; John Carlisle was twitching on the ground, blood pouring from his ruined face, while Alex Jacobs was being manhandled by the vampire like a squirming, protesting puppet.

This isn't right, she had time to think. *Not right at all.*

Too strong.

Too fast.

She raised her T-Bone and saw immediately that she had no clear shot; there was no way to fire the metal stake into the vampire's body without hitting Jacobs. She slammed the T-Bone back into its holster, drew her UV beam gun, aimed it at the vampire and thumbed the button in one fluid motion. A beam of bright purple light burst across the car park and engulfed him; he had no time to react before his body erupted into flames.

Purple fire licked across the vampire's skin, scouring it black, and blood began to spill from a spider's web of cracks. He howled in agony, but did not release his grip on Jacobs's hands; the Operator was protected from the flames by his uniform, but they billowed over and around him, and his screams matched the monster's. Angela watched, her eyes wide with horror beneath her visor, as the burning, howling vampire dragged Jacobs forward until his body was at a right angle, then brought his burning arm down across both of the

Operator's. Jacobs's arms broke with a terrible crunch; his screams reached an inhuman pitch as the vampire threw him aside and turned to face her.

Angela risked a glance at her fallen squad mate; his arms were both snapped mid-forearm, his hands pointing uselessly upwards at a grotesque angle. Then she returned her attention to the flaming monstrosity that was shambling towards her. Burning lumps of the vampire's body were falling to the concrete floor as he moved, hissing and steaming, on the cold ground. Angela backed slowly away, keeping a wide distance between them; she had seen the vampire's speed twice now, and would not take any chances. Without taking her eyes from the disintegrating face, she drew her MP5 and emptied it into the vampire's legs, blowing out his knees and shattering the long, thick bones. He slumped to the ground, no longer making any sound, and swayed on his ravaged knees, his arms wide, his mouth open and full of fire.

Jesus Christ, she thought. *Oh Jesus Christ.*

Angela Darcy had seen a great many terrible things in the course of her highly classified career, but this was one of the very worst. She took a deep breath, dropped the MP5, and drew her T-Bone again. The vampire appeared to look at her, but there were purple flames where his eyes had been, so she couldn't be sure. Her T-Bone felt heavy as she aimed it at the heart of the twitching, burning thing and pulled the trigger.

What was left of the vampire exploded in a thud of boiling blood, splattering across the dirty concrete floor. Angela was already moving, sprinting across the car park and yelling into her helmet microphone, demanding emergency medical evacuation for her fallen squad mates.

10

IN CONVERSATION

Jamie Carpenter stood outside a door on Level C and took a deep breath, trying to slow his racing heart.

He had left Ellison and Morton absorbing the detail of their briefing, what little there was. Of the five vampire targets they had been given, only one had so far been identified: Eric Bingham, a paranoid schizophrenic who had been caught attempting to strangle his infant niece, had wandered past a police station in Peterborough and been captured on CCTV. The Surveillance Division's facial recognition system had instantly identified him, logged his location into their system, and tracked him as he moved slowly south. The other four targets were mysteries, nothing more than heat blooms on satellite screens. Every effort would continue to be made to identify them before Jamie's squad moved against them; knowing whether they had been violent men before their turnings could prove vital.

They were scheduled to depart in just over an hour and a half, so Jamie had ordered his squad mates to meet him in the hangar in seventy-five minutes. He had been about to head down to the dining hall to grab a late breakfast when Jack Williams called and told him the news.

Angela Darcy's squad mates were both in the infirmary, being tended to by the Blacklight medical staff; Jacobs's arms had been set and splinted, and Carlisle's wounds had been treated and stitched. They were both going to recover, but Jacobs was going to be inactive for several months, and Carlisle had required surgery to remove a shard of plastic that had stopped a millimetre short of his left eyeball.

"One vamp put them both down," said Jack. "Angela said she'd never seen anything like it."

Jamie thanked him for passing on the news, and warned him to be careful out there. Jack told him to do the same and cut their connection.

The door in front of him was no different from any of the hundreds of others on B and C, the residential levels of the Loop; what lay behind it was why his heart was accelerating so sharply. He reached out a gloved hand, noted with anger its visible tremble, and knocked heavily on the door.

Silence.

Jamie knocked again, and was about to turn and walk away when he heard a deep voice emerge from inside the room.

"Who's there?"

"It's me," he replied. "Jamie."

For a long moment, nothing happened. Then the door unlocked with a series of smooth clicks and swung open a fraction. Jamie reached out and pushed it inwards, revealing a spacious room, far larger than his own quarters. It was sparse and scrupulously neat; the surface of the desk was clear, the bed was neatly made, the floor was clean and polished. A pair of armchairs sat opposite the desk. One was empty; the other was straining under the weight of its occupant.

The monster, now once again going by the name Victor Frankenstein, looked up as Jamie walked into his room. He was wearing a white shirt, open at the neck, and black trousers and boots; a thick multi-coloured beard sprouted from his cheeks and chin, and his hair fell carelessly across his forehead and below his ears. His appearance was not against regulations – Blacklight operated a far looser dress code than the regular military, just as the special forces did – but it worried Jamie nonetheless. On a small table beside the armchair stood a glass, a bottle of whisky and a bowl of ice, and these items worried him too, given that it was barely noon.

"Hey," said Jamie, settling into the empty armchair.

"Good evening," replied Frankenstein.

"It's afternoon," said Jamie, forcing a smile. "Early afternoon."

"I don't care," replied Frankenstein. He reached for the bottle and refilled his glass. "How are you, Jamie? Looking after yourself?"

"I'm trying," he replied. "It was easier with you looking after me as well." He smiled again, trying to encourage the monster, to flatter him. "A lot easier."

"I'm sure it was," said Frankenstein. "It's a shame you've had to grow up so fast. You didn't deserve it."

"I know," said Jamie. "But that's the world, isn't it? Bad things happen."

Frankenstein nodded. "Bad things happen."

The monster's free hand slid to the middle of his chest and rested there. Beneath the material of his shirt was a long pattern of scars, far more recent than the many others that covered his uneven flesh. They had been carved into him with a scalpel by Dante Valeriano, the self-styled vampire king of Paris, whom Frankenstein had injured terribly almost a century earlier, and who had spent the subsequent decades focusing on nothing except his insatiable desire for vengeance. In truth, he had been a fraud, a working-class boy from Saint-Denis called

Pierre Depuis who had asserted dominance over the Parisian vampires with little more than bravado and a compellingly fictional history. Jamie and a small squad of Operators had destroyed the vampire king in the theatre where he lived, and brought the captive Frankenstein home, but not before Valeriano had begun to exact his revenge.

He doesn't know he's doing it, thought Jamie. *Doesn't realise how often he touches his scars.*

Jamie felt his own hand twitch towards his neck, where an ugly red patch of skin stretched from his jaw to his shoulder, a memento of the search for his mother, what now felt like years ago.

You're not the only one, he thought. *We've all got scars.*

"How's your girlfriend?" asked Frankenstein. "What's her name? The vampire?"

"Larissa," said Jamie, through a suddenly clenched jaw. "She's fine. Thanks."

Frankenstein nodded. "Is she still in America?"

"Yes," said Jamie.

"Best place for her," grunted the monster.

Jamie bore down on the fury that was rising up through him with all his strength and somehow managed to push it back.

Be calm, he told himself. *It's not his fault. Be calm.*

Frankenstein's hatred of vampires was long-standing and potent. He had made his feelings on them as a species clear to Jamie the very first time they had gone out on an operation together; he believed them to be aberrations, creatures that had no right to exist in the world. His encounter with Lord Dante had not improved his opinion of them, and he had still not forgiven Larissa for wasting their time during the search for Marie Carpenter, despite Jamie's repeated pleas for him to do so.

"She seems happy," he said, as brightly as he was able. "So maybe it is."

Frankenstein stared at Jamie with his misshapen, multicoloured eyes, his gaze heavy and unblinking, and momentarily full of warning. "What about your other friend?" he asked. "The girl from Lindisfarne? Kate, was it?"

"She's fine," said Jamie, grateful for the new topic of conversation. "She's getting stuck into this new project she's running with Paul Turner. I hardly see her at the moment."

"That's life inside the Department," said Frankenstein. "There's always something going on."

"Tell me about it," said Jamie. "I've just come from a Zero Hour briefing. You're not going to believe what—"

"I don't want to know," interrupted the monster.

"I know, but—"

"Jamie," said Frankenstein, his voice like thunder. "We've been through this before. Cal offered me a place on the Zero Hour Task Force and I turned it down. You know that. I don't understand why you find it so difficult to respect my decision."

They looked at one another for a long, silent moment.

"You're still on the inactive list," said Jamie, eventually. It was a statement rather than a question.

"That's correct," replied Frankenstein.

"Why?"

"I would have thought that was obvious. I'm dangerous. I'm of no Operational use to anyone."

"You're dangerous three days of the month," said Jamie. "And I'm obviously not suggesting you go out during them. But the rest of the time—"

"I'm sorry," interrupted Frankenstein. "As always, I'm curious as to why you think this is any of your business?"

Jamie felt his face fill with angry heat. "I'll tell you why it's my business," he said. "It's my business because I risked my life, and the lives of four other people, to drag you out of that theatre in Paris and bring you home safe. *That's* why."

"Why did you do it, though?" asked Frankenstein. "Why did you risk so much to rescue me?"

"Why?" asked Jamie, leaning forward in his chair. "What the hell do you mean, why? Because we're on the same side. Because I thought we were friends. Because I didn't want you to die. Take your pick from any of those. Dante would have killed you if we hadn't got there when we did, and now all you can do is drink whisky and ask me stupid questions? What the hell is wrong with you?"

"You're lying to yourself, Jamie," said Frankenstein. The monster's tone was even, maddeningly so. "*Why did you rescue me?*"

"Because what happened to you was my fault," shouted Jamie. "If I hadn't listened to Tom Morris, then everything on Lindisfarne would have happened differently. You wouldn't have fallen, or been bitten, or lost your memory. So when we found out you were still alive, I couldn't let you die, OK? I had to find you and bring you home. Do you understand? I *had* to."

Frankenstein smiled at him, an open expression that seemed full of genuine warmth. "I know, Jamie," he said, his voice low. "And if you think I don't appreciate what you did, then you're sorely mistaken, I promise you. I owe you my life, truly I do. But we both know why you did what you did. Because you felt guilty, because you believed that rescuing me would atone for the mistake you believe you made last year. Which, as I've tried to tell you a thousand times, was never your fault in the first place. Bad things happen, Jamie. They do. You trusted a senior Operator that you had no reason not to and things went wrong. You blamed yourself and I understand that. But you rescued me, you brought me home, and now you can put down that weight you've been carrying around with you since I fell. I meant it when I said I owed you my life, Jamie. But that doesn't mean you get to tell me how to live the rest of it."

Jamie felt his anger dissipate, and slumped back into his chair.

"I get it," he said. "I get how bad Paris was. I mean, I don't really, but I can guess."

"It's not just Paris," said Frankenstein. "Dante, Latour, they're only part of it."

"So what is it?" asked Jamie.

"It's impossible for you to understand," said Frankenstein. "I'd buried so many of the things I've done, buried them so deeply that I'd been able to convince myself that maybe I wasn't the monster everyone claimed, that maybe the good I've done could outweigh the bad. But it can't. It doesn't work like that."

"Why not?" said Jamie. "Why shouldn't it?"

"Because it doesn't. You can never truly bury the past. I thought I had and, when it all came back to me, it was like experiencing it all again for the first time. It was like having my soul torn to pieces in front of me. I don't expect you to feel sorry for me, Jamie, or pity me. But I need you to understand that I can't go back out there. I just can't."

Jamie felt his heart go out to the huge grey-green man, who had once sworn a solemn oath to protect the Carpenter family. It was obvious to him what the missing word in Frankenstein's explanation had been.

He's ashamed. Of the things he did. Of himself.

"The thing you don't want to know about is big," Jamie said. "There's a new type of vamp out there. Really strong. Really fast. Angela Darcy's squad took one down last night and two of them ended up in the infirmary, so I'm going to say this for the last time. We could really use your help out there."

"I'm sorry," replied Frankenstein. "I can't. What about you? Are you going out?"

Jamie checked his console. "In just over an hour," he replied. "The entire active roster is going out today or tonight."

"You're taking your rookies?"

He nodded. "Holmwood has temporarily activated all the trainees. They go back to the Playground as soon as this is dealt with, but as of right now, they're officially Operators."

Frankenstein poured himself another glass of whisky. "Are they ready?" he asked.

"No," said Jamie, honestly. "But I think they'll do OK. And, to be honest, they're going to have to. This is pretty much the definition of in at the deep end."

The monster took a sip of his drink. "Keep a close eye on them."

Jamie forced a laugh. "Both of them are older than me; one was some kind of SIS assassin and the other was a Para on the verge of SAS selection. I'm hoping they're going to keep an eye on *me*."

Frankenstein put his drink down and leant forward.

"I'm serious," he said, his voice rumbling like an earthquake. "I don't care what they did, where they did it, or for how long. They've never seen the things that you and I have seen. So I'll say it again: keep a close eye on them. Do you hear me?"

"Yeah," replied Jamie. "OK, sure, I hear you. I'll be careful."

Frankenstein sat back. "I'm sure you'll try," he said. For a brief moment, his eyes seemed to sparkle with laughter and Jamie felt the atmosphere in the room lift. "Now let's talk about something less gloomy. How is Matt enjoying being asked to save the world?"

Jamie opened his mouth to answer, then felt his console vibrate once in its loop in his belt. It was the alarm he had set for himself, to make sure he had enough time to do everything he wanted to do before meeting up with his squad.

"Matt's fine," he replied, standing up. "I'll tell you next time, I promise."

"You have to leave?"

"I do," he said. "I'm sorry."

"I thought you weren't heading out for an hour?"

"I'm sorry," repeated Jamie, noting the expression of sadness that had flickered across the monster's face. "I'll come down tomorrow, OK?"

"All right," replied Frankenstein. "Good luck with the op. Be careful. And remember what you promised me. Stay away—"

"I know," interrupted Jamie, a smile breaking out across his face. "I know what I promised you. You remind me every time I see you. I'll see you tomorrow."

"All right," said Frankenstein, the sad ghost of a smile on his face. "Tomorrow."

"Really?" asked Valentin Rusmanov, placing two cups of tea on the low table that sat in the middle of his cell. "That's really what he made you promise?"

"Stay away from Valentin," said Jamie, grinning. "He reminds me every time I see him."

"How perfectly lovely," replied Valentin, settling easily on to the *chaise longue* that stood against one of cell's bare concrete walls. "Under normal circumstances I would not consider myself easily flattered, but I must confess it gives me a rather warm feeling to know that the monster considers me worthy of such warnings. Has he explained *why* you should stay away from me?"

"He says you can't be trusted," replied Jamie, sipping his tea. "He doesn't believe your reasons for being here."

"Well, I suppose I can't really blame him for that," said Valentin. "Although I am glad you choose to ignore his warnings. And I do rather resent his hypocrisy."

"What do you mean?" asked Jamie, glancing round the cell as he spoke.

Lamberton, Valentin's long-serving butler, was in his own cell next door, but was liable to appear at any moment. The ancient vampires could pass through the UV walls that were supposed to contain them with casual ease, and did so whenever they chose to. Jamie assumed that Lamberton was providing the illusion of privacy while his master spoke with his guest, although he knew full well that the servant would have been able to hear every word from a far greater distance than the neighbouring cell.

Several items had been added to the room since Valentin had arrived at the Loop, offering to help Blacklight defeat both his former master and his older brother. The elegant *chaise longue*, the rosewood coffee table, the matching pair of green leather chairs: all were new additions. Jamie didn't know where they had come from; they were presumably the result of discussions between Valentin and Cal Holmwood, discussions that Jamie would have loved the opportunity to listen in on.

The vampire was still a deeply polarising figure within the Department, even after his actions during his brother's attack on the Loop. He had fought Valeri to a standstill in front of everyone, and had given his own blood to help Larissa in the moments before the base's final defence mechanism, a ring of incredibly powerful ultraviolet bombs, had reduced them both to little more than burnt husks.

But to many Operators, he was still nothing more than a vampire, an old and incredibly dangerous one; he had been turned by Dracula himself and they simply could not bring themselves to believe that he was truly on their side. Some act of betrayal was widely expected, and the prospect contributed greatly to the oppressive air of anxiety within the Department for a very good reason: no one inside Blacklight was remotely confident of stopping Valentin if he decided to turn on them.

Jamie was unsure of his own feelings regarding the ancient vampire. Valentin was unquestionably a provocateur, and it was not in his nature to provide reassurance; he had refused all requests for some form of collateral to back up his words, whether it be wearing a limiter belt, allowing the insertion of a locator chip, or anything else. He maintained that his word should be sufficient, taking great delight, Jamie was quite sure, in the knowledge that there was no good reason for it to be. But he had fed Larissa his own blood after Valeri pulled her throat out, and for that Jamie would always be grateful. He wasn't stupid; he knew it was highly likely that Valentin had merely seen an opportunity to increase his standing within the Department. But there were so many potential levels of bluff, double bluff and counter bluff that it would never be possible to know why he had done what he did with any degree of certainty. Jamie had decided simply to take Valentin at face value, while never lowering his guard for a second or letting his hand drift too far from the grip of his T-Bone.

Doing so had proved easier than expected, because above and behind and beyond all the rational analysis of the situation lay a simple truth, a truth that it would have broken Frankenstein's heart to hear.

Jamie liked Valentin.

He liked him a lot.

The vampire was supernaturally full of life: cheerful, arrogant, funny, and endlessly charming. His appetite for the world around him was infectious, even though it had led him to commit atrocities that turned Jamie's stomach, and he found his spirits lifted merely by being in the vampire's presence. The same, he noted with a mixture of sadness or guilt, could not be said of Frankenstein.

"The monster has done things over the course of his long life that even I would have thought twice about," replied Valentin. "I know he's a loyal little Blacklight puppy now, but he wasn't always so tediously wholesome. So for him to judge me seems rather hypocritical. Wouldn't you agree?"

"I don't know," replied Jamie. "He regrets the things he did. You don't. Isn't that a pretty big difference?"

Valentin smiled broadly. "*Touché*, Mr Carpenter. But answer me this. Do his regrets undo any of the pain he caused?"

Jamie shook his head.

"Quite right," said Valentin. "Regrets and guilt and self-flagellation are all well and good, but they cannot change what has already happened. A murderer may find God in prison, or undergo therapy and come to regret his crimes. It may well mean he never kills again. But it won't bring his victims back to life."

"True," said Jamie. "But it's better than the alternative."

"The alternative, in this case, being me?"

"That's right."

"I suppose from your perspective that's true," said Valentin. "From mine, there is nothing more cowardly than pretending to be something you are not. If the day comes when someone puts a stake through my heart to punish me for the things I've done, I will bear them no ill will. By the standards of what passes for morality in this day and age, I'll deserve it, for having lived my life as I chose. Which is why it frustrates me to know that your superiors still cannot bring themselves to trust me. I have never claimed to be anything other than that which I am, and I have no intention of starting now. Can you see why it annoys me so?"

"I can," said Jamie. "But if it surprises you, then you're nowhere near as clever as you think you are."

There was a moment's silence, before the ancient vampire burst out laughing and Jamie joined in. The joke had been risky, but he believed he had acquired a pretty good feel for Valentin's boundaries, such as they were, and had been reasonably confident of getting away with it.

"I do enjoy talking to you, Mr Carpenter," said Valentin, once their laughter had faded. "There is more life in you than in a dozen of your black-suited friends."

"Thanks," said Jamie, smiling broadly.

I like talking to you too. I look forward to coming down here.

"You're most welcome," said Valentin. "So. What's currently occupying your time, Mr Carpenter?"

"You know I can't tell you," replied Jamie. "Although I'm sure you know."

Valentin smiled. "I do hear the occasional murmur, even all the way down here. Emptying the jails was a clever move on my former master's part. Very clever indeed."

"You think it came from Dracula?" asked Jamie. "Not Valeri?"

Valentin snorted. "Please," he said, his voice thick with contempt. "Although getting others to fight instead of him does indeed sound like the work of my dear brother, this is too bold, too smart a move for his tiny little brain to have devised. This is Dracula beginning to assert himself, I'm sorry to say."

"That's what I thought," said Jamie, and sighed, deeply.

"I hear the escaped vampires are unusually powerful. How perplexing."

Jamie narrowed his eyes. "What do you know about it?" he said.

"Nothing," said the ancient vampire, with a glint in his eye that Jamie didn't like. "Absolutely nothing. I assume you and your colleagues are no closer to locating my former master?"

"You know I—"

"Can't tell me, yes, of course," interrupted Valentin. "So I will just assume that's the case, and you need neither confirm nor deny. Which is a shame, especially given that I've told your superiors on a great many occasions that there is a solution to your problem."

Jamie sat forward in his chair. "What solution?"

"Me, Mr Carpenter," said Valentin. "Sorry, I rather assumed that would have been obvious. I can find them."

"How?"

"I know the dark corners where my brother hides. I know the men and women with whom he associates. I can extract information from people who would not even tell you their names. And more than that, I can *feel* them. We're linked, by blood. I can find them, but I am not allowed to do so."

"Why not?" asked Jamie.

"Your superiors do not trust me, Mr Carpenter, as I have lamented so many times. They believe that my being here is a ruse, a sham of some kind, and that if they allow me to leave, I will return to my brother and my former master and tell them everything I know about this place and its inhabitants."

"That's stupid," said Jamie. "What could you tell them that they haven't already got from Valeri's spies? We barely survived his attack as it is."

Valentin raised his hands and spread them wide. "I've made that point quite vociferously," he replied. "Unfortunately, they are less capable than you of seeing the simple logic of the matter. So here I remain, unable to help, and getting more and more bored with each day that passes."

Jamie considered the stupidity of the situation that had just been described to him. "Can't you just go?" he said, eventually. "Do you really need their permission to leave?"

"My dear Mr Carpenter," replied Valentin. "I'm flattered by your faith in my abilities, I truly am. And yes, I probably could make my way out, if it became necessary to do so. But once out of this cell, there are only two options: break through the airlock and fight my way to the surface, or dig through several hundred metres of concrete and earth. Either one would likely involve killing the majority of the men and women in this base, which is not a prospect that particularly appeals to me."

"I'll talk to them," said Jamie.

"I'm sure you will, Mr Carpenter. As always, you have my gratitude."

"Cool," said Jamie. He was dimly aware of the fact that Valentin had not actually asked him to do anything, that he had, in fact, volunteered to speak to his superiors on the vampire's behalf, but he pushed the thought aside. What he had said made sense, surely anyone could see that?

His console vibrated against his hip; he reached down and dismissed the alarm again.

"Time for work?" asked Valentin.

"Almost," said Jamie, standing up and stretching his arms over his head.

"Those newly-turned vampires aren't going to destroy themselves, are they?"

"I doubt it," replied Jamie, a smile rising on to his face.

"That's a real shame," said Valentin, and stood up. "It's been a pleasure to see you, Jamie, as always." The vampire extended his hand and he shook it with a thick band of confusion rippling through his head. It was how he always felt when he left Valentin's cell, as though he had somehow only heard half of the conversation, that what was actually important had taken place without him noticing.

"You too," he said.

Valentin smiled a final time, then floated back on to the *chaise longue* and opened the battered paperback copy of *The Count of Monte Cristo* that had been lying on the coffee table.

Jamie watched him for a second or two, then walked through the UV wall, feeling the familiar tingle on his skin. He turned to his right and walked quickly towards the cell at the end of the block.

It was always a strange moment for Jamie when he stepped out in front of the UV wall that enclosed the square room his mother now called home.

The warm, comfortable space she had made was in such stark contrast to the austere grey concrete of the other cells that it always made him want to laugh. Marie Carpenter was standing in the middle of the spotlessly neat room, smiling nervously at him as he appeared. He walked through the ultraviolet barrier, hugged her, and felt her reach carefully around him and link her arms at his back. This too made him want to laugh; his mother was so worried about accidentally hurting him with her vampire strength that she held him as though he was made of glass.

"How are you, Mum?" he said, pulling back. "Everything OK?"

"Everything's fine," she said. As they always did, her eyes flicked to the scar on his neck. "How are you, love?"

"Surviving," replied Jamie, smiling at her. She frowned, and he instantly regretted the small joke. "I'm fine, Mum," he said. "I'm all right."

"Good," she said. "That's good."

They stood, looking at each other, for a long moment.

"I might sit down, Mum," said Jamie, eventually. "What do you think?"

"Yes," she said. "Yes, sit down. Definitely. Would you like tea?"

"I'm fine, thanks," he replied, and flopped down on to the brown leather sofa that had stood for years in the living room of their house in Kent.

"Sorry," said Marie. "I forgot you just had one."

Jamie looked confused for a moment, then laughed. "You heard me talking to Valentin."

"I wasn't listening," she said, quickly. "Not on purpose. I couldn't help overhearing."

"It's OK, Mum," he said. "It's not your fault."

"Do you want something else?" she asked, eagerly. "I've got some biscuits."

"I'm fine, Mum, honestly. I can't stay long."

Her face fell. "Are you going on a mission?" she asked.

Yet again, Jamie fought back the urge to laugh. It was ludicrous to hear his mother talking about missions, although no more ludicrous than the fact that she was now a vampire, the result of Alexandru Rusmanov's last attempt to hurt the Carpenter family, or the fact that she had fought against Valeri's army during the attack on the Loop, committing acts of violence that were so out of keeping with her gentle nature.

"I am," he replied. "I can't tell you what it is, though."

"Is it dangerous?" she asked, nervously, holding a packet of Rich Tea biscuits in her hand.

"They all are, Mum," he replied. "Forget the biscuits. Come and sit down."

She nodded, replaced the packet on the table that had once stood in their kitchen, and sat down next to him on the sofa.

"Are you OK?" he asked. "Have you got everything you need?"

She nodded.

"I'm sorry I can't stay," he said. "I'll come down and see you tomorrow, OK? I promise."

"You said that two days ago," she replied. "And the day before that too."

Jamie felt heat rise in his cheeks. But this was not the anger that had filled him as he talked to Frankenstein; this was the dull bloom of shame. He *had* promised his mum he would come and see her two days ago, and the day before that, and a great many days before that as well. Somehow it always slipped his mind; things happened, and he forgot. She never complained, or made him feel bad about it; she had never even mentioned it, until now.

"I know," he said, softly. "And I'm sorry. It just... gets a bit crazy up there sometimes."

There was a long moment of silence. The expression on his mother's face made Jamie want to cry; it was so full of unconditional love.

No matter how often I let her down, he thought. *She always forgives me. I don't deserve her.*

"Do you ever get scared?" asked Marie, her tone gentle. "It's OK if you don't want to tell me."

The question cut right through him. He considered lying to his mother, but quickly decided against it; he had promised himself that he wouldn't, regardless of what it might mean he had to tell her.

"Sometimes," he said. "Not usually. But right now..."

Marie frowned. "I heard you and Valentin talking about some new vampires. Are they worse than the usual ones?"

"I haven't seen them in the flesh," replied Jamie. "But yes, it sounds like they're pretty bad."

"Do you have to go?" she asked.

Jamie nodded.

"Can't somebody else deal with them? Why does it always have to be you?"

"It's not just me, Mum. Everybody is going out."

"It really must be serious," said Marie. "Promise me you'll be extra careful?"

Jamie smiled. "Don't worry, Mum. I'll come down tomorrow so you can see I'm OK. I promise."

She smiled at him, and he suddenly felt as though his heart might break. "Don't make promises you can't keep, love," she said. "I'm not trying to make your life harder, I'm honestly not. It would just be nice to see you now and again. That's all."

"I'm sorry, Mum," he repeated. "I really am. I'll come down tomorrow."

"OK," she said, squeezing his hand briefly. "I'm sure you will."

He felt a lump rise in his throat and got to his feet. She floated up with him and he hugged his mother again; she gave him a tight squeeze, then floated off across the cell and began to make tea for herself. Jamie watched her for a moment, his heart aching, then walked away down the corridor.

Marie Carpenter listened as her son's footsteps echoed away.

When he reached the airlock, she let out the breath she had been holding, a tremulous expulsion of air that was close to a sob. It hurt her to know that Jamie was in danger every day, but what hurt her even more was that she saw him so rarely; she had thought that the only upside to the terrible series of events that had befallen their family would be that she got to spend time with her son, the way they had before Julian had died, leaving her a widow and Jamie a fatherless teenage boy. But he was always busy, and he never came to see her when he said he would, and she tried so hard not to show him how much it hurt her, to not be a burden, or give him anything else to worry about when all he should be concentrating on was keeping himself safe. Sometimes she got so angry with herself; she tried to focus on the fact that he had bigger concerns than coming to see his mum, tried to just be proud of him and support him, but she couldn't help it.

She missed her son.

"Am I interrupting?"

Marie spun round and saw a tall, strikingly handsome man standing casually on the other side of the ultraviolet barrier. He was dressed in a beautiful dark blue suit and his skin was incredibly pale, almost translucent; it seemed to shimmer beneath the fluorescent lights.

"Of course not, Valentin," she said, with a wide smile. "It's lovely to see you, as always."

The ancient vampire smiled back at her, then slid through the UV barrier as though it was the easiest thing in the world. Marie had tried to do it herself, after the first time Valentin had come to see her, and burned her arm an agonising black. She was quicker now, however, gaining speed and strength with the assistance of her new friend, and she thought the day that she could step safely out of her cell might not be too far away. He appeared at her side, and his proximity made her feel like it always did; as though someone had turned her internal thermostat up by a couple of degrees without warning her.

"Did I hear you mention tea?" he asked, his smile dizzying.

"You did," she managed. "Go and sit down."

He stayed where he was for a long moment, then floated gracefully across the cell and settled on to the sofa.

"How was Jamie?" he asked.

Marie smiled at the mention of her son's name, and started to talk as she set about making the tea.

11

TIME TO GO HOME

EIGHT YEARS EARLIER

Johnny Supernova closed the door of his flat behind Albert Harker, then slid the chain into place and turned the deadlock.

He had been in the company of madness before, of all kinds. He had once helped talk a pop star down from the roof of her house in St John's Wood when she was threatening to jump with her two-year-old niece in her arms, had been one of the first into the bathroom of a party in Camden in which a teenage boy had carved most of the skin from his arms with a razor blade, babbling about the spiders that were crawling beneath his skin. He had seen paranoia fuelled by drugs and fame, violence and horror and abuse of all kinds, sadism, viciousness and, on one occasion that still chilled him to remember it, the blank, empty eyes of a psychopath as she stood beside him at a hotel bar and talked in a dead monotone about the weather.

But he had never, in all his travels through the dark underbelly of the world, seen madness as plausible and self-contained as he had in the face and voice of Albert Harker. What the man had told him was nothing short of lunacy, the fantasies of a child or a conspiracy fanatic, but there had been absolutely nothing crazy about the man's delivery. He had, in fact, been horribly convincing.

A shiver ran through Johnny as he walked slowly back into his living room and looked at the tape recorder lying on his coffee table. The small black machine seemed disconcerting, almost dangerous, and, for a moment, he considered smashing it to pieces, ridding himself of it, and the story it contained, forever. But something made him hesitate. His last commission had come in almost three months earlier, and the money he had been paid for it was long spent. He doubted anyone would take Albert Harker's clearly delusional story seriously, but he had learnt never to say never; maybe he could work it up into something about fathers and sons, about brothers and the upper-class obsession with family and tradition.

Johnny picked up the tape recorder and ejected the tiny cassette. He placed it in one of the two slots on the recording deck that stood on a shelf beside the window, inserted a blank tape into the other, and pressed record. His friends and acquaintances were often surprised to discover that Johnny Supernova was extremely diligent where his interviews were concerned; paper notes were scanned and backed up on his laptop, and tapes were duplicated and labelled with his own code, meaningless to anyone else.

The tapes whirred inside the high-speed deck, until a loud beep announced that the copy was complete. Johnny ejected the new tape, scrawled an apparently random combination of letters and numbers on its label, and placed it on to a shelf below the deck containing several hundred identical-looking cassettes. He put the original back into his portable recorder, then made his way to his flat's small kitchen. He brewed a pot of tea and was carrying it back into the living room, intending to listen to the interview again, when his doorbell rang.

Johnny frowned. He wasn't expecting anyone, and made a point of keeping his home address a closely guarded secret. There had been too many crazy fans over the years, people who turned up on his doorstep at the end of some weird pilgrimage, wanting to party with him, or in many cases just be in his presence. In the early days, he had invited these men and women in, given them beer and wine, occasionally drugs, and let them hang out for as long as they liked. In later years, he had given them a cup of tea, let them get warm for a few minutes, then sent them on their way. Now he simply told them they had the wrong address and closed the door in their faces.

He set his tea aside, walked down the stairs and out into the communal corridor that served the whole house. Johnny suddenly wished, not for the first time, that he had an entry-phone system; he could have checked who was outside from behind the safety of two heavy locks. But he didn't. He reached the front door and leant his face close up against the wood.

"Who is it?" he shouted, and felt a stab of shame as he heard the tremor in his own voice. "Who's there?"

"Metropolitan Police, sir," replied a flat, metallic voice. "Open the door, please."

Johnny paused. It was far from the first time the police had been at his door.

"How can I help you?" he shouted.

"We need to talk to you regarding a matter of national security, sir," replied the voice. "You can help by opening your door."

National security?

Still Johnny hesitated; something didn't feel quite right. He wracked his brains, trying to identify the source of his unease; when he failed to do so, he took a deep breath and opened the door.

It was barely clear of its frame before it burst open, sending

Johnny stumbling backwards. He lost his balance, twisted round, and planted one hand on the worn carpet of the hallway. By the time he had pushed himself back to his feet, the front door was closed and locked, and two figures in black uniforms were standing in front of him. Their faces were hidden by purple visors that emerged from the black helmets they were wearing; Johnny couldn't see a single millimetre of exposed skin. One of them stepped forward, raising a gloved hand, and terror exploded through him. He turned and ran for the open door of his flat.

He didn't make it.

As Johnny stretched for the door frame, intending to fling himself through the gap between it and the door, fingers closed in the hair at the back of his head, then whipped him sharply to the right. His balance left him and his head thudded into the wall. He saw stars and fought to stay upright, his brain screaming a single coherent thought.

Have to get away. Have to get away. Have to get away.

He threw himself forward, feeling an explosion of pain as a handful of his hair and scalp tore loose, and staggered through the door. He pushed weakly at it, but a heavy black boot had already been wedged against the frame, and it wouldn't close. He turned and stumbled up the stairs towards his kitchen, his mind reeling with panic. Footsteps thudded on the stairs behind him, horribly slow and calm, and Johnny realised there was nowhere to go. Then hands grabbed at him again; he was pushed through the kitchen and into the living room, where he was thrown on to his battered sofa. He stared up at the black figures. One of them appeared to be looking down at him from behind its impenetrable purple visor, while the other had picked up his tape recorder and pressed play. Albert Harker's voice instantly emerged from the small speaker.

"... is the biggest secret in the world, a secret that my family and others have kept for more than a century. And I'm telling it..."

The figure clicked the stop button, opened the recorder and took out the tape. It passed it to its colleague, who held it up in front of Johnny's face.

"This is the recording of your interview with Albert Harker?" it said, in the same empty voice he had heard through the front door.

Johnny nodded. He was literally too frightened to speak.

The figure slid the tape into a pouch on the side of its uniform.

"Where are your notes?" it asked.

He pointed with a trembling finger. His notebook was lying where he had left it, on the arm of his chair. The second figure picked it up, leafed through it, then pocketed it.

Johnny managed to find his voice. "Hey," he shouted. "There's other stuff in there."

"Other stuff?" asked the figure.

"Normal stuff," replied Johnny. "Work stuff. The Harker notes are only the last two pages. Let me keep the rest. Please?"

There was a long pause. Then the dark figure pulled out the notebook, tore out the last written pages and threw the rest down on to the coffee table.

Johnny was about to crawl across the floor and grab it when a black gloved hand gripped his face and turned his head. The purple visor was millimetres away from his face and he fought back a new torrent of panic.

"Mr Supernova," said the black figure, and the flatness of its voice made him want to scream. "It would be extremely inadvisable to attempt to publish what you heard today. The unsubstantiated ramblings of a man with both a long-standing substance addiction and a well-known grudge against his family will be of little interest to anyone, and cannot possibly be claimed to be in the public interest. To publish such a story would in all likelihood result in the death of your career, a career that is already ailing badly. Do you understand what I am saying to you?"

Johnny nodded rapidly. For a long moment, the visor didn't move; he could see his own terrified face reflected in the purple surface. Then the figure released its grip and stood up.

"We're done here," it said. The second figure nodded, strode back into the kitchen, and opened the door.

A second later they were gone.

He stared after them for a long moment, then burst up from the sofa. He ran across the room, his steps short and unsteady, and clattered down the stairs.

The corridor was empty.

The front door was shut.

Johnny let out a high, childlike sob and slammed his door shut, locking it and sliding the chain into place. He ran back up the stairs, scrabbled at the shelf of tapes beside the window and clutched the copy of the Harker interview in his shaking hands. Gripping it tightly, he slid to the floor, turning his back against the wall. He drew his knees up to his chin and began to weep.

A mile away, Albert Harker walked up on to London Bridge wondering why he had lied to the journalist.

No, that wasn't right.

He hadn't lied; everything he had told Supernova was the truth. But he *had* omitted something from his account of his refusal to join Department 19.

*

On New Year's Day 1980, Albert's twin brother Robert had taken him aside, sworn him to secrecy, and told him about Blacklight.

He was as animated as Albert had ever seen him, bursting with excitement at what the New Year had in store for them both. Albert listened, then asked him how he had come to know about the organisation he was describing. Robert frowned; it was the look of someone who has got carried away with something and hasn't thought the potential consequences through.

"Dad told me," he said, eventually. "On our birthday, when he was drunk. He said it was only one more year until we could start our real lives. I asked him what he meant and he told me."

"Where was I?" asked Albert. A familiar sensation had begun to creep into his chest, as though his heart was being packed in ice.

"It was late," said Robert. "You were asleep."

"So how come you're only telling me now?"

Robert's gaze flicked momentarily to the floor and Albert knew the answer before his brother spoke it aloud.

"He told me not to tell you," said Robert, with the decency to at least look apologetic. "The next morning. He said he shouldn't have told me and that I wasn't to tell you. So I told him I wouldn't. I'm sorry, Bert."

Albert pushed the hurt aside, something he was vastly experienced at doing, and tried instead to focus on what his brother had said; there was a future in which they would be together, would do something incredible, and exciting, and dangerous. The New Year, which usually brought him nothing but gloom, suddenly seemed bright and full of possibility.

"Don't worry about it," he replied, and smiled. "Although it sounds like you're going to have to get a lot better at keeping secrets."

Robert grinned. "So should Dad. You know who he told me works for Blacklight?"

"Who?"

"Frankenstein."

"Piss off. Doctor Frankenstein is real?"

Robert shook his head. "Not the doctor, the monster. Apparently, he took his creator's name. Some sort of honour thing."

"Frankenstein's monster is real and works with our dad? That's what you're telling me?"

"Yep," replied Robert. "And in a year's time, so will we. Try and get your head round that."

"I need a drink," said Albert, then grinned at his brother. "A big one."

Robert laughed, a noise that was high and loud and full of happiness. The two brothers threw their arms round each other's shoulders and rejoined the party as the crowd began their joyous countdown to midnight.

For eight long months, Albert looked forward to his birthday with an excitement he hadn't felt since he was a little boy. Spring and summer passed with agonising slowness, until finally, at long last, the day arrived. He journeyed from his halls in Cambridge to his parents' home the afternoon before, enjoyed the atmosphere of palpable anticipation that surrounded the table as they ate dinner, then bade his family goodnight.

It took him a long time to get to sleep.

When he awoke the next morning, he made his way excitedly down the stairs, and found his parents and brother in the midst of breakfast; he joined them, in what he would come to remember as the last moment of genuine happiness they experienced together. After the plates were cleared and the champagne was drunk and the presents were opened, Albert's father asked Robert if he could see him in his study. Robert agreed, tipping his brother a wink as he followed their father out of the kitchen and up the stairs.

The two men returned fifteen minutes later. Robert wore a remarkably smug expression, while their father looked as though he might burst with pride. Both men appeared to have been crying, and Albert felt a surge of love rush into his chest as they retook their seats at the kitchen table.

My turn, *Albert thought, excitedly.* Any second. My turn next.

But nothing happened.

The usual chatter resumed and Albert realised, with slowly dawning horror, that his turn wasn't coming. He tried desperately to catch his brother's eye, but Robert studiously avoided his gaze, looking in every other possible direction. When breakfast was over, the family went their separate ways, heading into the living room or out into the garden.

Albert remained where he was, unable to believe that this was really happening to him, to believe that anyone, even David Harker, could be quite so cruel. Eventually, he heard his father call for Robert. A moment later he heard the jeep's engine roar into life, heard the rattle of tyres across gravel, and knew it was real. He got up from the table, packed his bags, and left the house without saying a word to anyone.

Back in Cambridge, he got drunk for three days, and on the fourth he called his brother. Robert told him he didn't know what was happening, and that he couldn't talk about it even if he did. He was playing under a new set of rules, he said, and Albert wasn't to ask him about the organisation they had discussed on New Year's Eve. It would be for the best, Robert said, if he forgot about what he had been told.

Albert fought back the urge to shriek down the phone.

This isn't fair! This isn't fair! You get everything and now you get this too and I get nothing! IT'S NOT FAIR!

Instead, he told Robert he never wanted to see him again and hung up on the first syllables of his brother's protest. Then he opened a bottle of vodka and waited to see whether or not his father would put him out of his misery.

Weeks passed without word from home until, one baking hot afternoon in late August, Albert returned from a drunken stroll in the park to find his father standing outside the door to his room. His face curdled with obvious distaste as he took in his son's dishevelled, unshaven appearance, but he said nothing. He merely waited for his son to open the door and followed him through it.

Albert sat in the chair beneath the window, while his father remained standing. He didn't offer to make tea, or coffee, or anything else; he was only interested in what they both knew his father was there to say, which he proceeded to deliver in a flat, emotionless tone of voice that made Albert want to cry. David Harker explained quickly that there was an organisation called Blacklight, which every male member of the Harker family had been a member of, all the way back to his great-grandfather, who had helped found it. He, Albert, was entitled to join, if he wanted to.

And that was it.

Albert stared up at him for a long moment, realising with sudden certainty what had happened: his father had not wanted to invite him to join, had clearly had no intention of ever doing so, but had been told by someone, presumably his superiors, that it was mandatory. So he had driven to Cambridge and made the offer to his son in the least enthusiastic way possible, hoping against hope that he would say no. For a moment, Albert thought about saying yes, out of nothing more than pure, hateful spite. But the thought quickly passed.

"I don't want to join," he said, looking his father directly in the eye and seeing exactly what he was expecting: a momentary bloom of uncontrollable relief. He felt something break in his chest and told his father that he could see himself out. Without waiting to see if he did so, Albert walked stiffly into his bedroom and lay down on his bed.

He lay there for a long time. Eventually, he heard the click as his father pulled the door shut behind him.

The wind whipped up from the river below and Albert pulled his coat tightly round him as he made his way across the bridge.

He had let Johnny Supernova believe that he had never wanted to join Blacklight, that he had rejected his father's offer out of calculated malice. In truth, his twenty-first birthday had been the day his heart had closed to the rest of the world. It had been cold confirmation of all his deepest fears about himself: that he was no good, that he was inferior to his brother, that his father had never wanted or loved him. The reality was simple, and endlessly painful: he had rejected his father's offer because he couldn't bear the thought of seeing the disappointment in his eyes every day.

Albert was halfway across the bridge when a black car pulled to a halt beside him. He stopped and looked at it; the windows were the same impenetrable black as its body and the number plate on the front bore the legend DIPLOMATIC VEHICLE. The passenger door swung open and he leant down to look inside. A man in a black suit stared out at him, his eyes hidden behind a pair of sunglasses.

"Took you long enough," said Albert. "I didn't think I'd get this far, to be honest. Standards must be slipping."

"Will you come with us, please, Mr Harker?" asked the man. He gave no indication of having heard Albert speak.

"Come where?" he asked.

"There is someone who wants to speak to you, Mr Harker," replied the man. He shifted slightly in his seat and his suit jacket slid open far enough for Albert to see the black pistol hanging beneath the man's armpit.

"I can't imagine who that might be," said Harker, with a gentle smile.

He took a quick look around. The grey mass of the Thames moved sluggishly beneath him, as sunlight gleamed off the stone and glass and metal of the buildings on either side of the river. The sky was bright blue overhead, the clouds the purest white. It was a fine day, the kind that you hope for every morning when you force yourself out of bed. Albert Harker took a sweet, lingering breath and climbed into the back of the car.

They accelerated smoothly north, leaving the river behind.

Albert watched the passing city with an odd sensation of grief filling him; he felt like he was never going to see it again. The fact that the man in the sunglasses had not felt the need to blindfold him suggested that the journey was one-way; they clearly didn't care if he saw where they were taking him.

The car ploughed through the thick traffic at the Aldwych, crawled up Kingsway and Woburn Place, and emerged on to Euston Road. Beyond the filthy, litter-strewn streets that surrounded King's Cross Station, an area of London that Albert remembered being far, far worse as little as a decade earlier, they turned north on to York Way, past the goods yards and the sticky, almost stationary canal. The car's big engine purred as it made its way on to Camden Road, where it pulled into the driveway of a tall, narrow house.

The man in the sunglasses told Albert to stay where he was, then climbed out of the car. A second later the door beside him opened, to reveal the man holding it with such stolid politeness that Albert fought back the urge to laugh. He eased himself out of the car and looked up at the house. The door stood at the top of five stone steps, open to the warm afternoon air. Albert looked at the man in the sunglasses, who didn't move.

"Aren't you coming?" he asked.

The man didn't respond. Albert stared at him for a moment that seemed to last forever, then crossed the drive and slowly climbed the steps, one at a time. Beyond the door, he saw a man standing in a long, narrow hallway. His black suit was identical to the one worn by his colleague outside, and he gave no indication of having seen Albert Harker; he stood perfectly still, his hands clasped before his groin, the plastic earpiece behind his ear clearly visible. On the opposite side of the corridor was an open door. Albert approached it slowly, trying to slow his racing heart, and stepped through it.

The room was long and tall, with a semi-circular set of bay windows beneath which sat an empty sofa. Standing in front of it was Albert's father.

"Hello, son," said David Harker. He was wearing his Blacklight uniform, his hands dangling loosely at his sides, his face expressionless. Albert opened his mouth to reply, but then a second voice spoke from behind him, a voice that froze him where he stood.

"Hello, Bert."

Albert turned slowly and saw his brother standing at the far end of the room. He too was all in black, and standing beside him was a man that Albert didn't recognise.

"Robert," he said. "What are you—"

"Look at me, Albert," said David, sharply. "Your brother asked to be here, but it's me you're dealing with."

He forced himself back round. To Albert's well-practised eyes, two thin patches of pale pink were clearly visible high up on his father's cheeks. He had come to know them very well as a child; they were a clear warning that his father's patience was nearing an end, and that his temper, a great and terrible thing, was very close to the surface.

"Hello, Father," he said, as calmly as he was able. He suddenly felt incredibly alone among these three men, whose loyalty to each other, he knew, far superseded the loyalty that either of the members of his family felt towards him. "What can I do for you?"

David took a step forward. "What did you tell him, Albert?" he asked, his voice low and cold.

"Tell who?"

"The journalist. What did you tell him?"

Albert shrugged. "Everything," he said.

"Why?" growled David Harker. "For God's sake, why?"

"Because I knew it would make your life difficult," replied Albert, and smiled at his father.

David crossed the distance between them in the blink of an eye. There was a blur of black, before his fist crashed into his son's mouth, driving him to the ground. Albert felt pain explode through his head, felt his lip tear and his mouth fill up with blood. His stomach churned and he put his hands on the floor, trying to steady himself. He spat blood on to the wooden floorboards of the living room, then rocked back on his knees, staring up at his father. Behind him, from some great distance, he heard a vaguely familiar voice shout for someone to control themself, but paid it little attention. His gaze was fixed on the twisted crimson of his father's face, at the expression of pure hatred that blazed there.

"You stupid boy," breathed David Harker. "You stupid, pathetic little boy. He'll never print a word of what you told him. So all that you've done is embarrass your family, yet again. Why couldn't you just have stayed in that rathole in Southwark, with your junkie friends? Or just died, like most of your kind already have? It would have saved us all so much trouble."

"I'm... happy," said Albert, grinning through teeth smeared with blood, "to have... disappointed you... Father."

David Harker raised his fist again, but this time Albert's brother was there, grabbing his arm and holding it in place.

"No more," said Robert, casting a brief, disgusted glance down at his kneeling twin. "Not like this, Dad. This isn't how we do things."

David glared at Robert for a long moment, then his face softened into a look of such obvious pride that Albert felt it as a stabbing pain in the middle of his chest, like an icicle skewering his heart.

"You're right, of course," said David. "Thank you." He clapped his son on the back, then the two men looked down at Albert. An enormous quantity of blood had run from his mouth, soaking the front of his shirt red. He stared back at them with fear and loathing in his eyes.

"This is long overdue," said David. "I should have done this more than a decade ago. Your mother persuaded me to let you be, convinced me that you might eventually work out what it means to be a man, to be a Harker. Letting her do so was my mistake, and I see it now." He looked up towards the door and gave a nod. "Get him out of my sight," he said. "I don't ever want to see his face again."

Albert's mind was suddenly overcome with terror.

They're going to kill me, he thought. *They're going to kill me, oh God, I didn't mean it, I didn't think they'd really do it, oh God, I didn't know. I didn't know.*

Hands grabbed his arms and he began to scream, thrashing wildly in the grips of the men who held him. He screamed for his brother, for his father, screamed that he was sorry, screamed for another chance, one last, final chance. But Robert and David merely watched, their expressions calm, as Albert was dragged out of the room.

He fought them all the way to the front door, kicking and bucking and howling his head off, and when one of the hands released its grip on his arm, he redoubled his efforts. Then something huge and heavy crashed into his lower back and all the fight went out of him. The pain was monstrous, indescribable, and he vomited helplessly as his suddenly limp body was dragged from the house and towards the idling car.

The man in the sunglasses was waiting for him, leaning against the wide black boot with something in his hand. As they approached, Albert saw that it was a hypodermic needle, half full of a clear liquid. He tried to force his reeling limbs to move, to propel him away from the man and the syringe, but nothing happened; the combination of the blows to his face and kidneys had rendered his body unresponsive. He was hauled upright as the man in the sunglasses stepped forward, the faintest flicker of a smile on his face.

"Don't..." managed Albert, his voice little more than a plaintive croak. "Please... don't..."

The man didn't respond and, as the needle slid into his neck, a single thought filled Albert's mind.

This isn't real. None of this is real.

His eyes closed and his body went limp as he was bundled into the back of the car.

When he awoke, it was dark outside.

As his eyes fluttered open, Albert tried to lift his arms and found that nothing happened. His mind was thick and fuzzy, a state of being he knew very well from years of heroin addiction, but this was something else. Something unfamiliar. He concentrated hard and managed to slowly bring his shaking hands up to his face. His mouth was swollen and covered with blood that had dried to powder. He rubbed his eyes with the heels of his palms and looked around. He was alone in the back of the car, which was stationary. In the front, the driver stared rigidly forward; beside him, the passenger seat was empty. Albert shuffled across the seat to his left and peered through the windscreen.

A large building loomed in the distance, lit by circles of yellow light set into brick walls. In front of the car, the man with the sunglasses was standing beside a chain-link gate, talking to a woman in a white coat. As Albert watched, the woman gestured animatedly, waving her hands and shaking her head vehemently back and forth. The man in the sunglasses appeared to let her finish, then leant in close and talked for almost a minute. When he pulled away, the woman looked utterly deflated, her face pale, her shoulders slumped. The man pulled a sheaf of paper from the inside pocket of his suit jacket and handed it to her; she gave it a cursory scan, took a pen from one of the pockets of her white coat, and signed each page. She handed them back, turned, and walked away without a backward glance. The man in the sunglasses watched her leave, then walked briskly back towards the car. He opened the passenger door, slid in next to Albert, and gave him a wide smile.

"Welcome to your new home, Mr Harker," he said, his tone smooth and oily. "Driver, carry on."

They crept forward and, as Albert watched, the chain-link gate slid open. The big car passed through the widening gap and, as it did so, Albert saw a white rectangle moving slowly past his window. He slid away from the man in the sunglasses, fear and misery clawing at his drifting, reeling mind, pressed his face against the glass, and read the two words that were printed on the sign in bold blue letters.

BROADMOOR HOSPITAL

12

READY TO ROLL

As Jamie expected, Morton and Ellison were waiting for him in the hangar.

On time, he thought. *That's a good start, at least.*

The two freshly commissioned Operators were standing at the rear of the black van that had been assigned to Operational Squad M-3. He walked over to them, his boots thudding on the concrete floor, readying himself to say what he needed to say. He had spent the journey up to the hangar trying to decide whether to tell his rookies what had happened to Angela Darcy's squad; he was far from sure that the extra pressure would be helpful, but was also reluctant for them to start their first mission in the dark about what they were really facing.

"Operators," said Jamie, stopping in front of them.

"Lieutenant," they replied.

"Weapons and kit prep complete?" asked Jamie, eyeing their uniforms. He could already see that they were perfect, the result, no doubt, of dozens of checks and re-checks in the dormitory on Level C, but there were protocols to be followed.

"Yes, sir."

"Intelligence analysis complete?"

"Yes, sir."

"Operational parameters clear?"

"Yes, sir."

"Good. Operator Morton, who is our target?"

"Eric Bingham, sir."

"Operator Ellison," said Jamie, turning to face her. "What intelligence has the target's identification provided?"

"A long history of violence, sir," replied Ellison. "Paranoid schizophrenia, diagnosed more than ten years ago. One conviction for attempted murder, numerous previous incidences of assault."

"All of which means?"

"Shoot first, sir. And keep shooting."

"That's exactly right. Listen to me, do what I tell you, don't waste time trying to talk to him or bring him in alive. We track him down, destroy him, and move on. Clear?"

"Yes, sir."

"Good. Now listen carefully. An experienced squad, led by one of the finest Operators in this Department, returned to the Loop this morning with two seriously injured members. They were both hurt by a single vampire, one of the escapees from Broadmoor. The squad in question were not in possession of the full facts and paid the price. We will not make the same mistake. Is that clear?"

Neither Ellison nor Morton replied. Their faces had paled slightly and their mouths were set in thin lines.

This is it, thought Jamie. *They can handle this or they can't. They're ready or they're not. Time to find out.*

"OK," he said, hauling open the rear door of the van. "Let's move out."

The van sped through the thick forest that lay beyond the perimeter of the Loop, its powerful engine humming beneath its passengers' feet.

Operational Squad M-3 were strapped into three of the moulded seats in the vehicle's rear, their weapons and kit stowed safely in the slots between them. Jamie sat upright in his seat, his feet flat on the floor; he had been in this position dozens of times, and under normal circumstances his faith in the van's tracking and weapon systems meant that he was almost able to relax. But these were far from normal circumstances; he found himself concentrating on projecting calm to his new squad mates, even though his mind was still reeling at what had been done to Alex Jacobs and John Carlisle.

He had tried several times to start a conversation with his rookies, but had received only one-word answers; he had eventually given up, leaving them to their thoughts. As a result, the atmosphere inside the van was tense, dangerously so for the early stages of an operation; his new squad mates were obviously wound too tight, but Jamie thought drawing attention to the fact was only likely to make it worse. Instead, he had lowered the van's control screen and called up a map of eastern England, marked with two moving dots. The black dot was them as they accelerated south.

The red dot was Eric Bingham, their target.

He was still in Peterborough and appeared to have gone to ground in the hours since his escape from Broadmoor. He was moving, but within an exceedingly small range, and the Surveillance Division had pinned his location down to a warehouse on a long-derelict industrial estate on the edge of town, a warehouse that he had now not left for more than six hours. This was the first bit of genuinely good news that Jamie had heard all day; a disused warehouse meant no civilians, no potential hostages, and almost no risk of collateral damage. As squad leader, he had been given a clearance of five for the mission at hand, a concept that he would never, ever get used to.

If we get the vampires on our list and no more than five innocent people die, then everything's cool. That's the equation. One of ours for every one of them. Maths, written in blood and human lives.

The collateral damage allowance was one thing Jamie had felt no guilt about keeping from his rookies; he figured they had more than enough to worry about. Instead, he watched the screen, feeling an unsettling sensation of inevitability as they approached their target.

An hour later their driver's voice emerged from the intercom that linked the cab to the body of the vehicle.

"We're a mile out, sir. Do you want me to proceed?"

"Roger that," replied Jamie. "Go silent and get us one hundred metres out."

"Roger," replied the driver.

The rumble of the van's engine died away, leaving silence behind. It sounded as though the vehicle's power had been cut, but the lights and the screen remained bright, and it continued to move steadily forward.

"Weapons prep," said Jamie, looking at his squad mates. Calm appeared to have settled over them both, a state of being that he wanted to believe was genuine. Away from the Loop, in the real world with weapons to fire, a mission to carry out and a target to destroy, he was hopeful that Morton and Ellison had reverted to what they were: highly trained men and women who had been in situations where their lives were in danger dozens of times before. This was the moment of truth, where training and experience would hopefully overwhelm trepidation, where they would realise that they *could* do what was being asked of them.

As one, Morton and Ellison began to clip their weapons and kit into place. Jamie did the same, keeping his gaze fixed on them;

there were cold looks in both of their eyes that he liked. When the squad was fully equipped, he forced a smile.

"This is it," he said. "We stay calm, we do our job, and we go home. It's as simple as that. Clear?"

"Clear, sir," they replied.

Operational Squad M-3 ran across the cracked tarmac in a five-metre spread with Jamie in the middle.

The van had pulled away as soon as their boots hit the ground; even in a place as desolate as this, the vehicle was likely to draw unwanted attention, so their driver would move it to a less visible location until he was called back to collect them.

They were on their own.

The industrial estate was as bleak and lifeless as the surface of the moon. The roads and pavements were strewn with litter, and empty offices, factories and warehouses stood dark and brooding on all sides. There was broken glass in several of the windows, but the buildings were not falling down; they simply looked abandoned. Jamie wondered what had brought about the exodus that had clearly taken place here; had the companies that had once inhabited these buildings gone out of business? Downsized? Sent their operations abroad? The place felt sad and pointless, built for a purpose that was now gone and would likely never return.

Looming before the squad was the two-storey factory that was their destination; the sign on the approach to the building announced it as the home of MCM FROZEN FOODS. The front doors, through which workers had presumably once streamed in and out in the mornings and evenings, had been locked with a sturdy length of chain and a shiny steel padlock, both of which were now lying on the ground, bent and twisted. The doors themselves were standing slightly open as the three Operators reached them.

"Christ," breathed Morton. "Takes a lot of strength to do that."

"That's right," said Jamie. "It does. Stay calm."

"Not too subtle," said Ellison. "Doesn't look like he cares if he gets caught."

"I doubt he's thinking that clearly," said Jamie. "If he didn't feed in time, the hunger has probably driven him mad. If he did, if he's still himself, he has a long history of mental instability. I'm not expecting predictable behaviour from any of our targets, and you shouldn't either."

"So what's the plan?" asked Morton.

"We find him," said Jamie. "Which shouldn't be hard. Thermal imaging will make him look like a firework. Then we destroy him."

"OK," said Morton.

"Good," said Jamie. "Follow me."

He reached out, pushed open the doors, then slipped through, disappearing into the darkness. Morton and Ellison followed, their T-Bones drawn and resting steadily in their hands.

The reception that had once welcomed visitors to MCM FROZEN FOODS was no longer welcoming. The desk was empty apart from a small cluster of wires that had been left behind, and the fluorescent lights on the ceiling above it were dark. To the right of the desk stood a single door that presumably led into the warehouse itself. It too was standing open.

Jamie moved quietly across the reception and peered through the door. A cavernous black space stretched up and away from him. There was no movement, no sound of any kind. The warehouse, which would have once been piled from floor to ceiling with pallets of food awaiting despatch, appeared to be empty.

"Thermals," whispered Jamie. "He's in there somewhere. Ready One."

The phrase was Blacklight code that authorised the use of weaponry. Morton and Ellison set their T-Bones against their shoulders, as Jamie drew his from his belt and led his squad into the warehouse. In an ideal world, it would not be him that ended Eric Bingham; it was vital that his new squad mates got used to destroying vampires as soon as possible. But this was far from an ideal world, and he was not prepared to take any chances, not after what he had seen in the Zero Hour Task Force briefing; if the opportunity to make the killing shot came his way, he would take it without hesitation.

Jamie turned the dial on his belt that controlled his helmet's visual modes and watched as the cold concrete walls and floor of the warehouse disappeared in a great wash of dark blue and black. An instant later he saw that he had told Morton the truth.

Eric Bingham wasn't hard to find.

At the far end of the warehouse, a tight ball of bright yellow and orange was curled into the corner where the walls met the ceiling.

"There," said Ellison, the word appearing directly into his and Morton's ears.

"Got him," confirmed Jamie. "Ellison, take point. Morton, next to me."

Ellison moved past him and walked slowly towards the vampire. Morton fell into position beside him and they followed their squad mate, stepping quietly through the empty building. When they were still five metres away from their target, a strange noise began to be picked up by the speakers in Jamie's helmet, a low, rattling sound that he suddenly recognised.

Eric Bingham was growling.

"What the hell?" asked Ellison.

Jamie opened his mouth to answer her, but then the yellow and orange ball moved, bursting out of the corner and rushing down towards them.

"I see you!" screamed Bingham as he hurtled through the air, the heat from his body blinding them. Jamie recoiled, fumbling for the dial on his belt, shouting for his squad to open fire.

"Jesus," yelled Ellison, and fired her T-Bone. The projectile rocketed past the onrushing vampire and hit the wall with a metallic crunch. Morton did nothing; Jamie could hear his panting breath over their comms link and knew he had frozen.

Jamie yanked the barrel of his T-Bone round to where the vampire should have been and pulled the trigger. The metal stake burst from the barrel, but disappeared away into the darkness. Jamie swore, reached up and shoved his visor out of the way. The darkness of the warehouse pressed in on him, and his vision filled with expanding dots of grey and black. With a loud whir and a heavy thud, the metal stake flew back into the barrel of his T-Bone and locked into place.

"Where is he?" yelled Ellison. "I've lost him."

"Regroup," shouted Jamie, squeezing his eyes shut, trying to clear them. "On me, now."

The ghostly faces of his squad mates seemed to materialise as they pushed their own visors clear. They arrived beside him, their eyes wide, their skin pale.

"Where is he?" repeated Ellison, her voice low. "I can't see him."

"Quiet," whispered Jamie. "Both of you." He flicked his visor down and swore again; the blazing heat that had been emanating from Bingham had blown out his helmet's sensors. His visor was clearing, but slowly, ever so slowly; he shoved it back out of the way and drew his torch from its loop on his belt. A wide beam of white light burst from the LED; he swept it quickly across the wide dark space of the warehouse.

Nothing moved.

Ellison and Morton turned on their torches and two more beams appeared; they swooped and crossed, illuminating small circles of the huge room. Jamie could hear both his squad mates, the fear in their breathing, the rapid in and out.

"Easy," he whispered. "Take it easy."

"Is he still here?" asked Morton. He swung his torch as he spoke, aiming it into the distant corners.

"I don't know," hissed Jamie. "I can't see any better than you can." He flicked down his visor, desperate for it to be clear, then pushed it back up. His torch picked out a flash of something that skittered away from the beam, a long pink tail trailing behind it. He circled slowly, trying to keep his torch steady, trying not to let his hand shake.

"What do we do?" whispered Ellison. "Sir? What do we—"

Jamie felt the air shift behind him, a millisecond before Eric Bingham thundered through the middle of his squad, sending the three of them crashing to the ground; he hit the concrete hard and saw the vampire disappear away into the darkness. He leapt back to his feet, ignoring the pain that was shooting through his shoulders, and shone his torch in the direction Bingham had flown, heart pounding in his chest, blood roaring in his head. He saw something move, tried to follow it with his beam of light, but lost it.

Ellison and Morton climbed to their feet and closed in around him.

"We're sitting ducks," hissed Morton. "He can see us, but we can't see him. We need to pull back."

"Calm down, Operator," said Jamie. "Just find the target."

"We need to pull back," repeated Morton, his voice low and unsteady.

"You heard him, John," said Ellison. "Let's do our job."

"I see you!" screamed Eric Bingham. His voice echoed round the warehouse, seeming to come from everywhere at once. "I see you very well!"

Jamie tried to ignore the adrenaline that was pulsing through him, to push away the terrible screeching voice of the vampire and focus on the task at hand. He took a long step in the direction he had seen Bingham disappear, controlling his breathing, letting the darkness flow over him, willing it to reveal its contents.

"We need to pull back," said Morton again, but Jamie ignored him. He was waiting for the telltale shift in the air that meant the vampire was moving. He pulled the MP5 from his belt, pressed his torch against its barrel and stopped, listening to the silent warehouse, feeling the air on the skin of his face.

Movement.

Behind him.

Jamie spun on the balls of his feet, raising the MP5 and pulling its trigger as he turned. Fire licked from the barrel as deafening reports crashed through the enclosed space of the warehouse. His torch beam illuminated his squad mates as they threw themselves to the ground, then picked out something moving at head height, twisting and fluttering, trailing sprays of gleaming red blood behind it. He heard a guttural scream, then silence.

Morton was first to his feet, his eyes blazing, his torch beam blinding as he pointed it at Jamie's face. "What the hell are you—"

Jamie reached out and knocked the torch aside. "Look," he said, and shone his own light on to the warehouse floor, where splashes of crimson appeared in the beam. Jamie followed them towards a dark patch of the warehouse floor, the contents of which became horribly clear in the bright beam of the torch.

"Christ," breathed Ellison.

Eric Bingham was lying in a rapidly spreading pool of blood, staring up at them with wide, frightened eyes. He was middle-aged, probably nearer to fifty than forty, and looked remarkably small on the wide expanse of concrete. His chest was a ruin of bullet holes and his right arm lay shattered at his side.

"Please," he said, the words sending blood cascading down his chin. "I don't know. I told them. Please."

Beams from Morton's and Ellison's torches joined Jamie's own, illuminating the sorry sight before them.

"I missed," said Ellison. "When he charged us. I missed my shot."

"So did I," said Jamie. "It happened fast. It nearly always does."

"Jamie—" began Morton.

"Don't worry about it," interrupted Jamie. "It's done. Ellison?"

"Yes, sir?"

"Finish it."

"Yes, sir," repeated Ellison. She stepped forward, drawing her stake.

Bingham watched her with uncomprehending eyes. "Please," he repeated. "I told them. I promise. Please."

Ellison paused for a moment, beyond the reach of his one functioning arm. Then she darted forward and planted the stake in the vampire's chest. There was a loud crunching noise, before Eric Bingham exploded in an eruption of flying blood. Ellison leapt backwards, avoiding the worst of the mess, and placed the stake back in its loop on her belt.

*

"That was all wrong," said Morton.

The three Operators were back in their van, strapped in and ready to move on. Jamie had ordered the driver to wait while he requested an Operational update from the Surveillance Division, hoping that one of their remaining targets might have been identified since they had departed from the Loop. The connection had been established and he was waiting for any new information to be transmitted to them.

"What was?" asked Jamie. He had been staring at the touch screen, but something in his squad mate's voice made him turn his head.

"That," replied Morton. His face was pale, almost grey, and his eyes were glassy. "The vampire. Bingham. It... wasn't right."

"We did what we needed to do," said Ellison. "Nothing went wrong."

"I'm not saying it did," said Morton.

"Why did it feel wrong?" asked Jamie.

"I'm a soldier," said Morton. "Or at least I was. I've fought enemies in every corner of the world, but nothing like that. That wasn't human."

"It was," said Jamie. "Don't let yourself start to think otherwise. It was a human being with a disease, a disease that gave him unnatural power. It wasn't a monster, or a demon, or anything like that."

"It was all wrong," repeated Morton. He stared at Jamie, who didn't look away; he believed he knew what his squad mate was really saying.

He was scared. I think he'd forgotten what it feels like.

"I'm not a soldier," said Ellison. "I never have been. But I'd be willing to bet I've killed more living things than the two of you put together. Was Bingham stronger and faster than them? Yes. Was he more frightening? Definitely. But he was still just a target, one that needed taking down. Think of it that way, John. Trust me, it helps."

Jamie glanced over at Ellison, whose attention was fixed on her squad mate.

I got lucky here, he thought. *With her. Very lucky.*

On the control screen, a grey download bar was replaced by a window containing two lines of text. He glanced up and read them.

M-3/FIELD UPDATE RESPONSE
NO NEW INFORMATION AVAILABLE

Jamie returned his gaze to John Morton, and made a decision. "I'm pulling the rest of this operation," he said. "We're going back to the Loop."

Ellison frowned. "We've got five and a half hours until our window closes, sir."

"I understand that," said Jamie. "But I'm not going after unidentified targets with a newly commissioned Operator who is having trouble. It isn't safe."

"I'll be all right," said Morton, instantly. "Really. I just need to get my head round it."

"I know what you're going through," said Jamie. "And believe me when I tell you this doesn't have to be a big deal. But we're going home."

"Don't do this," said Morton. "Please. We'll be a laughing stock before we even finish our first operation."

"That's enough, John," said Ellison, shooting him a sharp sideways glance. "If he says we're done, we're done."

"It's all right," said Jamie. "This is on me, I promise you."

I hope that sounded convincing, he thought. *Because I'm really not sure it is.*

Jamie addressed his squad as soon as they stepped down on to the concrete floor of the Loop's hangar.

"Good work," he said. "Honestly. There's one less vampire out there and we came home in one piece. That's a good day around here, trust me. Go and get some rest and I'll message you as soon as I have tomorrow's schedule. Dismissed."

His new squad mates faced him. Ellison's skin was pale, but her eyes were sharp, and Jamie already found himself full of admiration for her; she nodded, gave him a quick smile, and headed for the elevators. Morton lingered a moment longer; his face was tight with anger, his jaw clenched, his mouth squeezed shut.

"Something you want to say, Operator?" Jamie asked.

Morton held Jamie's gaze for a long moment, then shook his head. "No, sir," he said, then turned and strode away across the hangar.

Jamie watched him go, guilt churning in his stomach.

He had lied to Morton, lied to them both; what their squad had done was far from good work. They had destroyed the first of their targets, but cancelling an operation once it was under way was going to mean questions from his superiors. He had turned it over and over in his head on the way back to the Loop, and was already second-guessing the decision he had made.

Maybe Morton had been right, and the rookie Operator had just needed some time to get his head round what had happened with Bingham, to face his fear and deal with it. Maybe he had overreacted, panicked at the first sign of potential trouble. But in the short time Jamie had been a member of Blacklight, he had seen too many people hurt, too many people killed, to take chances; the stakes were simply too high.

He *had* told the truth about one thing; he would make sure any negative fallout from the aborted mission fell squarely on him. He would not let Morton or Ellison take the blame for his decision.

Jamie scanned the hangar for the Duty Officer and signalled him over.

"Is there a debrief?" he asked.

"No, sir," replied the Officer. "Written reports only, sir."

"OK. Thanks."

The man nodded and went back to what he was doing. Jamie set off in the other direction, heading towards the lift at the end of the Level 0 corridor. He was relieved that he was not required to brief the Interim Director; he had no desire to explain what had happened now.

It could wait until the morning.

Two minutes later Jamie was standing outside the door to his quarters, almost exactly halfway along the long, curving corridor on Level B. He pulled his ID card from its pouch in his uniform, unlocked the door, and pushed it open. A pile of divisional reports teetered on the surface of his small desk, but he didn't so much as glance at them. Instead, he dragged his uniform from his body, hung it on the hooks behind his door and flopped down on to his bed. His eyes closed, and thirty seconds later he was asleep.

Thud.

Jamie's eyes fluttered and an involuntary groan emerged from his lips. His brain swam slowly into action, feeling thick and heavy.

Thud. Thud thud.

The noise reverberated through his tired skull as he forced his eyes open. He reached for his console and read the white numbers at the top of the screen.

02:32:56

Thud thud thud thud thud.

He swore loudly, swung his legs down from his bed, and made his way across his quarters. He pulled his uniform back on, then opened the door.

Standing outside in the corridor was Jacob Scott, the veteran Australian Colonel. Behind him, their faces pale, were the members of the Zero Hour Task Force.

"Lieutenant Carpenter," said Colonel Scott. His usually warm tone was curt and businesslike. "You need to come with us."

"Am I in trouble?" asked Jamie. He couldn't think of anything he had done that would warrant such heavyweight attention, but nor could he think of any other reason why most of the senior Operators in the Department would be knocking on his door in the middle of the night.

"Nothing like that," replied Colonel Scott. "There's a situation that requires our attention."

Jamie groaned. "You couldn't have messaged me?"

"Not while ISAT is ongoing," replied Scott. "Until they're finished, we can't assume electronic communications are secure."

Jamie glanced at Paul Turner. "This is serious, isn't it?" he asked.

"Yes, Lieutenant," said Colonel Scott. "It's serious."

13

SOCIAL NETWORKING

STAVELEY, NORTH DERBYSHIRE
ONE WEEK EARLIER

Greg Browning put on his headset and prepared to talk to a man he had never met.

He was sitting at the desk that had been his son's, in the room where Matt had slept until he was taken away by the government and their faceless, terrifying men in black. It was now almost a month since Matt had disappeared for the second time, and three weeks since his wife had taken his daughter and left him. If their son returned, he supposed there was a chance that she might come back, but he didn't really care, one way or the other; something had broken inside his wife when her son went missing for the second time, and he no longer recognised the woman she had become. In truth, Greg had been relieved when she finally packed her bags. With her gone, there was nothing to distract him from the only thing that still interested him: making the government pay for what they had done to his family.

His boss had tried several times to talk to him about what he referred to as his obsession, but Greg had refused to discuss it.

When he had eventually been called into the office and told that he was being let go, he had not been surprised; his work had been slipping for months, since the first time Matt had been taken. He bore his boss no ill will; the man was incapable of seeing the truth of the world around him.

A mental-health worker from the local authority had visited him several days later, presumably at his former employer's suggestion, and he had answered her questions with unfailing politeness. Shortly afterwards, a Disability Living Allowance cheque had arrived, followed by another a month later. The cheques were proof that the council had categorised him as mentally ill, but he saw no need to correct them; there was a pleasing symmetry to local government financing his crusade against the government.

It was like a snake volunteering to eat its own tail.

Three days after the government had stolen his son away in the night for the second time, Greg had defied his wife's hysterical protests and started a systematic search through the history on Matt's computer. He had immediately found a long list of sites about vampires and the supernatural, but nothing he considered out of the ordinary; it was mostly kid's stuff, about blood and fangs and things that went bump in the night. But, as he had been about to close the machine down, an instant message had appeared in the corner of the screen. He had followed the instructions it contained, not really knowing why he was doing so, and found himself looking at a website that felt like the first genuinely real thing he had ever seen.

The site, which had no name and a URL that was a seemingly random string of numbers and letters, was devoted to a simple concept: that vampires were real, that the government was aware of their existence and maintained a top-secret force to police them. It contained written accounts, blurry photographs, snippets of crackly audio recording; nothing that would have convinced the casual observer. But Greg Browning was far from a casual observer; he had watched an unmarked helicopter land in the middle of his quiet suburban street, stood aside as men dressed all in black forced their way through his house, pointing submachine guns at him and his son. And in his garden, he had seen a girl whose body was so severely injured that she could not possibly have been alive rear up to bite a man wearing a biohazard suit, before tearing his son's throat out in front of his eyes.

The website didn't possess the smoking gun that would be needed to blow a big enough hole in the government for the truth to leak out, but Greg saw immediately that it was close.

Tantalisingly close.

Almost without thinking, he had opened his son's word-processing program and started to write. He poured every detail he could remember about the night his life was changed forever on to the page, writing at furious speed, ignoring his wife's pleas for him to leave Matt's room, to just leave everything alone. It took him most of the night; the sun was peeking its head over the horizon when he hit SAVE for the final time. With a trembling hand, he copied and pasted the text into the box on the website's posting form, then paused, as a terrible thought belatedly occurred to him.

What if this wasn't real? What if it was all a trap?

He had followed the instant message's instructions and used a proxy server to access the website, but he had no idea how secure such things really were. What if the website was nothing more than an elaborate snare, designed to trick people who knew the truth into admitting it, so they could be disappeared? What if he was about to paste a huge target on to his own forehead?

Greg closed the browser and turned off the computer. He sat staring at the dead monitor screen for a long time, waiting to hear the sirens in the distance that would mean they were coming for him, until he eventually flopped down on to his son's bed and fell into a light, uneasy sleep. When he awoke the following morning, he turned the computer back on, intending to delete the browser's history and maybe destroy the machine itself.

That'll be the end of it, he thought. *Case closed.*

But he quickly discovered that he couldn't do it.

Instead, he yelled for his wife to bring him his breakfast and settled in to read the entire website, from start to finish. When he was done he was a changed man, full of a fire he had never previously known and the desire to do something, anything, about what was going on around him. He understood that what had happened to Matt was no isolated incident; there were accounts of missing children from all around the world, children who had disappeared from quiet streets or been dragged from their beds by faceless black shapes. He started checking the website on an hourly basis, and continued to do so as his marriage, his job and his life collapsed around him.

As the days passed, however, the fire that had burned so suddenly and fiercely inside him began to dwindle. The site was understandably updated extremely infrequently; the kinds of incidents that merited inclusion were, by their very definition, remarkably rare. Greg read every post and user comment dozens of times, searching for something new, something to get his teeth into. His own account of vampires and the men in black was burning a metaphorical hole in his son's hard drive, but he could not summon up the nerve to post it. Instead, he watched, and waited, and hoped.

The post that changed everything appeared overnight.

It was anonymous, as they all were, but claimed to have been written by a survivor of the attack on Lindisfarne by a doomsday cult called the Children of God that Greg vaguely recalled seeing on the news several months earlier. His account opened with a series of short paragraphs that made Greg want to cry.

THE ATTACK ON THE ISLAND OF LINDISFARNE WAS NOT CARRIED OUT BY 'THE CHILDREN OF GOD', AN ORGANISATION THAT I DON'T BELIEVE HAS EVER ACTUALLY EXISTED.

THE ATTACK ON LINDISFARNE WAS CARRIED OUT BY A LARGE ORGANISED GROUP OF VAMPIRES. I KNOW, BECAUSE I WAS THERE.

THAT NIGHT, I SAW MY FRIENDS AND NEIGH-BOURS TORTURED AND KILLED. THAT NIGHT, MY DAUGHTER WAS LOST. THE AUTHORITIES HAVE REPEATEDLY TOLD ME THAT SHE IS DEAD. I CANNOT LET MYSELF BELIEVE THAT.

The post went on to describe the attack on the tiny island in stunning, horrifying detail: the red eyes and gleaming fangs, the blood and helpless screams, the fervent desire on the part of the attackers to violate and murder. It explained how the author escaped with a small number of others on a boat belonging to one of his neighbours, how his daughter was stopped in her tracks by the lifeless body of her best friend, and how the boat had left without her. The last thing the author had seen, as the boat pulled away from the dock, was his daughter's blonde hair flying out behind her as she ran back on to the island.

The account continued beyond the attack itself, describing how the author had been visited multiple times in the aftermath by the local police, and by a number of men and women who presented no identification. He was told that his daughter was missing, presumed dead, and warned not to talk to anyone about what had really happened to his home. The Children of God story was given to him and the other survivors wholesale, with the consequences for deviating from it made crystal clear. After a month had passed, he had been told that his daughter was officially dead, although no body had ever been found, and that the matter was now permanently closed.

To Greg, the post was nothing short of the Holy Grail.

There was no mention whatsoever of the men in black, as the author had not seen them. But he *had* seen the vampires, of that Greg had no doubt. The descriptions matched exactly what he had seen in his garden, and he didn't believe that the government would let such accurate information be posted online, even if the website was a trap. There would be no reason for them to take such a risk.

He immediately posted a response, thanking the author for his bravery and honesty, and informing him that he was an inspiration. Then he did what he now knew he should have done the day he was first directed to the hidden website: he pasted his own story into the submission box and hit POST.

Greg had no way of knowing how many people had access to the website, but over the following forty-eight hours it seemed as though every single one of them posted comments on the two new accounts. Between them, they provided descriptions of both sides of the hidden world the site was devoted to exposing, the vampires and the men in black who hunted them, that were vastly more detailed than any of the others. They contained no visual evidence, but the words were more than compelling enough; praise for the authors' courage and commitment to the truth flooded in, as discussions sprang up about the likely fates of Greg's son and the man from Lindisfarne's daughter. In among it all, the two men who had sparked the firestorm of activity began to correspond; tentatively at first, in the comments sections of the opposite number's post, then more regularly, via the encrypted instant messaging feature that the website provided.

Now they were about to speak for the first time.

Greg ran a program he had downloaded from a deeply paranoid Usenet board that he had also begun to frequent; when it was finished, he was safely hidden behind a labyrinth of proxies and IP diverters that would have taken the finest analyst at GCHQ an hour to unravel. Satisfied, he opened Skype, disabled video access, and waited for the call to come through.

Less than a minute later the computer's speakers rang into life. Greg clicked the green ACCEPT button and watched as the connection was established and the counter began to run, indicating that the call was live. A second later a voice spoke to him across the internet.

"Hello?"

Real, thought Greg. *He's real. Thank God.*

"Hello," he replied. "It's good to talk to you, mate. Really good."

"You too," said the voice. It was warm and friendly, with a thick north-east accent. "Wasn't sure what to expect, to be honest. Part of me thought my door was going to get kicked down as soon as I clicked on your username."

Greg laughed. "Me too, mate. I've still got half an ear out for helicopters."

The man on the other end of the line laughed heartily.

"What should I call you?" asked Greg. "I'm happy to do real names, if you are?"

"Not yet," replied the other man. "No offence."

"None taken," replied Greg. "What then?"

"Call me North," said the voice. "And I'll call you South. How about that?"

"Works for me," said Greg.

"Great," said North. "I don't really want to be on for more than five minutes, if that's all right with you? I'm about as well hidden as it gets, but I don't think we should push our luck. So shall we get down to it?"

"Let's do that," said Greg, smiling in the empty quiet of his son's bedroom.

"I'm sorry about your boy," said North. "I can't believe they put a helicopter down in the middle of your street. That's incredible."

"Cheers," said Greg. "And I'm sorry about your daughter, I really am. As for the helicopter, I couldn't believe it either. I thought I was dreaming. Thought it for a long time afterwards, actually. When my son didn't come back, I asked all our neighbours about the helicopter. None of them would even admit they'd seen it."

"Bastards," said North.

"They were just scared," said Greg. "Like the government wants us all to be. What about the others who saw what you saw?"

"Same thing," replied North. "If I ask any of them about it, any of the ones that are still here that is, they tell me exactly what the cops told us to say. And you want to know the really screwed-up thing? They believe it. They really believe it. Like they've deleted the memory of what actually happened."

Greg was extremely familiar with what North was talking about;

he and his wife had done exactly the same thing when Matt had been returned to them, erasing the men in black and the girl and the helicopter from their previously well-ordered life.

"I know what you mean, mate," he said, softly. "Trust me."

There was silence for a long moment, but it was far from uncomfortable; it was the easy quiet of two people who are beginning to think they have found a kindred spirit.

"It's weird," said North, eventually. "I don't talk much to anyone these days. It doesn't seem worth the effort when I don't trust anything I hear. Cops, government, TV, the papers. It's all bullshit. I'm not saying I trust you, because I don't, not yet. But even if you are just one of the men in black waiting to arrest me when you've found out how much I know, it's good to be able to talk to someone. Do you know what I mean?"

"Yes," replied Greg, instantly. "Part of me will always wish I didn't know the things I know. I never wanted to. It all got dumped on me, and then I was told to shut up and forget it all ever happened. So this is good, mate. It's a good thing."

"I go to the mainland every week or so," said North. "You know where I live, so that shouldn't be a surprise. I go to Keswick, or up to Alnwick, sometimes all the way to Berwick, and I watch people. I watch them doing their shopping, holding hands, shouting at their kids, running for buses, and I feel jealous. I *envy* them for the things they don't know, for the way they just live their lives one day to the next, not knowing the dangers that are all around them. I sometimes wish I could go back to that, like you said. But I know I can't."

"Neither can I," said Greg. "We play the cards we've been dealt, right?"

"Right," replied North. "I don't care what happens to me any more and that's the truth. My life ended when my daughter was taken away. But that doesn't mean I *want* to die, at least not yet. What I *want* to do is get even, figure out a way to pay them back for what they did. And I want to warn everyone that what happened to you and me could happen to them next."

"How?" asked Greg. "I want that too, mate, but how? If we start telling people, we'll disappear. You know that as well as I do. And no one will believe us anyway."

"I know," said North. "We need someone with a bigger voice than ours, someone it won't be so easy for them to shut up."

"And we'll need proof," said Greg, thinking about the blank faces of his neighbours, the scared expression of the policeman who had told him that there was nothing he could do about Matt's disappearance, that an order had come down from the highest levels telling him to drop it. "If we had proof, maybe we could find a journalist who would do something. I mean, it's the biggest story in the world, mate. If we could persuade someone to run it, that is."

"What proof could we get?" asked North. "I've got nothing apart from what I saw. Have you?"

"No," replied Greg. "Nothing."

There was a second silence, longer than the first, which only ended when Greg's mobile phone began to beep. He picked it up from the surface of Matt's desk and saw that it had been four minutes since they had started talking.

"I'm going to get off," he said. He could hear the sadness in his own voice; he knew that when the connection was cut, he would be on his own again. "But we need to speak soon. We need to work out what the hell we're going to do."

"Agreed," said North. "I'll be in touch. Good to talk to you."

"You too, mate," said Greg. He reached out and clicked the red button marked END, his hand trembling slightly as he shut down the computer.

He'd taken the first step. There was no going back.

14

GIRLS VS BOYS

The waitress set a bowl of chicken salad large enough to feed a family of five down in front of Larissa, rousing her from her thoughts and returning her to the fluorescent surroundings of Sam's Diner. She thanked the woman and began to eat.

Her mind, as it often did, had drifted to Jamie. She was looking forward to calling him, once the time difference allowed it; it was the middle of the night in the UK, and she didn't want to wake him up. They had last spoken three days earlier and things had seemed fine, superficially at least; she had asked about Kate and Matt, about his mum, about Frankenstein and the Department he had been born to be a part of, and Jamie had answered her with his usual enthusiasm, updating her on the new Lazarus Project, on Kate's painful decision to join ISAT, and the ongoing efforts to bring Blacklight back to full strength. He had told her he missed her and she had replied in kind, instantly and truthfully.

But in the middle of the conversation there had been a space, a hole that they both seemed to be aware of, but which neither of them mentioned. Larissa knew it came from her, from the same issue she had been wrestling with since shortly after her arrival in Nevada, that she could still not yet bring herself to raise with her boyfriend.

Or with anyone else.

She finished her mouthful of food and took a long swallow of her root beer, the dark pungent liquid that was just one of the many small delights that NS9 had to offer.

"You still with us, Larissa?" The voice was gentle and full of mockery, and she smiled. Kara, one of NS9's squadron of helicopter pilots, was looking at her with a quizzical expression; her bright green eyes, full of humour, shone out against her dark brown skin and jet-black hair.

"Sorry," she replied, her smile widening. "I was just wondering what the chances were of me finding some more interesting dinner company."

Kara burst out laughing as Danny and Kelly, both Operators in their second years of service with NS9, bellowed in mock offence. Kelly, the tall, heavy-set Tennessee girl who had grown up on the banks of the Mississippi, pounded her hand on the table, her face a mask of perfect outrage. Danny, the loud, gregarious Virginian son of parents whose exploits in the CIA were still classified at the highest level, made as if to stand up and leave, so disgusted was he by Larissa's insult.

Aaron, the pale, quiet Israeli intelligence analyst who looked like a librarian but refused to talk about the things he had done as a member of Mossad before coming to Nevada, grabbed Danny's shoulders and pulled him back down into his chair, laughing as he did so. Larissa observed this pantomime with a comforting warmth spreading through her chest.

173

Her secondment to NS9 was a bridge-building mission, part of the new commitment made by the supernatural Departments of the world to pool their resources and intelligence, a commitment forged in the aftermath of the attack on the Loop and the abduction of Henry Seward. She had been ordered to spend two months in Nevada, during which time she was to select six American Operators who would help fill the holes left by Valeri Rusmanov's assault. Operators had been despatched to every Department in the world, with similar assignments; when they were complete, Blacklight would be the first fully multi-national Department, staffed by men and women of every race and nationality.

Out of the corner of her eye, Larissa noticed Tim Albertsson looking at her. Tim had been the second person she had met when she arrived in the western desert, and was technically her direct superior for the duration of her stay, although he had never given any impression that he thought of them as anything other than equals, and tended to phrase his ideas for how she should spend her time as requests, rather than orders. The Special Operator was immensely popular within NS9: polite, gregarious, effortlessly charming.

And clearly, obviously, attracted to her.

Larissa was not by nature an arrogant person, but she was sure that her reading of the situation was correct. She was mostly flattered, although part of her found it slightly disconcerting; Tim Albertsson was twenty-five years old and, although she was twenty herself, almost twenty-one, she still looked like she was seventeen.

I always will, thanks to Grey, she thought. *Stuck at seventeen while everyone around me gets old. Brilliant.*

Nonetheless, she liked Tim. He was open and positive and generous, and she couldn't resist flirting with him, just a little. She certainly wasn't encouraging him to do anything about the feelings she was sure he had for her, at least not consciously; she was in love with Jamie and would never do anything to hurt him. But he was a long way away, and she couldn't help enjoying the fact that Tim liked her.

The fact that they spent most of their time together did not help the situation. Tim had asked her to help him train a new intake of NS9 recruits, which was apparently one of the areas of responsibility that came with his mysterious rank. They had been working on the same group of nervous, eager men and women for more than a week now, and today had been the day that Tim had asked her to show them what they were really dealing with.

Nine nervous faces stared at Tim and Larissa.

The recruits were in a line at one end of the NS9 physical training facility, the round room that had been the direct inspiration for the Loop's Playground. For eight days, they had been put through their paces under Tim's watchful eye, while Larissa observed from behind the one-way glass of the observation gallery, offering comments and suggestions when it seemed appropriate. The recruits had run, and fought, and run, and fought. They had been dragged through the endless gleam of the White Sands desert for forty-eight punishing hours, forced to endure the sucking anguish of sleep deprivation, challenged to improvise and plan as their minds and bodies screamed for rest. They had practised endlessly with the tools of their new trade: the T-Bone pneumatic stake launcher, the Heckler & Koch MP7 submachine gun, the HK416 assault rifle, the Glock 17, the UV beam guns and grenades. They had been taught strategy and tactics, urban and rural pacification, use and maintenance of vehicles, and hand-to-hand combat, with no credit given for whatever training they had done in the past. Every one of them was bruised and every one of them had bled on the dark blue floor of the room they were standing in.

None had quit.

Now, for the first time, Larissa was standing before them, listening as Tim introduced her.

"Larissa Kinley is a Department 19 Lieutenant, ladies and gentlemen. She's also a vampire. If anyone has a problem with that, raise your hand now and I'll be happy to show you exactly how much patience I have for ignorance in my recruits. Anyone?"

No one raised their hand, but Larissa felt nine pairs of eyes settle on her. She knew part of it was the mention of Department 19; Blacklight was the original supernatural Department and was still revered by the Operators of its global counterparts. But mostly it was the word vampire; she knew that she was the first member of her species that these men and women had ever seen, and that they were curious to see exactly what she was capable of. She could tell from their expressions that several of them were afraid of her. She took no pleasure in it, although she was glad, for their sakes; being scared of vampires was, as far as she was concerned, the only rational response.

"All right," said Tim. "Larissa has very kindly offered to help with today's combat training. I don't like your chances, I'll tell you that now, but maybe one or two of you will surprise me. Larissa?"

"Thank you," she said, stepping forward. "Get your T-Bones."

The recruits glanced at each other; they were wearing their training uniforms, but were carrying no weapons.

"This is an unarmed session, Larissa," said Tim. "Non-lethal."

"Don't worry," she replied, glancing over at him. "Tell them to get their weapons. It'll be OK."

Tim shrugged and gave her an I-hope-you-know-what-you're-doing look. Then he turned back to the recruits, who were staring at each other uncertainly.

"You heard the Operator!" he yelled. "Weapons and kit, on the double! Move!"

The recruits scattered away to the far end of the training room and began attaching belts and weapons to their training uniforms. It took a long time, Larissa noted; it was not yet a process that had become second nature. Eventually, they reformed their line, T-Bones resting awkwardly in their gloved hands.

"That's my first lesson to you," said Larissa, walking down the line. "Never, ever get into physical proximity with a vampire unless you don't have a single weapon left. T-Bones, guns, beams, grenades: use them all before you even think about going hand to hand. Is that understood?" The recruits nodded. "OK," she said, smiling encouragingly at them. "Try to shoot me."

The trainees looked uncertainly at each other. "Who are you talking to?" asked a female recruit at one end of the line, who had presumably summoned up all her courage to do so.

"All of you," replied Larissa. Then she flexed a muscle that, of all the people in the room, only she possessed. Her fangs slid down from her gums and her eyes flooded a deep, glowing crimson. The recruits took a communal half-step backwards, their eyes widening and shifting as one to Tim. The Special Operator shrugged, trying not to let his emotions show on his face; he was worried, as this was far from an authorised training session, but part of him was telling him he didn't need to be. The recruits nervously raised their T-Bones and pointed them at Larissa.

"Do it," she growled, and they opened fire.

Nine stakes screamed through the air. Larissa leapt from the ground, quicker than human eyes could clearly follow, and pirouetted backwards, spinning through the air as a black blur and two trailing lines of red. As she shot towards the wall, her hands flew out and caught the T-Bone wires; she gave them a sharp yank and the weapons flew out of the recruits' hands, sending several of them crashing to the floor. Larissa stopped spinning and floated in the air above their heads, looking down at them with red eyes and an expression of disappointment.

"Guns," she growled. "Beam torches. Come on, for God's sake."

The trainees redoubled their efforts, pulling beam guns and assault rifles and opening up in the enclosed space, the reports of the guns deafeningly loud. Larissa moved again, darting elegantly around the room at far below her top speed, and easily avoided everything. Nothing got close to her: not a bullet nor the purple beam of a UV torch. She danced through the air until the guns were empty and the batteries of the beam guns were exhausted.

Finally, the trainee who had spoken up raised a UV grenade and pitched it towards her. Larissa twisted in the air, batted it down towards the floor, then rocketed after it. She slid to the ground and brought her foot down on the glass and metal ball an instant before it fired; it burst with a fizz and a shower of sparks.

"So," she grunted. "No more weapons. Who's first?"

A hulking male recruit shouldered his way forward. On his face was an expression of great contentment; this was clearly a form of combat with which he felt far more comfortable. He cracked his knuckles and moved towards her, light on the balls of his feet, his arms loose at his sides. When he was almost in range, he threw a sharp decoy left, then skipped forward and launched a sweeping overhand right. The punch got closer than Larissa had been expecting, but nowhere near close enough. She slid to her left, bending at the waist, then reached up and grabbed the man's wrist. His expression of contentment faltered, then disappeared entirely as she spun him easily around and clenched her fingers. As Larissa felt bones creak beneath her grip, the recruit turned shockingly pale, tipped back his head, and screamed at the ceiling.

She lifted him into the air with one slender arm, his wrist bent halfway up his back, then threw him back to the ground an instant before it broke. He hit the floor hard and stayed down, grunting in pain. The other recruits *looked at her with absolute terror. This was exactly what Tim had wanted: for his vampire colleague to throw open the doors and show the recruits exactly what their new world was really like. But Larissa knew deep down that she hadn't, and didn't want them to be too discouraged.*

"Take a knee," she said. The words sounded weird coming out of her mouth; the phrase was an Americanism she had heard Tim use several times. But it had the desired effect: the trainees slowly hunkered down, even the one who had tried to hit her, who rolled to a sitting position, holding his rapidly swelling wrist.

"I'm not normal," she said, and smiled at them. "I've had military training and I use my powers every day. I'm faster and stronger than almost any vampire you'll ever encounter. Most of the ones you'll come across will be quick and savage, but they don't know how to fight, to use their environment, or repel your weapons. Listen to Tim, listen to your instructors, watch each other's backs once you're out there, and you'll be fine. OK?"

A collection of very small smiles emerged on the faces of the recruits, and several of them nodded.

"Cool," said Larissa. "Come and find me in the bar later. The first round's on me. Dismissed."

The smiles widened into grins. As the recruits began to chatter animatedly among themselves, she walked over to Tim Albertsson.

"How'd I do?" she asked.

"Terrifyingly well," replied Tim, smiling at her. "They're not going to forget that in a hurry, I can promise you that much."

"Brits are vicious," said Aaron, still holding Danny's shoulders. "Don't you know that?"

"I know," said Danny, then grinned at Larissa. "I've seen her fangs, man, trust me, I know."

The table burst out laughing again and Larissa joined in, happily.

She attacked her salad, listening contentedly as Kara lamented the recent collapse of her relationship with a Navy Air Corps pilot called Bobby that she had begun to tentatively believe might have had a chance of turning serious.

"How do you manage it, Larissa?" she asked. "I know you and Jamie are normally in the same place, but still. It must be hard."

"Sometimes it is," she replied, honestly, putting down her knife and fork. "To be honest with you, there have been times when it felt impossible. When things got really bad a couple of months ago, before the attack on the Loop, when everything was happening with Valentin and Frankenstein, I didn't think we were going to survive it. I really didn't. It's weird, you know, I only met him six months ago, so we don't have that history behind us that makes you work hard when things get rough. But we got through it. And if there's ever an end to all this, if that day ever comes, I think we'll be fine. Because I doubt any two people have waded through as much shit in the first few months of being together as we have."

"I think it's awesome," said Kara, with a broad smile. Out of the corner of her eye, Larissa noted the absence of a similar smile on Tim Albertsson's face. "You know how lucky you are to fall for someone who does what we do? Someone you never have to lie to about your life?"

"I do," replied Larissa. "I really, really do. I spent the first two years after I was turned lying every single day, just to try and stay alive. I don't want to go back to that."

"Don't you worry about him, though?" asked Tim. "It's all very well not having to lie to each other, and I see how great that must be, but the flipside is that you know exactly how dangerous it is every time he leaves the Loop. Isn't that hard?"

"Of course it is," replied Larissa, turning to face the Special Operator. "I know that every time he goes out might be the last time I ever see him. But he can handle himself. He's already survived situations no one would have given him a hope of surviving, and we both knew the risks when we signed up. What it comes down to is this. I know that if he *can* come back to me, he will."

Tim nodded, and said no more on the subject.

"Anyway," said Kara, casting a sideways glance at him. "What's the deal with Dominique Saint-Jacques? Larissa, you know him, right? I saw his picture in the report on the Paris mission and I feel like he could be just the thing to help me get over Bobby."

"I've met Dominique," said Tim, breaking into a smile. "We did a thing in Somalia a couple of years ago. You should probably take a number."

"What are you saying?" demanded Kara. "He's out of my league?"

"Did I say that?" asked Tim, his smile widening. "*You* said that, not me. I just said you should take a number. He's a very popular young man."

Larissa let her attention drift as Kara and Tim descended into bickering about a man who was five thousand miles away. On the other side of the table, Kelly, Danny and Aaron had huddled together and were talking to each other in low voices, but as far as Larissa, with her supernatural hearing, was concerned, there were no such things. She could hear whispering as loudly as most normal humans could hear shouting. And what she had heard was Aaron saying "... if I knew, I'd tell you. But I don't. No one knows who he is."

"What's the gossip?" asked Larissa, abandoning the analysis of Kara's attractiveness and leaning forward. "No one knows who who is?"

"The man in the cell," said Aaron, his expression of mild surprise making it clear to Larissa that he thought she should have known that. "The one that no one is allowed to see. You haven't heard about him?"

"I guess not," said Larissa. "Who is he?"

"*We don't know,*" said Danny. He spoke very slowly, as if to a child, then grinned at her. "That's sort of the point."

"Screw you," said Larissa, smiling back at him. "What's the story?"

"No one knows much of that either," replied Kelly. "About a month ago there was a general alarm for a breach of the perimeter that got overridden about ten seconds after it started. Nothing got announced, nobody got called out, and then..."

"... and then my Department issued a memo," continued Aaron, "listing the entire cellblock as DO NOT HANDLE, and making entry without direct authorisation from General Allen a punishable offence. The story got around that there's a man in one of the cells, but nobody knows who he is, or if there's actually anyone in there at all. It's a black hole."

"It's weird," said Danny. "Really weird."

Larissa considered this. "It's a regular cell, though, right?" she asked. "Not a supernatural?"

"Regular," replied Aaron. "Just a standard concrete box."

"That is weird," said Larissa. "What are the theories?"

"I heard it's Allen's brother," said Kelly. "Someone in the mess was saying he got compromised and the General brought him in until things calmed down."

"Why would he put his own brother in a cell?" asked Aaron. "What would be the harm in letting him live in quarters?"

"Who knows?" said Danny. "Maybe it's some human informant, someone the Director doesn't want the rest of us to know about."

"Why wouldn't he want the rest of us to know?" asked Kelly.

Aaron looked over at Larissa, who nodded her head. "Because even places like this have unfriendly eyes and ears," Larissa said, softly. "I know. Believe me, I know."

The four of them sat in silence for a moment, allowing the implication of Larissa's words to wash over them. The betrayals of Blacklight by two of its own members had caused great disquiet throughout the other supernatural Departments of the world. The idea that there could be traitors within their own ranks, on top of all the dangers they faced in the outside world, was a deeply unsettling one that no Operator liked to dwell on for too long.

"Thanks for that, Larissa," said Danny, pushing his half-eaten burger away. "I just lost my appetite."

"That's not the worst thing that could happen," said Kelly, eyeing her friend's stomach theatrically. "You're going to need a bigger uniform any day now."

"You absolute—"

Whatever colourful insult Danny had been about to throw at Kelly was lost in the bellows of laughter that burst from Larissa and Aaron. Tim and Kara immediately stopped sparring and demanded to be let in on the joke; as Aaron brought them up to speed, Larissa smiled as she looked at her friends. But at the back of her mind, she was still thinking about the anonymous man in the cell, and wondering how she might find out who he was.

51 DAYS TILL
ZERO HOUR

15

ONE OF OUR OWN

Jamie fell in beside Jack Williams as the Zero Hour Task Force
followed Jacob Scott along the Level B corridor.

"Do you know what's going on?" he asked.

Jack shook his head. "I know as much as you, mate. Jacob's got
something he wants to tell us. I don't think anyone knows what it
is."

"Is it a Dracula thing?"

"I don't think so," said Jack. "I think it's something else."

The two Operators walked on in silence for a few moments, until
Jamie spoke again. "How'd you get on today?"

"OK," replied Jack. "Got the first two on our list. Tried to press
for the third, but he was moving so I called it a night. What about
you?"

"Got the first," replied Jamie.

"Your rookies make out all right?"

"Kind of," said Jamie. "Ellison's going to be great, I can already
tell. She's ice-cold. Morton sort of freaked out, to be honest with
you. I think coming face to face with an actual vamp scared him
more than he was expecting it to. But considering they should still
be in training, they did all right. Yours?"

"Better than I expected," said Jack. "Didn't panic, didn't freeze, did what I told them. Did you hear about Angela?"

"I got in and went straight to bed," replied Jamie. "What's she done?"

"She told Holmwood she wanted a new squad," smiled Jack. "Both of hers are in the infirmary, but all she wants to do is get back out there. Cal had to give her a direct order to go to bed."

Jamie grinned. Nothing about Angela Darcy, the beautiful, terrifying former spy, could ever surprise him; he had seen her at work in Paris, after she volunteered to help him rescue Frankenstein, and had been impressed and intimidated at the same time. The only other person he had ever seen who was so casually, elegantly lethal was Larissa, who had being a vampire as an excuse. That Angela was as friendly and flirtatious as she was dangerous only added to her appeal, and it was a well-known fact that at least a dozen of the Department's men were in love with her.

"I'm not even surprised," he replied.

"Me neither," said Jack. "I'm amazed Cal had the balls to tell her no."

Jack laughed and Jamie joined in, enjoying the easy friendship that had bloomed since the first time the two men had met. They had fought together many times in the six months since Jamie had arrived at the Loop, and Jack had been one of the Operators who volunteered for the Paris rescue mission. Jamie had been delighted to have him; he was a fine Operator and leader, as well as a good friend.

The group paused at the end of the corridor as they waited for a lift to arrive, then piled into the metal box and ascended to Level A. Jacob Scott led them along the central corridor and stopped outside the suite of rooms that made up the Interim Director's quarters. He rapped on the door, then waited. After a minute or so, it swung open and a bleary-eyed Cal Holmwood peered out at them.

"What's going on?" he asked. "Jacob? What is this?"

"I need to show you something, sir," replied Colonel Scott. "Can we come in?"

A flicker of obvious annoyance passed across Holmwood's face. "This needs to happen now, Jacob? It can't wait till morning?"

"No, sir," replied Scott. "I'm afraid it can't."

The Interim Director sighed. "Fine. Come in then, the lot of you." He pulled the door to his quarters open. Jacob Scott stepped inside and the Zero Hour Task Force followed him. Once the last man was in, Holmwood pushed the door closed and demanded to know what the hell was going on.

"It'll be easier if I show you, sir," said Jacob. "Can you call up the security footage of the Broadmoor escape?"

"Why?" asked Holmwood. "It's still being analysed. We don't even have a preliminary report yet."

"Like I said, sir," said Colonel Scott, "it'll be easier if I show you."

Holmwood looked at the rest of the men standing silently in his quarters. "Paul," he said, his gaze coming to rest on Major Turner. "Do you know what this is about?"

"No, sir," replied the Security Officer. "This is Jacob's show."

Jamie glanced at Jack, who widened his eyes in a gesture that conveyed exactly what it was meant to.

Holy shit. This must be serious.

Holmwood considered for a moment, then sighed. "Fine," he said. "I'll load the footage. Care to tell me what I'm looking for?"

"If you run the view of the courtyard as the hospital is breached, sir," replied Scott, "I'll tell you as soon as I see it."

Holmwood grunted, then flopped down into the chair behind his long wooden desk. He woke up his console and tapped in a series of commands. A wide screen lit up on the wall opposite, and the Operators shuffled to either side so that everyone could see. Holmwood navigated through the Blacklight network and dragged a file labelled EXT_COURTYARD out of a folder containing hundreds of gigabytes of footage of the Broadmoor escape. He double-clicked it and black and white video filled the screen.

The camera was positioned on the back of the gatehouse, directly above the entry arch; it looked across the courtyard towards the main door of the hospital building itself. As the footage began, a Range Rover was sitting in the middle of the frame with its driver's side door open and a man standing beside it. Beyond the car, on the ground in front of the hospital, lay a figure in a white hospital gown that suddenly leapt to its feet, causing several of the audience to gasp. The patient sprinted across the courtyard and leapt on to the bonnet of the car, thrashing and clawing and hammering at the windscreen, managing to get one hand through the glass. Then the car accelerated backwards, passing beneath the camera and out of view.

"Who was that in the car?" asked Brennan. His voice was low and shaken.

"Benjamin Dawson," replied Paul Turner, without taking his eyes off the screen. "And Charles Walsh. Both residents of Crowthorne, the village below Broadmoor. Both deceased."

Jamie said nothing. His eyes were locked on the awful events playing out on the wall screen. The video had no sound, which, if anything, made it worse; the horror seemed unreal without the screams that would have inevitably accompanied it in real life. The courtyard was still for a few moments, until a second white figure fell from somewhere above the camera's range. It thudded to the ground, one of its legs visibly breaking, then dragged itself in the same direction the car had gone. Seconds later another patient dropped into frame, followed by another, and another. Several of them ran for the gate, while others simply stood in the courtyard, seemingly unsure of what to do next.

Then the hospital door burst outwards, breaking and splintering on to the cobblestones of the courtyard. A huge man in a white gown appeared in the doorway, his eyes glowing; they showed up on the monochrome footage as bright, flickering white. He walked slowly forward, stopped, then threw back his head and screamed silently at the night sky. All at once the courtyard was full of movement, as the newly-turned patients of Broadmoor spilled into it; dozens of them, then what seemed like hundreds, running and leaping and pushing at each other, a wide stream of vampires revelling in the glory of freedom. They began to run across the courtyard, disappearing beneath the camera and flooding out into the night.

"Freeze it there!" shouted Jacob Scott. "Right there!"

Jamie looked over at the Australian Colonel; his eyes were fixed on the screen, his weathered face pale and drawn. Cal Holmwood hit a key on his console and the footage stopped moving. He rewound until Jacob told him to stop, then tapped at his console again. The still image sharpened until it looked like a photograph.

"What are we looking at?" he asked.

Jacob Scott got slowly to his feet and walked across to the wall screen. He reached out a trembling hand and pointed at a man walking calmly across the courtyard.

"Him," said Scott. "He's who I wanted you to see."

"Who is that?" asked Jamie.

"That's one of us," replied the Colonel. "That's Albert Harker."

16

CLASSIFIED MEANS CLASSIFIED

TWENTY MINUTES LATER

"I can't believe it," said Cal Holmwood. "I knew David Harker. I can't believe he'd do that to his own son."

"He did it, sir," said Jacob Scott, his voice low and unsteady. "I was there. I saw."

Jamie had listened with slowly dawning horror to the long, sad tale of Albert Harker. Colonel Scott had told it carefully, leaving out nothing, allowing the cruelty that had apparently lurked at the heart of the Harker family to be fully revealed; how his father and brother had committed Albert to Broadmoor under an assumed name, to languish there in secret until he died.

How could they do it? he thought, his mind struggling to process such horror. *How could anyone do that?*

"I don't know these men," he said. "They're not still Operators, are they?"

"They're both dead," replied Holmwood. "David died more than a decade ago, Robert, what, getting on for two years?"

Paul Turner nodded. "About six months after his sons passed," he said.

Jamie's mind was filled with an image of the bronze plaque in the rose garden at the edge of the Loop. "The Harker brothers who died when the first *Mina* went down," he said, slowly. "John and George. They were Robert's sons?"

"David's grandsons," said Holmwood. "And Albert's nephews, although I doubt they even knew he existed. I can't imagine their father mentioned his brother very often."

"But *you* knew Albert existed," pressed Jamie. "You knew David Harker and you must have known he had two sons. Didn't you ever wonder about him?"

"We knew Albert was... different," said Holmwood. "I mean, everyone did. It was no secret. It was a scandal when he turned us down and we all knew David was furious. But I had no idea about the rest."

"No one knew, sir," said Jacob Scott. "David and Robert knew, and I knew. That was it."

"How did you know?" asked Paul Turner. "Why were you even there, Jacob? This was clearly a family matter."

"Robert asked me to go with him," replied Scott. "He told me he needed someone he could trust. So I went."

"I don't understand why Robert wanted anyone there apart from himself and his father," said Holmwood.

"I've thought about that, sir," said Scott, his eyes flicking momentarily to the floor. "I've thought about it a lot, over the years. I've come to the conclusion that Robert didn't trust David not to go too far if it was just the three of them."

The implication of the Colonel's words hung in the air, clear to everyone in the room.

Jesus, thought Jamie. *Jesus Christ.*

"Are you saying that—" Jack Williams began, but was interrupted by the Interim Director.

"I think we all know exactly what Jacob is saying, Jack," said Holmwood. "And before we crucify the memory of a loyal member of this Department, I would remind you all that Jacob is telling us what he believes, rather than what he knows for certain. Is that clear to you all?"

"That's right," said Scott. "You asked me what I thought. I don't know for certain what was going through David's mind."

"But you were happy to go along with it?" said Paul Turner, his voice like ice. "Happy to help your friend commit his brother to a mental hospital for the rest of his life for no reason?"

"I wasn't happy about it!" shouted Colonel Scott. "Not then and not now! And neither was Robert, or David! It broke their hearts to see what Albert had become, how much he hated them, wanted to hurt them. But they put their feelings aside and they did what needed to be done, for all of us. For the good of the Department."

"For the good of the Department," repeated Turner, slowly. "Is that what you tell yourself, Jacob?"

"Go to hell, Paul," spat Scott. "Don't you judge me, not after the things we both know you've done. You think I don't remember Serbia? Or Belfast?"

"Enough!" shouted Cal Holmwood, slamming his hand down on the top of his desk. "Jacob, why are we only hearing about this now? Why didn't you tell us yesterday morning at the Zero Hour briefing?"

Scott met the Interim Director's eyes for a brief moment, then looked down at the floor.

"I know why," said Paul Turner. "Do you want to tell them, Jacob, or should I?"

Scott gave the Security Officer a look of pure venom. "You tell them," he said. "I can see you're dying to."

"Fine," said Turner. "We sent out the ISAT interview orders for tomorrow about an hour ago. Jacob's name is third on that list. By now, every Operator in the Loop knows at least some of the questions we're asking. One is whether there are any incidents in which the subject believes he may have compromised the security of the Department, intentionally or otherwise."

"You knew you were going to get caught," said Holmwood, looking at Colonel Scott. "So you decided to come clean first. Is that it?"

Jacob stared at the Interim Director, anguish written plainly across his face, and nodded. "I didn't think it mattered," he said, hoarsely. "Until yesterday, I really don't think it did. It wasn't Blacklight business, Cal. It was family."

"It was despicable," said Jack Williams.

"I'm inclined to agree with you," said Holmwood. "But regardless of how any of us may feel about David Harker's decision, the fact remains that he has left us a situation that needs dealing with. Firstly, I want a Field Investigation Team to find the journalist that Harker spoke to in 2002; he may well be in danger. Andrews, scramble a team and have him brought in."

"Yes, sir," replied Amy Andrews.

"All right," said Holmwood. "Secondly, I want a squad despatched to find Albert Harker. Ideally, I'd like him brought here and placed in custody, but if that proves to be impossible, then SOP applies to him in exactly the same way it does every other vampire."

"Let me do it," said Jacob Scott. His jaw was set in a straight line, and his voice was firm and steady. "I can bring him home, sir. I know I can."

"Not a chance, Jacob," said Holmwood. "You are hereby confined to quarters, and I'm suspending your position on this Task Force, pending a full Security Division investigation. Do you understand what I'm telling you?"

Scott's eyes had widened enormously and he appeared to be on the verge of tears. "Yes, sir," he managed, his voice little more than a croak.

"Good," said Holmwood. "Jack, I want you to take care of Albert. I'm going to make finding him Surveillance's top priority. When they do, we'll move him to the top of your target list under a fake name. Clear?"

"Yes, sir," said Jack Williams. "Thank you, sir."

"All right," said Holmwood. "The rest of you, carry on as normal. I'm sure I don't need to tell you that not a single word of this goes beyond this office? If I so much as hear the name Albert Harker anywhere in this base, I swear to God I will court-martial every single one of you and to hell with the consequences. Please tell me you understand?"

"Yes, sir," chorused the group of Operators.

"Good," said Holmwood, and sighed deeply. "It's at times like these that I remember exactly why I never wanted this bloody job. Lieutenant Carpenter, I need to speak to you, please. The rest of you, get the hell out. Dismissed."

Jamie groaned inwardly. Jack Williams gave him a quizzical look as he got to his feet; he gave his head the tiniest shake in response. Jack jerked his thumb towards the door and gave a brief nod. The meaning of the two gestures was clear.

I'll wait for you outside.

Then Jack was gone, and he was alone with the Interim Director.

"What happened yesterday, Lieutenant?" asked Holmwood, leaning back in his chair.

"Sir, I haven't had a chance to write my—"

"Cut the shit, Jamie," interrupted the Interim Director. "Just tell me what happened."

Jamie took a deep breath. "I terminated our Operation early, sir. I didn't think it was safe for my squad to remain in the field."

"It's never safe out there," said Holmwood. "What was different yesterday?"

"One of my new squad members reacted badly to his first encounter with a vampire, sir. He froze, and almost got hurt. The rest of our target list was still unidentified, so I made the decision to return to the Loop."

"Without authorisation?"

"Yes, sir," said Jamie. "I'm sorry, sir."

Cal Holmwood rubbed his temples and closed his eyes momentarily. "Your rookie," he said, eventually. "What's his name?"

"Morton, sir. John Morton."

"Morton," repeated the Interim Director, and sighed again. "Not everyone is cut out to be an Operator, Jamie. What they did before they got here doesn't guarantee anything."

"That's what I'm saying, sir," said Jamie, keeping his voice calm and even. "I don't think he's a lost cause, not at all. But I don't think he's ready to be out there."

"He's going back into training as soon as this crisis is over," said Holmwood. "Him and all the other rookies. When he does, I'll order Terry to keep a closer eye on him, but until then I don't know what else you want me to do."

"I want you to put him on the inactive roster, sir," said Jamie.

"Out of the question," said Holmwood, instantly. "We need all the men we can get. You know that."

"Sir, if we—"

"Lieutenant Carpenter," interrupted Holmwood, a weary expression on his face. "Do you understand what is happening right now? What we're facing?"

"Yes, sir," said Jamie. "Of course I do. I just think that—"

"There are still more than two hundred Broadmoor escapees out there, Jamie, and you've seen with your own eyes exactly what they're capable of. The normal vamps are getting bolder by the minute, Dracula is getting stronger and stronger, and we have no idea where he is, or whether Henry Seward is even still alive. So I hope you can understand why I cannot authorise having an able man sitting in this base twiddling his damn thumbs."

Jamie tried one last time. "I understand, sir. Will you at least let me send him down for psychological assessment? That might be enough. Sir."

"Fine," said Holmwood. "Do whatever you need to. But the next time you go out, he goes with you."

"Yes, sir," said Jamie, through gritted teeth. "Thank you, sir."

Jamie pulled the door to the Interim Director's quarters shut behind him and saw Jack Williams leaning against the opposite wall, an expression of mild concern on his face.

"Everything OK?" asked Jack.

"Fine," he replied, forcing a smile. "It was just the Morton thing. No big deal."

"You sure?"

"I'm sure," said Jamie, and started to walk down the corridor. "Don't worry about it, seriously. Especially right now. Can you believe Jacob? It's incredible."

Jack widened his eyes exaggeratedly as he fell in beside his friend. "No shit," he replied. "I don't think this has ever happened before."

"A descendant being turned?" asked Jamie. Jack had joined the Department in more peaceful times and had completed the entire thirteen-month-long training programme that all Operators were supposed to pass; as a result, his knowledge of Blacklight's history was usually far greater than Jamie's.

"I'm pretty sure," said Jack. "And no active descendant has ever been turned, I'm absolutely sure of that. A lot of them have died, but none have been turned."

A lot of them have died, thought Jamie, himself a descendant of the founders. *Thanks for that, Jack. Seriously.*

"It's big," he said. "Holmwood sending you after him. That's big."

"I guess so," replied Jack. "It shouldn't be any different really. He's an escapee like any other. I just have to keep my mouth shut about it."

"Still," persisted Jamie. "Of all the people in the room, Cal picked you to take care of it. You should feel great about that, mate. Really you should."

Jack smiled. "I am pretty pleased," he said. "It must mean I've been doing something right these last few months."

Jamie, who knew exactly how highly regarded Jack Williams was by every single member of the Department, refused to dignify his friend's comment with a verbal response; he merely tilted his head and raised his eyebrows.

"Yeah, all right," said Jack, a wide grin on his face. "My squad are super-cool vampire-destroying ninjas and Holmwood would have been crazy to pick anyone else. Better?"

"Better," said Jamie, returning his friend's smile. They walked on until they reached the lift at the end of the Level 0 corridor. Jack pushed the button and they waited in comfortable silence for it to arrive.

"We don't see each other very often, Jack," said Jamie, suddenly. "It's not surprising, given everything that's going on around here, but still. It's a shame."

"It is," said Jack. The lift arrived, and the two Operators stepped inside. "I don't feel like I see anyone apart from my squad these days. It's hard."

"I know," said Jamie. "I get back from operations and all I ever want to do is sleep."

"Do you miss Larissa?" asked Jack.

"Of course I do," said Jamie. "But even when she was here, it was getting harder and harder to find time to see her. And now she's on the other side of the world. I get why she's there and I'm happy she seems to be having a good time. But yeah, I miss her."

"She'll be home soon, though, right?" asked Jack. "And in the meantime, we need to hang out. Let's make it happen. Breakfast, or lunch, or something. Maybe tomorrow?"

Jamie nodded. "Definitely. Tomorrow."

The lift slowed to a stop and opened its doors on Level B. Jamie considered giving Jack a brief hug, but decided against it. "See you later," he said instead, and headed for his quarters.

"See you, Jamie," shouted Jack, as the lift doors closed.

As the members of the Zero Hour Task Force headed for the lifts that would take them back to their quarters, Paul Turner strode away in the opposite direction.

He had been asleep when Jacob Scott knocked on the door to his quarters, but now he was wide awake: the sad, sordid business of Albert Harker had banished the last of his tiredness. Turner found it hard to sleep at the best of times, more so than ever following the death of his son; where he had once taken advantage of every furlough to drive home and spend the night with Caroline, he now refused to leave the Loop except on Blacklight business. There were too many things that required his attention, too much to do if he was to make sure that what had happened to Shaun never happened to anyone else's child.

Caroline was bearing up as well as could be expected, given the catastrophic double loss she had suffered during that one terrible night, and was beginning to slowly resemble her former self. She was a Seward and had known more than her share of hardships, although losing both her son and her brother had tested the limits of her endurance. Paul knew that neither of them were truly dealing with Shaun's death; their grief was still too fresh, too vast. But they were united by a shared sense of duty that got them through each day.

There was work to be done. Mourning would have to wait.

Paul Turner loved his wife more deeply and completely than any Operator in the Department would have believed, and had loved his son exactly the same way. The loss of Shaun was a yawning hole in the very centre of his being, one that continually threatened to pull him down; only his remarkable reserves of willpower kept him moving, kept him putting one foot in front of the other, as he was doing now.

The Security Officer strode through the noisy, bustling Intelligence Division and keyed open the door that led into ISAT. The reception desk was manned, as always, and he nodded at the Operator behind it; the man straightened up in his chair and nodded in return. Turner walked across the small reception area and pushed open the door to the lounge, intending to spend the quiet hours until the day's interviews commenced drinking coffee, reading over the previous day's reports, and avoiding thinking about his wife and son. As a result, he was surprised to find Kate Randall lying on the lounge's sofa when he pushed open the door. She put down the folder she was reading and smiled broadly at him.

"Couldn't sleep?" she asked.

"I was, actually," he replied. "Jacob Scott woke me up."

Kate frowned. "What did he do that for?"

Turner considered the implications of her question. If he told her it was classified, he knew she wouldn't complain; the nature of Blacklight meant that some Operators always knew things that others didn't. But he had no desire to lie to her. He knew exactly what she had risked by volunteering for ISAT, and knew exactly why she had done it: because she had cared about his son and wanted to honour his memory. He opened his mouth to answer her question and realised he was about to break one of the Department's most fundamental rules, one that he, as the Security Officer, should have treated as nothing less than sacred; he was going to tell her what had just happened in Cal Holmwood's quarters, in a meeting that was Zero Hour classified, the highest security level the Department possessed.

"We don't lie to each other, Kate," he said. "Am I right about that?"

"Yes," said Kate, instantly. "That's right."

"Good. Do you remember the speech Interim Director Holmwood gave after the Loop was attacked?"

"Of course."

"Do you remember him saying that he would be setting up a Task Force to dictate strategy for dealing with the rise of Dracula?"

"The Zero Hour Task Force?" asked Kate.

Turner blinked, then allowed a small smile to creep on to his face. "I should have known you would already know," he said. "Can I assume that Lieutenant Carpenter told you about it?"

A worried expression appeared on Kate's face.

"It's OK," said Turner. "I'm not going to discipline him for doing what I was about to do myself. Jamie told you, didn't he?"

"Yes," said Kate. "Before Valeri's attack, when everything was going bad, we promised each other no more secrets. So he told us."

"Us?"

"Matt and Larissa and me."

Paul Turner's smile widened. He knew full well that Jamie Carpenter believed that he hated him, was unfair to him and singled him out, and it satisfied him to let the young Operator think so. The truth was very different; there were few Operators in the entire Department that he admired more than the youngest Carpenter, a boy whose stubbornness, temper, and absolute loyalty to his friends reminded him so much of his younger self that it was almost painful. Of course Jamie had told his friends about the Zero Hour Task Force; he knew exactly what the boy's thought process would have been.

He knew something that he thought his friends needed to know. Something he thought they would be safer knowing. So he told them. Simple as that.

"That's why Jacob woke me up," said Turner. "He's on the Task Force, or at least he was until about ten minutes ago. He had something he wanted to show us."

"What?" asked Kate.

"Footage from the Broadmoor escape. It turns out that Albert Harker, one of the very few descendants ever to turn down the chance to join us, had been locked up in there for almost a decade. And now he's out there somewhere, turned into a vampire like all the others."

"Jesus," said Kate. "That's awful."

Turner nodded. "I knew Albert's brother, Robert. And I *worshipped* his father. When I came in, David was the Operator everyone wanted to be, me included. Yet, according to Jacob, it was David who had Albert committed to Broadmoor, while Robert stood by and did nothing."

"Why?" asked Kate. "What did he do?"

Turner shrugged. "Gave an interview to a journalist. About the Department. Seems like he was angry at his dad, or his brother, or maybe both of them. I don't know. A breach that a Security Operator could clean up in ten minutes on his first day in the Department. But Albert's father clearly thought it was serious."

He walked across the room, lowered himself into the chair that stood by the small desk, and rubbed his face with his hands. He felt empty, like he had nothing left.

"Thank you for telling me," said Kate.

"You're welcome," replied Turner, then started to laugh, low grunts without any humour in them whatsoever; if anything they sounded, to Kate's ears at least, as though they were dangerously close to sobs.

"Go and get some sleep, sir," she said. "There's still time. Our first interview's five hours away."

"That's the other thing I wanted to talk to you about," said Turner, lowering his hands and looking at her. "You've seen the schedule, right?"

"I've seen it," said Kate.

"Are you going to be OK?"

"I'll be fine," she replied. "It was going to happen sooner or later. Weird they both came up for this morning, but I'll be glad to get them out of the way, to be honest with you."

"Good," said Turner. "And you're not going to be doing them on your own. I'll be right there."

"I know that," said Kate. "So I'll see you here at seven thirty, yes? After you get some sleep."

Turner laughed. "That really isn't necessary."

Kate put the folder aside and got up from the sofa. She walked across the lounge and held the door open, a wide smile on her face.

"I insist, sir," she said.

17

OLD SCORES

YESTERDAY

Albert Harker strode through the streets of Clerkenwell, marvelling at the power he could feel coursing through his body. Every ten steps or so, he lifted himself into the air and floated above the cracked squares of pavement, relishing the indescribable sensation of no longer being tethered to the earth.

The streets around him were empty. The sun would be coming up in less than ninety minutes, and the men and women who had packed the local bars and restaurants had long since wandered off in search of taxis and night buses, blissfully unaware of the monster in their midst. They would not be so innocent for long, if Harker had his way; they would not thank him for what he was planning, he knew that much, but he believed that, in time, they would come to see that he had only their best interests at heart.

Forewarned is forearmed, he thought, as he pushed open the gate that led to Johnny Supernova's front door. It had been almost a decade since he had last visited this place, on his final evening as a free man. During his years in Broadmoor they had tried to convince him that the things he knew were nothing more than delusions, and when he refused to show even the slightest inclination to believe them, or work with them, they had tried to drive them out with every means at their disposal. They had tried hypnosis, cognitive therapy, and course after course of electro-shock treatment as they attempted to erase his own memories from his head. He had clung to them as tightly as a drowning man clutches a lifebelt; his memories were all he had left and he knew they were real, no matter how many times he was told the opposite.

The house before him was dark and silent. Harker peered up at the windows of the flat on the first floor and saw empty squares of glass, without curtains or blinds. He pushed himself into the air, marvelling at how easy it was to do so, how utterly natural it felt, and floated outside the windows.

The room beyond them was empty. The jumble of furniture and books and records that he had once tiptoed round was gone, the walls and floorboards were bare, and a thick layer of dust lay on every surface. Harker let gravity exert its pull on him and descended slowly to the ground, his mind racing. He had allowed for the possibility that Supernova might no longer live at the same address; the journalist was flighty and unpredictable at the best of times. Harker was disappointed, as he would have liked this first part of his quest to have gone smoothly, but not undeterred. After glancing quickly around to make sure there were no witnesses to his presence, he swung a leg that felt as powerful as a steam piston and kicked the front door clean off its hinges. It broke as it flew into the dim corridor beyond, shattering into pieces that spread across the threadbare carpet. He stepped inside and looked around.

The hallway was clean and almost empty. But on a shelf beside the door, as is the case in most shared houses, there stood a thick stack of unopened post. Harker leafed through it and found what he was looking for immediately: three thick cream envelopes, stamped with the logo of **CHESNEY, CLARKE, ABEL & WATT** and addressed to **The Executor of the Estate of Mr J. Bathurst, Esq**.

Panic exploded through Albert Harker. He had been prepared for the fact that it might take some time to track his old acquaintance down, but he had not allowed for the fact that Johnny Supernova might no longer be alive. The journalist was central to his plans, to everything he intended to achieve, to all the good he meant to do for the world.

Calm down, he told himself. *Calm down. His flat is empty, which means all his possessions have gone somewhere. There'll be next of kin. Someone will know.*

He tore open the first of the letters and scanned its contents. A smile of pure relief lit up his face as he read, his eyes settling briefly on the name at the bottom of the letter, then on the address printed at the top. He read it a second time, then slipped it into the pocket of the overcoat he had pulled through the smashed window of a tailor's shop near Liverpool Street, and headed back out into the early London morning.

Tom Clarke parked his car in front of the house he was going to spend the next twenty years of his life paying for, turned off the BMW's engine, and sighed deeply.

It had been an awful day and he wanted nothing more than to lie in the bath for an hour while his wife put their kids to bed, then open a bottle of wine. His secretary had phoned in sick, an inconvenience he knew he had no right to be annoyed about, given Janet's impeccable attendance history and the generally exceptional quality of her work. But today had been one of those days; there had been two client conferences before lunch and a partners' meeting afterwards, and without her he had been woefully unprepared for all three. He knew it wasn't her fault, but that didn't stop him blaming her.

He climbed out of the car, locked it, and crunched across the drive to his front door. The house was Bonnie's dream home: a huge, detached, four-bedroom on one of the best streets in Hampstead that they had bought the year he made full partner. It had been a reach even then, but they were surviving, more or less, and as long as big companies kept buying little companies and needing lawyers to help them, they would probably continue to do so. But it was tight, and he had come to see the house in precisely the opposite way that Bonnie viewed it: as a millstone, a weight round his neck that threatened constantly to drag them down.

Tom turned his key in the lock and pushed open the door. Instantly, he could hear what had become the regular soundtrack to his life: James and Alec shouting over one another, as Bonnie tried half-heartedly to calm them down.

He put his briefcase on the table in the house's wide hallway and walked into the living room. The chaos was familiar; a bright, garish DVD boomed deafeningly from the television as James and Alec rolled and wrestled on the thick carpet, managing to somehow avoid the huge number of toys that had been scattered across the entirety of the room. Bonnie was sitting in her favourite chair, beaming at their sons with such inane pride that it made Tom want to vomit. He was about to say hello when the doorbell rang and he headed back into the hallway, grateful for the distraction. The outline of a dark shape was visible through the frosted glass of the door. Tom turned the handle and pulled it open, concluding that a chat with Jehovah's Witnesses or some door-to-door charity worker was a far more pleasant prospect than going into the living room with his family.

The door was barely halfway open when a fist looped through the gap and crashed into Tom Clarke's nose. It broke with a loud crunch; blood sprayed up and out as he staggered backwards. A bolt of pure agony sliced through the centre of his forehead, his feet tangled, and he fell heavily to the floor, his hands going to his face as crimson pumped out between his fingers.

"Honey?" called Bonnie. "Are you all right?"

Tom's throat worked convulsively and he fought for breath as the dark figure stepped silently into his house, locking the door behind him. He tried to focus, tried to get a clear look at the person who was invading his home, but his eyes were full of blood and tears. The figure walked past him without even looking down; Tom tried to reach out and grab its ankle, but it kicked his feeble grip away and disappeared into the living room.

A second later the screaming started.

The high-pitched noise hit Tom like a bucket of cold water, instantly clearing his head and galvanising his limbs. He rolled over on to his stomach, forced himself first to his knees then up on to unsteady legs, and staggered for the living-room door. He lurched through the open space and saw something from his worst nightmares made real: Bonnie was lying on the floor, screaming her head off, as a man with a terrible smile on his face stood over her, holding their sons by their throats. The boys' faces were twisted with fear, and Tom could see that James had wet himself; the dark patch on his pyjamas reached almost down to his knees.

"Don't hurt them," shouted Tom, his voice cracking and muffled by the blood that was running down his throat. "Please. We have money and jewellery. Just please don't hurt them."

"Mr Clarke?" asked the man, his voice well-spoken and remarkably calm. "Thomas Clarke?"

"That's me," replied Tom, staring at the stranger. He was wearing an expensive overcoat over a suit and shoes that would not have looked out of place in the office where Tom went to work every day. His hair was thinning and his skin was pale, but his eyes danced with terrible lividity.

"We have business to discuss, you and I," said the stranger. "Private business. I would assume that such a lavish house as this is equipped with a cellar?"

"We have a cellar," said Tom, his voice trembling. Bonnie was staring up at the boys, her eyes wide and frantic. James and Alec were looking at him with terrible faith in their eyes, the unquestioning belief that their daddy would make everything all right.

"Is there a phone down there?" asked the stranger. "Or any other means of communication? Don't lie to me."

"No," said Tom. "There's wine and our safe. There's money—"

"I'm not interested in your wealth, Mr Clarke," interrupted the stranger. "I'm here for a higher purpose than petty burglary. If you suggest otherwise again, I'll make you choose which one of these two fine young boys I kill. Maybe that will make you pay attention."

Bonnie shrieked in terror, and James and Alec began to thrash and squirm in the stranger's grip. He looked utterly unmoved by the reaction his words had caused.

"OK," said Tom, holding his hands out wide in a gesture of utter submission. "Whatever you say. Just tell me what you want."

"The cellar," said the stranger. "Does it lock?"

"Yes," replied Tom.

"From the inside or the outside?"

"Outside."

"Excellent. Where is the door?"

"In the hall."

"Mr Clarke," said the stranger. "I want you to go and open the door. Then nice and quietly, nice and peacefully, we're going to lock your family in the cellar. Then you and I are going to talk. Is that all clear?"

"Yes," replied Tom. "It's clear." His heart was racing and his stomach was churning, but the thought of putting his wife and sons in the cellar, putting at least some distance between them and the stranger, ignited a flickering flame of hope.

Maybe they'll get out of this, he thought. *Even if I don't.*

"Good," replied the stranger. "Before we go, I'd like you and your wife to empty your pockets. Just in case you happen to have any mobile phones you forgot to tell me about. I'd like you to do that now, please."

Tom immediately fished his mobile phone from the inner pocket of his jacket and threw it down on to the cream leather sofa. He dug into the pockets of his trousers, pulled out his wallet and the entry card for his office, and tossed them down beside the phone, praying that the single remaining item wouldn't be visible through the material of his suit.

"Thank you," said the stranger, before turning his attention to Bonnie. "Mrs Clarke?"

Tom watched as his wife, who was now weeping steadily, emptied the pockets of her jeans. They contained her mobile phone, chewing gum, and nothing else.

"Good," said the stranger. "Lead the way then, Mr Clarke. And please, for your family's sake, don't do anything stupid."

Tom nodded, then walked slowly out of the living room, casting a final desperate glance at his sons as he did so. The cellar door stood near the end of the hall, just before the kitchen; it was plain wood, locked by a single sliding bolt. He slid it back, hauled open the door and stood stiffly beside it. A moment later Bonnie emerged from the living room and came towards him, her face wearing the look of a woman who is trapped in a nightmare from which she has no idea how to wake up. She walked unsteadily down the first few steps, then turned, waiting for her boys. The stranger carried them down the hallway as though they were weightless, and put them down before their father.

"Go with your mother, boys," said Tom, in a strangled tone. "Go on now."

James and Alec ran through the cellar door and flung themselves against their mother; she almost overbalanced, but managed to right herself. Then the three of them were sobbing, clutching at each other and whispering incoherently.

"Close the door, Mr Clarke," said the stranger. "If you told me the truth, then they will be quite safe down there."

Tom pushed the door slowly closed; the last things he saw before it clicked into place were the faces of his family, staring pleadingly up at him from the darkness.

"Do you mind if I sit?" asked the stranger. Tom had led them back into the living room as soon as the cellar door was bolted, and had taken a seat on the sofa, as instructed.

"No," he said, slowly. "That's fine."

"Thank you," said the stranger, settling himself into the armchair that Bonnie spent the majority of her evenings in. Tom hoped he might get to see his wife sitting there again. But, as he looked at the stranger's pale, smiling face, he didn't think the chances were good.

"Now," said the stranger, casually crossing one leg over the other, "I am very interested, Mr Clarke, in the death of a man who went publicly by the name of Johnny Supernova. Particularly the circumstances of his death and any will he may have left behind. Would you kindly tell me everything you know about these matters?"

Tom stared blankly at the stranger. *This* was why he had broken into his home? Not for money, or jewels, or even for the information that actually *was* valuable, on oil futures and offshore cash dumps? But to ask about Johnny Supernova?

"It was a heroin overdose," he replied. "He died in a flat in Clerkenwell. He didn't leave a will."

"What a waste," said the stranger, shaking his head sadly. "Although I can't say I'm entirely surprised. What about family? Did anyone survive him?"

"There's a sister," replied Tom. "She didn't want anything to do with him. The last piece he wrote was about her. It wasn't flattering to say the least. Apparently, she refused to lend him money shortly before he died."

"What about his possessions? His personal effects?"

"Everything is being held in trust," replied Tom. "It's being sold next month to pay off his credit cards and settle a number of unresolved advances. There was only a single specified bequest, delivered through me to an old friend of his."

"What was the bequest?" asked the stranger, suddenly sitting forward.

"An envelope," replied Tom. "A tape of an interview, a transcript, and a folder of notes."

"Did you read them?"

"I did."

"What was it?"

"Nonsense," said Tom. "Kid's stuff, about vampires and secret agencies."

"Who was the interview with?"

"I don't remember," replied Tom.

"Was it Harker?" asked the stranger. "Albert Harker?"

Tom stared, as his memory jogged into life. "How do you know that?" he asked, slowly.

The stranger smiled. "It was the only interview I've ever given, Mr Clarke. It sticks in the mind."

"My God," said Tom, his eyes widening. "Oh my—"

Albert Harker's eyes bloomed a terrible glowing crimson and he slid out of his seat with a speed that defied reason. He gripped Tom Clarke by the throat, cutting off his words, then lifted the squirming, struggling lawyer into the air as though it was the easiest thing in the world.

"Who did he leave the envelope to?" asked the vampire, drawing Tom forward until their faces were only millimetres apart. "Who has the tape now?"

"McKenna," spluttered Tom. His head was starting to pound as Harker's fingers cut off the oxygen supply to his brain. "Kevin... McKenna... He's a... journalist... for *The... Globe*." Panic swept through his body, filling him with a terror like nothing he'd ever known, and he dug his hand into his trouser pocket, his eyes wide and frantic.

"Thank you," said Albert Harker, breathing out heavily. "Thank you very much, Mr Clarke. You have been most helpful."

He was about to drop the lawyer on to his sofa when Tom Clarke pulled out his car key, and buried it in his eye.

The pain was enormous, bursting through his head like a mushroom cloud. Harker threw back his head, feeling his eyeball rip as the key tore through its soft surface, and howled at the living-room ceiling. Half his vision was instantly gone, a dark red cloud in its place; Harker dropped the lawyer and clamped his hands to his face, gripping the skin as if he could somehow squeeze out the pain. His head screamed with hurt and anger; as he tried to clear it, he heard a rough, scrabbling sound and forced himself to open his remaining eye.

Tom Clarke was crawling out of the living-room door, dragging himself determinedly towards the hallway. Harker bellowed with rage and lurched across the room, yellow fluid spilling from his ruined eye and pattering to the carpet as he reached down and took hold of the back of Clarke's neck. The lawyer screamed, struggling against the vampire's grip. Harker bore down, lifting the man to his feet as he kicked and flailed, squeezing his neck with both hands. He dug his fingers into the man's flesh, sending blood spilling from the lawyer's throat and down his arms. Clarke's eyes widened; he opened his mouth and let out a silent scream of pain as the fingers pushed deeper, before the vampire jerked his hands towards the ceiling with an almighty cry of fury.

Tom Clarke's head tore free of his neck with a terrible ripping sound, like a sheet of paper being torn in half. Blood exploded into the living room, drenching the ceiling and walls and carpet, raining noisily down on the leather furniture. Harker threw the head aside, paused for a long, pregnant moment, then clamped his mouth over the spouting stump of the man's neck; he drank long and greedily, feeling a pleasure so great it was overwhelming pump through his body, filling him with a burning, electric sensation, as though his flesh was being consumed by glorious fire. He felt his eyeball refill and heal, his vision returning in a moment of shocking brightness, like a window being opened on a dark room.

When he was sated, he let the corpse fall from his grip and rose into the air. He threw back his head, his throat convulsing, his body trembling uncontrollably, and waited for the rush to pass. After several minutes, it began to: his heart started to slow; sensation began to return to his fingers. He breathed deeply, in and out, like a man on the verge of a panic attack, then descended slowly to the blood-soaked carpet, understanding rushing through him.

That was why vampires killed: that glorious, Godlike ecstasy.

Trembling, Harker walked across the living room, stepping round the worst of the mess, and out into the hallway. His legs seemed to move on autopilot and his eyes burned a terrible, lustful red as he slid back the bolt that locked the cellar door. He stared down the dark staircase, his supernatural hearing picking up heavy breathing and whimpering from the underground room, his breath coming deep and slow. He took a step forward, then paused as he heard a female voice whisper below him.

"Don't be scared," it said. "I won't let him hurt you. I promise."

Oh God. Oh dear God.

The glow died in Albert Harker's eyes as he realised what he had been about to do. His stomach lurched and his head swam; he shoved the cellar bolt back into place, ran down the hallway on suddenly unsteady legs, smashed the front door open and fled out into the night.

18

THE MOST IMPORTANT MEAL OF THE DAY

Kate Randall stared at the day's ISAT schedule and tried to ignore the tension swirling in her stomach.

You knew this was coming, she told herself. *Everyone is going to end up here eventually. It's just the same as any of the others.*

After a bad start, the first day's interviews had been entirely successful; they had uncovered no evidence of any treason against the Department, and no significant incidents of an Operator attempting to lie to them. Stephen Marshall's admission that he had used his position in the Surveillance Division to eavesdrop on his girlfriend had been reported to his superior for appropriate disciplinary action, but was not ultimately what ISAT was concerned with; what they *were* concerned with, they had so far failed to uncover.

Kate read the first line of the schedule again and felt her stomach churn.

0800. Browning, Matt.

Behind her, the ISAT lounge door clicked open.

"Morning," she said, swinging her chair round.

Paul Turner, looking visibly invigorated by the extra hours of sleep that she had insisted he take, smiled at her. "Morning," he said. "Are you ready for this?"

"Absolutely," Kate replied, instantly. "If we don't treat everyone the same way, then there's no point in doing this. Right?"

"That's right," replied Turner. He was looking at her with an expression so obviously full of pride that she felt herself begin to blush. "Exactly right."

"I know," said Kate. "That's why I said it."

There was a long moment of comfortable silence, punctured only when Turner's radio buzzed into life. He plucked it from his belt and lifted it to his ear. After a second or two, he said, "Understood," and placed the handset back in its loop.

"He's here," said Turner. "I'll get him wired in, you get yourself up to speed on his file, then meet me inside in five minutes. OK?"

"Got it," replied Kate.

Turner nodded and left the lounge. Kate watched him go, then went to the filing cabinet that stood against the wall beside the desk. The cabinet contained the personnel files of every single Operator in the Department, from the rookies that were currently undergoing training to Interim Director Holmwood himself. She placed her hand on a black panel on the front of the cabinet and a lens rose out of the top on a plastic stilt. Kate lowered her eye to the level of the sensor and let the red laser beam slide across her eyeball. There was a series of clicks as the cabinet's locks disengaged, before Kate hauled open the second drawer and flicked through the files. She found Matt's, and settled on the sofa to read it.

Four minutes later she set the file down and made her way to the interview room. She was smiling as she walked; the story of how Matt had ended up working for the Lazarus Project was one she knew very well, having lived through most of it, but she still wanted to laugh at its sheer reckless audaciousness. Matt had put himself in danger, far more danger than she suspected he had actually realised, just for the chance to return to the Loop, to a place where he honestly believed he could be useful. He was never going to be half the Operator that she or Jamie were, nor probably a quarter of the terrifying force of nature that Larissa was becoming, but in his own way, he was every bit as brave and resilient as anybody in the Department, even if he would have protested vehemently at such a suggestion; his modesty was one of the things she loved most about him.

Kate pushed open the interview-room door and saw that the Intelligence Division technicians had finished their prep; Matt was sitting in the chair at the far end of the room, attached to the trolleys of monitoring equipment by a series of sensors that had been placed on the skin of his chest, arms and neck. She smiled at him as she took her seat beside Paul Turner and he smiled back, without much conviction. Turner glanced over at her and she nodded.

Let's get this over with.

"Lieutenant Browning," said Paul Turner, his tone warm and polite. "Do you understand why Lieutenant Randall and I are carrying out this process?"

"Yes, sir," replied Matt. "You're looking for traitors."

Turner smiled. "That's correct, Lieutenant. Answer our questions truthfully and you have nothing to worry about."

Matt nodded. Kate gave him a moment, then cleared her throat and began.

"This is ISAT interview 057, conducted by Lieutenant Kate Randall, NS303, 78-J in the presence of Major Paul Turner, NS303, 36-A. State your name, please."

"Matt Browning."

Kate looked down at the screen set into the table and watched the two grey boxes turn bright green. "Please answer the following question incorrectly," she said. "State your gender, please."

Matt grinned. "Female."

The boxes on the screen turned red.

"All right," said Kate. "Mr Browning. Are you a Lieutenant in Department 19?"

"Yes."

Green.

"Are you currently working for the classified section of the Science Division known as the Lazarus Project?"

"Yes."

Green.

"What does that work entail?"

"That's classified," said Matt.

Green.

"Not to us, Lieutenant," said Paul Turner. "Please answer the question."

"Lazarus is classified to everyone, sir," said Matt, his tone apologetic. "Unless you get Interim Director Holmwood in here to tell me otherwise."

Green.

Kate grinned. She was suddenly very proud of Matt; she knew how intimidating the surroundings of the ISAT interview room were, having been the second person to go through the process herself. And she knew full well that Matt was at least as terrified of

Paul Turner as most people in the Loop, possibly more so. But his loyalty to the Lazarus Project, and what it was trying to do, had apparently overwhelmed his nerves. She continued with the interview, which passed without incident.

When the technicians finished unhooking Matt from the monitoring equipment, he stood up, massaging the places where the sensors had been, and smiled at Kate. They were alone in the interview room; Paul Turner had disappeared into the ISAT lounge, having ordered Kate to go and get breakfast before they resumed their interviews.

"That wasn't too bad," said Matt. "I hope I did OK?"

"You did fine," replied Kate, smiling back at him. "I knew you would."

"Good," said Matt, a tiny bit too eagerly. "That's good. I was really nervous. Even though, you know..."

"Even though you had nothing to hide," finished Kate. "It's OK, Matt, really it is. Everyone who comes in here is nervous. That's sort of the point."

Matt nodded. "I suppose it would be."

Kate checked her watch, then looked at Matt with a cheerful expression on her face. "I'm starving," she announced. "I'm going to get breakfast and you're coming with me. We haven't talked in ages."

"I should get back to work," said Matt. "We're on the verge of isolating—"

"If they cure vampirism in the next half an hour," interrupted Kate, smiling broadly, "I'm sure Professor Karlsson will message you. Now come on. I simply *must* have coffee."

Matt broke into a grin. "All right," he said. "Let's do it. I haven't had a breakfast that didn't come out of a vending machine in weeks."

Kate put her tray down on one of the tables at the far end of the canteen, away from the line of Operators queuing in front of the hotplates and fruit bowls and coffee machines. She had a bowl of grapefruit, a plate containing brown toast and two badly poached eggs, a tall glass of orange juice and two mugs of steaming coffee. She hadn't lied to Matt; she was drinking probably a dozen coffees every day at the moment, just to keep her brain firing and her limbs moving. The Shaun-shaped hole at her centre was always threatening to pull her backwards, to drag her under, and caffeine was one of the ways she stayed beyond its reach.

Matt's tray thudded on to the table and Kate laughed out loud at the sight of it. He smiled with embarrassment and took a seat behind a towering, unstable mountain of bacon, eggs, sausages, mushrooms, baked beans and toast. He had a mug of tea and a glass of water and attacked his breakfast with the urgency of a starving man who has just wandered out of the desert.

"Are you sure you've eaten *anything* in weeks?" asked Kate, only half serious. "They do feed you down there, right?"

Matt nodded, fighting to swallow his mouthful. "Don't worry, they do," he said, reaching for his tea. "It's pretty good too. There's a cook whenever you want something, no matter what time it is."

"No wonder you hardly ever come out. Twenty-four hours a day?"

"Yeah. It's kind of intense down there, Kate. Everyone works long hours."

"How long?"

"Long," said Matt, then dug back into his food. Kate watched him eat; he didn't look like he'd lost much weight, so she wasn't worried about his physical health. But her friend looked absolutely exhausted; his skin was pale, almost ashen, and the bags beneath his eyes were black and swollen.

"So how's it going?" she asked. "Lazarus, I mean. What's the news?"

Matt looked up and smiled with his mouth full. He would have sat in the ISAT interview room until the end of time before he told Paul Turner anything about the Lazarus Project, but Kate was a different matter. When things had seemed at their worst, before Jamie went to Paris and the Loop was attacked, the four of them, Kate, Jamie, Larissa and himself, had sworn that they would tell each other everything from then on; secrets and hidden agendas had been on the verge of tearing them apart, and they had vowed not to let such a situation arise again.

"There's not much to tell really," he said. "We're making progress on mapping the vampire DNA strand, and we've isolated some of the elements of the protein that triggers the turn. We've got a theoretically viable carrier enzyme in the early stages of development, and we're continuing our analysis of the data Jamie recovered from Christopher Reynolds."

Kate nodded. She had barely understood a word that Matt had said, but she didn't want him to know that; instead, she struck out for the one subject he had raised that she felt confident in discussing.

"Is Reynolds' data helping?" she asked. "Even though he was working on the opposite of what you're trying to do?"

"Oh, it helps," said Matt. "Trust me. The processes aren't the same, but the steps he took have given us a road map we can use. Professor Karlsson thinks we've saved at least a year by having access to his work."

His work, thought Kate, with disgust. *Torture is all it was. Murder.*

"He was a genius," continued Matt. "Evil. But a genius."

"Maybe so," said Kate. "I'm still glad Jamie shot him."

Matt grinned broadly. "Me too," he said. "Very glad indeed."

"So everything just carries on then?" asked Kate, slicing open one of her eggs and smearing it across a piece of toast. "No major breakthroughs, no big eureka moments?"

Matt shook his head. "I'm afraid not. The truth of the matter is, we get fractionally closer every day. But unless we get some magic shortcut, or someone takes an incredible leap of deduction that turns out to be correct, it's still going to take a long time. Years, maybe."

"Even with all of you killing yourselves every day," said Kate. "Shows what I know. I don't understand how *anything* can take years to work out."

"The cleverest people in the world have been trying to prove string theory for the last half a century," said Matt, sipping his tea. "And I'm sure they all work pretty hard."

"Have you told Jamie?" asked Kate.

Matt shook his head again. "No. I haven't seen very much of him lately, to be honest with you. But he knows it's going to take a long time; Reynolds explained it to him, when he was still pretending to be Talbot. It must have been one of the few times he told anyone the truth."

"It must be killing him," said Kate, softly. "His mum *and* his girlfriend."

"I suppose so," said Matt. "He's got more invested in Lazarus than most of us who actually work there. And if there was anything I could do to speed it up, to accelerate a cure for Larissa and Marie, you know I would. Right?"

"Of course I do," said Kate. "And so does he."

Matt smiled briefly, then set about demolishing the remainder of his breakfast. Kate did the same; when their plates were empty, she sat back in her chair and started on her second coffee. Matt had drained the last of his tea and was looking at her expectantly.

"What?" she asked, frowning. "Have I got egg on my face?"

"No," said Matt. "I told you about Lazarus. It's your turn."

"ISAT?"

Matt nodded.

"Not much to tell either," she said, putting down her mug. "We're only one full day in. Nothing to report yet."

"Nothing?" asked Matt.

Kate considered telling him about the Surveillance Operator and his girlfriend, but decided against it; she didn't believe their promise to tell each other everything covered the personal indiscretions of others.

"Nothing," she repeated. "Which is good, obviously."

"When are you doing Jamie?"

"I don't know," lied Kate. "The schedule is randomly generated every night."

"So Reynolds was the last leak?"

"We don't know that yet," said Kate. "But we haven't found anything so far that suggests a security threat."

"What about Major Turner?"

"What about him?"

"Working with him," said Matt. "What's that like?"

Kate took a long sip of her coffee and considered the question. "It's... remarkable," she said, eventually. "I've never seen anyone more dedicated to what they do than Paul. It's inspiring, to tell the truth."

"And that's not because of... well, you know, because of..."

"Shaun?" said Kate, putting her friend out of his misery. "That's definitely part of it. He lost his son because the Department wasn't

227

secure, because we'd stopped looking at ourselves, I mean *really* looking at ourselves, and neither of us wants what happened to Shaun to happen to anyone else. But it's not a personal crusade, whatever anyone thinks. It's about the Department. For both of us."

"Well, rather you than me," said Matt, smiling gently. "He still scares the crap out of me."

"Don't worry," said Kate, returning his smile. "He has that effect on most people."

"But not on you?"

"Not any more," she said. "We've... well, I guess we've become pretty close. Very close, actually. I'd trust Paul with my life."

"So would I," said Matt. "He still scares me, though."

Kate laughed and, after a second or so, Matt joined in. There was warmth in the laughter, a sense of comfort in each other's company, and a familiar thought appeared in Kate's head.

We need to do this more often. Jamie too, and Larissa when she gets back.

Matt's laughter subsided and he opened his mouth, before appearing to think better of whatever he had been about to say. Kate was a remarkably observant girl, who rarely missed anything, especially not something as obvious as Matt's aborted gesture, and she immediately leant forward in her chair.

"What is it?"

"Nothing," said Matt, flushing bright red. "I was just going to... it's nothing."

"It's clearly not nothing, whatever it is," said Kate, her voice gentle. "Tell me."

Matt swallowed hard. His face appeared to be on the verge of bursting into flames. "There's... a girl," he said, eventually. "She works downstairs. Her name's Natalia."

A girl, thought Kate, grinning inwardly. *Of course there's a girl. Well, whoever she is, she has to be a better bet than the last girl he had a crush on. Angela Darcy would have torn him to pieces. Probably literally.*

"All right," said Kate. "A girl called Natalia. I don't think I know her."

"You don't," said Matt. "She lives in the Lazarus quarters and she hardly ever leaves the lab."

"Where's she from?"

"She's Russian," said Matt, and Kate saw his eyes light up as he thought about her. "The SPC pulled her out of university a couple of years ago and sent her to us when we were re-staffing Lazarus. She's only eighteen, but she's smarter than almost anybody in the Project. I think maybe only Professor Karlsson..." Matt trailed off and blushed again at the realisation that he had been gushing.

"Have you talked to her?" asked Kate, trying not to openly grin. Matt was so utterly adorable, so enthusiastic and shy and unsure of himself.

"I talk to her every day," said Matt. "We work five desks apart."

"No," said Kate, patiently. "Have you *talked* to her?"

"Oh," said Matt, and looked down at the table. "No."

"Maybe you should?" suggested Kate.

For a long moment, Matt's gaze remained fixed on the surface of the table. Then he looked up with a delicate, beautiful smile on his blushing face. "Let's change the subject," he said. "How do you think Larissa is getting on at NS9? I haven't even spoken to her since she left. Do you think she's keeping out of trouble?"

19

THE WAR ON DRUGS, PART ONE

Larissa ducked her head beneath a stream of bullets, threw herself back against the low ornamental wall, and grinned at Tim Albertsson. The Special Operator stared back at her, his mouth open, his eyes bright.

"How many?" he asked.

Larissa raised her head above the wall and lowered it again in a blur of movement that Tim could barely see; not a single shot was fired, such was her supernatural speed.

"Four," she said, calmly.

Tim looked down the wide expanse of grass that had, until very recently, been an immaculate lawn. At the bottom of the gentle slope, taking cover behind the low walls and outbuildings that stood inside the estate's open gates, he could see the black shapes of the other four members of their squad. They were perhaps fifty metres away, too far to be of any real help if the vampires above them charged, but Larissa didn't seem remotely concerned. The vampire girl was positively beaming, her eyes crimson, her fangs fully extended, her usually pale skin flushed pink.

Bloodlust, thought Tim. *I've never seen it up close before, but that's what it is. Her vampire side has taken her over.*

"Ready to do this?" she asked, fixing him with her glowing eyes.

Tim nodded. "I'll call the others up," he said. He reached for his radio, but Larissa gripped his wrist and held it. Her touch was gentle, but he was very aware that he could not move his hand a millimetre unless she let him.

"They'll follow," she said. "I'm talking about you and me, right now. Are you ready?"

Tim stared at her, utterly bewitched. Then he nodded. "Let's roll," he said.

They had been in the gym, putting the new intake of recruits through their paces yet again, when the session had been interrupted by General Allen.

There had been a heavy atmosphere of unease throughout Dreamland since the compulsory briefing several hours before, during which the NS9 Director had informed the entire Department that the Florence Supermax, the Colorado prison that was generally acknowledged to be impregnable, had not only been broken into, but that the prisoners it had held had all been turned and released. The determination that Larissa had seen on the faces of her new colleagues as the briefing began had rapidly evolved into something very different as General Allen played a piece of police surveillance footage taken above the outskirts of Denver.

The camera was looking down on the aftermath of a crash that had taken place on a wide, four-lane highway.

Several cars, perhaps as many as eight or nine, were strewn across the tarmac, crunched together into sculptures of twisted metal, at least one of them flipped on to its roof. The traffic that had managed to stop before becoming part of the carnage was backed up for what looked like miles in either direction, and the source of the incident was clearly visible; he was standing in the middle of the road wearing a prison jumpsuit pushed down to his waist.

The man was striding back and forth across the road, punching out the windows of crashed cars and screaming soundlessly at what appeared to be nothing. His head was bald, and his heavily tattooed body rippled with muscle; it gleamed under the glaring spotlight shining down from the police helicopter, a blinding beam of light that he suddenly seemed to become aware of. The prisoner stopped in the middle of the road and stared directly up at the camera. Then, with casual, almost nonchalant power, he leapt into the air, rising towards the screen like a shark emerging from the depths.

There was a crash of noise as the man disappeared from the frame, and then the footage began to shake wildly. The pilot and the occupants of the helicopter could be heard screaming and yelling, and the watching audience of Operators gasped as a flailing shape fell away from the camera, crashing on to the surface of the road, where it lay still. The movement of the frame became more and more violent, before the video and audio finally cut out. The last thing that could be heard before it did was a desperate voice screaming, 'Mayday!'

Larissa looked round the briefing room as the video ended and the wall screen went back to displaying the NS9 crest. Her new colleagues were pale, their eyes wide and staring. Unsurprisingly, Tim Albertsson was the first to break the silence. "He shouldn't be that strong," he said. "Not if he's new."

"No," said General Allen, from his podium at the front of the room. "He shouldn't be."

"So what's going on?" asked an Operator that Larissa didn't know.

"We have no idea," replied Allen. "But similar reports are coming in from Departments around the world. We will find out what has happened in Colorado, but, in the meantime, I want you all to be aware of what is out there. These vampires appear to be more powerful than most of you have ever faced, and you will prepare yourselves accordingly. Do I make myself entirely clear?"

There was a murmured chorus of agreement. General Allen stared at the massed ranks of his Department for a long moment, then nodded and continued with his briefing.

Larissa had left the assembly hall with her stomach churning, but desperate to be given a mission; she wanted to help, to make a genuine contribution to the Department she was a temporary part of.

As a result, she had been expecting to be reattached to one of the Operational Squads she had gone out with in recent weeks; she was extremely disappointed when the message that arrived on her console was the same one she had received almost every day during her time in Nevada: an order to report to the training facility and continue working with the new intake of recruits. Tim Albertsson had said nothing, but it was clear to her that he was equally annoyed by the situation. So when General Allen walked into the gym and told them he needed to speak to them, she saw the same excitement on his face that she could feel burning in her chest.

"I'm hearing good things about this intake," said the General, casting a glance in the direction of the recruits. "Ahead of schedule, they tell me. That true?"

"Yes, sir," replied Tim. "They're responding well, sir."

"Responding well to what?" asked Allen, a smile emerging on his face. "Having their asses kicked by a teenage girl?"

"Yes, sir," replied Tim, fighting back a smile of his own. "That certainly made an impression, sir."

"I bet it did," said Allen, turning to face Larissa. "Did you take it easy on them, Lieutenant Kinley? Be honest with me."

"Yes, sir," replied Larissa, not sure whether she was saying the right thing. "I didn't want to hurt them, sir. Well, not too badly, anyway."

General Allen burst out laughing and a second later Tim joined in. Larissa didn't, as laughing at her own jokes was not in her nature, but she allowed herself a small smile.

"All right," said General Allen, composing himself. "I need you both in Briefing Room 3 in fifteen minutes. We've got new intel that needs immediate action. Find someone to cover the rest of your schedule and meet me there. Clear?"

"Yes, sir," said Larissa.

"Yes, sir," said Tim, less than a second later. "Although you could have just messaged that, sir."

"I like to come down here now and again," said Allen, looking round the circular room. "This room brings back a lot of memories. Fifteen minutes, Operators."

The Director turned and strode out of the gym. They watched him go; as soon as the door closed behind him, Tim clapped his hands together.

"All right," he said, his voice full of excitement. "Time for me to see what you can really do."

"Maybe," she replied. "We don't know what the mission is yet."

"Almost the whole Department went out this morning chasing down the Supermax escapees," said Tim. "They're the worst of the worst, the most violent, dangerous, anti-social prisoners we've got, and you and I have been down here, training kids. So if we're finally going out, this must be something big."

Larissa nodded; she knew what he was saying made sense. Tim's squad were all Special Operators, the somewhat nebulous term that she had heard many times since arriving in Nevada; truth be told, she was rather looking forward to seeing exactly what made them so special.

"I guess so," she said. "Meet you there in ten minutes?"

"See you there," said Tim, smiling broadly.

Larissa opened the door to Briefing Room 3 eight minutes later and saw, to her complete lack of surprise, that Tim was already sitting in one of the chairs arranged before a wooden lectern. He turned his head as she entered and nodded, his mouth set in a straight line.

All business, thought Larissa. *No smiles and flirty comments now. Just business. Good.*

General Allen didn't keep them waiting long.

After no more than a minute, he entered through a side door, nodded curtly at them both, and strode up to the lectern. The Director pressed a button on the console he was holding in his hand, turning on the screen fixed to the wall behind him. It lit up, displaying a thermographic satellite image of a large house, surrounded by gardens and walls. A number of figures could be seen moving through the grounds and the many rooms, the majority of them a bright, burning yellow.

"Operators," said General Allen. "What you are looking at is the Nuevo Laredo residence of Garcia Rejon, formerly a General in the Mexican Army and the current head of the Desert Cartel. He was discharged from the Army six years ago, after his unit was discovered to have been providing security for Cartel shipments and bodyguards for its high-ranking members. Five years ago the former head of the Cartel, his wife, his mistresses, his children, his domestic staff and his bodyguards, were all murdered by Garcia Rejon's men in a single night. One of the men who carried out the murders was a former Army Captain by the name of Roberto Alaves, whose wife was an enthusiastic consumer of the Desert Cartel's primary product. Three years ago we caught her with eight grams in her purse during a weekend trip to San Diego, flipped Alaves, and got him to roll over on Rejon. The DEA made it stick, even though half the witnesses ended up dead, and Rejon got four consecutive life sentences in Federal prison. The Mexican authorities waved him goodbye and he was shipped up to Colorado. End of story."

"Until last night," said Larissa. "Right, sir?"

"Right," confirmed General Allen. "Rejon wasn't caught in the initial round-up after the Supermax break, nor were any of his former lieutenants. We've been watching the border, in case they tried to get home, but we can't watch every inch of it, especially when you're looking for men who can fly. This morning, the good citizens of Nuevo Laredo woke up to this charming image on the local news."

Allen pressed a key and the screen changed. Larissa gasped, and heard Tim Albertsson let out a deep breath beside her. The photo showed what Larissa assumed was Nuevo Laredo's business district; the road was four lanes wide, the bridge running over it looked new, and tall buildings of glass and metal rose up in the background.

Hanging from the bridge were twelve dead men, their bodies naked and mutilated.

Wire had been wrapped round their necks and tied to the concrete rail of the bridge; beneath them, on the grey tarmac, lay a wide puddle of blood, dotted with lumps of pink and purple. The high-definition photo gave terrible clarity to the men's wounds, and Larissa saw something that turned her stomach: the pool of blood was heavily tracked with the paw prints of dogs, and smeared where their tongues had lapped at the gore.

Beyond the hanging men, three large vans stood stationary beneath the bridge, their rear doors open wide. Inside, piled high and tangled together, were more bodies than Larissa could count. Blood soaked the interiors of the vehicles, coating arms and legs and hands and faces. Several of the bodies had spilled out on to the road – *were dragged out by the dogs, more likely*, she thought – and lay twisted on the tarmac, their faces contorted in the agonies of their deaths.

"Sixty-eight dead men and women," said General Allen. "All of them Desert Cartel, including the entire leadership. Eyes put out, fingers and toes cut off, tongues missing, genitals in their mouths. All done pre-mortem."

"Jesus," said Tim. "Cause of death?"

"Blood loss," said Allen. "They were tortured and left to die. No gunshots, no clearly fatal wounds."

"No mercy," said Larissa. "This wasn't just about getting these people out of the way. This was a statement."

"What sort of statement?" asked Tim, glancing over at her.

"I'm back," replied Larissa. "And everyone better accept it. That sort of statement."

"Intelligence coming across the border suggests that what you're saying is correct," said General Allen. "The situation is somewhat chaotic, as you might expect, but what we do know is that the sixty-eight Cartel members who are now dead were all taken from their homes at approximately four o'clock this morning and dumped just before dawn. One of the DEA's agents within the Cartel, who luckily for us, and him, operates at a level below those who were killed, reported this morning that he was called, along with everyone else, to Garcia Rejon's home to be informed of the change of leadership. He saw Rejon in person, with his own eyes. Then he and the rest of the soldiers and street dealers were sent home, with orders to carry on with business as normal."

The Director paused, and looked down at his two Operators, who were hanging on his every word.

"I'm sure I don't need to tell you that a group of vampires at the head of one of the largest and most violent drug cartels in Mexico represents a serious threat to the national security of the United States, especially when those vampires can be assumed to be in possession of the same exceptional power that we saw on the Denver footage. Which is where the two of you come in. Tim, you're going to take your squad across the border this afternoon, with Lieutenant Kinley as a temporary attaché. Insertion into Rejon's compound is scheduled for 8:48pm, ten minutes after sundown. No special SOP, no op-specific restrictions. Destroy every vampire you find and come home. Clear?"

"Clear, sir," replied Tim. "Although I have to ask, sir, whether it might be wiser to insert in daylight?" He shot Larissa an apologetic glance as he spoke, and she did her best not to let her eyes burst red with anger.

"Surveillance confirms that the windows of Rejon's compound have all been painted out," replied General Allen. "And intelligence suggests that a number of his bodyguards have been left unturned. The advantage of being able to use Lieutenant Kinley outweighs the disadvantages of working in darkness."

"Understood, sir," said Tim. He glanced at her again, a pained expression on his face. Larissa knew exactly what it was meant to convey.

Nothing personal. I had to ask.

"Excellent," said General Allen, and tapped his console again. The screen changed to a wide pyramid of photographs, each with a name printed beneath it. At the top was General Garcia Rejon, a handsome, thin-faced man with a covering of dark stubble and piercing dark brown eyes. Under him were three men listed as Colonels, and below them were widening rows of Lieutenants and soldiers. "This is what we believe to be the new Desert Cartel leadership," said Allen. "Intelligence suggests that the majority of these men, all of whom we suspect have now been turned, are currently residing in Garcia Rejon's compound. The General and his Colonels are Priority Level 1, the rest Priority Level 2. The preferred outcome of this Operation is that none of these men survive."

"Collateral?" asked Tim Albertsson. "You said there were unturned guards?"

"Not a consideration," replied Allen, and Larissa felt a chill run up her spine. "Your objectives are the Priority Level targets. Clear?"

"Yes, sir," said Tim, firmly.

"Lieutenant Kinley?" asked the Director, turning to her. "This is a Priority Level operation with Presidential approval. Can you handle it?"

I don't know, thought Larissa. *I'm not a murderer. But there's no way I'm telling you that.*

"Yes, sir," she said. "I can handle it."

"Good," replied General Allen, and smiled at her. "I'm glad you're going along on this one, Larissa. I wish I could be there to see it."

"Thank you, sir."

"You're welcome. I want wheels up at 1900. The Operational briefing has been sent to both your consoles; study it, prep your team, then go and get this done. I want a full report as soon as you're back. Dismissed."

Tim tensed the muscles in his legs; he was about to jump over the low wall that they had taken cover behind, when Larissa disappeared into the evening sky in a silent streak of black.

He gasped at her sheer speed; before a second had passed she was gone, lost in the gloom overhead. A nervous babble of Spanish floated through the air, confirming that Rejon's men had seen something, although they appeared unsure as to exactly what. Tim crouched behind the wall, adrenaline coursing through his body, uncertain what to do. He raised his head and peeked over the top of the wall; the garden beyond was perhaps fifteen metres square, with two rings of flower beds and a round pond in its centre. Beyond it, atop the gentle rise, was Garcia Rejon's home, a sprawling mansion with blacked-out windows and blast-proof concrete walls, its outline silhouetted against the rapidly darkening sky. On the far side of the garden, a low wall divided it from the gravel drive that wound up to the front of the house. Behind it, crouched in the darkness with AR-15s in their hands, were four of Rejon's newly-turned vampires.

Tim braced himself. He had no idea what Larissa was doing, but he knew he couldn't just crouch behind the wall indefinitely, waiting for her to make her intentions known. The muscles in his legs tensed as he readied himself to move out from behind the wall; he took a deep breath, and then a high whistling noise filled his ears. He raised his head just in time to see a black shape drop out of the sky on the other side of the garden.

An explosion of dirt and shimmering blood erupted from behind the wall, which cracked and fell heavily forward on to one of the flower beds. As he stared, incredulous, two large shapes flew through the air and crashed on to a strip of lawn. The vampires twisted and writhed on the grass, digging brown furrows with their elbows and heels, both of them bleeding from so many places it looked as though a grenade had gone off beside them.

The sight of the blood cleared Tim's head and he threw himself over the wall; grunts of exertion and screams of violence rang out across the garden, but he ignored them, focusing only on the two injured vampires. He drew his stake as he ran and plunged it into the chest of the nearest man; he burst with a deafening bang, spraying Tim's uniform with blood and meat, but the Special Operator barely noticed. He was already moving, raising his stake and bringing it down on the second man; he exploded with a thick, wet pop as Tim raced across the lawn towards where Rejon's men had been taking cover.

Dust swirled in the air beyond the collapsed wall. Tim raised his T-Bone to his shoulder and flipped down the visor of his helmet, twisting the dial on his belt as he did so. The thermographic filter activated, and the scene before him shifted to a swirl of pale yellow as hot dust floated through the air. In the middle, standing quite still, was a single figure, coloured dark red and bright pulsing white. Tim pushed his visor back up and inched forward, his finger resting on the T-Bone's trigger.

"Larissa?" he shouted. "That you in there?"

"It's me," shouted the vampire girl. "Catch!"

Something flew out of the dust towards him. Tim removed his left hand from the barrel of his weapon and grabbed for it; he felt something coarse and slippery, and looked down to see what Larissa had thrown him. It was the severed head of a man in his late teens, his glowing eyes wide and staring, his mouth still opening and closing, trying to speak. Tim stared at it, revolted.

Does she know? he thought. *Does she know that she gets like this?*

The sound of metal crunching through bone shook him from his thoughts, and he dropped the head a millisecond before it burst like an overfilled balloon, splattering his uniform from ankle to knee.

"Nice catch," said Larissa, strolling calmly out of the dust. Her eyes blazed red and her fangs gleamed as she smiled at him.

"Thanks," he managed. Behind him he could hear the rest of his squad approaching. "You could have let me put it down before you staked the rest of him."

Larissa leant towards him, so close that he could feel her breath hot in his ear. "Don't be such a baby," she whispered. Then she pulled away, and went to meet the others as they skidded to a halt in the middle of the ornamental garden. Tim remained where he was for a long moment, his mind wiped temporarily clear by the vampire girl; he was utterly intoxicated by her, had known as much for several weeks now. Since the day she arrived, if he was honest with himself. But now he felt something new; he felt fear.

He was scared of her. And, to his surprise, he realised it didn't change the way he felt. If anything, it only made it stronger.

Snap out of it, for Christ's sake, he thought, and shook his head briskly, trying to clear it. *You're in the middle of a Priority Level operation. Get your shit together, right now.*

Tim took a deep breath and turned to address his squad. The words died in his throat as a hand, tanned and lined and incredibly strong, closed round his neck.

20

THE SLEEP OF THE JUST

Jamie Carpenter's head spun as he walked the familiar corridor of Level B.

A descendant of the founders. Jesus.

He pressed his card against the panel outside his quarters, pushed open the door, and walked inside. The assault on Broadmoor, and the similar attacks on prisons and hospitals around the world, had clearly been designed to keep the supernatural Departments of the world busy, distracting them from the most pressing matter at hand: finding Dracula before it was too late. But now it seemed as though the plan had delivered a bonus that neither Valeri nor his master could have anticipated: the reopening of an old wound that went to the very heart of Blacklight.

I wonder what he wants, wondered Jamie, as he removed his uniform and pulled on a pair of shorts and a T-shirt. *What would I want if I'd been locked in a hospital for almost a decade for no reason?*

Jamie considered the question as he brushed his teeth in the small sink in the corner of his quarters, looking at his reflection in the mirror as he did so. His eyes were bloodshot and the bags beneath them were heavy and grey. The scar on his neck had faded in the months since his skin had been burned by acid in the chemist's Bliss laboratory, but it was still clearly visible: a pink patch of rough skin and shiny scar tissue that he had come to accept as a permanent part of himself. He drank two glasses of water and, as he lay down on his bed, realised he knew the answer to his own question. It was a single word.

Revenge. If I was Albert Harker, I'd want revenge.

The thought chilled him and when his console beeped into life in the darkness he jumped, ever so slightly. He lifted it from his bedside table, glad that Larissa hadn't been there to see him so easily scared, and saw an overdue message waiting for him. He thumbed it open, read the contents, and groaned.

Brilliant timing. Just bloody fantastic. Thanks very much.

Five hours later Jamie opened his eyes.

The thick fog of tiredness that he had to fight his way out of most mornings was strangely, wonderfully absent; his mind was clear and his body felt more rested than it had in months. He checked the digital clock that stood on his bedside table and was astonished to see that it was 8:45am. It was incredibly rare for him, or any other Operator, to sleep so late. Alarms, console messages, unscheduled briefings: any or all of these interrupted sleep in the Loop on an almost nightly basis.

Jamie swung himself out of bed and flicked on his little plastic kettle. He made a steaming mug of coffee, left it cooling on his desk, and headed for the showers. In the wide block in the middle of the Level B corridor, he stepped under the water, letting the heat burn away the aches and pains that always gradually resurfaced, no matter how well he slept, and thought about John Morton.

Most Department 19 Operators were already highly experienced when they arrived at the Loop to begin their training, either in the military, the intelligence services, or the elite regiments of the police; it tended to count for very little, however, when they were first confronted by a live vampire. So it had been with Morton; the reality had clearly shaken him and made him immediately begin to question everything. This was natural, in Jamie's experience, possibly even healthy, but it presented him with a problem. The situation they found themselves in, with hundreds of particularly dangerous new vampires on the loose, didn't permit the shallow learning curve that was preferred for rookie Operators, which meant that he was going to have to have a conversation with John Morton that he was not looking forward to.

Jamie towelled himself dry and made his way back to his quarters. A message had appeared on his console while he was in the shower; he pressed READ with his thumb.

M-3/AWAIT_FURTHER_INSTRUCTIONS/ MAINTAIN_READINESS

He breathed a sigh of relief.

That buys me some time. Enough, hopefully.

Morton and Ellison would by now be awake, in the dormitories on Level A where all rookie Operators were housed. For a moment, Jamie considered giving them the morning off, but decided against it. Going easy on them would do nobody any good, least of all them; a couple of hours in the Playground with Terry would sharpen them up. He sent a quick message to that effect, then pulled the most overdue report from the teetering pile on his desk, settled into his chair, and began to read.

An hour later his console beeped into life again, rousing him from the report. He rubbed his eyes with the heels of his palms and opened the message, although he was already sure he knew what it was going to say.

NS303,67-J/ISAT_INTERVIEW/SURDIV/1100

He checked his watch. It read 10:36.

For Christ's sake. As if there's nothing important going on right now.

The same message had been waiting for him when he returned from the Interim Director's quarters in the early hours of the morning. Part of him had been hoping that either Kate, or Paul Turner himself, might have moved his appointment back, given the demands of MOVING SHADOWS and the implications of Jacob Scott's revelation.

Too much to ask, clearly.

Jamie closed his eyes and tried to imagine answering Kate's ISAT's questions. Then he stood up, gave his head a quick shake, and started to pull on his uniform, dragging the black jumpsuit over his body, doing up the zip and folding the flaps into place. He pushed his feet into boots that had once been so hard they made his toes bleed, but which were now as soft as silk, and laced them tight. His Glock 17 went into the holster on his right hip, even though he wasn't leaving the Loop, and his belt was fastened tightly round his waist. He checked his appearance in the mirror and exited his quarters, walking quickly towards the lift at the end of the curved corridor. When it arrived, he stepped inside and hit the button marked G, checking his watch yet again as he did so.

Twenty minutes. Enough time for breakfast before I go up to ISAT.

The lift slid smoothly to a halt. Jamie set off for the dining hall, his boots clicking rapidly along the corridor floor.

I'm not doing this on an empty stomach, he thought. *It might not be Kate asking the questions. If it's Paul Turner, I'm going to need to be at my best.*

21

THE WAR ON DRUGS, PART TWO

Larissa spun, drawing the stake from her belt faster than the human eye could follow, and threw. It accelerated through the air in a silver blur, slamming into the head of the vampire that had seized Tim. It fell back, blood gushing from a hole in its forehead, its glowing red eyes wide and incredulous. Larissa leapt forward as Tim's hands went to his uninjured neck, pulled the stake out of the vampire's skull and plunged it into its heart. Blood thumped into the warm evening air, pattering to the ground as thick crimson rain.

Tim slowly lowered his hands and turned to face her. Larissa's head was pounding with the scent of freshly spilled blood; she could hear her own roaring through her veins, could feel burning heat emanating from her eyes and cheeks. She was breathing heavily, but not as the result of exertion; it was something primal, the panting of an animal in the middle of a hunt. She was still capable of rational thought, still knew who she was, where she was, and what she was doing, but that information seemed dull and distant compared to the bright red immediacy of violence.

Her squad leader glanced down at the remains of the vampire who had grabbed him, then returned his gaze to her. "Thank you," he said.

"Don't mention it," she said. "Try not to be so easy to sneak up on next time."

Tim narrowed his eyes and stared at her for a long moment. She held his gaze until he turned away and addressed the rest of the squad. "We go in the front door," he said, his voice low. "We're going to empty it out, room by room. Overlapping, flanking formation. Anything that moves gets destroyed."

"Yes, sir," growled Larissa, as the rest of the squad voiced their agreement.

"OK," said Tim. "Follow me."

He dropped into a low crouch and they followed him up the driveway to the front door of the house. It was ominously quiet in the aftermath of all the shooting and screaming. Tim raised his right hand and jabbed two fingers in the direction of the door; Anna Frost, the quiet, serious Canadian Special Operator whose name suited her perfectly, and José Rios, the handsome, relentlessly charming Dominican who had been a Recon Marine sniper before his recruitment to NS9, ran forward and set themselves on either side of the door, their backs to the wall, their HK416s raised.

"Larissa," said Tim, his voice low. "See if anybody's home, would you?"

Larissa grinned and floated forward. She slid silently to the ground in front of the large, ornate wooden door, feeling her fangs pressing against her lower lip; she took a deep breath, then slammed the palms of her hands against the door. It exploded inwards, the heavy wood splintering as though a bomb had been detonated against it.

From inside the house there came screams of terror and the rattle of panicked Spanish. Larissa leapt backwards, landing behind Tim; the squad leader was flanked by Jill Flaherty, the tall, powerful former NSA agent who served as his second-in-command, and Pete Rushton, a loud, relentlessly optimistic Californian who had served in Delta Force for almost a decade before being summoned to Nevada. Frost and Rios swung themselves around the shattered door frame and disappeared into the house, their rifles at their shoulders.

"Clear," yelled Rios.

"Go," bellowed Tim. Flaherty and Rushton ran through the empty doorway, their weapons drawn, overlapping Frost and Rios, who had already checked the corners and exits. Tim ran forward and Larissa followed him. A second later the squad regrouped in the middle of a vast entrance hall, a tight cluster of black, bristling with weapons.

"No welcome party," said Rushton. "That's just rude."

Larissa smiled at him, her eyes full of heat.

"I want a fast sweep of this floor," said Tim, ignoring his squad mate's comment. "Room by room. No surprises."

"Yes, sir," said Flaherty. She stepped forward, her MP7 in one hand, her console in the other. On its screen was an architectural blueprint of the house they were standing in. "Three rooms in the centre of this level. Eighteen around the outer wall, sir."

"Don't we have a satellite overhead?" asked Larissa. "There's no time for a twenty-one-room sweep."

"I've requested sat coverage," replied Tim. "Surveillance is telling me we'll have overlook any minute. Until then, we're on our own."

"But twenty-one—"

"You heard me, Lieutenant Kinley," said Tim. "We'll just have to move quickly. Frost, take point."

Anna Frost nodded, and walked silently across the wide entrance lobby to where a dark wooden door stood closed. She settled her HK416 against her shoulder as the rest of the squad formed up a short distance behind her, took a deep breath, then kicked the door open, darting back behind the cover of the wall as it swung on its hinges. There was no movement inside the room, no rattle of gunfire. Frost checked over her shoulder for confirmation and saw Tim pointing a finger silently towards the open door. She nodded and stepped noiselessly into the room. As she did so, Larissa heard something, something inaudible to anyone without her supernatural hearing.

A tiny inhalation of breath.

"Wait!" she yelled.

But she was too late.

As Frost stepped into the room, something silver whistled out from behind the door and crashed into the side of her helmet, sending sparks flying into the air and driving her to her knees. She twisted as she buckled, pulling the trigger on her HK416 instinctively. Fire burst from the end of the barrel as the rifle thundered deafeningly in the enclosed space of the house.

"Move!" yelled Tim Albertsson, and ran forward.

Larissa beat him to it. She blurred through the space between where she was standing and where Frost was lying on the floor, and scooped the Operator easily into the air with one hand, drawing her T-Bone with the other. She pushed Frost behind her, pointed her weapon into the space behind the door, and froze.

Slumped on the ground was a woman, no older than twenty or twenty-one. She was wearing an orange bikini, and bleeding from at least a dozen bullet wounds. Crimson covered the wall and pooled on the ground beneath her. Resting limply in one of her hands was a long machete. Her eyes were wide and staring, devoid of life.

The rest of the Special Operations Squad burst into the room, their weapons drawn, skidding to a halt as they followed Larissa's gaze.

"Christ," said Flaherty. "What the hell is this?"

"Anna," said Tim, taking hold of the Canadian's shoulders. "Are you hurt?"

Larissa released her grip. Frost staggered slightly, but managed to stay upright.

"I'm OK," she said. "Stupid of me. I'm sorry, sir."

"It's OK," replied Tim. "You're all right."

"Sir," said Flaherty, and Tim turned towards her. "This girl wasn't a vampire. She's human, sir."

Anna Frost pushed back her visor. "Human?" she asked, her voice unsteady.

"Human," confirmed Flaherty. She was crouched beside the dead girl, running the beam from her UV torch over her skin.

"She's dead?" asked Frost. "I killed her?"

Tim turned sharply back to face her. "She attacked you, Operator. Remember that. You did your job."

Frost nodded, but the sickly grey-green colour of her face suggested that she was far from convinced. Larissa stared helplessly at her, then heard something else, from beyond the closed door at the far end of the room. It was a soft scratching sound, like bare feet shuffling across wooden floorboards.

"We're about to have company," she whispered.

Tim took one look at the expression on her face and ordered his squad to take cover. Rushton pulled Frost and Flaherty down behind a huge leather sofa that sat in the middle of the room, as Tim and Rios took cover behind a heavy wooden desk beneath the window. Larissa floated silently up into the air, spreading herself easily against the ceiling, and trained her T-Bone down at the closed door.

There was a long, pregnant silence. Nothing moved, nothing made a sound, until Larissa heard a sharp intake of breath from the other side of the door, a millisecond before it was kicked open.

It slammed against the wall with a deafening crash as a stream of figures burst through the empty space, screaming and yelling and waving their hands above their heads, hands that were full of metal.

"Freeze!" bellowed Tim Albertsson, rising up from behind the desk, his rifle locked against his shoulder. The rest of the squad rose as one, their weapons pointed at the mass of screaming humanity, which stopped dead at the sight of the black-clad figures before them.

Standing inside the doorway were seven women in bikinis. The oldest appeared to be in her late twenties, and several appeared to be little more than teenagers. In their hands they carried an array of kitchen knives, machetes, and other sharp pieces of household metal; one girl was carrying a garden trowel.

"Drop the weapons!" shouted Tim Albertsson. "Drop them now!"

The women instantly threw what they were holding to the ground; the makeshift weapons clattered against the floorboards, one of the knives digging into the wood and vibrating. They wore expressions of fear and misery on their faces, and several of them clutched at their almost naked bodies, covering their chests and crotches to the best of their ability. At the front, a tall, dark-skinned woman stared at the black figures, her arms hanging loosely at her sides. She looked as though she was about to speak when her eyes flicked to the corner of the room and what lay there. Her hands flew to her mouth and she screamed through her fingers. She stumbled forward, until Rios yelled at her to stay still.

"*Bastardo!*" she cried. "*Asesino! Olivia, mi pobrecita, mi querida ángel...*"

Her voice trailed off in a paroxysm of sobbing.

"Tim," said Larissa, speaking through the comms link that only their squad mates could hear. "Get hold of this. This is going to get out of hand quickly."

Tim nodded, then turned his attention back to the women, all of whom were now in tears, trembling and shaking and pointing at the dead girl. "Ladies," he said. "Identify yourselves."

The girl who had screamed stared at him with open loathing. "I am Eva," she spat.

"Eva," said Tim. "Can I talk to you? Can we talk calmly?"

"I do not talk with murderers," said Eva. "With cowards."

"She attacked me," said Frost, her voice low. "I was defending myself."

"With your gun and your helmet and your armour," said Eva, looking at Frost with open contempt. "She had a piece of metal that wasn't even sharp. How much of a threat was she to you?"

"Eva, look at me," said Tim. Behind her, the rest of the women were beginning to mutter in Spanish, and he was keen to try and neutralise the situation. If they attacked, his squad would be in no real danger. But he knew that not all of the women would survive if his team were forced to defend themselves; possibly none of them would.

"Why are you here, Eva?" he asked. "Why are you all here, in this house?"

She looked at him for a long moment. "We cut," she said, eventually.

"Cut what?"

"The product," she said. "In the basement. We cut and wrap and parcel."

"Why are you dressed like that?" asked Larissa.

One of the younger-looking girls spoke up. "So we not steal," she said, her voice wavering. "They no trust us."

Jesus Christ, thought Larissa. *How humiliating.*

"And because they like to look," said Eva. "The men. They like to look." Behind her, the rest of the women murmured their agreement.

"Why are you up here on your own?" asked Tim. "Where is General Rejon?"

"Downstairs," replied Eva. "When the shooting start, he sent us up here. Told us to fight."

"Does he know who we are?" asked Tim. "Why we're here?"

Eva shook her head. "General thinks you are from other cartel." She examined their uniforms. "But I am thinking not."

"So he sent you all up here with lumps of metal to fight with?" asked Larissa, her voice vibrating with fury. "Dressed in nothing? After he had heard with his own ears that whoever was up here had guns?"

Eva shrugged. "It not matter if we die. There are eight of us cutters, seven now, after Olivia. We all die, tomorrow a hundred girls ask for jobs. If we say no, we will not fight, the General will kill us himself. So we fight."

"No, you don't," said Tim. "You take your friend's body and you find some clothes and you get the hell out of here as quickly as you can. Do you understand me, Eva?"

"What we tell General tomorrow?" asked one of the women, her face a mask of worry. "How we explain?"

"You don't need to worry about that," said Tim. "Eva, you said General Rejon is downstairs?"

She nodded.

"That's dumb," said Flaherty, frowning. "There's only one entrance to the lower level. Next door, in the library."

"The General will not run," said Eva. "He told us he will not go back to prison. He will die first."

"Then let's give him what he wants," spat Larissa. "Why are we standing around up here when they're down there?"

"How many of them are downstairs?" asked Tim, shooting a glance full of warning at Larissa.

"Eleven including the General."

"Are you telling me the truth, Eva?"

"Yes."

"She's telling the truth, sir," said Flaherty. "We just got overlook. Twelve humans and one vampire on this level, eleven vampires downstairs."

"Good," said Tim. "Thank you."

"Yeah, great," said Larissa. "Pity we didn't have that information before we killed an innocent girl."

"Larissa?" said Tim, softly.

"What?"

"Shut the hell up. That's an order."

Larissa stared at her squad leader for a long moment.

It's not his fault, she told herself. *Not anyone's fault. Bad things happen. Bad things happen.*

"Yes, sir," she said, without dropping her gaze.

"Thank you," said Tim, and returned his attention to Eva. "The General and his men. What weapons do they have?"

"Knives," said Eva. "And guns. Many, many guns."

The Special Operations Squad stood in General Rejon's library, facing the door that would take them down to the building's basement level. The room was dark, with a wooden floor and ceiling-height bookshelves covering three of the walls. The fourth was dominated by a vast picture window, which looked out over the sloping gardens and grounds towards the distant front gates, a view that would normally have been idyllic, but which was now dotted with patches of spilled blood, still visible in the last of the evening light.

Eva had led the terrified, grief-stricken cutters out of the house, two of them carrying the body of the woman named Olivia between them. They had gone without a word, although Frost had been unable to meet any of their eyes as they departed; her face was pale and drawn.

"Anna," said Tim. "I want you guarding this door. Anything comes up the stairs that isn't one of us, kill it."

"I'm fine, sir," she said. "You don't need to leave me up here."

"I know," replied Tim. "But I need this door covered and I want you to do it. Is that clear?"

"Yes, sir," replied Frost. Her face wore an expression of abject misery.

"The rest of us are going down there," said Tim, nodding towards the door. "There are eleven vampires waiting for us, none of whom the world is going to miss. I want visors down and weapons ready. Let's get this done and go home. José, you're on point."

Rios nodded and walked across to the door; he kicked it open and leapt backwards, creating separation between himself and the empty space. The satellite imagery indicated that all eleven of the vampires were in one place, a long room in the centre of the basement, but it was impossible to be too careful when you were dealing with vampires.

"Clear," said Rios. He stepped through the door and started

down the stairs towards the basement. Larissa watched as Flaherty and Rushton followed him, her stomach churning with boiling acid, her eyes burning with a heat she had never felt before.

She was angrier than she had ever been in her life.

The opulence of the house and its grounds, the art and the cars and the fine decorations, were an insult to the overwhelming majority of human beings, the men and women who scraped by and tried to live decent lives. The house was a palace built on death and misery, on the expendability of men and women like Olivia, who had attacked a soldier wearing only a bikini and carrying a dull machete because her employer had promised to kill her if she didn't.

All their money and their guns aren't going to help them now, she thought, her mind so flooded with the bittersweet desire to commit violence that she could barely form the words.

Nothing can help them now.

They went silently, taking the stairs one at a time, and emerged into a wood-panelled corridor.

The long wall to their left was covered in framed posters of old Hollywood films: *Tarzan, The Adventures of Robin Hood, King Kong, The Magnificent Seven.* To their right, the wall was covered with black and white photographs of film stars, politicians, musicians and models. A handsome man sporting a thick moustache and wearing military uniform smiled out from the middle of every frame; the man who was no longer a man, the vampire the Special Operations Squad was there to destroy.

"Flaherty," said Tim, across their comms network. "Do we still have overlook?"

"Yes, sir," she replied.

"Talk us through the layout of this level."

"One room to our left," said Flaherty, pointing at a door set in between two of the posters. "To the right, there's one large room on the other side of this wall. Small rooms along the edges, but the central space is open. The vamps are gathered at the far end."

"OK," said Tim. "Stay on it. Let me know if they move."

"Yes, sir," replied Flaherty.

The squad leader raised his hand and pointed at the door set into the left-hand wall. Rios and Rushton moved silently along the corridor until they were standing either side of it. Tim and Flaherty moved up behind them, their T-Bones raised to their shoulders, Larissa watching their backs. There was a moment of silence before Rios reached down, gripped the handle, and threw the door open. Tim led them in, Flaherty behind him, Rios, Rushton and Larissa bringing up the rear.

The room was long and wide, full of metal benches beside which stood a number of stools. On the bench tops sat plastic tubs full of white powder, along with metal spoons, wooden sticks, and a pair of ancient-looking scales. A set of shelves contained rows of rectangular parcels, wrapped in brown paper and layers of clear plastic. A digital radio was plugged into a wall socket in the corner, the single concession to levity in this severe, businesslike room.

"This is where those women worked," said Larissa. "The cutters."

Tim nodded. "Set a UV grenade on that bench," he said. "Motion sensitive. I don't want any surprises down here."

"Yes, sir," said Larissa. She pulled a UV grenade from her belt, placed it in the middle of one of the piles of powder, and twisted its dial three clicks to the right; it began to flash steadily as the squad made their exit. Larissa cast a final glance into the room as she pulled the door closed and felt the fury in her chest, hot and sharp and comforting.

Time's almost up, General, she thought. *I'm going to carve Olivia's name into your heart before I crush it with my bare hands.*

They regrouped in the corridor, their weapons raised.

"Overlook?" asked Tim.

"No change," said Flaherty.

"OK. Once we go round this wall, is there anything between us and them?"

"Structural pillars," said Flaherty. "Furniture. Tables and sofas by the look of it."

"All right. I want an even spacing as we move up. Once we engage, Jill and Larissa break right, Pete and José to the left with me. Clear?"

Rushton and Rios nodded.

"Let's do this quick and clean," said Tim. "Remember that these are not the same vampires we're used to dealing with; they're stronger, and faster, and most of them have military experience. Get them in your sights and put them down. Don't let yourself get cut off, and fall back if you find yourself in a changing situation. This is no time for heroics. Are you listening to me, Larissa?"

She grunted and nodded her head. Fire was coursing through her veins, demanding violence, urging her to spill blood and tear flesh.

"All right then," said Tim. "Let's move out."

Larissa followed her squad mates round the corner at the end of the wooden corridor, bracing herself for the rattle of gunfire, her MP5 resting easily in her hands.

Nothing moved. Nothing made a sound.

The room they found themselves at the edge of was long and wide, as Flaherty had suggested; wood panelling covered the walls, polished floorboards the ground. Pillars that presumably held the basement ceiling up stood at wide intervals, with tables, sofas and chairs arranged between them. All the surfaces had a dull dusting of white powder; beer bottles and wine glasses were everywhere, beside ashtrays overflowing with the discarded ends of cigarettes and cigars. The smell of tobacco and whisky mingled in the air with something acidic, something that smelt almost like petrol. At the far end of the room, where Flaherty had told them General Rejon and his soldiers would be waiting for them, there was a long wooden bar full of glass bottles, and a semicircle of empty sofas facing a huge wall-screen TV. A small fridge stood on top of the bar, which Larissa was willing to bet was full of blood.

"What the hell?" asked Tim. "Flaherty?"

"I don't know, sir," she replied. "The satellite's showing eleven subterranean vampire heat signatures. They should be right in front of us."

"Can you see any vamps?" asked Tim. "Because I can't."

"No, sir," replied Flaherty. Her tone was ice-cold.

"Good," said Tim. "I'm glad it's not just me. Move up."

The Special Operations Squad stepped silently into the wide-open area at the end of the room. A large rug covered much of the floor, woven with an intricate pattern of loops and zigzag stripes. On the wooden surface of the bar, three glasses sat half full of clear liquid, beads of condensation rolling slowly down their sides. Smoke rose lazily from an ashtray, the crushed remnants of a cigar still glowing inside it.

"They were here," said Larissa. "Recently."

Tim pushed back his visor and glared at her. "That's helpful," he said, colour rising in his cheeks. "Do you have any other observations?"

Larissa didn't reply; she merely lifted her visor and fixed the squad leader with a long, flat stare. After a second or two, he looked away.

"All right," said Flaherty, pushing back her own visor. "Let's just try to—"

The deafening clatter of automatic gunfire filled the air, thundering against the wooden walls and crashing into the Operators' ears. The wide rug bucked and twisted as a hail of bullets pounded through it, filling the air with flying pieces of hot, deadly lead. One slammed against the side of Larissa's helmet, sending her stumbling backwards as her squad mates dived for cover. She shoved her visor down, feeling her fangs sliding down from her gums, her eyes filling with blazing heat.

"Back against the walls," yelled Tim.

Larissa flung herself up into the air, the smell of gunpowder threatening to overwhelm her, then swooped forward, ignoring Tim's order completely. She skimmed the ground, moving at dizzying speed, and dragged the rug up and away. Beneath it, now almost obliterated by gunfire, was a wide trapdoor.

"They're under the floor," she yelled, her voice booming directly into the ears of her squad mates. She spun upwards, hovering in the thick, smoky air, and threw the rug aside. Then she drew her MP5 from her belt and emptied the submachine gun into what was left of the wooden floor. The rest of the squad followed suit; the gunfire howled and bellowed for what felt like an eternity, then stopped, leaving only silence in the acrid, smoke-filled room.

"Hello, my friends," shouted a deep, distant voice. "I am General

Garcia Rejon, and you are most welcome in my home. Why don't you come down here and introduce yourselves?"

Larissa growled, the noise rumbling up through her throat. "Why the hell didn't we know there was a sub-basement down here?" she asked.

"It's not on the plans," said Flaherty. "I'm sorry."

"I can see you, my friends," shouted General Rejon. "But I cannot hear you. Don't you want to talk to me? Is that not why you are here?"

Tim twisted the dial on his belt. "I'll talk to you, General," he said, his voice echoing through the basement. "What do you want to talk about?" As he spoke, he pulled a pair of UV grenades from his belt.

"How about trespassing?" shouted General Rejon. "Or unlawful entry? Or murder?"

"You want to talk about murder?" asked Tim. "Fine. Let's talk about that."

He crouched down and pitched the two UV grenades towards the trapdoor; they rattled across the uneven, shattered surface, then dropped out of sight. There was a moment of absolute stillness, before the grenades exploded in a silent, blinding burst of purple light that blazed up through hundreds of jagged bullet holes.

A chorus of deafening agony immediately filled the air, as the basement floor erupted upwards in an explosion of flying wood and burning, screaming vampires. The purple light died away and a smile burst across Larissa's face as she threw herself into the battle.

General Rejon and his men fled in every direction, purple flames billowing from their bodies, their faces twisted in expressions of pain and surprise.

Didn't expect that, did you? thought Larissa, savagely.

Two of the burning shapes made for the exit, weaving through the basement in shambling, stumbling steps. Larissa slipped easily through the smoke and carnage as her squad mates engaged the reeling, terrified vampires, drawing her T-Bone as she flew through the thick, bitter air. She sighted down the barrel of the weapon and fired it into the back of one of the fleeing vampires. The metal stake struck him between his shoulder blades and exited through his breastplate, whistling away towards the far wall. The vampire staggered, clutching at his chest, then exploded in a burst of black and crimson.

The second escaping figure cried out as blood sprayed across his face; Larissa saw panic in the man's eyes, saw his tongue flick out involuntarily and lick his friend's blood from his lips; he turned to face her, his face a mask of utter terror. She swooped lazily down towards him, drawing her stake from her belt. The vampire raised a burning, ruined arm in a futile gesture of resistance; she knocked it aside and buried the stake in his heart. The vampire's eyes bulged momentarily, before he burst across her helmet and uniform.

Larissa felt the satisfying thud as her T-Bone's stake wound back into the barrel and turned back towards the bar. Her squad mates were engaging the rest of the vampires, keeping their distance and picking them apart with bullets and T-Bone stakes. Her smile widened; the escapee vampires might well be stronger and faster than most of the newly-turned, but with their bodies burnt and ravaged by ultraviolet fire, they were no match for the Special Operations Squad.

As she flew back to help, Flaherty staked a vampire that had been driven back against the wall by a careful volley of fire from

Tim's HK416; he exploded, leaving a huge dripping splash of blood on the wall. The scent of burning flesh and boiling blood filled Larissa's nostrils, intoxicating her, calling her forward. She was about to join the fight when water exploded from the ceiling of the room, spraying out of the building's sprinkler system. The last of the purple flames disappeared, and great clouds of steam rose from the roasted flesh of the vampires.

"Hold," said Tim, his voice appearing in her ear. "This is over."

The steam cleared, billowing away to reveal a scene of horror, as the seven remaining vampires hauled their devastated bodies across the shattered wood of the floorboards. Their bodies were burnt black and they seemed to crawl aimlessly, their eyes gone, their limbs continuing to move on instinct alone. Some were on their hands and knees, the rest dragging themselves along with their elbows. They swivelled their heads at the sound of the approaching Operators, but made no noise apart from the occasional guttural grunt.

Larissa could not bring herself to feel any sympathy for them; if anything, she felt that they had got off lightly. She floated to the ground beside Tim Albertsson, who drew his stake and plunged it quickly in and out of the chests of the two nearest vampires; they exploded with pitifully small sprays of blood. Larissa watched, feeling nothing. Rios staked two on the far side of the room, then joined the rest of the squad in the centre, where the trapdoor had been. On the floor, the last three vampires crawled in aimless circles.

"Clear," said Flaherty. "Good job, everyone."

"Finish them," said Tim, nodding down at the vampires. Rushton darted forward and staked them in quick succession. They burst, splattering the shredded floorboards with gore. Larissa let out a deep breath, then removed her helmet and checked it as her squad mates looked at each other, smiles rising on their faces; there was a long groove where the bullet had hit it.

Lucky, she thought.

Then, as Tim opened his mouth to speak, Larissa heard a soft click beneath them.

She moved in the same moment that Garcia Rejon burst up through what was left of the floor, a huge black shotgun in his hands. His eyes glowed a furious red and his mouth was twisted into a terrible grin as he pulled the trigger. There was a deafening blast and Larissa felt a bolt of white-hot fire stream past the side of her head. Pain bloomed there instantly and she twisted away, grabbing for the site of the agony with her hand. Her fingers touched the side of her head and she recoiled; her ear was missing. She brought her gloved hand in front of her face; it was slick with blood.

A guttural roar burst from Larissa's mouth as her squad mates opened up on the General with their rifles, driving him across the basement, the shotgun spilling from his hands. She ran forward, reached down, and picked up the shotgun as Rejon hurled himself upwards and disappeared through the ceiling of the basement with a loud, splintering crunch. She growled again, her vampire side in almost total control, and gave chase, ignoring Tim Albertsson's shouted demands for her to stop.

Larissa burst through the hole the General had made, like a corpse rising from the grave.

The air around her was thick and hot, and a mixture of scents filled her nostrils: blood, sweat, burnt flesh, electricity. She was floating above a wide lawn at the back of the sprawling house, walled on three sides; in front of her stood a dark grove of trees, the trunks widely spaced, the darkness between them absolute. From somewhere among them, a warm, friendly voice floated on the warm air.

"Where are your friends, bitch? Scared to face me in the open?"

Larissa laughed, despite the pain radiating from the side of her head. "They're scared," she said. "But not of you."

Rejon laughed. "What then? Some little girl in a uniform?"

"That's right. And I don't think they're the only ones."

A growl reverberated through the trees. "You watch your mouth, bitch."

"I'll watch nothing," growled Larissa. "I don't take orders from someone who sends unarmed girls up to face soldiers while he hides underground."

"Whores come and go," said Rejon. The friendly tone was back. "Sometimes they die, and I go out the next day and get new ones. They beg me for jobs. They do anything. Just like you would."

"You're scum," spat Larissa, her eyes flaring. "You're an animal, hiding from a little girl. You're pathetic."

"You think I'm hiding, bitch? I see you where you stand. Do you see me?"

She peered into the darkness. Even with her supernatural eyesight, she saw nothing but columns of wood and dense patches of dark green.

"I'm right here," said the General, his tone almost gleeful. "Come closer."

Larissa knew that she should be careful; Garcia Rejon was far more powerful than a new vampire should have been, and had been a violent, sadistic man long before he had been turned. But she simply didn't care; *her* vampire side was pleading for violence, and what remained of rational, human Larissa was desperate to make Rejon pay for what had happened in the house, to a girl whose life had been considered literally worthless. She floated forward to the treeline, waiting for the attack, ready for it, relishing the prospect.

Garcia Rejon didn't make her wait.

A fist blurred out from behind one of the thick tree trunks and crashed into Larissa's chin, sending pain bursting through her skull, driving her backwards. The smile on her face didn't falter, even as blood began to pour from her bottom lip, but a cold shiver fluttered up her spine.

Strong, she thought. *So strong. I've only been hit harder than that twice, by Alexandru and Valeri Rusmanov. Jesus.*

Larissa wasn't scared; she was confident she was more than a match for the General. The raw power the vampire possessed had taken her by surprise, and the thought that there were hundreds like him out there in the world chilled her. But there would be time to worry about that later. The General swooped out from behind the tree and smiled at her; his military tunic was covered in blood, but his arms hung easily at his sides, his boots floated above the lawn, and his eyes blazed dark and bright.

"Looks like you're missing an ear," said Rejon, his tone friendly and conversational. "That must hurt."

"It's nothing," said Larissa. "Like you."

Rejon tilted his head to one side. "Maybe," he said. "What I'm going to do to you, though? That won't be nothing."

Larissa stared at him, the smile on her face broadening, then threw the shotgun down to the grass. She raised a pale, delicate hand, extended a finger, and beckoned him forward.

Rejon grinned, then flung himself towards her, his arms wide. Larissa leapt backwards into the air, feeling the air rush around her, and rammed a booted foot into the approaching vampire's face. His nose crunched, the dry snap echoing round the garden, and his smile disappeared. He tumbled to the ground, his hands cupping his nose, and howled into the night air.

"You broke my nose, you BITCH!"

"That must hurt," said Larissa, dropping gracefully to the lawn. She doubted it really did, certainly not in comparison to the injuries the General had sustained both as a soldier and a cartel boss, but she had a sense that the physical pain wasn't the issue; the fact that a teenage girl had injured him was the problem.

That does hurt, she thought. *I'm sure of it.*

Rejon let go of his squirting nose and glared at her with burning hatred. He growled and came for her again, swinging his fists in two arcing blurs. Larissa danced backwards, but he was faster than she expected, faster than almost any vampire she had encountered. One of his fists swooped through the air and crashed against the wet hole where her ear had been, and she screamed, the electric bolt of agony driving her down to one knee. The scream was still rising from her mouth when Rejon's other fist thundered through the darkening air and connected with her throat, knocking her backwards across the lawn. The pain was overwhelming, and a terrible realisation flooded through her as she tried to drag air into her lungs.

I can't breathe.

She lay on her back, her chest convulsing, her eyes widening, fighting back the panic that was threatening to explode through her. Garcia Rejon walked towards her, an awful smile on his face, and looked down at her with an expression that seemed close to pity. She opened her mouth, but only a barely audible wheeze emerged; her head was pounding as her lungs screamed for oxygen;

her hands gripped her damaged throat, trying to massage it back into working order.

The General stepped over her, then dropped to his knees, straddling her thighs and pinning her to the lawn.

"Pathetic, am I?" he said. "An animal? I'll show you what an animal does."

He reached for her face, his hands huge and dark in the night air; she watched in slow motion, saw the calluses on his thumbs as they moved towards her eyes. Larissa opened her mouth, hauled in possibly her last breath, and felt something shift in her throat; air whistled down into her constricted lungs and she felt strength burst through her as her panic evaporated. Her hand shot out, sliding down her body, and grabbed the General between his legs. There was just enough time for Rejon's eyes to widen before she squeezed with all her might, feeling something burst beneath her grip.

The noise that erupted from Garcia Rejon's mouth was otherworldly, an ear-splitting howl rising from the deepest, darkest corner of his soul. He tried to pull away, but she held her grip tight, and winced as she heard something tear. Rejon's scream reached a terrible new pitch, then cut out, replaced by a low scratching noise as his vocal cords ripped apart. Larissa released her grip as she swung her other hand, crunching her fist into the General's broken nose, spreading it across his twisted, agonised face and knocking him into the air. He thudded to the ground as Larissa got to her feet, hatred boiling through her mind, and walked towards him.

Rejon stared at her, and Larissa saw fear in his eyes, bright and shining. He pushed himself back across the grass, his face covered in blood, his body shaking with pain. She moved towards him, not hurrying, letting him experience every second of his terror, his powerlessness; she wanted him to feel it all. Then the General stopped, and his eyes narrowed as a smile began to rise on to his face.

Larissa threw herself through the air, determined to end him before whatever had caused that smile could be brought to bear. She was barely a metre away, her eyes blazing in the darkness, when the General swung the shotgun up from the grass where she had dropped it and pulled the trigger.

The noise of the shot was deafening, even in the open air of the garden. Something punched Larissa in the stomach, something vast and made of fire, and pain pounded through her as she landed on Garcia Rejon's chest and yanked the gun from his hands. She swung it through the warm air on a low, flat arc that ended on the side of the General's head. The wooden stock of the shotgun shattered, and blood gushed out of the hole it had made; Rejon's eyes rolled backwards in his head and his limbs began to spasm. Larissa rolled on to the grass, pushed herself away from the stricken vampire with her legs, and dragged herself to her feet, her eyes blazing with righteous fire.

She racked the shotgun, her mind empty of everything but violence.

"Look at me!" she screamed. "Look at me, you monster!"

Garcia Rejon's eyes rolled, then focused unsteadily on her face. He pushed himself slowly up to his elbows, blood spraying from the side of his head, his mouth working silently. Larissa pulled the shotgun's trigger; the bullet blew out his shoulder and drove him back on to the grass where he writhed, screaming hoarsely, barely audible. She stepped forward, pumping the shotgun again. The second bullet shattered the General's left leg, almost severing it, and his eyes bulged until it seemed as though they must fall out of his head. The third bullet destroyed his right knee, and the fourth and fifth obliterated his arms. What was left of the General spasmed and croaked on the sodden grass as Larissa put her foot on his chest.

Despite the catastrophic damage done to his body, Garcia Rejon managed to fix one of his eyes on hers. As his life ebbed away, he opened his mouth, releasing a torrent of blood, and tried to spit at her, creating little more than a bubble of red on his lips. Larissa raised her foot, then brought it crashing down on his chest. Her boot smashed through the General's breastplate and mashed his heart against his ribs. He burst, what little blood there was left splashing wetly across the lawn and soaking Larissa's legs.

She let out a deep sigh, tipped back her head, and closed her eyes. Her vampire side was sated, and what was left was pain, and sadness. She let them flow through her, embracing them; her biggest fear was that the day might come when violence no longer felt wrong to her.

"Jesus Christ."

It was Tim Albertsson's familiar voice, and she turned to face him, opening her eyes as she did so. He was standing on the grass beside Flaherty; as she watched, Rushton hauled Rios up through the hole in the lawn.

"Do me a favour," said Larissa. "Next time, let's count the dead before we relax. What do you say?"

Her squad mates stared at her with wide eyes.

"Larissa..." Tim managed. "Your..."

"What?" she asked.

"Your stomach," he said.

Larissa frowned and looked down.

Above her belt was a gunshot wound the size of a dinner plate, a gaping hole from which blood was pumping in dark rivers. The sight of the injury caused the pain to appear, all at once.

"Oh," she said, distantly. "That."

She felt her eyes roll back as her legs gave way beneath her, and then all was cool, empty darkness.

22

ON THE TRAIL OF THE DEAD

FIELD INVESTIGATION TEAM D9
REPORT 6931/H:
SUBMITTED: 0745
BY: MAJOR ALAN HARDY/NS303,41-C
FAO: INTERIM DIRECTOR CALEB HOLMWOOD/
NS303, 34-D
SECURITY: ZERO HOUR CLASSIFIED

BEGINS.

As ordered, I assembled a Field Investigation Team comprising myself and Operators Andrew Johnson (NS303, 55-R) and Katherine Elliot (NS303, 62-J). Our orders were to locate John Bathurst aka Johnny Supernova and take him into protective custody.

We left the Loop at approximately 0250 and proceeded to 162B Clerkenwell Road, London, Mr Bathurst's last registered address. While in transit, we received updated intelligence informing us that Mr Bathurst was deceased (see attached coroner's report) so I requested clarification of our objective.

I received new orders to investigate whether Albert Harker had attempted to make contact with Mr Bathurst since his escape from Broadmoor Hospital, operating on the assumption that Harker would have been unaware of Mr Bathurst's death. I requested a list of known associates of Mr Bathurst, and proceeded as ordered.

We arrived at 162B Clerkenwell Road to find the front door broken. It had been removed from its hinges by a blow of significant force, which initial analysis suggested had been delivered by a human foot wearing a leather shoe.

In the hallway of the residence we found two letters addressed to Mr Bathurst's executor from the law offices of Chesney, Clarke, Abel & Watt, and a discarded envelope similarly addressed. The contents of that envelope were missing, presumably removed. We opened the two remaining envelopes and found them to be identical requests for clarification of a particular bequest, signed by a Mr Thomas Clarke. We requested his home address from the Surveillance Division and proceeded.

We arrived at 67 Frognal Lane at approximately 0410, and found several rooms within the residence illuminated and the front door unlocked. Upon receiving no response to repeated door knocks, we accessed the residence and found the body of Thomas Clarke in the living room. He had been decapitated, and a large amount of his blood was missing, presumed ingested. I ordered Operator Johnson to document the scene while Operator Elliott and I searched the residence.

The remainder of the rooms on the ground and first floors were empty, with no signs of intrusion. Operator Johnson rejoined us, and we searched for evidence of any subterranean level. We found a door at the rear of the main hallway and proceeded into a cellar, where we found Bonnie Clarke, James Clarke and Alec Clarke. All three were suffering from shock, but were physically unharmed. We instructed them to remain in situ, alerted local police, finished documenting and surveying the scene.

As we exited the residence, we received a list of John Bathurst's known associates. It contained a single name, a journalist named Kevin McKenna. We proceeded to Mr McKenna's last known residence at 62A Kilburn Lane, arriving at approximately 0700 and made contact with Mr McKenna.

We informed him that a recently released prisoner with a grudge against John Bathurst may attempt to contact him, as per the active cover story, and instructed him to contact the police immediately if such a situation arose.

Awaiting further instructions.

23

TRUTH OR CONSEQUENCES

Jamie made his way into the Intelligence Division and found Kate Randall waiting for him in front of the door that led into ISAT. She smiled as he approached, and he resisted the overwhelming urge to hug her.

"Are you ready for this?" she asked.

"The timing could be better," Jamie replied. "But at least it'll be done with."

"It's just routine, Jamie," said Kate. "Answer the questions honestly and we'll get you out of here as quick as we can."

"No problem," he replied. "Lead the way."

Kate nodded and tapped a series of numbers into the panel that controlled the security door. It unlocked with a series of heavy clunks, and he followed her inside. An Operator was seated behind a small reception desk; he looked up at Jamie and nodded in recognition. Jamie nodded back, then stepped through a second door and into the interview room. Kate closed the door and motioned him towards the chair at the far end of the room; he settled uneasily into it as his friend spoke quietly into her radio.

Moments later the door opened again and two Intelligence Division Operators entered. They said nothing as they began to attach a number of sensors to his chest and neck; they seemed unwilling to even look at him.

"What's all this?" Jamie asked.

"Standard lie-detector stuff," replied Kate. "Nothing to worry about. I'll be back in a couple of minutes and we can get started."

"Take your time," said Jamie. "I'll just wait here." He grinned, and she smiled over her shoulder at him as she left the room.

Kate pushed open the door to the ISAT lounge and stepped inside. Paul Turner looked up from his copy of Jamie Carpenter's file, which was remarkably thick for someone who had been an Operator for less than a year.

"Three minutes," said Kate. "At least this one should be quick."

"We'll see," said Turner, and returned his attention to the file.

The technicians pressed the final sensor into place and exited the room, leaving Jamie alone. He tried to find a comfortable position in the chair, pushing himself against the shiny plastic, but quickly abandoned the effort; the furniture in the room had clearly not been selected with relaxation in mind. His heart was thumping in his chest and he focused on trying to calm it, taking long, deep breaths. His eyes remained fixed on the door, his mind on what Kate might be about to ask him.

Paul Turner closed Jamie's file, then led Kate out into ISAT's small atrium, unlocked the interview room door and held it open. She took a deep breath and walked through it. Jamie smiled at her, although the expression didn't appear wholly genuine; she smiled back in what she hoped was a reassuring fashion and took a seat at the desk. Paul Turner closed and locked the door, before settling into the empty chair beside her.

Ten minutes, she thought. *Yes, it's weird, yes, it's awkward. Just be professional and get it done as quickly as possible.*

"Lieutenant Carpenter," said Paul Turner. "Do you understand the importance of the process that Lieutenant Randall and I are carrying out?"

"Yes, sir," replied Jamie, and gave Kate a brief glance full of pride. "I do."

"Excellent. Be honest and this will be over soon."

Jamie nodded. Kate waited a moment, cleared her throat, and began.

"This is ISAT interview 068, conducted by Lieutenant Kate Randall, NS303, 78-J in the presence of Major Paul Turner, NS303, 36-A. State your name, please."

"Jamie Carpenter."

Green.

"Please answer the following question incorrectly," said Kate. "State your gender, please."

Jamie smiled. "Female."

Red.

"OK," said Kate. "Let's get started. Mr Carpenter, are you currently a Lieutenant in Department 19?"

"Yes."

Green.

"Do you understand that every aspect of your role within Department 19 is classified at Top Secret or higher?"

"Yes."

Green.

"Do you understand the necessity for the general public to remain unaware of our existence?"

"Yes."

Green.

"Have you ever done anything to jeopardise that state of affairs?"

Jamie fell silent for a long moment. "Yes," he said, eventually.

Green.

"Please explain what you were referring to in your previous answer."

"I allowed a Department helicopter to make an emergency landing on a residential street in Paris."

Green.

"Why did you make that decision, Lieutenant?"

"Colonel Frankenstein was injured and in a condition likely to draw attention. I didn't believe we had time to reach our scheduled extraction point."

Green.

"Did you consider the possible implications of your decision?"

"Yes."

Green.

"And what did you conclude?"

"That Colonel Frankenstein's life was worth the risk."

Green.

Kate smiled inwardly. This was the first incident in Jamie's file that Intelligence had flagged, even though he had included it in his report at the time. She was relieved to see him deal with it head-on.

"Lieutenant Carpenter," she continued. "Have you ever engaged in activities with the intention of damaging or hindering this Department?"

"No."

Green.

"Have you ever passed information regarding this Department to anyone who was not a member?"

"Yes."

Green.

"To whom did your previous answer refer?"

"Matt Browning."

Green.

"Please explain what you are referring to."

Jamie cleared his throat. "When Matt came out of his coma, I told him where he was and some of what we do here. He told me he wanted to help, and I told him that he should try to get back here if he was serious."

Green.

Kate felt the tension in her shoulders relax, just a little. The incident involving Matt was the second, and most serious, flag in her friend's file, and she was glad to hear him volunteer the information.

"Why did you pass on classified information to a member of the public?" she asked.

"I don't know," replied Jamie. Colour had risen in his cheeks, which Kate guessed was embarrassment at the memory of what he had done. Either that or anger; if that was the case, she hoped it wasn't directed at her. "There was just something about Matt that I trusted. I believed he was faking his amnesia, which would mean he was already aware of the existence of vampires, and had seen Operators with his own eyes. Mostly, I believed his desire to help was genuine."

Green.

"Were you aware that you were breaking a number of Department regulations by giving Matt Browning classified information?"

"Yes."

Green.

"Lieutenant Carpenter, have you ever conspired in any way to harm this Department?"

"No."

Green.

"Have you ever discussed this Department with any supernatural being beyond the execution of orders given to you by your superiors?"

"No."

Green.

"Would you ever betray the trust of this Department?"

"No."

Green.

"Are there any incidents in which you believe you could have compromised the security of this Department, whether intentionally or otherwise?"

"Yes."

Green.

"Please explain your previous answer."

"Matt could have told people what I told him," said Jamie. "He couldn't have damaged the Department with the information I gave him, but I suppose he could have asked some awkward questions."

Green.

"Any other incidents?"

"No."

Green.

Kate let out a deep breath. "Thank you, Lieutenant Carpenter," she said. "We're—"

"Lieutenant Carpenter," interrupted Paul Turner. She looked over at him, a frown emerging on her brow.

"Yes, sir?" replied Jamie. His eyes narrowed slightly as he shifted his gaze to the Security Officer.

"Do you consider yourself a descendant of the founders?" asked Turner.

Jamie frowned. "I don't see what that—"

"Answer the question, please, Lieutenant."

"Yes," said Jamie, after a long pause. "I consider myself a descendant of the founders."

Green.

"Do you believe that makes you better than the rest of this Department?"

"Of course not," said Jamie, his face like thunder.

Green.

"Are you proud to be a descendant?"

"Yes. I am."

Green.

"Why?"

"Kate," said Jamie, looking over at her. "Is this really—"

"Lieutenant Carpenter," said Paul Turner, his voice low. "I'd ask you to direct your attention to me when I'm talking to you. And I'd like you to answer my question, please."

Jamie stared at the Security Officer, his expression unreadable. "Fine," he said, eventually. "What was the question?"

"Why are you proud to be a descendant of the founders, Lieutenant Carpenter?"

"Because I'm proud of the men my ancestors were," said Jamie. "I'm proud of the things they did. They make me feel like I'm part of something special."

Green.

"It makes you feel special?" asked Turner.

"That's not what I said."

Green.

"I heard what you said, Lieutenant. Does it make you feel special?"

"No."

Green.

"Do you blame yourself for the condition that Colonel Frankenstein now suffers from?"

"Yes."

Green.

"Explain."

"Because if I had trusted him before I went to Lindisfarne, he wouldn't have been attacked by the werewolf."

Green.

"You can't know that for certain," said the Security Officer. "Don't you consider it egotistical to believe that everything happens because of you?"

"I don't think that everything happens because of me."

Green.

"Do you wish your mother wasn't a vampire?"

A long, heavy silence filled the room, as Jamie stared at Paul Turner with open, blazing fury.

"Of course I do," he said, the words emerging from his mouth like pulled teeth.

Green.

"Do you wish that Colonel Frankenstein wasn't a lycanthrope?"

"Yes."

Green.

"Do you love your mother?"

"Paul," said Kate, sharply. "Stop this." Her face was pale, her eyes wide, but Turner didn't so much as glance in her direction.

"Do you love your mother, Lieutenant Carpenter?"

"Yes," said Jamie, his voice laced with venom. "I do. Very much."

Green.

"You would do anything to return her to normal, correct?"

"No."

Green.

"You wouldn't?"

"No," repeated Jamie.

Green.

"Why not? You just told me you love her. Very much, in fact."

"I know what you're trying to do," snarled Jamie. "You think you're so clever, don't you? But you're wrong. I love my mother more than anyone else alive, and I wish every day that what happened to Colonel Frankenstein hadn't. But I still wouldn't betray the Department for them, no matter what anyone offered me."

Green.

"Why not, Lieutenant Carpenter?"

"Because neither of them would want me to."

Green.

"Is that the only reason?"

"No."

Green.

"Why else?"

"Because I'm not a traitor, Major Turner. It's as simple as that."

Green.

For several seconds, it seemed as though everyone in the interview room was holding their breath; the air felt poisonous, thick and heavy with tension. When it felt as though the pressure had reached the point where it must surely explode, Paul Turner spoke.

"Thank you, Lieutenant Carpenter," he said, calmly. "That will be all."

Jamie stared at the Security Officer, then slowly turned his head to look at Kate. She could feel her face burning with embarrassment and anger, and found that she couldn't meet his pale blue gaze; she dropped her eyes to the table, ashamed.

"All right then," said Jamie, slowly. "Thank you."

Paul Turner got up and unlocked the interview room door. The Intelligence Division Operators reappeared; they began to disconnect Jamie from the monitoring equipment as Turner held the door open, waiting for Kate. She climbed slowly to her feet and exited the room, taking great care not to make eye contact with Jamie as she did so. The Security Officer stepped past her, held open the door to the ISAT lounge, then followed her inside.

"He's clean," said Turner, as soon as the door was closed behind them. "Who's next?" His tone – businesslike, almost casual – was utterly maddening.

"What was that?" Kate asked.

Turner frowned. "What was what?"

"You know what," she said, her voice rising. "*That*. All that stuff about his mother and Frankenstein. Why the hell did you bring all that up?"

Turner looked at her, and seemed to suddenly notice just how angry she was. His eyes widened and his expression softened.

"It wasn't anything personal, Kate," he said. "I know Lieutenant Carpenter and I haven't always seen eye to eye, but I have no secret desire to torment him, I promise you. I know he doesn't believe that, but it's the truth."

The Security Officer poured himself a cup of coffee from the pot on the desk, then poured a second and handed it to Kate. She took it without a word and waited for him to continue.

"ISAT isn't only about finding out what people might have done in the past," he said, lowering himself on to the sofa and sipping his coffee. "It's also about the future. Part of the purpose of this project is to assess whether any Operator presents a potential security risk, and the questions I asked Jamie were with that purpose in mind. I don't believe for a second that he is, was, or is ever likely to be a traitor. I never doubted he would pass his interview, and I'm glad he did. But his circumstances present possible opportunities for leverage and I had to investigate them. Tom Morris betrayed us because Alexandru was able to offer him something that was more important to him than Blacklight. It didn't matter that he couldn't actually deliver it. There are things that our enemies could offer Jamie that he might want, possibly desperately, and I needed to make it clear that we know what they are."

"I get it, sir," said Kate. "But that doesn't mean I like it."

"I don't either," said Turner. "I warned you they would hate us for this, Kate. Did you think I was joking?"

"No," she sighed. "I knew you weren't."

Turner looked closely at her. "We've got three more interviews before lunch," he said. "Then eight more this afternoon. Once they're done, I want you to take the evening off. And I mean *off*, you understand? Go to the mess, go for a run, go and get some sleep. Go and do anything you want, as long as it has nothing to do with all this. Now go and get your head straight; we start the next one in twenty minutes."

Kate nodded and headed straight for the door. She was intending to head up to Level 0 and grab a few lungfuls of fresh air, perhaps even stretch her legs for a minute or two, so she let out an audible groan when the receptionist called her name as she laid her hand on the handle of the security door.

"Yes?" she said, turning back.

"Someone's asking to see you," said the Operator behind the desk, an apologetic look on his face. "I told her you were busy, but she wanted to wait. I'm sorry, Kate."

"It's OK," she said, and forced a smile. "I'll see her. I need a break anyway."

On the level below, a dark figure crouched in the centre of room 261.

On the floor sat a plastic tub filled with a precise mixture of diesel and farm fertiliser, a combination familiar to terrorist groups throughout the world. Hanging from a metal tripod were the explosive charges of half a dozen hand grenades, carefully spaced and resting in the clear liquid. Wires ran from them to a simple trigger: a piece of copper on a hinge that would close an electrical circuit and allow current to pass into, and fire, the charges. The trigger was attached to a radio receiver; when it detected a particular aural input, it would wait three seconds, before closing the circuit.

The dark figure armed the device and turned on the receiver. Then it slipped silently out of the room and disappeared along the corridor.

Ninety minutes later the lift doors at one end of Level B slid open.

The corridor in front of her was long and curved, and it took several minutes to reach the door. She unlocked the door, then paused for a second, considering, not for the first time, what a strange series of turns her life had taken in the last few months.

She pushed the door inwards. Blinding white light filled her eyes, a tidal wave of heat and noise threw her backwards across the corridor, and everything went dark.

24

THE WAR ON DRUGS, PART THREE

NUEVO LAREDO, MEXICO
YESTERDAY

"Larissa."

The voice was distant, floating towards her from somewhere in the emptiness. She tasted copper as she drifted back into herself, felt solid ground beneath her, and forced her eyes to open. A dark shape filled her vision, before gradually coming into focus. It was Tim Albertsson; he was looking down at her with worry on his face.

"Tim?" she managed.

"You're OK," he said, relief rippling across his features. "You're fine, don't worry. It's OK."

Behind him, Larissa saw the rest of the Special Operations Squad. They were gathered round their squad leader, staring down at her. She pushed herself up on to her elbows and looked slowly around. She was lying on the warm grass of the walled garden, the night sky hanging low above her; she smelt the thick, coppery scent of blood, and then everything came back to her.

The cutters. Rejon. The shotgun.

Her eyes widened, and panic rose through her as she looked down at herself. Her uniform was shredded, blown open by the shotgun's heavy shell. But beneath the torn fabric was only the skin of her stomach, flat and white. She touched it hesitantly with one pale hand, feeling its firm surface beneath her fingers.

"What happened?" she asked. She felt as though she might cry with relief.

"You passed out," said Tim, smiling at her. "There was a hole right through you, Larissa. I've never... none of us has ever seen anything like it. We could *see through you.*"

"Lovely," said Larissa, softly.

"Thankfully, Rejon had a fridge full of blood in his bar," said Tim, holding up two empty plastic bottles. "I tipped them into your mouth. You were unconscious, but you managed to swallow it. Automatic, I guess. And then..."

"The hole just closed up," said Flaherty, her eyes wide with wonder. "Everything grew back, all the bones and the organs and the muscle, then new skin, and it was suddenly like nothing had ever happened."

"Yeah," said Larissa. "It does that."

"That shot should have killed you," said Tim.

"But it didn't," said Larissa, pushing herself up on to slightly unsteady legs and smiling at her squad mates. "Believe it or not, I've had worse." She was remembering the sensation of being burned alive by the ultraviolet bombs that had risen out of the grounds of the Loop when Valeri Rusmanov's attack had seemed on the verge of success.

"Christ," said Rushton. He was looking at her with an expression that she thought was weirdly close to adoration. "I would *not* want to see what that looks like."

Larissa's smile widened. "It wasn't pretty."

Tim grinned, as the rest of the squad seemed to visibly relax before her eyes; their concern for her now allayed, they could belatedly enjoy the success of their mission.

"Let's get out of here," said Tim. "Flaherty, take Rushton and Rios back downstairs and clean up. I want no trace that we were ever here. Then go up the way we came and relieve Frost. Rendezvous in the lobby in four minutes."

"Yes, sir," said Flaherty, and led Rushton and Rios back down through General Rejon's improvised escape hole. The second they were gone, Tim stepped forward, took Larissa's face in his gloved hands, and kissed her.

For a long moment, she was too shocked to respond; his lips mashed furiously against her own, and she felt heat begin to creep into the corners of her eyes once more. Then clarity rushed through her and she pushed him away, harder than was necessary. He stumbled backwards, but quickly righted himself and looked at her, his cheeks flushed a deep pink.

"Don't do that," she warned, her voice low.

"I'm sorry," he replied, staring hungrily at her. His breath was short and his eyes gleamed. "Actually, I'm not. Not in the slightest."

"Well, you should be," said Larissa. "Don't do it again, Tim."

"All right," he said, but didn't drop his gaze. The intensity of his stare caused a flickering warmth to bloom in her stomach, which she instantly extinguished.

Jesus Christ. What the hell are you thinking?

"Is this going to be a problem?" she asked, as calmly as she was able.

"Not for me," replied Tim. "I can't speak for you."

You arrogant prick.

"Good," she said, fighting to keep her temper. "In which case, it's probably time to head home."

"Let's do that," replied Tim, smiling broadly at her.

25

FROM BEYOND THE GRAVE

WAPPING, LONDON

Kevin McKenna was in a foul mood as he made his way down to the garage beneath *The Globe*'s offices.

His day had started with the police at his door, warning him that an escaped prisoner might try to contact him, and ended with his editor calling him into his office just after five o'clock, a classic end-of-the-day ambush that he had seen coming a mile away, and telling him that while his general reportage was as bitchy and lowbrow as ever, two adjectives that Colin Burton meant as compliments, both the investigative pieces he had turned in the day before were unacceptable. McKenna had asked why, although he already knew the answer.

"Because you're not hot shit any more, Kev," said Colin. "I know you were once, and I know you wish you still were, but you're not. You don't work for *The Gutter*, you work for me. And my readers don't give a damn about any of this bollocks." He picked up one of the pieces, entitled DIY ART INVADES MOSCOW, and waved it in McKenna's face. "Celebrities, tits, gossip, crime, football. They're our bread and butter. Got it?"

"Got it," said McKenna. "Sorry, boss."

"It's all right," said his editor, and sighed. "The writing's bloody good, Kev, I'm not saying it's not. But our readers don't give a toss about good writing, and they're going to be bored shitless by the end of the first paragraph. Spice it up a bit, all right? Arty blonde birds with their kit off, a bit of Russian gang violence, something like that. You know?"

"I know," said McKenna, his stomach churning with self-disgust. "I'll get on it. Cheers, Col."

In truth, he had known the pieces weren't really *Globe* material as he was writing them; they were too like his old work, the kind of stuff he had long since given up trying to get past *The Globe*'s editorial board. In his first year on the job the editor at the time, a kindly old alcoholic called Bob Hetherington, had taken him aside and told him not to bother.

"I don't need anyone trying to reinvent the wheel," Hetherington had said. "Just keep ours turning. That's your job."

In the subsequent years, he had thrown in the occasional feature on fashion or music, but had never really fought for them, or protested when they got spiked. He knew he was really writing them for himself, in the hope that whatever remained of his talent might not fade away completely.

It was quiet in the garage when McKenna exited the lift; the heels of his shoes clicked loudly on the concrete ground, as the cars and pillars and posts that separated the bays cast long shadows beneath the bright yellow lights. He was halfway to the black BMW he had treated himself to after he had been promoted to associate editor two years earlier, when an odd sensation filled him: an unmistakable certainty that he was not alone in the garage.

He stopped walking and stood absolutely still, listening intently.

Nothing.

There were no more than a dozen cars in the garage, which had been built to accommodate ten times that number; the wide space was almost empty. But there were plenty of places where a mugger or a crackhead could hide themselves from view if they wanted to, in the shadows behind the pillars, or crouched beside the cars.

"Hello?" he shouted. "Who's there?"

Silence.

McKenna felt a chill creep slowly up his spine. He was suddenly scared; the feeling that he was not alone twisted in the centre of his gut, cold and determined.

An awful sensation of vulnerability overcame him and he ran for his car, his footsteps echoing loudly through the concrete space. Part of his brain, the rational part, shouted at him as he ran, branding him a coward, but he ignored it; he was focused only on getting into his car and locking the doors, shutting out whoever was in the garage with him, crouched low behind one of the cars or standing statue-still behind one of the concrete pillars, listening and watching and waiting.

McKenna pulled his keys from his pocket as he ran and pressed the button on the plastic fob. The BMW's locks disengaged with a beep that sounded loud and inviting, an announcement of his location and his intention. He grabbed for the car's door, felt the reassuring smoothness of its plastic handle, and was about to pull it open and throw himself inside when cold fingers closed on the back of his neck and lifted him into the air.

He screamed long and loud, his legs kicking beneath him, and felt his bladder let go in a warm rush of shame and terror. Then he was airborne, his body seeming to float momentarily as whatever had grabbed him threw him across the garage. He watched the floor rising up to meet him, his mind paralysed by crashing waves of terror. He saw white ovals of discarded chewing gum, a small patch of oil, and a discarded paper coffee cup. Then he hit the concrete, his shoulder exploding with agony, and skidded across the ground, the heels of his shoes squeaking.

McKenna slid to a halt in a crumpled heap beside the emergency door that led to the stairs, his shoulder on fire, the air driven from his lungs. His first thought, the only cogent thought in his reeling, panicking mind, was to drag himself through it and up the stairs towards the office. But he made the mistake of looking behind him; what he saw froze him where he lay.

Gliding towards him, his feet a clear ten centimetres above the ground, was a man in an elegant navy-blue suit. His face was pale, his hair thinning, but his eyes glowed the colour of burning coals and his mouth was open in a wide smile of pleasure.

Not real, he screamed, silently. *Can't be real. Not real.*

The man cocked his head slightly to one side, then shot forward at a speed that McKenna could not comprehend; one second there was five metres between them, the next his hands were gripping the lapels of his suit jacket and lifting him easily into the air. He tried to turn his head away from the terrible red gaze that was now only millimetres in front of him, then cried out as he was driven into the concrete wall of the garage. The back of his head cracked against it and his vision greyed. When it cleared, the man was peering at him with an expression that seemed almost curious, the way a spider might regard a fly that has become stuck in its web. The dreadful red eyes roiled and burned, and McKenna felt consciousness start to slip away as his mind shut down, unable to process the horror that confronted it.

One of the man's hands appeared from nowhere and slapped him hard across the face; the impact sounded like a rifle shot in the empty garage, reverberating around the thick concrete walls. McKenna's eyes flew open and his mouth formed a perfect O of shock.

"Are you Kevin McKenna?" asked the man.

He stared, tears gathering in the corners of his eyes, incapable of speech. The man slapped him again, harder, and McKenna tasted his own blood as it spilled from the corner of his mouth, galvanising his paralysed brain.

"Yes," he gasped. "I'm Kevin McKenna."

"A pleasure to meet you," said the man. "Did you receive an envelope from a lawyer acting on behalf of the late John Bathurst?"

Dear God. Oh my dear God.

"Johnny?" asked McKenna, smiling drunkenly. "Johnny's... dead."

The man with the red eyes growled, a guttural noise that rose from somewhere deep inside him, and bared his teeth. Two long, razor-sharp fangs emerged from the man's gums, sliding down over his canines.

"I'll ask you once more, Mr McKenna," said the man. "Then I'm going to tear your face from your skull. Did you receive a letter?"

Kevin McKenna fought to clear his reeling mind as terror more profound than anything he had felt in his entire life gripped him. *True*, whispered a distant voice. *What Johnny sent you. All true.*

"Yes," he said, his voice cracking. "I got... a letter. From Johnny."

The man broke into a huge, cheerful grin. "Splendid," he said, his voice suddenly as light and jovial as a daytime newsreader's. The grip on McKenna's chest was released; he slid to the ground in a heap and began to cry, as the man stepped back and looked down at him.

"No more lies, Mr McKenna," he said. "There should be no lies between friends, which I am sure you and I are to become. May I help you to your feet?"

McKenna tried to compose himself, to halt the crying that felt on the verge of becoming hysterical; he failed, but managed to force himself to nod. The man strode forward, still smiling broadly, and extended a thin, pale hand. After a long moment, McKenna reached out and took it, his mind screaming warning after warning. But the man merely pulled him gently to his feet; he stood on unsteady legs, his chest heaving up and down from the sobs that had wracked his body, and stared into eyes that glowed far less fiercely than they had only minutes earlier.

"Good," said the man. "No harm done, eh? My name is Albert Harker and we have already established that you are Kevin McKenna. We are well met, are we not?"

McKenna nodded again. The tears were slowing and the pain in his shoulder had faded to a dull ache. His shell-shocked mind was still piecing itself back together, but managed to come up with a best course of action.

Do whatever it says. Don't make it angry. Do whatever it tells you.

"I have clearly startled you somewhat," said Albert Harker. "For that, I can only apologise. Perhaps a stiff drink is in order?"

"OK," said McKenna, his voice trembling.

"Excellent," beamed Harker. "Your place it is."

26

TOO CLOSE TO HOME

Matt Browning was sitting at his desk in the Lazarus Project when a muffled thud ripped through the Loop, shaking the floors and ceilings. There was an uncomprehending moment of silence before the general alarm screamed into life, its ear-splitting whine echoing through concrete and steel.

Matt clamped his hands over his ears and leapt to his feet. The rest of the Lazarus Project staff did likewise, their faces contorted with pain; they stared desperately around, looking for someone to tell them what to do. Matt empathised; his colleagues were scientists and doctors, with no real understanding of how dangerous the situation beyond the laboratory really was. He had no such illusions; he had almost been killed by a vampire girl he now called his friend, the first director of the Lazarus Project had been about to murder him until Jamie intervened, and he knew from the stories his friends told just how bad it was outside the Loop. As his colleagues began to shout over the din of the alarm, speculating that a generator had blown or a fuel store had been breached, Matt kept what he was sure would turn out to be the truth to himself.

That was an explosion. A big one.

He looked around the room at the frightened men and women, wondering how best to help, and froze.

Natalia Lenski wasn't there.

Fear trickled through him, chilling his spine like a bucket of ice water. There was no reason to panic; there were any number of reasons why Natalia might not be in the lab at that precise moment. But something, some primal instinct buried deep in his gut, began to insist that something was wrong.

Matt ran across the lab, ignoring the nervous stares of his colleagues, and twisted the handle on the main door.

Nothing happened. The keypad beside it glowed a steady, mocking red.

He shouted with fury and grabbed the handle again, twisting it, hauling on it, beating the surface of the door with his other fist. Hands grabbed at his shoulders, spinning him round, and he found himself facing the worried gaze of Professor Karlsson.

"Calm down!" yelled the Lazarus Project Director, straining to make himself heard over the din of the alarm. "They're sealed automatically! It's all right, Matt!"

Matt pushed the Professor's hands away. "Where's Natalia?" he yelled.

Professor Karlsson turned then and scanned the room. When he returned his attention to Matt, his forehead was furrowed by a deep frown.

"I don't know!" he shouted. "Where is she?"

"I don't know!" yelled Matt, pulling his radio from his belt. His mind was pounding with concern for Natalia, who would be absolutely unprepared if there was an attack taking place above their heads. A single coherent thought made its way to the surface.

Call Jamie. He'll know what to do.

Matt raised the radio and looked at the screen.

It was blank.

He twisted the power switch backwards and forwards, but nothing brought the handset to life. Matt bellowed again and hurled it against the wall. Karlsson recoiled, shielding his face as shattered plastic and severed metal wire flew through the air, then grabbed hold of Matt.

"You have to calm down!" he shouted. "We're safe in here, Matt!"

"That's great!" yelled Matt. "What about Natalia? What about my friends? They're out there somewhere and we have no idea what the hell is going on!"

Four floors above the Lazarus Project, Jamie Carpenter was in his quarters when the explosion thundered through Level B, shaking the walls of his small room so violently that his desk toppled over, spilling its mountains of files and folders across the floor.

He was lying on his bed, still seething at the humiliating ordeal that had been his ISAT interview. His hatred for Paul Turner, a complex emotion that never lay far below the surface, blazed more potently than ever before. And although he knew the second part of the interview, the unfair, vicious line of questioning that seemed to have been designed specifically to antagonise him, had been the work of the Security Officer, he was struggling to spare Kate the anger and disappointment that was boiling through him.

He knew it wasn't her fault, but she was part of it; she was the other half of ISAT, and even if she had not been complicit in the ordeal he had been subjected to, her attempt to stop it had been half-hearted at best. When she had told him she was going to volunteer for ISAT, he had told her to think long and hard about it, as it was a decision that was bound to make her unpopular. Now, having been through the invasive, demeaning process himself, he was beginning to think he had been too kind.

They're going to do more than dislike her, he thought, with a bitter mixture of concern and spite. *It's going to be much worse than that.*

Everyone's going to hate her.

This thought was filling his mind when the deafening roar tore through Level B. Jamie leapt up from his bed as the room shook and rattled, his hand going instinctively to the grip of his Glock 17. A second later he yelled in pain as the alarm screeched into life, but the paralysis that had gripped Matt and his colleagues did not lay a hand on him; he was up and across his quarters and twisting the handle of his door before the first peal had even died away.

Nothing happened.

Jamie turned back into the room and slid to his knees, digging through the spilled contents of his desk, looking for the Director override code that Henry Seward had given to him and Paul Turner, the night that Shaun Turner had died and Seward himself had been taken by Valeri Rusmanov. He found the laminated card, ran back to the door, flipped down the panel that concealed his quarters' emergency controls and keyed the code into the touchpad. For a long moment the bar at the bottom of the panel glowed yellow, and Jamie allowed himself to believe that it was going to work. Then the panel turned solid red and he hammered on the immovable door in frustration.

He knew without looking that his console and radio would be dead; the protocol for any kind of internal attack on the Loop called for a complete lockdown, which only Paul Turner, as the Security Officer, and certain members of the Security Division would be exempt from. He checked them anyway and saw the blank, lifeless screens he had expected.

Jamie walked back across his room, his heart racing. Surely there was no way that the base could be under attack again? The frontal assault by Valeri and his vampire army had been successful because they had been supplied with information by Christopher Reynolds, the original head of the Lazarus Project who had been working for the eldest Rusmanov his entire life; his information had enabled them to evade the surveillance and warning systems that protected the base. They had all been reset and improved, and access to their specifics was now one of the most heavily guarded secrets that Blacklight possessed; if they had been compromised again, the implications would be unthinkable.

The pounding alarm stopped abruptly and was replaced by a familiar voice, amplified and broadcast via the speakers that sat above the door of every room in the Loop.

"Attention," said Paul Turner. "There has been a security incident which has resulted in this facility being placed into lockdown. Please do not attempt to leave your location. The Security Division are investigating and the lockdown will be lifted as soon as possible. Thank you."

Jamie waited for the alarm to begin again; if it did so, he intended to put his helmet on and set its exterior volume control to zero. But thirty seconds later the silence in the Loop remained total, so he poured himself a glass of water and sat down on the edge of his bed. His heart was racing, but he tried to ignore it, as he did his best to ignore what the voice at the back of his head was whispering.

It was telling him that the explosion had sounded like it had been on his level, from the far end of the curved corridor.

Where Kate lived.

*

Paul Turner was alone in the ISAT lounge when the explosion shook the floor beneath his feet; he had sent Kate for lunch ten minutes earlier, and was reading through the file of the first of the afternoon's interviewees. He was on his feet instantly, throwing the file aside, sprinting across the room and grabbing the door handle, which refused to turn.

He swore, pulled his ID card from its slot on his belt, and pressed it against the panel beside the door. His role as Security Officer allowed him to override almost every lock in the Loop; the plastic square turned bright green as the general alarm burst into deafening life, and he hauled the door open. The Operator behind the ISAT reception desk looked at him with wide eyes as he strode across the semicircular space.

"Stay here," he barked. He ran his card against the panel that controlled the security door, waited impatiently for the heavy locks to disengage, then stepped out into the chaos of the Intelligence Division.

Operators were on their feet beside their desks, shouting and gesturing, trying to make themselves heard over the siren. Their computer monitors had all gone dark, Turner was relieved to see; in the event of a security breach inside the Loop, access to the Blacklight system was instantly cut to everyone apart from the Security Division to protect the terabytes of sensitive information it contained. He pulled his console from his belt and saw its screen light up.

Good. That's good.

He tapped the screen as he walked, asking the system to pinpoint the location of the explosion and provide a preliminary report, and trying to ignore the shouted questions from the Operators of the Intelligence Division.

"Stay at your desks!" he yelled, as he reached the door. "And stay calm, for God's sake!"

His console beeped as he stepped out into the Level A corridor. He tapped the screen, opening the information he had requested.

PRELIMINARY INCIDENT REPORT

INITIAL CONCLUSION: DETONATION OF CHEMICAL MATERIALS (SPECTROANALYSIS IN PROGRESS).

CHARACTERISTICS: EXPLOSIVE TEMPERATURE RISE. HIGHEST RECORDED TEMPERATURE 812 DEGREES CELSIUS. CONCUSSIVE BLAST WAVE. DURATION 1.09 SECONDS. RANGE 112.2 METRES.

DAMAGE REPORT: SUPERFICIAL DAMAGE TO LEVEL B CORRIDOR. LEVEL B POWER SYSTEMS INTERRUPTED (BACKUPS ACTIVATED). LEVEL B ATMOSPHERIC CONTROL INTERRUPTED (BACKUPS FAILED). LEVEL B MONITORING SYSTEM INTERRUPTED (BACKUPS FAILED). LEVEL B FREQUENCY SPECTRUM INTERRUPTED. BACKUPS WORKING AT 46% CAPACITY.

CONTAINMENT: FIRE EXTINGUISHED BY HALON SYSTEM.

LOCATION: LEVEL B, ROOM 261.

Turner read the report, his stomach churning with cold, furious outrage.

A bomb. A bomb inside the Loop. How dare they?

He typed a new request into the console, asking who lived in Level B, room 261. The system returned the information immediately.

OCCUPANT: RANDALL, KATE (LIEUTENANT)/ NS303,78-J.

27

DORMANT FOR TOO LONG

McKenna walked down the short corridor that connected his kitchen to the living room of his small flat with a four-pack of lager in his hand, flopped down into the armchair beneath the window, and opened a new can.

"So that lot that visited me this morning," he said, taking a long swig. "They weren't the police, were they? They were the ones you told Johnny about. The secret department."

Albert Harker nodded at him from the sofa on the opposite side of the room. "Department 19. Or Blacklight, as they are often called."

"So how come they came to see me?"

"I presume they visited the last known address of Mr Bathurst, found the same correspondence that I found, and made the same enquiries that I made. And since you are the sole named beneficiary of Mr Bathurst's estate, they likely assumed that I would attempt to make contact with you."

"They told me a released prisoner might try to contact me. They said I should phone the police."

Harker smiled. "Of course they did. That's what they do, Mr McKenna. They lie."

"Why?"

"To keep you and everyone else in the dark, under the guise of keeping you safe."

McKenna drank deeply from his can and levelled his gaze at the vampire. "And what is it that you want, Mr Harker?" he asked. "You've got the tape and the transcript, and I give you my word that I won't tell anyone about you. I don't have anything else."

Albert Harker smiled broadly. "Mr McKenna, that is exactly the opposite of what I want from you. I *want* the world to know about me, and others like me. I want to expose Blacklight and all its lies, and I want you to write the story that pulls back the curtain. How does that sound?"

"It sounds nuts," said McKenna. "It sounds like the craziest thing I've ever heard."

Harker's face darkened and a red flicker appeared in the corners of his eyes. "It's the biggest story in human history," he said, his voice low. "The greatest exclusive in the history of journalism, and I am giving it to you. I would expect you to be more grateful."

Grateful, thought McKenna. *Sure. There's a vampire sitting in my living room. An actual real, walking, talking, breathing vampire, who threatened to tear my face off my skull less than an hour ago. And I'm supposed to be grateful?*

Then his eyes narrowed.

A vampire. An actual vampire, because they're real. A real vampire.

Despite himself, his mind started to turn it over.

Forget long-lens tits and cheating celebrities. He's crazy, but he's right about one thing. This could be the biggest story ever. And I could be the one to break it.

"It's a big story," he said, carefully. "I'm with you there, no argument whatsoever. But you have to see that there's not a chance in hell anyone would ever print it. You're sitting right there on my sofa and I only half believe it. My editor is going to laugh his arse off for about a minute and then he's going to fire me. I'll never get another byline as long as I live."

"I understand your concern," said Harker. "And you're right, we will need more than the word of one man if we are to be convincing. We need evidence, testimonials from men and women who have encountered my kind, or the men who are supposed to protect them from us."

"How do we do that?" asked McKenna. "Where are we going to find these people?"

Harker smiled. "We don't need to find them, Kevin. They'll come to us, willingly. You have a blog, yes?"

"You know what a blog is?"

"I was in a hospital, Kevin, not on the moon. I am familiar with the internet. Do you have a blog or not?"

"Yeah."

"Good. You will write a post asking for people who have lost friends and family members, but who have been threatened not to talk about what happened to them. Ask for their stories, of figures dressed all in black, or men and women with sharp teeth and red eyes, and guarantee their anonymity."

"And you want me to do this when?"

"Immediately. There is no time to lose."

McKenna considered the vampire's plan. His initial reaction was that most people would laugh their heads off at him if he wrote the post that Albert Harker had described, and the ones who didn't laugh would feel sorry for him. Then, for the first time in a very long time, he pushed his self-loathing aside and was honest with himself.

What the hell are you worrying about? People laugh at you now, behind your back. You know they do. You're a joke. And worst of all, you're a joke that pretends he isn't. You're nothing. You're nobody. Why not go out with a bang, one way or the other?

He finished his beer, opened yet another, and reached for his laptop. It was sitting on the coffee table where he had left it that morning, when the world had been a different place, far smaller and safer than it now seemed.

Then a dreadful thought occurred to him. "So I write this blog," he said, slowly. "And let's say you get what you want, and we bring it all down. What happens then? You kill me?"

"Of course not," said Harker, placing a hand across his chest. "I am not a monster, Kevin. I have no intention of hurting anybody."

McKenna laughed, a short sound that was little more than a grunt. "It didn't feel like that when you were throwing me across the garage."

"I needed to get your attention," said Harker. "If you refused to help, I had to make sure you were too scared to go to the authorities. I meant you no harm, I assure you."

"How can you expect me to believe that?" asked McKenna.

"I can do nothing more than give you my word. Whether you believe it or not is up to you."

"So what would happen if I decided to get up and walk out of here right now?"

"I would attempt to persuade you not to."

"And if I insisted?"

"I would... prevent you from leaving."

"How?"

"My friend," said Harker, spreading his hands wide in a gesture that Kevin felt sure was meant to portray honesty. "Let us not dwell on such things. Can we not just say that we are here, and there is work for us to do? Great work, that future generations will thank us for?"

McKenna stared at Albert Harker for a long moment, trying to shake the feeling of dread that had taken up residence in his chest.

I don't believe a word you say, he thought. *I've known violent men, I've been around them. They have this look, this aura about them. Just like the one you've got.*

"All right," he said, eventually. "So I post a blog. Then what?"

Harker smiled. "Then we wait."

"What if nobody replies?"

"Do not worry," replied Harker. "If we are forced to do this alone, I have a plan for that eventuality. But I think it is remarkably unlikely that we will need to. I have faith that our call will be answered."

McKenna opened his laptop, logged in, and accessed the dashboard of his blog. He was about to start typing when he paused, his fingers hovering over the keys.

"This matters to you, doesn't it?" he said, looking at the vampire. "This isn't just about revenge for what they did to you, or getting back at your family. You really want the public to know what's going on."

Albert Harker regarded him with an expression of naked determination. "You are quite correct, my friend," he said, softly. "I was incarcerated for almost a decade with no hope of release, by people acting with total impunity from the law, but this is not about vengeance. This is nothing less than a crusade, against everything that Blacklight has done in the shadows, on behalf of all the men and women who died because they weren't allowed to know the truth that might have saved them. And I promise you this, Kevin, right here and now. The day will come when you will be proud to tell people that you were there when it began."

McKenna nodded, and began to type. As the words began to flow, more easily than they had in a long time, a tiny part of the fear that had filled him ever since he stepped into the garage beneath *The Globe*'s offices evaporated. It was replaced by something else; something his long-jaded system found unfamiliar.

Excitement.

28

WHERE IT HURTS

For a terrible moment, Paul Turner was completely unable to breathe; his eyes remained fixed on his console's screen as his heart froze in his chest and his insides turned momentarily to water. Then his long years of experience kicked in; his fingers flew across the screen, ordering it to find Kate Randall's locator chip. The console worked as Turner screamed silently for it to hurry, then returned the result of its search.

RANDALL, KATE (LIEUTENANT)/NS303, 78-J/LOCATOR CHIP NOT FOUND

Turner shoved the console into its loop on his belt and took off towards the Level A stairwell at a flat sprint.

It doesn't mean anything, he told himself as he ran. *Monitoring is down on B. If she's there, then her chip won't show up. It doesn't mean anything.*

As he pounded down the corridor, his boots echoing against the hard concrete floor, Paul Turner pulled his radio from his belt and entered his code on to its screen. The small rectangle lit up and he tapped a series of commands, activating a Security Division interrupt;

this would cause the handsets of his Operators to act like speakers, broadcasting his voice whether they were switched on or not.

"Security breach on Level B," he said, his voice perfectly steady even as he ran. "Sections A, B and D, implement Security Protocol Alpha 7. Section C, convene on Level B room 261. Full medical and forensic tech. Out."

Protocol Alpha 7 would see three-quarters of the Security Division pair up into two-man teams and station themselves outside the most sensitive areas of the Loop: the hangar, the Lazarus Project, the Interim Director's quarters, and a long list of others. The remaining quarter of the Division would meet him at the site of the explosion.

Kate's room. Where the bomb went off. Kate's room.

Turner knew he should not be thinking about the situation in such terms; the entire Department could be in danger, the bomb merely the precursor to a larger attack, and the fate of a single Operator should not be a priority under such circumstances. But as he skidded to a halt in front of the access door to the emergency stairs and pressed his card against the panel beside it, he found himself unable to view the situation in such objective terms.

Not her. Anyone else. Just not her.

The door unlocked and he pushed it open. The emergency stairs ran down the outer edges of the sprawling base, a seemingly endless column of concrete steps that doubled back on themselves between each level. He leapt down them three at a time, his heart thumping in his chest, and pressed his ID against the door that led into Level B. Turner pushed it open and immediately smelt smoke, along with a bitter chemical undercurrent that made his eyes water.

The alarm was still sounding its endless two-tone whine. Turner paused, accessed the security override controls on his console, and turned it off. He replaced the console with one hand as he drew out his radio with the other and switched it to the Loop's global frequency. He walked slowly into the northern Level B corridor, speaking into his radio as he did so, telling everyone in the Loop to remain where they were and wait for further instructions. The Security Officer knew that there would be panic in certain sections of the base, but that was the unavoidable result of a lockdown; the purpose of containing everyone where they were was to allow Turner and his team to do their job, and to prevent potential enemy operatives or suspects from escaping.

The damage report had been correct; the fires that the explosion had caused had been extinguished, as it had claimed. But the smoke that had billowed from them had far from dissipated; it quickly began to burn his nose and throat as he made his way forward. His helmet was in his quarters on Level C, so he pulled his field survival kit from his belt, extracted the air filtration mask and the plastic goggles, and put them on. The goggles did nothing to clear the drifting smoke, but they protected his eyes from the acrid air, and the mask would keep out any toxins that had been let loose in the blast.

Paul Turner walked slowly through the smoke with his Glock drawn. He doubted that whoever was responsible for the explosion would be nearby; he fully expected to find out that the bomb had been detonated either remotely or automatically. He also had no intention of being unprepared if his assumption turned out to be wrong.

The numbers on the doors to his left climbed steadily – 235, 237, 239, 241 – and the smoke thickened as he approached number 261. He walked silently, his breathing shallow, his senses heightened; when the distant thud of boots on concrete became audible behind him, he settled his back against the wall and levelled his Glock in the direction of the sound. Moments later a cluster of ethereal black shapes became visible through the smoke, shapes that seemed to solidify as they neared him, their purple visors lending them a familiar robotic, anonymous appearance. Turner lowered his pistol and stepped into the middle of the corridor to meet them.

"Section C reporting, sir," said the nearest Operator, his voice flattened by the filters in his helmet.

"Is that you, Bennett?" asked Turner.

"Yes, sir," replied the Operator.

"Good," said Turner. "Fall in behind me. Ready One for supernaturals, anyone else I want alive. Anything that moves, anything that shows up hot, I want to know about it immediately. Clear?"

"Clear, sir."

"Then follow me."

Less than a minute later Turner began to see the carnage described in the damage report with his own eyes. The corridor had been stained white by the billowing clouds of carbon dioxide released by the fire-suppression system. A blackened piece of wood lay in the middle of the floor, surrounded by chunks of plaster and scraps of twisted metal. The debris mounted up as Turner led Section C past rooms 257 and 259, then stopped.

The entrance to room 261 was entirely gone.

The door itself had been blown across the corridor and was lying on the ground beneath a pile of debris; much of its wooden surface was missing, revealing the metal skeleton beneath. The doorway had been destroyed, leaving a ragged hole where there had once been a rectangular frame. Smoke plumed from the room as thin white foam poured out into the corridor.

"Jesus," said Bennett. "I hope there wasn't anyone in there."

The Security Officer turned his head and stared at him. He wanted to reach out and crush the Operator's throat with his bare hands, as punishment for giving voice to what Turner had already realised: if Kate had been in her room when the bomb went off, there was no chance of finding her alive.

"Bennett, with me," he said, summoning all that remained of his legendary self-control. "The rest of you, check the remainder of the corridor and double back. Then seal off a ten-metre perimeter and see what you can do about getting rid of this damn smoke."

"Yes, sir," said one of the Section C Operators, and led the rest away down the corridor. Bennett stood silently at Turner's side, facing the remains of the entrance to room 261; he appeared to have concluded that the best course of action was to keep his mouth shut.

Paul Turner took a deep breath. The air in the corridor was slowly beginning to clear, but the dark interior of the room was still thickly clouded with smoke and spent chemicals. He drew his torch from his belt and flicked it on; a bright white beam burst from the bulb.

"Careful," he said. "Don't touch anything."

"Yes, sir," replied Bennett.

Turner nodded, then walked into Kate Randall's quarters.

The small room had been utterly destroyed.

The wardrobe, desk and bedside table had been blown to splinters and blasted against the walls and ceiling, leaving scratches and gouges across the plaster. The bed was ruined, torn to shreds and scorched by both the explosion and the fire that had burned fiercely until the Halon system had activated. A pitch-black depression in the centre of the floor suggested the likely location of the bomb; of the device itself, there remained nothing that the naked eye could discern.

Attached to the door, Turner thought. *I'd bet my life on it. Triggered as it opened, then a second or two delay to make sure she was in the room before it fired.*

He looked round the devastated room. The walls were scorched and blackened, as were the floor and ceiling; it was like standing inside an enormous oven. The residue coating the surfaces was thick and lumpy, and impossible to identify. It could be manufactured or biological; Turner could not tell with any degree of certainty whether what he was looking at were the charred remains of Kate Randall.

"There's no one here, sir," said Bennett. "We need to seal this for forensics."

"Wait," said Turner. He was not ready to leave just yet; if Kate had been in here when the bomb detonated, if she was, in fact, all around him, on the walls and the ceiling, then this would be the last time he was ever close to her. Forensics would analyse the room, then tear it down and send it piece by piece to the labs for chemical and spectral analysis. Whatever was left of Kate would end up in Petri dishes and specimen jars.

"Sir!" shouted a voice from the corridor. It awoke him from his thoughts, and he turned towards the ragged hole where the doorway had stood. Section C had returned and were crouching beside the shattered door of room 261.

"What is it?" he asked, walking towards them.

"There's someone here, sir," replied the Operator. "Under the door."

Paul Turner's heart stopped in his chest. For a moment, he just stared at the pile of rubble atop the ruined door, his eyes wide and uncomprehending. Then his paralysis broke and he ran forward, sliding to his knees beside his men.

"Are they breathing?" he asked, peering down at the door. Beneath it, through a gap between the frame and a jagged lump of wall plaster, he could see pale human skin.

"There's a pulse, sir," confirmed the Operator.

"Let's get this off them," said Turner, and gripped the edge of the door with both hands. One of Section C took hold of the other side and the two of them hauled the heavy metal frame up and back, sending it clattering to the floor. A cloud of dust billowed up from where the door had lain; Turner waved it away, almost frantically.

Let it be her. Please let it be her.

The dust dispersed and they crowded in to look.

Lying on the floor, covered in broken plaster and splintered wood, was a tiny girl with blonde hair and pale skin. Her eyes were closed, a thick smear of blood ran down the wall above her head, but her chest was rising and falling steadily.

"Who is she?" asked Turner. He was overcome with disappointment, for which he truly hated himself; he had wanted it to be Kate Randall so badly that the sight of anyone else was terrible. It meant that Kate could still be in her room, smeared across the walls.

It meant she could still be gone.

One of the Operators placed his console against the girl's forearm and typed a command. The locator chip that was surgically implanted beneath the muscles of every Operator's forearm was scanned, and a name appeared on the screen.

"Her name is Natalia Lenski," said the Operator. "She's Lazarus, sir."

"Then what the hell was she doing on Level B?"

The Operator shook his head. "No idea, sir."

29

DROWNING OUT

Larissa Kinley stared through the hole in the wall and wondered who she was going to have to explain it to.

She had hit the gym as soon as the Special Operations Squad returned from Nuevo Laredo. The ride home in the helicopter should have been triumphant, and for most of the squad it clearly was; they were basking in the afterglow of a job well done, joking and laughing among themselves. Tim Albertsson had joined in, although she didn't believe for a minute that his focus had truly been on his squad mates and what they had achieved; instead, it had been where she now belatedly realised it had for several weeks.

On her.

She had asked for permission to fly home on her own, knowing he would not grant it, but hoping that the question would reinforce what she had told him in the walled garden behind Garcia Rejon's mansion, after Tim had kissed her.

He kissed me. That's what happened. He kissed me. I didn't kiss him back.

Tim had refused her request, as expected, so she had strapped herself into the seat furthest from his and stayed silent the entire way home. She didn't trust herself to speak, unable to predict with sufficient accuracy the words that might come out of her mouth. Tim had been either astute, or oblivious, and had left her alone. She had still caught him looking at her, though; tiny glances, barely more than flicks of his eyes, but there nonetheless, and obvious once she knew what to look for.

How long has he been looking at me like that? Why didn't I notice before?

Larissa excused herself the instant the helicopter set down on the tarmac outside the NS9 hangar and made for the safety of her quarters. Once the door was locked behind her, she turned on the screen that hung on the wall opposite her bed, loaded NS9's secure video link application, and sat with her finger hovering over the button that would send a message to Jamie's console informing him she was trying to reach him, for almost five minutes. Her mind was racing, thoughts and feelings jumbling and rolling together; and at the very back of her mind a voice, the one she hated, that told her she was ugly and stupid and no good, whispered to her.

Maybe you did notice how Tim looked at you. Maybe you didn't say anything because you didn't mind. Maybe you liked him looking at you like that.

She pushed the voice away as far as she was able, and closed the application. Then she pulled off her uniform, threw on a pair of shorts and a vest, and headed for the gym, her feet floating above the ground.

That's not true, she told herself, as she began to work the heavy bag. She was pulling her punches, but it nonetheless began to swing back and forth rapidly, her knuckles thudding against it with a noise like the crack of a bullwhip. *I didn't know he liked me, I swear I didn't. I didn't encourage him. I really didn't.*

But the voice at the back of her mind wouldn't leave her alone; it dripped poison into her ears as she swung her fists, harder and harder.

Why don't you talk to Tim about Jamie? You're so quick to tell everyone else about him, you normally won't shut up about him. Why is it different with Tim?

The bag swung higher and higher, creaking on the chain that connected it to the ceiling.

Didn't you notice how he always sits next to you at dinner? Of course you did, you're a smart girl. You noticed and you liked it, didn't you?

Puffs of dust began to burst from the seams as her fists pounded the bag; it was now little more than a red blur, hurled backwards and forwards by her supernatural strength.

Why haven't you mentioned Tim to Jamie? You've worked with him almost every day since you've been here, but you never thought he was worth telling your boyfriend about? Why didn't you want them to know about each other?

"Shut up," whispered Larissa, and felt familiar red heat spill into the corners of her eyes. The heavy bag whipped back and forth, impossibly fast, and she felt the muscles in her shoulders ripple as she increased the power of her swings.

Maybe that's why you don't want to go back to Blacklight. Maybe it's got nothing to do with how they treat you or how they look at you. Maybe that's why you asked General Allen about transferring Jamie here, because you knew he'd never do it. Maybe that's what you're hoping for, that you can stay here with Tim.

"SHUT UP!" she screamed, a guttural roar that seemed to rise from the pit of her stomach and erupt from her mouth. Her eyes blazed under the fluorescent lights of the gym, and she felt her fangs burst into place, cutting her lower lip. She swung her fist with every shred of power she possessed, crashing it into the side of the heavy bag with the force of a wrecking ball. The chain snapped and the bag itself rocketed across the gym, crunching a hole in the opposite wall before bursting in a great cloud of sand.

Instantly, the rage left her. She stared at the hole, embarrassment rising quickly through her as a memory surfaced from her old life, the life before she needed to drink blood to survive; her fourteen-year-old self hurling a glass against the wall of her bedroom, a disproportionate response to some long-forgotten parental slight. Her mother had said nothing, just stared at her with an expression of such deep disappointment that Larissa had burst into tears, screaming for her mum to get out of her room, to leave her alone, before hurling herself on to her bed and covering her head with a pillow, unable to meet her mother's gaze. She felt similar shame now, although there was one major difference between what was happening now and what had happened when she was fourteen.

I haven't done anything wrong, she thought, fiercely. *I love Jamie and I'd never betray him, but that doesn't mean I have to tell him everything. I'm allowed a life of my own. Friends of my own. And to hell with anyone who thinks differently.*

Larissa felt the heat in her eyes ebb away and breathed out heavily. She was coated in a light film of sweat and was suddenly exhausted; her bones felt heavy, her skin thin and brittle. As she made her way towards the showers, she realised that there was something she had to do: she needed to talk to Tim. She felt no obligation to tell Jamie what had happened, but she *was* going to have to talk to her colleague, for one simple reason: she had seen in his eyes, as clear as day, that there would come a time when he would try to kiss her again. She wanted to avoid that situation for the same reason that she avoided all other dangerous situations: because you could never be absolutely sure what might happen in the heat of the moment.

Because, despite all the best intentions in the world, sometimes bad things happened.

30

PRELIMINARY CONCLUSIONS

Paul Turner tapped rapidly on the touch screen of his console. He was standing in the centre of the Level B corridor, his outer appearance betraying not the slightest hint of the turmoil inside.

Come on. Come on. Come on.

The screen glowed as the console returned the results.

CARPENTER, JAMIE (LIEUTENANT)/NS303, 67-J – B171
BROWNING, MATTHEW (LIEUTENANT)/NS303, 83-C – B173

As the door was being lifted, Turner had felt panic threaten to overwhelm him; the thought of losing Kate Randall, the girl upon whom he had come to rely far more than he hoped she knew, who represented one of the few remaining links to his late son, was unimaginable.

The sight of Natalia Lenski, injured but clearly still alive, had wiped the rising panic away and returned his icy, analytical brain to something resembling its normal mode of operation; emotion had receded, replaced by problems that needed solving, situations that required handling. The most pressing of these was the need to update Cal Holmwood on the situation, but that was not what the Security Officer had turned his attention to.

Kate Randall was missing. That was his priority.

He was already sure that the bomb had been detonated by the door to her quarters being opened, which meant that it was extremely unlikely she was dead; the door had been blown outwards, crashing into the Lenski girl who had obviously been standing in front of it at the time. Even if Kate had been standing beside her as the explosion tore through the small room, there was very little chance that she had been obliterated so completely that no visible remains had been left behind.

No, the Lazarus girl went into the quarters on her own and triggered the bomb. The bomb that was meant for Kate.

Exactly why Natalia Lenski had been entering Kate's room was a question for another time. Right now, there was a far more pressing one that needed answering.

Where the hell is she?

Her chip wasn't showing up on the grid, which meant that, assuming he was right about her not being dead, she had to be somewhere on Level B, where the explosion had knocked out the monitoring equipment. The level was almost entirely residential and normally home to more than seventy Operators, although in the aftermath of the attack on the Loop, it housed fewer than forty. But of those that remained, two were Kate's best friends in all of Blacklight, the two teenage boys whose room numbers he had just asked his console for.

171 and 173. That's right. They live next door to each other.

Turner strode down the corridor, holding back the urge to run; it would not do for the Section C Operators to see how unsettled he really was. Identical doors passed by on both sides, until he found himself standing outside the one marked 173. He pressed his card against the black panel on the wall, and heard the locks disengage. At the last second, when it was far too late to do anything about it, he suddenly wondered whether the bomber might have also booby-trapped the quarters of Kate's friends, and marvelled at such an unthinkably junior error. But the door merely swung open, revealing not a ball of expanding fire, but a small room that seemed to be almost full of files and folders. The bed was the only surface not covered in teetering mountains of paper, and it was empty. Turner hauled the door shut and moved on to room 171.

Jamie Carpenter's room.

He overrode the door lock, this time taking the precaution of moving three quick steps away along the wall. The door swung open and a familiar voice shouted through the opening.

"Who's out there? Show yourself."

Turner suppressed a tiny smile, and stepped out in front of the open doorway. Jamie was standing in the middle of his quarters, his legs shoulder-width, his MP5 resting easily against his shoulder.

The teenage boy who came here is gone, he thought. *For better or worse, he's gone.*

"Lower your weapon, Lieutenant Carpenter," he said, his voice level. Jamie did so as Turner stepped into the small room, instantly realising that Kate Randall wasn't there.

"What's going on, sir?" asked Jamie.

"Nothing you need to worry about, Lieutenant," replied Turner. "I'm looking for Lieutenant Randall. Do you know where she is?"

Jamie frowned. "Kate?" he asked. "Isn't she in ISAT?"

"If she was in ISAT, I wouldn't be asking you if you knew where she was."

"I don't know where she is," said Jamie, his eyes narrowing. "Have you run her chip?"

"Of course I have," replied Turner. "Stay here until you are told otherwise, Lieutenant Carpenter." He turned and headed for the door.

"Hey!" shouted Jamie.

Turner stopped and faced him. "What is it, Lieutenant?"

"Why don't you know where Kate is?"

"Don't worry about it," said Turner. "Just stay here. We'll be lifting the lockdown as soon as we can."

"Don't give me that," said Jamie, fiercely. "I heard an explosion that sounded like it was on this level. So if something's happened to Kate, you'd better tell me right now or—"

"Or what, Lieutenant Carpenter?" interrupted the Security Officer. "What exactly do you intend to do about it?"

Jamie stared at him, and Turner felt the usual mixture of admiration and irritation that filled him whenever he looked at Julian Carpenter's son. Then the teenager's face softened.

"Is Kate OK, sir?" he asked. "Just tell me. Did something happen to her?"

Jamie's face was suddenly so full of obviously genuine concern that Turner felt his heart go out to him.

"I don't know, Jamie," he replied. "Someone put a bomb in her quarters, but I don't think she was there when it went off. Her chip isn't showing up, but the blast knocked out the monitoring systems on this level, so that doesn't necessarily mean anything. I'm working on the assumption that she's somewhere else."

Jamie's eyes had widened as Turner spoke. "A bomb?" he asked. "In Kate's room?"

Turner nodded.

"Was anyone hurt?" asked Jamie.

"A girl from the Lazarus Project."

"What was she doing in Kate's room?"

"I don't know, Jamie. She could have been planting the bomb for all I know. It detonated about nine minutes ago, so I don't have the answer to every single question just yet."

"So Kate has to be on this level?"

"That's the most likely explanation."

"Have you checked next door? In Matt's room?"

"Yes. She's not there."

Jamie stared for a long moment, seemingly at nothing; for some reason, it was a moment that Paul Turner felt compelled to let him finish, even though he knew he should be on his way up to Cal Holmwood's quarters by now.

Then Jamie broke into a small, sad smile. "I know where she is," he said.

"Where?" asked Turner. "Tell me."

The young Operator shook his head. "I'll show you."

The two men walked along Level B in silence, until Jamie stopped outside one of the hundred or more identical doors that lined the corridor. Turner read the number printed on the flat surface.

059

It felt familiar; he frowned as he stared at it. He had seen it before, that combination of three numbers, but couldn't remember where, or why the feeling that they were important was rising through him. Then understanding hit him like a punch to the stomach.

This was Shaun's room. 059. This was my son's room.

Without a word, Turner reached out and ran his card across the black plastic panel. His stomach churned, he could feel blood pounding through the veins in his head, but he forced his hand not to tremble. The locks released and the door slid open. Jamie didn't give any indication of movement, so he stepped forward and pushed the door wide, his heart full of a swirling mixture of longing and dread. It swung back against the wall of the small room, and Paul Turner found himself looking at Kate Randall, who was sitting on the edge of the bed that had once been Shaun's.

It had been stripped down to the mattress, and the rest of the room was similarly bare; the bedside table and desk were clear, the wardrobe was empty, the walls had been given a fresh coat of whitewash. Once the Security Division had completed the mandatory examination that followed the death of any Operator, Shaun's possessions had been handed to him in a single cardboard box. He had taken them home to his wife, placed them on the kitchen table, and let her see them; he had been unable to speak, to soften the blow for her in any way.

"Paul?" said Kate. "Jamie? What are you doing here? What's going on? I heard something that sounded like an explosion."

For a second or two, Turner just stared at her. Then he strode forward, pulled her to her feet, and enveloped her in a crushing bear hug. Kate laughed involuntarily, although her face wore an expression of confusion. "Hey," she said. "It's OK. What's wrong?"

"There was a bomb, Kate," said Jamie, softly. He was still standing in the doorway, watching the embrace taking place before him with a mixture of happiness and unease. "Someone planted a bomb in your room."

"What?" asked Kate, her eyes flying wide. "Let go of me, Paul, for God's sake. What happened?"

Turner released her, with obvious reluctance, and stepped back. "Jamie's telling the truth," he said. "An explosive device was placed in your quarters. It detonated when the door was opened."

"Was anyone hurt?" asked Kate.

"A girl from the Lazarus Project," said Turner. "Her name is—"

"Natalia Lenski," said Kate, distantly. "Oh Jesus. Is she OK?"

"She's going to be fine," said Turner, and smiled as relief flooded Kate's face. "She was still outside when it blew. The door shielded her from most of the blast."

"What was she doing going into your room?" asked Jamie. "I didn't think you knew anyone in Lazarus apart from Matt."

"I don't," said Kate, sitting back down. "I'd never spoken to her until this morning."

"Lieutenant Carpenter," said Turner. "I'm going to ask you to step out into the corridor. This is an active Security Division investigation. I'm sorry."

Jamie stared. "You're kidding?"

"No, Lieutenant," said Turner, holding out his ID card. "I'm not. Please step outside."

Jamie fixed his gaze on the Security Officer for a long moment, then got up and took the plastic rectangle from Turner's fingers. He used it on the black panel on the wall and stepped out into the corridor, casting an unreadable glance at Kate as the door swung shut.

"What happened?" asked Turner, as soon as the locks thudded into place.

Kate took a deep breath, and began to talk.

Kate took a deep breath and pulled open the ISAT security door.

Standing outside, perched on one of the Intelligence Division desks, was a tiny blonde girl wearing a white lab coat. Her pale face was tight and her eyes were wide and full of nervousness.

"Hello," she said, walking over and extending a hand. "I'm Kate Randall. I was told you wanted to see me?"

The blonde girl nodded. "My name is Natalia Lenski," she said. "I work downstairs, in the... well, you know..."

"I know where you mean," said Kate, smiling. "It's nice to meet you."

"You too," replied Natalia. "I have heard many things about you."

"That's nice," said Kate. "I think. So what can I do for you, Natalia?"

"Can we go somewhere else?" replied Natalia. "Somewhere quiet?"

"Of course," said Kate. "Let's go up top for a few minutes."

I don't know what the hell this is, she thought, but at least I'll get some fresh air.

Two minutes later, the two girls walked through the huge double doors of the hangar and out on to the grounds of the Loop. Kate led Natalia across the runway and the wide field that lay beyond it, and into the rose garden that had been built in memory of John and George Harker, brothers who had died in the blazing wreckage of the Mina, the original Blacklight jet. At the rear of the beautiful, fragrant garden stood a wooden bench; Kate took a seat, motioned for Natalia to do likewise, and waited; eventually, the blonde girl spoke.

"I feel awkward coming to you like this," she said. "I know you are very busy. But I cannot pretend that I am not worried about him."

"Worried about who?" asked Kate.

"Matt Browning," replied Natalia. "He is the one who speaks about you. He told me you are friends, yes?"

"That's right," said Kate. "Are you his friend too?"

"I think so," said Natalia, a tiny frown creasing her forehead. "It is difficult. That is why I wanted to talk to you."

"Is something wrong?" Kate asked. "Is Matt OK?"

"I am not sure," said Natalia. She lowered her eyes and picked nervously at her fingernails. "He works so hard. It is like he carries everything on his shoulders, the entire Project. He cares so much, and he is so desperate to help his friends."

"He told me what you're looking for could take years," said Kate.

"He is right," said Natalia. *"And I think it will kill him if it does. Robert has talked to him, tried to make him slow down, but he does not seem to hear."*

"Who's Robert?"

"Professor Karlsson. Our Director."

"Oh. OK. Go on."

"That is all," said Natalia. *"I wondered if you might talk to him, make him see that he is being too hard on himself. Maybe he will listen to you, because you are his friend. And I... am not."*

There's more to this, *thought Kate, suddenly.* There's something else going on here.

"Natalia," she said, *gently. "Do you like Matt?"*

"Of course," replied Natalia, *lifting her head and smiling broadly.* *"Everyone likes him. He is very popular."*

"No, I mean, do you like *him?"*

Natalia didn't answer, but she blushed deeply, soft red suffusing her beautiful pale face.

There it is. Wow. This definitely won't be complicated. Not at all.

"Right then," said Kate, *checking the time on her console.* *"We need to have a proper conversation about this. I have to go back to ISAT, but I should get some time off for lunch in about an hour or so. Can you get away for a little while?"*

Natalia nodded.

"Great. In which case, why don't you go to my quarters in an hour? If I'm not there, you can let yourself in and I'll be there as soon as I can. We can talk about Matt." She left this last comment intentionally ambiguous; she didn't want to embarrass a girl she found herself already starting to like.

"Yes, please," said Natalia. *"That will be very kind of you."*

"No problem," said Kate. "My quarters are on Level B, room 261. The override code for the door is 2TG687B33. Can you remember that?"

"I can," replied Natalia.

Of course she can, *thought Kate*. She works for the Lazarus Project. She's probably a certified genius.

"OK," she said. "If I'm not there, wait for me. Now I have to get back to ISAT. Are you coming back inside?"

Natalia shook her head. "I will stay here for a little while."

"OK," said Kate. "I'll see you downstairs. 261." With that, she got up and jogged back towards the distant doors of the hangar.

"She should be in the infirmary by now," replied the Security Officer. He got up and thumped on the door, and immediately heard the locks start to disengage. "Her pulse was strong, her heartbeat regular. She's got some cuts and bruises, she's lost some blood, and I wouldn't be surprised if she's broken a rib or two. But she'll be fine. I wouldn't have said so if I thought otherwise."

"Good," said Kate. Her face was almost translucent, as though the colour had been drained from her skin. "I would hate to think that... something that was meant..." She burst into tears as the door opened and Jamie walked back into the room. He frowned, and Turner stood aside as he went to her, sitting beside her on the bed and putting his arm round her shoulder.

"Hey," said Jamie, squeezing her shoulders. "It's all right. There's nothing wrong with being scared, Kate. We're all scared."

"I'm not scared, Jamie," she said, shrugging his arm away and looking at him with eyes full of fire. "I'm bloody *furious*. How dare they? Who the hell do they think they are?"

Turner felt something huge move inside his chest. *I couldn't love this girl more*, he thought. *No matter how hard I tried.*

Jamie grinned at her and stood up. Turner stepped forward and took back his ID card as Kate got to her feet.

"What can we do?" she asked, her eyes shining. "Tell us how we can help, Paul."

"You can help me by doing nothing," said Turner. "This is a Security Division matter. I'm going to escort you back to Lieutenant Carpenter's quarters and you're going to stay there until we lift the lockdown. You will not tell anyone that we ever had this conversation; as far as everyone else is concerned, you were in Jamie's room the whole time. Is that clear?"

The two Operators opened their mouths to protest, but Turner cut them off. "I've told you what I need you both to do," he said. "So do you actually want to help, or do you just want to be the centre of attention, as usual?"

Kate and Jamie glanced at each other; something unspoken passed between them, something that Turner couldn't read.

"Fine," said Jamie. "We'll go to my quarters."

"Excellent," said Turner. "I'm so grateful that you have chosen to obey my direct order. How very kind of you."

Jamie's face flushed, but he said nothing as the Security Officer stepped aside and motioned towards the open door; he walked through it without a word, Kate following behind him. Turner took a last look around the room that had been his son's, a room that he had spent far too little time in when it had been occupied, and stepped into the corridor, closing the door behind him.

As the three Operators made their way back to Jamie's quarters, Paul Turner asked the question that was burning away inside him.

"Kate," he said, his voice low. She turned to look at him. "How did you get into Shaun's room?"

She blushed a deep, delicate pink. Jamie didn't so much as twitch;

he continued to walk steadily down the corridor, his gaze fixed forward, and Turner felt gratitude.

"He gave me the override code," said Kate. "I thought it would have been changed by now, but it hasn't. I go there sometimes, for a bit of peace and quiet. And because... well, you know." She smiled, a small, empty expression. "It feels like a bit of him is still there. Like it's all that's left of him. Do you know what I mean?"

Turner nodded.

I do. I know exactly what you mean.

Kate looked relieved and turned back to face in the direction they were walking. He stared at her, wondering whether to tell her that for a few awful seconds he had not recognised the number on his son's old room. He knew she would not judge him, and it might prove cathartic to admit to someone what he knew in his heart: that he had not always been the father he should have. But he decided against it; it would not help Kate to hear him give voice to his self-doubt, to the guilt that ate away at him every night, when sleep refused to come.

"Has anyone checked out your quarters?" asked Cal Holmwood.

The Interim Director of Department 19 was sitting behind his desk, his fingers laced together, his chin resting against them. He looked tired, the deep tiredness that comes from more than just lack of sleep, that settles into the bones and soul. Turner had been giving the Interim Director a preliminary report on the bombing and its aftermath, and had reached the location of the explosion when Holmwood interrupted him.

"No, sir," he replied. "Why?"

"What if this is about ISAT, Paul? What if it has nothing to do with Dracula or Zero Hour? If so, Kate might not have been the only target."

Turner stared at Holmwood. He hadn't considered that. Why the hell hadn't he considered that? He had been so caught up in trying to find Kate Randall that a motive for attacking her room had not really crossed his mind. He grabbed the radio from his belt and ordered Security Division Section B to make an immediate check on his quarters, exercising maximum caution.

"I'm sorry, sir," he said. "That should have been obvious. I don't know what's wrong with me."

"There's nothing wrong with you, Paul," said Holmwood, firmly. "You're doing the work of about five people and you're trying to keep us afloat while we put ourselves back together. Give yourself a break. And continue."

"Yes, sir," he replied. "Most of the monitoring systems on Level B are still down, but we've had a preliminary report from Surveillance. Their cameras don't show anybody entering or exiting room 261 since Operator Randall left it this morning, although the door does appear to open and close on two occasions. The device itself appears to have been made from readily accessible ingredients, detonated using the charges from standard-issue grenades and triggered using parts from a standard-issue radio handset. I'm afraid that's everything we have right now, sir."

Holmwood breathed out, deeply. "Not much to go on," he said. "Are you prepared to draw any conclusions at this time?"

"Nothing that I can back up, sir," replied Turner. "But one explanation does suggest itself."

"What explanation?"

Turner opened his mouth to answer, but a loud buzzing from his radio interrupted him; he looked enquiringly at the Interim Director, who nodded. The Security Officer thumbed the RECEIVE button on his radio and said, "Go ahead."

"Operator Grant, Security Division Section B reporting in, sir," said a crackling voice. "An explosive device was attached to the door of your quarters. We've disabled it and sent it to the labs for analysis. Over."

"Well done, Operator," said Turner. Familiar fury rose in his chest and settled there, as comfortable as the company of an old friend. "Carry on. Out."

"Yes, sir. Out."

Turner twisted the radio off and set it down on Cal Holmwood's desk. The Interim Director leant forward in his chair, an unreadable expression on his face. "What are your recommendations, Paul? Tell me what you need."

"I want authorisation to keep the lockdown in place overnight, sir," said Turner. "I want to know where everyone is while my team does its work. Squads in the field can be held in the dormitories as they come home. I know this means we will lose a number of Operations, but..."

"Authorised," said Holmwood. "We cannot fight vampires if we are under attack in our own base."

"My thoughts exactly, sir."

There was a long moment of silence.

"You said an explanation suggested itself," said Holmwood, eventually. "Tell me, although I'm sure I already know what it is. And what its implications are."

Turner nodded. "We'll know a lot more if we can salvage the data from the monitoring system," he said. "But the surveillance camera evidence is pretty damning on its own. As far as I'm concerned we're looking for a vampire."

31

FROM ANCIENT GRUDGE BREAK TO NEW MUTINY

TWELVE DAYS EARLIER

"So this is where they keep you?"

Valentin Rusmanov looked up from the book he was reading and smiled broadly. Standing on the other side of the ultraviolet barrier that formed the front wall of his cell, peering in at him with open loathing, was Frankenstein's monster.

"Indeed, it is," he replied, rising elegantly to his feet. "Do you approve?"

"Not really," said Frankenstein, his voice reverberating against the concrete walls. "If it was up to me, you'd be nothing more than a smear of blood on the floor."

"How vivid," said Valentin. "Can I assist you with something, Mr Frankenstein, or did you come all the way down here just to make insipid threats?"

For several long moments, Frankenstein didn't reply; his large grey-green face was still, his misshapen eyes narrow, his huge hands clenched into fists by his sides. His hair was long, and a beard climbed his cheeks towards his eyes. He was wearing a suit over an open-necked shirt, and a metal stake on his belt that looked tiny against his oversized frame.

"I want to talk to you," he said, eventually. "About why you're here."

"Here in this cell or here in this building?"

"In this building," said Frankenstein. "I want to know why you're keeping up the pretence of being on our side. My assumption is that it amuses you to do so."

"Interesting," said Valentin. "I can think of several thousand things I would prefer to do with my time than conversing with a recycled coward, but as none of them are available to me at this precise moment, I see little alternative. So come in, by all means, and make yourself at home."

Frankenstein bared his teeth momentarily, but stepped through the shimmering ultraviolet light and into the cell, his face like thunder.

"Have a seat," said Valentin. "Can I get you anything? Tea? Wine? Blood? Oh, I'm sorry, you don't do that sort of thing any more, do you?"

"There are limits to my patience, vampire," growled Frankenstein, lowering himself into one of the two chairs that stood beside the narrow bed. "It is far from endless."

"I'm sure that's true," said Valentin. He floated effortlessly into the empty chair and rested an ankle on his knee. "Although I suspect you will somehow manage to keep your temper, no matter how much it pains you to do so. I don't imagine you would be thrilled by the prospect of explaining to your superiors why you made an unauthorised visit to the detention level and ended up in the infirmary."

Frankenstein said nothing; he merely stared at the ancient vampire, one hand moving slowly to the centre of his chest and resting there.

"Well, this is invigorating, I must say," said Valentin, after a silent minute had passed. "I do so enjoy the cut and thrust of debate. It seems to have fallen to me to perpetuate this farce, so let me attempt to find a new topic for discussion. How about the effects of opium on the barely human body? Or the decor and music of Jazz Age New York? Or—"

"I want you to stay away from him," said Frankenstein. His voice rumbled like an earthquake, and his eyes burned with loathing.

Valentin smiled. "To whom are you referring?"

"You know damn well," replied Frankenstein. "Jamie Carpenter. And his friends. Stay away from them all."

"Why on earth should I do that?"

"Because I'm telling you to," said the monster, his face twisted with obvious disgust. "I may not be able to make them see your charade for what it is, but I will not have them caught up in the betrayal that you and I both know is coming."

"I see," said Valentin. "Let's imagine, just for a moment, that I choose to completely ignore you. What would be the consequences of such a decision?"

"Your destruction," said Frankenstein. "And your servant's."

"Interesting. And how exactly would you explain that to Mr Holmwood?"

"There would be no explanation necessary. Cal shares my opinion of you."

"Which is what?" asked Valentin, his voice smooth and polite.

"That you're an animal," said Frankenstein.

"I see," said Valentin. He leant back in his chair, laced his fingers together and set his thumbs against his chin. "Then let me ask you something else. Setting aside both your opinion of me and your annoying tendency to make threats that you are entirely incapable of carrying out, what makes you think that you, of all people, should have any say in who Mr Carpenter chooses to associate with?"

"I made a promise to his grandfather," said Frankenstein. "That I would protect his family. Jamie is all that's left."

"Interesting," said Valentin. "It would appear that John Carpenter was a man who liked entering into agreements. He and I struck a deal of our own, in which we agreed to let each other go about our lives unmolested, a deal I extended to cover his descendants."

Frankenstein's eyes narrowed. "You're lying."

"Believe whatever you wish," said Valentin. "I have no interest in trying to persuade you. I gave a detailed account to Major Turner when I first arrived in this most charming of places, so I'm sure there will be a transcript somewhere, if you have the clearance required to access it."

"Don't worry about my clearance," said Frankenstein.

"Really?" asked Valentin, cocking his head to one side. "I was told that you turned down the chance to sit on the Task Force that is committed to dealing with my brother and his master, and that you rarely leave your quarters. If I have been misinformed, and you are actually an active participant at the very heart of Blacklight, then you have my apologies."

Frankenstein didn't respond, but the colour drained from his face, leaving it a sickly pale green.

That struck home, thought Valentin. *Glass houses, my friend. Glass houses.*

"Can I assume from your silence that the information I received was accurate?" he asked.

"Yes," grunted Frankenstein. "You speak the truth, although God knows who told it to you. But that doesn't change what I came down here to tell you."

"Fair enough," said Valentin. The conversation was beginning to bore him; teasing and tormenting the monster was almost too easy. "You've had your say. I listened, even though there was absolutely no need for me to do so. Now I will have mine."

"I don't—"

"Be quiet," said Valentin. He felt heat in the corners of his eyes and admonished himself to remain calm. "If you know what's good for you, you will be quiet and listen. Telling me to stay away from Jamie Carpenter is not the same thing as protecting him. I understand why you cannot accept that, but it is the truth. Protecting him would mean leaving your quarters, strapping on your weapons, and standing by his side as he risks his life fighting vampires. You are clearly unable, or unwilling, to do so. I'm sure you have your reasons, reasons that I imagine have their roots in a certain European capital city, but they do not excuse you being angry with me because you are no longer capable of fulfilling the promise you made. So understand this: I will associate with whomever I want, whenever I want. And, given that I am confined to this concrete box, you may want to ask yourself who is initiating the contact between Jamie and I that you are so terribly concerned about. Now. Was that sufficiently clear for you? Or do you need me to use smaller words?"

"Perfectly clear," growled Frankenstein. "Thank you for that assessment of matters you know absolutely nothing about."

Valentin shrugged, and smiled at the monster. "Enlighten me then," he said. "Tell me why you're too scared to be of any use to Jamie and his friends."

Slowly, like an avalanche in reverse, Frankenstein rose to his feet. Valentin didn't move; his smile remained in place, although he tensed his muscles, ready to react if the monster was stupid enough to attack him.

"If Jamie needs me," said Frankenstein, his voice low, "I'll be there. As I promised."

"And how will you know if he needs you?"

"He'll tell me."

Valentin's smile widened into a grin. "Are you quite sure about that?"

Frankenstein turned away and walked slowly across the cell. When he reached the ultraviolet barrier, he looked back at Valentin.

"I don't want Jamie to know this conversation ever happened," he said. "If you truly mean him no harm, you will understand why."

"My lips are sealed," said Valentin. "And do feel free to drop by any time. I'd forgotten the thrill of having empty threats thrown my way."

Frankenstein stared at him for a long moment, then walked through the barrier without a backward glance. Valentin listened as the heavy steps echoed away towards the airlock, then let out a long, slow breath.

The monster's attempts to intimidate him had been laughable; he had no doubt that, for all Frankenstein's size and experience, he could tear him to pieces with one hand tied behind his back. But he was deeply relieved that it had not come to that; a physical altercation with the monster would have instantly drawn the attention of Lamberton, with the Blacklight Security Division not far behind, and he had no desire to fight for his life against highly armed soldiers in a long concrete tube.

Not unless he made the decision to do so.

Valentin pirouetted gracefully up into the air, enjoying its cool resistance against his skin, and lowered himself slowly back on to his bed.

It's rarely dull around here, he thought, as he picked up his book. *I'll give them that.*

50 DAYS TILL
ZERO HOUR

32

CLOSING THE NET

Jamie Carpenter looked round the Ops Room as Cal Holmwood called the meeting to order. The familiar faces that he had seen in this room dozens of times looked different: older, more drawn.

Tired.

The lockdown had been lifted an hour earlier, and since then the Loop had been consumed by tight, suffocating paranoia. Operators, scientists, intelligence staff, civilian workers, all were huddled in small groups throughout the base, their faces wearing expressions of open worry. It was not quite a full-blown panic, not yet, but a deep sense of unease had unquestionably settled into the bones of the Department. Men and women regarded each other nervously, uncertain of who they could trust, who they could truly believe was on their side. If the bomber's intention had been to spread fear and distrust throughout Blacklight, then they had succeeded admirably. Although a theory was gathering momentum among the senior Operators that it had been planted for a different reason.

"Zero Hour Task Force emergency meeting in session," said Cal Holmwood. "All members present. As you will all be aware, the Loop was placed into lockdown yesterday afternoon, after an explosive device was detonated in quarters on Level B. I'm going to ask Major Turner to bring us up to speed. Paul?"

"Yes, sir," said Turner. "The investigation is ongoing, but there is a certain amount I can tell you. The device was built with materials available inside the Loop, including its trigger and explosive core. We have been able to find no visual evidence of anyone entering room 261 after Lieutenant Randall exited it yesterday morning. A forensic investigation is ongoing and, as a result, the evidence so far does not support a conclusion."

"Of course it does," said Patrick Williams. "A vampire planted the bomb in Kate's room, one that moved too fast for our cameras to see it. Which narrows down the field of suspects to one, as far as I'm concerned."

"The investigation is ongoing," repeated Paul Turner, his voice full of warning. "All possibilities, both human and supernatural, will be fully examined. Now, the next—"

"Why are we putting ourselves through this charade?" asked Andrew Jarvis, his face suddenly white with fury. "Everyone knows that Valentin Rusmanov planted the bomb, but instead of going down to the cellblock and destroying him, like we should have done weeks ago, we're going to investigate each other and look for some complicated answer when the truth is staring us in the face. We're going to do exactly what he wants."

"Operator," said Turner, in a low voice. "Please do not interrupt me again." He stared at Jarvis with grey eyes as cold as the surface of the moon and, after a second or two, the Operator dropped his gaze. "Valentin Rusmanov is obviously a suspect," he continued, looking around, daring anyone else to interrupt him. "I'm sure half the men and women in this base are already convinced of his guilt, and if he turns out to be behind this, I will fire a stake into his heart myself. But there are other factors at work here which suggest that this was not an attack designed solely to cause panic."

"It *has*, though," said Amy Andrews, softly. "Everyone I've talked to since the lockout was lifted is scared out of their minds. They want to know how we're supposed to stop Dracula when we can't even feel safe in our own base. I've even heard rumours of desertions. Can you confirm them, Major Turner?"

Turner looked at her. "Three Operators were picked up ten miles beyond the perimeter of the Loop. They are now in custody. I can tell you no more than that."

"Jesus," muttered Brennan. "Deserters. I've never heard of anything like that before."

"What are the other factors?" asked Jamie. He had not taken his gaze from Paul Turner, who now turned to look at him.

"I'm sorry, Lieutenant Carpenter?"

"The factors that suggested this wasn't an attack designed to cause panic."

An expression flickered briefly across Turner's face, an expression that it took Jamie a moment to recognise.

Gratitude, he thought. *How about that?*

"Firstly, Lieutenant," said Turner, "we have the location of the device that was detonated. If the culprit is apparently undetectable by our security cameras, why place a bomb in Lieutenant Randall's quarters? Why not place it in the Ops Room, or the dining hall, or underneath the *Mina II*? Any of those targets would have caused far greater damage. What is it about Lieutenant Randall that made her worth targeting?"

"ISAT," said Angela. "You're saying this is about ISAT."

"Oh, come on," said Brennan. "Jarvis is right, this has Valentin written all over it. I don't know whether he was working on his master's orders or on his own initiative, but this was definitely about Dracula."

"Kate doesn't have anything to do with Dracula," said Jamie. "Or Valentin."

"She was there when he defected, wasn't she?" said Brennan. "Or when he supposedly defected, at least. You both talked to him. Maybe she said something he didn't like. Or maybe he just picked a room at random and she was unlucky."

"In which case, Operator Brennan," said Paul Turner, "perhaps you can tell us why an identical explosive device was found in my quarters?"

There was a chorus of gasps from all sides of the table, although Jamie noticed that Cal Holmwood didn't move a muscle.

They were already sure what this was, he thought. *Turner and Holmwood. They already knew. They just let us get there on our own.*

"I don't know," said Brennan. "I can't explain that."

"Lieutenant Darcy already did," said Cal Holmwood. "I'm not going to say that this attack had nothing to do with Dracula, because whoever carried it out may well have a connection to him that becomes clear in due course. And I assure you that *nobody* is ruling out Valentin Rusmanov as a suspect. But the ISAT investigation, the timing, and the locations of the devices add up to a clear picture. This was not a direct attack upon us by the vampires. It was about ISAT. It was someone with something to hide trying to protect themselves."

"So what do we do?" asked Angela Darcy.

"ISAT finishes its investigation," replied Paul Turner. "We are almost a quarter of the way through the roster. Whoever did this has to be someone we haven't questioned yet."

"Agreed," said Holmwood. "I want you to conclude ISAT as

quickly as possible. There's someone extremely dangerous inside this base and we need to find them before they get the chance to act again."

"I have a request," said Jarvis. "I'd like to have Valentin Rusmanov moved to the top of ISAT's interview list. I take your points, both of you, but I don't care, frankly. I don't trust the vampire."

"I'm fine with that," said Holmwood. "If you are, Major Turner?"

"Of course, sir," said Turner, casting a brief, deadly glance in Jarvis's direction. "Interviews will recommence this afternoon and I'm perfectly happy to bring Valentin in first. Maybe then we can stop chasing shadows."

"What about the rest of us?" asked Jack Williams. "What do you want us to do?"

"Carry on," replied Holmwood. "I'll be reactivating all squads within a couple of hours. You have your target lists. Nothing changes."

"Neither of my squad have been through ISAT," said Brennan. "Nor have I, for that matter. Do we still go out?"

"Absolutely," replied Holmwood. "We can't make everyone who hasn't been interviewed inactive, not with what's going on out there. Just be vigilant. Anything out of the ordinary, you call it in. Understood?"

Brennan nodded.

"OK," said Holmwood. "Anything else?"

"Yes, sir," said Angela Darcy. "What about Albert Harker, sir?"

"We believe Harker may be responsible for the murder of a lawyer named Thomas Clarke in north London last night," said the Interim Director. "Clarke was the executor of the estate of John Bathurst, also known as Johnny Supernova, the journalist to whom Albert gave an interview before he was committed. We are still attempting to ascertain whether there was something in Bathurst's estate that Harker may be trying to acquire."

"Maybe he blames the journalist for what happened to him," said Patrick Williams. "With Bathurst dead, maybe he's taking his revenge on people with connections to him."

"That thought has occurred to us," said Turner. "Fortunately, Bathurst's list of known associates only contained one name, a former colleague of his called Kevin McKenna. He has been informed that a recently released prisoner with a grudge against John Bathurst may attempt to make contact with him, and that he is to call the police if so. We're monitoring his mobile phone as a precaution."

"OK," said Patrick. "So we have no idea where Harker is."

"It's highly likely that he has gone to ground," said Turner. "He must know we'll be looking for him."

"I tend to agree," said Cal Holmwood. "Nonetheless, he remains a priority and I'll keep you updated as new information becomes available. As for the rest of the Broadmoor escapees, we're making solid progress. We have seventy-two confirmed destroyed, leaving two hundred and six unaccounted for. All target lists have been updated and the SOP remains in place until this is over."

"Admiral Seward?" asked Jamie, quietly.

"Major Landis has reported no progress on that front, Lieutenant Carpenter. Is there anything *else*?"

There was silence around the table.

"Then that's all," said the Interim Director. "As always, everything that has been said here is Zero Hour classified. However, I would urge you to try to find ways to reassure your teams. We all have jobs to do and this is no time for panic, or for people making mistakes because they're scared. Dismissed."

*

Jamie made his way along the Level B corridor and pressed his ID card against the panel beside the door to his quarters, smiling as he heard the sound of familiar voices from inside his room.

He knew who they belonged to; after the message had come through ordering him to attend the emergency Zero Hour meeting, he had sent one of his own.

No secrets, he thought, and pushed the door open.

Sitting on his bed were Kate Randall and Matt Browning; they had used the override code that opened his door, which both of them knew by heart. They looked up as he entered, narrow smiles on their faces.

"Hey," he said. "What's going on?"

"Not much," said Matt, brightly. "Apart from one of my colleagues getting blown up by a bomb that was meant for one of my friends. How are you?"

Jamie laughed. "Never better," he said, flopping down into the chair beside his desk. "The cameras don't show anyone going in or out of Kate's room yesterday morning, there was a second bomb in Paul Turner's room so he and Cal are convinced that this is all about ISAT, whereas the rest of Zero Hour think it was Valentin. Oh, and nobody has any idea where Albert Harker is. So, yeah, everything's awesome."

"Jesus," said Kate. "There was a bomb in Paul's room?"

Jamie nodded. "They defused it last night."

"Well, that seals it, surely?" said Matt, looking at Kate. "You *and* Major Turner? If this isn't about ISAT, that's an astronomical coincidence."

"I suppose so," said Kate. "Does anyone have any theories?"

Jamie shook his head. "Just that someone has something to hide and is willing to try and kill two Operators to keep it hidden."

"Jesus," said Kate. "I just keep thinking about Natalia. If she'd been badly hurt or—"

"She wasn't, though," interrupted Jamie. "She's going to be fine."

"I know," said Kate. "But the bomb wasn't meant for her, Jamie. She had nothing to do with any of this."

"That's a point," said Matt. "Why *was* she there when it went off? Was she coming to see you or something?"

"I don't know," said Kate.

"OK," said Matt. "But if the bomb went off when your door was opened, then she must have opened it. How did she do that?"

"How am I supposed to know?" snapped Kate. "Ask her yourself when she wakes up."

Take it easy, thought Jamie. *Don't bite his head off.*

"So," he said. "That was the Zero Hour meeting. What's next?"

"I've got to get back to Lazarus," said Matt. "We're short-staffed with Natalia in the infirmary."

"I thought as much," said Jamie. "What about you, Kate?"

"ISAT," she said. "Paul sent me a message telling me we're restarting this afternoon. Although he didn't mention the bomb in his quarters, unsurprisingly. So it's going to be a long day. What about you?"

"I've got to go and have a conversation I really don't want to have," said Jamie.

"With who?" asked Matt.

"One of my rookies," said Jamie. "John Morton."

"I heard you brought your squad back early," said Kate. "Is everything OK?"

"I don't know," said Jamie. "He missed a shot when we were taking out our first target, then started talking about vampires, how they aren't right, how what we did wasn't right. I asked Holmwood to bench him, but he wouldn't go for it. I got him to authorise a psych evaluation, though, so now I have to go and tell Morton. Which should be fun."

"I bet," said Kate.

"Speaking of fun," he said, smiling broadly, "you're in for a treat this afternoon. You and Major Turner."

Kate frowned. "What are you talking about?"

"You'll find out soon enough," said Jamie.

33

PLAYING WITH FIRE

Larissa knocked on the door of Tim Albertsson's quarters and waited for the Special Operator to appear.

She had slept well, surprisingly; tiredness had apparently overwhelmed the unease that had filled her in the aftermath of Tim's attempt to kiss her. She had looked at her body in the mirror after getting out of the shower, seen the round patch of new skin on her stomach that was paler than the rest, and forgiven herself for the exhaustion she had felt in the gym. She sometimes forgot that her body regularly endured extremes that would kill a regular human being; to her, it had come to seem bizarrely normal.

There was no response to her knock, and no sounds of movement from within Tim's room, so she gave up. Her console displayed no orders, and there were no training sessions scheduled for the day, so she had intended to clear the air with Tim, then round up the others and enjoy a few hours of well-earned time off. She tapped a message into her console as she walked along the corridor of

Level 3, asking her friends where they were. As she waited for the elevator, the first reply beeped on to her screen.

> Morning, gorgeous. In San Diego till early afternoon checking out the new SEAL intake. Kara and Danny here too. Be good without me. Tim

Larissa winced as she read it.

On the one hand, the tone of the message was no different to the dozens of others Tim had sent her, suggesting he was not annoyed with her, as she had feared he might be. On the other, the message was so blatantly flirtatious that she was instantly furious with herself for having taken so long to understand the situation.

I have to talk to him when he gets back, she thought. *As soon as he gets back.*

Her console beeped again and she thumbed the screen. Two more messages appeared, one above the other.

> In Intelligence training. Might see you later. Aaron

> Still in Colorado. Leaving soon, God willing. Kelly

Larissa smiled, and slipped the console back into its loop on her belt.

Kelly had been part of the response team despatched to Colorado to deal with the aftermath of the Supermax breakout; she had been due to come home the previous day, but her orders had been changed at the last minute. She hadn't been able to tell them why – everything to do with the prison break was Zero Hour restricted, a classification that all the supernatural Departments of the world had adopted – but her demeanour had suggested that it was not something she was relishing.

Larissa sent a group message telling them to look after themselves, then stepped into the lift and pressed the button marked 0. A minute later she stepped into the wide, semicircular hangar and looked out across the long-dry expanse of Papoose Lake. It was barely eight thirty in the morning, but the temperature outside was already in the high nineties and rising. By lunchtime it would be well into three figures, the sun beating down with such ferocity that it would burn regular skin within minutes; her own vulnerable flesh would erupt in an inferno of purple fire if a single ray of the bright desert light touched it.

The shade extended a metre or two beyond the edge of the hangar; its shimmering edge marked the border of her habitable world. She stared at it, painfully aware of the limitations that had been imposed upon her; she had made peace with her condition, had even managed to find ways to enjoy certain aspects of it, but the rational part of her still ultimately viewed it as a curse, a prison cell that followed her wherever she went. Her vampire side, the part of her that she increasingly thought of as almost a different person, cared little about such things, was interested only in blood and violence. She tried not to spend too much time thinking about it, and was grateful for the thought that suddenly arrived in her head, lifting her heart and brightening her mood.

I've got a day off. For the first time in what feels like forever, there's absolutely nothing I'm supposed to be doing.

The realisation washed over her like cool water. She knew there was a good chance that orders would appear on her console later in the day, but she would deal with them if and when they arrived; as of right now, she was free. And, as she stared at the burning white salt of Papoose Lake, she realised there *was* something she wanted to do.

Ten minutes later she was back in her quarters, logging in to the NS9 network. She had been given access the day she arrived, a gesture she had taken as a somewhat surprising show of trust, even allowing for the new spirit of togetherness among the supernatural Departments. She had expected to find her access limited, the way a guest user is restricted to certain areas of a system, but had been pleased to find the entire NS9 network open to her. She had barely used it, as her time had been spent largely either in the training rooms or with her friends. But she was using it now, to search for any information on the prisoner in the cell, the prisoner whose existence was not officially acknowledged.

Larissa had talked to an Operator from the NS9 Security Division at the bar in the bowling alley that sat on the other side of the mountain, and asked him about the prisoner outright. The man's eyes had widened, before he quickly denied the existence of any such prisoner. Larissa had persisted, applying a combination of her English accent and several deep glasses of rye whiskey to the increasingly helpless Operator. She reassured him that she didn't expect him to tell her *who* the prisoner was, as she moved her stool so that her leg rested against his. She didn't want to get anyone into trouble. All she wanted to know was the date the prisoner had arrived at Dreamland. Anyone could have told her that. No one would ever know it had been him. Eventually, the Operator had given in; she had thanked him, kissed him on the cheek, and left him staring at his glass with a look of profound confusion on his face.

Larissa opened the security logs and entered the date the Operator had given her. The prisoner had to have arrived at the base somehow and had likely not been expected, given the general alarm that Kelly had told her had sounded briefly on the day in question. She was hopeful that the records of the unscheduled arrival might still exist.

The system returned the results, for a Wednesday fourteen weeks earlier. There were two main columns, for arrivals and departures to and from the base, each containing a list of entries. Most appeared in both columns; these were squads departing on Operations and returning home when they were done. There were several entries in the departures column that had no counterpart in arrivals; these, Larissa assumed, were Operators being sent on longer-term missions, such as the one that Kelly was currently on in Colorado. She was sure that if she checked the subsequent days, the listings would eventually reappear in the arrivals column.

On the day she was interested in there were only two entries in the arrivals column without counterpart departures. One looked the same as almost all the rest: a string of Operator identification numbers, an operational reference and the access code and entry vector used by a vehicle entering the restricted airspace around Dreamland. This was most likely a returning mission that had departed on a previous day. The other entry, however, was quite different.

Where there should have been at least one ID number, there was merely an empty space. Where the Operational reference should have been was also blank, and instead of an entry vector, the word GATE 1 had been entered into the record. The access code that had been recorded was also different, unlike those recorded in every other entry for that day.

That's him, she thought, excitedly. *Whoever he is, that's him. That's when he arrived.*

Larissa wrote down the access code on a scrap of paper, closed the logs, and opened the security rota schedule. This was a large spreadsheet, listing every guard point and security position across the entirety of the Dreamland site; it was a vast document, as it applied not just to NS9, but also to the Air Force detachments at Groom Lake and throughout the entire White Sands Missile Range. There were more than a hundred entry points listed, ranging from traditional barriers and guard houses to underground sentry posts that watched over the subterranean installations where the truly unpleasant work was being done: chemical and biological weapons, low-yield nuclear research, next-generation fission weapons, all of it in direct breach of dozens of international treaties, all of it carrying on far beyond the range of even the most sophisticated satellite.

She was looking for the rota for Gate 1, the guard post and barrier that controlled access from the long road that led west from highway 375 and was referred to by Area 51 conspiracy fans as the Front Gate. It was on government land, hidden from the public beyond signs that warned the curious not to go any further.

He came in there? wondered Larissa. *By road? That's weird.*

She found the right column and scrolled down until she reached the date she was looking for. On duty at the Front Gate that day had been an Air Force Senior Airman named Lee Ashworth. Larissa closed the spreadsheet and entered Ashworth's name into the personnel directory; it returned his file immediately. She scanned quickly down to the key line of information: Senior Airman Ashworth's current posting.

Please don't let him have moved. Please.

POSTING: Edwards AFB Detachment 559. GOLD
SQUADRON. Groom Lake.

Larissa looked at the man's photo, memorised his face, and logged out of the network. A minute later she was standing at the end of the Level 3 corridor, floating impatiently up and down as she waited for the elevator to arrive.

She got out on Level 1 and walked quickly down its main corridor; her destination lay at the opposite end of the base, beyond a heavy metal door.

Tim Albertsson had shown her the tunnel on her second day in the desert.

He had been ordered by General Allen to show her around and let her get a feel for the place. The functional stuff had taken barely half a day: the dining hall, the gym, her quarters, the Briefing Rooms and the hangar. With the official tour concluded, Tim had shown her what he called "the fun stuff": the weapons ranges, the creepy, long-abandoned research labs sealed away on the lower levels, and the tunnel.

It was more than half a mile long, running directly beneath the mountain range that separated Groom Lake from Papoose Lake, and emerged inside the complex of buildings the outside world referred to as Area 51. It was part of a wide network of tunnels, covered walkways and canopies that had been installed to shield the installation's men and women from the increasingly advanced eyes of the spy satellites that orbited overhead, and now served a purpose that its designers would likely never have envisaged: allowing Larissa to move around the vast majority of the two bases in broad daylight.

She reached the heavy door and ran her ID card over the panel beside it. Electromagnetic locks disengaged and the door swung open on well-oiled hinges. Larissa stepped through, pulled it shut behind her, then rose into the air and accelerated. She shot forward with a speed that would have been dizzying to any watching human eyes; one moment she was motionless in the air, the next she was a streak of black and glowing red. The half-mile of tunnel passed below and around her in less than five seconds; she slid gracefully to a halt in front of a door that was the mirror of the one she had just come through, unlocked it with her ID card, and emerged into a circular holding area made of flat, gleaming metal.

"Remain still," ordered an electronic voice.

Larissa did as she was told; in the walls and ceiling machines were scanning her identification chip, taking photos, and logging the time of her entry.

"Proceed," said the voice, after a short pause. She fought back the ridiculous urge to say thank you and walked through the door that had slid open in front of her.

This led her into Groom Lake Central Control, a large round room full of radar monitoring equipment, seismic read-outs and screen after screen of satellite imagery. One of the Duty Officers looked up as she entered, and nodded; the staff of Central Control had become quite used to her arriving this way. She nodded back, and asked the woman where she might find Gold Squadron.

"Building B12," replied the Duty Officer. "Do you know where that is?"

"I'll find it," she replied.

B12 was a low, rectangular building near the centre of the complex and posed no access problems for Larissa; the route to its door was entirely covered by a wide central canopy, shielding her from the blazing late morning sun. Gold Squadron occupied a wide arrangement of open-plan desks and a row of offices that ran along the back wall of the building. There was a hum of activity as Larissa pushed open the door, a steady stream of radio chatter and the steady beeping of a number of radar screens. She walked up to the nearest desk and said hello to the woman sitting behind it.

"Oh, hi," replied the woman. For a second, she seemed startled, then extended her hand. "You're Larissa, aren't you? I'm Carla Monroe."

She shook the hand and nodded. "Larissa Kinley," she said.

"Good to meet you," said Carla. "Can I help you with something? I don't mean to be rude, but we're pretty swamped right now. We're live testing today."

"What are you flying?" asked Larissa.

"F-71 prototypes," replied Carla. "We're opening them up to fifty per cent, so everyone's a bit on edge."

"How fast is fifty per cent?"

"About Mach 5.3."

"Wow."

"Yeah."

"In that case," said Larissa, smiling broadly, "I won't take up any more of your time. I'm looking for Senior Airman Ashworth."

"Second office on the left at the back," said Monroe, pointing towards a wooden door near the far end of the room. "He's our Air Force Test Centre liaison, so I wouldn't disturb him unless it's urgent. He gets a bit short-tempered when we're live."

"I'll bear that in mind," said Larissa. She gave Carla Monroe a final smile and set off across the long room. When she reached the door, she knocked sharply on it and pushed it open; she didn't want to give the Senior Airman the option of refusing to answer.

"Who the hell are you?" demanded a loud voice before she had even closed the door behind her. Lee Ashworth was sitting behind his desk beneath a narrow window; he was a slender man in his mid-twenties with a shock of unruly black hair, a flushed face, and eyes that seemed full of instant dislike. He looked, in her opinion, like a man who was extremely stressed.

"I'm Larissa Kinley," she replied. "NS9."

"Is that supposed to impress me?" snorted Ashworth.

"No," said Larissa. "You asked, so I told you."

Ashworth eyed her for a second or two, then grunted. "What do you want, Kinley?" he asked. "We're in the middle of a live flight test and my shift ends in exactly two hundred and four minutes, so you'll forgive me if I'm not in the mood to chat."

"This won't take long, I promise. I just wanted to ask you about the man that came through Gate 1 on January 22nd. As soon as you tell me who he was, I'll be on my way."

Ashworth's eyes widened, and the red in his cheeks deepened alarmingly. "How do you know about him?" he asked.

"I don't," replied Larissa. "That's why I want you to tell me."

"Is this some kind of joke? Do you know what they'll do to me if they find out I talked about that?"

"They won't find out," said Larissa. "I'm not trying to cause trouble, I just need to know who he is. I think he might be important."

"I don't know who he is," said Ashworth. "That's the truth."

"I believe you," said Larissa. "I just want you to tell me what you *do* know. I'll find out the rest myself."

"Maybe you will," said Ashworth. "But you won't get any help from me. Now get the hell out of my office."

Larissa didn't move; she merely stared at the Senior Airman, allowing an uncomfortable atmosphere to steadily build. Ashworth's desk was neat, almost obsessively so; the files and folders and sheets of paper were equally spaced, their edges perfectly aligned. The only concession to anything personal was a photograph of a pretty blonde woman with her arms round two grinning children.

"All right," she said, eventually. "We'll talk soon."

"Not if I have anything to say about it," said Ashworth.

She gave him her best smile, then turned and left the small office.

Getting closer, she thought, as she left building B12. *I'm on to you, whoever the hell you are.*

Larissa was so lost in thought that she didn't hear the chorus of voices shouting her name from across the central plaza of the complex. She didn't become aware that there was anyone near her until a hand dropped on to her shoulder and her vampire side reacted. Her eyes flooded red, her fangs burst in place, and she grabbed the hand and threw whoever it belonged to through the air. Before they had even hit the ground, she had spun round, eyes blazing, teeth bared, to find herself looking at three of her friends.

"Jesus Christ, Larissa," said Kara, her eyes wide with shock.

Larissa looked at Kelly and Danny, who were standing beside their friend, and saw similar expressions on their faces. Then she heard a low groan from behind her; she felt the red disappear from her eyes and her fangs retract as she turned to see what she had done, to see who she had hurt this time.

"That's quite an arm you've got there," said Tim Albertsson, a smile rising on his face. He was sitting on the tarmac, rotating one of his shoulders, checking the range of movement. His uniform was covered in dust, but he was looking at her with bemusement, rather than the anger she had been expecting.

"Jesus," she breathed, hot shame flooding through her. "Tim, I'm so sorry. I was in a world of my own and then you... I'm really, really sorry."

"It's OK," he said, getting slowly to his feet. "No harm done. My fault anyway, I shouldn't have surprised you like that. I wasn't thinking."

I'm like a wild animal, thought Larissa, through a dark fog of self-loathing. *There are rules for handling me.*

Tim stepped forward, threw an arm round her shoulder, and faced the rest of her friends. Kara's eyes had returned to normal, as Kelly and Danny began to smile, but there was still palpable unease in the air.

"No harm done," repeated Tim. "Don't sneak up on her, that's my advice to the three of you. You'll be taking your lives in your hands." He grinned, and Larissa felt a wave of gratitude crash through her. Kara laughed, Danny and Kelly's smiles turned into grins and, just like that, everything was all right.

Thank you, she thought, casting a glance at Tim. His arm was still round her shoulder, but she thought she could tolerate it, for a little while at least.

"How was Colorado?" she asked.

"Cold," replied Kelly, shaking her head. "Full of vampires."

"San Diego was sunny and full of barely dressed Navy SEALs," said Kara. "In case that makes you feel any better?"

Kelly flipped her friend the finger and smiled.

"So," said Tim, his attention still focused on Larissa. "Now that we've found you, we need to get you back to Dreamland asap."

"Orders?" she asked.

Kara shook her head. "We've been given a forty-eight-hour furlough."

"Furlough?"

"Forty-eight hours off, Larissa," said Tim, and checked his watch. "Which officially started seventy-three minutes ago. So we need to hurry. It's almost a two-hour drive to Vegas."

"Vegas?" asked Larissa. "We're going to Las Vegas?"

"Well, *we* are," said Kelly, looking round at her colleagues. "But we were hoping you might want to come with us. What do you say?"

Larissa frowned. "Why would General Allen give us two days off? There are still Supermax escapees out there, we're right in the middle of training the rookie intake, and—"

"Who cares?" interrupted Kara. "Let's just get the hell out of here before he changes his mind."

"It doesn't make any sense, though," persisted Larissa. "You don't even work together. Why would the five of us get furlough at the same time?"

"You know why," said Tim, smiling gently at her. "You're just not saying it."

Larissa thought it through. If Allen had given Tim and his Special Operations Squad time off after Nuevo Laredo, it would still have surprised her, but it would have at least made sense. But there was nothing that united the four people standing in front of her, apart from the fact that they were—

"This is because we're friends," she said, slowly. "Isn't it?"

"Of course it is," said Tim. "You know the Director adores you and you're not going to be here for long. This is a gift, from him to you. We just get to come along. So, as you can imagine, we're pretty keen for you to agree to our plan."

"But there are things that need doing," said Larissa. "I don't see how we can—"

"Look, it's really simple," said Kelly, cutting across her. "If the Director didn't think the Department could survive without us for two days, he wouldn't be letting us go. So why don't you trust him to know what he's doing, come with us to Vegas, and thank him when we get back. What do you say?"

A grin emerged on Larissa's face, huge and happy. "I say yes."

34

THE SUM OF OUR PARTS

"Are you benching me?" asked John Morton. "You are, aren't you?"

Jamie shook his head, trying to buy time. He hadn't expected the rookie to so quickly work out why his squad leader had come up to the Level A dormitory to see him. "No," he said. "That's not what's happening. But you should know, because I wouldn't want you to hear it from anyone else, that I asked the Interim Director to place you on the inactive roster. He refused."

Morton stared. "You don't want me on your squad?"

"That's not true," said Jamie. "What I want is you at your best, ready to face what's out there. And I don't think that's where you are."

"I'm fine," said the rookie. He pushed his chair back from his desk and turned it to face his squad leader. "Really, sir. I'm fine."

"I don't think you are," said Jamie, softly. "I think you're scared." He saw colour begin to rise in Morton's cheeks and moved to defuse the situation. "It's not a criticism, John. It takes people different amounts of time to adjust to being part of Blacklight, to come to terms with the reality you get shown. There's no shame in it."

"I've been scared, Jamie," said Morton. "I *know* scared. This is something else."

But you admit there is something, thought Jamie. *That's a start, at least.*

"What is it then?" he asked. "It will stay between us."

Morton looked down at his hands for a long moment. "Afghanistan," he said, eventually. "Last summer I was attached to a Recon Marine battalion, working the mountains in Helmand. I saw everything you can imagine, and probably stuff you can't. Dead kids, men who'd been tortured over hearsay, women who'd been gang-raped for teaching girls to read. We came into this village one morning, where three Taliban fighters were supposed to be holed up. We'd pounded the area all night, drone strikes from twenty miles away. I don't know how many missiles, maybe fifty, maybe a hundred. I don't know. We had air surveillance at both ends of the valley and they confirmed that no one had got out, in any direction.

"So, when dawn came, they sent the six of us in. We came over the rise at the head of the valley, and where the village had been there was just rubble and dust. Nothing standing, nothing moving. We just walked right down the middle of the track, because there was no way anything could have lived through what the drones had done, and we found the first body about twenty metres outside the village. It was an old woman, gone below the waist, just a spray of blood. She was face down in the dust. There was a square in the middle of where the village had been, a little patch of dust not much bigger than this room. Two kids were lying on the ground, holding hands. Both dead. In the ruins of the buildings we found more bodies, bits of bodies really, almost all of them children, some women. Maybe two or three men, old and grey, beards down to their knees.

"We finished our sweep on the other side of the village, where we found a dead teenage boy and the only thing that had survived, this mangy little dog. It was eating the dead boy, chewing at a hole in his stomach. One of the Marines, a guy called Brody, shot the dog and we headed back to our extraction point. Thirty-four dead was the final count. Thirteen women, four men, counting the teenager, and seventeen kids. No sign of the fighters, and when we got back to Bastion no one could show us the intelligence that had suggested they were there. So it got written up and the CIA redacted most of it and suppressed what was left, and two days later they gave me a medal and a week later I came home. That was seven months ago."

"Jesus," said Jamie. "That's awful."

"Right," said Morton. "I saw other stuff that was almost as bad, but that was the worst. It was like they weren't people any more, and I don't just mean because they were dead. They weren't whole, they were broken. Do you know what I'm trying to say?"

Jamie thought of the terrorised, mutilated monks of the Lindisfarne Priory, the men and women who had been abused and tortured for the entertainment of the membership of *La Fraternité de la Nuit*, and nodded his head. "I know," he said, softly. "Believe me."

Morton stared at him for a long moment, then smiled a thin, painful smile. "I do," he said. "You can tell when people have seen things they can't forget. It does something to their eyes. Yours have it. I was scared in Afghanistan, and in Iraq before that. If you weren't scared, you were either an idiot or you were lying. But that wasn't the problem yesterday. I can't explain it."

"Try," said Jamie.

"The vampires," said Morton, slowly. "They're... wrong. That's the best I can do. I've faced people who wanted to kill me, and I've been in situations where I could have died, more than I can count. I'm not afraid of dying. But with them... it's like they're not

373

real. Or they shouldn't be. But they are, and it doesn't seem right. None of this feels right, sir."

"You just need more time," said Jamie. "You'll get your head round it, I know you will."

"Ellison already has," said Morton. "She was born to do this, like you. Maybe I wasn't. Maybe that's just the truth of it."

"No one was born to do this," said Jamie. "You're being too hard on yourself, John. You missed a shot, you started beating yourself up about it and you overthought everything. It happens. It won't be the last shot you miss, and that's not what worries me. What worries me is what you said afterwards. I can't have someone on my squad who is conflicted about whether destroying vampires is a good idea."

Morton nodded. "I get that," he said, his voice low.

The two Operators sat for a long moment. Eventually, Jamie broke the silence. "Do you think you should be on the active roster? Be honest with me."

Morton looked at him. "I don't know. What do you think?"

"You know what I think."

"I want to help," said Morton. "I don't want to be sat here while everyone else is out there fighting. That's not me, sir."

"You're not helping if I have to worry about you every second we're out there," said Jamie. "You can see that, can't you?"

"I can," said Morton.

Jamie stared at the rookie, then rubbed his eyes and sighed. "The Director says you stay active," he said. "So you stay active. That doesn't mean I won't leave you in the van if I think it's necessary."

"I understand, sir."

"And I'm sending you down to the Science Division for a psych evaluation. Non-negotiable."

"When?"

"Right now. As soon as we're done here. They're expecting you."

"OK," said Morton. "Anything else?"

"No," said Jamie. "We'll talk again when the psych results come back. As for right now, you're still in my squad. Is that what you want?"

"Yes, sir," said Morton. "Thank you. Sir."

Jamie was waiting outside the Level A lift when his console vibrated in his pocket. He fished it out, grateful for the distraction from his own thoughts; he had been expecting Morton to get angry, to threaten him, possibly even try to attack him. The rookie's quiet, uncertain demeanour had somehow been far more troubling.

He saw the message icon glowing on the console's screen and thumbed the screen into life.

ALL/OPERATIONAL_SQUADS_REACTIVATED/ SCHEDULES_TO_FOLLOW

About time, thought Jamie. *The lockdown already cost us a whole night.*

The console beeped again in his hand and a second message appeared. His squad's updated schedule flashed up and he read through it quickly. The Surveillance Division had identified the second vampire on their list as a middle-aged escapee by the name of Alastair Dempsey, and pinpointed a probable location in Central London. Operational Squad M-3 were scheduled to depart at 1600 hours to continue their mission.

Jamie checked his watch and saw that he had almost five hours to kill. He forwarded the schedule to his squad mates with a note telling them to meet him in the hangar at 1545, thought about reminding Morton that his involvement was conditional on the results of his psych evaluation, and decided against it. The rookie's confidence was already shaken and he didn't think any good would come of labouring the point. When the lift arrived, he pressed the button marked H, leant against the wall and closed his eyes.

A minute later Jamie stepped out of the airlock that controlled access to the Blacklight detention block. He nodded to the Operator sitting inside the control station and set off down the long corridor, his boot heels clicking against the smooth surface of the floor.

He fixed his gaze on the wall at the far end of the block as he passed the cells that held Valentin and his valet, Lamberton. Out of the very corner of his eye, he noticed the youngest Rusmanov watching him as he passed, but forced himself to keep going.

Not today. Go and see your mum, for God's sake.

As he approached the last cell on the left, the sweet smell of raspberry tea floated through the ultraviolet wall and into his nostrils, triggering a wave of nostalgia so sharp it was almost painful; it carried memories of the kitchen in their old house, the table where he had done his homework while he and his mum waited for his dad to come home from a job at the Ministry of Defence that had never actually existed. What his father had actually spent his days doing had been very different, a reality neither he nor his mother had become aware of until long after Julian Carpenter was dead.

Jamie stepped out in front of the UV wall and smiled. His mother was sitting on the sofa, sipping her tea from the cup and saucer he had bought her for Christmas when he was twelve and working on a crossword. She looked up before he said a word and smiled at him.

"Hello, love," she said. "Come in."

Jamie stepped through the barrier, feeling the familiar tingle on his skin as he did so. "How are you, Mum?" he asked. He leant down and gave her a hug that she returned in her usual careful manner. "You OK?"

"I'm fine," she replied, letting go of him and clearing the space beside her on the sofa. "How are you? Is everything all right upstairs?"

"Just about," said Jamie, flopping down next to her. "I can't tell you what happened, but I'm fine. So are Kate and Matt."

"The walls shook," said Marie. Her face was suddenly pale with worry. "It sounded like a bomb going off."

"I can't tell you anything, Mum," said Jamie, his tone a little sharper than he had intended. "You know that."

"I do," replied Marie. "I thought you might have let me know you were all right, though. I was worried."

Jamie felt heat rise in his cheeks, as shame and guilt fought for position in the pit of his stomach.

The blast shook the entire base, he thought, *and she's been down here on her own wondering what happened. I could have been dead for all she knew.*

"I'm sorry," he said. "I didn't think."

"You never do," replied Marie. Her tone was cool, but not angry; it sounded full of disappointment. "I love you Jamie, more than anything in the world, and I know you're busy and I know how important what you do is. But I'm your mum and I worry about you. I'm sorry if that's a burden."

Jamie felt tears threatening to well up in the corners of his eyes. "It's not," he said, in a strangled voice. "I really am sorry, Mum. They locked the base down overnight, but I should have come down first thing this morning. I didn't mean for you to worry."

She smiled at him, an expression so full of love that his heart felt like it would burst from his chest. "I know you didn't, Jamie," she said. "I never think that you don't care, I promise you I don't. And I'm *so* proud of you. Just spare me a thought now and again, OK?"

"I will," replied Jamie. His insides felt like they were on fire, set ablaze by a volatile combination of shame, self-loathing and unconditional love. "I'll try harder, Mum. I promise."

35

GOING UNDERGROUND

FOUR HOURS LATER

"Jesus," said Lizzy Ellison. "I wish I hadn't read that."

The van containing Operational Squad M-3 was cruising south, eating up the miles that lay between it and the capital. Ellison and Morton had both finished scanning through copies of their target's Broadmoor file, their faces turning increasingly pale as they did so. Jamie was still attempting to process both his conversation with his mother and the results of Morton's psych evaluation, and had been glad of something to keep his squad mates occupied, even something as grisly as the story of Alastair Dempsey.

Eighteen years earlier, Dempsey's sister and her husband had taken a two-week holiday on Fuerteventura, leaving their eight-year-old daughter in his care. This was a regular occurrence, and both Sharon and Nick counted themselves lucky to have a relative who was not only willing to babysit Beth, but who was also both a primary school teacher and a St John Ambulance volunteer. They had returned home, rested and relaxed, and picked their daughter up from her uncle's house. She seemed a little quieter than usual, but Sharon put it down to sadness at being made to come home; Alastair had always been his niece's favourite.

The following morning, Beth told Sharon that there was a ghost lady living in the walls of her uncle's house, and that she must be sad, because she cried at night when Beth was in bed. Sharon asked her if she was pretending and Beth swore on the life of her hamster that she wasn't. She asked her daughter if she had told her uncle about the ghost lady in the walls and Beth said no, because she could only hear her through a crack in the floor beneath her bed and she didn't think her Uncle Alastair would believe her.

When he got home from work that night, Sharon told her husband, who laughed. Beth had an active imagination, sometimes annoyingly so, and Nick believed this was nothing more than one of her stories. Sharon told him he was probably right, but couldn't quite put it out of her mind; the image of a woman trapped inside the walls of her brother's small detached house was such a horrible one. Two days later she had lunch with Alastair and told him what her daughter had said. They laughed about it, and agreed that Beth should be a writer when she grew up. Sharon didn't give the ghost lady another thought until the following Sunday, when she went to collect Alastair for their monthly visit to the nursing home where their mother lived, and found his house empty.

After twenty-four hours, in which a series of increasingly anxious calls to her brother's phone went unanswered, and his neighbours, with whom he had been friendly, confirmed that he hadn't mentioned any upcoming trips away, Sharon rang the police, who broke down the door of the small house he had lived in for almost twenty years. Inside, they found a hidden door standing open in the hallway, a door leading down to a basement that neither Sharon nor Nick had known existed. The small underground space was painted black, lined with cameras and recording equipment, and home to several racks of medical implements and power tools. In the centre of the room, hanging from an intricate arrangement of harnesses and pulleys, they found a young woman.

She was long dead and he was long gone.

Within six hours, Alastair Dempsey was the most wanted man in the country. His photo was plastered across every evening newspaper and television bulletin, and the following morning the tabloids exploded with an avalanche of outrage and fury, demanding that he be caught, warning the public over and over that there was a monster out there, searching for his next victim.

Six days after the hidden basement and its contents were discovered, Dempsey was caught at Dover, trying to board a ferry to France. He ran when he saw the armed police, but cornered against a freight container, with guns pointing at his chest, he gave up and went quietly.

His trial the following year was a media circus; twice he was attacked in the dock, leading the judge to take the extraordinary step of banning the public from his courtroom. Alastair Dempsey was charged with a single murder, that of the woman found in his basement, eventually identified as a prostitute named Anna Bailey, but was investigated in connection with more than thirty-five other missing persons, all women, all of whom had disappeared in the fifteen years prior to his arrest. And although none were conclusively linked to him, the Senior Investigating Officer on the case made it clear, in a number of classified memos, that he believed Dempsey had been involved in as many as twenty of them.

The man himself spoke only twice during the trial, to confirm his name and address. He refused to answer any questions, by either the prosecuting or defending QCs, and showed no emotion whatsoever when he was committed to a secure psychiatric unit for the rest of his life, a sentence that provoked the famous THROW AWAY THE KEY headline that filled *The Globe*'s front page the following morning, and which had now been cut short by supernatural intervention.

The three Operators sat in the back of the van, watching evening arrive in the capital via the cameras that were hidden in all four sides of the vehicle's bodywork.

In front of them stood the glass and concrete of King's College London; through the van's external microphones Jamie could hear the laughter and chatter of students leaving the building and making their way along the Strand, and the steady thud of music from the students' union at the bottom of Surrey Street.

"I can't stay here, sir," said their driver, over the intercom. "Not for more than a couple more minutes."

"No problem," said Jamie. "Just waiting for a clear moment to deploy."

He sympathised with the driver; the large black vehicle was far too conspicuous to park on a busy Central London street. As soon as his passengers disembarked, he would take the van to a less busy part of the city, and wait for the order to return and pick them up. The problem facing Jamie was that he and his squad mates were also highly visible, and he had no desire for them to be on the street for a second longer than was necessary. He checked the screens again, waiting for the foot traffic to die down, for a gap in which they could approach their destination.

Aldwych station, which still bore its original name, Strand station, had been part of a branch of the Piccadilly line that had closed in 1994. The station itself was now a listed building, and the tunnels and platforms that lay intact beneath it were regularly used as locations for films and television programmes. It had been the subject of several reinvention and reinvigoration schemes, none of which had made it through the labyrinthine mess of bureaucratic red tape that stymied so many of the capital's projects. "Surveillance are sure he's in there?" asked Ellison.

"So they say," said Jamie.

"How do they know?" she asked. "I get that our satellites can track vampires by their heat signature, but almost three hundred escaped from Broadmoor in about half an hour. There can't be that many satellites up there."

"There aren't," said Jamie. "Surveillance logged every escapee, but there's no way they can track them all. They'll be following as many as they can, at least one from each squad's target list, and checking back in with the rest, cross-referencing them with hits from CCTV cameras around the country. When a squad destroys a tracked target, Surveillance will search for another one from their list and do a search based on last sightings, or on the direction they were headed last time they were logged. As soon as they find them, they'll start tracking them."

"So they tracked Dempsey all the way here from Broadmoor?" asked Ellison.

Jamie shook his head. "They tracked Eric Bingham all the way to Peterborough," he said. "When we destroyed him, they tried to identify another one of the vamps on our list. Alastair Dempsey showed up on CCTV about a mile away from here last night, but we were locked down, so they tracked him here. They lost him when he went underground, but the plans show a closed system of tunnels, making this the only way in or out. They'd have seen him if he came back up."

"There's no such thing as a closed system," said Morton. "There'll be escape hatches, and air vents, and emergency staircases. He could be anywhere by now."

Jamie gave his squad mate a long look. "You may be right, Operator," he said. "But Surveillance has got this area covered for ten miles in every direction, and there's only a mile of tunnel down there. So—"

"Those tunnels lead into other tunnels," interrupted Morton. "And those lead into others, and so on and so on. He could be anywhere in London by now and you know it."

"If you think going down there is pointless," said Jamie, his voice steady, "you're more than welcome to stay in the van."

The rookie stared at him, then shook his head, slowly.

Morton had been cleared for Operations by the Science Division psychiatrist little more than an hour before the squad headed out. The assessment that had arrived on Jamie's console had been frustratingly brief, and seemed more interested in the need for able bodies to take part in Operations than the mental state of its subject. He had requested more detail and eventually received a radio call from the psychiatrist who insisted that the rookie was fine. Morton was apparently a deep thinker with an unusually well-developed conscience, attributes, the psychiatrist suggested in a maddeningly patronising tone, that Jamie should perhaps be looking to harness rather than complain about.

The man himself had been sullen ever since arriving in the hangar, and had said very little during the journey from the Loop to London. He had not been rude or genuinely insubordinate; he had answered questions, although his answers had largely been limited to single words, and he had given the appearance of listening to the briefing update. Jamie believed his pride had been dealt a blow by the psych evaluation, which could end up being a good thing; if it made him determined to prove Jamie wrong, it could work to the squad's advantage. But, as he looked at Morton, sitting stiffly in his seat in the back of the van, he was far from sure.

"We work with the information we have," he said, forcing as much calm into his voice as he possibly could. "And Surveillance says he's down there. So until we've checked every inch of those tunnels and found nothing, we're going to assume they're right. Is that clear?"

"Yes, sir," said Morton.

"Good," said Jamie. "Are you ready?"

"Yes, sir."

"Ellison?"

The third member of Operational Squad M-3, who had been watching the conversation between Morton and Jamie with gathering unease on her face, nodded. "I'm ready, sir. What's the plan?"

"Right through the front door," said Jamie. He had turned his attention back to the monitors and seen what he was looking for: a moment in which the pavement outside their vehicle had fallen quiet. "Move out."

He threw open the van's back door; cool air rushed in as Morton leapt out on to the temporarily empty pavement. Ellison went after him, the flicker of a smile on her face as she did so. Jamie followed them, slamming the door shut behind him, and strode quickly across to the pale stone façade of the station where his squad mates were waiting for him.

The two padlocks hanging from the security grille covering the station's red metal doors were intact, and covered with a thin layer of dust; it was clear that no one had entered the station by conventional means in at least a number of weeks. Jamie glanced upwards and instantly saw what he had been expecting: a broken window on the third floor.

That's how he went in. So he was here, even if Morton is right and he's gone.

Ellison pulled a small cylinder from her pocket and sprayed liquid nitrogen over the padlock. There was a crackling sound, like milk hitting breakfast cereal, before she reversed the cylinder and brought its pointed end down on the centre of the lock. The metal shattered, tumbling to the pavement in a hundred jagged pieces. Morton reached between the bars, unwound the chain, and pushed one of the doors open.

The ticket hall had once been grand, and some of that grandeur still remained in the green and cream tiling, the carved wood around the ticket windows, the high ceilings and arched openings. But dust now covered everything, and evidence of the functional use of the building was everywhere: piles of cables, extension leads, yellowed printouts of script pages and call sheets.

Jamie called for torches and ordered Morton to lead them through the empty ticket barriers and towards the long-stationary escalators that would take them underground. A single lift remained in working order, for transporting equipment and lazy actors and directors down to the platforms, but it was sealed shut. Jamie would not have used it in any case; he wanted to be able to see his surroundings at all times.

Jamie followed Morton, with Ellison close behind, her MP5 in her hands. He had not drawn a weapon, but his fingers were resting within easy reach of the grip of his T-Bone. They rounded a sharp corner, the beams from their torches sweeping from side to side, illuminating the green tiles of the old station walls. Then Morton raised a single clenched fist, ordering them to stop.

"What is it?" asked Jamie, his voice low.

"Door," replied Morton. "Broken open."

He stepped forward, pointing for Ellison to stay where she was. The corridor widened to accommodate the three escalators that filled it, and white wooden doors were set into the walls on both sides. One of these was hanging open, its lock splintered and dangling by a few narrow splinters.

"Check it," said Jamie.

Morton nodded, drew his T-Bone, and crept silently forward. He reached the door and pulled it towards him with the barrel of his weapon. It creaked once, then swung on its one remaining hinge, revealing a storeroom full of empty metal cages. Jamie stepped up to the doorway, his T-Bone against his shoulder, as Morton entered the storeroom, twisting and crouching to shine his torch up at the ceiling and the high corners of the room.

"Door," he whispered.

Jamie nodded and stepped through the doorway. At the end of the storeroom was a second door, also open. Footprints had been left in the thick dust in front of it, footprints that led towards where he was now standing. Morton edged forward and craned his neck through the door.

"Spiral staircase," he said. "Heading upwards. It must come out on one of the floors above the station."

Jamie nodded. "This is how he came in," he said. "Through the window, down the stairs, and—"

"What window?" asked Ellison, from out in the corridor.

"There's a broken window on the third floor," said Jamie. "I saw it as we came in."

"Thanks for telling us," said Morton.

"Sorry," said Jamie. "I thought you might have noticed it yourselves."

He shone his torch across the floor, following the footprints. They ended at the broken door, but that was far enough; they all knew where Alastair Dempsey had gone.

"The escalators are twenty-one metres," said Jamie, walking back out into the corridor. "There are two platforms, one on each side. If there's no sign of him, we'll check the east platform first. The tunnel was closed in 1917 and it's sealed at both ends."

"What about the west tunnel?" asked Morton.

"It was closed in 1994," said Jamie. "The tracks are still there and the tunnel is clear. It runs north for about half a mile."

"Half a mile?" repeated Morton. "Don't you think there might be one or two places to hide in half a mile of tunnel?"

"We'd better get on with it then," said Ellison, glaring at her squad mate.

Jamie shot her a quick smile. "Agreed," he said. "Morton, you stay on point."

"Yes, sir," he replied, and started down the middle escalator, his boots thudding on the metal stairs. The beam of Morton's torch rested steadily on the distant floor; Ellison's and Jamie's swept slowly in wide arcs as they followed him down towards it.

At the bottom, Jamie immediately saw that there was no need to check the east platform. A thick layer of dust and dirt covered the floor tiles, in which Dempsey's footprints were clearly visible; spaced widely and evenly apart, they disappeared through the arch that led to the west platform. It was darker at the bottom of the escalators; the lights in the station still worked, but Jamie had not asked for them to be turned on. He did not want to make it obvious to Alastair Dempsey that someone was coming.

The three Operators stepped silently through the arch and emerged on to a perfectly preserved platform. The tiling on the walls and ceilings was immaculate, and a tube train sat silently on the tracks before them, its doors open, its seats empty.

"What the hell?" asked Morton, his voice low.

"It must be used for filming," said Ellison.

"It's creepy."

"Tell me about it," said Ellison, and smiled at her squad mate.

The footprints headed north, then disappeared at the end of the platform. Jamie led his squad in the same direction, their T-Bones drawn, their torches casting bright white light before them. It was hot on the platform, and humid; the air was warm and musty, and seemed thick, almost solid. It smelt faintly rotten, and Jamie felt his nose wrinkle in mild disgust as he reached the end of the platform. He lowered his visor, twisted the dial on his belt to thermographic and looked down the tunnel; it appeared as a flat tube of dark red, with no detail whatsoever.

The humidity's blowing out the sensors, he thought, pushing the visor back up. *Awesome. No thermographics, no satellite overlook, no console signal. Welcome back to the dark ages.*

A concrete walkway extended about three metres, until four wide steps led down to the tunnel floor. The train loomed over them, incredibly tall when viewed from the same level as its wheels. It seemed oddly threatening, as though it was merely sleeping; Jamie imagined its engines suddenly roaring into life, the flat metal front lurching after them in the darkness as they fled along its rails, and shivered. He turned his back on the train, felt his shoulders tense slightly, and shone his torch down the dark abyss of the tunnel.

The tracks gleamed in the torchlight. Between and beyond the silver rails, the tunnel floor was dust and dirt. Toppled piles of crumbling bricks stood against the walls, and plastic bags full of goodness knows what were piled in shiny, sweating mountains. Rats scurried away from the beams, their feet clicking across the floor, their tails leaving trails in the dust and soot.

"This way," said Jamie, his voice sounding far less confident than he would have liked. He was suddenly very conscious of where they were, who they were looking for, and how far away help would be if something went wrong in this old, forgotten place.

"Let's do it," said Ellison.

Jamie nodded, and led his squad into the dark maw of the tunnel.

They swept the wide space with their torches, swinging them in slow, overlapping arcs. Water dripped from the ceiling, creating dark puddles topped with an oily film. The cables that powered the lights ran in thick bunches on the ceiling above their heads, black snaking tubes that reflected their torches back at them. They moved at a determinedly slow pace: the rails were slippery, the floor unsteady, studded with cracks and holes. It would be very easy to twist an ankle, and a long way back to the surface to have it dealt with.

"Question," whispered Morton.

"What is it?" asked Jamie.

"Has anyone actually thought about why Dempsey would be down here?"

"What do you mean?" asked Ellison.

"Exactly what I said," hissed Morton. "It's not like Dempsey worked for the tube, or was an engineer or a town planner. He didn't even live in London, for Christ's sake. So how come he knew about this place?"

"Why don't you ask him when we find him?" whispered Jamie. "Enough talk now. Let's keep moving."

They passed several emergency exit doors, as Morton had predicted, but all of them were locked and none looked like they had been opened in the last hundred years. The squad moved steadily,

390

all three silently aware that they would soon be reaching the end of the tunnel. Jamie could feel tension wriggling into his stomach, where it curled up in a tight little ball; he had expected the confrontation with Alastair Dempsey to have come by now, that the newly-turned vampire would have merely been hiding from the sun in the old tunnels, and therefore easy to find.

He was certain they hadn't missed him: the tunnel was simply not wide enough. Instead, he was starting to believe that Dempsey had flown back over his footprints and into the east tunnel, hoping that anyone who came looking for him would blindly follow the footprints half a mile in the wrong direction. Jamie didn't give voice to this awful possibility; doing so would cement it in his mind, would force him to explain why he had led his squad the wrong way. He was trying to force down his anger at himself – *arrogant, stupid, useless* – when they reached the end of the tunnel and saw what was there.

The circular passage had been sealed with a concrete plug that filled it to the edges on all sides. The grey wall was speckled black with dust and dirt, stained green by dripping water; its surface was still smooth, except for one small area near the right-hand wall of the tunnel. There, a dark hole absorbed the light of their torches, large enough for a grown man to squeeze through.

"OK," said Ellison, slowly. "I wasn't expecting this."

Jamie didn't respond. He walked forward, carefully stepping over chunks of fallen concrete, crouched down in front of the hole and shone his torch through it. The white beam illuminated nothing more than a few metres of identical wall, but picked out a splash of colour on the jagged edge of the hole itself. He shuffled forward and touched it with a gloved finger; it came away red.

"There's blood here," he whispered. "This is where he went."

"Through there?" asked Morton. "Are you kidding me?"

Jamie stood up and faced his squad mates. "No," he said. "I'm not."

"What's on the other side?" asked Ellison. "Could you see anything?"

Jamie shook his head. "More tunnel, as far as I could tell."

Morton laughed, a strange, high-pitched grunt of a sound. "More tunnel? The whole tube network is on the other side of this thing. He's *gone*."

"Maybe so," said Jamie. "But I want to know where this leads."

"He's gone," repeated Morton. "Why can't you just accept that?"

"Why are you fighting us on this?" asked Ellison, fiercely. "What's wrong with you?"

"What's wrong with me?" shouted Morton, his voice deafening in the quiet tunnel, his eyes wide with incredulity. "I don't want to waste our time stumbling around under half of London and there's something wrong with *me*? What's wrong with the two of *you*? This is RIDICULOUS."

Jamie stared at his squad mate. The rookie's eyes were wide and his skin was deathly pale; he looked like a ghost in the harsh light of the torch.

"Operator Morton," he said, as evenly as he was able. "If you don't calm down, I'm going to send you back to the surface. Is that what you want?"

Morton stared at him with resentment shining in his eyes. "Of course not," he spat. "Sir."

Jamie took a step towards him. "Tell me the truth, John. Right now. Can you handle this?"

"I'm fine," said Morton. "I just think this is a bad idea."

You don't look fine, thought Jamie. *You look like you're hanging by a thread. I nearly left you in the van and now I really, really wish I had.*

"You've made that clear," he said. "I'm going to do it anyway, so can we count on you? That's all I'm interested in right now."

Morton took a deep breath, and glanced over at Ellison. She was staring at him with huge concern on her face.

"Yes, sir," he said, looking back at his squad leader. "You can count on me."

It was tight, but the three Operators made it through the hole without tearing their uniforms or breaking any of their equipment.

The tunnel beyond the concrete wall was structurally identical, but Jamie realised within ten paces that this was a very different space to the one they had just walked through. The walls of this new section of tunnel were covered in paint; graffiti had been sprayed from floor to ceiling, wild patterns of pink and green and white, loops of yellow and gold. Faces stared down from the curved walls, grotesque figures with huge, gaping mouths and staring eyes. Letters emerged from beneath layer upon layer of aged paint, creating words that were not words at all. The three Operators scanned their torches slowly over the chaotic mural, taking it in.

"This is crazy," said Ellison, her voice low. "Who did all this?"

Jamie shook his head. "I don't know," he said. "It must have taken years."

Morton said nothing; he was staring at the graffiti with wide eyes, his mouth hanging open.

"Come on," said Jamie. "Let's keep moving."

They pressed on, spaced out across the tunnel. The tracks came to an end about a hundred metres from the concrete wall, prompting Ellison to point out that this could not be part of the main tunnel system. Her comment hung ominously in the air; Jamie could not think of a single reassuring response. As they made their way down the tunnel, his torch picked out a cylindrical object leaning against the wall and he stopped to look at it.

It was a large metal drum, scorched black on the inside by fire. There were lumps of charred wood in the bottom, and the surrounding floor was covered in ash and scraps of newspaper. Jamie reached down, picked up a handful, and let it drift away between his fingers. Ellison and Morton had carried on down the tunnel, their torch beams glowing beyond them. He watched them, his mind working, then shone his torch into the drum. The beam picked out something white and he leant down to get a closer look.

It was a small pile of chicken bones, picked clean of all their meat. Jamie stared for a long moment, then realised what he was looking at. He was looking at the remains of someone's dinner.

His eyes widened. Then he took off after his squad mates, his boots thudding across the floor, his torch beam jerking up and down as he ran. Ellison and Morton heard him coming and turned to face him, questioning expressions on their faces.

"Ready One!" yelled Jamie. "There are people down here! Ready One!"

He skidded to a halt and shone his torch past them, down the dark tunnel. And, at the edges of the beam, he saw shapes start to move.

Lots of shapes.

36

SIN CITY

LAS VEGAS, NEVADA, USA

Larissa had been in Las Vegas for just over eighteen hours.

After her friends told her the amazing news about their furlough, she raced to her quarters, threw the small collection of civilian clothes she had brought with her across the Atlantic into her gym bag, and arrived in the hangar almost five minutes early. Tim appeared a few moments later, a wide smile on his tanned face, closely followed by the rest of her friends. They piled into one of the black SUVs that lined the wall of the hangar, Tim in the driver's seat, Kelly beside him, Larissa sandwiched between Kara and Danny in the back.

"Music," demanded Kara, before Tim had even turned on the engine.

"I'm on it," said Kelly, pulling a wire out of the car's centre console and plugging it into her phone. She hit shuffle and pounding drums and juddering bass thudded through the car as Tim turned the key in the ignition.

"Where's Aaron?" asked Larissa. "Isn't he coming?"

"Didn't get a pass," said Tim. "I checked with the Director, but he said they can't spare him right now."

"Unlike the rest of us," laughed Kara. "We're clearly all expendable."

"*You* definitely are," said Tim, peering round and grinning at her. She aimed a half-hearted punch in his direction, but he dodged it, put the car in gear, and pulled out of the hangar. Fifteen minutes later they passed through the Front Gate; ten minutes later they were speeding east along Highway 375, the big car steadily eating up the miles that lay between them and Las Vegas.

Larissa spent the first hour of the journey overcome with a guilt that was almost physical. She had reconciled herself with Kelly's logic, that if General Allen was trying to do something nice for her, she should just be grateful and accept it. But that acceptance had been quickly replaced by worry over what Jamie and Kate and Matt would think about what she was doing. She hoped they would be pleased for her, that they would not resent her taking the opportunity to have some fun, but couldn't quite convince herself; they would be working and fighting while she drank and danced and gambled. By the time the Vegas skyline appeared on the horizon, she had pushed her concerns deep down inside herself. They were still there, however, twisting gently, seemingly indestructible.

They checked into a vast hotel with three towers and its own beach. Kara had called ahead and Larissa quickly found herself in an express lift, her bag in one hand, a plastic key card in the other. She emerged on the twenty-seventh floor and followed the long, winding corridor until she found her room. She pushed open the door, reaching for the light switch even though her supernatural eyes could see perfectly well in the gloom, then noticed the view from her window, and stopped.

Wow, she thought. *That's pretty amazing. Fair enough.*

The Strip stretched away below her, flanked on both sides by ludicrous recreations of landmarks of the world: the Eiffel Tower, the

Statue of Liberty, the Sphinx of Egypt. Cars cruised along the eight lanes of tarmac, thick beams of multicoloured light blazed into the night sky, and everything was bright and loud and full of life.

Larissa tore her gaze away from the view, which was so uniquely, brilliantly American that it brought a wide grin to her face, and returned her attention to the light switch. She found it on the wall beside the door, spent several minutes wondering why it was refusing to turn the lights on, and was on the verge of smashing it to pieces when she noticed a slot intended to house her room key; she slid it into place and warm yellow light filled the room. She unpacked her bag, hanging her clothes in the vast wardrobe and arranging her toiletries on the huge granite sink in the bathroom, then pulled her phone out of her pocket and called Kara. The helicopter pilot told her they were meeting downstairs in five minutes, outside the sports book. Larissa had no idea what a sports book was, but told her friend she would see them there.

Since then, it had all been a bit of a blur.

Larissa found the sports book, which turned out to be nothing more than a huge version of the betting shops that were found on every English high street, and met up with her friends. They were full of the laughter and happiness that came with being able to temporarily put down the enormous weight of NS9 and the permission to have fun without feeling guilty about it. Tim led them straight to the nearest bar and the drinks began to flow; they continued to do so as they set up camp at one end of a craps table, as Kara ushered them first into a cab and then into a restaurant inside a hotel that had been built to resemble Venice's Grand Canal. More drinks, a brief introduction to the world of blackjack, then another cab back to their hotel and a club that was little more than a large black box. Then dancing.

So much dancing.

By this point, Larissa had also made a startling, wonderful discovery; flexing the muscle that made her fangs descend and her eyes begin to flood red also sobered her up, instantly. Her friends, on the other hand, were not so lucky; Danny was the first to go, staggering away into the night, promising to meet them all for breakfast. Kelly was next; one minute she was sitting on a leather sofa in the corner of the club, chatting away amiably to anyone who would listen, the next her eyes had closed and she was snoring gently.

"She needs to go to bed," said Kara.

"Agreed," replied Tim, then cast a long look at Larissa.

This is it, she thought. *Kara will take Kelly back to her room and it'll just be you and Tim left and he'll suggest you get more drinks and you won't have a good reason to say no. Then he'll suggest you dance. And then you know what he'll try and do. Again.*

She stared at him for a long moment, their eyes locked on each other. Then Tim dropped his gaze and looked at Kara. "I'll take her back," he said. "You two have fun. I'll see you both in the morning."

Kara grinned happily and kissed Tim on the cheek as he scooped up the sleepy, protesting Kelly and guided her towards the club's exit. He nodded at Larissa as he left, an unknowable smile on his handsome face. She watched him go, unsure of exactly what she was feeling: relief, unquestionably, but also a cold sliver of something it took her a second or two to put her finger on.

It was rejection.

Maybe he's not going to try again, she thought. *Maybe he doesn't want me any more.*

Then Kara handed her a terrifyingly green shot and Tim Albertsson disappeared from her mind as she tipped the bright liquid down her throat. Moments later she and Kara were back on the dance floor, where they remained until neither of them could stand upright any longer, and they fled for the comfort of their beds.

Eight hours later they regrouped for breakfast in one of the hotel's many restaurants.

Four pairs of tired, bloodshot eyes stared enviously at Larissa, who was feeling not the slightest bit worse for wear, and had been informed by all four of her friends that they now hated her with a deep, abiding passion. She merely grinned, and sipped happily at her coffee.

Larissa was experiencing a contentment that she had not felt in a very long time. The weight that she carried around with her, a crushing combination of loathing of her own vampire self, concern about Jamie and her friends, desperate curiosity about the family that had rejected her, and the constant, lurking presence of Dracula, was gone. She was not stupid enough to believe it had left her forever, but she was incredibly grateful for the respite.

She ate heartily, watching her friends move their food listlessly round their plates, until they eventually admitted defeat and Tim called for the cheque.

"So what's the plan?" she asked, as everyone threw bills into the middle of the table. "What does everyone want to do today?"

"I want to die," said Kelly. Her skin was pale and a light sheen of sweat covered her forehead. "Can you arrange that for me?"

"Sleep," said Danny, from behind sunglasses that were shielding his bloodshot eyes.

"Sleep," echoed Kara. "I want to lie by the pool and sleep until I feel better. I reckon it'll only take three or four days."

Larissa laughed. Kara scowled at her, but couldn't keep it up; her face twisted into a broad smile, before she groaned again, loudly.

"What do you want to do?" asked Tim, looking at Larissa.

"I can't lie by the pool, I'm afraid," she said. "I don't think any of you could handle seeing me burst into flames this morning."

"Oh, hey," said Kara, sitting up and frowning. "I wasn't thinking. We don't have to go to the pool, Larissa. We can go somewhere—"

"Don't be silly," she interrupted. "It's fine. You guys hit the pool. I'll be totally OK inside."

"Are you sure?" asked Danny, lowering his sunglasses and peering at her. "Kara's right, it's not a big deal."

"I'm sure," replied Larissa. "Let's do our own thing for a few hours then meet up for an early dinner. Say six?"

"Sounds good," said Kelly. "There's a chance I might feel human by then."

"All right," said Larissa. "Six o'clock. Let's stick with the sports book."

"Agreed," said Tim. "We'll see you later then."

"Yep," she said, getting up from the table. "Have fun. Maybe a cocktail or two?" A chorus of groans rose from her friends and Larissa smiled to herself as she walked away from the table. She left the restaurant and headed directly down on to the casino floor, feeling the temperature of the air drop slightly, smelling the underlying scents of tobacco and sweat that the huge ceiling fans were never able to get rid of entirely. She strolled across the vast gaming area, skipping easily between crowds of frat boys and bachelor parties, around families on holiday, past old men and women feeding the slot machines, and the suited men with the flesh-coloured earpieces who watched over them all.

Larissa found a blackjack table with an empty seat, ordered a coffee from the waitress who instantly appeared beside her, and placed a fifty-dollar bill on the green felt. She had no idea how long she had been playing when Tim Albertsson eased himself into the seat next to hers.

"How's it going?" he asked.

"Not bad," she replied, smiling at him. "How was the beach?"

"Hot," said Tim. "Far too hot for me."

"So why did you go?"

"Because I didn't want to give the rest of them something else to gossip about."

Larissa's smile faded. "They talk about you and me?"

"Of course they do," said Tim.

"What do they say?"

"Nothing bad," said Tim, starting to look as though he regretted raising the subject; there was a chill to her voice that was clearly audible. "They know I like you. That's the long and short of it. And they think that maybe you like me. A little bit."

Jesus. What a mess.

"How do they know that?" she asked.

"How do they know what?"

"That you like me."

Tim shrugged. "Because I told them I do." Larissa opened her mouth to protest, but he cut her off. "I told them because it's true and because they're my friends. I know you're with Jamie and I respect that, whether you believe me or not. But I also think that you do like me, maybe more than you want to admit. Maybe things would be different if you were single, or if you were staying here permanently. But they aren't, and I don't want it to be weird when I come to Blacklight with you next month. That's why I came to find you. You're my friend, Larissa, and I don't want there to be a problem between us."

"Do you actually mean that?" asked Larissa. "If you don't, then tell me now because I'm going to be seriously pissed off if you let me think we're OK then try to kiss me the next time you see an opportunity. Which was a really shitty thing to do, in case you didn't realise."

Tim nodded. "I know," he said. "That's not really me, I hope you know that. It was just a heat of the moment sort of thing."

"I believe you," she replied. "It's fine. As long as it doesn't happen again."

"It won't," replied Tim. "I've no desire to get on your bad side, Larissa. I've seen what you can do, remember?"

She laughed, and felt some of the tension dissipate from where it had gathered in her shoulders.

"So we're cool?" he asked. "I won't do anything else that's stupid and inappropriate, and you'll still take me to Blacklight with you when you leave. Deal?" He extended his hand; Larissa rolled her eyes at his attempt at formality, and shook it.

"Deal," she said. "Now shut up and play your hand."

They played happily for a couple of hours, until Larissa announced that she was going to go and get ready for dinner.

Tim nodded, and told her he was going to play a few more hands. She left him at the table, made her way through the casino, and into one of the lifts. When she was back in her room, she drank two litres of blood that she had brought with her from Dreamland, undressed, and stepped into the huge walk-in shower that took up half of the bathroom. She let the pounding heat of the water clear her head, hoping that it would wash away the promise that she now deeply regretted making.

Tim Albertsson was obsessed with Blacklight. His grandfather had been a soldier in the Swedish army and a member of the FTB, the

German Office of the Supernatural, for more than two decades. When Tim had been recruited into NS9, his grandfather had filled his head with grand tales of the European Departments, whose history and proximity to the birthplace of vampirism lent them an aura the Departments in other continents could never hope to match. And, above all, he had told his grandson about Department 19, the place where legends had walked: Van Helsing, Harker, Seward, Holmwood.

Tim had applied for a transfer to Blacklight three times in five years, and on each occasion had been deemed too valuable to NS9 to part with. But General Allen had guaranteed Larissa free rein in picking the six Operators she took back to England with her, provided they were ranked below Major, which seemed fair; she could not expect the NS9 Director to let her gut the senior ranks of his Department, no matter how much he wanted to help Blacklight get back on its feet. This guarantee, which she had told Tim about one evening in Sam's Diner, represented the answer to his prayers, a way for him to fulfil his one great ambition.

I can't take him with me, she thought. *To hang out with me and Jamie and Kate and Matt. I just can't. It won't do anyone any good. I just have to hope he can understand that.*

Larissa turned off the shower, dried herself, and put on the pretty grey dress her mother had bought her the Christmas before she had been turned. It was one of a small bag full of things she had managed to grab from her room as her mother screamed into the phone downstairs, demanding that the police come and take her daughter away. It still fitted her, as she had essentially stopped growing the moment Grey sank his fangs into her neck. She adjusted it in the mirror, feeling a pang of painful nostalgia as she thought back to the Christmas morning when she had first worn it, an excited sixteen-year-old girl whose whole life was ahead of her.

She's gone now, thought Larissa. *Long gone.*

She dried her hair, letting it fall around her face and down to her shoulders, applied a tiny amount of make-up, and headed downstairs to meet her friends, wondering what the night had in store for them.

The club was quite simply the most ridiculous thing Larissa had ever seen.

It was a vast semicircle, full to capacity with barely clothed figures writhing and gyrating to a pulsing house track that vibrated through the floor and into her bones. A ring of tables, surrounded by red leather benches and topped with stripper poles, encircled a sunken dance floor. Away to the left, a long bar dispensed drinks of every conceivable size, shape and colour.

Tim shouted something over the music, but even her supernatural hearing was unable to pick it up. He tried again, and she shrugged and shook her head. Eventually, he tipped a cupped hand towards his mouth and pointed at the rest of their friends, who responded with nodded heads and raised thumbs. He wrestled his way towards the bar with Kelly following closely behind him, as Danny pointed towards the dance floor, his eyebrows raised. Kara and Larissa nodded, and the three of them began to make their way down towards it, Larissa holding her coat tightly in her hands.

They became separated almost immediately.

One second Larissa was right behind her friends, the next she was standing by herself. She scanned the steaming mass of bodies, searching for Kara or Danny, but could see neither of them. She decided to try a different angle, and began to work her way slowly towards the wide pool that lay beyond the open doors at the edge of the club's main room.

She stepped out into the warm evening air and surveyed the

scene. The pool had a wide ledge that was barely fifteen centimetres deep; men and women were dancing furiously in the shallow water, splashing and stomping and occasionally falling flat on their backs. Many of the women had stripped down to bras and bikini tops, and had acquired an admiring audience. Larissa left them to it and made her way round the pool. A ring of two-storey cabanas were full of men and women drinking bottles of beer and smoking cigars, while to her left an island in the centre of the pool was full of slot machines and gambling tables. Larissa grinned; in Las Vegas, the opportunity to gamble was never more than a few seconds away.

She was about to walk towards it, thinking that she might play a hand or two while she waited for her friends to find her, when a scent filled her nostrils that made her force her eyes to remain normal and her fangs to stay in place: a powerful aroma that she was unused to experiencing without her weapons and uniform.

The scent of another vampire.

Larissa stopped where she was and surveyed the crowd. There were less people out by the pool than inside, but the area was still busy; people strolled across the wet stone and huddled round the cabanas, laughing and chatting and shouting. She paid them all no attention; she was looking for someone different. And then, as though a spotlight had been suddenly shone down from the hotel that towered above the club, Larissa saw her.

The vampire was a woman in her early twenties, wearing a blue sundress and carrying a tall drink in a glass the shape of a test tube. She had long, honey-coloured hair, smooth, pale skin, and was wandering slowly along the edge of the pool, her bare feet in the shallow water. There was nothing to obviously single her out from all the other beautiful women in the club, but Larissa had no doubt: somehow, she just knew.

She made her way towards the woman, never taking her eyes off her. She closed the distance quickly and spoke in a low voice.

"You're like me."

The woman turned, a look of annoyance on her pale face, and for a split second Larissa saw red flicker in the corners of her green eyes.

"Do I know you?" she asked.

Larissa shook her head. "No," she replied. "But you know what I am. We're the same."

The woman narrowed her eyes and looked about to protest, when a smile emerged on her face, and she laughed instead. "How did you know?" she asked.

"I'm not sure," said Larissa. "I picked up the scent of another vampire, but I don't know how I knew it was you. I could just see it."

"You could smell me?" asked the woman, her smile fading. "What are you saying?"

"It's not a bad smell," said Larissa, quickly. "It's just... well. Can't you smell it? When there's another vampire around?"

The woman tipped back her head and breathed in sharply. "There is something," she said, eventually. "Sort of at the edges, if that makes sense? Is it you?" She nodded. "That's weird. How come I've never smelt that?"

"I don't know," said Larissa. "Maybe you've never been around another vampire before?" The idea seemed ludicrous even as she said it; she could not conceive of a world in which other vampires were not a constant feature.

"I used to date one," said the woman. "A guy in LA. But he's the only one I've met, as far as I know."

"Wow," said Larissa. It was all she could think of to say.

"Why?" asked the woman. "Have you known a lot of vampires?"

Larissa smiled. "That's a bit of an understatement."

"Really?" said the woman. "I'm Chloe. Do you want to get a drink? I feel like we might have some stuff to talk about."

"I think you might be right. I'm Larissa. And I could definitely do with a beer."

Chloe smiled, and took Larissa's hand; the sensation was odd, but she let the woman lead her towards the bar on the gambling island, where she ordered a beer and a refill of her own enormous cocktail. When the drinks arrived, Larissa followed her between the craps tables to the edge of the island, where Chloe sat down and dangled her feet in the water. After a moment, Larissa pulled off her shoes and sat down, putting her coat on the ground beside her.

"So how long have you been turned?" she asked.

"Turned," said Chloe, rolling the word round her mouth. "Is that what it's called? Like, the official term?"

"There aren't any official terms," said Larissa. "Turned is what some people call it."

"About a year," said Chloe. "Someone bit me in a club in New Orleans, on Super Bowl weekend. I didn't think much of it until the next morning when I opened the curtains and my arm caught on fire." She smiled, and Larissa returned it with one of her own.

"How did you get through the hunger the first time?" she asked.

"I killed a dog," said Chloe, matter-of-factly. "It belonged to this gay couple who were in the bungalow next to ours. It was a small dog, a yapping little thing, but it was enough. What about you? When were you turned?"

"Nearly three years ago," replied Larissa. "An old man bit me at a funfair in England, where I'm from. I think he meant for me to die, but I'm not really sure. One of his associates took pity on me, gave me some blood, and told me there was a place I could go, but I turned it down. I thought my parents would help me."

"They didn't?"

"No," said Larissa, a small smile on her face. "I lived on the streets for six months."

"It's weird," said Chloe. "Until I met Derek – he was the guy I mentioned – I just kind of had to work it out for myself, you know? The blood, the sunlight, the floating. But I got through it."

Floating, thought Larissa. *She said floating. Not flying.*

"I'm sorry," she said. "It's hard being on your own."

They sat in easy silence for a minute or so, Larissa swinging her feet gently in the water, feeling the ripples move against her skin.

"Have you ever had any trouble?" she asked, eventually. "Since you were turned, I mean."

"What kind of trouble?" asked Chloe.

"People trying to kill you. That kind of trouble."

Chloe laughed. "I don't hurt anyone, so why would anybody have a problem with me? And anyway, who would they be? The cops?"

"Sort of," said Larissa. "There are people that destroy vampires. Military organisations, secret ones. You've never heard about them?"

"Nope," said Chloe. "Never heard about anything like that. How come you know about them?"

I assumed all vampires did, thought Larissa.

"Someone told me," she lied. "A man I knew in Rome. Like us."

Chloe smiled. "Sounds to me like maybe he was trying to impress you a little bit. Tell you a far-fetched story, make it all seem hot and scary and dangerous."

"You're probably right," said Larissa, smiling. "He told me Dracula was real too."

Chloe burst out laughing. "Dracula?" she asked. "The old guy from the movies? With the cape?"

"That's the one. I think he could turn into a bat."

"I wish I could," giggled Chloe. "That could be super-useful."

Larissa laughed, and drained the last of her beer. She set down the empty bottle and looked at the woman beside her. "It's been nice talking to you, Chloe," she said. "I'd better go and find my friends."

"That's cool," said Chloe. "I'm going to stay here for a while. You take care of yourself."

Easier said than done, Larissa thought. *But I'll certainly try.*

She left Chloe with her feet in the water and headed back towards the main room of the club. She squeezed her way through the open doors and walked straight into Tim Albertsson, who was carrying two beers in his hands. He smiled, shouted her name just about loud enough for her to hear it, and handed her one of the bottles. She shouted her thanks, and didn't protest as he took her arm and led her back outside.

"Sorry," he said, once they were clear of the doors. "I couldn't hear a damn thing in there. About half the Air Force just turned up, rolling drunk. Took me about half an hour to get through them. Have you seen the others?"

"Danny and Kara were heading for the dance floor the last time I saw them," replied Larissa. "I thought Kelly was with you."

"I lost her before I even got to the bar," he said. "Looks like it's just you and me." He smiled, and Larissa took a long pull from her beer, leaning back so her eyes stared up at the ceiling. When she lowered her head, Tim had closed the distance between them; his face was barely five centimetres from her own, his eyes locked on hers, and Larissa felt a shiver hurtle up her spine.

"Don't," she warned, staring into his eyes. "You promised."

"I'm not going to kiss you again," he breathed. "But I want to. And I know part of you wants me to."

They stood motionless, locked in suspended animation; time appeared not to be passing, each second stretching out for an eternity. Then Larissa's phone burst into life in her coat pocket, breaking the spell of the deadly, dangerous moment. She blushed deeply and fumbled the phone out of her pocket, taking a step backwards, a step away from Tim, as she did so. The screen glowed with a single word.

JAMIE

Shame, hot and bitter, flooded through her as she stared at her boyfriend's name.

I didn't do anything. I didn't do anything.

She pressed the REJECT button on the phone's screen and stuffed it back into her coat. Then she stepped forward, feeling familiar heat in the corners of her eyes.

"Enough," she said, trying not to let her voice turn into a growl. "That's enough now."

Tim stared at her for a long moment, then nodded. "I'm sorry," he said. "Let's go find the others, OK?"

Larissa made him wait. "OK," she said, eventually. "Let's do that."

Tim set off towards the club's dance floor. She followed him, looking round at the garish opulence of the club with fierce disgust, as though she was suddenly seeing the place, *really* seeing it, for the first time. Her phone rang again and she fought the urge to scream with frustration. She pulled it out, saw Jamie's name on the screen, and pressed REJECT again.

What's wrong with me? she thought, the words hot and sharp. *Why am I in this awful place while my friends are trying to save the world? What the hell am I doing?*

She pushed through the crowd, not caring when her elbows and shoulders thudded into the people around her, relishing the cries of pain and shouted insults that followed her. Occupying half a dozen tables at the edge of the dance floor were the group of Air Force men Tim had mentioned; there seemed to be dozens of them, most in their dress uniforms, yelling and shouting and doing shot after shot after shot. They had attracted a huge crowd of gawking girls, who were clambering on and over the tables to join them, their exposed stomachs and thighs gleaming under the spinning lights of the club. Larissa stopped and watched, disgust rising through her. Then the sea of navy-blue uniforms parted and she gasped.

In the middle of one of the red sofas, holding a half-empty vodka bottle in one hand and a pretty brunette who looked barely old enough to drink in the other, was Lee Ashworth. The Senior Airman was chatting happily to one of his friends as the girl kissed his neck, taking the occasional swig from the bottle, completely oblivious to his surroundings.

An image appeared in Larissa's mind: a photo of a blonde woman and two smiling children, sitting on the Senior Airman's desk.

She pulled her phone out of her pocket, pressed the camera icon, zoomed in on Lee Ashworth, and snapped a quick series of pictures.

Got you, she thought.

Larissa turned away and closed the gap on Tim, who was still wrestling his way down towards the dance floor, her mind pulsing with a single thought, one that she knew had not crossed her mind as often as it should have in the last few weeks.

I miss you, Jamie. I wish you were here.

37

BY A THREAD

Jamie Carpenter skidded to a halt between his two squad mates, pulling his MP5 from his belt and snapping his visor into place as he did so. The two rookies looked at him with wide eyes.

"What the—" began Morton, but Jamie cut across him.

"Shut up," he hissed. "Visors. Weapons. We're not alone down here."

Morton's eyes widened even further, then training and instinct took over. He lowered his visor, swept his MP5 out of the loop on his belt, raised it to his shoulder, and pressed his torch tight against the submachine gun's barrel. Ellison did the same; the three Operators moved in close together, back to back in a tight triangle, three piercing beams of light scanning the darkness.

Jamie swung his torch slowly left and right, illuminating nothing but the graffiti-covered wall of the tunnel. Movement seemed to flicker at the edges of the beam, but when he swung his light towards it, whatever had moved was gone.

"There's nothing here," whispered Morton. "You're seeing things."

"I know what I saw," said Jamie, staring intently into the pitch darkness. "Something moved."

"It's not moving now," said Morton.

Jamie ignored him. He *had* seen something move, he was sure of it; more than one thing in fact. And they hadn't been rats, or stray dogs, or urban foxes; they had been far too big for that.

"What do we do, sir?" whispered Ellison. "We can't just stand here."

Jamie swore heartily. "I know that," he said. "Just let me think."

I did see something, he thought. *I know I did.*

From somewhere ahead of them – it was impossible to accurately judge distance in the deep darkness of the tunnel – there came the heavy clang of metal and a low fizzing noise. Then the tunnel's maintenance lights flickered into life and Jamie saw that he had been right.

Surrounding his squad was a crowd of men and women, perhaps thirty in total. Several were carrying weapons – lumps of wood, metal bars, in one case what looked like the skeleton of an umbrella – but they were not what Jamie noticed as his eyes adjusted to the sudden brilliance of the lights. What caught his attention was a simple, undeniable truth: the men and women who had appeared out of the darkness were, by some distance, the strangest-looking collection of humanity he had ever seen.

Most of them were filthy, their faces and hands black with dust and dirt, their clothing little more than rags, but bright paint shone from their skin and their ragged clothes, loops and swirls that looked as though they had been carefully applied. Their hair, which in most cases was long, had been twisted up into spikes and waves, and accented with flowers and feathers and pieces of foil that looked like sweet wrappers. Half a dozen of the crowd were naked, their entire bodies painted. One man, whose face was painted bright red and green, wore a dark blue suit and carried a tan briefcase. His hair was wild and colourful, but his eyes were distant; he looked lost, as though he had gone for lunch one day in 1986 and woken up underground a quarter of a century later.

"Lower your weapons," said Jamie, speaking via the comms system that only his squad could hear. "Don't do anything unless I tell you." Ellison and Morton made no response, but did as they were ordered, letting their guns hang at their sides, the barrels pointing at the floor.

A woman stepped forward, holding a wooden stick in her hand. Her face had once been pretty, that much was obvious, even through the layers of grime and flaking paint. She wore a short, floaty dress that might once have been yellow, but was now a deep, dirty grey, streaked with brown and black. One of her feet was bare, the other clad in an old sandal. She looked at the three Operators with open suspicion.

"Are you police?" she asked. "Don't lie, mind. I know liars."

"No," said Jamie, twisting the dial on his belt so his voice was audible. "We're not police."

"Soldiers?"

"Of a sort," said Jamie.

"You got a face under there?"

Jamie hesitated, then reached up and raised his visor. After a second or two, he heard Morton and Ellison do the same.

"Young," said the woman. "What you doing down here?"

"We're looking for someone," said Jamie. "He probably came in last night."

The woman shrugged. "Lots of people come down here at night."

"You wouldn't have seen this one before. And he'd have probably stood out. Moved faster than most people, maybe had something wrong with his eyes?"

"Vampire, is he?" asked the woman. "We get them down here,

from time to time. They ain't allowed to stay, though. Can't be trusted to control themselves." The look on Jamie's face made her cackle with laughter. "There's plenty that knows about the vamps, young soldier man. Live in the shadows long enough, you get to know things."

"You live down here?" asked Ellison.

"Something wrong with that?" asked the woman.

"No," said Ellison, quickly. "I was just curious."

"Curiosity did something nasty to the cat, young miss. Remember that."

"We're not here to cause trouble," said Jamie, shooting a sharp glance at Ellison. "The vampire we're looking for is a convicted criminal. If you take us to him, we'll be on our way."

"I don't care what he did," spat the woman. "Most of us that's down here done things they wish they hadn't. Why should we let you take this man? If he's even here, that is."

Because the three of us could kill you all without breaking a sweat, Jamie thought. *And there isn't a damn thing you could do to stop us.*

"Because he's dangerous," said Jamie. "You don't want him in your home, believe me. How many women do you have down here?"

"Some," she replied, narrowing her eyes. "What of it?"

Jamie said nothing; he let her put two and two together, and was gratified to see a ripple of unease cross her face as she made the connection.

"Could be that I can help you," she said, slowly. "What's your name, mister soldier?"

"Jamie."

"Jamie what?"

"Jamie's going to have to do, I'm afraid."

"Aye, I thought as much. Mine's Aggie. If you was to say I was in charge down here, well, you wouldn't be right, but you wouldn't be all wrong neither. Jackie?"

A girl who looked to be in her late teens or very early twenties stepped forward. She was wearing battered blue jeans and a giant fox fur coat, into which had been twisted hundreds of thin pieces of metal.

"You seen him that came in early this morning, didn't you?" said Aggie.

"I saw," said Jackie.

"He still here?"

"I ain't seen him leave," she replied. "He was down with the others, last I saw."

"How many of you are there down here?" asked Jamie.

"Depends on the day, mister soldier man," said Aggie. "Some days there might be a hundred, some days five. We don't take no registers."

"You all come in and out through the station?" asked Ellison. "How come no one notices that?"

Aggie laughed. "Ain't no one comes in that way. That's the last way *out*, in case we get trouble. There's ways all over the city, more than even I can remember."

"Why are you dressed like that?" asked Morton, suddenly. "Does everyone down here have to?"

"Dressed like what, soldier man?"

"The paint and the feathers and the bits of foil."

Aggie looked down at herself, then laughed. "That black's your uniform, right? Well, this is ours. We're the protectors of this place. They call us the Guardians."

"The Guardians of what?" asked Jamie.

"Of whatever needs guarding," said Aggie. "What else?"

Jamie fought back the urge to laugh; these people were the strangest thing he had seen since joining Blacklight, which was genuinely saying something. And he was already starting to like Aggie; she was blunt to the point of rudeness, but there was a wicked intelligence beneath her grimy exterior and he found himself beginning to enjoy it.

"Will you take us to where he is?" he asked. "Please?"

Aggie cocked her head to one side and narrowed her eyes, clearly considering his request. Eventually, she nodded. "We'll take you, soldier man. I don't know if I believe he's as bad as you say, but if you're here for him, he has to answer for that. Anyone brings the law down here puts it on themselves. You walk with me, and tell your friends to keep them guns pointing down. I don't want no shooting."

"Neither do I," said Jamie.

The procession making its way along the abandoned tunnel beneath the heart of Central London would have looked ridiculous to anyone who witnessed it.

Aggie and Jamie were at the front, walking steadily side by side. Behind them came Ellison and Morton, looking utterly bemused as they followed their squad leader through the darkness. After the two rookie Operators came the rest of Aggie's Guardians: two wide lines of remarkable-looking men and women who strolled easily across the uneven surface, their twists of foil and slivers of metal sparkling as they passed beneath the tunnel's maintenance lights.

Jamie kept his eyes peeled as they made their way forward. The mission had turned from what he had expected into something very different, and he was determined to stay focused on what had become an evolving situation. He thought there was very little chance that Alastair Dempsey would go down without a fight, but he hoped that, by arriving with Aggie and her odd band of painted Guardians, they might be able to take him by surprise and destroy him before he had either the chance to flee or to hurt anyone who lived down here.

He had asked Aggie about the lights, but she had just grunted that a big boy like him ought to know what made lights work, so he had dropped it. He assumed someone had run cable up to an electricity source on the surface, a feat that must have taken a huge amount of daring and a significant amount of technical expertise. He wanted to know about this strange place, but didn't want to annoy Aggie any more than he already had by bringing his squad into her home.

I don't blame her for not wanting to tell me, he thought. *She probably already thinks I'm going to bring a hundred Met officers back here and chase them all out.*

If she did think that, however, she was wrong; Jamie had already made up his mind that he would not be including this place in his report. It did not need bringing to anyone's attention; it wasn't a haven for vampires, or any other kind of supernatural, and therefore not his Department's concern. It was merely home to a group of people who presumably had nowhere else to go.

"How much further?" he asked. The tunnel seemed endless, the yellow lights illuminating little more than the ten metres directly in front of them.

"Ain't far," grunted Aggie. "Soon enough we'll be there. Then you can take your vampire man and leave us in peace."

I don't think it's going to be that simple, thought Jamie. *Although I hope I'm wrong. I really do.*

"It might be for the best," he said, carefully, "if you let the three of us confront him on our own. If you tell us when we're nearly there, then the rest of you can stay back."

"Piss on that," said Aggie, mildly. "We're the Guardians of this place, not you and your little friends. You do what we say, not the other way around."

Have it your way, he thought. *For a little bit longer, at least.*

After a period of time that Jamie could not have accurately estimated, but which he thought had to have been less than fifteen minutes, perhaps no more than ten, the tunnel suddenly expanded to twice its width, and Aggie stopped.

"This here's the junction," she said. "Two lines used to cross here, although both of them are gone now. Straight ahead, where those fires are, that's where we'll find your vampire."

Jamie stared into the darkness. After a few seconds, his eyes were able to pick out the faintest orange glow, what seemed like miles away.

Her eyes are incredible, he thought. *I doubt even Larissa can see that well.*

"What's over there?" he asked.

"It's a dead end," said Aggie. "Kind of a circle, although it ain't really, not any more. There's some shelters been built, and other bits and pieces."

"How many ways out?"

"If he runs before we cross the junction, then too many," she said. "If he don't, then two. There's a door on the left-hand wall, leads up to an old power exchange. It's one of the main ways in and out. Once we cross, the rest'll all be behind you. If you don't let him get past, and you don't let him get out the door, there ain't going to be nowhere for him to go."

A dead end, thought Jamie. *Excellent.*

"Did you get all that?" he asked, turning to face his squad mates, who both nodded. "Ellison, I want you to get in front of that door as soon as we're across. Morton, you stay with me. We finish this down here. Clear?"

"Clear," said Ellison. Morton merely nodded, staring directly at Jamie.

"OK," he said. "Aggie, do you want to lead us in? If we mix in with your people, then he's less likely to see us."

"Aye," said Aggie. "That seems like sense."

Jamie nodded and stepped back into the brightly painted crowd. Ellison and Morton did the same, holstering their MP5s and drawing their T-Bones. The three Operators kept their weapons low, where they would be less obvious to anyone watching the crowd approach.

"Let's do this," said Jamie. Aggie nodded and led them out across the junction.

The space was huge; the tracks were long gone, but the places where they had once intersected were still clearly marked by patches of the tunnel floor that were paler than their surroundings. Jamie found himself standing at the nexus, with four tunnel openings surrounding him. To the rear was the one they had just walked down, to the front their destination, where he hoped Alastair Dempsey was relaxing, unaware of their presence. To the left and right the tunnels disappeared into darkness, their destinations unknown.

Aggie's right, thought Jamie. *If he gets past us, he's gone.*

His heart was starting to beat more rapidly in his chest; he made no attempt to slow it, preferring to let its steady thud focus his mind on what was about to happen. If all went to plan, it would be over in a matter of seconds, but experience had taught him that things rarely did where vampires were concerned, particularly vampires as dangerous as Alastair Dempsey.

Jamie looked round and saw his squad mates walking steadily among the colourful throng of the Guardians. Both of them appeared calm, their eyes clear, their shoulders low, their progress quiet and steady.

Good, he thought. *Morton's got himself under control. About time too.*

He looked back just in time to see them pass beneath the entrance of the tunnel they were heading into. He could now see the fires clearly; there were two, built on opposite sides of the wide space. Figures huddled round them or wandered between them; he was just starting to be able to make out individuals when a voice echoed through the tunnel.

"Who's that?" it shouted. "That you, Aggie?"

"Aye," she shouted. "Me and mine."

"Find anything?"

"Nothing," she shouted. "Looks like someone did come through, but they ain't there no more."

"That ain't good, Aggie."

"What do you want me to do about it?"

The other voice fell silent.

"Visors," Jamie whispered over the comms link, and flipped his down. He glanced over his shoulder, saw that both his squad mates had done as they were told, and turned back as they approached the fires. The flames cast a beautiful orange glow, and his eyes widened as he saw the number of people the dead-end tunnel contained: there had to be a hundred and fifty men and women, maybe more. He was starting to wonder how they were going to go about finding their target without giving themselves away, when he saw the man they were looking for.

Alastair Dempsey was leaning against the wall on the other side of the fires. He was wearing a dark shirt and a pair of black jeans, and was standing on his own, his attention fixed firmly on the approaching group of men and women; there was an expression on his face that Jamie didn't like.

This one's a wild animal, he thought. *He can sense something is wrong, even though he doesn't know what yet.*

He was about to whisper their target's location to his squad mates, when Morton's voice boomed out, amplified by the microphone in his helmet, deafeningly loud in the enclosed space of the tunnel.

"Alastair Dempsey," shouted Morton. "Come forward with your hands up."

Dempsey was still more than ten metres away, but Jamie saw his eyes instantly flood a deep, glowing red, as a dreadful smile burst across his face.

"You—" began Ellison, but the insult she had been about to level at Morton was lost forever, as everything turned to chaos.

Jamie raised his T-Bone, his eyes fixed on Dempsey, determined not to let the vampire out of his sight while simultaneously trying to ignore the fury that had rushed through him as Morton gave away their element of surprise, but saw instantly that he had no shot.

People were running blindly, crashing into and over each other, sending huge showers of sparks into the air as they trampled through the fires. Men and women stumbled to the ground and Jamie heard the terrified screams of children beneath the roar emerging from the adults. Aggie turned and looked at him with terrible reproach, but he forced himself to ignore her; he was trying to focus on Dempsey, trying to keep their target in front of him, but realised with rising horror that he could no longer see the vampire.

"Sir?"

"What is it, Ellison?" he snapped, scanning the writhing mass before him.

"He's got me, sir."

Jamie felt the blood in his veins turn to ice. Slowly, he turned to face Ellison, who was standing as still as a statue. Looming over her right shoulder was the face of a middle-aged man, his mouth wide and grinning, his eyes smouldering red.

"Don't move," he growled. "I'll kill this one if you move."

Jamie let his T-Bone fall from his hands, drew his Glock, and levelled it at the vampire; there was a blur of movement as Dempsey pulled Ellison's head back and pressed his fingernails against her throat. He shook his head in gentle warning. Jamie didn't move, but nor did he lower his gun; he kept it trained directly on the visible portion of Dempsey's face.

"Stay calm," he said, over the comms link. "You're OK, stay calm."

"Yes, sir," replied Ellison, her words silent to everyone apart from her squad mates. "What's the plan?"

"Give me a second," he replied. "Morton, where the hell are you?"

There was no reply.

Cursing inwardly, he risked a glance to his right. Morton was facing the vampire, his weapon resting uselessly in his hands. Men and women were streaming around him, but he appeared not to even notice; he seemed to be frozen to the spot.

"Morton!" Jamie bellowed. His words burst directly into Morton's ears and the rookie yelled in pain, shoving his visor up as he stumbled backwards, his eyes squeezed tightly together. When they opened again, they were clear, and he turned towards his squad leader, his face flushing the deep red of shame.

"Go and cover the door," said Jamie, trying to control the anger that was filling him. "Don't say a word without your visor down. Just do it. Now."

Morton nodded and circled towards the wall, his eyes wide, his T-Bone locked against his shoulder.

Alastair Dempsey frowned; he was breathing heavily, his eyes flicking right and left, the eyes of a cornered animal.

Jamie looked quickly around the wide space and saw there were perhaps forty people still there, watching with open terror on their faces. He twisted the dial on his belt.

"Nobody move!" he shouted. "This has nothing to do with any of you. None of you are in any danger, unless you move now that I've told you not to." He refocused his attention on the vampire. "Alastair Dempsey," he said. "Surrender yourself to our custody. There's nowhere for you to go."

An expression of surprise flickered across the escapee's face, then he grunted with laughter. "Not a chance," he spat. "I'm not going back there. Not a chance in hell."

"Just give yourself up," said Jamie. "There's no way out of here."

The vampire shook his head. "Who are you?" he growled. "Special Branch?"

"It doesn't matter who we are," said Jamie.

"It does to me," he said, dragging Ellison backwards. "Do the doctors want me back this badly? Or are you just here to kill me?"

"We're here to kill you," said Morton, from his position in front of the door.

"SHUT THE HELL UP!" shouted Jamie, his voice echoing through the wide tunnel as his frustration with his squad mate finally got the better of him.

"Why?" asked Dempsey, glancing at Morton with an expression

of apparently genuine curiosity. "What have I done that I haven't already paid for?"

"You're a vampire," replied Morton.

Dempsey laughed. "And that gives you the right to kill me?"

Morton didn't respond.

Jamie twisted the dial on his belt again and spoke to Ellison in a voice that only his squad mates could hear. "When I say go, whip your head to the left as hard as you can. Clear?"

"Yes, sir," replied Ellison.

Dempsey took another step backwards, dragging Ellison with him, his gaze flicking between the two dark figures. Jamie tracked him with the Glock, silent and unmoving.

"Go," he said.

Ellison jerked her head to the left with all her strength. Dempsey was taken completely by surprise; his grip on her neck slipped, his fingers sliding across her uniform as she threw herself away from him. As Ellison hit the floor, her shoulder crunching into the ground, Dempsey's head became fully visible and Jamie emptied his Glock into it.

The reports were deafening in the confined space of the tunnel. The men and women he had ordered to stay still screamed in terror, clapping their hands to their ears and diving for the ground. Dempsey, who had an instinct for survival that far predated his being turned, flung himself back through the air, twisting as he did so. The first two bullets slammed into his face, tearing off his left ear and destroying his left eye in a shower of yellow fluid. The rest thudded into his shoulder and arm, sending the vampire crashing to the ground as the Glock's hammer closed on an empty chamber with a dry click.

Jamie ran forward, scooping his T-Bone up from the ground as he did so, but Dempsey leapt to his feet before he could take aim. With a screeching howl of anger and pain, his blood spraying in high-pressure jets from at least a dozen bullet holes, he hurled himself towards the door set into the far wall.

"Incoming!" Jamie yelled, racing after him. "Morton!"

Morton stepped forward, his finger tightening on the trigger of his T-Bone. The blood-soaked monstrosity shambled towards him, screaming and bleeding and howling, its remaining eye glowing red, its mouth wide and full of fangs. He took an involuntary half-step backwards and pulled the trigger. The metal stake erupted from the weapon's barrel with a burst of exploding gas and rocketed across the cavernous space.

But the half-step had been just enough to disrupt his aim; the stake ploughed through Dempsey's shoulder, tearing loose a chunk of meat the size of a grapefruit, causing a fresh bellow of agony to issue forth from the vampire's mouth. Morton grabbed for his stake, but was too slow; Dempsey thundered past him, sending him crashing into the wall before the weapon was even free of its belt loop.

Jamie sprinted across the wide tunnel and leapt through the doorway, his T-Bone pointing up the stairs that lay beyond it. He screamed an appalling torrent of abuse after the escaping vampire and stuck his head back through the door.

"I have to call this in," he yelled. "Follow me up." He disappeared back through the door, his footsteps clattering away up the stairs.

Ellison watched him go, then turned and looked for her squad mate.

Morton was sitting on the ground, staring across the echoing tunnel. He was perfectly still, his eyes wide, almost uncomprehending.

She hauled herself to her feet, wincing at the pain pulsing through her shoulder, and looked in the direction of his stare.

Her breath stopped in her chest.

"Oh shit," she said.

Lying on the floor, Morton's T-Bone stake sticking out of her throat, was Jackie, the girl who Aggie had asked about Alastair Dempsey. The orange glow of the fires lit her pale face; her eyes stared up at the ceiling and her mouth worked silently. Blood poured out of her neck, spilling across her fur coat, staining it black. Her hands clenched and unclenched weakly at her sides, as a crimson pool spread steadily beneath her.

Ellison ran across the chamber, forgetting about Morton entirely. She slid to the ground beside the stricken girl, pushing her helmet from her head, and examined the damage. The wound was deep and wide; the metal stake had been slowed by Dempsey's shoulder, but had still torn almost all the way through her neck, stopping only when it hit her spine. Ellison stared helplessly, knowing there was no help she could offer. If they had been within a minute's run of a hospital with a world-class trauma centre, then maybe, *maybe* something could have been done. But down here, in the tunnels below the city, there was nothing.

Jackie's eyes met hers. Ellison stared at the dying girl, forcing herself not to look away, not to fail at the only thing she could do: let the girl know that she was not alone. She took Jackie's hand, held her gaze, and watched her breathe her last. Her chest fluttered once, twice, then was still. A bubble of blood formed on her lower lip. After a second or two, it burst, and Ellison felt tears spill from her eyes.

"Leave her," said a voice.

Ellison turned and saw a man standing over her. His hands were tightly clasped in front of his chest, as if in prayer, and he was looking down at Jackie's body with disbelieving horror.

"Leave her," he repeated, his voice quavering. "Please. I'll take her."

Ellison stared up at him, then nodded. She turned back to the dead girl, pulled the metal stake gently out of her throat, then moved aside. The man knelt down, laid his head on Jackie's chest, and began to weep. She watched him for a long moment, then forced herself to her feet and staggered back towards her squad mate.

Morton hadn't moved; he was still staring blankly at the horror unfolding before him. Ellison crouched down and took hold of his shoulders.

"Look at me," she said, as firmly as she was able. "Look at me, John. It was an accident. An accident. It could have happened to any of us. Do you hear me?"

Morton stared at her, uncomprehending. She hooked her hands under his armpits and tried to lift him to his feet, but nothing happened; he was immovable, a dead weight.

"John," she said. "Get up. Come on, John."

She was suddenly aware of movement behind her and looked round; the inhabitants of the tunnel were slowly approaching, looks of abject misery on most of their faces. Aggie was at the front, her eyes narrow.

"Get out of our place," she spat. "Leave us our dead. Don't come here again."

Ellison looked at Aggie, trying to convey without words even a fraction of the sorrow she was feeling. Jackie had not deserved the fate that had befallen her; she had simply been caught up in the tornado of blood and death that seemed to follow Blacklight around. Aggie stared back at her, her expression not moving so much as a millimetre, until Ellison nodded.

"OK," she said. "It's time to go, John. Get the hell up. Right now."

Morton said nothing; he climbed slowly to his feet and looked at Ellison with a broken expression on his pale face.

"This is the second time we've talked about John Morton, sir," said Jamie. He was standing in front of Cal Holmwood's desk, his helmet under his arm. He had messaged the Interim Director before their van was even out of London, telling him he needed to see him the moment they got back to the Loop. "And this time a civilian girl died. It was an accident, but it happened because he panicked. I'm telling you for the second time, sir, that he can't handle this. Not yet anyway."

Holmwood closed his eyes for a long moment, then regarded Jamie with a weary expression. "Did Surveillance pick Dempsey up when you called it in?"

"Yes, sir," he replied. "They've still got him."

"Good," said Holmwood. "That's something at least."

"It's something," agreed Jamie. "What about Morton, sir?"

The Interim Director sighed. "You still want him placed on the inactive roster?"

"Yes, sir. More than ever."

Holmwood said nothing for a long moment. He looked barely awake, like a man running on empty. "OK," he said, eventually. "Do what you think is best. If that means making him inactive, then you have my authorisation."

"Thank you, sir," said Jamie, feeling relief wash over him.

"That's OK. Is there anything else?"

"No, sir. There's nothing else."

"Thank God for that," said Holmwood, and produced the thinnest smile Jamie had ever seen. "Go and get some sleep."

38

JOINING UP THE DOTS

LINDISFARNE, NORTHUMBERLAND

Pete Randall walked along the edge of the cliffs at the northern edge of the island that he had called home his entire life, lost in a world of his own.

In the distance, rising up against the afternoon sky, stood the stone buildings of the Lindisfarne monastery. The ancient seat of religious learning had withstood two Viking invasions, but had been destroyed in a single night by monsters that Pete Randall was forbidden from ever talking about, that he had been told repeatedly that he had never seen, despite the evidence of his own eyes.

The small number of monks who had survived the night his daughter was lost had left the island in the days that followed. Now the ancient building stood empty; it would probably still be standing long after the last of the houses built above the harbour had fallen into ruin. Pete inched his way to the cliff top and sat down, his legs dangling over the edge. Below him, the North Sea crashed against the cliffs; spray, cold and salty and sharp, was thrown up in great explosions, dampening the legs of his jeans. He barely noticed.

His mind was lost in the past.

When Kate had been six, he had brought her up here on a cold January night to watch the plumes of fire that rose from the distant oil rigs. The Lesters had recently moved to the island and Kate had immediately become best friends with their daughter Julie, a friendship that would last until Julie was left lying on Lindisfarne's dock with her mouth full of blood and her head twisted almost all the way round.

Andy Lester worked the rigs; every three months or so he flew by helicopter to Aberdeen and made his way down to Lindisfarne to spend two precious weeks with his family, before heading back out to sea again. This lifestyle, which Pete knew was a hard, dangerous way to make a living, had seemed almost unthinkably glamorous to Kate, a girl who, at that point, had only left Lindisfarne a handful of times. When he had told her that on a clear day you could see the rigs themselves, that on a clear night you could see great pillars of fire as the waste gas was burned away, she had refused to believe him, demanding to see for herself. He had waited for a clear night, the kind of night where the dark water seemed to go on forever, got permission from his wife, who was unwell again with what would eventually turn out to be the cancer that killed her, wrapped his daughter in warm clothes and led her across the island.

They had sat roughly where he was sitting now, drinking hot chocolate out of plastic cups he filled from a flask, and watched the horizon. For ten minutes or so, nothing had happened. Then a pillar of orange burst up from the horizon, a flare of crackling fire that seemed impossibly huge, even across the miles of freezing water. Kate had screamed with delight; he had taken a tight grip on the back of her jacket, in case her excitement took her too close to the treacherous, crumbling edge. They had stayed for more than an hour, Pete waiting for the novelty to wear off, before gradually realising it wasn't going to; Kate greeted each flare with the kind of joy that he had only seen from her on Christmas morning.

He had never known why the distant fires had filled her with such pleasure, and now he would never get the chance to ask her. He had come to believe that she saw them as proof of things happening beyond their small island, things that were different and bigger and brighter than those happening around her. There was something in her bones, a wanderlust that he had been proud to see grow and flourish, but which had nonetheless filled his heart with sadness.

He had always known that his daughter would eventually leave, that Lindisfarne would never be big enough for her. He and his wife had reconciled themselves to that awful prospect: Kate would visit and they would still have each other. But then Annie had died, and he and Kate had been left alone, and he had come to realise that her plans, her desire for a bigger, wider life, had been put on hold, possibly indefinitely. He knew she would not leave him on his own, and that realisation had filled him with a sadness far greater than he had felt at the prospect of her doing so.

But now she was gone, and he *was* alone.

His mobile phone buzzed and he pulled it out of his pocket. The screen showed a text message from SOUTH and he felt a small tingle of excitement flutter up his spine. They'd been emailing all week, several times a day, and had finally plucked up the courage to exchange numbers.

He thumbed open the message.

LOOK AT THIS ASAP.

http://www.kevinmckenna.wordpress.com/blog/news/032154

Pete read the text twice, searching for any hidden meaning, then pocketed the phone and headed for home. He didn't hurry; he doubted the link would contain anything life-changing.

He had no way of knowing exactly how wrong he was.

KEVINMCKENNA.COM – the online home of award-winning journalist Kevin McKenna

RED EYES AND BLACK UNIFORMS
Posted by KEVIN

I thought long and hard before writing this post. Believe me, I did.

I thought about the risk, about whether I might be endangering myself by writing it. I thought about the men and women who might read it, and whether they're better off in the dark. I thought about the government and the security of the country, although I understand if you don't believe me. I thought about it all, and I arrived at the most unshakeable conclusion of my life.

It's worth the risk. It's too important.

Right now, I'm not going to explain anything more than I have in the title of this post – if you don't know what I'm talking about, be grateful, carry on with your day, and don't give this a second thought. But if you do...

If you do, I want to hear from you. I want your stories. I want to know how many of you are out there.

Proxy up and post your stories in the comments below – I guarantee your anonymity. No one else needs to put their head above the parapet, at least not yet. If I get the response

I'm expecting, if people are brave enough to talk about the things they've seen, I think we'll see this start to move fast. But let's wait and see.

Red eyes. Black uniforms.

Tell me. I believe you.

Kevin McKenna

39

PRIME SUSPECT

Valentin Rusmanov's appearance at the ISAT compound caused exactly the reaction among the men and women of the Intelligence Division that the ancient vampire lived for.

He walked through the open-plan desks of the Division as though he was taking a casual morning stroll, despite the Security Division Operators flanking him with their T-Bones drawn. Valentin was a superstar, one of the oldest vampires in the world, turned by Dracula himself, and opportunities to see him up close did not come along very often.

He was as immaculate as ever, the result of the attentive skills of Lamberton, his valet. His pale, handsome face was smooth, his charcoal suit crisp over a bright white shirt, his shoes gleaming like mirrors. Every single member of the Intelligence Division stopped what they were doing when he entered and stared openly at him; Valentin smiled back expansively, nodding at the Operators whose desks he passed closest by. He loved few things in the world more than attention, and the rapt expressions on the faces of the men and women sitting at their small grey workstations were an utter joy.

Kate Randall was waiting for him outside the security door that controlled access to ISAT. She watched him make his way towards her, disgusted by the reactions of her colleagues.

He's a rock star, she thought. *Despite all the thousands of people he's killed. They're like star-struck kids.*

Valentin picked his way through the last of the desks and favoured her with a wide, dizzying smile. "Miss Randall," he said, extending his hand. "What a pleasure it is to see you again. I trust you're well?"

Kate shook the offered hand briefly. "I'm very well, thank you, Mr Rusmanov. If you'd like to follow me, we'll get this over with as quickly as possible."

"How professional you are," said Valentin, his smile widening even further. "Even though one of your colleagues tried to kill you yesterday. Bravo, Miss Randall. Bravo."

Don't rise to him, she told herself. *Don't give him what he wants.*

"As I said, Mr Rusmanov," she replied, forcing a narrow smile, "if you'd like to follow me." She typed a code into the panel beside the door, which unlocked with a series of clicks and thuds. She pulled it open and Valentin stepped through, followed closely by his guards.

Kate closed her eyes and took a deep breath, steadying herself in preparation for what she had to do. When she opened them, she saw the silent ranks of the Intelligence Division staring at her.

"Haven't you got any work to do?" she snapped, then walked into ISAT, pulling the door shut behind her.

Kate showed Valentin and his escorts into the interview room, and left the technicians wiring him into the chair. The vampire appeared to be taking it all in good humour, viewing the whole thing as little more than an amusing diversion, but she wasn't quite convinced;

she believed that, deep down, Valentin had to be finding this demeaning, or at the very least annoying.

I hope so, she thought. *I hope it's really pissing him off.*

She pushed open the door to the lounge and nodded to Paul Turner. The Security Officer was sitting on the sofa, reading Valentin Rusmanov's file. The document had been compiled from the interrogation that had been conducted when the vampire first defected to Blacklight and was almost as thick as a phone directory.

"Two minutes," said Kate.

Turner closed the file, and smiled at her. "Good," he said. "You don't mind me taking this one, right? I think it's for the best."

"It's fine," said Kate. "How deep are you going to go?"

"We've covered everything useful that he's prepared to tell us," said Turner, tapping the cover of the file. "Double-checking it all would take about a week. There are a couple of things I want to ask him again now that he's hooked up, but mostly it's about yesterday."

"Do you think he did it?" asked Kate.

"No," said Turner. "I don't. Do you?"

Kate shook her head. "Part of me hopes that he did," she said. "It would be a lot easier for everyone if his defection was a lie and he was still working for Dracula. But I don't believe that's the case."

"Me neither," said Turner. "If he was still working for Dracula, I don't believe that he would waste his time targeting you and me. But a lot of Operators do, for now at least. So we need to get this done and get on with our job. Someone out there is hiding something and we need to find out who."

Before they attack someone else, thought Kate, and shivered.

"All right," she said. "Let's get on with it."

"Before we go in there," said Turner, standing up, "I want you to promise me something."

"What?"

"That you won't let him get inside your head," said Turner. "Whatever he says, whatever he asks you. Don't give him what he wants."

"Don't worry," said Kate, with a tight smile. "I won't."

Valentin was sitting in the chair as they entered the interview room, one foot resting casually on his other knee. His escort stood on either side of him, their T-Bones raised.

"Major Turner," said the vampire, smiling broadly. "I honestly believe that, with the exception of Lamberton, I have conversed more with you than I have with anyone else in the last century or so. Surely there can't be anything *else* you wish to ask me? My sexual proclivities perhaps? The regularity of my bowels?"

"Mr Rusmanov," said Turner. "Thank you for coming."

"You're most welcome," replied Valentin. "Although your thanks imply that I had some kind of choice in the matter. If so, it wasn't made clear to me."

"We both know full well that if you had refused to leave your cell, there would have been very little we could do to compel you," said Turner. "I was being polite. I can stop, if you would prefer?"

Valentin grinned. "Politeness is a rare commodity in this day and age, Major Turner, and I respect you enormously for keeping tradition alive."

"Thank you," replied the Security Officer. He took one of the seats at the desk, as Kate slipped into the other. She looked down at the screen set into its surface and saw the system was live.

"This is ISAT interview 072," said Turner, his voice flat and even, "conducted by Major Paul Turner, NS303, 36-A in the presence of Lieutenant Kate Randall, NS303, 78-J. State your name, please."

"Is this it?" asked Valentin. "Are we officially under way?"

"We are," replied Turner. "State your name, please."

"Valentin Rusmanov."

Green.

"Please answer the following question incorrectly," said Turner. "State your gender, please."

"Female," replied Valentin.

Red.

Kate took a deep breath.

Let's go, she thought. *Let's do this.*

"Mr Rusmanov," said Turner. "Yesterday afternoon explosive devices were planted inside two rooms in this facility, with the clear intention of causing harm to members of this Department. Did you plant the devices in question?"

"Do you actually think I did?" asked Valentin, frowning. "Would you think so little of me, Major Turner? After all the time we have spent together?"

"Answer the question, please. Did you plant the devices?"

"Of course not."

Green.

"Do you know who did?"

"No."

Green.

"Do you have any information that could be relevant to identifying the perpetrator of this attack?"

"I'm afraid not."

Green.

Kate breathed out heavily. The results were exactly what she had expected, but it had still been a relief to see the green lights on the screens; there had been an elephant in the room since the Zero Hour Task Force meeting the previous day.

If it had been him, what the hell were we supposed to have done about it?

"Thank you, Mr Rusmanov," said Turner. "Now. I want to ask you about—"

"You didn't think I did it, did you?" asked Valentin, stretching his legs out and crossing them at the ankle.

"Mr Rusmanov, I am not—"

"I'm sure many of your colleagues think I did," continued Valentin. "For no other reason than it's the obvious conclusion, and the majority of them are not terribly bright. So I understand why I was summoned to answer your questions, but I must confess I'm now somewhat intrigued as to why you had already concluded I was innocent. Would you indulge me? For politeness' sake, if nothing else?"

"Mr Rusmanov," said Paul Turner. "We are not here to satisfy your curiosity. We're here to—"

"Excuse me, Major Turner," interrupted Valentin. "But I'm afraid I wasn't talking to you. I was talking to Miss Randall."

Kate frowned. "Me?" she asked. "Why would you care what I think?"

"Because I know why Major Turner didn't believe I was the culprit," said Valentin. "He is a man of evidence, of probability, and I have no doubt he concluded that I was innocent by applying sound, no doubt deeply boring, logic. You, on the other hand, have not yet had the life drummed out of you by this drab, grey place. So you interest me, just as your colleague bores me to tears."

"It might be wise for you to remember that you are a guest in this facility," said Turner, his voice low. "And that I do not have infinite patience."

"Then destroy me, by all means," said Valentin, spreading his arms wide and pushing his chest forward. "Then go and explain to dear old Mr Holmwood that you did it because the nasty vampire was rude to you. I'm sure he'll understand."

Turner didn't reply, but a narrow smile emerged on his face, and his gaze didn't leave Valentin's.

If the time ever comes when we don't need him any more, thought Kate, *Valentin will regret some of the things he's said. Paul isn't going to forget them, I know that much.*

"It didn't seem like something you would do," she said. "That's why I didn't think you did it."

"Explain," said Valentin.

"I thought exactly the same thing Major Turner did. If you were here on false pretences, if you were still working for Dracula, I thought you would have probably done something a lot worse than planting two bombs. And..."

"Go on," said Valentin, his smile wide and unsettling. "Please."

"It didn't seem like your style," said Kate. "Booby traps and home-made bombs. I suppose I felt you would consider that sort of thing beneath you."

Valentin's smile broadened into a grin. "Very good, Miss Randall," he said. "Very good indeed. You are quite the insightful little thing, aren't you?"

"I don't know," said Kate. "I've never thought about it."

"Oh, but of course you have," said Valentin. "Everyone constantly thinks about themselves. We think about what we're good at, and what we're bad at, and we compare ourselves endlessly to those around us. You, for example. Do you think of yourself as the great

Jamie Carpenter's faithful sidekick? Of course you don't, even though that is how the rest of the world sees you. You see yourself as an intelligent, insightful girl, cleverer than most, and you resent the fact that you are forced to live in Mr Carpenter's shadow. Or am I wrong?"

"That's enough," said Turner. He cast a glance in her direction, a look she instantly understood.

Don't give him what he wants.

"Did I offend you?" asked Valentin, his voice dripping with insincerity. "If so, forgive me. It was not my intention."

"Yes, it was," said Kate. "But that's OK. And you're right about some things, Mr Rusmanov. I guess that when you've lived a life as long as yours you become pretty good at reading people. But you're wrong about Jamie. I don't resent him and I'm proud to be his friend. And I really don't care whether you believe that or not."

"I do believe you," said Valentin, softly. "And I know he feels the same about you."

Kate knew she was doing exactly what she wasn't supposed to by letting Valentin draw her into a conversation about herself and her friends. He was interested only in pushing her buttons, in eliciting the reactions he was looking for; it was nothing more than a game to him, a cruel entertainment.

"Did he tell you that?" she asked, unable to stop herself.

"Indirectly," replied Valentin. "His mother was kind enough to pass the information on."

Kate frowned. "When did you talk to Marie?"

"Oh, I drop in on her every now and then," said Valentin. "I am somewhat starved of company downstairs, and it turns out that Mrs Carpenter loves few things more than a pot of tea and a civilised conversation. She and I have become rather close as a result."

"If you hurt her," said Turner, his voice like polar ice, "if you upset her, or scare her, or in any way attempt to manipulate her, I will kill you, and I promise you that Cal Holmwood will not say a word. *She* is not part of this."

"Part of what?" asked Valentin, in a low voice.

"Of what we do. She's a civilian. She's innocent."

"Your opinion of me really cannot be rehabilitated, can it?" said Valentin. "Major Turner, you are aware that I made a promise a long time ago not to hurt any member of the Carpenter family, although I feel the need to point out that there is precisely nothing you could do about it if I changed my mind. I enjoy Marie's company and I know the feeling is mutual. I have done nothing more than attempt to teach her about what she has become and offer her a shoulder to cry on when she is worried about her son. I am still capable of emotion, Major Turner, and of associating with humans without the desire to torture and kill them. I am not the monster you think I am."

"No," said Turner. "You're worse. *You* hide your cruelty behind a mask of friendship. A convincing mask, at that. But still just a mask."

"I would not presume to try and change your mind, Major Turner," said Valentin. "You will believe what you believe."

"You're right," said Turner. "I will."

"Very well. In which case, let us leave Major Turner's beliefs where they are and return to the matter in hand," said Valentin, smiling broadly at Kate. "I know that Jamie is proud to be your friend because you are a subject which endlessly delights his mother. Marie practically falls over herself to tell me how fond of you she is. She also has a tendency to tell me things she has kept from Jamie, things that—"

"Don't," said Kate.

"Don't what?" enquired Valentin.

"Don't try to play games with me. I don't need to know what Marie has told you."

"If I was attempting to play games with you," said Valentin, pleasantly, "I would have told you how much Marie hates your friend Larissa, and how fervently she hopes her son will come to his senses and fall hopelessly in love with you. But I didn't tell you that, did I?" Then the ancient vampire's smile disappeared and, for the briefest of moments, a flicker of red flared in the furthest corners of his eyes. "Oh dear," he said, softly. "Now that was careless of me."

A chill ran up Kate's spine, then spread slowly through her entire body.

I didn't want to know that. I really didn't.

"Mr Rusmanov," growled Paul Turner. "This interview is over. Thank you very much for your time."

"So soon?" sighed Valentin. "I was just starting to enjoy myself."

"You don't know Jamie," spat Kate. "You don't know anything about him, or me, or Larissa. You don't know anything."

"Lieutenant Randall," said Turner, fixing her with an ominous stare.

"You don't care about anything," she continued. "You're only here because you don't like the idea of having to do what Dracula tells you, but you're too scared to face him on your own. You're just a coward."

"Kate—"

"You're clever, and you've been around forever, and you think it's fun to screw with people, to tell them things and see what happens. But it's not fun. It's pathetic. Jamie goes out there every day trying to stop the darkness from taking over and what do you do? You sit in your cell and you think up little schemes and tricks and pat yourself on the back for being *so* clever. You're nothing. I know it, you know it, and Jamie knows it."

Valentin frowned for a moment, before his eyes widened and he burst out laughing, a high, feminine sound that raised the hairs on the back of Kate's neck. "Oh dear," he said. "I honestly believed you knew. But you don't, do you? Neither of you do."

"Know what?" asked Paul Turner.

"Mr Carpenter has made rather a habit of spending time with me in my cell," said Valentin. "I assumed he was doing so with permission, but now I see that I was wrong. How awkward."

Kate stared at the ancient vampire. "You're lying," she said.

"I'm sure you think so," said Valentin. "But I'm equally sure that a clever girl like you can see that there's a very easy way for you to check. Ask him yourself, the next time you see him. Ask the friend that you clearly know so, so very well. But don't be surprised if you don't like what he tells you."

Major Turner stood up, his chair scraping across the floor with a noise like nails down a blackboard.

"For the last time," he said, his voice low and full of fury, "this interview is over. Operators, take Mr Rusmanov back to his cell. If he speaks, or so much as breathes in a way that you don't like, you have my direct permission to destroy him where he stands. Now get him out of my sight."

40

PAVED WITH GOOD INTENTIONS

Pete Randall read Kevin McKenna's post, read it again, then read it a third time. His heart pounded in his chest as his brain screamed for him to be careful, to think it through, to not walk blindly into a trap.

He googled McKenna and immediately breathed a sigh of relief. The man was clearly real; the range of articles by and about him was too voluminous to have been faked. But there was also nothing to suggest that he would write such a post; he was not an investigative journalist, the kind who seeks to trap corrupt politicians and financial fraudsters, and he appeared to have done nothing of note for many years.

He knows, though. Somehow, he knows. And he's saying so, in public.

Pete sat with his laptop on his knees, paralysed by the thought of what to do next. What he *wanted* to do was click on the comments box at the bottom of McKenna's post and start spilling his broken heart out on to the screen.

But he didn't.

South will know. I'll ask him what to do.

He started typing a text message, then paused as the man's number glowed on the screen. He stared at it, then gently pressed the tip of his finger against it.

The phone rang and rang, and Pete's heart sank.

Of course he won't answer. He's not that stupid. I bet he doesn't even have voicemail.

"North?"

Pete almost dropped the phone. "Yeah," he said. "It's me."

"What are you playing at, mate?" asked South. He sounded angry. "We didn't agree to this. Mobiles are the easiest thing in the world to trace, you know that."

"I know," said Pete. "I'm sorry, I just... I can't believe that post. I don't know what to do about it and I needed to talk to someone."

There was a pause.

"It's OK," said South, his tone of voice fractionally warmer. "Don't worry about it. So you read it?"

"Yeah," replied Pete. "I can't quite believe it. Do you think it's legit?"

"I think so," said South. "I'm not sure, but I think so. I've been turning it over and over, and I can't see why the government would do this. I'm assuming that they've got us, and anyone else like us, under surveillance, so what would be the point? To try and trick us into talking about what we know? To get us out into the open? Why bother? If they've decided we're a potential problem, why not just make us disappear?"

A chill rattled up Pete's spine. "That's what I thought," he said.

"If it *is* real," said South, "then the balls on this guy..."

There was silence for a long moment.

"So what do we do?" asked Pete, eventually. "I mean, my first instinct is to tell him what happened to me and my daughter. What are you thinking?"

"The same," said South. "I was just checking through what I wrote for the other site. I'm going to post it as soon as I'm done."

"Are you sure?" asked Pete. "That it's the right thing to do?"

"I don't know," replied South, the heat returning to his voice. "And to be honest with you, mate, I don't give a shit. If I post it and they catch me and throw me in some cell somewhere, or put a bullet in the back of my head, then so be it. There's nothing left they can take from me. So, if this guy is going to try and do something, then I want to at least try and help him. Don't you?"

Two hours later, a long way from Lindisfarne, Kevin McKenna sipped a can of lager while Albert Harker read over his shoulder, his fangs visible beneath a top lip that was curled into a wide grin of pleasure.

The journalist and the vampire were huddled round McKenna's laptop in an anonymous room in a chain hotel in the west London suburbs. They had left his house in Kilburn less than an hour after the blog post went live, Harker in the clothes he was wearing, McKenna with a sports bag full of hastily gathered clothes, notebooks, pens and toiletries. He had no way of knowing whether the vampire was right, that Blacklight would come for him when they saw the blog, but he had found himself unwilling to take the chance.

"Wonderful," said the vampire. "Just wonderful. Less than six hours and already we have two highly detailed eyewitness accounts of both vampires and Blacklight. I could not have hoped for better."

McKenna nodded as Harker floated across the room and picked up a steaming mug of coffee. He had been astonished to see the stories appear beneath his blog, stories that were full of helicopters and soldiers and death and blood, but were nonetheless horribly, compellingly convincing. He was trying to stay calm, to not get too carried away, but was not completely succeeding.

If this is all true, he thought, *then he's right. This is the story of the century.*

"So what now?" he asked, carefully. "We've got two people who say they saw vampires, and one who saw the men you told me about. It's a start, but it's only two people."

Harker sipped his coffee. "There'll be more," he said. "A lot more, I suspect. As for what now, you need to get to work."

"On what?"

Harker smiled. "Your finest hour, my dear Mr McKenna."

41

UNDERCURRENTS

"I'm sorry," said Kate. "I let you down."

"Nonsense," replied Paul Turner. "You were provoked by someone who has been manipulating people for more than four centuries. You stood up to him, and for your friends."

"But that's what he wanted," said Kate.

"It doesn't matter," said Turner. "You should still be proud of yourself."

They were sitting in the ISAT lounge, Kate on the sofa and Paul in the plastic desk chair. Kate was so furious with herself for having risen to Valentin's bait that she was physically shaking; she had tried to drink a glass of water to calm herself down, but had spilled most of it on the carpeted floor. She had been expecting her boss to be every bit as angry with her as she was with herself; as a result, part of her was almost disappointed by his response.

"You told me not to let him inside my head," she said. "You said those exact words."

"I know what I said," replied Turner. "And I wish you hadn't. But I don't believe he can use anything you said against you, or us. I imagine attempting to upset you amused him."

"He succeeded," said Kate.

"So I could see," said Turner. The sight of his colleague shouting at one of the oldest vampires in the world had warmed his heart considerably; it had been all he could do to stop himself grinning like an idiot.

Kate managed a small smile. "What are you going to do?" she asked. "The things he said about Jamie and Marie?"

"I don't know," said Turner. "Jamie's Zero Hour cleared, so I don't think he's breaking any regulations by visiting Valentin. But if it's happened more than once, if it's become some kind of regular thing, then it will have to stop. As for Marie, I don't really see what I can do about that. We can't put her anywhere else, and Valentin can go through the UV barriers at will."

"You don't think he'd hurt her, do you?" asked Kate.

"I don't know," said Turner. "I hope not. But there isn't much I consider beyond Valentin Rusmanov, if the wrong mood were to take him."

"Don't tell Jamie that," said Kate. "He's got enough to worry about."

"We all have," said Turner. "But I won't concern him with something we can't do anything about."

"I can't believe he's been going to see Valentin," she said, in a low voice. "If he needed to talk to someone, why not me or Matt? Or his mum? Or Colonel Frankenstein, for that matter?"

"I wish I knew," said Turner. "Maybe he wanted to know more about his family. Valentin knew his grandfather, maybe that's what they talk about."

"Frankenstein knew John Carpenter," said Kate. "Why not talk to him?"

The Security Officer didn't answer and she found herself suddenly, painfully angry; despite the promise she, Larissa, Matt and Jamie had made to each other months earlier, the world was still riddled with secrets, with lies and hidden motives.

Paul Turner's console beeped into life. He pulled the plastic square from his belt and checked it. As Kate watched, his eyes widened momentarily, before his face brightened into a smile.

"Natalia Lenski is awake," he said. "No permanent physical damage, no memory loss. Excellent."

"Good news," said Kate, feeling her anger subside as the weight of her guilt over what had happened to the young Russian girl was lifted from her shoulders. "That's really good."

"Agreed," said Turner, getting up from his chair. "I need to send a Security Division team down to question her. We'll push the next interview back an hour. Go and get a coffee, forget about Valentin Rusmanov, and come back ready to work. OK?"

"Paul," she said. He paused, his hand resting on the door handle, and turned back to look at her.

"Yes?"

"Do you think you could do me a small favour?"

Kate and Matt walked quickly along the Level C corridor towards the infirmary.

Paul Turner had not been thrilled by her request to let Matt see Natalia before she was officially interviewed, but had agreed after only a small amount of pleading; he understood why it was important to her, and why it would be to her friend. She had thanked him and immediately messaged Matt. Ordinarily, she would not have expected a reply: Jamie, Larissa and herself had all become accustomed to Matt being extremely difficult to get hold of. But in this case, she had not been surprised to receive a message from him less than a minute after she pressed SEND, agreeing to meet her at the Level C lift.

"So she's really going to be OK?" he asked. "That's what Major Turner said?"

"For the fifth time," she said, smiling at her friend. "Paul said she's going to be fine."

"That's good," said Matt. "That's really great."

You've got it bad, my friend, she thought, happily. *If only you knew what I know.*

They reached the infirmary and stepped through the double doors. The long white room was almost empty; only a single bed, halfway down the left-hand wall, was occupied. Natalia Lenski raised her pale, pretty face from her pillow and peered at them as they approached, a small smile of recognition appearing as she did so.

"Matt," she said. "Kate. It is very good to see you both."

Matt blushed ever so slightly as she said his name, a tiny bloom of pale pink. He pulled slightly ahead as they neared Natalia and arrived at her bedside first. Kate slowed her own pace fractionally, hanging back to give them the briefest of moments alone.

"Are you all right?" asked Matt. "How do you feel?"

Natalia Lenski was a mess. Her face was bruised black and yellow, and covered in small scratches and cuts. A thin rectangle of bandage covered a patch of skin just above her ear, and her left eye was swollen almost shut. But she smiled at his questions, her face lighting up beautifully as she did so.

"I am not too bad," she said. "I was lucky, I think. Very lucky."

"Hi, Natalia," said Kate, stopping beside Matt. "Good to see you again."

Matt frowned. "Do you two know each other?" he asked.

"Not really," said Kate. "Right?"

"That is right," replied Natalia, and smiled again. The girl's injuries made Kate's heart hurt, but her smile was a lovely thing to see.

"Do you remember what happened?" asked Matt. "The explosion?"

"I remember a sound," said Natalia, frowning. "A very big sound. Then nothing until I woke up here and the doctors told me the door had hit me. They said it kept the fire away."

"Wow," said Matt, softly. "I can't believe you survived a bomb blowing up right in front of you. You're like a superhero."

Natalia smiled, and Matt blushed again, more obviously.

I should go, thought Kate. *I'm in the way here.*

"I have to get back to ISAT," she said. "I just wanted to see if you were OK, Natalia, and I'm really glad you are. Matt, you can stay for about ten minutes before Security gets here. If you want to, that is?"

"I'll stay," said Matt, then looked at Natalia. "I mean, if that's OK with you?"

"Stay," said Natalia. "It will be nice."

"OK," said Kate. "I'll see you both later." She turned to leave, but Matt said her name and she stopped.

"I wanted to ask Natalia something," he said. "It might be better if you're here."

"OK," she said. "What is it?"

Matt turned his pale, earnest face towards the girl lying in the bed. "Why were you going into Kate's room, Natalia? When the bomb went off. What was going on?"

Natalia blushed deeply. "I cannot tell you that," she replied. "It is private."

"Private?" asked Matt, glancing at Kate. "Between the two of you? How does that work?"

"You heard her, Matt," said Kate. "She said it's private."

Matt frowned and looked about to protest, but saw the gentle warning in his friend's gaze. He looked at her for a moment, then turned his attention back to Natalia.

"I have to go," continued Kate. "Lunch tomorrow. One thirty. No excuses."

Matt nodded. "OK," he said, then began to tell Natalia about the developments at the Lazarus Project in the last thirty-six hours. Natalia's smile slowly returned and Kate left her listening happily to Matt's increasingly excitable narrative. She closed the infirmary door behind her, knowing full well that she would not see Matt in the dining room the following afternoon, and forgiving him in advance. She walked along the corridor, her mind full of hope at the fragile, bittersweet prospect of two people finding happiness amid the darkness that surrounded them all.

Christ, I hope he works out what's going on, she thought, pressing the button that summoned the lift. *There's no way she's going to tell him and I promised her I wouldn't. It's so obvious, though, surely he'll see it for himself? He is a genius after all.*

The lift arrived and she stepped inside, a big smile on her face.

Although for a genius, she reminded herself, *he sometimes isn't very bright.*

As Kate Randall and Matt Browning were opening the door to the infirmary, Major Paul Turner was stepping out of the airlock at the end of the cellblock on Level G. His stomach was twisted into an unpickable knot, a hard ball of cold, raging fury.

Stay calm, he told himself. *For her sake, if not for your own. Stay calm.*

The guard post to his left was occupied by an Operator from the Security Division that Turner commanded. The protocol was for every visitor to the block to sign in and out, but the Security Officer didn't so much as glance in the man's direction as he strode down the corridor, even when the Operator plaintively called his name. He kept walking, forcing himself not to run, his boots clicking loudly on the floor of the corridor.

Stay calm. Stay calm.

He had told Kate Randall he wasn't angry with her, wasn't disappointed in her, and he had been telling the truth.

He wasn't angry with *her*.

Turner reached Valentin Rusmanov's cell, took a deep breath, and stepped out in front of the ultraviolet wall that was supposed to keep the ancient vampire contained.

The cell was empty.

Turner stared for a long moment, and was about to reach for the radio on his belt when a blur descended from the ceiling. An arm shot out, inhumanly fast, hauled him through the purple barrier and slammed him against the flat concrete wall. He gasped as the blur solidified into the familiar shape of Valentin Rusmanov, his fangs gleaming, his eyes blazing red.

"If you're planning to kill me, Major Turner," said the vampire, "I suggest you learn to be a little lighter on your feet."

"I didn't come here... to fight," croaked Turner. "If I had, I wouldn't... have come... alone."

"Fair enough," said Valentin, and released his grip. Turner fell to the floor, clutching at his neck. "In which case, what can I do for you, Major Turner? Given that we had the pleasure of each other's company barely an hour ago?"

The Security Officer forced himself to his feet.

"I want to know why you did it," he said. His voice was low; it was taking every ounce of his strength to keep his temper, to not let the humiliation Valentin had just dealt him mix fatally with the fury that was already roaring inside him. "I want to know why you did that to Kate."

458

"What did I do to her?" asked Valentin, floating effortlessly backwards through the air and coming to rest in one of his two chairs.

"You know exactly what you did," said Turner. He picked up the other chair, set it opposite the vampire's, and flopped into it. "She's nothing to you. She didn't even know you existed until three months ago. Why torment her?"

"Major Turner," said Valentin, lacing his fingers together behind his head. "Do you truly understand the prospect we are facing here? What will happen if my former master is allowed to rise?"

"I do," said Turner.

"If you truly did, then you wouldn't be here asking me that question."

"Listen to—"

"No, you listen to me," interrupted Valentin, his eyes flaring a terrible, oily red. "If Dracula rises, then everything that this Department has ever faced is going to seem like a happy memory. And these children, in whom you and Holmwood have placed so much of your faith? They aren't ready for what is coming, not ready in the slightest. You treat Jamie as though he is the reincarnation of Quincey Harker, Kate like a favourite daughter, and young Matt as though he is the magical key to a cure that you and I both know will probably never exist. I know you think you're helping them. But you aren't. You are failing them, Major Turner. This whole Department is failing them, and before long it will be too late."

Turner felt as though he had been punched in the stomach. He tried to tell himself that what Valentin was saying was wrong, but couldn't make it sound convincing; the vampire's words had the terrible ring of truth.

"So what are you saying?" he asked, slowly. "What are—"

"I told you all when I arrived here that I did not want to see

Dracula rise," said Valentin. "That was, and continues to be, the truth. I am on your side, Major Turner, whether you believe that or not. But if our side consists of young men and women who fall to pieces when someone tells them something they don't want to hear, who are so very easily unsettled by their little secrets and petty jealousies, then what chance are we likely to have?"

Turner was silent for a long moment. "You did it to help her?" he asked, slowly. "Is that what you're telling me?"

Valentin smiled. "Of course not," he replied. "I'm a monster, remember?"

42

FATHERS4TRUTH

From: kevinjmckenna@googlemail.co.uk
To: north3571@hotmail.co.uk; 6589south@gmail.com
Sent: 21:06:54
Subject: Your comments on my blog post

Hello,

Thank you both very much for your comments on my recent blog post. I'm extremely grateful to you for sharing your stories, and I'm deeply sorry for the losses you have suffered.

I am writing to you to ask for your permission to use your accounts in the story I'm currently working on, one that I'm sure will be very close to both of your hearts. You will be credited as anonymous sources, and your email addresses will be kept completely secret.

Please let me know whether this is OK with you, and whether you are happy for me to proceed.

Best wishes,
Kevin

From: north3571@hotmail.co.uk
To: kevinjmckenna@googlemail.co.uk
Cc: 6589south@gmail.com
Sent: 21:23:07
Subject: Re: Your comments on my blog post

Dear Kevin,

Thank you for your email – I'm very happy for you to use what I wrote in your story, as long as my anonymity is guaranteed.

Please do keep me up to date on the story as it develops – I suspect that you're right, and I will be very interested in reading it when it's done.

Cheers,
north3571

From: 6589south@gmail.com
To: kevinjmckenna@googlemail.co.uk
Cc: north3571@hotmail.co.uk
Sent: 21:29:41
Subject: Re: Your comments on my blog post

Dear Kevin,

I too am very happy, excited even, for you to use what happened to my family in your story. It will be nice for me to think that I've helped, even in some small way, to prevent what happened to north3571 and me from happening to anyone else.

Best wishes,
6589south

"What did I tell you?" said Albert Harker, a smile rising on his pale face. "Easy."

"OK," said McKenna. "So they agreed to let me use what they wrote. I still don't get why you're so excited."

"It's simple, my friend," said Harker. "This is the beginning of a crusade, a movement, and it's possible that you, or I, or both of us, will not be around to see its conclusion. If we succeed, if we alert the public to the monsters in their midst, do you really think that will be the end of it? Blacklight is violent, and vengeful, and has a long memory; I am living proof of that. As things stand now, if we were to be found and killed, that would be it. The story would die with us. We are going to need help and I think these two men would be happy to fill that role."

"All right," said McKenna. "But why these two? We've had more than thirty comments on the blog now. What makes them so special?"

"They were the first," said Harker, looking down at the laptop's screen. "Look how quickly they posted. They've been waiting for something like this, I guarantee it. Look how detailed their stories are, how full of rage. They want to do something about this; they've just been waiting for someone to tell them what. They just need the right push."

"Push?" said McKenna.

"Email them back," said McKenna. "Tell them we want their help. I'll bet you any amount they come."

"And then what?"

"We put them to work," said Harker, smiling. "If your editor turns the story down, which I think we both suspect he might, then we're going to need to take a more direct course of action. If it comes to that, four of us will be better than two."

A more direct course of action? thought McKenna. *What the hell does that mean?*

"All right," he said. "I'll email them. But don't be surprised if they think it's some kind of trap. I would."

Harker uncorked a bottle of red wine and poured himself a glass. "Don't worry," he said. "They'll come. How's the story coming?"

McKenna opened a window on his laptop. "It's done," he said.

"Let me see."

He gestured towards the screen. Harker walked back to the desk and McKenna rolled his chair out of the way, giving the vampire space. He opened another can of lager as Harker began to read, and lit a cigarette.

The story was crazy; there was simply no doubt about it. But it was big, it contained some of the best writing he had done in years, and he was surprised to realise how much he wanted Albert Harker to like it.

The vampire scared him; there was no sense in pretending otherwise. But his arrival, and the mad, furious cause that he had brought with him, had lit a fire underneath McKenna, something he hadn't known since the old days. It was little more than a faint flickering, but it was there; he could feel it. And he liked it. He was beginning to allow himself to believe that he might, just might, be able to say goodbye to the mindless, soul-destroying work that filled his days and once again be someone who mattered, who could look himself in the mirror. He didn't know how all this was going to end, but until it did, he was going to play his part to the best of his abilities.

Harker's cause would not fail because of him.

There was one thing he did know, however. The quality of the prose wasn't going to matter to Colin Burton; it would be a miracle if his editor read more than an inch or two beyond the headline. If he was lucky, Burton would think it was some kind of elaborate practical joke; if he wasn't, the reply was likely to come complete with an invitation for him to find a new job.

"It's good," said Harker, turning his head and smiling warmly. "It's very, very good. It's exactly what we need."

"I'm glad," he replied. "They're not going to run it, though, Albert. You know that, right?"

"Maybe," said Harker. "Maybe not. Let's send it and find out."

McKenna rolled back to the desk and brought up his email client. He opened a new message, attached the file, and wrote a short paragraph to his editor. He hit SEND and sat back in his chair, blood thumping in his veins. He wondered how slight the chances were that Colin would see his story for what it was and print it. Then an unexpected word appeared in his mind, unbidden.

Salvation, he thought to himself. *This could be my salvation.*

"Well done," said Harker, squeezing McKenna's shoulder. "Let's hope that he has more sense than you give him credit for. And if he doesn't, well, as least we're prepared. Email our two new recruits, then try to sleep. I have a feeling it's about to get very busy."

The vampire withdrew his hand and headed back to the sofa. McKenna sat for a long moment, his mind racing with prospects he had not considered in years.

Respect. Acclaim. Credit. Fame.

From his desk at *The Globe*, covered in photos of celebrities in bikinis and footballers snorting drugs in nightclub bathrooms, such concepts had seemed as distant and unattainable as the moon. But now, with this story in front of him, a story so explosive that it might genuinely change the world, his mind was tormenting him with what it could mean for his career.

For his life.

McKenna drained his beer, stubbed out his cigarette, and started to write the second email that Harker had asked for.

From: kevinjmckenna@googlemail.co.uk
To: north3571@hotmail.co.uk; 6589south@gmail.com
Sent: 23:19:02
Subject: Re: Re: Your comments on my blog post

Hello,

Great news – I'm honoured that you would let me use your words to help tell my story (I know it's all of our story really, that's just the journalist in me coming out...) and trust me to treat them with the dignity and respect they deserve.

As a matter of fact, I've been thinking about something a bit radical since I received your replies. As before, please do not even hesitate to say no if it isn't something you're interested in. But here it is.

I want you to consider coming down to London to help me open this huge can of worms. The time may come soon when a few brave souls are required to stand up and be counted. Let me know if I'm talking to the wrong people.

Best wishes,
Kevin

From: 6589south@gmail.com
To: kevinjmckenna@googlemail.co.uk
Cc: north3571@hotmail.co.uk
Sent: 23:52:33
Subject: Re: Re: Re: Your comments on my blog post

Dear Kevin,

We have discussed your proposition and we accept.

We will be travelling to London tomorrow – no further details
at this stage, I hope you understand.

Please let me know where we should meet.

Best wishes,
6589south

Kevin McKenna turned his laptop and showed the message to Albert
Harker. The vampire smiled, red light flickering in the corners of
his eyes.

"It's all falling into place," he said. "Just as I told you it would.
Well done, my friend. Well done."

49 DAYS TILL
ZERO HOUR

43

THE DARK HORIZON

CHÂTEAU DAUNCY
AQUITAINE, SOUTH-WESTERN FRANCE

Henry Seward spat a thick wad of blood into the sink and looked at himself in the mirror.

His nose had been broken and reset that morning, sending blood pouring down his throat and leaving a hot island of pain in the middle of his drawn, exhausted face, but he didn't think that was what he had just spat on to the white porcelain. The blood was almost black and he felt sure it had come from somewhere deeper, from the depths of the body that was steadily beginning to fail him; his gut maybe, or his lungs. He coughed now, loud, wet barks that pounded his chest, and his lower back was a perpetual sheet of agony where the worst of Valeri's beatings had been focused. His skin had a yellowish sheen to it, and his eyes were sunken and small.

I'm dying, he thought, with an absence of emotion that surprised him.

He had always believed that he would die either in the heat of combat or as an old man at home in his bed. This scenario, being slowly tortured to death on the orders of Dracula himself, had never occurred to him.

Seward dressed himself carefully. His fingers and limbs were slow to respond to commands these days, as if the lines of communication between them and his brain were beginning to erode. He buttoned up his shirt, then slowly slipped his jacket over his shoulders. He had been invited to take drinks with Dracula in the vampire's study, and he knew from painful experience that the penalties for tardiness were severe.

With his jacket in place, Seward faced himself in the mirror and smoothed down his hair. It was greyer than it had been, and there was significantly less of it; clumps had fallen out in the aftermath of one of the worst sessions of torture, when his body had still been vibrating from the current that had been passed through his wet skin. He looked as though he had aged ten years in the three months he had spent as Dracula's guest; he was absolutely certain that he would not last another three, and probably a lot less than that.

If you're going to come for me, Cal, he thought, *I hope it's soon. Otherwise you're going to be wasting your time.*

Ten minutes later Seward knocked on a door on the top floor of the chateau.

He had been escorted up the stairs by one of his guards, a female vampire whose husband had been destroyed by a Blacklight Operator five years earlier, and who seemed to be constantly trying to restrain the urge to tear out his throat with her bare hands. She left him at the end of the corridor and he walked the last few steps alone; the vampires in the chateau were scared of Dracula and seemed to avoid being in his presence wherever possible, despite the love they all professed to have for him.

"Come in," called the rich, smooth voice that had become so familiar. Seward took a deep breath and pushed open the door.

The room was beautiful, a wide, wood-panelled space that occupied the south-western corner of the grand old building's top floor. It had been Valeri's private sanctuary in the years after the destruction of his wife, but had been immediately claimed by the convalescing Dracula. Bookshelves and paintings covered the walls and a low coffee table sat between two enormous green leather sofas. In the corner of the room was a wooden door, standing open to the cool night air.

"Out here," called the voice. "Do join me, my dear Admiral."

Seward walked slowly across the study and stepped through the door. A wide stone balcony ran all the way round the uppermost floor of the chateau, from where it would have once been possible to see approaching Spaniards when they were still half a day's ride away. He turned to his left and saw Dracula reclining in an elegant wooden chair, his legs stretched out before him. A delicate wrought-iron table stood beside him, on which rested an ice bucket and two glasses of pale, bubbling liquid. The vampire picked one up and held it out, smiling warmly. Seward took the glass from his captor's long, pale fingers, trying not to let his hand shake.

"Thank you," he said.

Dracula smiled, and nodded towards the empty chair. "You're most welcome, Henry. Take a seat. You look as though you might fall over if you don't."

Seward forced down the shame that swam up from his stomach and settled himself into the chair. He sipped the champagne, which was exquisite, and looked out across the vast, dark forest that extended to the west. The air was cool and clear, and it seemed to soothe the pain that had become his constant companion.

"How are you?" asked Dracula. "I heard you had an uncomfortable night."

On your orders, you bloody monster.

"You heard right," said Seward. "You know it would be easier for you just to kill me."

Dracula took a sip from his glass. "Indeed it would," he said. "But that is what you want, yes? And I cannot give you what you want."

"Why not?" asked Seward, realising that he was suddenly on the verge of tears. "Why not just have done with it?"

"Because you are the commanding officer of an organisation that has dedicated itself to destroying my kind," said Dracula. "How would it look if I were to grant you mercy, or allow you the release of a quick death? What is being done to you brings me no pleasure, but even you must see that it is necessary. An example must be made, I'm sorry to say."

Seward knew full well that his suffering gave the ancient vampire great pleasure, but he forced himself to ignore the lie and returned his gaze to the stone wall that encircled the balcony and the horizon beyond it. Somewhere, in the deepest, darkest corners at the back of his mind, an idea had begun to form.

"How does this all end?" he asked. "After all the blood and the screaming and the fighting. What happens then?"

Dracula refilled their glasses. "When I was a man," he said, eventually, "I had no desire to rule the world, despite what the histories may claim. I was Prince of Wallachia, the country of my birth, and that was all I had ever aspired to. I fought to keep her safe, to repel those who would take my throne from me, and I did so with great vigour. But I never wished to be Alexander, with an empire that spanned the globe. My own country was enough."

"You invaded Transylvania," said Seward, mildly. "And Hungary."

Dracula laughed. "Transylvania was in the pocket of the Turks and they deserved no less than they received. I took no pleasure in raiding Hungary, or Serbia for that matter. They were not moves of ambition, of invasion. They served only to keep the Turks at bay. I did nothing during any of my reign that was not solely intended to keep my country safe and free."

Seward said nothing. He took a long sip of champagne, glanced again at the stone wall surrounding the balcony, then returned his attention to his captor.

"Once I became what I am," continued the vampire, "after my throne was stolen for the final time, I withdrew from public life altogether. For a long time, many decades, in fact, I lived in something close to isolation, with only my Generals and their wives for company. My appetite for war and bloodshed had died with my human self, and I was content to let humanity fight and squabble among themselves."

"So what changed?" asked Seward, draining his glass.

"Men from your country chased me to my castle and stuck their blades into my flesh. That's what changed."

Seward didn't respond.

"You want to know how this ends?" asked Dracula. "It's extremely simple. Every human being on this planet will be given the opportunity to pledge their unending loyalty to me, and their complete obedience to my everlasting rule. Those who do so will be spared. Those who do not will die."

"And if everyone were to refuse?" asked Seward, his voice low. "What then?"

"I believe I made myself clear, Henry. What you are suggesting will never come to pass, for once the dying begins, the cowards will beg for the chance to kneel before me. But if it did? I would kill every living soul on this planet."

Seward stared at the vampire; deep, dark red was creeping into the furthest corners of his wild, flickering eyes.

Madness, he thought. *Nothing but madness.*

"Those who do kneel," he said, carefully. "What world will they get the privilege of continuing to live in?"

"A far better one than this," said Dracula. "Without wars, or borders, or religions. A world where the only law is my word, and the only requirement is that they obey."

"It sounds delightful," said Seward, smiling widely.

He was hoping for a laugh and got one; Dracula tipped back his head and roared, a full-throated, guttural blast of amusement. For the briefest second the vampire's eyes closed, and he made his move.

Seward launched himself up out of his chair, reached the stone wall in two faltering steps, and threw himself over it, feeling cool air billow around him as he tumbled towards the distant ground.

Henry Seward fell, watching with complete detachment as the stone wall at the top of the chateau shrank away above him. He had time to wonder whether hitting the ground was going to hurt before a dark shape burst over the wall and rocketed towards him.

Dracula thundered into him in mid-air, his face twisted in an inhuman snarl of rage, his fangs bared, his eyes boiling with red-black fire. He gripped Seward's shoulders with both hands, his nails sinking deeply into the flesh beneath the jacket, and he cried out with new pain. The vampire grinned in triumph, although the smile began to fade as quickly as it had arrived; Seward stared into the ancient, hateful face and realised what was happening.

They had stopped moving when Dracula had taken hold of him, but now they were descending again. He twisted his head around and saw two things: they were still six or seven storeys up, and they were accelerating. He looked back at Dracula, a bitter smile rising on his face, and saw uncertainty on the old monster's.

"Can't hold me, can you?" spat Seward. "Not strong enough. Let me go or I'll take you down with me and we'll find out what the courtyard does to that new body of yours."

Dracula gritted his teeth, and Seward felt their descent slow once more. But it was a brief respite; as he watched, blood began to bubble out of Dracula's nose and fall steadily on to Seward's chest and upturned face. A savage elation filled him.

Not strong enough. Nowhere near. You're one bit of heavy lifting away from falling apart.

"Let me go!" he bellowed, and began pounding at the vampire's arms with his fists. "Let me go!"

Dracula redoubled his efforts and hauled them a few metres back towards the increasingly distant roof of the chateau. Blood was starting to appear at his hairline and run down his forehead, spreading in patches across the front of his crisp white shirt. Seward watched him struggle, his mind still full of hope that he might be allowed to fall, that Dracula's ego would prevent him from calling for help. But then the vampire threw back his head and screamed Valeri's name, dashing Seward's hopes to pieces.

From far below the two twisting, writhing figures, there came the sound of breaking glass; a second later Valeri Rusmanov appeared beside them, his eyes blazing red, and swung a gnarled fist through the air. It crashed into Henry Seward's jaw; a jolt of shuddering pain burst through his head and everything turned grey. He felt new hands take hold of him, hands that were impossibly strong, and, as his vision cleared, he heard Valeri ask his master what had happened.

"The coward jumped from the roof," said Dracula. He was

floating under his own power, smeared and soaked with blood, and was looking at his guest with a fury that seemed to burn into his skin. "I caught him before he was able to take the easy way out."

"You should have let him fall, master," said Valeri, staring at Seward with open loathing. "He is not worth exerting yourself for."

"Do not presume to tell me what I should do, Valeri," said Dracula, his voice full of fire. "He dies when I say he dies, not a second before or after. Is that clear?"

"Perfectly clear, master," said Valeri, and Seward fought back the urge to laugh in the face of the craven, servile vampire.

You could tear his heart from his chest before he even saw you move, he thought. *But you would rather take his orders and insults. How pathetic you truly are.*

"What would you like me to do with him?" asked Valeri.

"Take him back to his room," said Dracula. "I have lost my appetite for his company. Then have a girl brought to my study. Two of them in fact. I feel the need to take my disappointment out on somebody."

"As you wish, master," said Valeri.

Dracula began to ascend, painfully slowly, towards the distant roof. Blood continued to fall steadily from beneath his clothes as he disappeared in the darkness.

I reckon that's set him back at least a couple of days, Seward thought, as he hung in Valeri's grip. *Maybe that'll help you, Cal. I hope so. It's not much, but it was all I could do.*

I hope you know that one day.

I hope you know I tried.

44

THREE MUSKETEERS

Jamie awoke in his bed with a clear conscience.

He had done as Cal Holmwood had told him: gone straight to his quarters and tried to get some sleep. But he had lain awake for a long time, his gaze fixed on the grey ceiling of the small room, his mind turning the Morton problem over and over.

The man had been an outstanding soldier and Jamie believed he could be just as good an Operator, in time. But time was what they didn't have: the situation unfolding around them required every Operator to pull their weight, and Jamie had already lost a highly dangerous vampire because of the actions of his rookie. It wouldn't be fair to Ellison, or to the rest of the Operators who were risking their lives chasing down the Broadmoor escapees, if he allowed the same thing to happen again because he was unwilling to make a hard decision. Although, as he lay on his bed, he had realised that it actually wasn't all that hard; it was, in fact, barely a decision at all.

Now he just needed to work out how to tell John Morton.

Jamie climbed out of bed and made his way to the shower block. The hot water was soothing and he stayed beneath its pounding heat for a long time, feeling his muscles relax, the knots in his shoulders and thighs slowly loosen. When his skin was pink and tingling, he shut the shower off, towelled himself dry, and headed back to his quarters. He dressed quickly, grabbed his phone from his desk and did some calculations in his head.

Nevada is eight hours behind. So it's just after midnight yesterday.

He deliberated for a minute, then scrolled down to Larissa's name and pressed CALL. There was a pause as the connection was made, before the phone started to ring. It rang twice before stopping dead. A second later Larissa's recorded voice invited him to leave her a voicemail.

Jamie frowned. If his girlfriend was asleep, or on Operations, her phone would either be switched off, in which case it would have gone straight to voicemail, or on silent, when it would ring a dozen times or so before cutting out. He took the handset away from his ear and pressed CALL again. Larissa's phone rang for slightly longer this time, almost four rings, before cutting out again. He considered leaving a message, but decided against it; instead, he put the phone in his pocket and took out his console. A press of his thumb activated the screen and another opened the messaging app. Jamie typed out a short message to Ellison and Morton, telling them to report as normal for training in the Playground, then looked with deep resentment at the mountain of files and reports towering on his desk. With a deep sigh, he settled himself into his chair, and pulled the first one down from the top of the pile.

Five hours later Jamie pushed open the door to the dining room and felt his heart sink.

It was lunchtime and the long, wide room was almost full: Operators, scientists, doctors and civilian staff filled the tables, and queued along the length of the serving counters, laughing and chatting to each other at what seemed like a deafening volume.

He stood at the entrance to the room, trying to decide what to do; his head was pounding from catching up on the reports, and the prospect of the conversation he knew he had to have with John Morton was starting to loom large in his mind. But he was here and it would be stupid not to eat. His squad's orders had not yet arrived, but he assumed they would be going out again in a few hours; he was going to need to be at his best, especially in light of the fact that there would only be two of them leaving the Loop.

"Looking for someone?" asked a familiar voice.

Jamie turned to find Kate Randall standing outside the door, a big grin on her face. He stepped forward and pulled her into a bear hug, almost lifting her off her feet; she gasped, then started laughing and pounding on his back, demanding that he put her down. He did as he was told and she stepped back, her face flushed.

"It's good to see you too, Jamie," she said. "Have you eaten already?"

"No," replied Jamie, smiling happily. "I was just deciding whether or not to bother."

"I'm supposed to be meeting Matt," said Kate. "But we both know how likely that is to actually happen."

Jamie laughed. "Right," he said. "He lives next door to me and I see him about once a week if I'm lucky."

"Well, if we're assuming that Matt isn't going to show," said Kate, "I suppose you would just about do as a substitute lunch companion. Fancy it?"

"Absolutely," he replied.

The two Operators made their way across the dining hall and joined the back of the queue for the food counters. Jamie surveyed the wraps and brimming bowls of salad, before ordering an enormous burger, groaning with bacon and cheese, and a pile of fries to go with it. Kate shook her head at him as she selected a tuna baguette; he flipped her a casual finger and pushed his tray away along the counter, leaving her staring after him with a perfect O of mock outrage on her face.

They found an empty table in the far corner of the dining hall and sat down. Jamie was about to take the first bite of his burger when he spotted a skinny figure in civilian clothes standing by the dining-room door.

"Wow," he said. "Who would have believed it?"

Kate frowned and turned her head towards where he was looking. Then she was waving her arms in the air and shouting across the dining hall. "Matt! Over here!"

Matt flinched at the sound of his name, then grinned when he saw his two friends. He raised a hand in acknowledgement and began to pick his way through the maze of tables and chairs towards them. His foot caught an outstretched leg at the last second and he stumbled, arms wheeling furiously for balance, before righting himself and crash-landing in the empty chair beside Kate.

"This place is a death trap," he said. "It's safer out there than in here."

"It's safer anywhere you aren't," said Jamie, grinning.

"Really?" replied Matt. "Is it my fault that everyone decides to constantly put things in my way. If I could fly like Larissa, there wouldn't be a problem."

"Maybe we can persuade her to bite you when she gets back," said Kate. "I think she'd agree it's for the greater good."

"You are both terrible people," said Matt, smiling. "It's good to see you."

"You too," said Jamie. "How're things downstairs?"

"They're OK," said Matt. "We're making progress."

"How are the team settling in?" asked Jamie, finally taking an enormous bite of his burger.

"They're great," said Matt. "They're so committed, even though they're trying to find a cure for a disease that none of them knew existed three months ago. It's pretty inspiring."

"Right," said Kate, grinning wickedly. "I'm pretty sure I know which one of them inspires you the most."

Matt flushed bright red. "I don't know what you're talking about," he said.

"What's going on?" demanded Jamie. "Kate?"

"Ask Matt," she laughed. "Ask him about a pretty Russian girl called Natalia. I'm sure he'll have plenty to say on the subject."

"You're dead, Kate," said Matt, grinning evilly. "I'm going to kill you with your fork."

"The girl who got hurt in the blast?" asked Jamie. "The one who was going into your room, Kate?"

"That's the one," she replied. "Matt?"

"She's just a girl that sits near me in the lab," said Matt. "She's a geneticist from Leningrad. The SPC sent her."

"And you love her," said Kate, her face rigid with fake seriousness. "You love her and you want to marry her and have lots of little genius children with her."

Jamie burst out laughing. Matt gave him a look that, if facial expressions could kill, would have tortured him for several days before slowly dismembering him.

"I do *not* love her," he protested. "I barely know her. I just like her, that's all."

"And she likes you?" asked Jamie.

"I don't know," said Matt. "I wouldn't have thought so."

Kate groaned. "You are absolutely the stupidest genius I've ever known," she said. "I told her I wouldn't say anything, but I suppose our pact comes before everything else. She was going into my room when the bomb went off because I told her to. She came up to ISAT to ask me about you, and I told her to go and wait in my room so we could talk properly."

Matt's eyes widened. "She came to ask you about me? What did she want to know?"

"She was worried about you," said Kate. "She thought you were working too hard, which you quite obviously are. But she could have talked to Professor Karlsson about that. She came to see me because she likes you, and she wanted to ask someone who knew you what she should do about it."

"So what did you tell her?" asked Jamie, his burger completely forgotten.

"I told her she should talk to Matt," replied Kate. "But then the bomb happened and she ended up in the infirmary."

"Jesus Christ," said Jamie. "I'm just putting this together now. This is what you told Major Turner when he made me leave the room yesterday?"

Kate nodded. "We went to see her yesterday. She's going to be fine, thankfully." She turned her attention back to Matt. "Why do you think I got out of there so quickly? So I could leave the two of you alone."

Matt stared. "I didn't know that," he said. "I didn't know any of this. She likes me? She told you she does?"

"She did," said Kate. "So unless the bomb scrambled her brain, it's probably a pretty safe bet that she still does."

"Tell her you like her," said Jamie, firmly. "As soon as she's out of the infirmary. No sense in waiting around."

"I agree," said Kate. "It looked like it took all of her courage to come and ask me what she should do, so grow some balls and give her a break."

Matt stared at his friends, his immensely powerful brain completely overwhelmed. "OK," he said, eventually. "I'll think about it. And I'll talk to her when she gets out. Everyone happy?"

"Very," said Kate. "She's a sweet girl, Jamie. You'll like her."

He smiled. "I don't doubt it. She's clearly got good taste."

Matt grinned, the wide, naughty smile of a schoolboy.

It's good to see him smile, thought Jamie. *To see them both smile, and laugh, and talk about something that isn't vampires and cures and traitors.*

"So," said Kate, "let's move the spotlight before our friend explodes with embarrassment. What's going on with you, Jamie?"

He groaned. "Nothing half as much fun," he said. "Everyone is still chasing down the Broadmoor escapees and we're only on to the second of ours. We missed him yesterday."

"*You* missed him?" asked Kate. "That's not what I heard."

"No," admitted Jamie. "Not me. One of my rookies. Morton."

"Is she the woman?" asked Matt.

"No, *he's* the man," said Jamie. "John Morton. He missed a shot his first time out, a hard shot in pitch darkness, but it made him start questioning stuff. Then yesterday a civilian died and he's blaming himself for her. The worst thing is, he isn't totally wrong. If he hadn't choked, she'd still be alive."

"Should he be active?" asked Kate, a deep frown on her face.

Jamie shook his head. "No," he replied. "I'm benching him until this Broadmoor thing is all sorted. I'm not giving up on him, not by any means, but I can't have him in my squad right now. It's too dangerous."

"I'm sorry," said Kate. "That's hard."

Jamie shrugged.

"What about the other one?" asked Matt. "What's her name?"

"Ellison," said Jamie, breaking into a wide smile. "Lizzy Ellison. She's awesome. I couldn't have asked for anyone better. So that's something, at least."

"You be careful," said Kate. "Your mum isn't the only one who worries about you when you're out there. You know that, right?"

"I know," said Jamie. "But there's no need. I'm always careful."

"How is your mum?" asked Matt. "Is she OK?"

"She's all right," he replied. "At least I think she is. I don't go and see her as often as I should. I know I don't. She doesn't say anything, but I know she thinks the same. But she's safe down there, and that's the main thing."

"Do you think she knows who's in the cell on the other side of the corridor?" asked Matt. "Does she have any idea?"

"Not in the slightest," said Jamie, shaking his head. "She doesn't know any vampire history and, even if she did, she wouldn't care. She's not their biggest fan, let's put it that way."

The implication of Jamie's words was not missed by any of them, and suddenly the chair beside him seemed particularly empty. Kate, who knew full well that Marie Carpenter had become quite familiar with the ancient vampire who lived opposite her, and exactly what she thought of their absent friend, held her tongue.

"Anyway," he said, forcing a thin smile, "enough of that cheery subject. Let's talk about something light and fluffy. Kate, what's going on with ISAT?"

His friends burst out laughing and he joined in, relishing the sound.

"It's fine," said Kate, once the laughter had subsided. "We're making progress, everybody hates us for what we're doing, and hopefully we won't find anything. But, given the bomb, that seems less and less likely."

"Because it was in your room?" asked Matt.

"And because there was an identical one in Major Turner's," said Jamie. "Right?"

"Right," said Kate. "We're about a quarter of the way through the interviews so if there's something there, if someone we haven't talked to yet is hiding something, we'll know soon enough. The obvious suspect was Valentin, but we interviewed him yesterday and he passed."

"What was that like?" asked Jamie.

"What was what like?"

"Interviewing Valentin."

"It was... enlightening," said Kate, and gave him a strange look, one he wasn't sure he liked. He considered pressing her on the subject, but something made him hold back. Instead, he pushed his plate to one side and sat back in his seat.

"Look," he said. "We all know we should do this more often, but we all know how difficult it is to make it happen. So all I'm going to suggest is that we try a bit harder. How does that sound?"

"It sounds good," said Kate, instantly. "I miss the two of you."

"Me too," said Matt. "I know I'm not around much at the moment, what with Lazarus and everything, but I'll try harder. I promise."

"It's OK," said Jamie. "Everyone knows how important what you're doing is, and no one takes it personally. It would just be good to see you more often."

Matt nodded. "It would," he said, softly. "It really would."

Jamie looked at his two friends for a long moment, and made a decision.

"I have something to tell you," he said. "It's nothing major, but it's something I've been keeping to myself, and we promised each other we wouldn't do that. So here it is. I've been visiting Valentin in his cell, even though I promised Frankenstein I wouldn't."

Kate smiled and, in that moment, Jamie realised she had already known; clearly, that had been the enlightening part of her conversation with the vampire.

She didn't say anything, he thought. *Didn't tell me off or try to trick me into confessing.*

"Should you be doing that?" asked Matt, his face clouding with concern. "Is it safe?"

Jamie shrugged. "Valentin's pretty much unstoppable," he said. "If he wanted to hurt me, he would. So being in his cell is no more dangerous than anywhere else."

"What do you talk to him about?" asked Kate, the same smile on her face.

You know this too, don't you? I'll play along, though.

"My family," he replied. "Valentin knew my grandfather, knew him better than I think anyone in the Department realises. He tells me about him."

"That sounds good," said Kate. "As long as you're being careful?"

"Like I said," smiled Jamie, "I always am."

Matt started telling Kate something that Professor Karlsson had said the previous day. Jamie was half listening when Lizzy Ellison walked into the dining hall, a look of intense concentration on her face.

He sat up in his chair and waved to her. She didn't respond, but headed towards him in a straight line that was the opposite of Matt's clumsy, circuitous route. Whatever the Director of the Lazarus Project had said had clearly been extremely funny, as his friends had both fallen about laughing, but Jamie had stopped listening entirely. His attention was focused on his approaching squad mate.

Ellison arrived at their table and Jamie saw that her face was noticeably pale. Kate and Matt had finally stopped laughing and were now looking at the new arrival with obvious interest.

"Ellison," said Jamie. "Do you know Matt Browning and—"

"I'm sorry, sir," interrupted Ellison, glancing at Jamie's friends. "I need to talk to you. In private."

"Whatever it is," said Jamie, "you can tell me here. I don't keep secrets from Kate and Matt."

"Yes, sir," replied Ellison.

"Do you want to sit down?" he asked. "You look like you're about to burst."

"I'm fine, sir," she replied, then looked at him with an expression of such awful distress that he felt a chill crawl up his spine.

"No, you're not," he said. "What is it? Tell me."

Ellison glanced over at Kate and Matt again. "It's John, sir."

"Morton?" asked Jamie. "What about him?"

"He's gone, sir."

The chill spread across Jamie's shoulders and up the back of his neck. "What do you mean gone?" he asked. "Gone where?"

Ellison pulled her console from her belt, thumbed it open, and held it out. Jamie took it from her and read the short message that glowed on its screen, his eyes widening as he did so.

From: Morton, John/NS304, 07-B
To: Ellison, Elizabeth/NS304, 07-C

Gone after Dempsey. Don't follow me. Need to do this myself.

Oh Christ, thought Jamie. *Oh Jesus Christ, what have I done?*

45

FINAL EDITION

As the train pulled into Darlington station, Pete Randall suddenly found himself on the verge of a panic attack.

He had driven across the Lindisfarne causeway in beautiful pale sunshine and made his way up to Berwick without incident; the roads were clear, and it was one of those fresh, clean mornings, where the world felt as though it was brand-new. It felt like the beginning of some great adventure, a journey into the unknown, the destination uncertain.

Pete parked his car at Berwick station, wondering idly whether he would ever see it again, and bought his ticket. The train creaked and squealed up to the platform, miraculously on time, and he climbed into coach D on legs that were unsteady with excitement. Tucked under his arm was a copy of *The Globe*, its brightly coloured front page screaming with outrage about a footballer who had been photographed leaving a nightclub with a woman who was most certainly not his heavily pregnant wife. He found a seat, bought a cup of tea from the trolley, and carefully coloured in *The Globe*'s white logo with a black felt-tip pen. Then he sat back, stared out of the window at the North Sea as it rushed past, and waited.

A small number of people crowded coach D's aisle as the train pulled into Darlington, pulling bags and cases down from the overhead shelves, putting on coats and scarves, and making their way towards the doors. Pete watched them leave, cursing silently that he had unwittingly sat on the wrong side of the train, and therefore been unable to get a look at the people waiting on the platform; he had never met the man he knew only as South, never seen a photo of him, but had a curious sense that he would recognise him. He would certainly recognise the uniforms of the police he was still partly convinced were *actually* going to be waiting for him.

As the aisle cleared, people began to board the train. Pete sat back in his seat and raised his copy of *The Globe* with trembling hands, pretending to read it as he scanned the new arrivals.

A woman walked through the carriage with a screaming baby in her arms and a look of profound exhaustion on her face. Two teenage boys followed her, huge headphones resting around their necks, as an elderly woman struggled into the carriage behind them, dragging a suitcase so enormous that a kindly man sitting near the door got to his feet and helped her wrangle it on to the luggage rack.

No one else appeared.

Pete's heart thumped in his chest; he was suddenly overcome with the desire to run to the end of the carriage and pull the driver alarm, stopping the train before it left the platform. He could get off and run, and keep running until he worked out what to do next. But he didn't; panic paralysed him, freezing him in his seat.

He looked at the other people in coach D, eyeing them all with new suspicion. Were any of them police? Were *all of them* police?

Or if not police, then something worse? Men and women who would not think twice before making him disappear?

"North?" said a low voice, and Pete Randall clamped his teeth together so he didn't scream. He whirled round in his seat and saw a middle-aged man standing beside him with a deeply nervous expression on his face.

"South?" he asked, his voice high and unsteady.

"That's right," nodded the man, a tentative smile spreading across his face. "It's good to finally meet you, mate. Really good."

"You too," Pete replied, his heart still pounding in his chest. He extended a hand. "I guess we're done with this North and South thing, right? I'm Pete Randall."

South took his hand and shook it fiercely. "Greg Browning," he said.

From: colin.burton@mailserver.theglobe.co.uk
To: kevinjmckenna@googlemail.co.uk
Sent: 11:05:42
Subject: Re: Urgent submission

Kevin,

If this is a joke, it's a pretty good one. If it isn't, you need psychiatric help.

Colin

"I told you he wouldn't go for it," said Kevin McKenna. He watched as Albert Harker read the email, and waited for the explosion he was sure this setback was going to provoke.

"I know what you told me, Kevin," replied Harker, softly. "My memory is perfectly functional. This reaction was only to be expected, as you yourself suggested. Reply to him, telling him that you are quite serious. Tell him you want pages one and two of tomorrow's edition, and that your story is to run uncut."

McKenna grinned with relief. "Anything else?" he asked. "Shall I ask him to send us a suitcase full of money and a case of champagne to toast our success with?"

Harker turned to him and smiled. "I think that might be pushing our luck, Kevin. Don't you?"

From: kevinjmckenna@googlemail.co.uk
To: colin.burton@mailserver.theglobe.co.uk
Sent: 11:09:16
Subject: Re: Re: Urgent submission

Dear Colin,

No joke. This is the biggest story of both of our careers, the one that you'll thank me for when they give you your knighthood. I want it to run on pages one and two tomorrow, and I want it to run uncut. Send me the layouts once they're ready.

Cheers,
Kevin

From: colin.burton@mailserver.theglobe.co.uk
To: kevinjmckenna@googlemail.co.uk
Sent: 11:12:13
Subject: Re: Re: Re: Urgent submission

Kevin,

I can take a joke, and I've put up with a lot of your shit over the years. This takes the piss, though. It really does.

I want you to take two weeks off and think about your future. Unpaid, before you ask. I don't want to see you in the office during that time.

Take a good look at yourself, then let me know whether you still want to be a journalist. I'm saying this as your friend. Because this is not how serious people behave.

Colin

"What now?" asked Kevin. His editor's reply had come quickly, and was even worse than he had expected; he was trying to keep his tone of voice light, in the hope of keeping Albert Harker calm.

"As I told you," replied the vampire, "I prepared for this eventuality. This makes our path slightly harder, Kevin, nothing more."

"Feel like sharing this grand plan of yours?"

Harker shook his head. "In time. Although, as a hypothetical, imagine we paid a visit to your editor in his home and I pulled his fingernails out one at a time until he agreed to run the story. Do you foresee any major flaws in such a plan?"

"I wish I didn't," said McKenna. "Because I'd pay money to see that. I really would."

"But you do see a flaw?"

McKenna nodded. "Colin has a video conference with New York

every evening, where they sign off the next edition. Getting him at home wouldn't work. We'd have to hold him prisoner in his office while he spoke to his boss."

"How many people would be in the office at that time?" asked Harker.

McKenna shrugged. "Forty? Fifty? Maybe more?"

"I suspected as much," said the vampire. "No matter. We will continue with the plan as I devised it."

"All right," said McKenna. "I've got faith, you know. I'm not worried."

"Nor should you be," said Harker, smiling. "Everything is going to be absolutely fine."

Then someone knocked on the door.

Greg Browning stood in the dim corridor with Pete Randall beside him. His stomach was churning; this was the address that Kevin McKenna had sent them the night before, and was the last point at which the rug could be pulled out from under their feet.

The train journey had passed quickly and uneventfully. His legs had barely been able to carry him as he climbed aboard coach F of the stationary train; when he had made his way to coach D and found the nervous-looking man holding a copy of *The Globe* that he clearly wasn't reading, Greg had been so relieved that he almost burst into tears.

He had been equally relieved to discover that he liked Pete Randall immediately; the friendship that he had felt begin to kindle as they spoke anonymously online had blossomed quickly in the flesh. They had spent the journey chatting as if they had known each other for years, talking mainly about their families and their children, even though it hurt both men to do so.

Greg heard voices on the other side of the hotel room door and felt his muscles tense.

Here it is, he thought. *Here's where we find out whether this is real.*

The door opened, revealing a man he didn't recognise, but who smiled at them with immense warmth.

"Gentlemen," said the stranger. "My name is Albert Harker. Please come in. We have been so looking forward to your arrival."

Harker stood aside, beckoning them into the room. Greg cast the briefest of glances at Pete, who gave the tiniest of shrugs.

We didn't come all this way to turn back now.

He took a deep breath that he hoped wasn't obvious, and walked slowly into the hotel room. Out of the corner of his eye, he saw Pete Randall follow.

The room was exactly what he expected: a small box with cream walls and a headache-inducing green and yellow carpet. A table in the centre of the room was covered with a mass of papers and notebooks, and a man was standing beside the room's single small window.

He recognised Kevin McKenna from the photos he had searched for on the internet when the blog post that had started all of this had gone live. He looked much as he had on his son's computer screen; he was a little thinner, perhaps, but the smile on his face was wide and welcoming.

He must be under so much stress, thought Greg, admiringly. *It takes true bravery to do what he's doing.*

The man stepped forward and extended his hand. "Kevin McKenna," he said.

"I know who you are," he replied, gripping the hand and shaking it vigorously. "I'm Greg Browning. This is Pete Randall. We're glad to be here."

"Thanks for coming," said McKenna. "We weren't sure if you would."

"I'm not sure we were," said Pete, stepping forward and shaking McKenna's hand. "I was half expecting to find a room full of men in black ready to take me away."

"I know what you mean," said McKenna. "I've felt the same thing. But we're still here. And now you are too."

"Quite so," said Albert Harker. He had closed the door and stepped forward into the room. "Gentlemen," he said, smiling broadly. "The four of us represent the beginnings of a movement that Kevin and I have no doubt will one day number in the thousands. Men and women who are tired of being lied to, tired of watching their government put them in danger by refusing to acknowledge the monsters that walk in their midst."

Greg felt like his heart was expanding in his chest. This was exactly what he had been hoping to hear.

"Kevin is the bravest of us all," continued Harker. "He stood up when no one else dared to do so, and all it has got him is derision and mockery. We wanted to bring what we know to the public's attention by traditional means, but Kevin's paper has refused to run the story. This was a disappointment, but not an unexpected one. So now we are forced to use other methods, which *I* would call civil disobedience, but which the courts of this land may well consider industrial sabotage. As a result, we will think no less of you if you choose to walk away now, if this is not what you believed you were signing up for. But if you still want to help, we, and the parents of every missing child, will be in your debt."

"What about you?" asked Pete. "Why are *you* doing this?"

"Because of what was done to me," replied Harker. "Please brace yourselves, gentlemen, and try not to panic."

Greg frowned, and was opening his mouth to ask Harker what he was talking about, when the man's eyes flooded a dark, glowing red. His heart stopped dead in his chest as terrible memories flooded through him, carrying with them emotions he had tried to suppress: fear, panic, and dreadful, awful helplessness. They galvanised his limbs and he fled for the door, his eyes wide and staring, his mouth opening and working soundlessly. He was reaching for the door handle when he felt a rush of air above his head and suddenly Albert Harker was standing in front of him, blocking the door.

"Kevin could not have told you," he said, his eyes burning. "You would not have come. But I believe there should be no secrets between us. Yes, I am a vampire. I never wished to be one, but I am. I am the victim of a crime for which there can be no justice. And, when our task is complete, I will be the irrefutable proof the public needs. Will you stay and help us? I promise you, there is nothing more you do not know. Please?"

Greg stared at the vampire; it was only the second one he had ever seen in the flesh, after the girl who had landed in his garden months earlier, triggering the collapse of the life he had taken so wastefully for granted. Fear was roaring through him, but something else was making its presence known beneath it: a deep, burning sense of outrage.

This is it. This is what we're fighting against, in the flesh. This is what we're trying to stop happening to anyone else.

"I'm still in," he heard himself say, and looked over at Pete Randall. His companion looked as though he was reliving his worst nightmare, his eyes bulging, his throat swallowing convulsively. But he managed to force his vocal cords into action and tell Harker that he was still in too.

"Thank you," said the vampire. The red was fading from his eyes; it was now little more than a pink glow in the corners. "I promise you that neither one of you will live to regret your decision. Kevin will fill you in on everything that has happened, and then I suggest you both get some rest. We have a busy night ahead of us."

46

IT NEVER RAINS...

"Jamie?" asked Kate, her voice full of concern. "What does it say?"

"Show them," said Jamie, handing the console back to Ellison and grabbing his own from his belt. He slid its screen into life with his thumb and opened the location tracker. As he typed Morton's name into the search field, he heard Kate gasp as Ellison did as she was told.

"Oh no," he heard Matt whisper. "That's awful."

Jamie didn't respond; his mind was pounding with a single thought: that they had to go and help Morton, had to go and save him from himself. The console beeped as its screen lit up, displaying the location of the rookie Operator's chip.

It was in the northern outskirts of London, moving south.

Jamie opened the Surveillance Division menu, his fingers flying across the console's touch screen, and opened the satellite tracking record for Alastair Dempsey. The satellites had followed his heat bloom from the substation near Holborn where he had escaped their squad the previous day to a disused warehouse in the middle of Soho. Dempsey had entered it an hour before dawn that morning, and there was nothing to indicate that he had left the building since then.

"He's nearly in London," said Jamie, looking up at Ellison. "There's no way we can get there before he gets to Dempsey."

Ellison looked absolutely heartbroken. "What do we do, sir?" she asked, her voice cracking. "We can't leave him out there on his own."

"Of course not," said Jamie.

"I'll come with you," said Kate, scrambling to her feet.

"Me too," said Matt.

"No," said Jamie. "Thank you both, you know how much that means to me. But we'll do this ourselves."

"What happened to sticking together?" asked Kate. There was a ghost of a smile on her face, just enough to let Jamie know that she wasn't really serious.

"We'll be fine," he said, glancing at Ellison, who nodded. "You're needed here. I'll let you know as soon as we find him."

"See that you do," said Kate. "And be careful. Both of you."

"We will," said Jamie, then turned to face his squad mate. "Ready?"

"Ready, sir."

"OK then," he said. "Let's go."

Matt watched his friend stride out of the dining hall, his face a mask of helpless concern.

"Jesus," whispered Kate. "I can't believe this."

"It'll be OK," said Matt, trying to sound a lot surer than he felt. "Jamie can handle it. It'll be OK."

"Paul showed me the footage of the escapees," said Kate. "They're brutal, Matt. Strong and fast and vicious."

"I know that, Kate," snapped Matt. "I saw the footage too. But they're still just vampires, and Jamie knows what he's doing."

"I'm sorry," said Kate, turning her head and giving him a thin smile.

"I'm just worried about him. These new vamps are dangerous. They really are."

"I know," said Matt. "I'm sorry too. I didn't mean to snap." He sighed deeply. "Why hasn't Science come up with anything yet? They've had captive escapees for almost four days and they still have no explanation for why these new vamps all look like they were turned by—"

He stopped dead.

Something had flickered into life in the back of his mind, and Matt knew from long experience to simply shut everything else down and see if his brain could fan the flames. For several agonising moments, the idea danced out of reach, slippery and elusive, but then it caught and burst into bright, burning life.

"My God," he whispered, and stood up from his chair.

"What's going on?" asked Kate. "Matt? Where the hell are you going?"

"I have to check something," he replied, then turned and ran off without a backward glance.

47

TIME WAITS FOR NO MAN

EDWARDS AIR FORCE: DETACHMENT GROOM LAKE
NEVADA, USA
FIVE HOURS LATER

Larissa had been perched on a stool at the bar in the Groom Lake officers' mess for almost forty minutes when Lee Ashworth finally made his way into the building. She was practically vibrating with excitement; she was ready to get the answers she was looking for.

The mess was a square building that had been built in the 1950s and expanded continuously over the subsequent decades; at its heart was an ornate dark wood bar, a varnished wooden floor and a collection of leather chairs and sofas that stood around low tables on which had been played innumerable hands of cards. But it had been added to and decorated with whatever could be scavenged from the surrounding towns and bases: a fluorescent sign announcing WELCOME TO TRINITY, a *Dark Shadows* pinball machine, a Mercury High School Football pennant, photos of atomic bomb tests, of the F-117A stealth fighter and the B-2 bomber, and a hundred other curios and mementoes.

Senior Airman Ashworth made his way to the bar, nodding at

a couple of his colleagues as he did so. He ordered coffee and a breakfast burrito, and hauled himself up on to a stool, barely even glancing in her direction.

"You've got some nerve," he hissed. "Some goddamn nerve."

"I don't know what you're talking about," said Larissa.

She had ambushed Lee Ashworth in his office an hour earlier and shown him the photographs she had taken in Las Vegas two nights earlier. She had placed her phone alongside the photo of his wife and children, to make sure her meaning was absolutely clear, then suggested that he might be more inclined to tell her about the day the stranger had arrived at Area 51 than he had been the last time they had talked.

He had unleashed a torrent of swearing and insults of such imagination and volume that Larissa, who had once spent more than a year in the company of Alexandru Rusmanov, one of the most dangerous and abusive creatures ever to walk the earth, was genuinely impressed. Then he had told her to meet him in the mess in an hour, and to get the hell out of his office before he called the MPs.

"You know exactly what I'm talking about," said Ashworth, his face red with anger. "So let's just get this over with. Sit there, shut the hell up, and listen. All right?"

Larissa smiled. "Fine by me, sir."

Ashworth gave her one final glare, took a sip of his coffee, and began to talk.

"I pulled guard detail that week because we had eight guys back at Edwards running models and it was Gold Squadron's turn in the rotation. So I ended up at the Front Gate. It's not a bad post, but it's boring. It's really, really boring. You get the call sheet for the day and that's all you normally see, unless some geek drives past the signs by accident, and even then the grunts normally grab them before they get anywhere near the gate."

"Grunts?" interrupted Larissa.

"Civilian security," said Ashworth. "They patrol the perimeter in their pick-ups and their Aviators, acting like they're the badasses of the world, when all they really do is drink coffee and listen to ESPN. Maybe once a month some hiker will lose track of the markers, and they get to swoop down all big and bad and hold them until the police get out here to take them away. But most of them, ninety-nine per cent of them, drive up to the signs, take some pictures, wait for the grunts to park their truck up on the top of the hill, then head home, happy with their Area 51 experience. And on the day you're interested in, that's what I assumed was happening. We picked up this crappy little jeep as soon as it turned off 375, and the system tracked it all the way along the road. Nothing out of the ordinary, no unusual speed, no explosives, no weapons.

"It makes its way up to the signs and it stops, just like all the others. I'm watching it on my screens in the guardhouse, and the grunts are in their usual spot on the hill, and there's no reason to think anything's wrong, right? I mean, this happens all the time. *All* the time. But then a minute or so passes, and the jeep just sits there, and whoever's driving it doesn't get out, and I don't see any camera flashes, and I start to get this weird feeling, you know? Not anything major, not any big thing, just like something is a little bit off.

"I'm about to radio the grunts and tell them to drive down and say hello to this guy, when whoever's in the jeep floors it. And for a moment I just stand there, staring at the screen, because what the hell is this guy doing? He's going to invade Area 51 in his jeep? I see the grunts haul their truck round and start down the hill, and that's when I snap out of it. I grab my M4 down off the wall, radio in that we've got an intruder, run outside to the barrier, and wait to see who gets there first.

"The grunts are hauling ass down the ridge, trying to cut him off, but he's really shifting, whoever he is. I figure he's going to roll it on the last bend, but he doesn't. He comes round the corner, going hell for leather, this huge cloud of dust blowing up behind him, and I see the grunt truck in the dust, and a bit of me is like, I want to meet this guy. Because he has balls, you know, if nothing else. And he can drive, no question about that. I raise the stingers and clear out to the side, because they're going to flip him about ten metres into the air the speed he's going.

"But he doesn't hit them. At the last minute, and I really mean the last minute, he hits the brakes, and there's this huge squeal of tyres, and the jeep starts to shake from side to side because he's dumping off the speed too quickly, and then it stops, about a metre in front of the gate and the stingers. The grunt truck screeches to a halt beside it and I'm running out with my M4 raised when the jeep's door opens and this guy jumps out, his hands in the air."

"What did he look like?" asked Larissa. Her heart was thumping in her chest; the prisoner, whoever he was, was real. The man sitting next to her had seen him with his own eyes.

"Tall, middle-aged. Pale, even though he was driving in out of the desert. In good shape. Hard eyes, like a soldier. I point my rifle at him and tell him to get down, but he doesn't move. He keeps his hands in the air and shouts a code at me—"

"Which code?"

"F-357-X. It's maximum clearance. Old, but still active. Then he shouts that he needs to see General Allen and that just floors me. This guy drives up to the Front Gate, outruns the grunts and then gives me a max code and tells me he needs to see the head of NS9? Refers to him by name? I mean, seriously, what the hell, right?"

"How did he speak?" asked Larissa. "Did he have an accent? Anything unusual?"

"English," replied Ashworth.

"I guessed that much."

"No, he had an English accent. The guy *was* English."

Larissa stared, attempting to process what the Senior Airman was saying. In the deepest corner of her mind, a thought occurred to her: a ludicrous, impossible thought that she quickly pushed away.

"I understand," she said, slowly.

"Good," said Ashworth. "Anyway. He's looking at me, and I'm looking at him, and then the grunts finally show up and they grab him and throw him over the hood of the jeep, and they're about to cuff him when I suddenly realise I have to call this in. The guy's used a max code, regardless of how he arrived, so I tell the grunts to stop, to go back to their post and forget this ever happened.

"The English guy watches them leave, then he thanks me and starts to tell me what he needs, but I tell him to shut up, tell him I'll shoot him if he moves, and he kind of shrugs and just stands there with his hands up, and that's when I start to think that maybe this guy is more than just a soldier, maybe he's SAS or something, because he doesn't even look like he's sweating, even though he's just raced through the desert and he's standing outside the most classified facility in the country with a gun pointing at his head. He looks like he's just out for an afternoon stroll in the desert.

"I grab my radio and give Central Control the code he gave me. There's silence, a long silence, which means you're getting transferred all over the base, and eventually this voice I don't recognise comes on the line and tells me they're sending a vehicle out, that I'm not to engage my prisoner in any way, not to even speak to him, but also not to let him out of my sight until he's been collected.

"So I keep my gun on the guy and we just stare at each other for a few minutes, until this NS9 Hummer arrives and one of you spooks gets out and tells me to stand down. I'm like, no problem, no problem at all, I don't want any part of this mess, so I head back into the guardhouse. The English guy gets into the Hummer and it drives off towards the lake. I haven't seen him since and I still don't know who he is. I've told you everything I know and I shouldn't have told you that. So now you're going to take your phone out of your pocket and delete those photos, then I'm going to sit here and eat my breakfast while you piss off and leave me alone. I'm all done talking."

Larissa pulled the mess door shut behind her and stood beneath the wide central canopy, her head spinning.

She hadn't expected Lee Ashworth to be able to tell her who the secret prisoner was, and she had believed him when he said he didn't know. But she had got what she wanted from him, and more. The man was real, that much was now certain; he had driven out of the desert in possession of a maximum security code, which meant that he was either directly or indirectly involved with the secret apparatus of the US military. He had asked for General Allen by name, which meant that he was aware of the existence of NS9. And he was English, which didn't in itself mean anything, but strongly suggested some connection to Blacklight.

Larissa wandered slowly back towards Central Control and the tunnel that would take her back to Dreamland. She was starting to think she might just take an elevator down to Level 8 and see if there was any way to see the prisoner with her own eyes. It would land her in serious trouble if she was caught, but at that moment she just didn't care.

I have to find out who he is, she thought. *I don't even know why it's become so important to me. I just have to know.*

Half a mile to the east and almost the same distance down, the prisoner Larissa was so desperate to identify was finishing his morning shave. Under normal circumstances, prisoners were not allowed anything they could conceivably do themselves harm with, especially nothing as obviously dangerous as a razor blade. But the circumstances surrounding Julian Carpenter were far from normal.

Bob Allen may have had no option other than to lock him up, but he had brought the contents of Julian's jeep down to the cellblock, and handed them over to him personally. He presumed they had been checked thoroughly first – his old friend was anything but stupid – but he was grateful nevertheless.

Changing his clothes every day, shaving his face in the morning, brushing his teeth in the evening: they were small things, but they made him feel as though he was still human, still himself. He laid the razor on the rim of the sink and looked in the polished sheet of metal that passed for a mirror. His face was paler than ever as a result of more than three months without exposure to natural light. His skin seemed loose; it hung from his cheekbones and beneath his chin.

He looked like an old man.

The situation he found himself in was almost blackly comic. He had overridden a lifetime of training, years and decades of forcing himself to make decisions based on logic rather than emotion, and handed himself over to NS9 because he had been desperately, terribly worried about his son. The vision he had seen in the desert cave with the cured vampire who called himself Adam had seemed terrifyingly real: his son as a vampire, with red eyes and gleaming fangs, telling him he was too late.

Despite Adam's pleading, his warnings that visions were unreliable, Julian's mind had been instantly made up. He had needed to know that Jamie was all right, and surrendering to NS9 was the only way he could think to do so; his last remaining contact inside Blacklight, from the time before he had been forced to fake his own death, was missing, presumed dead. And he had been right: Bob Allen had managed to persuade Henry Seward to tell him that his son was alive and well.

Julian's relief had been enormous, but short-lived. It was not enough to know that Jamie was all right; he wanted to help his son, wanted it more than anything else in the world, and he had put himself in a position from where it would be absolutely impossible for him to do so.

Stupid, he thought, staring at his reflection. *Weak. Stupid. Old.*

At the end of the corridor that ran down the centre of the detention block, the heavy metal door clunked open and footsteps clicked across the concrete, getting louder as they neared his cell. Julian dried his face with the thin towel that was standard issue for NS9 prisoners and waited for Bob Allen to arrive; there was no question of it being anyone else. The detention block Duty Officer brought food three times a day, but never spoke a single word; Julian could have tried to engage him, knowing he would be under orders not to respond, but he had no wish to make the man's life harder. It wasn't his fault that Julian was where he was; it was no one's fault but his own.

The footsteps stopped outside his cell. Julian heard a series of soft clicks as the access code was entered into the control panel, before the door swung open and the NS9 Director stepped into his cell, a tired half-smile on his face.

"Evening, Bob," said Julian. "Good to see you."

"You too," replied General Allen. "How are you doing, Julian?"

"I'm in jail," he said. "I'm having a ball. Yourself?"

Allen grunted with laughter, then flopped down into the plastic chair that was one of the cell's three pieces of furniture. Julian pushed himself across his bed and sat with his back against the wall.

"I'm tired, Julian," said Allen. "We've destroyed or detained about forty per cent of the Supermax escapees. Another fifteen per cent are under surveillance. We couldn't track the rest of them. So they're gone."

"That's good, Bob," said Julian. Allen had told him about the coordinated prison breaks and the frightening strength and speed of the newly-turned vampires, even though he was breaking about a dozen regulations by doing so. Julian had been full of grudging admiration for the tactics of the vampires. The chaos that had been created had sucked in every supernatural Department, and showed no sign of ending; it was a huge, audacious piece of misdirection, designed to keep them all busy with something other than looking for the still-recovering Dracula. "You'll have more than half of them by the time it's all said and done, and that's not bad. You had no warning, and no reinforcements you could call in to help you out. Half is good, Bob. Don't beat yourself up."

"Thanks," replied Allen. "I appreciate you saying so. And we got some of the very worst. My SpecOps team took down the entire leadership of the Desert Cartel in Nuevo Laredo, with a little help from our vampire guest."

"Larissa," said Julian.

The revelation that NS9 had a vampire working for them had been one thing, the fact that she was actually a member of Blacklight on secondment to the US was another, and the *further* fact, confirmed first-hand by his friend, that she was the girlfriend of his son, was the icing on the cake. He was desperate, truly desperate, to meet her. He had begged Allen for the opportunity to do so, for just five minutes to ask her about how Jamie was doing and the person he had grown up to be, but the Director had refused. Julian had seen on his face that it pained him to do so and hadn't pushed the issue.

Not yet, at least.

"Lieutenant Kinley," confirmed Allen. "Tim Albertsson, the SpecOps head, said he's never seen anything like it. Apparently the leader of the cartel shot her point-blank in the stomach with a shotgun and she didn't even notice it. I think he was a bit scared, to be honest with you."

"Any of your people get hurt?" asked Julian.

Allen shook his head. "Kinley lost an ear along with her gunshot wound, but they fed her blood and she was back on her feet a minute later. No other injuries and only one civilian fatality."

"After a night assault on the headquarters of a Laredo cartel," said Julian. "You've got to be pleased with that, Bob."

"I am," replied Allen. "To be honest, I wish we could keep her, and I'm not the only one who does. I think I could persuade Cal to let me have her, but she wouldn't come without her friends, and there's not a chance in hell that he would transfer your boy. Not after everything he's done."

Julian smiled. He was immensely proud of his son and would never be able to forgive either Thomas Morris or himself for conspiring to prevent him being able to share in Jamie's triumphs.

He was a man who had a great many regrets, so many that he had long since committed himself to not thinking about them unless it was entirely unavoidable, but none were greater than how he felt about his son having to fend for himself, having to fight and struggle and survive, without his father.

"That's sort of why I'm here, Julian," continued General Allen. "I spoke to Cal this morning. He's sending a team here overnight. They're taking you and Larissa home in the morning."

"Why?"

"I can't tell you that. They're working on something big and Cal says they need Larissa's help. To be honest, I think he wants to tie up any Blacklight loose ends."

Julian's expression didn't change. "Are they reinstating me?"

"I don't know," replied Allen. "But if you want my advice, I would suggest you prepare yourself for disappointment."

"I didn't do anything wrong," said Julian, his voice rising. "I didn't betray anyone and I didn't get the Harkers killed."

"A warrant was put out for your arrest and you faked your own death rather than answer it," said Allen, evenly. "I understand why you did what you did, and I'm sure Cal does too. But you died, Julian. Or at least you let everyone think you did. If you're expecting Cal to give you a big hug and hand you a new uniform, then you're delusional. You have to see that."

Julian slumped on the bed, his eyes downcast and red at the corners.

"So, what?" he asked, his voice now little more than a whisper. "What do you think is going to happen to me, Bob?"

"Best guess? They'll clear you of any wrongdoing and send you on your way. I think they'll let you have a life, Julian, but I don't think it will be inside Blacklight."

"And my family?"

Allen looked away.

"What about my family, Bob?"

"I can't tell you what Cal will do," said Allen, looking straight at his friend. "But I know what I would do."

"What would you do?"

"I'd forbid you from ever contacting either of them," said Allen. "Jamie is an Operator and Marie is in Blacklight custody, and they both think you're dead. I wouldn't let you anywhere near them, at least until the Dracula situation is resolved. *If* it gets resolved."

An uneasy silence hung in the air for a long moment, thick with the dismal prospect that Bob Allen had described. Julian couldn't believe that Cal Holmwood would do that to him, not after all the years they had fought alongside each other, but he knew that his friend was suggesting a genuine possibility. If they wanted to keep him away from his family, it would be easy for them to do so.

Their case for doing so would also be easy to make: that his return would provide a distraction to a serving Operator as they approached potentially the darkest period in their long history. He was sure that Marie and Jamie would be furious if they found out, but therein lay the central problem; with his son and his wife living inside the Loop, merely letting them know he was still alive would be almost impossible.

"I hope you're wrong, Bob," he said, eventually.

"So do I, Julian," replied Allen. "More than you know."

The two men sat in silence for a long while; both of them looked old and tired, the cumulative wear and tear of years spent walking into the darkest corners stood out in the deep lines on their faces.

"Is it worth it?" said Julian, suddenly.

"Is what worth what?"

"What we do," he said. "Everything we've done and everything we've given. Was it worth it? Did we ever do anything good, Bob?"

There was a long pause. "I don't know," said Allen. "There are people who are alive because of the things we did. That has to count for something."

"There are just as many who are dead, maybe even more," said Julian. "Men and women we killed because they were vampires, not because of anything they'd done. I think of some of the things I've done and I can't even begin to imagine how I justified doing them."

"Orders," said Allen. "Following orders."

Julian grunted. "Right," he said. "I've heard that excuse before, Bob. Heard it used to excuse the same thing in fact: destroying people because of what they are, not what they've done."

"Jesus, Julian," said Allen. "I get it, you're locked up down here and everything looks black. But don't do this to yourself."

"Do you remember Kosovo, Bob?" he asked.

"I remember."

"What was that, 1999? 2000? Christ, I can't even remember."

"It was '99," said Bob, his voice low.

"There was that Albanian girl in the square. Do you remember her? What the vamps had done to her?"

"Yeah," said Allen. "I remember."

"We found them up in that barn behind the church," said Julian. "The vamps and their women and their kids."

"Julian..." said Allen, helplessly.

"We started shooting, and then I grabbed my stake, and when it was over, I couldn't lift my arm above my shoulder for two days. I remember *that*, Bob. I've tried to forget it, but I can't. I just can't."

"We did what we had to do," said Allen. "What we were ordered to do. They were killers, Julian, we saw what they'd done with our own eyes."

"The men," said Julian. "But the women? The kids? What had they done to deserve a stake?"

Allen didn't answer.

"If Dracula rises," he continued, "then it's over for us, and everyone like us. But even if he doesn't, even if you manage to stop him in time, I think it might still be over. Nothing lasts forever. We keep the biggest secret in the world, and we've killed and killed and killed to keep it safe. But how long until someone finds out what we don't want them to know? Or until more people find out than we can lock up or kill? What happens when the world sees the things we've done?"

"I don't know, Julian," said Allen. "And neither do you."

The two men looked at each other, the weight of history bearing down on them.

It was a long time before they spoke again.

48

BEHIND THE CURTAIN

Matt Browning ran down the centre of Level D and skidded to a halt outside the entrance to the Blacklight Science Division. He pressed his ID card against a black panel on the wall and waited impatiently as a series of locks released. When the panel turned green, he pushed the heavy security door open and stepped through it.

He emerged into a large square room containing a wide reception desk and the open-plan workstations that were occupied by the Division's administrative staff. The woman behind the desk frowned at Matt as he approached: his arrival was unscheduled, and his eyes were a little too wide for comfort.

"Can I help you?" she asked.

"I'm Matt Browning," he replied, putting his ID on the counter. "Who's the Duty Officer? I need to speak to them, please."

"I'm sorry," replied the receptionist. "Dr Cooper is in the lab. Can I take a message?"

"No," said Matt. "I'm sorry, but you can tell him I need to speak to him right now, on Zero Hour Task Force business. I don't want to involve the Interim Director in this, but I will if you make me."

The receptionist narrowed her eyes and, for a moment, Matt

thought she was going to call his bluff; he suspected that Cal Holmwood would back his demand to speak to a senior member of the Department without notice, but that he would also not be thrilled about being forced to do so. The receptionist stared at him for a long moment, then lifted the telephone from her desk and dialled a number. She spoke quietly into the receiver, turning her head away from Matt and shielding her mouth with her hand, then replaced the phone in its cradle.

"Dr Cooper will see you," she said. "I'm to take you through."

She got up from behind the desk, her body language making it clear that there was literally nothing in the world she would less like to be doing than assisting him. Matt fought to keep his temper, which rarely showed itself, in check; when the receptionist waved her hand in a way that vaguely suggested he should follow her, he bit his tongue and did so.

In the wall behind the administrative desks stood three heavy white metal doors. Beyond them, the Science Division comprised three large research labs arranged in a semicircle, each one home to two of the Division's six primary areas of research: Computational and Information Sciences, Sensors and Electron Devices, Human/ Supernatural Research and Engineering, Survivability/Lethality Analysis, Vehicle Technology, Weapons and Materials Research. There was a large proving area at the southern edge of the Loop's grounds, as well as ranges and experimental chambers of all sizes and specifications spread throughout the underground levels, all of which were highly classified. Access to the labs was controlled by a series of double airlocks, and the entire Division was monitored at a microscopic level; the complex of rooms was fully automated and could be locked down instantly in the event of a breach or an accident.

The receptionist unlocked the middle door and led Matt into a short corridor. At the other end stood the entrance to a grey airlock, identical to the one that guarded the containment block four levels below. She gestured for Matt to step inside and was making her way back towards reception before the airlock door had even closed behind him.

Matt fought back claustrophobia as the light inside the tight space turned first red, then purple. A billowing cloud of gas rushed up from vents in the floor and he shut his eyes, waiting for it to be over. When the roaring ceased, he opened them in time to see the light turn green and the inner door swing open, revealing a tiny man in a white coat with a big smile on his face.

"Matt?" he asked, extending his hand. "Matt Browning?"

"Hello," said Matt. He took the outstretched hand; the man in the white coat pumped it up and down enthusiastically.

"I'm Mark Cooper, Director of the Science Division. It's great to meet you."

"Is it?" blurted Matt, slightly overwhelmed by the warmth of the greeting.

"Absolutely," said Cooper. "Cal Holmwood shares some of the Lazarus Project reports with me. Amazing stuff, truly. It's incredible what you're doing down there."

"Thanks," said Matt. He suddenly found himself trying not to laugh.

"You're welcome," said Dr Cooper. "I met Robert Karlsson a few years ago, in Geneva. A great man."

"He is," said Matt. "We're lucky to have him."

"No doubt. Now what can I do for you, Mr Browning? I'm guessing it has something to do with our recent arrivals?"

"It has," said Matt. "Can I see them, please?"

"Of course," said Dr Cooper. "Follow me."

The Science Division Director turned and strode away down the corridor, at a pace that surprised Matt; the man's legs were so short he would not have predicted such speed was possible. At the end of the corridor stood a pair of doors with round windows at head-height. A sign was fixed to the wall beside them:

RESEARCH LABORATORY 2
HUMAN/SUPERNATURAL RESEARCH AND ENGINEERING
SURVIVABILITY/LETHALITY ANALYSIS

Matt followed Cooper through the doors and into the lab.

It was huge: a rectangular space with a high, flat ceiling and tiled floor. The entire room was painted white; its walls and ceiling gleamed almost as brightly as the metal benches that lined the walls and the computer screens that sat atop them. At least a dozen men and women in white coats were bustling between a wide arrangement of desks, a long wall full of files and folders, and rows of machines that Matt recognised: gene sequencers, hologram projection units, powerful supercomputer cabinets, 3D virtual database racks. At the back of the room, a row of six cells was set into the wall, shimmering with the same ultraviolet barriers that restrained the occupants of the detention block.

"Welcome," said Dr Cooper. "I'm sure this must look pretty unimpressive compared to the Lazarus labs, but we call it home."

"It's great," said Matt. "What are your priority projects?"

"Right now, investigating the advanced physical attributes of the Broadmoor escapees," replied Cooper. "Generally, the same as always. Tactical analysis of vampire strengths and weaknesses, analysis of the

520

virus itself. We work in tandem with Lab 3. They apply our work to weaponry and defence development."

"You use live subjects?" asked Matt. A chill ran up his spine. "I mean, other than the Broadmoor escapees?"

"We do," said Dr Cooper. "Although I know what you're thinking and you don't need to worry. What we do here is nothing like what Professor Reynolds was up to."

Matt had seen the interior of the original Lazarus Project labs; they had been nothing more than sophisticated torture chamber, where vampires had been eviscerated, destroyed and revived, and treated as nothing more than animals, all in the name of Reynolds' headlong pursuit of a cure for their weaknesses, the precise opposite of what the rest of Blacklight had believed he was working on.

"I hope not," he said. "What he did was inhumane."

"I saw," said Dr Cooper. "I led the team that cleared out the labs after he was killed. It still gives me nightmares." He smiled, but Matt didn't think the doctor was joking; not entirely, at least.

"There were two survivors," said Matt. "A man and his daughter. Reynolds was about to destroy them when Jamie interrupted him. Do you know what happened to them?"

"Patrick and Maggie Connors," said Cooper, nodding his head. "They were released as soon as the investigation into Reynolds was complete."

"Really?" asked Matt. "We let two vampires go?"

Dr Cooper nodded. "The Interim Director ordered them released personally. Surveillance could probably tell you where they are, if you're interested?"

Matt shook his head. "That's OK. I just find it odd that they got released and now the whole Department is under orders to destroy the Broadmoor escapees. None of those men wanted to be vampires. It seems... inconsistent."

"It's a grey area," agreed Cooper. "Cal's doing his best."

"I'm sure he is," said Matt. His mind was threatening to run away with him, wanting to dig deeper at the moral questions that lay at the heart of Blacklight; he forced himself to focus on what he was there to do. "Can I see the escapees you're holding?"

"Of course," said Dr Cooper. "Follow me."

Matt did so, weaving through the rows of desks and benches. Several staff nodded at him as he passed, but most were engrossed in their work; the atmosphere was much the same as it was in the Lazarus Project complex where he spent the overwhelming majority of his time. Dr Cooper led him to the cell at the far left of the row and stopped outside the UV wall. Matt joined him, then looked into the sealed room.

It was sparse, but was still a far cry from the transparent cubes in which the unfortunate victims of Christopher Reynolds had been kept; there was a bed with sheets and pillows, a chair with a small table beside it, a sink, and a curtained-off area that Matt assumed contained a toilet. CCTV cameras peered down from all four corners of the room, presumably positioned to record the treatment of the cell's occupant. Which, in this case, was a man in his fifties, lying on his bed and reading a paperback book. He didn't look up at Matt and Dr Cooper, even as they began to talk about him.

"Christian Bellows," said Dr Cooper. "He was recovered in the Broadmoor grounds. Put up no resistance when they brought him in and has been no trouble since he got here. He just likes to be left alone."

"What did he do?" asked Matt. "To end up in Broadmoor in the first place?"

"Almost killed a postman," said Dr Cooper. "He had come to believe that the man was planning to kill him, so he attacked him with a kitchen knife."

"Jesus."

"He's a paranoid schizophrenic," said Dr Cooper. "We have his treatment records and his pharmaceutical schedule. Don't worry, we're looking after him."

"Does he understand what's happened to him?" asked Matt. Bellows looked calm and relaxed, like a man lying on the sofa in his living room.

"Yes," replied Cooper. "We had to tell him the truth. He has a long history of delusions and his new surroundings could have played dangerously into that. He understands that he is ill, with an extremely rare disease, and that we're treating him. He made peace with it quite quickly."

"So he's cooperating?"

"Yes," said Dr Cooper. "Which is more than I can say for the other one. Come on."

Matt followed the Science Division Director to the next cell. It appeared to contain the same furniture and fittings as the one Christian Bellows was lying in, but where his had been neat and tidy, this one was a wreck. The bed had been stripped and thrown against the wall, the table had been smashed to splinters, and the curtain surrounding the toilet had been torn down and shredded. In the far corner of the cell a figure was huddled, its arms wrapped round its knees, its head lowered.

"Alex Masterson," said Dr Cooper. "He was picked up breaking into a chemist's in a town about fifteen miles from the hospital. He fought, but they managed to subdue him. We've kept him sedated since he was brought in."

Matt surveyed the wreckage of the cell. "It doesn't look like it," he said.

"It's been rather difficult," said Cooper. "The standard dosages don't work, or at least not consistently. We've never had captive vampires as powerful as these two. I suspect we have nothing that would work on Valentin Rusmanov."

"Probably not," said Matt. "So you've examined them both?"

Dr Cooper nodded. "We've found no physical differences between them and other vampires. We think it must be the virus itself."

"What did he do?" asked Matt, his voice low. He was staring at the dark ball pressed into the corner of the cell. The vampire was motionless; it was impossible to tell whether he was even awake.

"Masterson?" asked Cooper. "He committed a series of rapes in the nursing home where he worked. He's a sociopath, pure and simple. Doesn't understand why what he did was wrong."

"Good job he was picked up," said Matt, his stomach revolving slowly.

"I suppose so," said Cooper. "Might have been better if they'd just destroyed him. But at least he can't hurt anyone if he's here."

Matt shook his head sharply, trying to clear it. Although this place was a far cry from the blood-soaked nightmare that had been the first Lazarus Project lab, the sense of sickness, of banal, miserable horror, was just as palpable.

"You said there are no physical differences?" he asked.

Dr Cooper nodded. "Like I said, we think it's something in the virus itself. There's a well-established correlation between age and power, and the theory has always been that the virus continues to mutate inside the carrier after they turn, increasing their strength and speed over time."

"Right," said Matt. "But that doesn't explain this."

Or explain Larissa, he thought. *She's frighteningly strong. And fast. And she's barely been turned three years.*

"I know," said Dr Cooper. "Do you have a theory, Mr Browning?"

Matt nodded. "I do," he said. "And if I'm right, it's bad. Really bad."

"How can I help?"

"You said you examined them," said Matt. He spoke slowly, as though carefully considering each word. "I assume you interviewed them as well?"

"We did."

"What do they remember? About the night they were released?"

Dr Cooper shrugged. "Very little. Doctors, nurses, needles. Violence. Red eyes. Neither of them could give any specifics."

"What about their bites?" asked Matt. "The ones that turned them. Were they still visible when they were brought in?"

"No," replied Dr Cooper. "But then they almost never are. If the newly-turned has fed, the bite will usually have healed."

"OK," said Matt. "Do you have a terminal in here I can use?"

"Sure," said Dr Cooper. "Over here."

He led Matt to one of the long metal workbenches, flipped a monitor up out of its surface and raised a keyboard into place. Matt lifted himself up on to a stool and logged into the Blacklight network; Dr Cooper watched silently as he accessed the Zero Hour restricted section and navigated into one of the many folders containing raw footage of the Broadmoor attack.

"Do you know which wings they were being held on?" asked Matt.

"Bellows was on D wing," replied Dr Cooper. "What are you looking for?"

"I'll show you," said Matt. He opened a file called D_WING_MAIN_CORRIDOR and watched as silent black and white footage

525

began to play. The camera was positioned above a long corridor, in the middle of which a male nurse was pinned against a wall as two patients tore at his throat and chest. Blood pumped out, horribly dark beneath fluorescent lights, as he was dragged to the floor and fallen upon. A doctor ran for his life, his eyes wide, pursued by a patient with a scalpel in his hand. The patient's eyes blazed almost white and his mouth was twisted in a snarl of pure joy.

"Christ," said Dr Cooper. "That's horrible."

Matt didn't reply; he was watching the footage closely, waiting for what he was looking for. Two naked patients strolled down the corridor, past the twitching remains of the nurse; their eyes glowed, and their bodies gleamed with sweat. Matt hit PAUSE, freezing the image in place.

"There," he said. "Look."

"What am I looking at?" asked Dr Cooper, leaning in closer to the screen.

"This is minutes after the attack happened," said Matt. "These patients have only just been turned. So where are the bites?"

Dr Cooper narrowed his eyes and leant in even closer. "I don't know," he said, eventually. "I can't see any."

"Me neither," said Matt, his voice trembling. "And I think I know why."

The doctor straightened up and looked at him. "Why?"

Matt turned away from the screen and faced him. "Because there aren't any," he said. "The Broadmoor patients weren't bitten."

Dr Cooper stared at him. "They... weren't bitten?"

Matt shook his head. "Look, we know the bite itself isn't what turns people. The plasma that coats their fangs initiates the genetic change; the bite is just how it normally gets introduced into the bloodstream. I think you're right about the virus, that it evolves and increases the power of the vampire it has infected, but I think there's more to it than that. I think that when older evolutions of the virus are introduced into a victim, the turn begins at a more advanced stage. My friend Larissa was bitten by the vampire who is supposed to be the oldest in Britain, and she's already stronger and faster than almost any other I've ever seen, even though she was only turned a few years ago. I think there is a direct correlation between the age of the attacking vampire and the speed with which their victims develop."

"So what are you saying?" asked Dr Cooper. His eyes were wide, his skin pale. "If they weren't bitten, what the hell happened to them?"

"I don't know for sure," said Matt. "My guess is they were injected. With plasma from a very old vampire, that had evolved to the point where it could make the newly-turned this powerful."

"Valeri Rusmanov?" asked Dr Cooper. He was visibly trembling, as though he was about to faint.

"No," said Matt. His voice was little more than a whisper. "I'm afraid not."

49

PIECES OF THE PUZZLE

Cal Holmwood looked up from the report he was reading as someone knocked on his door, and sighed. It often seemed as though there were simply not enough hours in the day for him to deal with everything that he was expected to deal with, and he found himself yet again full of admiration for Henry Seward, who had run the Department with a smoothness that he was only now beginning to realise had been remarkable.

"Come in," he called, and set the report aside.

The door opened and Andrew Jarvis stepped through it, his face tight and pale.

What now? wondered Holmwood. *It won't be good news. It never is.*

Jarvis was the Surveillance Division representative on the Zero Hour Task Force and was widely respected within the Department. He had been recruited from GCHQ, the agency that monitored communications and provided intelligence analysis for the Security Services, and had quickly risen to second-in-command of Surveillance; the Division's Director, Major Vickers, had joked on several occasions that he could almost feel Jarvis's breath on the back of his neck.

"Captain Jarvis," said Cal, forcing a smile. "What can I do for you?"

"I'm sorry to come unannounced," said Jarvis, stopping in front of his desk. "But I thought you should see what's just appeared on my desk."

Holmwood sighed. "What is it?"

Jarvis held out a folder. Cal took it and put it down on his desk.

"Just tell me," he said. "I've read enough reports today to last a lifetime."

"Yes, sir," said Jarvis. "Yesterday afternoon, Kevin McKenna published a post on his blog, which referenced red eyes, and men in black suits. He appealed for people who knew what he was talking about to come forward with their stories."

"Oh Christ," said Holmwood. "Where is McKenna now?"

"We don't know, sir. He's not at home and he hasn't used his phone or his credit cards since yesterday."

"Albert Harker has him," said Holmwood. "Find them, Jarvis. I don't care how you do it, just find them."

"We're trying, sir," replied Jarvis. "Unfortunately, that's not all."

"Go on."

"The first two comments on McKenna's blog were long, detailed accounts that set off about a dozen Echelon alerts. One appears to describe the incident that took place on Lindisfarne last year, while the other refers to a girl who fell from the sky into a garden, and a helicopter that landed in a suburban street."

Holmwood stared. "Kate Randall's father? And Matt Browning's?"

"Yes, sir," said Jarvis. "We've tracked the IP addresses from where the comments were posted. They were behind a maze of proxies and aliases, but we got the locations eventually. Lindisfarne, Northumberland, and Staveley, Derbyshire."

"Where are Randall and Browning?"

"Missing, sir. We found Randall's car at Berwick train station this morning. No tickets were bought using his name. We're working on the assumption that they are either with, or on their way to meet, Kevin McKenna and Albert Harker."

Holmwood stared for a long moment. "Why am I hearing about this now, Captain Jarvis?" he asked, his voice low and angry. "You were in the Zero Hour meetings. You know that Albert Harker is a priority."

"I'm sorry, sir," said Jarvis. "We're tracking more than thirty of the Broadmoor escapees and keeping tabs on the rest as best we can. We're badly understaffed, and this didn't appear important to anyone who isn't Zero Hour classified. It fell through the cracks, sir."

Holmwood looked at the Captain for a long moment. "All right," he said. "It is what it is. I'll bring Jack Williams up to speed. No one else needs to know about this. Is that clear?"

"Yes, sir," said Jarvis.

Kate Randall waited for the electronic locks to disengage, then pushed open the ISAT security door.

Her mind was full of worry – for Morton, for Jamie and Ellison, and for Matt – but not the anger she had felt only months earlier when Jamie had rejected her offer to help in similar circumstances. She was proud of herself for having reached a point where she no longer assumed the worst of her friend, no longer assumed that his decisions were designed to diminish or damage her, when, in fact, they tended to represent the opposite: a well-meaning, if slightly patronising, desire to protect her.

She headed for the lounge, where she hoped Paul Turner would be; she wanted to tell him what had happened to Jamie's squad.

She was so deep in thought that she didn't see the nervous-looking woman standing in the reception, and walked straight into her.

"Oh God," Kate said, stumbling and grabbing the reception desk to steady herself. "I'm really sorry." She looked round and found herself face to face with a glowing red gaze.

"Oh, Kate," said Marie Carpenter, her eyes instantly fading back to their usual pale green. "I'm so sorry. Did I frighten you?"

"No, Mrs Carpenter," said Kate, smiling. "I'm fine. Are you OK?"

Marie nodded, her usual nervous expression back on her face. "I'm fine," she said. "I'm sorry about my eyes. I can't... it just happens. I'm sorry."

"It's OK," said Kate. "Honestly. I've seen far scarier things than you, believe me."

Marie smiled. "I'm sure you have."

Kate looked at her friend's mother, deep affection rising in her chest. Marie was dressed in a pair of dark red slacks and a pale blue blouse. She looked every inch the middle-class housewife she had been, which made her seem incredibly out of place inside the Loop, a place of endless black and grey.

"Is this where you work?" asked Marie, looking around the small ISAT reception. "Jamie told me you were doing something important, but he said he couldn't tell me what it was."

"This is it," said Kate. "It's called ISAT. It's... sort of an internal affairs department."

"Is it dangerous?" asked Marie. "Sorry, silly question. Of course it is. Everything here is dangerous."

"I didn't think it was going to be," said Kate. "Unpopular, yes. But it's turned out to be more dangerous that I thought. Like you said, I probably shouldn't be surprised."

"No," said Marie. She had clutched her hands together in

front of her stomach and was wringing them gently. "Probably not."

"What are you doing here, Mrs Carpenter?" asked Kate, gently. "Did someone send for you?"

"Oh," said Marie, her face brightening. "A young man came down and told me I had to have an interview and brought me here. He was very polite."

"I'm glad to hear it," said Kate, smiling. "I'm sorry, the schedules keep changing at the moment. If I'd known, I'd have come down to get you myself. The interview is nothing to be worried about, I promise. I'll be there, so you won't be on your own. Just stay here and someone will come and get you."

"I'll do that," said Marie. She smiled, an open, lovely smile that warmed Kate's heart. "I'll wait right here."

"OK," said Kate. "I'll see you in a minute."

She left Jamie's mother standing beside the reception desk and walked into the lounge. As she had hoped, Paul Turner was there; he was sitting on the sofa, holding a piece of paper in his hands. He looked up as she entered, and the look on his face filled her with instant concern.

He looks like he's seen a ghost.

"Paul?" she said. "Are you all right?"

He nodded. "I'm fine."

"What's that?" she asked, pointing at the document in his hand.

"Security completed their investigation," he said. "Into the bombing. These are their conclusions."

"Anything we didn't know?"

"Yes," said Turner. "Sit down."

Kate frowned, but pulled the plastic chair out from beneath the desk and took a seat.

"There *was* a vampire in your quarters, Kate," said Turner, his eyes fixed on hers. "It's been confirmed. For four minutes, about two hours before the device exploded. More than long enough."

Kate felt cold spill through her. "How do you know?" she asked. "I thought there was nothing on the cameras?"

"There wasn't," said Turner. "And that was persuasive, although not conclusive. But the cameras aren't our only means of surveillance. We have a system that monitors the temperature of every room in the Loop and records even the smallest variation. That's how we know."

"I've never heard about that," said Kate. "Is it new?"

Turner nodded. "It was installed after Valentin's defection. After it became clear he could leave his cell whenever he wanted, we needed a way of tracking him. In case of something like this."

"Who knew about it?" she asked.

"The Interim Director, Security Section C, and myself," replied Turner. "It was decided that it was better for as few people as possible to know. It's easier to watch people who don't know they're being watched."

What a lovely concept, thought Kate.

"So it showed a rise in temperature in my room?" she asked.

"That's right," said Turner. "A spike, from the room's ambient temperature to several degrees beyond what humans are capable of producing. It's definitive."

"So why didn't it show up straight away? How come you've only just found out about it?"

"The monitoring systems on Level B were damaged in the explosion," said Turner. "We didn't know whether it was going to be possible to retrieve their data. A lot of it is lost, but they managed to extract the records for your quarters. And there it was."

"So we were wrong," said Kate, slowly. "This *was* a vampire attack. It wasn't anything to do with ISAT."

"I don't know," said Turner. "I still don't buy the idea that a vampire would attack you and me by pure coincidence, but I don't have an explanation yet. If nothing else, we've narrowed down our list of suspects."

The pieces clicked into place in Kate's mind. "Jamie's mother is in reception," she said. "Is this why?"

"Yes," said Turner. "Although I will be genuinely astounded if she turns out to be our culprit. I'm beginning to suspect that one of the many skills our friend Valentin has acquired over the centuries is how to pass a lie detector, even one as sophisticated as ours. I want him brought back up here as soon as we're done with Marie. Then, I suspect, we'll get some answers."

"I'll take care of it," said Kate. "I had something to tell you as well."

"What is it?"

"You know John Morton? Jamie's rookie?"

"I know him," said Turner. "I saw Jamie had sent him for a psych evaluation. He made a couple of mistakes in the field?"

"That's him," said Kate. "They've been chasing a vamp called Alastair Dempsey, a really horrible piece of work. They missed him yesterday and a civilian girl died. Apparently, it was Morton's fault."

"So?" asked Turner. "Jamie knows what he's doing. What's the news?"

"Morton's gone after Dempsey on his own," said Kate. "He left a note for Ellison – she's the other rookie in Jamie's squad. He went three hours ago."

"Christ," said Turner. "Has Jamie gone after him?"

"Yep. Him and Ellison left about fifteen minutes ago. She's out of her mind, thinks he's going to get himself killed."

Turner appeared to consider this for a moment. "Jamie's doing the right thing," he said, eventually. "One of your team gets in trouble, you try your best to get them out of it. That's all you can do."

"I know," said Kate. "I just thought you'd want me to tell you."

"I'm glad you did," said Turner. "We can't afford to lose anyone else, not with the Department as weak as it is. But Jamie will bring him home. I'd bet on it."

"I would too."

"OK then," said Turner. "Back to our own job. Let's see what Mrs Carpenter has to say. Quickly."

"This is ISAT interview 086, conducted by Major Paul Turner, NS303, 36-A in the presence of Lieutenant Kate Randall, NS303, 78-J. State your name, please."

"Marie Carpenter."

Green.

"Please answer the following question incorrectly," said Turner. "State your gender, please."

"Male," replied Marie.

Red.

Jamie's mother looked incredibly nervous and Kate felt deeply sorry for her. Marie Carpenter had only become involved with Blacklight by accident, as a consequence of a lie her husband had perpetuated throughout their entire marriage; now she was a supernatural creature, imprisoned indefinitely inside a military base, and subject to frightening and unpleasant episodes like the one she was currently undergoing.

"Thank you," said Turner, his voice level. "We have some questions we need you to answer, but we won't keep you a minute longer than we need to, I promise."

"It's OK," said Marie, forcing a small smile. "I want to help."

Green.

"Two days ago, an explosive device was detonated on one of the residential levels of this facility. Were you aware of that?"

"I felt the building shake," said Marie. "I knew something had happened. I didn't know it was a bomb, though."

Green.

"Thank you," said Turner. "Were you—"

"Was anyone hurt?" asked Marie. Her face was pale.

"I'm sorry?"

"When the bomb went off," said Marie. "Was anyone hurt?"

"That's classified information, I'm afraid."

"That means someone got hurt," said Marie.

"Mrs Carpenter, that isn't important right now. What is—"

"You're the one my son talks about," said Marie. Her voice had acquired an edge to it, a sliver of smooth steel. "The cold-blooded one. How can you say people getting hurt isn't important?"

"That's not what I meant," said Turner. "I meant it's not important to this process. I didn't mean to upset you."

"Oh," said Marie, her voice small once more. "I'm sorry. I just don't like the thought of people being hurt."

No surprise there, thought Kate. *Given who her son is.*

"I don't either," she said. "Are you OK to continue?"

Marie nodded.

"All right," said Turner, shooting a grateful glance in Kate's direction. "Mrs Carpenter, were you responsible for planting the explosive device on Level B of this facility?"

"No," said Marie, instantly. "Of course not."

Green.

"Do you know who was responsible?"

"No."

Green.

"Do you have any information that could be relevant to identifying the perpetrator of this attack?"

"Not that I can think of. I'm sorry."

Green.

"We interviewed Valentin Rusmanov yesterday, Mrs Carpenter. He told us that he has had a number of conversations with you in your cell. Is that true?"

"Yes," said Marie. "Am I in trouble?"

Green.

"Not at all," replied Turner. "Has Mr Rusmanov ever said anything that you believe could have been related to the planning of an attack on this Department?"

"No," replied Marie. "I'm sure he hasn't."

Green.

"What do the two of you talk about?"

"I'm not sure that's any of your business, Major Turner," replied Marie, politely.

Green.

Kate smiled. "You're probably right," she said. "But it could be really helpful. Anything you tell us will go no further than this room."

Marie looked at her with an expression on her face that Kate didn't like.

She's disappointed in me, she thought. *For being part of this.*

She was surprised to discover how much she disliked such an idea; it was similar to how she had felt on any of the many occasions that her father had caught her doing something she wasn't supposed to, or playing somewhere she shouldn't.

"Jamie," said Marie, eventually. "We mostly talk about Jamie."

Green.

"Is Valentin interested in your son?" asked Turner.

"Very," said Marie, proudly. "He told me that, out of all of you, he defected to Jamie because he was so impressed by what he had done to his brother."

"Jamie killed his brother," said Turner, softly.

"I know exactly what he did," snapped Marie. "I was there. So was Kate, for that matter. Where were you, Major Turner?"

Wow, thought Kate. *There are about three people in this whole building who would have had the balls to say that. Wow.*

Turner smiled. "I was in Russia," he said. "Cleaning up a different massacre. One carried out by the oldest Rusmanov."

"Oh," said Marie, colour rising in her cheeks. "I didn't know that."

"It's all right," said Turner. "There's no reason why you would."

"I'm sorry," said Marie. "I get a bit defensive about my son."

"Perfectly understandable," said Turner. "I had a son. He did a lot of stupid things, but I always took his side. I don't think parents can help it."

Kate felt a chill up her spine. *Don't talk about him,* she thought. *Not now. Please don't.*

"You *had* a son?" said Marie, slowly.

"Shaun."

"What happened to him?"

"He died," said Turner. "A few months ago. He was killed by Valentin's brother."

"I'm so sorry," said Marie, her voice thick and choked with tears.

"Thank you," said Turner. Kate looked helplessly at him; she wanted to reach out and put her hand on his shoulder, but knew she could not.

"So that's all you and Valentin talk about?" she asked, hoping to give Paul a moment. "About Jamie?"

"No," said Marie. "Sometimes he tells me about my husband's family. He knew Jamie's grandfather."

"John," said Turner.

"That's him," replied Marie. "He sounds like a remarkable man."

"I never met him," said Turner. "He retired before my time. But from everything I've ever heard, I'd say you were right."

"I told Valentin to tell Jamie about him. I think he'd like to hear about his grandfather."

"Maybe he will," said Turner. "Apparently, they talk quite often."

Kate watched Marie closely. There was no surprise on her face, but something flickered across it.

"They do," said Marie. "I can hear him as soon as he gets out of the airlock. I don't know if he knows that, but I can. So I hear them talking."

He doesn't always come and see you, does he? realised Kate, suddenly. *Sometimes he visits Valentin and not you. Jesus, Jamie.*

"Have you heard anything else from the other cells?" asked Turner. "Anything out of the ordinary?"

"No," said Marie, shaking her head. "People talking, laughing. Tapping away on those big mobile phone things you all carry. Nothing strange."

Both Kate and Paul Turner froze.

After a few seconds, Marie gave a nervous little laugh. "What did I say?" she asked.

"What did you hear, Mrs Carpenter?" asked Turner, recovering slightly faster than Kate. "What exactly? Tell me."

"Fingers tapping on a plastic screen," said Marie, frowning. "And that beep they make. Jamie is always playing with his when he visits me."

Turner grabbed his console from his belt. "Send me a message," he said, turning to face her. "Quickly."

"What message?" asked Kate, thumbing her screen into life.

"Anything," said Turner. "Nothing. It doesn't matter."

Kate tapped on the MESSAGING icon and pressed NEW. She searched Paul Turner's name, quickly wrote TEST in the subject line and hit SEND. There was a long, pregnant moment of silence, then the screen on Paul Turner's console lit up and a short, two-tone beep sounded in the silent room.

"Was that the noise?" asked Turner, turning back to face Jamie's mother. "The one you heard? Was that it?"

Marie nodded. "Yes."

Green.

Turner flicked a glance in Kate's direction; his eyes were wide, and the corners of his mouth were curling slightly upwards, in what appeared to be the beginnings of a smile.

"Let me get this straight," he said. "You're telling us that you've heard Valentin Rusmanov using a console like the ones that we carry, like the one you've seen your son use? And that you've heard it beep like mine just did? Is that what you're saying?"

"No," said Marie, frowning. "That's not what I'm saying at all."

"What do you mean?" asked Turner.

"It wasn't Valentin. It was the other one."

Turner stared. "His butler?" he asked. "Lamberton?"

Marie Carpenter nodded. "That's him."

50

DEADLINE

SPIRIT OF INNOVATION INDUSTRIAL PARK, READING, BERKSHIRE

The sun finally slipped beyond the horizon, plunging the industrial estate into the gloomy grey of twilight.

Four pairs of eyes watched from inside a rented van as the men and women who worked in the vast concrete boxes began to stream out, heading for the train station or the sprawling car parks. They went quietly, paying no attention to the small white vehicle parked in front of the glass reception of one of the largest buildings on the estate: the printing press that produced more than half a million copies of *The Globe* every night of the year.

Inside the van, Pete Randall was nervous.

Throughout the long, tense afternoon, Albert Harker had refused to tell them what he had planned; he believed it was vital that only he knew the details until it was absolutely necessary. His caution was extreme, bordering on paranoia; he had apologised, but would not be moved on the matter.

Pete and Greg had eventually been sent out with a handful of Albert Harker's money and instructions to rent a vehicle, a van with no windows in the sides or back, so the vampire could be safely transported inside it. They had found a place barely ten minutes' walk from the hotel. At first, Pete had been reluctant to hand over his driving licence, until Greg told him that, at this point, it no longer mattered. They were in too deep to worry about a paper trail or an electronic fingerprint.

The four of them had piled into the van and the vampire had given him the location that he was to drive them to. It had initially meant nothing to Pete: a nondescript industrial estate in a part of the world that was full of them. But as he had driven the van through the entrance, he had seen a familiar logo on the tall board listing the resident companies and felt his stomach tighten.

"This is where they print *The Globe*, right?" he said.

"Indeed," said Harker. "The printing presses that produce Kevin's former publication each night. *This* is where we will strike our first blow for truth."

Then he leant forward and explained his plan.

The side door of the van slid open and four figures emerged. They were dressed in black clothing, one of them carrying a black sports bag over his shoulder.

They walked quickly across the forecourt towards the printing press's entrance, Albert Harker in the lead. Through the glass, Pete could see the reception desk and the lone security guard sitting behind it. The man had noticed their approach and was watching them, but his face bore no trace of concern: out-of-hours visitors were presumably a common occurrence. As they neared the glass door, the guard reached out and pressed a button on his desk. A second later there was a loud buzzing noise and the door clicked open.

Albert Harker took hold of the handle and pulled it open.

"Thank you," he said, as Pete, Kevin and Greg followed him inside.

"No problem," said the guard. "Sign in—"

The rest of the sentence died in the guard's throat, as Albert Harker's eyes burst a deep, flaming red. He crossed the reception in a blur of black, grabbed the reeling guard by the back of his head, and slammed his face into the desk. There was a loud crunch as the man's nose broke; blood flew in the fluorescent brightness of the reception.

"Jesus," shouted Kevin McKenna.

Harker lifted the guard's head; his mouth hung open, his eyes rolled back.

"He'll be fine," said the vampire. "He's going to have a sore head when he wakes up, but we'll be long gone by then. Greg, tie him and bind his mouth. Make sure you leave his nose clear; we don't want him to choke."

Greg nodded, and shrugged the bag down from his shoulder. He unzipped it and pulled out a roll of black electrical tape and a length of plastic wire. Harker lifted the security guard over the desk with one hand and laid him flat on the floor; Greg quickly tied his hands behind his back and his legs together at the ankles. Then he tore a strip of tape and pressed it firmly over the guard's mouth.

"Well done," said Harker, and carried the man back behind the desk. He placed him on the floor beside his chair, hidden from anyone looking in from outside, then walked back to his companions, his eyes still blazing.

"That's it, right?" said McKenna. "No one else gets hurt?"

"As I promised you, my friend," replied Harker. "No one else gets hurt."

"OK," said McKenna. "Like you promised."

*

543

At the rear of the reception, a pair of doors led on to the printing press floor. Access was controlled by a key-card panel, but Harker simply pushed until their deadbolts gave way with a loud crunch of metal. Deafening noise spilled instantly out into the reception, an unholy cacophony of thundering metal pistons and giant spinning wheels.

"Follow me," said the vampire, and walked through the doors.

The printing press looked like something out of an industrial nightmare; it filled the enormous room from floor to ceiling, a series of innumerable machines connected by conveyor belts that snaked between them. An open area to their right contained a number of desks and computer screens; a sign that read EDITORIAL hung from the ceiling above it.

Five metres along the wall beside the door stood a large glass cabinet. Harker strode along the edge of the room and stopped before it. His companions followed, Pete scanning the huge room as they did so, his eyes peeled for any of the press's employees. McKenna had told them that the facility was almost fully automated; once it was running, only a skeleton maintenance crew stayed overnight, their job to fix the machines if something went wrong. He had estimated that there would be no more than ten men and women in the entire building.

Beside the editorial department, rolls of paper taller than the average man spun endlessly, feeding the hungry machines. At the far end of the room, Pete could see stacks of finished newspapers being automatically bundled, wrapped in plastic, and stacked on to pallets. Then one of the press's employees, a man wearing blue overalls, appeared, driving a forklift truck with a yellow light spinning on its roof. The distant wall contained a number of large rolling doors, most of which were open; these were where the lorries that delivered *The Globe* to distribution centres throughout the country parked, ready to be filled up with brightly coloured pages of gossip and sport.

As Pete watched, the man lifted a pallet into the open trailer of a lorry, before a second worker closed its doors and locked them. The lorry immediately pulled away from its berth, leaving a rectangular hole in the side of the building. The man reversed the forklift, until it disappeared behind the towering machines.

Harker pulled open the glass front of the cabinet, as his companions crowded round him. There were a number of illuminated switches on a metal panel, with a large red button in the middle marked ALL STOP.

The vampire reached out one thin, pale finger and pressed the button.

The cessation of noise was so startling it made them all jump. For a long second, all that could be heard was a high hissing as the presses ground to a halt. Then a number of alarms began to sound and shouted voices echoed through the cavernous space.

"Here we go," said Harker. "Let me do the talking."

The vampire's eyes bloomed red as his fangs slid into place. A second later two men in blue overalls appeared from between the rows of machinery, their faces red and frowning.

"Hey!" shouted one of them, pointing at Pete. "What the hell do you—" His voice died away as he caught sight of Albert Harker, a grinning, glowing thing from his worst nightmares. His eyes widened and he tried to turn back, but it was too late; Harker slid forward and lifted both men off their feet. He threw them almost casually into the editorial department, where they hit the ground hard. They screamed in pain and terror, their eyes wide and staring.

"Watch them," growled Harker, then disappeared.

Pete and Greg ran forward and stood over the cowering, terrified men. Seconds later Harker returned, holding two more workers in his supernatural grasp; after less than two minutes, eight men were huddled together between the desks, trembling with visible terror.

Albert Harker dropped out of the air and regarded them with his terrible glowing eyes. "Stay calm, gentlemen," he growled. "You will come to no harm as long as you do as I tell you. Do you understand?"

The men's panicked whimpering receded slightly, and three or four of them managed to nod their heads.

"Good," said Harker. "We are going to be making a late alteration to tomorrow's edition and you fine men are going to help us. You are not going to be blamed for this, and no one will think it was your fault. So please do not do anything stupid."

The men stared, uncomprehending.

"How many of you are required to run this press?" Harker asked.

There was silence from the huddled mass.

"I asked you a question," said the vampire, his voice rumbling with menace. "I expect an answer. You, tell me."

He pointed at a skinny, pale man at the front of the cowering group. He was barely more than a boy and his expression was one of utter terror, but he managed to find his voice.

"If nothing breaks..." he whispered.

"Speak up, for God's sake," snapped Harker.

The man gulped audibly and tried again. "If nothing breaks," he said, "you don't need anyone on the machines. Just loaders at the other end."

"How many of you to load the lorries?"

"Four," said the man. "Four of us can do it."

"Good," said Harker. "That's good. Greg, tie four of them up. Quickly, please."

Greg Browning stepped forward, enthusiasm radiating from his face. Pete watched, an odd feeling rising in his stomach; a sensation of being in the dark, of not being told all there was to tell. The vampire seemed to be taking unnecessary enjoyment from the fear of the men who were huddled before him.

I don't know if this is what we thought it was.

Greg stepped away from the group of men, leaving four of them tied and gagged. Harker dragged them easily away from their colleagues and laid them in a line against the wall.

"Watch them, Pete," he said. "They're your responsibility."

He nodded. "Got it."

Harker smiled, then turned to McKenna. "Kevin," he said. "Make us proud."

McKenna nodded, his face tight with concentration, and made his way past the bound men into the editorial department. He took a seat at one of the desks and woke up the computer that sat on it. The screen lit up, displaying the file that was currently running through the enormous press; the following day's edition of *The Globe*. The front page was a splash photograph of an American singer on a beach in a bikini, with a headline speculating as to whether she had been the recipient of surgical enhancement. The sidebar contained the apparently exclusive news that a Spanish footballer was about to make a multi-million-pound move to a team from the north-west.

McKenna pulled a memory stick out of his pocket and slotted it into the side of the monitor. He expanded the folder when it appeared and opened the only document. Working quickly, he deleted the edition's existing front page and pasted a huge headline and three short columns of text on to page one. He then wiped page two, pasted in the rest of the document, and saved the new version of the print file. He scrolled back to page one, before showing it to Harker and his companions.

It was far from a masterpiece of design: the fonts were boring, the text was small, and the formatting was simple at best. But there was no disputing the blunt power of the page that McKenna had created.

**VAMPIRES
ARE REAL.
THE GOVERNMENT
IS LYING TO YOU.**

"It's perfect," said Harker, his hand clasping the journalist's shoulder. "It's exactly right. Print it."

"I need one of them to do it," said McKenna, pointing at the four men who had not been tied up.

Harker nodded. "Who can start the process?" he asked, his eyes flaring red. "Don't make me ask twice."

One of the men put his hand up. "I can," he said.

"Then do so," said Harker. "Quickly."

The man nodded and got to his feet. He walked unsteadily over to where Kevin McKenna was sitting, gently taking the computer's mouse from his hand. Pete watched as the man ran through the pre-print checks, recalibrated the system to accommodate the new pages, and set the machine running. A rumble shook the ground beneath the men's feet, but the machines stayed still.

"Why is nothing happening?" asked Harker.

"It takes eight minutes to warm up," said the man, his voice shaking. "There's nothing I can do."

Harker gave a brief growl, but nodded his head. "So be it," he

548

said. "Eight minutes will make no difference. Kevin, stay here and carry out the second part of your task. Pete, you know what you're doing?"

"Watching them," he replied, nodding towards the bound men.

"Correct," said Harker. "Greg, you're coming with me, as are you fine gentlemen. As soon as copies start to come off the press, you go back to work. I don't want the delivery drivers to have the slightest idea that anything out of the ordinary is happening here. If you try to alert one of them, both you and he will wish you hadn't. Am I making myself clear?"

The four workers nodded furiously, their eyes full of fear.

"Good," said Harker. "Then let's go. Pete, Kevin, you shout if there are any problems this end. I can hear you quite clearly. Remember that."

Pete frowned.

Remember that? Was that a threat?

The vampire floated up into the air, provoking a new ripple of panic among the men in the blue overalls. They scrambled to their feet and staggered down the corridor between the machines with Greg Browning behind them, herding them back to the loading bays. Pete watched them go, unable to shake the feeling that something was wrong. He looked over at Kevin McKenna, trying to gauge the man, but the journalist was turned away from him, working rapidly at the computer.

Pete stared at the back of his head; the feeling in his stomach was getting stronger and more insistent by the minute. He had never been an arrogant man; he had, if anything, tended towards excessive modesty where his attributes and achievements were concerned. He had always known he wasn't the cleverest, the strongest, the best-looking or the most charming, and that was absolutely fine. The one thing he *had* always believed about himself, that he had given himself credit for, was that he was a good man, a man of integrity, loyalty and moral courage. He backed away from the journalist, giving himself distance from the four bound men laid out against the wall, and tried to reconcile what he was doing with the man he had always believed himself to be.

McKenna pushed his chair away from the desk and rubbed his eyes with the heels of his palms.

"Albert," he said, barely raising his voice. "Do you want to see this?"

There was a long moment of silence, before the vampire dropped silently out of the air beside McKenna and peered at the screen.

"It's live?" he asked, his eyes smouldering.

"Yep," replied McKenna. "It's up, for everyone to see."

Harker clapped him on the shoulder. "Well done," he said. "You have played your part perfectly, Kevin."

"Cheers," he replied. "So what now? The papers go out, then we're done, right?"

"Done?"

"Done," repeated McKenna. "The public will know everything. That's what we want."

"My dear friend," said Harker, a smile rising on his face. "This is not the end. Far from it. When we are finished here, you will start work on the follow-up story."

McKenna frowned. "What follow-up? What else is there for me to write about?"

"A personal description of the world we are showing them," replied the vampire. "The death, the horror, the blood. Families torn apart, innocent men and women caught up in the carnage. A crusade needs rallying points, images too sad and shocking to be ignored, that make people confront a reality that could happen to them. In short, Kevin, it requires martyrs."

A chill ran up McKenna's spine. "What do you mean, martyrs?" he asked, slowly. "You told me nobody was going to be hurt."

The smile on the vampire's face narrowed. "Don't concern yourself with the details," he said, softly. "Suffice it to say, you are perfectly safe."

"What about the others?" hissed McKenna. "Pete and Greg, and the print workers?"

"We will honour their memories."

McKenna stared at the glowing face of the monster, realisation spilling through him, turning his insides to ice.

"You planned this all along," he said, slowly. "That's why you wanted them to come. So they could die for your cause."

The red in Harker's eyes deepened to a swirling crimson. "I told you not to concern yourself with the details. Consider the concept of the greater good, if you must fixate on something."

There was a rush of air and the vampire was gone, swooping up towards the cavernous roof of the press. McKenna stayed where he was, frozen to his chair, his mind racing.

OhGodohGodohGodohGodohGodohGod.

His chest felt as though it was made of concrete; he tried to breathe, but couldn't force air into his lungs. Pressure built in his head, pounding at his temples as he realised what he had done.

You can't tell them. He'll hear you, even if you whisper. Think, for God's sake. How can you stop this?

He turned his head slowly and looked at Pete Randall. He was standing by the door, a thoughtful expression on his face as he surveyed the captive workers. McKenna watched him for a long moment, and the solution became suddenly clear.

He raised his hand and beckoned Pete towards him.

Pete Randall frowned as the journalist gestured at him. He made his way towards him slowly, staying on the balls of his feet; he was beginning to think that somehow the situation had changed, that the landscape had shifted beneath them.

"What is it?" he asked, drawing close to McKenna.

"Look," said Kevin, standing up and pointing at the screen. "I was just showing Albert. I've done it."

Pete eased himself into the chair and looked. The bar at the top of the screen was displaying the URL of *The Globe*'s website, but the photos and videos and forums were all gone from the page itself; all the screen contained now was Kevin McKenna's huge headline and the long text of his story.

"Holy shit," said Pete. "Is that live?"

"It's live," confirmed Kevin, from behind him. "Pretty cool, huh?"

"Pretty cool," said Pete. He turned his head to smile at McKenna; as a result, the journalist's fists crashed down on his cheek, rather than on the back of his head. Pain burst through him and he slid down on to one knee, his vision greying. McKenna grabbed the side of his head, then slammed him into the surface of the desk. He felt the skin above his ear tear like paper and a gush of blood, shockingly warm, pour down his face. Then his eyes rolled back and everything turned a deep, empty black.

When he came to, he was lying on the ground. He struggled to open his eyes; the lids felt as though they were made of lead, and his head was roaring with pain. He bore down, using what felt like all of his strength to force them open. The warehouse swam slowly back into focus and he found himself looking at the four men that Greg Browning had tied up; two of them were staring at him with wide eyes, but the others were crawling furiously towards the door that led to reception.

There was no sign of Kevin McKenna.

Pete sat up and pressed his hand against the side of his head. It came away covered in blood and he felt his stomach lurch violently. His head swam and he fought to clear it; he forced himself up on to unsteady legs and staggered towards the door. The crawling men froze, staring up at him, their eyes wide with looks of complete powerlessness. Pete ignored them. He lurched through the door into reception and saw Kevin McKenna standing behind the desk, a phone clamped to the side of his head.

"*The Globe* printing press," said the journalist, his eyes wide and staring. "No, I don't know the bloody address. Somewhere near Reading. Albert Harker is holding me and two other men hostage, Pete Randall and Greg Browning. He's an escapee from Broadmoor. For God's sake, just get here as—"

Pete staggered towards him, trying to call Kevin's name. But his mouth wouldn't work; all that emerged was a low croak. McKenna saw him coming and circled round behind the desk, putting it between the two men.

"Stay back," he shouted. "Stay back, Pete. I'm doing this for you."

He lurched onwards. The journalist backed away, the phone still pressed to his ear. Then his eyes flew open wide and the last of the colour drained from his face. Pete tried to turn his head; he knew he had not caused McKenna's reaction. But before he got the chance, a black blur rocketed past him.

It solidified into the roaring, demonic form of Albert Harker. He grabbed McKenna by the lapels of his jacket and jerked him into the air, screaming incoherently into the journalist's face. The phone tumbled from McKenna's hand as he fought futilely against the supernatural strength of the vampire.

"You traitor!" roared Harker, his eyes blazing, his mouth wide and foaming with spit. "You gutless backstabber!"

He threw McKenna against the glass wall of reception; it cracked from top to bottom, but didn't break. The journalist slid to the floor, his mouth hanging open, his eyes staring blankly up at the monstrous thing he had somehow found himself on the same side as.

Harker reached down and lifted him to his feet. Pete watched helplessly, screaming at himself to intervene, to say something, do something, but could not; his body was not obeying his commands, and all he could do was watch. For a long moment, McKenna thrashed in Albert Harker's grasp. Then the vampire sank the fingers of his other hand into the soft flesh beneath McKenna's chin and tore out his throat. It gave way with a terrible ripping noise; blood sprayed into the air, shockingly bright, and splashed across the glass windows and the bare concrete floor.

Harker dipped his face into the crimson geyser erupting from McKenna's neck and drank deeply, his eyes closed in ecstasy. Then he dropped the corpse of the man he had called his friend, lifted the phone, and smashed it against the desk, sending shards of plastic and coils of wire flying through air that stank of blood.

51

... IT POURS

"We've got him," said Paul Turner, his eyes flashing fiercely. "Lamberton. Not Valentin. We've got the bastard."

"Careful," said Kate. "Valentin could still be part of this. I don't think Lamberton does anything without permission from his master, and he lives in the cell next door. Wouldn't he have heard the same things Marie heard?"

The two Operators were sitting in the ISAT lounge, trying to process the bombshell that Marie Carpenter had inadvertently dropped on them. Jamie's mother had been unhooked from the monitoring equipment and given a Security Division escort back down to her cell. Before she left, Turner had impressed upon her the necessity that Lamberton must not realise that anything was wrong; she was to return to her cell and act exactly as she normally did.

"For how long?" she had asked. "I'm afraid I'm not a very good liar."

"Not long," Turner had replied. "We'll be down there before you know it."

Marie had nodded and followed her escorts out of ISAT. They had watched her go, still incredulous that the key piece of information had come from her, even if she hadn't known it was important.

"Maybe," said Turner. "But even Valentin has to sleep. How would he have got his hands on a console? Why would he bother? No, this is between Lamberton and whoever has been sending him messages."

"I'm sure you're right," said Kate. "I'm just asking you to be careful."

Turner looked at her and saw the concern on her face. "Don't worry," he said, and smiled. "I will be."

Kate smiled back. "So what happens now?"

"I have to tell Cal what we know," said Turner. "Then it's up to him."

Kate was about to reply when her boss's console buzzed into life. Turner swore, grabbed it, and thumbed the screen into life. He read the lines of text and groaned. "Echelon intercept," he said. "Zero Hour classification. Excuse me for a second."

The Security Officer set his console down and lifted his radio from its loop on his belt. He keyed a number into the pad on the front of the handset, then held it to his ear. "NS303, 36-A coding in for Echelon intercept assessment. Proceed."

Kate watched as Turner listened to the message that had been intercepted by Echelon, the vast monitoring system that constantly scanned electronic communication for words and phrases flagged by the Security Services: evidence of crime, of potential terrorist plots and attacks. But the system also scanned for a long list of words and phrases that would seem strange to anyone outside the Department: vampire, blood, fangs, red eyes, Blacklight and dozens of others.

Paul Turner had become very still, she noticed. He was staring straight ahead, his eyes widening visibly.

What now? she wondered.

"Understood," said Turner. "Forward me the transcript. Out."
He placed the radio back on his belt, then turned to her with a
stricken expression on his face.

Panic leapt into her heart.

"What's wrong?" she asked. "Paul, what is it?"

His console beeped with the same noise he had demonstrated
to Marie Carpenter only minutes earlier. He opened the message
and held it out towards her. She took it from him with hands that
had begun to tremble, and looked at the screen.

ECHELON INTERCEPT REF. 45110/4F
SOURCE. Emergency call (landline telephone 0118 974 6535)
TRANSCRIPT BEGINS. I need the police, right now. My
name is Kevin McKenna. My location? The Globe printing press.
No, I don't know the bloody address. Somewhere near Reading.
Albert Harker is holding me and two other men hostage, Pete
Randall and Greg Browning. He's an escapee from Broadmoor.
For God's sake, just get here as. TRANSCRIPT ENDS.
RISK ASSESSMENT. Priority Level 1 (Zero Hour classification)

Kate stared at the words on the screen. She read them a second
time, her brain desperately trying to make sense of them, trying to
find a way to tell her that what she was seeing was something other
than it was.

Dad? she thought. *Oh, Dad. What have you done? What the hell
have you done?*

She looked up at Paul Turner, who was staring at her with a
look of utter anguish. The sight of such naked emotion on the
glacial Security Officer's face brought tears instantly to the corners
of her eyes.

"What is this?" she asked, her voice shaking. "What does this mean?"

"I don't know," replied Turner, his eyes locked on hers. "I don't know, Kate. I'll find out, I promise. Just stay calm."

"My dad," she said. "And Matt's dad. And Albert Harker. I don't understand."

"Kate..."

"I have to go," she said, getting up from her chair. "I have to go right now."

"Kate, just—"

"You're not going to try and stop me?" she asked, staring at him. "Please tell me you wouldn't do that?"

"Kate, dammit, will you just stop for a second? I need to think."

She could see the cogs and wheels turning inside Turner's usually cool head, could see the dilemma he was trying to resolve: go to Holmwood with the news about Lamberton, or help her. "I don't have time for this, Paul," she said, her voice low.

"I'll come with you," he said. "We'll go right now."

"You can't," said Kate. "We both know you can't. You have to go and deal with Lamberton."

"Albert Harker is a Priority Level 1 target with a Zero Hour classification," he said. "Everything else can wait."

"No," she said. "It can't."

"Goddamnit, Kate, what the hell do you want me to do?" Turner shouted. "I won't let you go up against Albert Harker on your own. We don't have any idea what he's planning or what your father is doing with him."

"I know that," she said, smiling at his show of emotion. "But I'm going. If you were in danger, Shaun would have come for you. Nothing would have stopped him. You said it yourself, Paul; one of your team gets in trouble, you do your best to get them out of it. That's all you can do."

Turner stared at her. "That's not fair," he said. "Bringing him into this. It's not fair."

"I know," she said. "And I'm sorry. But you know I'm right. So please don't try to stop me."

"OK," he said. "Just hold on a minute." She could see him turning the situation over in his head, looking for an angle, for some way he could help. "I'm not going to stop you," he said, after a long moment. "And I'm not even going to try to persuade you not to tell Matt. I have to tell Cal what's happening, but you'll have a head start over Jack's squad. Just do one thing for me, OK? Give me ten minutes. Be in the Ops Room in ten minutes. Promise me."

"OK," she said. "I promise. Ten minutes."

Matt Browning stood stiffly in front of Cal Holmwood's desk, his hands clenched tightly behind his back. The Interim Director was staring at him with an expression of such abject despair that it made him feel guilty just to look at it.

"Let me get this straight," said Holmwood, eventually. "You're saying that every prisoner and patient that was released during the attack on Broadmoor was turned using a vampire virus that had been extracted from an extremely old and powerful vampire? Possibly even Dracula himself? Is that really what you're standing there telling me?"

"Yes, sir," replied Matt.

"Because of the correlation between the age of a vampire and the power of the men and women they turn. Am I understanding correctly?"

"Yes, sir. I'm sorry, sir."

"I'm assuming that this isn't in any way your fault?"

Matt frowned. "No, sir."

"Then don't apologise. You're the bearer of bad news, not the cause of it." Holmwood dragged his hands through his hair, then slammed them down on the surface of his desk, causing Matt to flinch. "Goddammit," he said. "You're sure about this? There's no chance you could be wrong?"

Matt considered this. He had come straight up to the Interim Director's quarters from the Science Division labs, his heart pounding in his chest, his palms clammy with sweat. He had examined his theory from every angle as he made his way up through the Loop, looking for a flaw in his logic, looking for an assumption that couldn't be supported.

He had found nothing.

"I could be, sir," he said. "But I don't think I am. It fits with the evidence we've seen of the power of the escapees, and it solidifies the connection between age and power, including from vampire to victim. The accepted wisdom has always been that older vampires just got stronger over time, like humans get stronger the more they exercise. And I think that *is* the case. But I now think that the virus in a vampire's system changes too. *It* becomes more powerful."

"Meaning that when an old vampire turns someone, that someone will be stronger than if they'd been turned by a younger vampire?"

"Yes. For instance, Valentin would create very strong vampires."

"Like Lamberton."

Matt nodded.

"But how could we not know this before?" asked Holmwood. "With all our research?"

"I don't know," said Matt. "But I have a theory."

"Go on."

"We never saw the connection because I don't think old vampires turn people very often. They feed and they kill. Which is logical – anyone they turned would be powerful. A potential threat. Look at Larissa; she's so strong, even though she's only been turned for a few years. Which makes sense because she was turned by Grey, who's supposed to be the oldest vampire in Britain. But according to her, he never meant to turn her. He *intended* to kill her."

"Jesus," said Holmwood.

"I hope I'm wrong, sir. Nobody will be more pleased than me if I am."

"I will be," said Holmwood, and forced a smile. "But I'd also be very surprised. Why do you think it's Dracula?"

Matt shrugged. "Theoretically, it could be any old vampire – Valeri, or someone else we don't know about. But if it's Dracula, then it fits, doesn't it? The graffiti we've been seeing doesn't say, 'He will rise.' It says, 'He rises.' Let's say we're right, and Dracula himself has not returned to full power; he can still send his servants out with syringes full of his plasma and infect all these prisoners. It takes up our time, when we could be looking for him, and it puts him out there in the world, causing chaos. It just... it feels like something he would do."

"It does, doesn't it?" said Holmwood, and sighed deeply. "So what do you want me to do about this?"

"I've no idea, sir," said Matt. "I just thought you should know."

"So should the rest of the Departments," said Holmwood. "Is there any way we can prove your theory? I mean, prove it beyond any doubt?"

"We could prove that the virus evolves if Larissa was here," said

Matt. "There should be similarities between the virus in her plasma and in that of the escapees."

"Larissa's in Nevada," said Holmwood.

"I know, sir."

"I could bring her home," said the Interim Director. "If it would help?"

"It would help," said Matt. "But that's not my decision, sir."

"OK. What about proving that Dracula was involved in all this?"

"That's possible too, sir," said Matt. "If we had a sample of his DNA. Even a partial one. I don't think we'd get a one hundred per cent match, because the vampire virus alters the victim's DNA rather than replacing it. But I would expect to see enough similarities between his DNA and that of the Science Division's prisoners for us to be pretty sure."

"All right," said Holmwood. "I'll see what I can do. I'm assuming I don't need to tell you that this goes no further than this room?"

"No, sir," said Matt. "I understand."

"OK. Good work, Mr Browning. Exceptionally good work. Dismissed."

Matt nodded, crossed the Interim Director's quarters and pulled open the heavy door. He stepped through it and was on his way back down to the Lazarus Project when his phone buzzed into life.

He pulled it out of his pocket and saw Kate Randall's name on the small screen. If he had been at his desk, he would not have answered it. But for once, her timing was perfect; he pressed the green ANSWER button and held the phone to his ear.

"Hi, Kate," he said. "I was just—"

"Matt, listen to me," interrupted Kate. "We've got trouble. Meet me in the hangar in five minutes."

Matt paused. Kate's tone was even and businesslike, but beneath it he could hear something that sounded horribly close to panic. "What's wrong?" he asked. "Kate, what's the matter?"

"My dad," she said. "And yours, Matt. Your dad. We got an Echelon intercept from someone calling himself Kevin McKenna. He said he was being held hostage by Albert Harker, with Pete Randall and Greg Browning."

For a long moment, Matt didn't respond; terror had struck him completely dumb.

My dad? With Kate's dad? And Albert Harker? How can that be possible?

"Are you sure?" he heard himself say.

"I'm not sure of anything," replied Kate. "But I can't take the chance. I'm going, Matt. I'm going now. Will you come with me?"

Fear crashed through Matt in a great, freezing wave. This was close to the worst thing he could imagine: his father, the man he had loved and hated in equal measure, in need of help. An opportunity for him to fail his father, to let him down yet again. Yet another chance to be the old, useless Matt he had started to believe he had left behind forever.

"Kate..." he said, helplessly.

"I won't think any less of you," she said. "I promise I won't. But I need to know right now, Matt. Are you coming with me or not?"

He squeezed his eyes shut.

Wimp. Failure. Disappointment. Mummy's boy. Coward.

"I'll see you in the hangar," he said.

Cal Holmwood watched Matt Browning pull the door to his quarters shut behind him and sat back in his chair. He had no doubt that the brilliant, nervous teenager's theory was correct; in less than three months, he had come to trust him completely.

Just under three hundred escaped patients effectively turned by Dracula himself, he thought, a chill running up his spine. *Thousands more around the world. So much worse than any of us thought.*

He sat forward and pressed a series of keys on his desktop terminal. The wall screen opposite lit up, displaying the Blacklight network. Holmwood opened the secure video messaging program and scrolled through his contacts list.

Matt's word is good enough for me. But the others are going to need proof.

He highlighted Aleksandr Ovechkin's name and clicked CALL. A few seconds later a young SPC Operator appeared on the screen, wearing an expression of surprise.

"Director Holmwood," said the man. "I am Yevgeny Alimov, Colonel Ovechkin's assistant. I'm very sorry, I do not have your call on my schedule."

"Don't worry, Operator Alimov," said Holmwood. "This isn't a scheduled call. I need to speak to the Director."

Alimov looked relieved. "Yes, sir," he said. "I will see if he is available. Excuse me."

The young man got up from his chair and disappeared from the frame. Holmwood waited as patiently as he was able; he was on the verge of shouting in frustration at the screen when the large grey-clad figure of Aleksandr Ovechkin settled into the empty chair and smiled at him.

"Cal," he said. "This is an unexpected pleasure. How are you?"

"I'm well, Aleksandr," he replied. "Yourself?"

"I cannot complain. Each night we destroy vampires, each night more are turned. Such things do not change."

"How are you doing with the Black Dolphin break?"

Ovechkin shrugged. "Half have been destroyed, although every single one of them has fought hard. We have surveillance on half of the remainder. The rest are gone. You?"

"Similar," said Holmwood. "The breakouts are why I'm calling you, Aleksandr. I've come into some information. It's only a theory at the moment, but I can prove it with your help."

"Where did it come from?" asked Ovechkin.

"From one of my Lieutenants. He works in the Lazarus Project, alongside the girl you sent us."

"Natalia Lenski," said Ovechkin. "Is she doing well? It was hard to part with her."

"Extremely well, according to Professor Karlsson. She was involved in an incident two days ago, which caused her some minor injuries, but nothing for you to worry about."

"That is good. So what is the information?"

Cal took a deep breath and began to explain Matt Browning's theory to the SPC Director. It took him several minutes; the concepts were neither as easy or as familiar to him as they were to Matt, so he forced himself to go slowly, to paint as clear and convincing a picture as possible for his Russian counterpart. When he was finished, Ovechkin fell silent for a long moment.

"You trust this boy?" he asked, eventually. "You think he is correct?"

Holmwood nodded. "I do. I'm going to order my Science Division to fully investigate his theory, but I need something from you first."

"Tell me and it is done."

Holmwood took a deep breath. "I need you to send me the DNA profile you extracted from Dracula's ashes. Matt thinks there should be a sufficient match with the DNA of our captive escapees to be sure."

Ovechkin stared at him. The Russian Colonel's face was monolithic, and not prone to displaying emotion; Holmwood was therefore surprised and relieved when a smile curled on to the SPC Director's face.

"You know, Cal," said Ovechkin. "If you had asked me that three months ago, I would have denied that we had ever been able to extract a profile from the ashes."

"And now?" asked Holmwood.

"I will have my geneticists send it over to you," said Ovechkin, the smile still wide on his face. "Providing that you share your results with us as soon as you have them?"

"Of course," said Holmwood. "Thank you, Aleksandr."

"It is not a problem. We are all on the same side now, are we not?"

I hope so, thought Holmwood.

"We are," he said. "I'll send you the results as soon as we have them."

"All right. *Do svidaniya*, Cal."

"Goodbye, Aleksandr."

Holmwood reached out, cut the connection, and released a long sigh of relief. A new spirit of cooperation had settled over the supernatural Departments of the world in the wake of the furious, damning speech he had made after Admiral Henry Seward was taken by Valeri Rusmanov. It had been a painful process, as historical rivalries and decades-old layers of mistrust were put aside in the service of a common goal, and Holmwood was far from naïve enough to believe that no secrets remained among them, but it was a vast improvement on the situation that had been the status quo.

He got up and walked across to his small kitchen. He pulled a bottle of water out of the fridge, carried it back to his desk, and scrolled up through his contacts. When he reached Bob Allen's name, he highlighted it and hovered his finger over the button.

She's going to hate you for doing this to her, he thought.

Holmwood hesitated, giving himself a moment to think through his decision. Matt said that having Larissa home would help, and he had no reason to doubt the young Lieutenant. But there was more to it than that; the darkness was gathering around his Department and Cal had a sudden desire to close ranks, to bring his people home.

She'll understand. It was never meant to be a holiday.

Then guilt flooded through him, as he remembered the man who was locked in the cell beneath Dreamland, the man he realised he had not thought about in a very long time. He had set Julian Carpenter aside, as there were far more important things happening; now, perhaps, it was time to deal with the man he had once called his friend.

Holmwood clicked CALL and waited for the connection to be established.

Two birds with one stone, he thought. *I hope they can both forgive me.*

Kate put her phone back in her pocket and shut her eyes for a long moment.

She was trying to think clearly, trying to sort out what she needed to be aware of and prepare for, but she could not stop picturing her father, her poor, dear father who had never hurt a fly, in the clutches of Albert Harker. How the vampire had found him, or Matt's dad, didn't matter now. All that mattered was destroying him and making sure her father was safe. Explanations, recriminations: they could all wait.

She grabbed her console from her belt and tapped rapidly on its screen. The message was short; it ordered the on-duty pilot to meet her in the hangar in five minutes, on Zero Hour authorisation. The high level of classification would ensure their departure was not challenged.

And to be honest, thought Kate, as she stowed her console and ran for the hangar, *I'm not even lying. This is the definition of Zero Hour business.*

She bolted through the open-plan desks of the Intelligence Division, oblivious to the curious looks she attracted from the staff. Kate pushed through the main door without slowing, cut right, and accelerated towards the double doors that opened on to the Blacklight hangar; they slammed open with a loud thud. She ran across the hangar, her boots cracking on the tarmac floor, and hauled open the door to the armoury. There was no time to go down to her quarters and retrieve her own gear, so the guns and equipment on the stainless-steel racks would have to do.

Thankfully, there was a locker at the end of the room that contained a number of spare uniforms. She stripped off her clothes, not caring in the slightest whether anyone was watching through the plastic window behind her, and pulled on the familiar black bodysuit. She zipped it up, and was attaching weapons and kit to her belt when Matt burst into the room, his face pale, his breathing hard and shallow.

"Get dressed," she said, barely looking round at him. "Uniforms there."

Matt nodded, squeezed past her, and pulled down a uniform in his size. He held it in his hands for a long moment, then began to undress.

Oh Christ, she thought. *He's never worn this stuff outside the Playground. I shouldn't be taking him. It isn't fair.*

"Matt—" she began, but he cut her off.

"Save it," he said. "I know what you're thinking. I'm coming."

She nodded and returned her attention to the task at hand. When her equipment was in place, she helped Matt attach his: Glock 17, Heckler & Koch MP5, T-Bone, ultraviolet grenades, ultraviolet beam gun, torch, radio, console.

"You know what you're doing, right?" she asked. "You can use all this stuff?"

"Don't worry about me, Kate," he replied.

She was suddenly full of fierce, fiery love for her friend; he was scared, it was clear in the pallid colour of his face, the wideness of his eyes, but he was here. And he was refusing to let her go alone.

"OK," said Matt, standing up and patting himself down. "I think I'm good."

"Grab one of those," said Kate, pointing at a row of gleaming black and purple helmets. "Pass me one too."

Matt nodded, then did as he was told. Kate took a helmet from him and slipped it over her head. She opened a panel on its underside, pulling out the black cable concealed behind it. It went into a port in her uniform, at the back of her neck; this connected up her uniform's control system, meaning she was able to change the visual and aural modes of her helmet using the buttons and pad on the side of her belt.

Matt watched carefully, then copied her. The two young Operators looked at each other for a brief moment, their visors raised, and Kate fought back the absurd urge to give her friend a hug. It was not the time for such things; they had a job to do.

"Let's go," said Matt, firmly. "I'm ready."

"One last thing," said Kate. "We have to go to the Ops Room. Just for a minute."

Matt frowned. "Why?"

"I promised Paul I would."

"Kate, there isn't time," said Matt. "We need to go."

"I promised," she said. "Wait here if you want. But I have to go."

Matt stared for a moment. "Fine," he said. "Let's make it quick."

"Agreed," said Kate.

She pushed open the armoury door and ran back across the hangar, Matt close behind her. They burst through the double doors, sprinted down the corridor, and stopped outside the door to the Ops Room, the oval space that was the tactical and strategic heart of the Department. Kate pulled it open; they stepped inside, then stopped dead in their tracks.

She had not wasted a moment wondering why Paul Turner had made her promise to go to the Ops Room before she left; there was too much else to think about. But even if she had, she doubted she would ever have guessed the truth.

In the middle of the wide room, leaning on one of the tables, was Colonel Victor Frankenstein.

The huge, misshapen man was wearing an Operator's uniform and casually holding the biggest shotgun Kate had ever seen; it dwarfed the T-Bone that hung from his belt. Frankenstein smiled at them as they skidded to a halt, their eyes widening; a narrow smile that didn't reach his eyes.

"Paul told me what's happening," he said, his voice like rolling thunder. "I'd like to help. If you'll let me."

Kate glanced over at Matt; her friend was still staring at the monster, his eyes wide with surprise. She looked back at Frankenstein, her heart filling with desperate gratitude.

"I thought you only protected Jamie's family?" she said, smiling round the lump that had risen in her throat.

"Isn't that what you are?" replied Frankenstein.

52

HEADLONG

The black van screeched to a halt outside the warehouse where
Alastair Dempsey had been located.

Rain was pouring from the skies above London, bouncing up
from the empty pavements and causing the gutters to run like rapids.
The deluge had forced the majority of the pedestrians off the streets,
sending them running for refuge in bars and restaurants, or the tube
stations that would take them home.

Jamie Carpenter sat in the back of the van, watching the feeds
from the external cameras. He stared at the crisp HD images, waiting
for the right moment for them to make their move.

He and Ellison had said little to one another on their flight from
the Loop. As soon as they were in the air, Jamie had requested
permission to make an emergency landing in Central London, on
the grounds that an Operator's life might depend on it. The
Communications Operator on the other end of the line had sounded
incredulous, and had instantly refused the request, ordering them
instead to London City Airport; it was the closest location where
they could set down the helicopter without attracting unnecessary

attention. Jamie held his tongue, resisting the urge to tell the Communications Operator exactly what he thought of him, and cut the connection as the dark vehicle thundered through the sky towards the capital. As they touched down in a secluded section of the airport, he asked their driver how long it would take to get into Soho.

"Thirty minutes," he replied. "Maybe thirty-five, allowing for traffic."

"Do it in fifteen," said Jamie.

The driver attacked his task with admirable commitment, sending the vehicle hurtling into Central London, weaving between the black cabs and crowds of tourists, the deafening siren and blinding blue light screaming on the van's roof.

They covered the distance from the Loop to Soho in less than half the time it had taken Morton, but it had not been fast enough; Jamie had called up the location of their squad mate's chip on the flat screen as they roared along the Embankment, and he and Ellison had watched it with a sense of utter helplessness, hoping for a miracle. It had been close, closer than Jamie had dared to hope, but in the end, it had been futile. Fifteen minutes before they had arrived on this dirty London backstreet, Morton's chip had stopped moving.

It doesn't mean anything, Jamie told himself, staring at the screen. *There's been no sign of Dempsey either. Surely he would have run.*

Ellison stared at him with professional calm on her face. The woman who had come to find him in the dining hall, who appeared on the verge of tears, was gone, replaced by the Operator that Jamie had told his friends about. She was waiting for him to tell her what to do.

As Jamie watched, a man who had been vomiting enthusiastically into the gutter behind the van staggered away into the night, and suddenly the screen was clear in both directions.

"Go," he said, throwing open the rear doors of the van. "Ready One as soon as we're inside."

Ellison nodded, and leapt out of the vehicle. Jamie followed, the rain and steam rising from the pavement instantly clouding his visor. He wiped it with the back of his gloved hand, slammed the van doors shut, and turned to face the warehouse.

The building loomed over them like some squat, hulking animal. It was made of the same pale stone as the rest of the old buildings in Soho, but had been stained dark grey by years of hard work and neglect. Its lower walls were plastered with posters for gigs, art installations, political rallies and pop-up shops, pasted over and over each other until they were millimetres thick in places. The entrance was set back from the street, up two wide stone steps, and covered with a steel security gate, the kind that is installed in the hope of keeping squatters at bay.

The gate and the door beyond it were standing open.

"Take point," said Jamie. "Carefully."

Ellison nodded, then ran up the steps and disappeared into the building. Jamie cast a final glance up and down the rain-sodden street, then followed her.

He pushed the door shut behind him and surveyed the area inside. A wall stood before them, covered in drawing pins and scraps of paper. It ran away to their left and disappeared in the darkness.

"Torches," said Jamie. "Thermo on your helmet, regular view on mine. Silent comms. If Alastair Dempsey is still here, he doesn't get out. I don't care if we have to blow this building to rubble with him inside it."

"What about Morton?" asked Ellison.

Jamie didn't respond. He pulled his torch from his belt and shone it along the wall; it ran for perhaps ten metres, before ending in a dark corner.

"This way," he said, drawing his T-Bone and holding his torch against its barrel. "Follow me."

He walked silently down the dark corridor, with Ellison close behind him. As they approached the corner, he spoke into his helmet's microphone. "Give me a thermal of whatever's on the other side of this wall."

"Yes, sir," replied Ellison. She stepped silently past him and slowly leant out beyond the end of the wall. "Nothing," she said. "Nothing warm, nothing moving."

"Understood," said Jamie, and stepped round the corner.

What had once been the main warehouse space was now a vast stone box. His torch picked out grooves in the floor that had presumably once held the foundations of shelving, and a pair of metal shutter doors at the far end. The floor in front of them was marked with a series of yellow lines.

"Loading bay," said Ellison, then flicked her torch to illuminate a door on the right-hand wall. "Stairs."

"OK," said Jamie. "Stay on point."

Ellison nodded and headed across the empty space, her boots thudding softly on the concrete floor. Jamie followed, his torch scanning the ground and the bare, peeling walls as she reached the door and pushed it silently open. His squad mate crouched down and peered through, her T-Bone raised.

"Clear," she said.

Jamie stepped through the door. His torch revealed a metal staircase that doubled back on itself, with a landing halfway up. He climbed it slowly, his T-Bone pointed steadily upwards. When he reached the landing, he trained his weapon on the open door that stood at the top of the stairs and motioned for Ellison to overlap him. As she climbed the stairs towards him, something floated momentarily into his nostrils: a bitter, oily smell that he could taste at the back of his throat. It was gone as quickly as it had arrived, and he refocused his attention as Ellison arrived at the door. She darted her head through it, then spoke into his ear.

"Three doors. Looks like offices. Nothing hot in the corridor."

"Understood," said Jamie. The smell came again, sharp and bitter, and he frowned behind his visor. "Can you smell something?"

"No," said Ellison. "Can you?"

"I thought I could," said Jamie, slowly. "It's gone now."

He stepped out into the empty corridor and felt his heart sink. *They're gone*, he thought. *Dempsey ran, and Morton chased him, and now they could be anywhere.*

He twisted the dial on his belt that controlled the radio in his helmet and pressed the button that triggered a connection to the Loop. "NS303, 67-J signing in," he said. "Requesting a surveillance update on the locations of Morton, John, NS304, 07-B and Priority Level target Dempsey, Alastair."

"Processing," said the voice on the other end. "No update to report."

"Understood," replied Jamie, and cut the connection.

"He's here?" asked Ellison. "They both are?"

"I don't think so," replied Jamie. "Something's gone wrong at Surveillance." He walked forward and pushed open the first door, revealing an empty office. "I don't think they have any idea where he is," he continued. "Maybe he's lost it completely and cut his chip out. I don't know."

He opened the second door, revealing another empty room. The smell came again, floating on the air, but he ignored it. Anger was bubbling through him, alongside something else: a deep sense of helplessness. He had no idea where John Morton was and no way to help him.

He's gone, he thought. *They're gone. They could be anywhere.*

He reached the final door and kicked it angrily open. Then the world turned grey, and ceased to turn.

The breath froze in his chest, as his eyes widened behind the purple plastic of his visor. He opened his mouth to scream, but all that emerged was a thin rush of air.

"Jamie?" asked Ellison. Her voice was full of sudden concern, and she ran across the corridor towards him. "What's the..."

She trailed off as she looked into the office. Then she *did* scream, a deafening, head-splitting howl that pounded directly into Jamie's ears and shook him from his paralysis; he looked into the office again and tried to process what he was seeing.

Hanging in the centre of the room, suspended from a web of thin white ropes, was John Morton. The ropes were looped round his arms and legs and had been tied to the metal beams that filled the triangular ceiling space, hauling him into the air.

There was a single rope round his neck, pulling his head up and back so he was staring at the door. His face was pale and lifeless, his eyes wide and bulging, his mouth contorted in a gaping scream of eternal pain and terror. In the centre of the floor, in a heaped mass of red and purple, lay Morton's internal organs; they had spilled out of a wide, jagged incision that ran from his neck to his groin.

The knife that had been used was still lodged in the bone at the base of his throat; it reflected the awful white light cast by his torch. The smell bloomed out of the last office, filling Jamie's nostrils again, stronger than ever, but he didn't even notice; he could not take his eyes away from the stricken, mutilated corpse that had been his squad mate.

Jamie stepped slowly into the room. Behind him, Ellison stood in the doorway, seemingly paralysed; she appeared unable to follow him inside. He circled round the hanging body, his heart racing in his chest, the contents of his stomach threatening to rise up and explode from his mouth.

Too much, he thought. *This is too much. Oh God, nobody deserves this.*

The smell intensified as he made his way slowly round the body and his eyes began to water. Still he ignored it; it was probably some gas that Morton's body had released, some acid that should still have been inside him, rather than pooling on the floor of an abandoned warehouse office. He was almost back at the doorway when movement caught his eye. He looked round, saw a dark shape looming behind Ellison, and opened his mouth to scream her name.

Before the word left his lips, she shot forward as though she had been fired out of a cannon. Ellison lost her footing and crashed heavily into Morton's corpse, sending it rocking backwards, then fell towards the pile of viscera beneath it. Somehow, Jamie didn't know how, she managed to pivot in mid-air and throw her weight towards him, crashing to the ground at his feet. Her grunt of pain echoed in his ear.

Jamie turned back to the door, raising his T-Bone. A white-hot fury was exploding through his body, a vengeful anger that buzzed and screamed and danced. There had been many occasions since he had joined Blacklight, and he had no doubt there would be many more to come, where the things that he and his colleagues did under cover of darkness had given him cause to wonder who

578

really were the good guys, and whether terrible things done in the supposed service of good were still just terrible things.

But this was not one of them. He had never felt more certain about what was expected of him. He would kill Alastair Dempsey and he would do it with a smile on his face: the smile of the righteous, of the just.

The dark shape was barely visible in the darkness of the corridor, but Jamie could see just enough of it to aim at. His finger was tightening on the trigger when the shape moved, like a shadow dissolving at dusk. A second later Alastair Dempsey's voice echoed through the empty building, seeming to come from everywhere at once.

"Stop following me," he shouted. "This is the last time I'm going to tell you."

Ellison leapt to her feet beside him, pushing her visor back to reveal a face twisted with hatred. "Never!" she screamed. "You monster! You coward! Never!"

"That's a shame," said Dempsey. There was a click in the corridor outside the office and a small yellow light flared in the darkness.

Jamie was suddenly filled with terrible clarity. All at once, he knew what the smell was, and what it meant.

"Out!" he bellowed. "Get out of—"

The rest of his sentence was lost as a cigarette lighter flew through the open doorway, its flame flickering, and the petrol that Alastair Dempsey had splashed across the walls and floor of the office caught fire in a roaring explosion of burning heat and blinding light.

53

LEAVING ON A JET PLANE

LINCOLN COUNTY, NEVADA, USA

Larissa had been about to head for the shower when someone knocked on her door.

She swore under her breath; the dust seemed worse on the other side of the mountain, and she had been looking forward to thinking through what Lee Ashworth had told her as she washed it from her skin. She threw her towel down on her bed, crossed the small room, and opened the door. An Operator she didn't know nodded politely at her.

"Lieutenant Kinley," he said. "Director Allen wants to see you."

"Now?" she groaned. "Right now?"

"I'm afraid so," said the Operator. "He's waiting for you in his quarters."

"Do you know what he wants?" asked Larissa, stepping out into the corridor and pulling the door shut behind her. "Is there something wrong?"

"I don't have any further information," said the Operator. "I'm sorry."

Don't shoot the messenger. Don't shoot the messenger.

"That's OK," she said. "Thanks."

She stepped round him, lifted herself effortlessly into the air, and flew towards the elevator at the end of the corridor.

The NS9 Director's quarters lay in the middle of Level 0. Larissa was floating outside the door in less than a minute and rapped on it hard with her knuckles.

"Come in, Larissa," called General Allen.

She dropped back to the floor and did as she was told. General Allen was sitting on one of the two sofas; he nodded at her as she entered, and gestured towards the other one.

"Have a seat," he said. "Drink?"

"Water, please," she said, settling on to the sofa.

Allen pulled a plastic bottle out of his fridge and tossed it to her. She caught it out of the air, twisted off the cap, and drank half the contents.

"How was Vegas?" asked Allen.

"It was crazy," she replied. "There's nothing like it in England."

"Good place to be a vampire, I would think?"

"Yes, sir," said Larissa. "Not bad at all."

"That's good," said Allen. "Really good."

Larissa looked closely at the General; his face seemed slightly paler than usual, and he appeared somewhat preoccupied.

"Did something happen while we were away?" she asked, setting the water bottle down on the coffee table. "Is everything all right?"

General Allen shook his head. "Nothing happened while you were away," he said. "But there is something I need to tell you."

"OK," said Larissa. "Am I in trouble, sir?"

"Not at all," said Allen, and sighed. "Larissa, I brought you here because I had a video call with Cal Holmwood about an hour ago. He's sending the *Mina II* here tonight. It returns to the UK tomorrow morning and he wants you to be on it."

For a long moment, she just stared. General Allen's words seemed like nonsense, like they had been spoken in a foreign language.

"I'm going home?" she said, eventually.

"You're going home," said General Allen. There was a look of genuine disappointment on his face.

"I'm supposed to have four more weeks," she said, slowly. "What changed?"

"I don't know, exactly," said Allen. "Your friend Matt Browning has come up with a theory about the escapee vampires. Cal wouldn't tell me exactly what, but apparently he needs your help to confirm it, and he wants you back at the Loop tomorrow."

"But... four more weeks," said Larissa. She felt as though she was on the verge of tears.

"I know," said Allen. "I made that point to Cal, made it very strongly. I'm sorry, Larissa, I really am. If it's any consolation at all, I'm incredibly sad to be losing you. But there's nothing I can do."

A number of emotions jostled for position inside her chest. There was relief, at the realisation that resolving the Tim Albertsson problem had been taken out of her hands. But there was pain, sharp and bitter, at the thought of leaving her new friends and the place she had already come to love, and something that was close to panic at the thought of confining herself again to the grey corridors and suspicious, distrustful eyes of the Loop. Finally, a bright plume of excitement burned in the middle of her chest, as she realised that it would be less than twenty-four hours until she would see Kate and Matt again.

And Jamie.

"Why didn't he just ask me to fly home?" she asked. "If there's such a hurry?"

Allen tilted his head slightly to the right. "Could you do that?" he asked.

"Do what, sir?"

"Fly home," said General Allen. "All the way across the country and the Atlantic."

"Yes, sir," she said. "No problem."

"Remarkable," said Allen, softly. "I assume he's sending the *Mina* because he wants whoever you're taking with you there as quickly as possible."

"That's still happening, sir?" she asked. "I assumed this meant my mission was cancelled."

Allen shook his head. "Nothing's been cancelled," he said. "Cal told me he's still expecting six of my Operators. I know you thought you had more time, but you're going to need to give me some names. Do you have anyone in mind yet?"

That's a good question. I thought I did. But do I?

"Do you need them now?" she asked.

"No," said General Allen. "By 0700 tomorrow. Is that enough time?"

Larissa nodded.

"Good," said Allen. He pulled a beer out of the fridge, flipped the cap off it, and took a drink. "It's going to be weird with you gone," he said, smiling at her. "I've gotten used to you being here."

"Me too, sir," she said, feeling a lump rise in her throat.

"A lot of people are going to miss you. I can tell you that much."

"That's nice to know, sir."

"It's the truth."

They sat in silence for a long while. General Allen sipped his beer and Larissa wondered what Matt could have come up with that meant Cal Holmwood needed to call her home early.

Then an idea struck her, like a bolt from the blue.

Could it be? Could that be what's going on here?

She looked at General Allen as he sipped his beer.

Can I ask him? I'm going home tomorrow anyway. How angry could he be?

Larissa sat forward and looked at the Director. "Can I ask you something, sir?" she said. "Even if I'm not supposed to?"

Allen frowned. "What is it?"

"Me going home," she said, carefully. "Matt coming up with some new theory, Cal sending the *Mina*. Is this really about the prisoner you're keeping downstairs?"

General Allen froze, his beer halfway to his mouth, his eyes widening. Then, ever so slowly, he lowered his beer to the coffee table and sat forward in his seat.

"What do you know about that?" he asked. "Tell me the truth."

"I don't know who he is," said Larissa. "But I do know some things."

"What things?"

"I know that he's English," she said, watching Allen's face drain of colour as she spoke. "I know he drove in out of the desert, used an old access code, and asked for you by name. I know that no one except you is allowed to see him."

"How?" asked Allen, his voice low. "How do you know all that?"

"I asked questions," she said. "I found the right people to answer them."

"Have you told anyone else what you've just told me?" he asked. "Tell the truth. It's incredibly important."

584

"No, sir," she said. "I wasn't trying to cause trouble. I was just curious."

"Curious?"

"Everyone knows there's someone down there, sir. They all talk about it, but no one knows anything. I wanted to know, sir."

"Why? What does it matter to you who we keep in the cells?"

Larissa shrugged. "Like I said, sir, I was curious."

General Allen appeared to have regained his composure. The colour was returning to his face, and he lifted his beer back to his lips and drained the bottle.

"I can't tell you anything about the prisoner," he said. "It's not that I don't trust you, but it's classified at Director level only. So don't ask me. You already know far more than you should."

"Do you think that's it, though?" pressed Larissa. "Do you think that me being called home has something to do with him?"

"I don't think so," said General Allen. "Cal was pretty clear that something new had come up. But the prisoner in question will also be leaving tomorrow, on the same plane as you, so you can draw your own conclusions. And that's the end of our discussion of the matter. Is that clear?"

"Yes, sir," said Larissa, her head spinning with possibilities. "Absolutely clear."

54

GUILTY PARTIES

Paul Turner took a deep breath and knocked on the entrance to the Interim Director's quarters.

"Come in," called Cal Holmwood.

The locks disengaged and Turner pushed the door. It swung open silently on its counterweight, revealing the Interim Director where he almost always was: behind the long wooden desk that groaned under the mountains of paper that were added to it each day. A glass of dark liquid sat on its surface.

"Paul," said Holmwood. "If you've got good news, get in here quickly. If you haven't, I'm afraid you enter at your own risk. I can't take much more today."

"I'm sorry, Cal," said Turner. He pushed the door shut and walked into the room. "There's something you need to see. Zero Hour level."

Holmwood's face sagged. "Dracula?"

Turner shook his head. "It's Albert Harker," he said, and held the Surveillance report out across the desk. Holmwood took it, then picked up a folder and handed it to the Security Officer. "In which case," he said, "you need to read that."

Turner frowned and opened the folder. He read the summary of Andrew Jarvis's report, feeling a chill rise up his spine as he did so.

"Why didn't I know about this?" he asked.

"Excuse me, Major?"

"I'm the Security Officer, Cal. I should have seen this as soon as it was written."

"This may be hard for you to hear, Paul," said Holmwood, "but you are not actually in charge of this Department. I am. And when it comes to sensitive information, I decide who sees what. Is that clear?"

"Of course, sir," said Turner, his voice low and tight. "I'm sorry."

"It's all right, Paul," said Cal. "I only got in a couple of hours ago. You haven't seen it because until Surveillance finds them, there's nothing we can do about it."

"Read what I gave you, Cal. The situation has changed."

Holmwood opened the folder and scanned it quickly. When he looked back up at Turner, his face was pale.

"What's Intelligence's take on this?" he asked. "Is it genuine?"

"They're still assessing credibility," replied Turner. "I suggest we operate under the assumption that it is."

"Jesus," said Holmwood. "What the hell is going on?"

"We don't know for certain, sir," said Turner. "But the fathers of two Operators of this Department, a journalist and the only descendant of our founders ever to be turned in a modern printing press represent a potential disaster, sir. The risk of public exposure alone is enormous."

"Thanks, Paul," said Holmwood, his voice dripping with sarcasm. "I hadn't realised that. Christ." The Interim Director pulled his console from his belt, typed rapidly on its touch screen, then looked at his Security Officer. "I've ordered Jack Williams' squad to the Ops Room in ten minutes for briefing. Is there anything I need to tell him apart from what you've given me?"

"No, sir," replied Turner. "That's all we know."

"Does anyone else know about this?"

This was the moment that Turner had been dreading: the moment that he knew, hyperbole aside, could signal the end of his Blacklight career. On his way up from ISAT he had considered lying to his friend, letting him find out once it was all over, but had decided against doing so. It would not be fair to let Jack Williams and his squad depart with incomplete intelligence; beyond that, it was simply not in his nature. He had made a decision, one whose consequences he would have to live with, and he would not lie to his commanding officer when he was asked a direct question.

"Yes, sir," he said, his voice as steady as he could manage. "Kate Randall and Matt Browning are already *en route*. Colonel Frankenstein is with them, sir."

For a long moment, Cal Holmwood didn't so much as blink. When he eventually spoke, his voice was little more than a growl. "Why would you do that, Paul?"

"I'm sorry, sir," replied Turner. "Lieutenant Randall was with me when I received the intercept. She would have gone with or without my permission, and she would have taken Browning with her. I thought it was pointless to delay them."

"She's a seventeen-year-old girl, Paul," said Holmwood, each word as heavy and dangerous as an avalanche. "Are you saying you couldn't have prevented her from going? Are you seriously asking me to believe that?"

"No, sir," said Turner.

"Lieutenant Browning was in here barely twenty minutes ago. He's a scientist, Paul. Not a soldier. I'm struggling to understand why you of all people would do something so utterly, criminally reckless."

"It's their families," said Turner, simply. "I had to. I would have done the same if I was them."

"Then you're just as stupid as they are," said Holmwood, his voice rising with anger. "You've let them put themselves in harm's way because you would have done the same thing? I don't know if it's slipped your mind, but when you were their age, you'd already been to Afghanistan twice with 2 Para. Browning isn't even an Operator, for Christ's sake, and Randall has only been one for a few months. I should bloody court-martial you for this!"

Turner stared into the rapidly reddening face of the Interim Director. *He's right,* he thought. *Everything he's saying is true. If Kate gets hurt, it's on you. Matt too, and Frankenstein for that matter. All on you.*

"I understand, sir," he said. "Give me an order."

Holmwood stared at him, his eyes blazing. He looked as angry as Turner had ever seen him, as though he was about to burst.

"Why didn't you go with her?" he asked.

Turner frowned. "Sir?"

"This is about you and Kate, Paul, and don't pretend otherwise. You and Kate and Shaun. If anyone else's father appeared in an intercept, you wouldn't even consider letting them go out there on their own, and we both know it. So why didn't you go and protect her? Why send Victor? Why the hell are you still here, Paul?"

"I wanted to go, sir," said Turner. "But I couldn't."

"Why not?"

"Because I know who planted the bombs, sir. I was on my way here to tell you when the intercept came in."

Holmwood stared for a long moment. "Who was it?" he asked, eventually.

"It was Valentin's servant," said Turner. "It was Lamberton, sir."

"How do we know? Are we sure?"

Turner nodded. "Yes, sir. Security confirmed the presence of a vampire in Kate's room about two hours ago. Valentin passed ISAT and we've just interviewed Marie Carpenter. She told us that Lamberton has been using one of our consoles in his room."

"What good would a console do him?" asked Holmwood, frowning.

"It wouldn't do *him* any good, sir," replied Turner. "But it would be very useful for whoever is giving him orders."

"One of us?"

"Has to be, sir. No one else would be able to get the console to him, and only an Operator would be at risk from ISAT."

"Do we know who?"

"Not yet, sir."

"Jesus Christ, Henry," whispered Holmwood, dropping his gaze to his desk. "You never told me this was what being Director was like."

"Excuse me, sir?" said Turner.

"Nothing," said Holmwood. "I wasn't talking to you." He got up from his desk. "Let's find out who was holding Lamberton's reins," he said, and headed for the door.

The two veteran Operators stood silently in the lift as it descended.

They had fought alongside each other more times than either could remember, had seen and done things that both of them wished they could forget, had suffered losses that would hurt until they stopped breathing in and out. But even as everything appeared to be collapsing around them, as revelation piled upon revelation and the pressure upon their shoulders weighed as heavily as it ever had, neither man would have changed a thing. They had lived lives of great wonder, lives that were varied and full, and they were proud to be what they were: soldiers of the light, descending into the darkness yet again.

"What if Valentin knew?" said Holmwood. "That could be a real problem."

"I know," replied Turner. "Can you see him taking orders from one of us?"

"No," said Holmwood. "But I don't know if I believe a word he's said since he's been here. Nothing he did would surprise me."

"I agree with the second part," said Turner. "But I believe he's here for the reasons he gave. I don't trust him, but I don't think he's trying to hurt us."

"Let's hope you're right," said Holmwood. "Because I can't see him being thrilled when we stake his servant."

There was a long pause.

"There's something else, sir," said Turner.

Holmwood laughed. "What else could there possibly be?" he asked. "Is an alien battle fleet about to enter the earth's orbit?"

"Not as far as I'm aware," said Turner. "It's Jamie's rookie."

"Morton?"

Turner nodded. "He's gone after the vamp their squad was chasing on his own. Kate told me. Jamie and his other rookie have gone after him."

"I gave Jamie permission to put him on the inactive list."

"Apparently, he was going to," said Turner. "Morton went before he got the chance."

"There's nothing we can do about it now," said Holmwood. "Jamie's a good Operator. He knows what he's doing."

"Yes, sir."

The lift slowed to a halt. Its doors slid open, revealing the airlock that controlled access to the cellblock. On the other side of it was the long corridor of cells, one of which, the ninth on the right, was the home of Lamberton, Valentin Rusmanov's oldest companion.

Cal's right, thought Turner, as they approached the airlock. *If Valentin stands by Lamberton, this could get ugly. Very ugly.*

Holmwood pressed his ID against the black panel on the wall. A green light appeared and he quickly tapped a series of numbers into its touch screen. The light changed to a bright purple, then both the inner and outer doors of the airlock slid open at the same time, in direct contradiction of the principle that governed them.

"There's no time," said Holmwood, noticing Turner's expression of surprise. "I have to be in the Ops Room in five minutes so I can send Jack Williams to clean up your mess."

"Yes, sir," replied Turner, and followed his commanding officer through the open airlock. The duty Operator, a member of the Security Division named Jess Nelson, had left her guard post when the airlock had hissed open and was staring at it with unease. Her face brightened as she saw the two men who stepped through it and on to the block.

"Who are you here—" she began, but Turner cut her off.

"Grab a Daybreaker and come with us, Operator."

Nelson's eyes widened; the Russian-made launcher was used in only the most dangerous of circumstances, and kept only in the hangar armoury and the cellblock guard post. But she did as she was told; she ran back inside and came out with the heavy black weapon settled against her shoulder, its wide barrel pointing at the ceiling.

"Ready, sir," she said.

He nodded. "Good. Follow us."

Holmwood strode down the corridor and Turner fell in beside him.

Nelson walked on the other side of the Interim Director, her eyes fixed on the cell that was home to Valentin Rusmanov.

Almost, thought Turner, following her gaze. *But not quite. Wrong vampire.*

The three Operators passed Valentin's cell without slowing. The ancient vampire was lying on his bed, reading a page of sheet music; he looked up and frowned as the three black-clad figures disappeared from his view.

They stopped outside Lamberton's cell and looked inside. The vampire was at the rear of the square room, shining a pair of his master's shoes with a pale cloth; his hands moved at such supernatural speed that the cloth was barely visible as it blurred back and forth over the leather.

"Lamberton," said Cal Holmwood.

The valet looked up and stopped what he was doing. He placed the shoes and the cloth aside, then approached the ultraviolet barrier that was intended to keep him inside.

It evidently poses him no more problems than it does his master, thought Turner. *Although I'm looking forward to hearing how he got out of this block.*

"Mr Holmwood, Mr Turner," said Lamberton, smoothly. "And I'm afraid I don't know your name, Miss. How can I be of assistance?"

"You can stand back," said Turner, raising his T-Bone and pointing it at the vampire's heart. "That will be a good start."

A flicker of annoyance crossed Lamberton's face, but he stepped back, staring at the three Operators.

"What is the meaning of this?" asked a smooth, friendly voice from the corridor beside them. Nelson spun round, saw Valentin Rusmanov leaning casually against the wall between Lamberton's cell and his own, and gasped in shock. Paul Turner merely glanced in his direction. "This doesn't concern you, Valentin," he said. "Go back to your cell."

"Oh, I hardly think so," smiled Valentin. "Not when you're pointing your little gun at my companion."

Turner glanced at Cal Holmwood, who nodded.

"All right," he said. "Go and stand with your man. You should hear what we have to say to him."

"I'm all ears, my dear Major Turner," said Valentin, and slipped effortlessly through the UV barrier and into his servant's cell.

"My lord," began Lamberton, instantly. "I'm afraid I don't—"

"Be calm, old friend," said Valentin, fixing his gaze on Paul Turner. "I'm sure our hosts will explain the meaning of this. Quickly."

Cal Holmwood cleared his throat. "Your associate is guilty of the attempted murder of Operators of this Department, Valentin. That's why we are here."

"I see," said Valentin, narrowing his eyes. "You have proof, I presume? I'm sure you do not expect us to take your word for such serious allegations?"

"The proof is in this cell," said Turner. Beside him, Nelson lowered her Daybreaker by a few degrees; it was not pointing at either of the vampires in the cell, but it was no longer pointing at the ceiling.

Valentin looked round the sparse room. "I must confess that I fail to see it, Major Turner."

"Maybe you aren't looking hard enough," replied Turner, and stepped towards the ultraviolet barrier.

A snarl emerged from Lamberton's throat.

Valentin looked at his valet, who was staring at the Security Officer with eyes that were now glowing the colour of old coals, and a tiny frown creased his forehead. "Present your evidence, Major Turner," he said, softly. "I would see it, if indeed it exists."

"By all means," said Turner, and stepped through the barrier. The shimmering wall of light tingled his skin as he passed through it and made his way towards Lamberton's impeccably made bed. He knelt down, thrust his hands beneath the mattress, and instantly found what he was looking for.

A hard rectangle, its size immediately familiar to his gloved hands. *Thank God for that.*

Turner felt along the edges of the mattress, searching for the opening. Behind him, Lamberton was emitting a steady growl, like the noise made by a cornered dog. Just before they reached the corner, Turner's fingers slipped through a neat slit and into the mattress itself; he shoved his arm in up to the elbow and felt his fingers close round the rectangle. He pulled it out, dragging strands of stuffing with it, then stood up and faced the two vampires, holding it out in his hand.

"What is that?" asked Valentin.

"It's a portable console," said Turner. He tried to suppress the elation he was feeling, tried not to let it show on his face. "They're issued to every Operator. But not to vampire prisoners."

"What does that prove, Major Turner?" asked Valentin. "If my associate has stolen one of your little machines, then by all means slap his wrist, with my full blessing. I fail to see how it is proof of attempted murder."

"The Security investigation into the explosion on Level B was concluded this afternoon," said Turner. "The results were unequivocal. A vampire spent approximately four minutes in the room in question, two hours before the device was detonated. There are only three vampires in this base at the moment. Valentin, you and I had a charming conversation yesterday morning, which cleared you of any involvement. And this afternoon, we interviewed Marie Carpenter, who was also cleared. She did tell us something interesting, though. She told us that on several occasions she had heard you, Lamberton, tapping on something that sounded as though it was made of plastic. She had also heard a beep that she didn't recognise. I played her the new message tone on my console and she confirmed that it was the noise she heard."

Turner thumbed open the console and entered the messages folder. There were two, both read, both from an unknown sender; a string of numbers and letters filled the space where a name was usually displayed.

"You planted the bombs," he said, staring evenly at Lamberton. The vampire returned his gaze, his eyes boiling with crimson. Behind him, Valentin Rusmanov's face had become even paler than usual; he was looking at his servant with an entirely unreadable expression. "You left your cell, left this block – although I must confess I have no idea how you managed that – and you planted two bombs. Bombs that were intended to kill Lieutenant Randall and myself. I challenge you to deny it."

Lamberton snarled again, but said nothing. Turner opened the console again and read the messages. One had been sent the previous morning:

TODAY/B261/A86

Mine and Kate's room numbers, he thought. *We've got you.*

The final one had been sent yesterday afternoon:

YOU FAILED

Damn right. Goddamn right you did.

Turner threw the console across the cell towards Cal Holmwood. It had barely left his fingertips when Lamberton moved, a guttural howl erupting from his throat, and snatched it out of the air. He raised it above his head, his face contorted with hate, and was about to smash it to pieces on the hard floor of his cell when a voice as old and cold as death spoke a single word.

"Lamberton."

The vampire froze, his arm raised. Then, ever so slowly, he lowered it, and turned to face his master.

Valentin Rusmanov was staring at his servant with the most terrible look of disappointment that Paul Turner had ever seen. His eyes burned a pale, melancholy red and his mouth was curled downwards, as though he had just tasted something unpleasant.

"Did you do these things?" he asked. "Do not lie to me, old friend. Not now."

Lamberton stared wretchedly at Valentin. His throat was working furiously, as though he was searching for some combination of words that would mean he could avoid lying to his master. In the end, what emerged was almost a shriek of misery.

"I did, my lord," he cried. "I'm sorry, forgive me, oh, forgive me, my lord. I did it for you."

Turner raised his T-Bone without realising he was doing so and levelled it at Valentin Rusmanov. Cal Holmwood, who had been watching the scene play out with a look of grim determination on his lined face, did the same, as Operator Nelson levelled her Daybreaker.

"For me?" asked Valentin. He ignored the arsenal of weaponry pointing at him; his focus was entirely on his servant. "What do you mean?"

"He came to me, my lord," said Lamberton. He had begun to cry, great sobs that shuddered through his narrow frame. "One of *them*, he came to me while you slept and told me what he wanted me to do. He gave me the materials to make the devices and the console, and told me to hide them until it was time. He would have destroyed you, my lord, he said he would destroy you in your sleep. I had no choice, my lord. I had to."

"Who came to you?" asked Valentin. His eyes were darkening, becoming the colour of molten lava. "Who told you?"

"I don't know his name, my lord. He was here when we arrived. He stood with these men, the first time they came to talk to you."

Oh Christ, thought Turner, his heart stopping in his chest. *The Zero Hour Task Force. We came down here together, the morning after they arrived. The morning I started the interrogation.*

"What did he look like?" asked Cal Holmwood. The ashen look on his face told Turner that the Interim Director had come to the same realisation as him.

"Tall," said Lamberton, between sobs. "Black hair. Stood at the back, near Mr Carpenter. That's all I know, I swear it."

"That's Brennan," said Turner, his voice little more than a whisper. "He's been in Zero Hour since the beginning, Cal. He knows everything."

Holmwood stared. "Has he been through ISAT?"

"No."

"Find him. Run his chip."

The Security Officer pulled his console from his belt and searched for Richard Brennan. The system returned a result almost immediately.

"He's here," said Turner, relief flooding through him. "On the grounds. Out by the runway."

An alarm rang out from Holmwood's console; he swore and

grabbed it from his belt. "I have to brief Jack," he said. "Finish this, then find Brennan. Don't let anyone else do it. You find him, Paul, and you bring him to me."

He turned and strode away down the cellblock without waiting for his Security Officer to answer. Turner watched him go, then pointed his T-Bone at Valentin's butler's chest.

"Lamberton," he said. "You are hereby sentenced to immediate destruction, for the attempted murders of members of this Department."

The vampire's sobbing intensified, and he threw a pleading look at his master. "My lord, I beg you. I did it for you, to protect you. I could not let anything happen to you, my lord, after all our time together. I beg you, my lord, don't let them kill me."

"You thought that I could not protect myself?" asked Valentin, his voice low. "You thought so little of me? You did not even think to tell me after you were approached?"

"I dealt with it, my lord," babbled Lamberton. "I did not want to trouble you, my lord, to bother you with something so trivial. I looked after you, my lord, like I always have, like I always will. What are two dead humans, my lord, what difference would they make? They are nothing, my lord, but you, *you* are my whole life, my lord, my everything. I could not take the risk, my lord. Forgive me, oh, forgive me."

"You were played," said Valentin. "Your loyalty to me was taken advantage of and so, so easily. You should be ashamed of yourself."

"I am, my lord," sobbed Lamberton. "I truly am."

"Stand clear, Valentin," said Turner, sighting along the barrel of his T-Bone. "I have a sentence to carry out."

An expression of naked despair rose on to Lamberton's face; he cast a final desperate glance at his master, who looked back impassively. Turner breathed out and squeezed the trigger of his weapon. The bang of exploding gas was deafening in the confined space of the cell, an echoing thunderclap that rang through his ears. The stake exploded from the T-Bone's barrel and rocketed towards the vampire butler. A millisecond later, the wire that trailed behind it went slack as Valentin plucked the projectile out of the air.

Oh shit, thought Turner.

Valentin turned the stake over in his hand. "I cannot allow you to destroy my servant, Major Turner," he said, without so much as glancing in the Security Officer's direction.

Lamberton breathed out a great bubbling mess of relief. "Thank you, my lord," he sobbed. "Oh, thank—"

Valentin moved.

The ancient vampire threw the metal stake aside, stepped forward and thrust his hand into Lamberton's chest. The servant's eyes flew open as it disappeared up to the wrist; from inside him came the sickening crunch of breaking bone. Lamberton threw back his head to scream, but no sound came out; instead, an enormous jet of dark red blood erupted from his gaping mouth, spraying against the ceiling before falling to the floor. With a grunt of effort, Valentin pulled his hand out of his servant's chest and held Lamberton's beating heart up before his staring, stricken face.

"You have disgraced yourself," he said, staring into his valet's wide, outraged eyes. "And, by extension, me. I am extremely disappointed."

Lamberton made a series of awful, strangled noises, as blood poured out of the gaping hole in his chest. Valentin held his gaze for a long moment, then crushed the slowing heart in his fist. The heavy muscle burst under the pressure and a millisecond later the rest of Lamberton did likewise; he exploded with a huge, wet bang, splattering across his cell and the pale face of his master.

For several seconds, the soft patter of falling blood was the only sound in the cell. Then Valentin turned to face Turner, soaked in the blood of his oldest friend.

"I'm afraid that was something I could only have allowed myself to do," he said. "I hope you can understand. And that you will accept my sincere apologies for the things he did in my name."

Turner stared at the gore-streaked figure before him and nodded slowly. He pressed the button that wound his stake back into his T-Bone and holstered it, his eyes never leaving Valentin's.

"This Brennan," continued Valentin. "The man my servant was in league with. He is still in the grounds of this facility?"

"Yes," said Turner. He was still attempting to process what had just happened before him. "Probably running for the fence."

"You are going to collect him?"

"That's right," said Turner. He could feel his equilibrium starting to return, feel his mind beginning to regain its sharpness.

"Major Turner," said Valentin. "I would very much like to accompany you. I feel that I must make amends for the crimes of my servant."

Turner opened his mouth to say no, then reconsidered.

He's here, he thought. *And he's just destroyed his oldest friend. We're going to have to start trusting him at some point. There's nothing we can do to him if he's lying, so we may as well start using him.*

"Nelson," he said. "Call for a Security Division Section and stay here until they relieve you."

The young Operator nodded, and he turned his attention back to the remaining occupant of the cell. "Come on then," he said. "Before he gets away.

Valentin blurred through the ultraviolet wall. Turner stared, marvelling again at the old vampire's astonishing speed.

"Ready when you are, Major Turner," said the vampire, and smiled.

Paul Turner looked at Valentin Rusmanov as the lift they were standing in ascended; the vampire appeared supernaturally calm considering what he had just done, and who he had done it to.

This could be the stupidest thing I've ever done, he thought. *Which is really saying something after today.*

The lift slowed to a halt, before the doors opened on the long Level 0 corridor. Turner set off at a flat sprint, pulling his console from his belt as he ran. Valentin flew effortlessly alongside him, peering down at the small rectangular screen.

"Where is he?" asked the vampire. "Is he gone?"

"No," said Turner. "He's still out by the runway. It doesn't look like he's moving."

They reached the wide double doors that led into the hangar. The Security Officer dipped his shoulder and burst through them without slowing; Valentin swooped gracefully through behind him.

The huge doors stood open to the night sky; the rippling underside of the vast hologram that shielded the base from enemy satellites and reconnaissance planes loomed overhead, blocking out all but the brightest stars. Turner banked like a sprinter entering the final bend and accelerated towards the wide grounds of the Loop, his console in one hand.

"How far?" asked Valentin.

"Six hundred metres," replied Turner. "Straight ahead."

"Forgive me, Major Turner," said Valentin, then he disappeared from Turner's view. The Security Officer skidded to a halt, shock barrelling through him.

No no no. You treacherous bastard.

He was reaching for his T-Bone when impossibly strong hands gripped him beneath his arms and lifted him effortlessly into the air.

Valentin Rusmanov rocketed forward like a bullet from a gun, sweeping Paul Turner along mere centimetres above grass and tarmac that were little more than a blur; the speed of the vampire was absolutely dizzying, impossible and unnatural. Less than two seconds later Valentin pirouetted upwards and spun back down to the ground, landing as gracefully as a butterfly. He released his grip on Turner, who staggered like a drunk.

"Where is he?" asked the vampire. "I can't see him. Or smell him."

With some difficulty, Turner focused his attention on his console. According to the map on the screen, they were less than fifteen metres away from Operator Brennan. In front of him, a wide black shape sat in the flickering darkness beneath the hologram.

"What's that?" asked Valentin. "It smells remarkable."

"It's a garden," replied Turner, pulling his MP5 from its holster. "A rose garden. It's a memorial to two Operators who died out here."

"Is he in there? This man we're looking for?"

"So my map says," replied Turner. He stowed his console and drew his torch from his belt.

"Come on then," said Valentin, and floated across the grass towards the garden. Turner strode alongside him, until they reached the opening in the stone walls that served as the entrance to the garden. He stepped up on to the wooden boards that ran between the huge rose beds, turned on his torch, and shone it round the dark garden, already certain of what he was going see.

Nothing.

There was no sign of Richard Brennan.

His torch beam picked out a splash of colour at the rear of the garden and he walked towards it. Valentin floated silently alongside him, having clearly also realised that their pursuit had been in vain. In front of them stood the wooden bench that had been dedicated to the memories of John and George Harker; their names were engraved on a bronze plaque bolted to the centre of the backrest. Turner shone his torch slowly across it and saw what his map had led him to.

A pool of blood lay on the wooden seat of the bench. It was almost dry, but it had run when it was fresh, spilling between the boards and dripping on to the ground. In the middle of the dark liquid, a small square of metal gleamed in the white beam of Turner's torch.

"He cut his chip out," said Turner, softly. "Cut it out of his own arm. He could be anywhere."

Valentin stood beside him, looking down at the gory present Brennan had left for whoever came looking for him. "There's something written on the bench," he said. "I can smell the paint."

Turner widened the beam of his torch, knowing what he was going to see.

Two words had been scrawled across the back rest, desecrating the bronze plaque with bright green spray paint.

HE RISES

For a long moment, neither man nor vampire said a word.

Paul Turner suddenly felt more tired than he could remember feeling at any point in his long, full life. There was a limit to how much any man could handle, could absorb and still continue to put one foot in front of the other, and he felt, for the first time, as though he was on the verge of reaching his. Everything seemed dark, a tunnel in which the light at the end was slipping further and further away. Brennan was gone and with him, presumably, every discussion they had ever had about Dracula: their theories, assumptions, and the beginnings of their strategy to attempt to deal with him.

This did not put them back to square one; it put them much further back than that.

"I can find them, you know," said Valentin. His voice was full of quiet fire. "Dracula. My brother. If you let me, I can find them. I can return and tell you where they are."

Turner shrugged. "If you decide to leave," he said, "I think we both know that I can't stop you."

"I suspect you would give it quite the try," said Valentin, a smile rising on his face. "But I'd rather I didn't have to find out. I'd rather go with your blessing."

Turner studied the ancient vampire's face for a long moment. "Go," he said, and smiled. "Go and find them. Then come back. Don't make me look stupid for trusting you."

"Count on it," said Valentin. He looked at Turner for a brief moment, then rose into the sky and was gone.

55

HOLD THE FRONT PAGE

Kate Randall sat on the bench in the back of the helicopter, her hands resting on her knees, and tried to still her racing heart. Matt Browning was beside her, his pale, gentle face set with determination, his gaze locked on the floor. On the bench opposite sat Colonel Victor Frankenstein, his huge grey-green head almost brushing the ceiling. He was watching them silently, his uneven eyes unreadable.

They had lifted off from the Loop twenty minutes earlier, their helicopter hauling itself into the darkening sky and heading south. The pilots had announced an ETA once they were airborne, and since then there had been silence in the passenger hold. That was fine with Kate; she had no desire to talk about where they were going or what they were going to do. This was not a normal operation, where intelligence could provide a reasonable understanding of the terrain, numbers and motives of the enemy they were about to face.

This was different.

They had no idea how many vampires were waiting for them; it could be Albert Harker on his own, or he could have an army with him. They had no idea what Harker was doing, although the location they were heading to, the printing press of one of the biggest tabloids in the country, certainly suggested that his plan involved the public exposure of something, whether it was vampires, or Blacklight, or both. And, crucially, neither of them had any idea how their fathers had become involved with whatever was happening.

Kate glanced over at Matt. She was trying not to worry about him, but failing; he had no Operational experience whatsoever, and had undergone only basic weapons and tactics training at the Loop. This was understandable, as Matt had been recruited to work for the Lazarus Project, not as an Operator; the only normal scenario in which he would be expected to take up arms was in defence of the Loop. Part of her was convinced that she should not have brought him, that if anything happened to him, it was going to be her fault. But she knew she could not have gone without him and lived with herself: there were certain things that you simply did not keep from people.

"Five minutes," called the pilot.

"OK," rumbled Frankenstein, then gave Kate a thin smile. "Are you ready?"

The monster gave her no cause for concern, despite his absence from active operations; he had volunteered, he had more experience than the rest of the Department combined, and she was absolutely delighted that he was there.

"I'm ready," she said.

Albert Harker smiled as he rounded the security desk, which was now soaked with Kevin McKenna's blood, and floated towards Pete Randall.

His terrible eyes glowed a red so dark it was almost black, and Pete found himself absolutely certain that his life was about to end. But rather than the agonising death he was expecting, Albert Harker merely clapped him hard on the back.

"No going back, Pete," he said. "We go all the way to the end."

Harker led him back into the main room of the press and turned his attention to the four men that Greg Browning had tied up earlier. The noise in the room was deafening; the machines had started to run again, pumping out copies of the vandalised version of the next day's edition of *The Globe* that carried Kevin McKenna's final story. The captive men looked up at the blood-soaked vampire with outright terror, as Pete tried desperately to clear his head; the unthinkable horror of McKenna's death and the heavy blow to the head had combined to render him barely functional.

The vampire approached the two nearest men, the ones who had tried to crawl away when Pete had been briefly unconscious, and pulled their throats out with two casual flicks of his wrist. Blood gushed out across the concrete floor, a pool of crimson that spread with nauseating speed. The two remaining men screamed and grunted behind their gags, their eyes bulging in their heads. They tried to squirm away as Harker approached them, his smile wide, his eyes blazing.

"Don't..." managed Pete. "Please..."

The vampire rounded on him. "Don't what?" he asked. "Do what needs to be done? Your courage may be failing you, but mine remains resolute."

"You said... no one... would get hurt."

Harker sighed. "That is how I would have had it, Pete. Believe me. Unfortunately, Kevin has changed that, for all of us. Now they will be coming, and we must be ready."

Pete stared, tears rising in the corners of his eyes. This was not what he had signed up for, what he had gathered his courage and travelled into the unknown to be a part of. This was the murder and terrorism of the innocent.

This was madness.

Harker lifted the two crying, thrashing workers into the air and turned to face Pete. "Go to the loading bay with the others," he said. "This will be where they come. Quickly, now."

Pete looked down the long room. At the far end, beside the rolling metal doors, he could see Greg Browning overseeing four men in blue overalls. Three of them were stacking a pallet with bundles of newspapers as they came off the press; the fourth was sitting in the cab of a forklift truck, waiting to load it into a waiting lorry. The driver was presumably safely in his cab, waiting for the word to go, with no idea of what was taking place less than fifteen metres behind him.

Pete wondered briefly whether he could run, whether he could hide in the tangle of machinery, but realised immediately that such a move would be futile; Harker could fly above the machines to look for him, could move many times faster than him, and could in all likelihood hear him breathing.

He was going to have to bide his time, and hope for a chance to atone for the horror he had helped unleash.

Jack Williams stood beside the open doorway of the helicopter, his static line fixed safely to the security rail. Behind him, Todd McLean, the Australian rookie who had replaced Shaun Turner, and Angela Darcy, whom he had temporarily recalled to his squad after her own had been decimated, were watching him carefully, waiting to see if he could control the anger that was raging inside him.

He was *furious* with Kate and Matt for going after Albert Harker, and incredibly disappointed they had not come to him and told him what was happening. He would have let them come with him, of course he would, and it hurt him to think that Kate hadn't known that. And part of him, the ambitious part that wanted to be the Blacklight Director one day, was terrified by the thought that they might succeed, might destroy Albert Harker before he could get there.

Mine, he thought, as the helicopter swept low across the landscape. *He's supposed to be mine.*

Pete Randall walked between the thundering machines of the printing press like a man going to the gallows.

Albert Harker flew easily above him, holding the bound men casually in each hand. As they reached the wide expanse of the loading bay, and Greg Browning and the four workers in blue overalls stopped to watch their approach, the vampire's eyes bloomed a bright, joyous red. He swooped down to the ground, dropped one of the two men to the floor, then turned and threw the other over the towering machines. The stricken man spun through the air, impossibly high, and disappeared from view. A second later there was an awful thud, like a bag of cement hitting the ground.

"Continue with your work," growled Harker, turning to face the staring, shell-shocked workers. "And you may yet live to see the morning. If you get any stupid ideas, of trying to run, or trying to oppose either myself or my companions, I suggest you think about what I just did and reconsider. There have been changes to our circumstances, but your roles remain the same. Untie your colleague, load the trailers, and send them on their way. Let nothing else concern you."

The four men stared at him, their faces slack with terror.

"Get back to work!" bellowed Harker.

The men scattered, three of them running back to their posts with their heads down. The other lowered his head, scampered forward, and untied the man that Harker had carried down the long room.

610

The huge press had continued to run as Harker spoke and a number of copies of *The Globe* had piled up on the floor at the end of the final conveyor belt. As the workers began to scoop them up, Pete looked at the front page full of the simple, awful headline that McKenna had written, and felt nothing. This was what he had dreamt of, a daring plan to alert the public to what they weren't being told, but the reality was awful; the papers turned his stomach to look at them.

He looked up and saw Greg Browning staring at him. The expression on his face was one of total dismay, and Pete knew that his new friend was feeling exactly the same things as him.

Betrayal. Disappointment.

Fear.

Albert Harker rose up into the air and hovered above the rolling doors, watching the men working below him. His red eyes kept glancing along the long length of the building and Pete knew why: the vampire believed they were about to have company.

Greg curled the fingers of his hand in a tiny, subtle 'come here' gesture. Pete walked slowly across to the conveyor belt, as casually as he was able, and pretended to examine the newspapers that were streaming past. Greg made his way to the opposite side and lowered his head, as if concentrating on the job in hand.

"Where's McKenna?" he whispered, his voice barely audible.

"Dead," said Pete, his voice low and trembling. "Harker killed him."

"Why?" asked Greg. "What the hell for?"

"He rang the police," said Pete. "Knocked me out, then rang the police from reception. So Harker tore his throat out."

"Jesus," whispered Greg. "Why did Kevin do that? This is his thing."

Pete shook his head, so slightly it was barely visible. "I don't think it is," he said. "To be honest, I don't think it ever was. I just don't think McKenna realised until it was too late. This is Harker's thing. You, me, McKenna, we're just pawns. And I'll tell you something else, Greg. I don't think you and I were ever meant to get out of here."

"What are you talking about?"

"Think about it. Why are we here? Harker doesn't need us to do what he's doing. He could do this on his own. And the last thing McKenna said to me, the last thing he said to anyone, was, 'I'm doing this for you.' I think he realised that he'd been lied to and was trying to do something about it."

"But Harker is doing what he told us he was going to do," said Greg. He reached out, grabbed one of the copies off the belt, pretended to examine it, then put it back. "It's happening, Pete. The public are going to know."

"And five innocent people are dead," said Pete. "He's doing it, but I don't think he's doing it for the same reasons as you and me, for the reasons he told us and Kevin. This is about revenge for him. He thinks Blacklight are on their way here right now and he isn't scared, Greg. He's *excited*."

"Why?"

"I don't know," hissed Pete. "But what do you think is going to happen to us if he's right and the men in black show up? We might not have killed anyone, but you tied those men up, and I stood still and did nothing when he tore two of their throats out. We have to get out of here."

"How?" asked Greg. He looked up for a split second and Pete saw the naked fear in his new friend's eye. "We can't fight him, not the two of us on our own. I doubt the seven of us can, even if we could persuade the others to try."

"I don't know," said Pete. "I don't have a plan. But we'd better think of something, because if Albert is right, this is only going to get worse."

The helicopter containing Kate Randall, Matt Browning and Victor Frankenstein touched down outside *The Globe*'s printing facility with a heavy thud.

The car park was deserted; scraps of litter, thrown into the air by the draught from the rotor blades, swirled across the tarmac, and street lights cast a pale amber glow. Frankenstein leapt easily down, then held out his hand. Kate took it and allowed herself to be helped to the ground, before Matt did the same. As soon as they were all safely clear, the helicopter roared back into the air, disappearing into the dark sky overhead.

Matt watched it go. His stomach felt as though it was filled with concrete: a painful, relentless pressure that made it difficult to put one foot in front of the other. He was scared; Kate knew it, and he was pretty sure that Frankenstein did too. That was fine. What he hoped they also knew was that he had no intention of letting them down.

The printing press loomed over them, a huge grey building with a glass reception. Even from where they were standing, perhaps fifteen metres away, Matt could see that at least one of the panes of glass was cracked and that red covered much of the small transparent area.

"Blood," he said, pointing with a gloved finger. "Lots of it."

"I see it," said Kate. "Let's move. Ready One from here on. Matt, visors at all times for you and me. We can't let anyone see who we are. Silent comms. Is that clear?"

"Clear," he said. He flipped his visor down, marvelling as ever at the technology contained within the thin sheet of coated plastic.

Kate did the same, then spoke into his ear. "Are you ready for this, Matt?"

"I'm ready," he replied, with as much conviction as he could muster. "Lead the way."

Kate did so, drawing her T-Bone as she walked and holding it before her, one hand resting beneath its barrel, the other curled round its grip. Matt did likewise, feeling the heavy weight of the weapon in his hands. Frankenstein left his T-Bone on his belt, but drew the enormous silver shotgun from its holster that ran down his long spine. They walked forward in a line, like gunslingers down the main street of an old Western town as the clock ticked towards high noon.

The reception door was controlled remotely, but Frankenstein simply pushed its handle until the lock gave way. Kate stepped inside, with Matt following close behind her. The smell hit him instantly: the rich, coppery scent of the blood that covered the floor, the desk, and ran in thick streaks down the glass walls. Frankenstein stepped round the desk and checked the security guard who was lying beneath it. There was no need to do the same for the other man; his throat had been torn wide open.

"Dead," said Frankenstein. "Tied up first, for a while at least. His hands are blue."

"Something went wrong," said Kate. "I doubt the plan was to decorate this room with blood. Anyone could have seen it."

"Agreed," said Frankenstein. "I want you both to be very careful. This thing, whatever it is, might be unravelling."

Matt nodded, his stomach churning. He had seen his fair share of blood, including a great spray of his own as it burst from the hole Larissa had made in his neck, but he was not as used to dealing with it as his companions.

"Come on," said Kate. "Let's find out what we're dealing with."

She crossed the blood-soaked reception and looked at the doors that presumably led into the facility proper. They were hanging slightly off their hinges, broken by a feat of unnatural strength. Matt took a deep breath, then stepped up beside her. Frankenstein brought up the rear, towering over them both.

Kate reached out, took the handle in her hand, and pushed the door open. A huge cacophony of noise rolled through the empty space and into their eardrums, and Matt winced behind his visor. Kate pushed the door wider and slipped through the gap. He followed, with Frankenstein close behind him.

The room they had entered was huge, a tangled labyrinth of metal and spinning rubber. Matt, whose heart always lifted at the sight of feats of engineering, especially on this sort of scale, stared with fascination, until Kate grabbed his arm and told him he was standing in someone's blood; he looked down and felt his stomach lurch.

"Jesus," he said, his voice low. He glanced around and instantly saw the source of the pool of crimson beneath his feet. Two men were lying by the wall, their throats torn open, their eyes blank and staring. Frankenstein knelt down beside them; he pressed two long grey-green fingers to each of their necks in turn and shook his head.

"Where are they?" asked Matt, his voice low. "Harker. Our dads."

"They're in here somewhere," said Kate.

"Don't tell me we're splitting up to look for them," said Matt. "Because that only ever seems like a stupid idea to me."

Kate smiled behind her visor and shook her head. "We stick together," she said. "Like we said we would."

56

WE TAKE CARE OF OUR OWN

The heat in the warehouse office was instantly overpowering, as flames exploded across the walls and floor.

Jamie felt the air burn his nostrils and his throat, and turned back into the inferno, grabbing for Ellison through the rising hurricane of fire. She had managed to lower her visor, but she was doubled over, coughing heavily into the speaker in his ear as flames billowed round her legs. The Blacklight uniforms were fire-retardant, but Jamie didn't think they had been designed with fire this intense in mind.

He plunged into the flames, shouting Ellison's name. She struggled upright and reached out a gloved hand; he grabbed for it, feeling the heat beginning to seep through his suit, feeling the sheen of sweat that was now coating him from head to toe. He closed his fingers tightly round hers and hauled her forward. She staggered through the fire, a dark shimmering shape in the inferno the small concrete room had become. Above his head, Jamie heard a terrible crackling noise, as a thick, fatty smell invaded his nostrils; John Morton's corpse was beginning to burn, suspended over the flames like a stuck pig.

Jamie grabbed his squad mate's shoulder and shoved her towards the open doorway with all his might. Ellison stumbled over her own feet, but she didn't fall, not until she burst into the cool darkness of the corridor. He ran for the door, feeling the heat at his back beginning to become unbearable, and slid to the floor beside her. She was coughing again, her body shaking as she wrapped her arms round her stomach. He lifted her visor and looked at her; her face was a bright shade of pink, but her eyes were clear, even as tears ran from their corners. She pushed him away, her eyes flashing with anger.

"Go after him," she croaked. "I'll be fine."

Jamie didn't waste a second checking whether she meant what she said; he leapt to his feet and sprinted away down the corridor, in the only direction Alastair Dempsey could have fled.

His boots thudded against the metal stairs as he took them two at a time. As he ran, he twisted the dial on his belt and changed his helmet's view to thermographic imaging. There was a faint haze of residual heat floating on the air as he dipped his shoulder, smashed open the door at the bottom of the stairs, and burst back into the cavernous empty space of the warehouse.

Jamie scanned it quickly, looking for the telltale pillar of white and yellow heat that the vampire could not disguise, but saw nothing. He twisted the dial again, switching his helmet's visual mode back to normal, and immediately saw something different; one of the metal shutter doors was standing halfway open. Rain was pouring through the empty rectangle and the dim glow of street lights illuminated its edges.

Jamie ran towards it, pressing the button that established a secure connection with the Loop as he did so. A second later an Operator from the Surveillance Division answered.

"Priority Level target Dempsey, Alastair," shouted Jamie. "He's moving. Tell me you've got him?"

"Code in," replied the voice.

"Carpenter, Jamie, NS303, 67-J," he yelled. "Give me his position, right now."

"Establishing," said the voice. "Three hundred metres south-south-west of your position. In motion."

Jamie ducked under the half-open door and skidded out on to the street. Rain poured down from the sky and was whipped against him by the gusting wind. He grabbed his console from his belt, checked his position on the map that lit up the screen, and set off down Bridle Lane at a flat sprint.

"Give me running updates," he shouted, his boots pounding the tarmac. "Don't you lose him."

Jamie ran as though his life depended on it, his arms pumping, his heart thundering in his chest.

Not this time, he thought. *You're not getting away again.*

Several men and women, huddled against the rain or drunkenly embracing it, stopped and stared at him as he ran, but he ignored them; he knew he was breaching a fundamental Blacklight regulation by exposing himself to such public scrutiny, but that didn't matter right now.

Nothing mattered beyond seeing Alastair Dempsey destroyed.

An alleyway opened up to his right and he headed towards it, his boots slipping and sliding on the wet ground. His balance shifted, and for a brief moment he thought he was going to fall, but then his momentum carried him round the corner, and he accelerated again.

"Distance?" he shouted. The alleyway narrowed alarmingly, but was open at the far end, and he sprinted towards the tall, tapering gap.

"One hundred and ninety metres," replied the Surveillance Operator. "Course unchanged."

Catching him. I'm catching him, he thought.

Dempsey was evidently not hurrying; Jamie wondered whether he was assuming that they had died in the fire trap he had set for them, but doubted that the vampire would be that complacent. More likely, he was unaware of the level of surveillance his pursuers were capable of bringing to bear. He probably believed that his head start, when combined with the darkness and the labyrinthine backstreets of this section of Central London, was enough to guarantee his escape.

Wrong, Jamie thought, baring his teeth in a smile so savage that anyone who saw it would have backed away immediately. *Dead wrong.*

Jamie reached the end of the alleyway and sprinted out across the street without slowing; if there had been a taxi making its way down the road, his pursuit of Alastair Dempsey would have ended with him in hospital, or worse. But the street was empty. Rising from the pavement on the opposite side was another narrow opening, cluttered with discarded rubbish and the dissolving remains of cardboard boxes. He ploughed through them and kept running.

"Position?" he yelled.

"Forty-five metres," replied the Operator, instantly. "Directly ahead of you."

"Jamie?" said Ellison's voice. It was raw, little more than a croak, but it was full of determination. "Where are you?"

"Surveillance," said Jamie, as he ran down the alleyway. "Give Operator Ellison my location."

The Operator immediately began to give his squad mate directions; he tuned them out, focusing entirely on the pursuit of Alastair Dempsey. The alleyway he was running down was long and empty, stretching all the way to the hustle and bustle of Lexington Street.

I should be right on top of him. Where the hell is he?

He twisted the dial on his belt back to thermographic, and saw him.

The vampire was making his way along the roof of the building that made up the right-hand wall of the alleyway, a bright blob of white and orange four storeys up that Jamie would never have seen without the visual enhancement his visor offered him. He skidded to a halt and pressed himself into the shadows on the wall to his left, watching to see whether Dempsey had heard his pursuit. The rain thundered down against the pavement, as dark grey clouds roiled against the black night sky.

Dempsey gave no indication that he had realised he was being followed. The vampire continued along the edge of the roof, gliding above the tiles at little more than walking speed, as though he was merely taking an evening stroll across the sodden canopy of the capital. Then, without warning, he floated into the air and across the alleyway, before resuming his course directly above Jamie's head.

Jamie crouched down and ran across the narrow passage. He looked up and saw the vampire continuing in the same direction, towards the busy road that was getting closer and closer. He followed Dempsey, matching his speed, then froze as the vampire leapt easily back across the narrow gap.

He's having fun up there, he thought, hatred spilling through him. *He's having a great time.*

His mind was racing, trying to work out how to bring Dempsey down to his level, where he might have the advantage. If they reached Lexington Street, it was over; no matter how angry he was, how hot and livid his desire for vengeance might be, he simply could not follow the vampire into a heavily populated area; the risk of exposure was just too great. As he stared upwards, an idea occurred to him; it was a long shot, but it was going to have to do.

Jamie reached down, never taking his eyes off Dempsey, and unclipped the ultraviolet beam gun from his belt. Then he ran forward, hoping that the drumming of the rain would hide the sound of his footsteps, that the monster above his head would not choose that particular moment to look down. He waited until he was fifteen metres ahead of the strolling, dancing vampire, then stopped and raised the beam gun.

One shot, he thought, feeling his body fill with a familiar icy calm. *If I miss, he's gone again.*

He stared up at Dempsey, still little more than a distant splash of bright white and yellow heat, and felt his heart slow down, his breathing become low and even.

One shot.

Four storeys up, Alastair Dempsey turned to his left and floated easily into the air. In the alleyway directly beneath him, Jamie Carpenter pressed the button on his beam gun, and hoped.

A bright shaft of purple light burst up through the rain, piercing the gloom of the night sky, and enveloped the vampire completely.

Dempsey erupted in purple fire, screaming with sudden shock and pain. His trajectory was fatally compromised; the vampire thrashed and screamed, beating at his own skin, trying to extinguish the roaring purple flames, and crashed into the side of the building, high above Jamie's head. He grabbed the wet bricks, screaming and fighting to stay in the air, but it was futile. With his flesh burning, with fire roaring down his throat and into his lungs, Dempsey descended towards the ground in a series of lurching drops.

Jamie kept the purple beam trained on him, his head roaring with savage delight, with the primeval desire to hunt and kill. The vampire made one final, doomed effort to postpone the inevitable, his burning fingers scrabbling at nothing, then fell to the soaking alleyway floor in a heap of blood and burning meat. A cloud of steam rose from him, and he lay still.

Jamie turned off the beam gun, placed it back in its loop on his belt, and breathed out a long, deep sigh. Nothing was going to bring John Morton back, or erase Jamie's memory of the horrors that had been inflicted upon his squad mate, so this was the best he could do: ensuring that the monster who had killed Morton would never get the chance to hurt anyone else. Revenge was not the same as justice, but in this case, it would have to do; it was all he had to offer.

He drew his Glock and quickly screwed a suppressor on to its barrel.

"Jamie?" said Ellison, her voice loud and harsh in his ear. "I saw the UV. What's going on?"

"He's down," he said, and heard the tremor in his own voice. "I got him."

"Don't destroy him," said Ellison, instantly, and he recoiled at the passion in her voice. "Wait for me. Please?"

"I'll wait," he said. "Hurry."

"I'll be right there."

Jamie looked down at the steaming remains of Alastair Dempsey. Most of his skin was burned bright red, although there were patches where it was either black or burned away entirely. It was peeling in sheets and covered in wide blisters; several of these had burst, sending thick whitish-yellow fluid running on to the pavement, where it was carried away by the rushing rainwater. The vampire wasn't moving; his eyes were closed, his mouth open and filling with rain.

Playing dead, thought Jamie. *Give me a break.*

He raised the Glock, pointed it at Alastair Dempsey's knee, and pulled the trigger. The gunshot cracked in the sodden night air and the bullet slammed into the wall where the vampire had been a millisecond earlier.

The burnt, ruined thing burst up from the floor of the alleyway, steam rising from his roasted body, a roar of rage emerging from his mouth. Jamie brought the pistol up, but Dempsey closed the gap before he could pull the trigger a second time. He swung a burnt, ravaged arm and connected with the thick plastic of Jamie's visor.

The impact was enormous. Cracks raced across his visor's surface, disabling its thermographic view as Jamie was lifted off his feet and sent tumbling through the air, his eyes rolling, his head a ball of agony. He landed hard on the tarmac and slid along the alleyway on his back.

Never been hit like that, he thought, as he tried to force his limbs into action. *So strong. So much power.*

He reached up with a shaking hand and pushed his visor back. His ears were ringing, and his brain felt slow and stupid, like it was no longer working properly. He forced his eyes open, looked down the alleyway, and felt fear tighten round his heart.

The blackened figure of Alastair Dempsey was walking towards him, a smile on what was left of his face.

He shouldn't even be able to stand. My God.

Jamie pushed himself backwards along the ground. His Glock had fallen from his hands as he was thrown into the air and he fumbled at his belt for something, anything he could use. He pulled the beam gun and saw glass fall from the end of the cylinder; he turned it round and stared numbly at the shattered remains of its bulb. His hand closed round the grip of his MP5, but even in his desperate state he could not bring himself to pull it free. Firing the submachine gun a stone's throw away from a crowded Soho street was far too dangerous to consider, no matter what it might cost him. Then his fingers brushed the handle of his T-Bone; he yanked it out of its loop and brought it round before him.

Dempsey wasn't hurrying. His expression was one of supreme enjoyment, the look of a predator as it approaches an injured animal. He walked steadily across the wet stone, his smoking, red-black arms hanging loosely at his sides. Jamie aimed the T-Bone and pulled the trigger. As the stake burst from the barrel, a single thought filled his mind.

This isn't going to work.

The stake rocketed down the alleyway on a direct collision course with the centre of Dempsey's chest, barely visible to Jamie's eye. A fraction of a second before it crunched home, the vampire moved, sliding to his left as though it was the easiest thing in the world, and plucked the trailing wire out of the air. Jamie saw burnt skin peel away from his hand as he grabbed the hurtling metal cable, but Dempsey seemed not to even notice. He looked down at the wire for a moment, then jerked it up and back with a flick of his wrist.

Jamie didn't even have time to think about releasing his grip on his T-Bone before he was wrenched up into the air again, his shoulders and forearms screaming in agony. He watched, almost incredulous, as the wet ground moved away from him, as his limp body seemed to float towards the waiting vampire, who reached up with what seemed almost like indifference and caught him by the throat.

His legs kicked and jerked, flailing away at nothing. He grabbed at Dempsey's arm, tearing at the burnt skin, feeling it come loose in his hands like barbecued meat, but the grip remained utterly implacable. He could feel his throat being constricted and panic burst through him; there were grey spots appearing at the corners of his vision and he was suddenly tired, so very tired. His hands fell away from the vampire's arm and dangled uselessly at his sides. As the darkness crowded in on him, as the last spots of light in the centre of his view of the world seemed about to turn black, Dempsey threw him against the alleyway wall, as casually as someone might throw a tennis ball.

The back of Jamie's head smashed into the wall, his helmet the only thing that prevented his skull from cracking like an egg. The impact cleared his vision, bringing the world back into shocking focus. There was a loud crunch as he hit the wet bricks, before pain, stabbing and urgent, filled his torso and shortened his breath to ragged gasps.

Ribs, he managed to think, as he slid helplessly to the ground. *Broken. Three or four of them. Maybe more.*

Then a simpler, more primal thought filled his head as he saw Alastair Dempsey walk towards him.

I'm going to die.

The vampire strolled across the alleyway, reached down, and hauled him to his feet. Jamie tried to will his reeling, damaged body into action, to raise his arms and fight, but couldn't do it; he had nothing left.

Dempsey peered at him, his burnt face even more awful close up; his eyelids were gone, as was most of his nose, and his lips were cracked and oozing in a dozen places. The skin itself was charred black, apart from in the places that it had peeled away, revealing mottled red beneath. The vampire smiled, his fangs emerging from behind his broken lips.

"You can't be my friend," he said, his voice a ragged growl. "I don't play with men. But you'll do for food."

Jamie watched, his mind so overwhelmed by fear that he was incapable of even closing his eyes, of shutting out the terrible thing that was about to kill him. The fangs were vast and otherworldly; he waited for them to pierce his skin, wondering if it would hurt.

Crack.

Something hot and wet sprayed into Jamie's face. Then the pressure holding him against the wall was gone, and he slid to the floor. He summoned some distant reserve of strength and wiped the liquid out of his eyes, in time to see Alastair Dempsey crumple on to the ground in front of him, a huge hole where one side of his head had been. Blood and brain gushed out, sliding across the wet ground, as the vampire's eyes, their crimson fire extinguished, rolled back in his head.

He tried to take a deep breath, grimacing at the pain from his broken ribs, and slowly turned his head. Ellison was walking down the alleyway towards him, her Glock raised, smoke curling upwards from its barrel. She didn't run, or lower her weapon; when she arrived in front of him and pushed her visor back, she kept the pistol trained on the motionless body of Alastair Dempsey.

"Are you all right?" she asked. "Are you hurt?"

Jamie grimaced, and forced out two words.

"Stake him."

Ellison nodded. She drew the metal stake from her belt with her free hand, keeping her gun on the vampire, then darted forward and slammed it into his chest. The charred remains of Alastair Dempsey burst with a wet bang, splattering them both with blood. For a long second, Ellison kept her gun pointed at the gore-soaked patch of ground, then holstered her weapon and came towards Jamie, concern written across her face.

Jamie felt his broken ribs scream with pain as Ellison helped him to his feet; he clenched his teeth and tried not to let it show. He leant against the wall of the alleyway and took a low, shallow breath. The pain was bad, but he didn't think the jagged end of one of his ribs had punctured a lung; he could breathe, just about.

Ellison took a half-step back, as he tried to force a smile on to his blood-smeared face. He felt no euphoria over the destruction of Dempsey. He just felt tired, and empty.

"Well done," he said, the words little more than grunts. "Are you OK?"

Ellison shook her head. "No, sir," she replied. "Not even close. Are you?"

"No," he said. "I'm alive, though. Thanks to you."

She managed a smile of her own, a fleeting expression that was quickly replaced by one of misery.

"Jesus, Jamie," she said, her voice choked. "John... poor John. I just..."

He reached out, wincing at the pain, and took hold of her shoulder. "I know," he said. "He was a good man and he deserved better. But we're still here, Lizzy. And we have to keep going."

"I keep thinking about it," she said. "What he must have gone through... you know... before he—"

Jamie felt his heart break for her. "You always will," he said. "You're never going to forget him or what was done to him. So you have to *use* it. Use it to stop it happening to anyone else."

She nodded. "Yes, sir. I'm sorry. I've seen awful things before, just nothing so..."

"I know," he said, softly. "It's OK."

"We need to get you to the infirmary, sir," she said.

Jamie nodded. He reached down and pressed a button on his belt, opening a line to the driver of their van. "Immediate extraction requested," he said, grimacing with pain. "My location." He twisted the dial and pressed the button again, re-establishing his connection to the Surveillance Division. "Clean-up required at previous location. Emergency services likely already in attendance. No supernatural exposure. Remains of Morton, John, NS304, 07-B require extraction and return to the Loop." He twisted his comms system off and looked at Ellison. "Two minutes."

Ellison nodded.

The two Operators stood in the darkness, their minds full of pain and loss, as the remains of Alastair Dempsey diffused into the rain and drifted towards the overflowing drains.

57

HOT OFF THE PRESS

Pete Randall was standing beside the final conveyor belt, pretending to keep an eye on the men packing the newspapers and loading them on to the pallets, when he heard a deep growl emerge from Albert Harker's throat. He looked up at the vampire and saw his eyes bloom their familiar glowing red, before he swooped down to the ground beside him.

"They're here," said Harker, a dreadful smile of anticipation on his face. "Three of them. They just arrived."

"What are you going to do?" asked Pete.

"Why, kill them, of course," replied Harker. "What did you expect?"

"You don't care about any of this, do you?" said Pete, his voice trembling. "Everything Kevin told us, what you told us once we got to London. None of it was real, was it?"

Harker snarled, then lifted Pete off his feet with one slender hand, holding him in the air without any apparent effort.

"Don't presume to tell me what I care about," said the vampire, his eyes burning with red fire. "You could never understand what this means to me, how much I have suffered at the hands of the men we have set ourselves against. The difference between you and

I is that I have the fortitude to do what needs to be done. I don't snivel and whine at the first sign of adversity."

"My daughter... died," gasped Pete. "Is that... not... suffering enough?"

Harker laughed, a short sound that was little more than a grunt. "People die," he said. "They die every day, when I was not even allowed that option. My life was stolen from me by the people who were supposed to care the most, men who I should have been able to trust unthinkingly. I would have traded death for the life I have lived, and traded it gladly."

He released his grip on Pete, who crumpled to the floor, massaging his constricted throat. Out of the corner of his eye, he saw Greg Browning watching the scene playing out in front of him. His new friend was as still as a statue, his eyes wide, but he said nothing.

"Keep loading the trailer," shouted Harker. "I will be watching. If you stop, I will kill you. If you try to run, I will kill you."

"We were never meant to survive this, were we?" said Pete. He was holding his injured neck, tears standing in the corners of his eyes. "Greg and me, and the rest of them. It doesn't matter now, so just tell the truth, you bastard."

Harker stared at him for a long moment, then raised a single finger to his lips. "Shhh," he whispered, then flew straight up into the shadows at the roof of the building and disappeared.

Pete climbed slowly to his feet and faced the workers in the blue overalls. There was nothing he could say to them, nothing that could make what was happening any better. The five men held his gaze, expressions of awful resignation on their faces, then returned to their tasks. Pete watched them, impotent misery coursing through him, as Greg Browning walked slowly over and stood beside him. There was a long, uneasy silence, until eventually his new friend spoke, his voice barely a whisper.

"We're going to die, aren't we. All of us."

"I don't know," said Pete. He was dimly aware that a role reversal had taken place, that Greg was now looking to him for answers. "Probably."

"I don't want to die," said Greg, his voice choked with fear. "I know I said I didn't care what happened to me, but I take that back. I don't want to die."

"Me neither," said Pete. "Not like this. But if I have to, I want to take him with me. That's all I can think of right now."

"How?" asked Greg.

"Just be aware," said Pete. "If a chance comes, it'll probably be the only one we get. Be ready to take it."

Kate led Matt and Frankenstein slowly between the towering aisles of machinery, the three Operators gripping their weapons tightly.

The noise was relentless; paper thundered through rollers and trimmers, as huge bars smoothed ink across it. The heat was overwhelming, and dust hung thickly in the air. Matt rested his finger nervously on the trigger guard of his T-Bone, glad his visor was hiding his face from his companions; he didn't think he would be able to hide his fear without it.

Something moved, in the darkness near the roof.

Matt froze.

"What is it?" asked Kate.

"I don't know," he replied. "I thought I saw something. Up there."

They waited, absolutely still, their T-Bones raised. Matt's heart thumped in his chest, as he stared up at the distant ceiling.

"OK," said Kate, eventually. "Let's keep moving."

They made their way slowly between the machines. Above their heads, a conveyor belt curved down and ran round a corner to their left. They followed it in single file, their weapons raised, and saw the huge room open up before them. The three Operators stopped, their uniforms disappearing into the shadows, and surveyed the scene.

Newspapers rolled endlessly down the conveyor belt, as men in blue overalls scurried to and fro, packing and bundling and loading them on to pallets. At the rear of the wide space, a row of rolling metal doors punctuated the wall; standing in front of one of them were two men in normal clothes. Their heads were inclined towards each other, as though they were deep in some vital conversation. Then one of the men looked up, and Matt heard Kate gasp.

"My God," she said. "I didn't really believe it."

Pete Randall frowned, as though he had heard something, and whispered to the other man, who stood up straight. Matt felt the breath catch in his chest and stop.

His father was standing less than ten metres away.

Greg Browning looked as though he had aged ten years since Matt had seen him last; his hair was streaked with grey, his face lined more deeply than ever, and his eyes had a sunken, haunted look to them.

Scared, thought Matt. *He looks really scared. They both do.*

He was suddenly overcome with the desire to rush across the open space and hug his father; it was something he would never have done when they lived in the same house, when the world had still been small and unkind, but the urge was almost uncontrollable.

"Oh Jesus," he said. "What are they doing here, Kate?"

"I don't know," she replied. It sounded like she was on the verge of tears. "They're both OK, though. That's the main thing."

"Agreed," said Frankenstein. "But where's Albert Harker?"

There was a fluttering noise, like the sound of a large bird beating its wings, and then a dark blur dropped from the ceiling above them. Something flashed out, impossibly fast, and caught Matt on the side of the helmet; the impact was unbelievable, like being hit with a sledgehammer, and he staggered backwards before stumbling to one knee. His head swam, and he watched with greying vision as the dark shape slammed Kate into the machine they were taking cover against. She folded to the ground, her finger tightening spasmodically on the trigger of her T-Bone. The stake exploded out of its barrel and whistled away towards the ceiling.

Frankenstein, whose instincts and reactions were honed by decades of experience, ducked the punch that was thrown his way and fired his shotgun. The report was deafening as fire licked from the gaping barrel. The dark shape leapt back into the air and vanished.

The monster reached down and hauled Kate to her feet.

"I'm OK," she gasped. "Matt?"

He struggled to his feet, his head still ringing from the force of the vampire's blow. "I'm all right," he said.

The men in the blue overalls had stopped working and were watching the violence playing out before them with wide eyes. Matt and Kate's fathers were staring directly at them, their mouths hanging open.

"Follow me," said Frankenstein.

The monster ran across the open space of the loading bay. The workers backed away, their faces blank. Pete Randall and Greg Browning simply stood and watched, resignation on their faces, as the three dark figures arrived beside them, setting their backs against the rolling door.

"I want to keep him in front of us," said Frankenstein. "He's much faster than he should be, but I've seen faster, believe me. Stay calm."

Matt adjusted his grip on his T-Bone and fought the urge to stare at his father; Greg Browning was standing less than five metres to his right, staring at him and his squad mates with an expression of pure terror on his face.

I bet this is bringing back some bad memories, thought Matt, unaware of just how right he was.

Greg Browning tried to drag his gaze away from the men in black, but found that he couldn't; he was transfixed by fear.

They were the bogeymen, the stuff of his nightmares, the dark agents of the government who had taken his son away from him. They had forced their way into his home, their faces hidden, and pointed their guns at his family. They were the very thing he and Pete had come south to try and expose, and now they were here, so close he could almost have reached out and touched their hateful black uniforms. Albert Harker had scattered them with his initial attack, but they had regrouped instantly; they appeared to be communicating with each other, even though none of them had said a word; their silence only served to make them more unsettling.

He looked over at Pete, who was also staring wide-eyed at the men in black; he wanted to shout that this was their chance, that they should at least try to get the workers out, but he couldn't make his throat work. Part of him was back in his garden, watching his son bleeding on the lawn, feeling again the terrible impotence that had been the very worst aspect of that awful day: the feeling of helplessness, of being small and scared and weak. So he watched, too scared to move, as the three men in black waited for Albert Harker's next move.

*

"The helmet and the uniform are all well and good," shouted a voice from somewhere above them. "And I must confess, I had come to believe my brother was lying when he told me you were real. But I know the shape of a legend when I see it. How are you, Mr Frankenstein?"

The monster twisted the dial on his belt that controlled his helmet's microphone. "I'm very well, Albert," he said, his deep voice booming out through the cavernous space. "I assume it would be pointless to ask you to stop this madness?"

Harker laughed, a high-pitched noise that was close to a scream. "You assume correctly," he said. "Although I must say, I am deeply flattered that Blacklight sent you to try and stop me. That is a far greater compliment than my family ever paid me."

"I'm glad you're happy," said Frankenstein. "Why don't you come down here so I can show you just how glad I am?"

"Oh, I don't think so," replied Harker. "I'm rather enjoying the view from up here. I see you so clearly and you see nothing. It suits my purposes rather well."

"Which are?" asked Frankenstein.

"Deciding how to kill the three of you," said Harker. "I would ideally like to let you experience a little of what your beloved Department did to me, but I'm afraid we simply do not have the time. Agonising pain will have to do."

Matt twisted the dial on his belt to thermographic and scanned the darkness above the machines, looking for movement, for the telltale points of glowing red, but could see nothing. His heart pounded in his chest and his legs felt like jelly.

"Where is he?" he asked. "I can't see him."

"I don't know," replied Kate. "He's going to have to show himself at some point. Keep your eyes peeled."

"I'm ready when you are, Albert," said Frankenstein. "In the meantime, I'm starting to find these machines annoying. I'm sure you understand."

The monster strode forward, raising his shotgun as he did so. He jammed its barrel into a vent on the side of the machine at the end of the press and pulled the trigger three times. The machine exploded, its panels buckling, its insides crunching as it ground to a halt. Copies of *The Globe* quickly piled up inside it, fouling the line and blocking the conveyor belt. All the way along the press, alarms began to wail as the machines shut down one after the other.

A scream of fury echoed from the darkness overhead.

Matt braced himself.

Here he comes.

But nothing happened. The scream died away, and from somewhere in the distance there came the tinkling of breaking glass.

"That *really* pissed him off," said Kate. "Was that a good idea?"

Frankenstein grunted. "Can't hurt," he said. "Angry people tend to make mistakes. And we can hear better without those damn machines running."

Matt opened his mouth to answer, but didn't get the chance.

With a huge screech of rending metal, the rolling door that the five of them were leaning against exploded inwards, sending them sprawling across the floor of the loading bay. The metal frame slammed into Matt's lower back, sending a bolt of agony shooting through him; he hit the ground and dragged himself forward, his teeth gritted, the blood pounding in his head. Around him, heavy thuds and cries of shock and pain rang out across the loading area.

Matt turned his head and saw his father roll across the floor, blood pumping from a gash across his forehead. Kate's dad was on his back, the buckled frame of the door pinning his legs. Matt used all his strength and flipped himself over on to his back; the metal sheet was lying across his thighs, but he could still move. He pushed himself backwards as Kate yelled in pain; he risked a glance in her direction and saw the door pressing down on her stomach. Frankenstein couldn't be seen at all; there was simply a large bulge in the metal at the edge of the fallen door, where he was presumably lying.

A dark rectangle stood open to the night sky where the door had been. For a second, there was silence, then Albert Harker dropped casually into it, his eyes blazing, a vicious grin twisting his face, and strolled into the loading area.

"All your training," said Harker, his tone warm and friendly. "All your weapons and your tactics and your experience, and you fail to be aware of your surroundings."

Matt pushed against the floor with all his might. The twisted metal of the door scraped down his shins, causing him to cry out with pain. His feet reached the edge of the frame and, for an awful moment, he was stuck; he bore down, ignoring the agony radiating from his ankles, and they slid out from beneath the door. He scrambled to his feet, pain stabbing at him from a dozen places, and backed away, his eyes fixed on the approaching vampire.

"Matt," screamed Kate, her voice loud in his ear. "Be careful, Matt."

"You have spirit," continued Harker, smiling broadly at him. "What a brave little stormtrooper you are. I bet Blacklight are terribly proud of you, aren't they? Not like me. I should have been like you, but I never got the chance."

The vampire walked across the fallen door, the metal creaking and bending under his weight. He reached the edge and floated down on to the concrete floor. Kate was still squirming, trying to lift the heavy frame. Harker looked down for a moment, then swung his foot against the side of her helmet. There was a sound like breaking pottery and she lay still. The vampire raised his head and resumed his course towards Matt.

"My own father didn't want me to join his precious Department," said Harker. "Did you know that? I bet you did. I'm sure you and your colleagues still laugh about what he did to me. After all, I deserved it, didn't I? I might have embarrassed him and my brother, and that could never have been allowed."

Matt raised his T-Bone with shaking hands. He had managed to hold on to it when the edge of the door had thrown him forward, but he had no idea whether it had been damaged as he fell. He kept backing away as the vampire came forward, his eyes burning red.

"I'm not going to kill you," said Harker, smiling at him. "Not immediately, anyway. I'm going to break your spine and let you watch while I kill your friends. That seems only fair."

The conveyor belt, full of copies of *The Globe*, thudded against Matt's lower back, leaving him nowhere to go.

Oh God. Do something, before it's too late. Oh God. Oh God.

He set the T-Bone against his shoulder, sighted down the barrel, took a deep breath, and pulled the trigger; the metal stake burst from the barrel with a loud bang of exploding gas. Harker's smile widened as he slid to his left, inhumanly fast. The stake rocketed past him and clattered uselessly against the wall.

Matt let the weapon fall to the floor and pulled the MP5 from its loop on his belt as panic barrelled through his system, gripping at his heart and threatening to reduce him to tears of abject misery. He raised it in hands that felt as weak as a newborn's, and was about to pull the trigger when a dark shape rose up behind Albert Harker, taller and wider than the vampire by far.

There was a blur of movement and a fist the size of a basketball crashed into the side of Harker's head, sending him flying across the loading bay. The vampire smashed into one of the machines with a deafening crash, then slid to the floor. Matt was still holding the MP5 in his hands and staring wide-eyed at the place where the vampire had been; it was now occupied by the giant figure of Frankenstein, his helmet gone, his grey-green face twisted with fury.

"Are you hurt?" he growled.

Matt shook his head, his eyes wide, his chest heaving up and down.

Frankenstein nodded, then strode across the floor and lifted Albert Harker into the air. The vampire's face came up and Matt gasped. His nose was squashed flat, his front teeth were shattered, and blood was spraying out of a gash that ran the width of his forehead. But what was worse was the noise emanating from Harker's mouth: a high-pitched, shrieking sound that Matt realised, a millisecond too late to warn Frankenstein, was laughter.

The vampire's fist thundered into the monster's stomach, driving the air out of him. His grip sprang open and Harker floated gently to the ground as Frankenstein staggered backwards.

"Nice punch," he said, rubbing the back of his head. "Would you care to bet that you don't land another?"

Frankenstein dragged in a deep breath, stood up straight, and looked at the vampire. "I don't gamble," he said. "I don't believe in chance."

"How interesting," said Harker. A smile spread across his broken face; in the same instant, he launched himself forward, his hands outstretched and grasping.

Frankenstein saw him coming; he twisted his body, impossibly fast for a man his size, and clubbed the vampire out of the air with a huge forearm. Harker's smile evaporated as he was driven into the concrete, digging a long furrow in the floor. A cloud of concrete dust exploded into the air, then swirled and billowed as Frankenstein ran through it. Incredibly, Harker was already on his knees by the time the monster arrived in front of him.

Frankenstein didn't even break stride; he swung one of his tree-trunk legs and kicked the vampire in the chest. There was a huge cracking sound and Harker screamed in agony as he was thrown backwards through the air, clutching at his shattered ribs and solar plexus. Blood rose up from somewhere inside him and erupted into the air as he screamed, his blazing eyes rolling wildly in their sockets.

He crashed to the ground and Frankenstein raised his foot again, apparently intending to stamp the vampire's head into the concrete and grind the life out of him. He brought it down, a terrifying look of rage on his huge, misshapen face, and connected with thin air as Albert Harker threw himself out of the way. He skidded across the floor, twisting on to his back as he went, then leapt to his feet. Frankenstein turned and the two men, who were in different ways both so much more, faced each other.

Matt stared, his weapons long forgotten, as the two monsters threw themselves towards each other, colliding with a noise like a train crash. In the corner of his eye he saw Kate's arms begin to move and heard a low, distant groan in his ear.

Frankenstein felt one of his ribs break as Albert Harker slipped beneath a long, looping haymaker and slammed his fist into his side. He clenched his jaw as the vampire circled away, trying not to show how much the blow had taken out of him.

He's strong. Really strong.

Harker moved in on him again, a dark, bleeding blur, and

Frankenstein feigned left then right. The vampire's fingers sliced through the air where his face had been; he reached out, lightning fast, and gripped one of Harker's wrists. He squeezed and twisted at the same time, and felt a surge of satisfaction as bones broke inside his fist.

Harker bellowed in pain, wrenched his shattered wrist free, and backed away. Frankenstein hauled in a deep breath, then felt it freeze in his chest as Harker leapt forward again, so fast, far too fast, and landed a catastrophic punch on the centre of his chin. Pain tore through his skull and darkness exploded around him as he fell backwards towards the floor. His last thought, as the ground rushed up to meet him, was a simple one.

Too slow.

Matt watched in horror as the monster fell to the concrete floor.

The groaning in his ears was becoming louder and more insistent, but he wasn't listening; his mind was reeling from the sight of the defeated Frankenstein. Albert Harker staggered, clutching at his chest; it looked as though the punch had taken almost as much out of him as it had its target. Then he spat a dark wad of blood on to the ground, stood up straight, and turned to Matt.

The vampire walked slowly towards him, a smile of inevitability on his damaged face. The noise in his ears had become louder and its rhythm had changed; as Matt stared desperately at the terrible figure approaching him, he realised it had become two words, spoken by a croaking, battered version of Kate's familiar voice. He focused his reeling mind, and heard them.

"Beam... gun."

Matt's eyes widened; he reached down and grabbed the heavy cylinder from its loop on his belt. A small frown crossed Albert

Harker's face a millisecond before Matt pushed his beam gun's button and pointed the wide ultraviolet beam directly at it.

Purple fire burst from the vampire's features and he screamed in high-pitched agony. Harker beat at his face with his hands, stumbling to his knees as he did so; the fire licked across his fingers, burning them red, as smoke began to plume from his body. Matt stared, his stomach churning, as Harker beat out the roaring purple flames and raised his head.

What looked at him was little more than a skull.

One of the eyes was gone; the other swivelled madly. The skin of Harker's face had dissolved, revealing thick muscle and gleaming white bone. His teeth were visible through ragged holes in his cheeks, and his scalp was burnt black where his hair had caught fire.

Then slowly, almost unbelievably, the vampire climbed to his feet.

The pain was beyond excruciating; Albert Harker felt as though he was being sliced to ribbons with a thousand razor blades.

His face burned with an agony he would not have thought possible, and his nostrils were full of the smell of his own roasted flesh. His mind was reeling with shock; he tried to form a single coherent thought and felt it slip away, over and over. Acting on nothing more than instinct, he lurched to his feet and looked around the loading bay with half of his vision dark. The printing press workers were staring at him with stricken expressions of horror on their faces. One of the Blacklight soldiers was still squirming beneath the fallen door, one was still backed against the conveyor belt, and the big one, the monster, was lying still on the floor. Pete Randall and Greg Browning were looking at him with disgust on their pale faces. And McKenna? Kevin McKenna was dead, his throat torn out by Albert's own hands; the journalist's blood had coated his skin until the purple fire had burned it away.

642

Clarity swept through his damaged, broken mind, carrying with it the voices of his father and brother.

Failure. Disappointment. Embarrassment.

Harker threw back his head and howled, a harsh, jagged noise that sounded far from human. He had controlled the pain of what had been done to him for so long, using it as fuel to keep his desire for revenge burning, but now it ran freely through him, threatening to drive him to his knees.

Useless. Black sheep. Second-best.

He looked at the conveyor belt, at hundreds of copies of the newspaper he had killed to produce, and felt something tear open inside him. It was as though the flames had scoured his soul, leaving behind an empty husk that had brought damnation upon itself when it had spilled innocent blood.

Godforsaken. Waste. Disgrace.

Harker howled again, as the voices of his father and brother screamed at him, telling him that he had done nothing less than prove them right, that he had deserved everything that had happened to him. Kevin McKenna rose into his mind, his nervous, open face now harsh and accusing, his ruined throat gushing blood as he asked the question that he had asked so many times, the question that Harker had answered every time with lies.

No one gets hurt, right?

The vampire staggered towards him, smoke rising from his head and neck. Matt dropped the spent beam gun and pulled his stake from his belt; he held it out before him in a shaking hand, his reason wiped away by the unrelenting horror that had unfolded around him.

Albert Harker stopped before him, his breath coming in ragged whistles, his one remaining eye spinning in its socket, the distance between himself and the stake in the terrified teenager's hand no more than a few centimetres.

"Make them proud," said the vampire, the words wet and strangled. "Tell my father and brother what you did. They'll be so proud of you."

Matt couldn't move. He was transfixed by the smoking, devastated chaos that had been Albert Harker's face; he could not tear his gaze away from it.

The vampire growled, then moved, his hands rising towards Matt's neck. His mind unfroze and he pushed the stake forward, but was too slow, much too—

Crunch.

Matt stared in amazement as his stake disappeared into Albert Harker's chest. Blood began to pour from the wound, running down the metal barrel and soaking his gloved hand, but the vampire seemed not to notice. He looked down, the white of his remaining eye now red, the iris black. Then he looked back up at Matt, his mouth twitching at the corners.

Smiling, thought Matt. *It looks like he's smiling.*

Then Albert Harker exploded, in a thunderclap of steaming blood that soaked Matt from head to toe.

Matt Browning looked round the silent loading bay. The spreading pool of blood that had been Albert Harker glistened beneath the fluorescent lights. Kate was still trapped beneath the fallen door, but was croaking an incoherent stream of cheers and congratulations into his ears. Frankenstein was flat on the ground, his chest rising and falling steadily. The printing press workers were gathered round the forklift, alongside—

His breath caught in his chest.

In the midst of all the screaming, the violence and the spilled blood, he had forgotten what had brought him and Kate on their headlong quest to confront Albert Harker. Now, as he looked at his father's pale, drawn face, he remembered.

Greg Browning was standing beside Pete Randall, identical looks of shock standing out on both of their faces. The urge to run over and hug his dad returned, hotter and stronger than ever, but he forced himself to slow down, to think clearly. He took a deep breath, then ran across to where Kate was wrestling with the fallen door; he gripped the edge, heaved with all his strength, and held it up as she wriggled free. She clambered to her feet, then grabbed him in a long, fierce hug.

"Amazing," she said, her voice inaudible to the other men gathered in the loading bay. "You're completely amazing. You got him, Matt. You got him."

"I don't know if I did," said Matt. "I think... I don't know."

Kate pulled away from him, holding his shoulders in her gloved hands. "What do you mean?"

"He said something to me," said Matt. "He said I should make his father and his brother proud. And then he lunged, and I..." He stopped and took a deep breath. "He could easily have avoided my stake if he'd wanted to. I mean, I barely even moved it. It was more like... I don't know."

"What are you saying?"

"I don't know."

"Why would he do that, Matt?"

"I have no idea. But just before he died, I could swear..."

"What? You could swear what?"

"I could swear he smiled, Kate."

"Jesus," she said, her voice still little more than a croak. "That's awful."

"I know," said Matt.

"But still," she said. "You're the Operator who destroyed Albert Harker. No one's going to care about the details. You're going to be a hero."

"I don't feel like a hero," he said.

There was silence between them for a long moment. Eventually, it was Matt who broke it.

"What do we do now?" he asked, then nodded at their fathers. "What do we do about them?"

"I don't know," she replied. "But there's someone else we need to deal with first."

She took his arm and led him across the loading bay to where Frankenstein was lying. They crouched down on either side of him, as Kate took hold of his upper arm and shook him gently. The monster's eyes flickered and a low groan emerged from his uneven mouth.

"Colonel?" said Kate. "Colonel Frankenstein? Can you hear me?"

The monster's eyes opened slowly. They revolved unnervingly, then fixed on the purple visors leaning over him.

"I hear you," he rumbled. "Where's Harker?"

"Dead," said Matt.

"Who got him?"

"It doesn't matter," said Matt. "He's gone."

Frankenstein pushed himself up to a sitting position and looked round the carnage of the loading bay. "Forgive me," he said. His voice was like distant thunder. "I let you down."

"Don't be ridiculous," snapped Kate. "We're all still here, aren't we?"

"Just about," said Frankenstein. He raised a hand to his chin and winced.

"Can you call this in?" asked Matt. "There's something we need to do."

Frankenstein frowned. Then he noticed the stationary shapes of Pete Randall and Greg Browning, and grunted with understanding.

"I'm not going to stop you," he said. "Go. I'll call it in."

Kate nodded, then reached out and took Matt's hand; she lifted him to his feet and led him slowly back across to where their fathers were standing. He saw his dad's eyes widen as they approached, saw him take an involuntary half-step backwards, and felt shame rise through him.

He's scared of me, he realised. *They both are.*

Beside him, Kate reached up and lifted off her helmet. She shook her head and her blonde hair fell down around her ears. She took a deep breath, and looked at her father.

The colour drained from Pete Randall's face, as though he had suddenly been switched to monochrome.

He clutched at his chest and, for a terrible second, Matt thought he was having a heart attack. His friend stepped forward, her eyes widening in alarm.

"Kate?" gasped Pete Randall.

She nodded. "It's me," she managed, her voice cracking. "How are—"

She got no further. Her father rushed forward and lifted her off the ground in an embrace that crushed her tightly against his chest.

Matt watched, tears rising in the corners of his eyes, as Kate's dad began to sob uncontrollably against her shoulder. Then he turned to face his dad, who was looking at his friend and his daughter with an expression full of more warmth and empathy than Matt had seen in the sixteen years they had lived under the same roof. He took a deep breath and lifted his helmet from his head. His father glanced in his direction, before returning his attention to Pete and Kate. Then slowly, ever so slowly, he turned back towards his son.

"Matt?" he asked. "My God. Is it really you?"

"It's me," replied Matt. "Hi, Dad."

Greg stared for a long moment, his eyes wide and unblinking. Then he stepped forward very slowly and wrapped his arms round his son.

58

AFTER THE HORSE
HAS BOLTED

Jack Williams led his squad through the blood-soaked reception and into the huge main room of the printing press.

"Two dead here, sir," said Todd McLean, pausing beside the bound and gagged bodies of the two in blue overalls.

"Leave them," said Jack, without even looking. "Harker is the priority. Ready One." He strode down the space between the silent machines, his T-Bone set steadily against his shoulder. Angela Darcy followed him and McLean brought up the rear, casting a final backward glance at the two corpses.

Jack was fuming as he made his way down the long room. Their pilot had pushed his helicopter to its limits, extracting every last bit of speed from its rumbling, protesting frame, but he was depressingly sure it had not been enough. He had been an Operator for a long time, and he trusted his instincts without question; those instincts were telling him that he was too late.

He rounded a corner at the end of the long, stationary conveyor belt and instantly saw that he was right. Colonel Frankenstein was standing off to one side of the wide loading bay that had opened up before him, while five men in blue overalls huddled round a forklift truck at the opposite end. In the centre, beside a huge spray of spilled blood, Matt Browning and Kate Randall were embracing two men he didn't recognise. There was no sign of Albert Harker.

"What the hell is all this?" shouted Jack, striding out towards them. "Browning, Randall. I want a report this instant."

Matt and Kate pulled away from the strangers and turned to face him.

"Jack," said Kate, frowning. "What's the—"

"I asked you for a report, Lieutenant Randall," said Jack, his voice seething with anger. "Start with the whereabouts of Albert Harker, then follow that with a damn good explanation for why you decided to go after this particular Priority Level 1 target without informing your superiors."

"Calm down, Jack," said Frankenstein, his voice low.

"I will not calm down!" shouted Jack, making everyone jump. "My squad were put in charge of destroying Albert Harker! Cal gave *me* the responsibility and... and..." He sighed deeply, the fire going out of him as quickly as it had flared up. "Just tell me what happened, Kate."

"Harker's dead," she said, pointing at the wide pool of blood. "Matt destroyed him."

"Matt did?" asked Jack, turning to face him.

"I suppose so," he replied. "He's dead, in any case."

"McKenna?"

"Dead," said Frankenstein. "That's his blood in reception. Harker killed him."

"OK," said Jack. "Harker's dead, McKenna's dead. Anyone else?"

"The security guard who was manning reception," said Frankenstein. "Three employees."

"At least you three are alive," said Jack. "Who are these two?" He pointed at the two men standing beside Kate and Matt.

"Pete Randall," said Kate's father, stepping forward. "Who are you?"

"Who am I?" said Jack, incredulous. "What the hell are you doing here, Mr Randall?"

"I thought I was helping Kevin McKenna expose vampires to the public," said Pete. "I didn't realise this was about Albert Harker's revenge until it was too late."

"*We* were helping him," said Greg Browning, stepping forward. "We both were."

"I'm assuming you're Matt's dad?" said Jack.

"Greg Browning. That's right."

"Of course," said Jack, feeling the absurd urge to laugh rising through him. "Of course you are. Great. Is there anyone else here? Anyone else who was involved in this complete and utter shambles?"

"No," said Pete. "Me and Greg, and McKenna, and Harker. These men had nothing to do with it." He pointed at the five men in the blue overalls, who were watching the conversation with complete confusion on their faces.

"OK," said Jack. "I'll have a Security Division team sent here to explain the situation to them. No harm done."

"I wouldn't say that," said Pete. "Not exactly." He walked across to the conveyor belt, picked up one of the vandalised copies of *The Globe*, and passed it to Jack; he frowned, read the front page, and felt his heart stop in his chest.

"Jesus Christ," he said, and held it up for everyone to see. "What the hell did you do?"

"It wasn't them," said Frankenstein. "It was Albert Harker."

"No," said Pete Randall. "We knew what we were doing. Nobody twisted our arms."

"Jesus Christ," repeated Jack. "I can't believe this. Are you telling me these are out there?"

Pete nodded.

"How many?" he asked, his voice rising. "How many copies have left this building?"

Pete looked over at the printing press workers. One of them shuffled forward, a nervous look on his face.

"Hundred thousand," he said. "Give or take."

59

WHAT MIGHT HAVE BEEN LOST

"When did the first lorry leave?" asked Jack.

"About an hour ago."

"Where was it going?"

The man in the blue overalls shrugged. "I don't know."

"You don't know?" said Jack. "Don't you have shipping records? Schedules?"

"Normally," replied the man. "Normally, there are eight of us, not five. And normally, there isn't a bloody monster flying around threatening to kill us."

"Goddammit," said Jack. "Are you telling me there's no way you can find out where the lorries you loaded are going?"

"I'm sorry," said the man.

"There's something else you need to see, Jack," said Frankenstein.

Jack looked at the monster. "What is it?"

"Come with me," said Frankenstein. "It's in the editorial department. I'll show you." He cast a sharp glance at Matt Browning, who nodded; he knew exactly what the monster was doing.

He's buying us time. He doesn't know what's going to happen to our dads, so he's buying us some time.

"Jesus," sighed Jack. "All right. Darcy, McLean, secure the perimeter.

Any new lorries turn up, stop them and hold them. Nothing else leaves this building unless I say so. Randall, Browning, you and your fathers wait here. Is that clear?"

"Yes, sir," said Kate.

Matt nodded, and waited as Operational Squad F-7 dispersed across the loading bay and Frankenstein led Jack Williams away between the silent machines. When they were gone, he turned to face his dad, anger bubbling up through him; he was intending to ask his dad exactly what the hell he thought he had been doing, if he understood quite how much damage he had done by helping to print the newspapers that were piled behind him, but the outrage died in his throat when he saw the look on his father's face.

Greg Browning was looking at him with an expression of utter fury.

"You left us," he said, his lower lip trembling. "Your mother, and your sister, and me. You left us and you didn't say a bloody thing. We thought you were dead."

"I'm sorry," said Matt, a lump leaping into his throat. "I really am, Dad. But I had to. I had a chance to do something important, and it was something I couldn't tell you about."

"I don't understand," said Greg. "You're one of them? One of the people that took you away?"

Matt nodded. "I'm really more of a scientist, but yes. I work for them."

"Who are they?"

"I can't tell you that, Dad. You already know too much."

"You couldn't tell us what you were doing?" Greg's voice was rising, reaching a volume and pitch that were very familiar to Matt. "You couldn't even say goodbye to your mother?"

"I'm sorry," said Matt. "There's nothing else I can say."

"Mr Browning," said Kate. "Matt never meant to hurt you or his mother. I can promise you that."

"How do you know what he meant to do?" asked Greg, turning on her. "You let your dad think you were dead. What do you know about compassion?"

"I did what?" asked Kate, her voice catching in her throat.

"You let me think you were dead," said Pete Randall. His voice was little more than a whisper. "They told me you were dead, Kate. I almost believed them."

Guilt so sharp it was physically painful spilled through her.

They told him I was dead? They promised me they would never tell him that.

She thought back to the conversation that had taken place on the morning she had agreed to join Blacklight; her only condition, the one thing she had asked for, on which she was completely immovable, had been that they let her father know that she was all right, that she was safe.

A pillar of cold fury rose inside her.

Major Gonzalez said they would tell him I was OK. He told me that to my face. He said they would wait a few weeks until things died down, then they would tell him that I was doing something secret, but that I was OK.

She suddenly understood why her father was here, why he had ended up in the company of a monster like Albert Harker, and the realisation threatened to overwhelm her. He had not spent the last few months quietly proud of a daughter who was doing something important and secret; he had spent the last few months wondering whether his only daughter was dead or alive.

He must have felt like he had nothing left to lose.

"I'm sorry, Dad," she managed. "I never wanted you to think that. I didn't know that's what you had been told."

"And that's supposed to make it all right?" asked Pete. "You left me without even saying goodbye and I'm supposed to be OK with that?"

"She really didn't know," said Matt, his stomach churning; this painful mixture of guilt and recrimination was not how being reunited with their fathers was supposed to be. "I know what she was told."

"I don't care what she was told," shouted Pete, and Matt flinched. "I've been on my own in an empty house on a dying island, wondering what happened to you, for three months. *Three months.* How could you do that to me, Kate? After what happened to your mother?"

Kate's eyes widened in shock. "Don't bring her into this," she said. "It's not my fault she died, Dad. You can't blame me for that."

Pete sagged, visibly. "I'm not," he said, softly. "And I don't. Never think that, not even for a moment. But I've *missed* you, Kate. I've missed you so much."

Kate took her father's hands and met his gaze with her own. "I've missed you too, Dad," she said. "I never wanted what I did to hurt you, although I suppose I knew it would. But it was an opportunity to *do something*, Dad, maybe the only one I was ever going to get. This was my chance."

"I would never have stopped you," said Pete. "I've known since you were five that I was going to have to say goodbye to you one day. Lindisfarne was never going to be big enough for you, and that's fine, that's great. I wanted you to go out and make a life of your own, and your mum dying didn't change that."

"It did for me," said Kate, her voice shaking. "I could never have packed a case and said goodbye and left you in that house on your own. I could never have done it."

"So you let me think you were dead? You thought that was kinder?"

"I didn't know that's what you were told!" shouted Kate. "I've told you that!"

There was a long moment of silence, deep and pregnant with tension. Father and daughter stared at each other, their chests rising and falling, the heat high and clear in their faces. Eventually, it was Pete who dropped his eyes first.

"So what is it you do?" he said, his voice little more than a whisper. "For these people you work for?"

"I can't—"

"You can't tell me," said Pete. "Right."

"I'm sorry."

"Do you kill vampires?"

"Dad," said Kate, helplessly. "You know I can't—"

Pete shook his head, then lowered it, as though he was deep in thought. "Is it right?" he asked, eventually. "What you do now. Is it right?"

"It's necessary," replied Kate.

"All right," said Pete. "All right then." He drew his daughter to him and threw his arms round her. Matt watched, relief spreading through him, before turning back to his dad.

"Your mother is going to be so happy," said Greg. "She... well. She's going to be very happy."

"How is she, Dad?" he asked. "How's Laura? I miss you all."

"They're OK," said Greg, his voice suddenly unsteady. "As far as I know, they're all fine. She's going to be so happy when she hears you're all right."

As far as you know? wondered Matt. *Why don't you know for certain?*

The answer hit him like a bucket of cold water.

She left him. After I went, she took Laura and she left him. Has he been on his own all this time?

Then he realised what his father had said, and his heart sank.

"You can't tell Mum about me, Dad," he said. "If they let you go, you can't tell anyone about any of this."

"What do you mean, *if* they let me go?"

"What did you think was going to happen to you if you got caught, Dad? You were just going to get a slap on the wrist and be sent home on the next train? This is classified government business, Dad, more highly classified than you can imagine." He was suddenly furious with his father for being so stupid, for having got himself mixed up in this bloody mess. "Why are you even here, Dad? What the hell were you doing with someone like Albert Harker?"

It was Pete Randall who answered; Matt's father looked so shocked he was incapable of speaking.

"We didn't know what he was," he said, letting go of his daughter. "We thought we were helping Kevin McKenna do something good, helping him warn the public about vampires. We didn't know this was what Harker really had in mind."

"I'm sure you didn't," said Matt. "I'm sure you were doing what you thought was right. But you were wrong. It won't help the public to know about this stuff. It won't do any good."

"We just wanted to do something," said Greg Browning, finding his voice. "We didn't want anyone else to go through the same thing as us. I lost my family and they told Pete he'd lost his. All because of vampires and the goddamn men in black. So what were we supposed to do?"

Kate looked over at Matt; he met her gaze, but said nothing.

He had no answer to his father's question.

60

HOMECOMING

LINCOLN COUNTY, NEVADA, USA

Larissa floated above her bed, her hands laced behind her head, and checked the clock on her bedside table for perhaps the hundredth time in the last hour.

6:42.

Eighteen minutes until General Allen is expecting me to give him my decision. And I still don't know what I'm going to tell him.

On her desk were two pieces of paper, representing two very different futures; she stared at them from across her quarters, and felt her stomach churn with uncertainty.

She had slept, although for a long time after leaving the NS9 Director's quarters she had not thought she was going to be able to, but when it came, it had been fitful and full of bad dreams. When she had woken up to see the clock telling her it was just after 5am, she had given up and headed for the showers. The pounding water had done nothing to clear her head, however; she had been no closer to a decision when she returned to her room than she had been when she lay down on her bed seven hours earlier, to consider a decision she had long thought would be easy.

Within a week of her arrival in Nevada, Larissa had been pretty sure who she was going to take back to Blacklight with her. Tim had asked her as soon as they began to work together and through him she had met four of the remaining five, the four Operators with whom she had become close: Kara, Kelly, Danny and Aaron. Her participation in the attack on General Rejon's compound had left her spoilt for choice as far as the sixth place was concerned, but she had taken an instant liking to Anna Frost, the quiet, elegant Canadian Operator who reminded her so much of Kate Randall.

And that should have been it. Six names, six men and women who would all be assets to Blacklight, and who she would be delighted to have in the Loop with her; the right choices, for herself and her Department.

Until Tim Albertsson ruined it.

That isn't fair, she told herself. *You both ruined it. You liked the attention and you misread the situation. It's your fault too.*

Larissa knew that was the truth and it made her furious with herself. She had started to wonder if there was something wrong with her, if she possessed some natural propensity for self-destruction. She wanted to take her friends back to Blacklight, where she knew they would be on her side, would defend her against the distrust and suspicion she still regularly encountered at the Loop, and now she wasn't sure if she could.

All because of stupid, handsome, arrogant Tim Albertsson.

Even after Mexico and Las Vegas, she had still believed there was time to make the problem go away. There was still a month left on her secondment; plenty of time to talk to him, to make it absolutely clear to him that nothing was going to happen between them, and for him to come to terms with that before the six of them departed for Britain.

General Allen's bombshell the previous evening had destroyed that hope; now there was no time, and the awkwardness and embarrassment that she felt was raw and powerful. She couldn't take Tim to Blacklight, not like this, not with the memory of his kiss so fresh in her mind, the memory of how he had looked at her in the club in Las Vegas, the naked hunger on his face. How could she introduce him to Jamie, and Kate and Matt? She would spend every waking minute on edge, waiting for Tim to say the wrong thing, either by accident or on purpose, to tear apart the fragile bonds that held Jamie and her together.

It was far too great a risk.

But she had made him a promise and if she didn't keep it, she knew full well that she couldn't take the others. There would be too many questions, too much animosity left behind; Tim would never forgive her if she compounded her change of heart by taking all of his closest friends with her when she left.

How did I make such a mess of this? she wondered. *How did I manage to let it all go wrong?*

Larissa rose up off her bed, feeling heat spill into the corners of her eyes, drying away the tears that had been starting to gather there. She hung in the cool air of her quarters, took a deep breath, let it out, and looked down at the two pieces of paper.

On one sheet were the names she had anticipated handing to General Allen when the time came. On the other was a second list, men and women she knew would be good for Blacklight, but who were not her friends. Taking them with her would mean she had done her job, done it properly and well, but would also mean that a real chance to improve her life had been left behind in the Nevada desert. She stared at the two lists of names for a long time, until the clock ticked over to 6:58.

All right, she thought. *All right then.*

Larissa floated down to the ground and picked up one of the pieces of paper. For a second, she stood absolutely still, her eyes fixed on some distant point beyond the wall in front of her; then she opened her door and flew down the corridor towards the elevator without a backward glance.

"Are you sure about this, Larissa?" asked General Allen. He was sitting on one of the sofas in his quarters while she perched on the other, her hands twisting nervously in her lap. "These aren't the names I was expecting."

"Are they a problem, sir?" she asked.

Allen shook his head. "No problem," he said. "They're just surprising. No Tim, no Kelly or Kara? None of your friends?"

"No, sir," said Larissa, trying to keep her voice as level as possible. "I was sent here to take six Operators back to Blacklight. Not to make friends, sir."

"I understand that," said Allen. He narrowed his eyes in obvious suspicion. "What aren't you telling me?"

Larissa felt heat threatening to rise in her cheeks and willed herself to remain calm. "Nothing, sir," she said. "These are the Operators I think will be the best fit for Blacklight."

General Allen picked the sheet of paper up and read it again. "Captain Van Thal," he said. "Operators Johnson, Schneider and Burgess. Trainees Gregg and O'Malley. They're from the class you and Tim have been training?"

Larissa nodded. "They're going to be good Operators, sir."

"I'm sure they are," said Allen. "James Van Thal I understand. He's spent time at Blacklight before. Did you know that when you chose him?"

"No, sir," said Larissa. "Although that's certainly a bonus."

"Johnson, Schneider and Burgess. Have you worked with them all? Be honest with me."

"I've worked with them all," said Larissa. "And I've gathered opinions from other members of the Department. Everyone rates them extremely highly."

General Allen set the list down on the sofa beside him and fell silent. Larissa studied his tanned, weathered face and wondered what he was thinking. She supposed there was nothing preventing him from rejecting her list and insisting that she take a different group of Operators back to England with her, but she was certain he wouldn't want to do so.

"I'm going to agree to this," he said, eventually. "And I'm not going to make you tell me what's really going on here, even though I know there's more than you're saying. I just want to make sure you know that if there *was* anything you wanted to tell me, it would stay between us. All right?"

Larissa's throat tightened; the General's voice was full of kindness and devoid of judgement. "I do know that, sir," she said. "Thank you."

"OK," he said, getting up from the sofa and standing in front of her. "You're cleared for departure at 10:00. I'll give them their orders and have them meet you in the hangar at 09:30. I imagine most of them are going to be a little bit surprised."

Larissa got to her feet. "Thank you, sir," she said. "And thank you for making me so welcome here."

General Allen smiled widely. "It's been a genuine pleasure, Lieutenant Kinley. I'm going to miss you."

"I'm going to miss you too, sir," she said. "I really am."

*

Six hours later the *Mina II* sped smoothly east, its supersonic engines propelling it above the flat blue-grey expanse of the Atlantic Ocean. Larissa sat strapped into one of the seats that ran along the walls of the aircraft's hold, her heart pounding in her chest.

She had been unprepared for the range of emotions that had spilled through her as the sleek jet sprinted along the Area 51 runway and leapt gracefully into the bright Nevada sky. Sadness she had been expecting, and it was there in spades; what she had not anticipated were the potent blooms of grief and loneliness, and a sharp, acidic burst of something that felt horribly close to despair. For a single, panicked moment she had considered shouting for the pilot to turn the plane around, to take them back so she could change her mind.

But it was too late for that; the six Operators she had selected were sitting in the *Mina*'s hold, looking at her with expressions of mild curiosity that hadn't changed since they had arrived in the NS9 hangar to report for a mission that none of them had been expecting to be a part of.

Captain James Van Thal was a tall, dark-skinned man in what Larissa guessed was his early forties. His head was shaved bald and his eyes were a beautiful pale brown. He had been a Recon Marine before being recruited into NS9; a stripe of pale pink rose up the back of his neck and on to his scalp, the result of a series of grafts to replace skin that had been burned away in the Iraqi desert more than a decade earlier.

He was soft-spoken and had been one of the first people to welcome Larissa to Dreamland, without making any mention whatsoever of the fact that she was a vampire; she had been impressed and grateful. Kelly and Danny had worked closely with him before he had been moved into the Intelligence Division, and both spoke of him in glowing, almost reverential terms. He had been born in Angola in the middle of the War of Independence, and his father had apparently died getting his infant son out of the country; Larissa's friends said that Van Thal was happy to talk about it in general terms, but would not be drawn on any details. His aura around Dreamland was similar to Paul Turner's around the Loop, although the two men could not have been more different; Van Thal was warm and friendly, unfailingly polite and gregarious.

Patrick Johnson and Mark Schneider looked so alike that they could easily have been mistaken for brothers, especially in their NS9 uniforms. The two men were in their early twenties, with closely cropped hair and the deep tans that came with being stationed in a desert where the daytime temperature regularly exceeded forty degrees. They were both former Navy SEALs and had both been leading Operational squads for several years; they were solid, experienced Operators, the kind of men that nobody at Blacklight would be surprised Larissa had brought with her.

Carrie Burgess was a tall, sharp-faced woman in her twenties with black hair and delicate features. She looked nothing like the CIA intelligence operative she had been before NS9, but had a reputation as one of NS9's sharpest intelligence analysts, for calm, level-headed thinking and strategic excellence. Larissa had only worked with her directly once, and had found her somewhat bland, but she worked closely with Tim Albertsson and the rest of the NS9 Special Operator programme, which was enough for her; the SO programme only utilised the very best of the best.

Tom Gregg was barely out of his teens, short and powerful with jet-black skin and huge, nervous eyes. He had joined the Army straight out of high school, and quickly made an impression on his superiors with his determination and tenacity; he had already been marked out as a future member of the special forces, most likely Delta, by the time General Allen had swooped in and recruited him for NS9. He had performed well during the training that Larissa had helped Tim Albertsson oversee, taking his knocks with quiet persistence, always eager to learn and improve.

Laura O'Malley was slightly older than Gregg, perhaps twenty-two or twenty-three. She was short and extremely pretty, her dark red hair as much a signifier of her Boston Irish roots as her surname, and had arrived at Dreamland from the NSA, the shadowy branch of the National Security apparatus, where much of what she had done was highly classified. Larissa was already looking forward to seeing her and Angela Darcy together; the two women's careers had been remarkably similar, and she suspected they were either going to become good friends or bitter rivals.

Larissa looked round the cabin at the men and women she was taking to join the Department she loved and hated in equal measure. She was sure they would do well, and she was excited at the prospect of working with them, but there was something far more interesting than them on board the *Mina II*; something to which her attention kept returning, and was the reason her heart was still pounding in her chest after the visceral, physical shock of leaving Nevada had worn off.

At the rear of the hold, two Blacklight Operators, visors down and MP5s in their hands, stood in front of a thick plastic barrier that stood flush against the walls, ceiling and floor, creating a sealed space beyond it. On a bench at the back of this space, a black hood over his head, his hands cuffed behind his back, sat the man Lee Ashworth had told her about.

The prisoner had been escorted through the hangar barely five minutes before the *Mina II* taxied out on to the Dreamland runway, flanked by the same Operators who were now standing guard outside his cell. They were members of Paul Turner's Security Division, and had spoken only to inform her that she and her NS9 recruits were forbidden from attempting to make any type of contact with the prisoner. It was infuriating to Larissa, who outranked them both, but she let it slide; Interim Director Holmwood had presumably made it clear to them that their orders superseded rank.

The prisoner himself had barely moved since the plastic barrier had been sealed, other than to occasionally stretch his legs and shift the pressure on his shoulders. His head was lowered almost to his chest, and Larissa couldn't tell whether he was awake or asleep. She stared at the man, who had been the focus of so much gossip inside Dreamland, and felt her skin tingle with excitement and frustration; he was now less than five metres away from her and she still did not know who he was.

Once they were back at the Loop, she had every intention of telling the Interim Director how much she knew and asking him outright who the prisoner was, a man important enough to have his identity protected not only by the hood on his head but by the two armed Operators guarding him. Far from being sated, her curiosity about the prisoner was hungrier than it had ever been.

"Three minutes," said the pilot, his voice emerging from speakers set into the walls.

Larissa's heart leapt in her chest as she pulled the safety harness round her shoulders and waist. Three minutes and she would be back at the Loop. And while the prospect of returning to Blacklight did not fill her with unequivocal joy, there were three reasons she was suddenly trembling with excitement.

Kate. Matt.

Jamie.

*

The *Mina II* slid down on to the Loop's runway with a low, rattling thud and a momentary screech of tyres.

Larissa unbuckled her harness as the pilot applied the brakes and steered the sleek supersonic jet towards the hangar; she flew easily through the air and floated beside the door-release handle, waiting for the light on its control panel to turn green. The deafening roar of the engines was diminishing, and behind her she could hear her recruits unfastening themselves, getting to their feet, and pulling their bags out from under their seats. She ignored them; her eyes remained fixed on the small glowing red circle. With a final shuddering lurch, the *Mina II* came to a halt, its engines letting out a long, low whine as the red light in front of Larissa turned green. She flipped open the plastic case that covered the panel, raised the safety handle, and pressed the flat yellow button.

There was an instant rumble of machinery as the ramp at the front of the aircraft began to slowly lower to the ground, letting a gust of cool evening air into the stuffy hold. Larissa breathed it in, relishing the smells of the Loop: petrol, grass, grease, sweat. The ramp thudded down on to the tarmac of the landing area and she swooped out through the open doorway, her supernaturally enhanced eyes searching the familiar landscape for familiar faces.

"Lieutenant Kinley."

She turned towards the source of the voice and felt a smile rise on her face. Cal Holmwood was standing on the wide landing area, Paul Turner at his side. He smiled back at her as she slid to the ground before him and snapped a sharp salute.

"Hello, sir," she said. "How are you?"

"As well as can be expected," said Holmwood. "How was the flight?"

"Short," she replied. "Longer than if I'd done it myself, though."

"I'm sure," said Holmwood. "Are these our new recruits?"

He nodded in the direction of the *Mina II*. Larissa turned to see the six Americans making their way down the ramp, staring around at the vast grounds of the Loop with wide eyes.

"Yes, sir," she replied. "Do you want to meet them?"

"I think I probably ought to."

Larissa nodded. "NS9 Operators," she shouted. "Over here on the double."

The men and women made their way across to where she was standing, incredulous expressions on their faces.

"Interim Director Cal Holmwood," she said. "May I introduce Captain James Van Thal, Operators Patrick Johnson, Mark Schneider and Carrie Burgess, trainees Tom Gregg and Laura O'Malley."

"Holy shit," said Burgess, then blushed a deep red. "Sorry, sir."

"Don't worry about it," said Holmwood, smiling broadly at the new recruits. "It's good to meet you. I'm grateful to you all for being here."

"It's an honour, sir," said Van Thal.

"It's nice to have you back, Major," said Holmwood. "Things have changed quite a bit since you were last here."

"I'm looking forward to getting started, sir."

"Glad to hear it," said Holmwood. "Major Turner, please will you show these men and women to their quarters and see that they have everything they need?"

"Yes, sir," said Turner, stepping forward. "Follow me, please."

The Security Officer turned and strode towards the open hangar; after a second or two, the NS9 Operators followed him. Holmwood watched them go, then turned back to Larissa.

"They're good people," she said.

"I'm sure they are," said Holmwood. "I wouldn't have sent you if I didn't trust your judgement. Or if I didn't think it would be good for you. How was it?"

"It was wonderful, sir," she said. "But it's over. I'm home."

Holmwood nodded. "Go and get yourself settled back in. I want a full debrief tomorrow morning. And I think there are a few people who are looking forward to seeing you."

"I hope so," said Larissa, grinning.

"Go on then," said Holmwood. "Dismissed."

She cast a final glance in the direction of the *Mina II*. The two Operators were standing at the bottom of the ramp, flanking the prisoner; he stood stiffly, his hooded head up, his back straight, his feet shoulder-width apart. She considered asking the Interim Director about him, getting it over with there and then, but decided against it.

It's not the time, she thought. *And I can't wait any longer to see my friends.*

Larissa set off towards the hangar. Without thinking, she floated into the air, then remembered where she was and let her feet sink back to the ground. Flying, which had been so glorious in Nevada, so wonderfully liberating, was a cause for suspicion and distrust among a significant number of her colleagues, and she felt her heart sink, just a little.

Her boots clicked across the concrete floor of the hangar as she headed for the double doors that would take her inside the Loop. She pulled her console from her belt and was about to type a message to Jamie, asking him where he was, when she heard three sets of footsteps come to a halt behind her and glanced back over her shoulder.

The prisoner and his escort had stopped in front of Cal Holmwood; as she watched, he waved a hand and the two Operators walked into the hangar, leaving the Interim Director alone with the hooded man. As Larissa turned away, she saw Holmwood take one of the prisoner's arms and lead him forward. She reached the double doors and was about to push them open when she heard three words that stopped the breath in her chest. Cal Holmwood whispered them at a volume that no normal person would have been able to hear, but to Larissa's supernatural ears they were as clear as a bell.

"Welcome back, Julian."

Larissa gasped. She pushed through the doors, not wanting to give any sign she had heard anything, and walked down the corridor beyond them. Her head was spinning; she told herself to calm down, to not jump to conclusions.

There are plenty of people called Julian. It doesn't mean anything. He's dead, for God's sake.

The possibility was so incredible that she couldn't allow herself to properly consider it; it was too big, too monumentally, earth-shakingly huge. It was a thought that had occurred to her momentarily in Nevada, but she had dismissed it then, as she was trying to do now.

Coincidence. It has to be a coincidence.

She stepped into a waiting lift and pressed the button marked B. The doors slid closed in front of her and Larissa leant against the metal wall of the car, her head pounding.

There was no way she could tell Jamie what she had heard, not without ironclad proof that the idea now churning in her stomach was true. If she let him get his hopes up and turned out to be wrong, it would destroy him, and them. But if there was even a chance that he had been lied to, that his father was still alive, how could she not? If the prisoner disappeared into some dark corner of

Blacklight, and she failed to tell him while there might be a chance to do something about it, how would she be able to live with herself?

She was deep in thought as the lift doors slid open, revealing the long central corridor of Level B; she turned left and walked along the grey semicircular path that led to her quarters, to the room that she had not seen for more than a month. Her mind was so full of dead men and secrets that she was completely unaware of the dark shape behind her until she unlocked the door and felt a tap on her shoulder.

Her eyes widened, then instantly bloomed dark red; she whirled round, fangs bursting from her gums, and stopped dead. Standing in front of her, a huge smile on his face, was Jamie Carpenter.

Larissa opened her mouth, but didn't get the chance to utter a single word. Jamie reached round her waist, lifted her into the air, and strode into the room, kicking the door shut behind them.

TWO DAYS LATER

61

POST-MORTEM

"This meeting is called to order," said Cal Holmwood. "All members of the Zero Hour Task Force present, Lieutenants Kinley, Randall and Browning, Colonel Frankenstein and Captain Van Thal present in addition."

Jamie looked round the Ops Room. The central table was full, men and women in black uniforms occupying every seat round its edge. The Interim Director sat at one end with Paul Turner on one side of him, Jack Williams on the other. He looked tired, as always, but his face wore a determined expression, and his voice was low and steady.

"The last week has been remarkable, even by the standards of this Department," said Holmwood. "This meeting has been called to update you on recent events. Minutes will be forwarded to your consoles afterwards, together with Security Division regulations regarding what you are authorised to tell your teams. Until you have them, please discuss nothing you hear in this room with anyone not present now. Is that clear to you all?"

There was a chorus of agreement and a ripple of nodded heads.

"Good," said Holmwood. "Before we begin, I'd like you all to join me in welcoming the new additions to this Task Force.

Lieutenants Kinley, Browning and Randall you all know, similarly Colonel Frankenstein, who has returned to the active roster. I'd like to introduce Captain James Van Thal of NS9, who has joined us for the foreseeable future. He and I have worked alongside each other several times, and I can tell you we're lucky to have him."

Kate and Matt blushed slightly, Frankenstein gave no visible indication that he had heard his name mentioned, and Van Thal nodded and smiled.

"To business then," said Holmwood. "I'm sure most of you already know, but I can confirm that Albert Harker, who escaped from Broadmoor during the mass breakout, was destroyed two nights ago in the printing presses of *The Globe* newspaper near Reading. He was destroyed by Lieutenant Browning, who was accompanied to the scene by Lieutenant Randall and Colonel Frankenstein. Interrogation of Harker's associates has confirmed that his stated intention was to alert the general public to the existence of vampires and this Department, although they have come to believe that gaining revenge against us was his true objective He was at least partly successful in terms of the public."

"How successful?" asked Angela Darcy. "What's the exposure?"

"Approximately one hundred thousand physical copies of the edition of *The Globe* that Harker and Kevin McKenna altered were despatched from the facility. We intercepted several lorries before they reached their destinations, and were able to remove a significant portion from retail outlets. But there are at least twenty thousand copies unaccounted for, which we have to presume were bought and read.

"In addition, *The Globe*'s website ran Kevin McKenna's story uninterrupted for more than an hour. It has been taken down, along with the blog that McKenna wrote, presumably on Albert Harker's orders, but pasted versions and caches of both appear on a daily basis. There is simply no way to make them disappear entirely, or make any accurate estimates about how many people may have read them in their various incarnations. The official response ran in *The Globe* yesterday, a retraction and editorial accusing Kevin McKenna of sabotage, of playing a practical joke on the country before killing himself. Early indications are that this story is holding, at least so far, although it has been roundly rejected in conspiracy theory circles. The Ministry of Defence have received more than three thousand phone calls and fifteen thousand emails enquiring about our existence, which have all been answered with firm denials. Beyond continuing to monitor the situation, there is little more we can do at this time."

"Jesus," said Jack Williams. "It's out there now, even if no one believes it yet. Harker got what he wanted."

"Lieutenant Browning shoved a stake into his heart until he burst," rumbled Frankenstein. "I doubt he wanted that."

I'm not so sure, thought Matt.

"The Security Division has concluded that there is no immediate danger of exposure," said Paul Turner, giving Frankenstein a sharp glance. "Although it goes without saying that it is now a significantly more likely prospect than it was a week ago. Harker may not have thrown the doors open as he intended, but he has opened them a crack. The likelihood of this Department, and the supernatural, remaining unknown to the public indefinitely is now almost nil."

Jamie listened to his colleagues, his eyes widening. He knew what had happened in the printing press, had heard the tale in great detail from both Kate and Matt, but until now nobody outside the Security Division had known the extent of the damage Albert Harker had caused.

"This could have all been avoided," he said, his voice low, "if we had known where Albert Harker was, if his family had treated him better. None of this needed to happen."

"Thank you, Lieutenant Carpenter," said Turner. "When the Science Division invents a time machine, I promise you it will be the first thing we go back and fix."

Jamie stared at the Security Officer, who returned his gaze, his expression as flat and empty as always.

"Moving on," said Holmwood, shooting them both a warning look. "We have an update on Albert Harker's fellow Broadmoor escapees. The Science Division has now been able to confirm the theory put forward by Lieutenant Browning, due in no small part to the cooperation of the SPC. The theory explains the unusual power of the turned escapees, and how such a widespread global action was able to be perpetrated at the same time."

Jamie glanced over at Matt, who had blushed a deep red, and saw Kate and Larissa do the same.

You didn't tell us this, whatever it is, he thought. *What happened to no secrets?*

"What has been concluded is that the Broadmoor patients were not turned via the traditional method that we are all familiar with. They were not bitten."

"So what the hell was done to them?" asked Larissa. She was looking at the Interim Director with a frown on her face.

"They were injected, Lieutenant Kinley. With the plasma that coats the fangs of every vampire. In this case, that came directly from Dracula himself."

There were gasps around the table. Jamie's eyes widened, and he looked at Frankenstein. The monster was as impassive as ever, but he thought he saw a flicker of surprise in the corners of his eyes.

"The SPC was able to map Dracula's DNA from the remains that were formerly in their possession," continued Holmwood. "A comparison with the altered DNA of two of the Broadmoor patients produced a partial match, with enough similarity to draw the conclusion I have just given you."

"That doesn't explain why they're so strong," said Angela Darcy. "I thought vampire power increased with the amount of time they're turned?"

"That was the accepted wisdom," said Holmwood. "And we believe it remains the case. But Lieutenant Browning's theory suggests there is more to it than we had believed. There now appears to be a clear link between the age of the vampire and the power of their victims. This explains why the escapees are so dangerous."

"Maybe it only applies to Dracula?" suggested Dominique Saint-Jacques. "Because he was the first?"

Holmwood shook his head. "There are other examples. Marie Carpenter, who was turned by Alexandru Rusmanov, is significantly stronger and faster than we would expect her to be, given when she was turned. And..." He paused, turning his attention towards Larissa.

She frowned, then blushed under the combined gaze of the Zero Hour Task Force. "Me?" she asked. "You mean me?"

Holmwood nodded. "General Allen has reported that you demonstrate abilities far ahead of the expected curve. He described you to me as one of the most powerful vampires he has ever seen. Is that the case?"

Larissa was silent for a moment. "I suppose so," she said, eventually. "I don't know. I have nothing to compare myself with."

"Well, let us assume that General Allen, who has seen many hundreds of vampires in his time, is correct. You were turned by

Grey, who is reputed to be the oldest British vampire. Which, again, would fit the pattern that Lieutenant Browning has uncovered."

There was silence around the table. Larissa looked deeply uncomfortable; Jamie tried to catch her eye, to give her a silent expression of support, but she didn't look his way.

"This is remarkable," said Major Van Thal. "Have you communicated these findings to the other Departments?"

Holmwood nodded. "The Departments have been made aware. Several are conducting their own research and will share their results when appropriate, but all have accepted the Browning Theory in principle."

Matt's eyes widened and he blushed again. Jamie smiled; his friend was so uncomfortable with praise or attention, despite his obvious gifts. He was so lacking in arrogance, or ego, and he found himself suddenly furious, not for the first time, with the bullies who had made his friend's life a misery for so long.

"So what does all this mean?" asked Kate. "Does this change anything?"

"Not in terms of our response," said Holmwood. "There are one hundred and twelve of the Broadmoor escapees still at large, and the Operational objective remains search and destroy. All Operators will be briefed to exercise increased caution when confronting them, but the plan doesn't change."

"Maybe it should, sir," said Larissa. Her face was pale, and Jamie could see a red flicker in the corners of her eyes that he knew all too well.

"You have something to say?" asked Holmwood, turning to face her.

"I've been thinking about something, sir," said Larissa. "Something that happened to me a couple of days ago."

"What is it?"

"I was in Las Vegas," said Larissa. Jamie's eyes narrowed slightly, but if she noticed, she didn't let it show. "In a nightclub. I was outside and I smelt another vampire, could smell her as soon as I was within about fifty metres of her, so I went over and said hello. Her name was Chloe and she'd been turned a year earlier, in a club in New Orleans."

"Why are you telling us this, Lieutenant Kinley?" asked Holmwood. "This isn't the time for holiday stories."

"Sorry, sir," she replied. "The reason I'm telling you is because she had no idea who we were. She'd never heard of Blacklight, or NS9, or the SPC. She didn't know that we existed, and even once I'd told her, she didn't seem to care. She'd only ever known one other vampire, a man she'd dated for a while in Los Angeles. She didn't kill people, or turn them. And she thought Dracula was a character from the movies she saw when she was a kid."

"What's your point?" asked Paul Turner. "I'm assuming there is one?"

"My point," said Larissa, fixing the Security Officer with an icy stare, "is that this was a perfectly normal girl, living her life, minding her own business, who just happened to be a vampire. She was no danger to anyone. But if some NS9 Operator sees her through their visor on an Operation in LA, they'll stake her without a second thought."

"So?" asked Holmwood.

"So how is that OK?" asked Larissa, her voice rising. "Killing her because of what she is? She hasn't done anything wrong and she never asked to be a vampire. Nor did any of the Broadmoor patients. They'd already been imprisoned for their crimes and now we've passed death sentences on them all for something that isn't their fault."

"What do you suggest we do?" asked Turner. "Build some giant facility to contain them all and cross our fingers that Lazarus comes up with a cure before we have another breakout to deal with?"

"I'm not suggesting anything, sir," replied Larissa. "I just think it's important for us to remember what we're really doing every time we pull the trigger of a T-Bone. We're not destroying monsters, or rats, or cockroaches. They're people with a disease, and we're killing them."

"That's enough, Lieutenant Kinley," said Cal Holmwood. "We're facing far more serious problems at the moment and we're barely managing to stay afloat. So I'm afraid questions of morality will have to wait."

Larissa nodded, although the look on her face assured Jamie that the issue was not dead; she would bide her time, but he had no doubt in his mind that she would raise it again when she felt the time was right.

Good, he thought. *She should. What she said is the truth.*

"All right," said Holmwood. "Again, some of you will already be aware of this, but the investigation into the explosion that took place in Lieutenant Randall's quarters is now complete. The device, together with an identical one that was safely defused in Major Turner's quarters, was placed there by Lamberton, the former valet to Valentin Rusmanov. He was blackmailed into doing so by a former member of this Task Force, who I'm sure you have all noted by his absence."

"Brennan," spat Patrick Williams.

"Richard Brennan," confirmed Holmwood. "His connection to Dracula, or more likely to Valeri Rusmanov, has not yet been ascertained, although it appears clear that it was the prospect of that connection being discovered that led him to take the action he did."

"Attacking ISAT," said Angela Darcy.

"Correct," said Holmwood. "Whether he assumed that the deaths of Major Turner and Lieutenant Randall would mean the end of the investigation, or whether he was merely trying to create enough confusion to cover his escape, we don't know. He's gone and we have no way of tracing him."

"How did he pull it off?" asked Jamie. "How did he get Lamberton out of the cellblock to plant the bombs?"

Holmwood glanced over at his Security Officer. "Major Turner?"

"Thank you, sir," said Turner. "Brennan took the components for making the devices to Lamberton himself, in a standard-issue holdall. We have security footage of him entering the cellblock three days ago carrying the bag, then leaving without it. It wasn't picked up by Surveillance. Brennan's Zero Hour classification meant that his visiting the captive vampires was not a noteworthy event."

"Perhaps more investigation should have been done before we handed out such freedom," said Frankenstein, his voice low and deep.

"Perhaps, Colonel," said Turner. "As far as releasing Lamberton from the cellblock, I am disappointed to report that Brennan successfully blackmailed a member of my Division, Operator Alex Lombard. Lombard was apparently conducting an extra-marital affair and Brennan had come into possession of a series of incriminating emails. Lombard was instructed to allow Lamberton out for a twenty-minute window during his shift in the cellblock guard post. Brennan apparently promised him that nobody would be hurt."

"Where is he now?" asked Captain Van Thal. "Lombard."

"He has been discharged from this Department," said Turner. "Dishonourably."

Van Thal nodded.

"What about Natalia?" asked Matt. "Is there a medical update?"

"As I'm sure you well know, Lieutenant Browning," said Holmwood, the ghost of a smile rising on his face, "Miss Lenski is recovering well and is expected to rejoin the Lazarus Project within the week."

"Good," said Kate. "That's something, at least."

Turner nodded. "Agreed. Now. I am pleased to be able to report the completion of the ISAT process that Lieutenant Randall and I have been conducting. We have now interviewed and assessed every serving member of the Department, including Captain Van Thal and his colleagues. It may be little consolation today, in light of recent events, but our preliminary conclusion is that the current roster of Blacklight is clean, for what we must regrettably assume is the first time in a very long while."

"Thank you," said Holmwood. "And thank you too, Lieutenant Randall. I know this was far from an easy assignment, and the whole Department owes you its gratitude."

Turner nodded and glanced at Kate, who smiled.

"Is there anything anyone wishes to add?" asked Holmwood.

"Valentin," said Jamie, instantly. He had gone down to see his mother following the doomed chase after John Morton, and noticed immediately that both the cells that had been occupied by the youngest Rusmanov brother and his servant were empty. "Where is he?"

"Mr Rusmanov has been sent in search of his brother and his former master," said Holmwood. "He will report back when he has information."

Frankenstein grunted with laughter. "I won't be holding my breath."

"Neither will I, Colonel," said Holmwood. "But I believe Valentin to be a man of his word, and that we will see him again."

"I'm sure we will," said Frankenstein. "Walking alongside his brother as his master leads them into battle against us."

"Time will tell," said Holmwood. "One of us will no doubt be right, and the other wrong. But only time will tell. Anything else, the rest of you?"

There was silence around the Ops Room table.

"We have been hurt," continued Holmwood. "By Valeri's attack and by the rot we have found at the heart of everything we thought we were. But we have won victories too, these past months, and we will win more of them. If I didn't believe that, I would not be standing here in front of you all, and I would not ask you to give as much as I do. I remain honoured to be your commanding officer. Thank you. Dismissed."

Larissa was last to leave the Ops Room; she watched with almost detached interest as the rest of the Zero Hour Task Force made their way out into the corridor.

Kate paused to talk to Paul Turner, before walking away alongside Matt, who checked over his shoulder to see if Jamie was following them. He was rising from his chair with a grimace on his face and a hand pressed against his damaged ribs.

Patrick Williams and his brother strolled out side by side, Jack unable to resist taking the briefest of glances at Angela Darcy, who was deep in conversation with Dominique Saint-Jacques and Andrew Jarvis. Amy Andrews left alongside Cal Holmwood, while Paul Turner and Frankenstein exited deep in conversation. She waited for a long moment, enjoying the quiet of the suddenly empty room, trying to let her anger subside.

There's a phrase for killing people simply because of what they are, she thought. *It's called ethnic cleansing.*

Larissa took a deep breath and crossed the room; she knew Jamie would be waiting for her in the corridor, and she knew they needed to talk.

They had spent most of her first day back locked in her quarters, emerging only to shower and eat. Jamie had told her about John Morton, and she had tried to make him see that it wasn't his fault. He had asked about Nevada, and she had told him that she had enjoyed it, without offering any further details. His eyes had narrowed with suspicion but they had not spoken about it again; instead, they had spent their time catching up on what had been happening at the Loop, a question that took a long time to answer.

Larissa opened the Ops Room door and smiled at her boyfriend. He was leaning against the wall and straightened up as she approached.

"Matt and Kate need to get back to work," he said. "But they're going to get something to eat first. I told them we'd join them."

"OK," said Larissa. "That sounds good."

They stood in the corridor, the silence between them uneasy.

"Are you all right?" she asked.

"I think so," replied Jamie. "Were you in Vegas when I rang you? I tried a couple of times."

Larissa nodded. "I was talking to Chloe," she said. "The vampire. I'm sorry I couldn't answer."

That's almost the truth, she told herself. *Almost.*

"It's OK," he said, his smile returning. "I know how it is."

"Right," said Larissa. The freedom of thought and deed that she had so enjoyed in Nevada was already gone; now her world was again full of guilt, and secrets, and darkness.

"I'm glad you're home, Larissa," said Jamie, softly. "It hasn't been the same without you."

"I'm glad to be back," she lied.

EPILOGUE:
THREE FAREWELLS

"I can't believe she didn't even say goodbye," repeated Tim Albertsson.

"Really?" asked Kelly. "You can't think of any reasons why she wouldn't? Not a single one?"

They were sitting in a booth in Sam's Diner with Danny and Aaron. The atmosphere was cool and tense; it was the first time the four friends had been together since Tim had sent them all a message telling them that Larissa was gone, and each of them was wrestling with things they wanted to say.

"Say what's on your mind, Kelly," said Tim. "Don't imply it."

"What she's implying," said Danny, tipping cream and sugar into his coffee and stirring it vigorously, "is that it's your fault she went like she did. And I agree with her."

"What are you talking about?" asked Tim. "I didn't do anything."

Kelly snorted. "Apart from make it obvious that you liked her, and flirt with her, and try to kiss her, and make her feel uncomfortable. You knew she had a boyfriend, but you couldn't leave it, could you, couldn't accept that maybe you couldn't have her? And you're surprised that she decided not to take you back to Blacklight with her, so you could hang out with her and Jamie? If so, you're an idiot."

Tim stared at his friend. He knew what she was saying was true, but he wanted to tell her she didn't know the full story, that Larissa *had* liked him back, he knew she had, and that she had liked his attention, encouraged it even. But he couldn't say so; it would only make him seem more arrogant, more self-obsessed.

"What really pisses me off," said Danny, looking evenly at him, "is that you didn't just screw it up for yourself. You screwed it up for all of us. She would have taken us with her, but you made her feel like she couldn't. So she's gone and we're still here."

"I don't blame her," Tim said, eventually. "And you're right, it's my fault. I'm sorry."

"That's great," said Aaron. The quiet Intelligence Operator was staring out of the diner's window, sipping from a glass of water. "It doesn't change anything, though, does it? She was only here for a few weeks, but she was part of us. I don't think I'm the only one who thought so. It's sad that you don't get to go to Blacklight, because I know how much you've always wanted to. It's annoying that we don't get to go either, as I for one was looking forward to the change of scene. But there's a bigger issue here, far bigger. I think we all know that Blacklight is going to be at the frontline of what's coming. And I'm sure we could help them, but we aren't going. And that's on you, whether you're sorry or not."

Tim was astonished; it was the most he had ever heard Aaron say in one go and the words cut him deeply. He was happy to accept the charge of having pursued Larissa when he shouldn't have, of causing her to run away from him and his friends, but what Aaron was suggesting was far, far worse.

He's saying that I hurt our chances against Dracula.

"I'm sorry if I let you down," he said. "All of you."

"Jesus, Tim," said Kelly. "We know you weren't deliberately trying to mess everything up, and we know this isn't how you wanted things to turn out. You just need to realise that you can't control everything, that everything doesn't always go your way. Bad things happen."

"Bad things happen," repeated Tim. "Amen to that."

A long way from Sam's Diner, in the north-east of England, a man and his daughter stopped beside a car in a station car park.

Kate Randall had spent much of the previous three days with her dad. She and Matt had pleaded with Cal Holmwood not to lock their fathers in the Loop's cells and the Interim Director had eventually relented, permitting them to sleep in one of the dormitories that usually housed new Blacklight recruits. They were locked in every night and confined to the Loop, although that was largely an unnecessary restriction; the two men were not soldiers, and were extremely unlikely to attempt to escape from a classified military base.

To begin with, their conversations had been awkward. She had talked to Matt and been relieved to hear that he was finding the same thing when he spoke to his dad. Pete Randall's relief, his utter joy at the discovery that his only daughter wasn't dead, had quickly given way to an annoyance that, from Kate's frustrated viewpoint, bordered on petulance. He kept returning to the same point, again and again, the one point that she did not have a reasonable answer for.

You let me think you were dead. How could you do that?

She had tried to explain it to him, tried to get him to see what had happened from her point of view: the lack of a future on

Lindisfarne, the chance to do something good, something worthwhile. And, most importantly, that Blacklight had promised her that they would *not* allow him to think that, a betrayal that she intended to take up with Cal Holmwood as soon as things returned to what passed for normal at the Loop. But it didn't matter; as far as Pete was concerned, she had abandoned him.

The situation had been worsened by the long wait for Cal Holmwood, in conjunction with Paul Turner, to decide what action he was going to take against her father and Matt's. Both men had broken civilian law, and were aware of the existence of both vampires and the agencies that fought against them; there had been rumours, many of which had reached Kate's ears, that they would be locked up for the rest of their lives.

When the judgement had finally come, Kate's first reaction had been to burst into tears. Her second was the understanding that she owed Paul Turner her thanks, yet again.

"So this is it," said Pete Randall. He had his car keys in his hand, and his face was pale and drawn. "This is where we say goodbye. Am I ever going to see you again?"

Kate took a deep breath. She had escorted her father in the van that had returned him to Berwick station, where his strange, awful odyssey with Albert Harker had begun what seemed like such a long time ago, but could go no further. Holmwood had given Pete and Greg permission to return home, in the knowledge that they would spend the rest of their lives under surveillance, but she could not take the chance that anyone she had grown up with might see her; Lindisfarne was a tiny community, and her appearance would raise questions that she didn't want her father to have to try and answer.

"I don't know," she said, honestly. "I hope so. There are things happening, things that I can't tell you about. But when they're over, if we're all still here, then I hope so."

Pete nodded. He was clearly reluctant to get in his car and drive home; for all his annoyance with her, it was obvious that he did not want to be parted from her again.

"I have to go, Dad," she said. Her voice sounded strangled and her chest was tight; if she didn't go quickly, she wasn't sure she would be able to do so. "Are you going to be all right?"

Pete smiled. "I'll be fine," he said.

Kate walked forward and threw her arms round her dad. He crushed her tightly against him, dipping his face down to her ear.

"I'm proud of you, Kate," he whispered. "I love you so much."

She felt tears spill from the corners of her eyes and a huge lump rise in her throat. "Thanks, Dad," she managed, the words mangled and crushed. "I love you too."

Pete Randall released his grip and stepped back. He looked at his daughter for a long moment, then opened the car door and climbed into the driver's seat. She stepped back as the engine rumbled into life, and watched as he pulled slowly away. As he reached the exit to the car park, she saw him twist in his seat and look at her. She raised her hand and saw him wave back. Then there was a rattle of gravel, and her father was gone.

She walked unsteadily back to the van that was idling behind her. She pulled open the passenger door, climbed in, and fastened her seat belt.

"Where to, sir?" asked the driver.

"Home," said Kate.

Less than a hundred miles to the south, a similar exchange was taking place.

Matt Browning was standing in the kitchen of the house he had grown up in, drinking the first cup of tea he could ever remember his father having made him. He was still in mild shock; he would not have claimed with any great conviction that his father knew where the kettle was, or how it worked. The house was spotlessly clean and tidy, which had been another surprise; he had expected the rubbish to have reached the windows in the time since he and his mother had been gone.

He had gone up to his room while his father made the tea and been struck by a feeling of nostalgia so huge it was almost physical. The room, in which he had spent so much of his life hiding away from the outside world, looked so small. His bed was made, and his shelves of books and comics were as he had left them, but they felt as though they belonged to someone else; he no longer recognised the inhabitant of this room.

"You want another?" asked Greg Browning. He nodded at the mug in his son's hand.

"No, thanks, Dad," said Matt. "I'd better get going."

His dad's face fell briefly, but he rallied quickly. "Of course," he said. "I understand. You've got work to do."

Matt nodded.

"I wish I understood it," said his dad, smiling gently. "But that's nothing new, is it? I never understood most of the stuff you were doing. You were cleverer than me by the time you were about five."

"I'm sorry, Dad."

Greg frowned. "Don't apologise, Matt. Don't you ever apologise for who you are. I'm the one who should be sorry. I should have tried harder when you were little, been more interested. It was hard for me, son. We never liked the same things and I didn't try hard enough to understand you. I was intimidated, to be honest with you, and I can admit that now. But it's no excuse. And I *was* always proud of you, whether you believe that or not. I was always telling people about my son the genius."

Matt blushed. He didn't know what his dad wanted him to say. Was he asking him to forgive him, to tell him it was all right? He'd happily do so if he thought it would help, but when he looked at his father, he was far from convinced that it would.

"Now look at you," continued Greg. "Working for the government, trying to save the world. I wish I could tell people that."

The colour drained from Matt's face, and his dad smiled again. "Don't worry, son," he said. "Your mother, no one else. I understand."

He nodded. "Are you going to ring her?"

"Yeah," replied his dad. "As soon as you go. Part of me wants to ring her now, let you talk to her, but I don't know if that's a good idea. To be honest, I don't know if she'd take my call."

"I'm sorry," said Matt, again. "I didn't mean to mess everything up."

"I know you didn't," replied Greg. "To be honest, things weren't great before you went. They hadn't been for years. You leaving for the second time was just the final straw."

"Do you think she'll come back?" asked Matt.

His father shrugged. "I don't know, son. I don't think so, to tell the truth. But it'll be better once she knows you're safe. It might make things easier."

"Do you miss them?" asked Matt, gently.

"Course I do," replied his dad. "I miss you too. To be honest, I'm not sure what I'm going to do now. Since your mum left, I've thought about nothing apart from trying to get back at the people I thought had taken you away from us, and I didn't care what happened to me in the process."

"You could go to Sheffield," suggested Matt. "Get a job up there. Be nearer to Mum and Laura."

"Maybe," said Greg. "You giving me advice now?"

Matt smiled. "Looks like it."

The two men fell silent for a long moment. Matt was aware that he should go, should head back to the Loop and to his desk at the Lazarus Project. They were busier than ever, as a result of what was now referred to as the Browning Theory; the revelation that the vampire virus continued to evolve with its host, was able to confer greater power on new victims the longer it had been allowed to grow, had implications for both their primary analysis and the wider security of the entire Department.

But he was surprised to find that he didn't want to leave. While he would not have gone so far as to claim that his dad was a changed man, the anger and frustration that had boiled endlessly inside him appeared to be gone, at least temporarily. Matt wondered whether the loss of his family had been the equivalent of what addicts referred to as reaching rock bottom, if his dad had finally been forced to turn his anger on himself, rather than blaming the disappointing world around him.

"You sure you don't want another tea?" asked Greg. "One for the road?"

Matt looked at his dad. "Sure," he said. "Tea would be great."

His dad nodded, a broad grin breaking across his face. He flicked on the kettle and began to rummage through the cupboards. After a second or two, Matt went to help him.

EPILOGUE: TWO PRISONERS

Henry Seward spat a thick wad of blood on to the floor between his feet and frowned; there was something white lying in the middle of the crimson puddle. He reached out with a hand that trembled visibly in the soft candlelight of his room, picked it up, and held it up in front of his face.

It was a tooth.

Seward's stomach lurched. He ran his tongue quickly along the rows of his teeth and found the gap; it was on the upper right, about halfway along. He pressed his tongue into the empty space, grimacing as the tip probed the soft hollow of his gum. He gagged, and looked at the tooth again. It appeared to be whole; the roots that had once nestled safely inside his jaw, thick and pale yellow, were intact.

It fell out, he realised. *It's not broken. It fell out.*

He was sitting on the floor of the small, elegant room that served as his cell, his knees raised, his arms folded across them. Through a window on the opposite wall, the first fingers of dawn were creeping over the horizon to the east, staining the sky purple. Seward still did not know exactly where he was; Dracula had told him they were in France, but that was the limit of the information the old vampire was prepared to reveal. On the clearest, darkest nights, Seward believed he could see the distant glow of electric lights, but what and where they were was a mystery.

There had been no torture since the night he had leapt from the chateau's balcony. Valeri's rage had been awesome and terrifying, and for the first time since he had been taken from the Loop, Seward had genuinely believed that his life was about to end. Dracula's servant had attacked him with a cold, vicious precision, drawing screams from him that had come to sound like animal howls. The following morning, when he had been deposited back into his room, bleeding and sobbing and barely breathing, two vampires had come and tended his wounds with far greater care than usual. Since then, he had been left largely alone; fed and watered in his room and provided with fresh dressings and powerful, numbing painkillers by vampires who were more polite and less hateful than usual.

Seward knew that these new modes of behaviour were not motivated by generosity or kindness; they were the result of Valeri's instinct for self-preservation. He had heard Dracula order his associate not to kill him, and he believed that Valeri had come far closer to doing so than he had intended. Consequently, he was being coaxed back to something approximating health, to ensure that the elder Rusmanov did not incur his master's displeasure.

Seward remained proud of himself for what he had done on the balcony. He didn't know how far he had set Dracula's recovery back, if at all, but it had felt so good to see the uncertainty on the old monster's face as his strength began to fail him; it had almost been worth the dark agonies that had followed it. He still didn't know what the vampire had meant when he claimed, over dinner, that he was everywhere, but in all honesty, he didn't really care. It was unlikely to be something he could do anything about from inside the tall stone walls of his prison, and was therefore not worth fixating on. He had faith in Cal Holmwood and the men and women of Blacklight, and he was sure they could deal with whatever was thrown at them. His one regret was his firm belief that he was not going to be there to see his friends wipe the smile off the faces of Dracula and Valeri.

He coughed again, his chest heaving, and spat out a smaller lump of congealing blood. He shook almost incessantly, one of his ears rang, and he was in constant pain, but he forced a smile, his bared teeth smeared red.

One of my friends is going to stab your heart out of your chest, you old bastard, he thought. *And, wherever I am, I'll be laughing my head off when they do. You can count on that.*

Several hundred miles to the north, Julian Carpenter sat up as his cell door unlocked with a muffled series of clunks and thuds.

He had been lying on his bed, trying, and failing, to get some sleep. The flight back from Nevada had been short, but remarkably uncomfortable; the physical pain in his wrists had been bad, as had the sense of claustrophobia that came with the hood he had been forced to wear, but the humiliation of being taken back to Britain like a common criminal had been worse. He had been loaded on to the plane in the dark, warned not to say anything to anyone, sealed inside a soundproof cell that he couldn't even see, then walked off at the Loop with Operators holding his arms. He had been on the verge of despair until he had heard Cal Holmwood's voice welcome him back; the familiar, friendly tone had been enough to allow him to keep his composure as he was taken down to the cell he was now sitting in.

His handcuffs had been removed and he had taken off his hood as soon as the door was closed behind him. The cell was slightly larger than the one he had spent the last three months in, but was just as sparsely furnished: bed, toilet, sink, chair. He was exhausted, but sleep would not come, for a single reason that pressed against the inside of his skull; somewhere, perhaps no more than a few hundred metres away from where he lay, were his wife and son.

The cell door opened and Cal Holmwood stepped through it. He nodded, and Julian gave him a thin smile in return; it was all he could manage under the circumstances.

"Julian," said the Blacklight Interim Director. "How are you?"

"What do you want me to tell you, Cal?" he replied.

Holmwood shrugged, and sat down in the plastic chair. Julian pushed himself across his bed and leant his back against the wall.

"I am sorry about this," said Holmwood. "I hate seeing you in here. I know it's not fair."

"There's an easy solution, Cal," he replied. "If you hate it so much."

"No," said Holmwood. "There isn't."

Julian felt his insides turn to water. "What's going on?" he said. "Tell me."

"Nobody can know you aren't dead, Julian," said Holmwood. "It causes too many problems. At least for the moment."

"Nobody?" asked Julian, quietly. "Including—"

"Including Marie and Jamie," said Cal. "I'm sorry, Julian. You died a suspected traitor and I can't afford to have all of that dragged back up. Not now. Thomas Morris admitted framing you, but faking your own death looks suspicious, Julian, you have to see that. There will need to be an enquiry, testimonies, interviews and investigations. And I cannot authorise that use of time and manpower. Not with everything else that's happening."

Julian felt numb. This was the possibility that Bob Allen had warned him about, had tried to prepare him for, but hearing the words emerge from Cal's mouth still felt like a punch to the gut.

"You're telling me I'm not allowed to see my family," he said, slowly. "Am I hearing you right? I want to be very clear on this."

"That's right," replied Holmwood. "As I said, I'm sorry."

"You're sorry? Is that meant to be a joke?"

"It's meant to—"

"I didn't do anything wrong," interrupted Julian. "Not then, and not since. I faked my death because I could see how well someone had framed me and I couldn't let Marie and Jamie pay for the things I'd supposedly done to this Department. In the years since then, I told nobody who I was. I told nobody anything about us, or the vamps, or anything else that's classified. I only broke cover when I believed my son was in danger, and since then I've been sitting in prison cells. So explain to me how your being sorry is supposed to mean anything to me?"

Holmwood said nothing.

"They're my family, Cal," said Julian, his voice on the verge of breaking. "My wife. My son. Please don't do this to me."

Holmwood looked at him. His eyes were bloodshot and the bags beneath them were dark and heavy. "It's done," he said, softly. "I'm sorry. But the decision is made."

Julian felt cold creep through him. It felt as though something inside him had died as his friend spoke, some essential part of himself. "So what now?" he said. "I stay here and hope you change your mind?"

"It's up to you," said Holmwood, sitting up in his chair. "You can stay here, in this cell. You'll be safe, and looked after, and I'll see about getting you some things to make it a little more bearable, some furniture, some entertainment. But nobody apart from me will know who you are, and you'll be forbidden from talking to anyone else."

"Or?" asked Julian.

"You can leave," said Holmwood. "We'll give you a new name, and a new life. But you can never come back. You can never attempt to contact anyone from this Department or any of our counterparts around the world. You'll be under surveillance for the rest of your life and the slightest transgression will see you arrested. But you *can* have a life. We owe you that much."

"Without my family?" asked Julian.

Holmwood nodded. "Yes. Without them."

"What kind of life would that be, Cal?"

"One that's better than you can have locked inside this room," said Holmwood. "One where you can go outside, see the sun, choose what you want to eat. Take it or leave it."

"Take it or leave it?" asked Julian. His mind seemed to be slowing down, as though the enormity of what his friend was telling him was cutting power to his vital systems. The cell seemed to be becoming even greyer, clouding at the edges of his vision and shrinking in on him, reducing his perspective to a dark tunnel.

"I'm afraid so," said Holmwood. He stood up from his chair, made his way across to the door, and banged on it three times. "I'll give you some time to think about it. And like I said, I really am—"

"Just get out, Cal," said Julian, and lay back on his bed.

The door unlocked and swung open. Holmwood looked at him

for a long moment, then turned and walked out of the cell, slamming the door behind him.

Julian stared up at the ceiling, his friend's words pounding through his head.

Take it or leave it.

Take it.

Or leave it.

46 DAYS TILL
ZERO HOUR